FOREVER YOUNG

Book Three of The Young Blood Trilogy

T. Marshall Bunn

Belief Creating Reality Publications

ROCKVILLE, MARYLAND

Belief Creating Reality Publications
Rockville, Maryland
www.youngbloodtrilogy.com

Publisher's Note: This is a work of fiction. Names, characters, places, and incidents are a product of the author's imagination. Locales and public names are sometimes used for atmospheric purposes. Any resemblance to actual people, living or dead, or to businesses, companies, events, institutions, or locales is completely coincidental.

Excerpt from *Dracula* by Bram Stoker, 1897, in the public domain

Excerpt from "His Eye Is on the Sparrow" by Civilla D. Martin and Charles H. Gabriel, 1905, in the public domain

Cover photo by Nicci Trent

Book Layout © 2014 BookDesignTemplates.com

Forever Young: Book Three of The Young Blood Trilogy/ T. Marshall Bunn. -- 1st ed.
ISBN 979-8-9861016-3-7

Library of Congress Control Number: 2022910507

Acknowledgments

It took me forever to get to this point, to finally translate the endless ideas I'd had for this story over the years into something in print. I want to thank everyone who encouraged me and helped along the way.

Also thank you to Fay Verburg and Carol Waggoner-Angleton from Augusta University's Reese Library for research assistance into my hometown's history, and thanks again to my friends Rachel Brune and Stephanie Stewart for their help with proofreading and editing.

When all the world is young, lad,

And all the trees are green;

And every goose a swan, lad,

And every lass a queen;

Then hey for boot and horse, lad,

And round the world away:

Young blood must have its course, lad,

And every dog his day.

— Charles Kingsley, 1862

CHAPTER ONE

I was crying. I was going to die, and I knew it. What was worse was that I deserved it. It was my fault that the girl I loved was now a monster, and she was going to take my life from me the same way I had taken so many others before. Things were always going to come to this. Turnabout is fair play, as my mother sometimes said, though I hadn't fully appreciated what that cliché meant until now.

I struggled on my back as Elizabeth, the beautiful girl I had wanted for so long and believed until only a few moments ago to be dead, held my arms to the ground. We were next to her grave, where I'd spent the past two hours pouring my heart out to her. She was a vampire, but that was supposed to be impossible.

There wasn't much time for me to ponder this, though, to try to comprehend how she was even here given that our victims didn't come back to life as vampires. That was one of the rules. But the rules kept changing, and someone had apparently neglected to tell me about this particular one.

These thoughts raced through my head in the few seconds it took for Elizabeth, smiling at me wickedly, to start leaning down over me, her face leaving my field of vision. I had seen her eyes — her piercing, deep blue eyes that I had daydreamed about so many times

— move from transfixing me with their gaze over toward the left side of my neck just a split second before I could no longer see her. I'm not sure if my inability to push her off of me was due to her supernatural strength or my sudden lack of motivation, the loss of my will to live. But I could still scream, and I did.

The scream stopped suddenly, replaced by a gasp, and a confused one at that. I had felt her breath as her mouth neared the skin above my jugular vein, the same vein I had torn open in so many people's necks all those years ago. I was certain that it was now my turn. But she didn't bite me.

Instead of the sharp pain I expected to feel, there was instead the sensation of something small and soft tapping my neck very briefly. A split second later, my skin in that spot felt slightly wet, then cold. Right in my ear, I heard Elizabeth giggle softly, followed by a short "Hmm" that left me further confused. "You taste nice," she said. I could hear the smile in her voice. Then I got it: She was toying with me.

"Please," I said, my voice quavering from fear, from grief, from so many desperate, painful emotions that I just wanted them all to stop. "If you're going to kill me, just do it." It wasn't that I was particularly brave or felt empowered by reciting a line I'd heard many times on TV or in the movies; I really had just accepted that she was going to kill me and wasn't too thrilled with the idea of her drawing it out.

Elizabeth straightened up, still holding me down, though by this point I was barely struggling because I knew it was hopeless. She looked down at me, and the expression on her face was hard to read. Her forehead wrinkled slightly, and she asked me with what appeared to be genuine sincerity, "Do you want me to kill you?"

"I… I…" I wasn't entirely sure.

"Because I could, you know," she said, raising her eyebrows. She seemed proud of this fact. She must have hated me for what I'd done to her, even though it had really been my clone who'd done it. I was still indirectly responsible. "Is that what you want?" Her smile broadened, and I could see her fangs again. The fact that she was still so impossibly beautiful hurt more than anything else. That smile in her eyes, the way they squinted and turned up on the ends slightly, was there again. It scared the hell out of me now.

"Your heart is racing," she said, and not only did her expression change, but so did her grip on my wrists. She still seemed very amused by everything, knowing that she was in full control of the situation, but her face became almost pouty. She cocked her head to one side as she spoke, rotating her upper body in the same direction, then looked down at my right arm. Her index finger, which had been pushing into my right palm, slowly moved its way down to my wrist, and I could feel her fingernail scratching me. No, not scratching. Just touching. And rubbing back and forth: towards my palm, back down to my wrist.

It was only at this point that I realized that the girl I had lusted after for so many years was lying on top of me, spread-eagle. How many times had I fantasized about that? How many other positions had I thought of, dreamed about? And now, it almost felt like she was flirting with me.

She giggled again, her face jutting forward and her long, straight blonde hair catching up with it a fraction of a second later, bouncing into place. Her face was one big smile, fangs and all, and she asked me, almost laughing, "So what do you want me to do?"

"What?"

"Do you want me to kill you or not," she said in a sort of sing-song way, almost condescendingly. She was having a great deal of fun with all of this. So much fun, in fact, that I found myself relaxing inside, despite my imminent death. Was she trying to give me a pleasant send-off before ripping my throat out like I deserved?

"Well?" she asked. The smile had gone away, but what replaced it wasn't fury or bloodlust, which honestly would have been less baffling. If anything, she seemed frustrated, perhaps impatient, the way one would act when talking to a small child who was too shy to answer a simple question.

"No," I said quietly. I was a little surprised to hear it come out of my mouth.

Her smile returned, and she straightened up again, finally releasing my wrists and rubbing her hands, looking away from me briefly as she did so. I made no move to get up. I still partly expected her to lunge forward again for the kill at any second.

"Good." She climbed off of me, positioning herself on the ground beside me, sitting on the lower half of her legs. Her hands were propping her up on either side, and she continued to look me in the eye.

Cautiously, I sat up, not taking my eyes off of her. Although I knew better, she looked like an ordinary girl, right down to the plain, white turtleneck sweatshirt and acid-washed blue jeans. "I don't understand," was all I could say.

"Understand what?" she said in that deadpan way a girl uses when she knows exactly what you're talking about but wants you to say it anyway.

"Why you didn't kill me."

She sighed audibly, rolling her eyes and shaking her head slightly. "Do we have to go through this again? I asked you if you wanted me to kill you. You said no. Have you changed your mind?"

Instinctively, I drew back from her, but she didn't follow my move. She just smiled, this time looking more evil. But I knew that expression. I'd seen it many times before. It wasn't really an evil look; it was her mischievous look. She had me. Now that the shock had worn off, I might have been able to fight her if she did make a move to attack. But what she said next intrigued me, more from the way she said it than anything else.

"I'm not going to kill you, Ray." Her tone was, while a bit terse, reassuring somehow.

"Okay, look," I said, slowly feeling more confident now that it looked like I might survive the night after all. "You're right. I don't want to die. But I don't understand why you don't want to kill me.

You're…" I realized what I was about to say, and it broke my heart. But I had to finish the sentence. I had to accept the reality of it. "You're a vampire," I practically whispered. I felt myself dying inside.

"And so that makes me a ruthless killing machine that runs around at night taking the life of anyone unlucky enough to cross my path." She said it as if she had just been given the most boring role in the school play and refused to commit to something so trite and mundane. I looked at her blankly. She looked to one side, raising her eyebrows and shrugging her shoulders slightly. "Maybe it does." She looked back at me, somewhat resigned. "And, apparently, there's somebody who looks exactly like you who is the same way. What I don't understand is why."

I struggled to take this in, trying to keep from withering under her piercing look. Her expression had changed again, looking slightly more angry, but not malevolent. She just appeared to be waiting for an explanation.

"What exactly…" I wasn't sure how to phrase my question. "What don't you know?"

"Hmm?" she said, looking down at her lap. "I don't know. Lots of things. Like how to play the piano. Always wanted to learn that." She smirked, looking back up at me. For a moment, she seemed like the same old Elizabeth I'd always known, clever and sweet and damn near impossible to figure out. But that couldn't be the case, not anymore.

"You know what I mean," I said, fighting back a nervous laugh.

"No, I don't," she said more firmly, sitting up and adjusting her position, her eyes transfixing mine again. I wasn't sure if it was the dim light or something else, but her eyes were different somehow, not quite the same as I remembered them. Then again, she and I had only talked at night one time before during a brief encounter in the parking lot after a science fair at our school. Maybe she just looked cuter in the dark.

I tried to gather my thoughts. "Okay," I said after a long pause. "You know about the other me. The vampire me."

"Yeah, we've met," she said pointedly. "Right before he killed me." I winced, then sighed. "But that wasn't actually you, right? He's like you, but *not* you. I thought he was at first."

I fought down the image that came to mind, my exact double surprising her and attacking her, taking her life. I then remembered the first time — the only time, in fact — that I had seen him, back when he first emerged from me in the hotel room. I'd spent the following weeks wondering just what he might be doing, and it was weird picturing someone who looked just like me doing things without my knowledge.

"What's he like?" I found myself asking.

Her expression hardened for a second, then became more thoughtful. "A bit of a dick, honestly," she said. I started to laugh, but I clammed up when she shot me a look.

"Sorry," I whispered, briefly feeling afraid again.

"You really don't know?" she asked.

"I… Well, not really. I assumed he was just like me, but a vampire. We only met once, and that was brief. Then he ran away."

"Well, that fits," she said, looking off to the side, but I wasn't quite sure what she meant. "But he was just… I don't know… kind of not all there. I mean you were always kind of weird…"

That stung, bringing back tons of memories of the times I'd tried to talk to her at school and failed miserably at coming across as cool, funny, or clever. Something on my face must have betrayed me, because she reached out with her hand and tried to reassure me.

"No, no, I just mean…" she began, then stopped, lowering her hand to the ground. "I guess I mean that it was kind of like he was you, but lesser. Like, missing something. Like he didn't have your sense of humor. I guess that's one example."

I still struggled to understand. "What's another one?"

She shook her head, looking frustrated, but then she brightened and pointed at me. "Okay, like there. What you did just there."

"What?"

"You asked me a question. Or, like earlier, when I was joking around, I saw you smile." I felt my face getting hot. "And that too!" she said eagerly, pointing at me again. "That's what I'm talking about. The other you wouldn't do that. He was just… well… *bluh.*"

"'Bluh?'" I asked.

"Dull. That's a good word for it." She folded her arms, and there was silence for a short time. We both seemed to be processing the things we'd been talking about, though I found my thoughts centering around the fact that I was sitting and having an almost normal conversation with someone who was a vampire. What was stopping her from lunging at my neck and killing me? And why was it that we were able to talk this freely now, but I'd never been able to carry on a normal conversation with her back when we were two ordinary teenagers at school?

"So," she said firmly, breaking the silence. "You still haven't told me very much. Like why he's here, why he exists. Why is there another you who happens to be a vampire?"

Brought back to the present, I again began to speculate. Why had my clone killed her in the first place, and why had he brought her back to life as a vampire? How was he even able to do that, when my friends and sisters and I never had been?

"I'm waiting," she said.

"Sorry," I said, shaking my head. "I'm still trying to figure all this out, too. But you're right. I do owe you some kind of explanation. As good as I can give one, anyway."

"Yes, you do." She raised her eyebrows, her smile beginning to return, which was a slight relief.

"Okay, okay. Let me think." I ran through all the stuff I had said at her grave earlier that night when I'd thought she was dead, everything about the vampire potion, how my sisters and friends had taken it when we were younger, causing us to become artificial vampires. Over the years, we had gone back and forth between being vampires and ordinary people, and that had eventually broken down to the point where we'd sworn never to do it again. The potion had somehow reasserted itself from within later, causing our vampire selves to emerge as separate beings, leaving us to either track them down and kill them or hide away and hope for the best. That had led to Elizabeth's death, but her reappearance this night had turned everything on its ear. Apparently, our clones were capable of making new vampires out of their victims, a development none of us had seen coming. It was a lot to take in.

But something was bugging me. Despite what Elizabeth had told me this night about my clone, I began to think that the reason he had killed Elizabeth must have been related to how I had felt about her before the emergence. I remembered Nick, my former friend who had also been one of the vampires, and how his clone had killed his ex-girlfriend. Whether the clone had done that out of spite or to protect us from being found out remained a mystery, but once I knew that my clone had killed the girl I'd always had a crush on, I'd kept wondering just why he'd done it. Unlike Nick's ex, Elizabeth hadn't known a thing about our past, and she and I had never been together even though I had spent years wishing desperately that we could. So did my clone turn her into a vampire hoping that doing so would make her become his lover?

The idea sickened me; I hated my clone. I regretted everything we had done as vampires and all the people we had killed, and the fact that our clones were out there doing the same thing was horrible to contemplate. I wanted nothing more than to wipe them all out, to finally put an end to all of the death and misery we had either directly or inadvertently brought upon our city. And now here I was having a conversation with another extension of that, the most beautiful girl I had ever seen transformed against her will into another instrument of death.

"Okay, look," I said, my voice deeper than usual. "Answer me two questions, and then I'll tell you everything I can."

Elizabeth straightened up, again positioning her legs beneath her. "Deal," she said simply.

I closed my eyes and looked down at my chest. "Did you kill someone tonight?" I asked the question as flatly as I could, almost as if it were a statement. I knew the answer as I asked it, or at least I thought I did.

"As a matter of fact, no," she said very firmly. I looked up at her, surprised. "Last night's feeding was enough for me." My face fell. "Yes, Ray," she said angrily, "I do kill sometimes. Just not all the time. Don't get all moral and judgmental on me. Don't you *dare.*"

My hair felt like it was standing up. "Okay. Sorry. You're… you're right. I guess I shouldn't be…" I trailed off, my eyes not leaving hers.

"Next question." It almost felt like we were back to our first encounter, with me feeling too terrified to speak. "Two seconds," she added.

"Are the two of you…" I started to blurt out, then froze mid-sentence. I was afraid to ask the question, more afraid of the answer. But she just continued to glare at me, not letting me off the hook. "You and the vampire me. Are you, well… together?" I finally managed to say.

She threw back her head and laughed, then struggled not to topple over as both of her hands went from supporting her upper body to covering her mouth. Recovering after a few seconds, she continued to smile, her eyes squinting similarly as she caught her breath. "I'm sorry," she said, still chuckling. She sighed comically, then said, "I think I liked the first question better."

The rest of the night was just as confusing, and it was cut short much sooner than I expected. We'd heard a bird start to chirp, which caused Elizabeth to swear as she looked up at the sky. She said that sunrise was coming, and she needed to get going quickly. I didn't want her to leave, and for more than one reason. First, I was so glad to have her back, plus it was nice to finally be able to talk to her, bizarre though the situation was. I also wanted to learn more about precisely what had happened to her and what was going on with my clone. I had been trying to give her the explanations I'd agreed to, but there just wasn't time.

We made plans to meet again the following night, and while I correctly assumed that she meant in this same place, the cemetery, it took me a moment to realize that this was where she was going to sleep during the day. Back when we were vampires — or as my old friend Carl had put it, "fake vampires versus real vampires" — we had slept either in the basement or in our house with garbage bags taped over the windows in order to hide from the sunlight. Had that or any of the other "vampire killers" (another term of Carl's) come into contact with us, the potion would immediately revert us back to regular humans.

But for Elizabeth, the situation was different. She was a real vampire, someone who had died and come back to life. And it wasn't like she could have just gone back to her parents' house and slept there. As far as they knew, she was dead, and I doubt they would have been happy to see her if she'd shown up as a monster. When I was younger, I'd known of the concept of vampires sleeping in coffins, but given my own less traditional experiences, that idea had faded to the back of my mind. So Elizabeth had to impatiently explain to me that yes, this was where she would in fact be sleeping.

Even more confounding was the manner in which she accomplished this. Given what I'd seen in movies and on TV, I assumed that this meant that she would have to dig back through the ground and make her way into her coffin. Presumably, that was how she'd gotten out in the first place. Instead, she did what looked like a cross between a magic trick and a special effect, and it freaked me out.

After saying goodbye to me, she turned her back, but as she did so, her entire body somehow warped and became flattened, then quickly slid downwards into the ground. It reminded me of something I'd seen in an old *Star Trek* rerun years before, where some evil alien woman disappeared by the use of special effects, which as near as I could figure out was done by the producers taking a freeze frame of the actress and rotating it until it appeared to vanish. To see something similar to this happen in real life was a bit too much to take, and I stood there for a few seconds, stunned.

Back in my mother's car, which I had "borrowed" in the middle of the night to visit Elizabeth's grave, I was surprised to find that the clock on the dashboard showed that it was only 5:40 a.m. Sunrise wouldn't be for another hour and a half, so apparently Elizabeth and I had been mistaken. Had we known that — and had I remembered to wear my watch when I was sneaking out of the house — we could have talked longer. I considered hurrying back to her tombstone, thinking that I could call out to her and bring her to the surface, but then I hesitated when my eyes fell upon the backpack that was on the passenger seat.

In it were, among other things, anti-vampire weapons, including a wooden stake. After Elizabeth had first pounced on me and pinned me down, and once I was able to think clearly enough after the initial shock of seeing her, I'd mentally kicked myself for not bringing that stake with me. I'd been defenseless, which by then I should have known better than to let happen. Our clones, the vampires, had been loose in Augusta for weeks, and going around at night without a weapon on me was a stupid move. Maybe I had just been too preoccupied with visiting the grave to realize my mistake until it was too late.

As I started up the car and headed home, I began to understand how lucky I had been. Had Elizabeth wanted to kill me, there would have been nothing I could have done to stop her. What's more, as upset as I had become that night, I was pretty much to the point where I was feeling suicidal enough not to put up much of a fight.

I probably could have gone back and talked to her more, but the thought of seeing her do that weird zooming effect again unsettled me. I had never seen a vampire do anything like that before, and it wasn't one of the abilities we'd had as vampires, at least as far as I knew. Susanna, my oldest sister and the one who had developed the vampire potion, had this annoying habit of not telling the rest of us all of our abilities and limitations at once, keeping some things to herself until she deigned it necessary to fill us in. And as for some of our other powers, such as being able to turn into bats, some of the other former vampires and I had begun to question the physical impossibility of such things, but Susanna wasn't very forthcoming. After things had fallen apart between us a couple of years earlier in 1987, she had become rather withdrawn and unhelpful.

Once back home, sneaking inside was a little more problematic than I expected. I cut the engine to the car and let it coast in neutral along the length of the driveway, carefully maneuvering it into position and parking it. As I crept toward the back door, our dog Scout woke up and, as usual, began to get excited that someone was around. He would bark at just about anything, and I did my best to placate him through the fence and keep him quiet.

I stealthily made my way in through the back door on the carport, turning the key as slowly as possible and then easing it out of the lock, but I almost dropped it when Scout let out one of his characteristic howls. I swore under my breath, afraid that he would wake my parents, and rather than gradually creeping back to my room as planned, I quickly tip-toed as lightly as I could, making it to my bedroom in a matter of seconds.

I locked my door and got into bed as fast as possible, hoping that I wouldn't hear my mother or father walking up the hallway to find out what was going on. After a few minutes, I hadn't heard them, and Scout had settled down.

It was difficult to process everything. Part of me was happy that Elizabeth was alive, but then, she wasn't really, was she? She was a vampire, which surely made her the enemy. At least, that was how I had gotten used to thinking of things ever since our clones had emerged from us. They were going around killing people, just as we had done when we ourselves had been the vampires, and the only way to make things right was to track them down and eliminate them. The guilt we had felt over what we had done only seemed assuaged by the notion that killing these murderous remnants of ourselves might somehow make up for everything.

But now, it was different. This unexpected development — that unlike us, our clones could actually create new vampires from their victims — meant that there could be countless monsters out there. The situation was much worse than we had imagined. I still felt the obligation to get rid of the vampires, and at least some of my friends felt the same way, I knew. We had to put an end to this nightmare somehow, and deep inside, I still felt that it was possible to do that.

What I didn't know at the time was that not all of us would make it out of this alive.

CHAPTER TWO

I was woken up the following day just a few minutes before noon by a knock on my bedroom door. My mother called out my name a couple of times before I groggily responded.

"Is everything okay?" she asked.

"Yeah," I groaned, projecting my voice towards the door. "Fine. I was just up really late last night." I flinched as the words came out, realizing that I shouldn't have admitted to being up at all. If she or my father had noticed any evidence of my sneaking out the night before and stealing the car, I had just blown my cover.

"Well, you can't stay up all night and sleep all day!" she said, her tone more resigned than harsh. Our relationship wasn't a close one; our conversations tended to be brief and without much depth. I was a sullen, morose teenager by this point, and I think that she and my father were used to us not connecting. Communication was never a very healthy thing in the Young household.

"Your dad and I are going out to Appling to see Eleanor and Howard," she said, referring to my aunt and uncle in the small Georgia town almost an hour's drive away from my native Augusta. "We can wait a little bit if you want to get up and come with us."

"No, that's okay," I said, sitting up in bed and stretching. "I've got some homework to do anyway." That was a lie; I really just needed some time to myself to work through everything that had happened. Lying to my parents wasn't difficult; I'd done it all my life, and I certainly never would have told them about the whole vampire thing. Those adventures always happened when they went out of town in the summer to attend the American Library Association conference. They both worked in libraries, so using such a scholarly excuse for staying home seemed legitimate enough.

The night before, I hadn't realized until I lay down just how exhausted I was, and despite how much my mind was racing, I'd fallen asleep pretty quickly. Truth be told, part of me was surprised that I was waking up on this day at all given what I had originally planned to do the night before.

As I ate lunch, I mulled things over, shuddering once when I remembered that my plan had included the possibility of committing suicide. The other former vampires and I had learned that the reason our clones hadn't attacked us was that if we were to die, the clones would die, too. They were some sort of weird manifestations of our vampire selves, an unexpected side effect of the potion, identical to us in both form and thought.

Somehow, they were linked to us, and the two of us whose clones had already been killed had described this strange sensation of feeling a thread detach from themselves at the moment of death. For Susanna, this had happened when some unknown person had killed her clone, possibly someone who had been attacked but had managed to destroy it instead. It might also have been the work of some anti-vampire vigilantes, the sort of which had risen up in the city back in 1987 to fight us when we were the vampires.

The other clone had been killed by its original "host" (as my friend Tim had once termed it), Nick. He had been a friend of mine in seventh grade at my previous school, a rebellious skater kid who listened to punk rock and had no patience for people he termed "posers," fake types who were only interested in being mainstream and popular. I'd liked him, but after I'd roped him into joining us as vampires and the subsequent fallout that culminated in all of us almost killing each other, he'd made it quite clear that he wanted nothing more to do with me.

Still, armed with the information Nick had passed on about how he killed his vampire self, I hoped to track down my own clone and eliminate him as well. This proved difficult, and after I found out that he killed Elizabeth, I concluded that the only way to get rid of him was to kill myself, therefore "erasing" him. As bad as things had gotten, I even felt I deserved that. After all, I had done horrible things during my time as a vampire, killing dozens of people. My clone was out doing the same thing, completely out of my control, and I needed to make it stop.

As I lay on my bed after lunch thinking through all of this, I felt frustrated over how confused and conflicted I was. Yes, killing myself might have eliminated my vampire double. But what about the bigger picture? I hadn't even thought about how upset my parents would have been had I succeeded, nor my sisters or anyone else. And even if I had gotten rid of the other Ray, that still left five other clones. One was based on my other sister, Carolyn, another on her ex-boyfriend, Damon. And then there were the ones who had come from my other old friends: Carl, Dennis, and Tim. Each of us had dealt with the situation in our own way, some by trying to engage the enemy, others by trying to avoid the situation and pretend that it would all go away. I had hoped to attempt the former.

This new development, the fact that the vampire Elizabeth even existed, threw a wrench into everything. How was it that my clone had been able to bring her back to life as a vampire? Back when my sisters and friends were vampires, we'd just flown around the city, killing as we wished, seemingly without any consequences. The people we killed didn't come back as the undead, unlike in traditional vampire lore. We had encountered some "real" vampires, people who had died and come back, so even though we knew that such a thing was possible, it wasn't supposed to apply to us or the clones.

I kept going in circles thinking about this, and eventually, I had to tell myself to stop. I realized that I was avoiding one big question: Should I kill Elizabeth now that she was a vampire? The idea was unbearable; I'd loved her more than anything when she was alive. I'd been too scared to tell her, afraid that she'd reject me, even afraid of how I would be ridiculed by my classmates if that happened. I'd seen it happen to a geeky kid I knew at school named Aaron after he'd tried to ask out Annie, one of the popular cheerleaders, how everyone had ragged on him for thinking he had a chance with such a pretty girl. I didn't want that to happen to me, so I stayed hidden, my desire kept secret.

Thinking of that now felt so strange, so small. I'd wanted Elizabeth so much, just as any 15-year-old boy would want to be with a girl. She wasn't part of the popular crowd; she and her two friends Melinda and Helen were some weird kind of off-shoot from both the pretty cheerleaders and the more mundane, well-behaved good girls. I didn't fit in with any of the boys at school either; I wasn't tough and jerky enough to hang with the bad boys, nor did I have any interest in being with Aaron and his nerdy friends. I could sometimes get along with any of these groups, but I never felt like I belonged. But again, all of this thought of high school cliques felt amazingly trivial to me now.

I was faced with a dilemma, one unprecedented in my life so far. A girl I'd liked at school had died and been brought back to life as a vampire, and this was a problem. I recalled the novel *Dracula,* how a girl in that book had been turned into a vampire and had to be killed. The idea was that once this beautiful, pure person had been turned into such a monster, it was better to destroy her rather than to allow her to continue on as an undead beast that fed on people night after night.

The noble men in that story had to do their duty, and I reluctantly began to accept that the same was true for me.

The more I pondered this, the more angry I got at myself, particularly for the way I had lost perspective. I was supposed to be tracking down my clone and killing him. That had been the plan the night before, and Elizabeth's sudden appearance had distracted me. I still needed to kill the vampire version of me, and with or without the others' help, maybe I could take down the rest of the clones, too. The fact that they could create new vampires made this all the more urgent, and Elizabeth having become one of those shouldn't have changed my mission. If anything, it reinforced it: I couldn't let what happened to her continue to happen to more people.

But there was one major difficulty, one that had plagued mine and my friends' efforts so far: Most of us were too young to drive. Stealing my mother's car wasn't something I had ever done before last night, and the only one of us who had recently turned sixteen, Dennis, seemed to have withdrawn from the rest of us and wouldn't return my phone calls. My two older sisters were no help, either: Susanna lived miles away in Columbia, South Carolina, and Carolyn had so far been too scared to get involved. So it was one thing to declare myself some kind of determined vampire hunter who was going to save my city from all of this death and destruction, but actually getting out there and accomplishing anything was another matter.

This limited mobility came into play after my parents came back late that evening. It was well after sunset by then, and while Elizabeth and I had agreed to meet up at the cemetery again, I had no way of getting there. But I was fine with that; I had no intention of continuing our conversation. She might change her mind and decide to kill me after all, or for all I knew, she'd been intentionally distracting me from killing my clone and was in league with him, despite the few things she had said to the contrary the night before.

"I just don't care," she'd said. "About him, I mean. He... How do I put this... I guess I just didn't really understand his intentions toward me." She'd paused, a quick smile flashing across her face as she continued to look at the ground. "Unlike you."

This had made my heart leap, mostly from embarrassment, which increased when she shot me an impossibly cute glance. Before I could interject, she pursed her lips as she fought down her smile, then quickly continued talking as she looked away. "But yeah, he just seemed... It was like he just wanted to order me around more than actually talk to me."

I had started to ask her what she meant by that, but that was when we had been interrupted by the bird chirping and mistakenly believed that sunrise was on its way. And since our encounter, I had run through that part of the conversation in my head several times, not entirely sure what to make of it.

This most recent time, I had been lying down on my bed again, and I was starting to daydream, maybe even to drift off to sleep. The scene of us talking played out in my mind again, but after her "unlike you" quip, she suddenly became fierce, her eyes lighting up like blue fire as she jumped at me, fangs extended.

I bolted awake, my heart pounding. I rolled over on the bed, wondering what to make of that. Had it been a premonition? I was psychic, though the intensity of that had varied over the years. I had first been introduced to my powers by Dennis, who had similar ones, and it later turned out that Tim had them, too. During our last summer as vampires, our powers had increased tremendously, probably because of something the potion had done to us. What had once been vaguely accurate premonitions and the ability to make small misfortunes happen to people we didn't like ballooned into massive abilities like clairvoyance and mind control. Those had died down once we were human again, but I still had some powers. The annoying thing was that I didn't always know when they were real or just my imagination.

My thoughts were interrupted when I heard a tapping sound come from my window, which was right next to my bed. Startled, I jumped up and threw back the corner of the drapes before I knew what I was doing. Had I been thinking more clearly, I might have hesitated, been more cautious. Focusing through my own reflection, I could barely make out Elizabeth's features, which became more visible as she leaned in closer. Her expression was hard to read; it seemed to be a mixture of playfulness and anger, maybe triumph. I wasn't sure what to do.

"Hi!" I barely heard her say through the glass, but even that barrier couldn't mask her tone. It wasn't a friendly "hi;" it was more sarcastic and impatient.

I pulled the curtain behind my head, then stood up between it and the window in order to undo the latch. I slowly lifted the frame, afraid that it might make too much noise and alert my parents. I was pretty sure that they had already gone to bed, but I didn't want to take any chances.

Once the frame was far enough up, I leaned on the windowsill and looked at Elizabeth through the screen. "What are you doing here?" I whispered.

"Looking for you," she said quietly. "I got tired of waiting." She didn't sound happy.

"Sorry," I whispered, unsure what to do next. I began to picture the wooden stake that was in the drawer of my night table just a few feet to my right. "I… I couldn't make it. My parents only just now went to bed." It was more or less true.

"I see," she said flatly, then looked down for a moment. Looking back up, she added, "Well?"

"Well…" I said uncertainly.

"Are you going to come out and talk to me or what?"

"How did you get here?" I asked.

"How do you think? I flew. Still getting used to the whole turning into and being a bat thing, though I have to admit that it's kinda neat."

The playfulness had returned to her voice, and she began to smirk. "Wanna see?" She began to step back from the window, turning her body slightly and lifting her arms from her sides theatrically, her smile broadening.

"No!" I said loudly, then caught myself, again trying to keep quiet. "No, really. It's okay. I don't." I realized that, like seeing her do that weird zooming effect down into her grave the night before, seeing her transform into a bat would really bother me. I wasn't entirely sure why; maybe it was just another reminder of what she had become.

She seemed disappointed, also confused. "Okay…" she said cautiously. "Again, are you coming out?"

"Give me a minute." I moved from behind the curtain, out of her sight. I sat on the bed for a moment and tried to figure out what to do. Part of me was glad to see her again, and it wasn't every night that a beautiful girl showed up at my bedroom window and asked me to come outside. But I was also scared of what she might do. Aside from the fact that she didn't seem happy about me standing her up, there was also my fear that she might be planning to kill me.

I leaned over and opened the drawer, pulling out the wooden stake. After putting on my blue denim jacket, I put the stake into one of the inner pockets and started to head for the window, then stopped and thought. I pulled back one drape and got a glimpse of Elizabeth, who was still crouching down close to the screen.

As she looked up at me, I said quietly, "Hang on. Gotta get something else. Back in a minute." I could just make out her impatient expression through the screen.

I made my way to the kitchen, not sneaking exactly, but still wanting to be quiet. It was only about 10:00 on a Saturday night, so even if my parents did hear me, that wouldn't be a big deal. But I didn't want them to get curious enough to get up and ask me what I was doing. I also didn't want to explain to them why I was taking the garlic powder from my mother's spice rack.

"Ray, please put that stuff back inside," Elizabeth said, drawing back from me. We were standing on my front lawn not far from my bedroom, just after I had clumsily made my way out of it. Sneaking out through my window wasn't something I had done before, and while I had managed to get outside eventually, I had also accidentally let the screen fall out from its hinges near the top of the frame, not used to how it worked. For now, Elizabeth and I had rested it on top of the large bush in front of the window, the idea being that I would figure out how to put it back into place once I was ready to go back inside.

"What?" I asked stupidly, surprised that she had sensed what I was carrying.

"The garlic," she said, pointing towards my jacket and looking both angry and scared. "I really don't..." She coughed suddenly, her forehead creasing as she covered her mouth. After shaking her head for a second and blinking back tears, she continued, "Please, just put it away. I can smell it. I really don't like it."

I was surprised that she could smell it through the plastic container it was in, but apparently she could, and I found myself feeling guilty. Back in the kitchen, I had popped the lid briefly to make sure that there was enough inside and that I could use it on her if necessary, and maybe that had contributed to my failed attempt at stealth.

"I just..." I didn't know how to continue.

"You don't need that, Ray. I promise I'm not going to kill you. I told you that last night. Please, just trust me."

She seemed sincere, even hurt by the notion that I might not believe her. And even in the pale, dim glow from the nearby streetlights, she looked as impossibly beautiful as ever, so it was hard for me to say no to her. Despite my fear of her, there was something deep down in me that knew that I probably wouldn't be able to kill her even if I needed to.

"You won't hurt me, either," she said, her thoughts echoing mine. "I know you won't."

This surprised me for half a second, and then I laughed slightly. "Well, I guess that still works, too," I said to myself.

"What does?"

"I'll explain in a little bit," I said, still smiling and turning back to look at my open window. Turning back to her, I said, "Okay. You win. Wait here." She nodded, looking relieved but still a bit angry.

Getting back into my room was easier without the screen in the way, but I worried briefly that I might have trouble getting it put back on. Once inside, I took the garlic powder out of my jacket pocket and placed it onto the floor near the window, just in case I wound up scrambling back inside for it later on. I then reached into my jacket and felt for the stake, which I decided to leave in there.

A memory sprang up in my head, and I winced, again feeling mad at myself for what may have been a past mistake. I had been wondering how Elizabeth had suddenly shown up at my house, and then I remembered that back when we were at school together, I had told her where I lived. I'd even told her the street names; we lived at an intersection in my neighborhood. It was just something that happened to come up in a conversation among me and some other classmates, including her, and at this moment, I regretted the fact that I'd given her that information. Apparently, she had remembered it, and that may have put me and possibly even my family in danger.

Back outside, seeing that she looked more relaxed now that the garlic was gone, I tried to gauge the situation. I still didn't trust her, and something else had been bugging me, too.

"How did you know how to find me?" I asked her, having directed her to follow me to the far end of the house and toward the driveway. There, we could talk more freely, my parents' bedroom being on the other end of the house.

"Well, you told me where you lived a while ago," she said, sounding innocent at first, but there was also a hint of haughtiness in there somewhere. I couldn't help but notice that once again, what she was saying was very close to what I had been thinking earlier. That was another one of my psychic powers, but it wasn't something I had much control over. Sometimes it seemed like I was thinking something because someone near me was thinking it, but more often, it was more like my thoughts were being projected, somehow broadcast outward. Back when we were closer friends, Dennis and I had many of these "I was just thinking that!" moments, well beyond the point where it could be dismissed as coincidence.

"Yeah," I said, "but how did you know which room was mine?"

She laughed a little, glancing down at the pavement. "I'm not entirely sure," she said, her tone having gone kind of musical. "It's…" She looked up at the sky. "I think it's some kind of vampire sense, if that makes sense."

I laughed a little at the way she emphasized that second "sense" because she knew it sounded redundant. "Are you…" I began, then hesitated as our eyes met. "Are you psychic?"

"No," she said, but she seemed unsure of herself, maybe even ashamed. "I mean, maybe. I didn't use to be. But maybe I am now. I really don't know." She shrugged, again looking and acting quite adorable. It was enough to make me forget my fear of her for the moment.

I scrutinized her for a few seconds, the conversation pausing long enough for her to look at me pointedly and ask, "What?"

"Just… Well, how do I put this…" I held back again, knowing how a normal person might react to what I was about to say. But Elizabeth was far from being a normal person, especially now that she had become what she was. So I gave up and blurted out what I needed to: "I actually am psychic. Like, in a real way."

I expected her to laugh at me; she probably would have if I'd said this to her before. But instead, she just squinted a little, then breathed in through her nose, her lips shifting to one side. "Really," she said or asked; it was hard to tell. "Okay." She swayed back and forth, holding her arms to her chest loosely as she looked to the side and said vaguely: "So…"

"So…?" I asked, not sure where this was going.

"So you're a psychic guy who used to be a vampire, and now there's a vampire copy of you running around the city killing people and turning them into vampires, including me, and here we are talking about this like it's perfectly normal, and…" She drew out that last word in a silly way, her eyes fixed on mine, then threw her arms out and spun around, again fixing me with a gaze once she'd done a full circle.

"I guess it is kind of insane, huh?" I said.

"Little bit." She said this with a slight narrowing of her eyes, which I realized looked smaller than I remembered. I must have started staring, which led her to ask, "What?"

"Nothing, nothing," I said, feeling embarrassed and looking down.

She sighed. "Well, when do I get the rest of my explanation?"

I sighed back. "I know, I know. I'm sorry. I guess I'm not really good at this. I've kept it secret for so long, and, well, the people who knew about it already knew about it, if that makes sense."

"Kinda," she said. "I suppose I can understand that."

And so we talked for a few hours, having relocated to the driveway of the empty house across the street because Scout had started barking at us. No one lived there; the owners were an extremely wealthy couple who had another house in a more affluent neighborhood, so well off that they hadn't bothered to sell their previous home for a few years now.

I told her everything I could, a more concise version of the big speech I'd made at her grave the night before when I'd thought she was dead. As I told the tale, though, I occasionally left bits out, saying that they weren't important or weren't interesting. Sometimes that was true, but what I found was that there were parts I was ashamed to tell her, like how much I had enjoyed being a vampire at the time.

I hated that so much now, the fact that I had those memories, how I had been such a merciless beast and been responsible for so many deaths. This led me to choose my words carefully, to try to gloss over some things, but Elizabeth didn't let me get away with that after a while.

"Ray, you can tell me the truth," she said once. "I do know what this feels like, you know."

"I know! And that's what sucks so much about it all! I never meant for you to get caught up in this! I didn't think you would end up being turned into…" I broke off, not wanting to say it.

"A vampire," she said, slightly stern. "That's what's happened. It's not something I asked for, either. But it is what it is."

I bowed my head; it touched my knees, which I had been holding up to my chest as we sat on the lawn by the driveway. Part of me wanted to cry, but I didn't want to look that weak in front of her.

"I still don't understand how that even happened," I said, my voice pitched lower than usual. "When we were vampires, the people… our victims didn't come back. They stayed dead."

"Is that what you wish had happened to me?"

"What? No! I mean… I mean, I hate the fact that you got turned into this… this thing…"

She sighed again, this time sounding more frustrated.

"Fine. Vampire. There, I said it." And I still hated it. After a long pause, I continued, "So, putting aside the fact that it should have been impossible… Well, see, that's another thing I wonder about. What did the other vampires have to say about the whole thing?"

"Who? Oh, them. I don't know; not much, I guess."

"And how did they figure out that they could make their own vampires? Did they just try it one time and then, boom, it worked?"

"I think that's what happened," she said. "I wasn't there at the beginning. I mean, I wasn't the first. I wasn't clear on the exact order of things, like who got made into a vampire when."

I considered this for a few seconds. "God, I wonder how many there are by now."

"Not a whole lot," she said, her eyebrows raised and her expression resigned. "Well, at least in Ray's group. No idea about the others."

"No idea?"

"The other people you've been telling me about. Carl, Tim, the other one, your sisters, all them. They weren't around."

"What? Why not? Where were they?"

"Like I said, no idea. That was something Ray — the other Ray — was so pissed about. None of them stuck around; they went off on their own and refused to do what he wanted."

"I see," I said. That wasn't how I had pictured things at all; I had assumed that all of the clones had stayed together and were a single unit, planning and plotting their evil deeds just as we had done in the past. But apparently, that wasn't the case.

"That makes sense, now that I think about it," I said. "It's not like we were all on the best of terms in the first place."

"Yeah," she said. "Given everything that you've told me, I can see that there was a lot of bad blood between you." After a pause, she added quietly, "Not sure if that was a pun or not."

I laughed, then caught myself, wanting to keep things serious. "There was some resentment from Susanna the older I got, how I tried to be more in charge, and Carolyn accused me more than once of..." Something else crossed my mind, and it baffled me that it hadn't occurred to me before. "And Damon! Her ex-boyfriend! By the time the emergence happened, those two hated each other. Or at least, she hated him. So I guess it wouldn't really work for their vampire selves to just hang around in a big happy group together. I never even thought of that. I just always assumed..." I trailed off. "Well, okay. So that's new."

"The vampire you was pretty much a control freak," she said, "that's for sure."

"That bad, huh?"

Her eyes went wide, but again, something about them looked strange to me, slightly off somehow. "Completely!" she said. "Finally

I was like, 'I'm not your little soldier, asshole,' and I was out of there." As she said this, she made an upward motion with her hand, I think to indicate flying. "Took a while to shake him off, too. He wasn't about to let it go. I think it was the others calling him back that finally got him to give up."

I pictured this scenario, then asked, "So, who were the others? Were they all vampires he made himself?"

"Yeah. There was a Chinese girl named Kay... or was she Japanese? Something like that." She then rolled her eyes and started to speak again. "Gh--" She stopped suddenly, appearing to choke as she mouthed another word or two, then stopped, holding a hand to her chest and shaking her head quickly.

"Are you okay?"

"Yeah," she said, laughing slightly. "Not sure what happened there. That's what I get for being racist, I guess."

"I didn't think you were."

"Well, it kind of was, what I was saying there. Like the whole 'all oriental people look alike' thing. That's just... tacky."

"I suppose." I didn't have much of an opinion when it came to race. Truth be told, growing up, I didn't have very much exposure to other races; my upbringing was mostly, though not exclusively, among white people. I didn't have anything against black people or Asians and such, but I also didn't know very much about them given my limited experience with them and beyond what I saw on TV. In fact, the family who owned the property where we were sitting was Korean, but I only knew that because my parents had told me. Like what Elizabeth had implied earlier, I had trouble telling the different varieties of Asian people apart, and I didn't learn until much later that referring to them as "oriental" was considered offensive to them. It was ignorance, but not in a malicious way. I didn't think of the people I was brought up with as better, just normal. Anything that deviated from that, whether it was race, religion, or even someone's accent, was strange and different, but not necessarily wrong.

"Oh, and that's another thing I wanted to tell you," she said, changing the subject. "Something interesting that happened with the other you. You remember that time back at school, the swimming party we went to at Chris's house?"

I certainly did. It was the first and only time I had seen her in a bathing suit, and given how attracted I was to her, it was a huge turn-on. I had been to pool parties with my classmates before when I was younger, but back then, there wasn't anything sexual about it; I was too young for thoughts like that. But by the time this particular party came around, it was near the end of eighth grade, my hormones were through the roof, and my crush on Elizabeth was in full swing. I'd wanted her, fantasized about her, and imagined all kinds of scenarios in which we might get together, some innocent in nature, some not. I didn't dare say any of this to her, though; I simply answered, "Yes."

"And Jay forgot to bring any sunscreen, so you let him use yours. I just always thought that was nice of you, especially given how Helen and Melinda were to him about it when he tried to ask them if he could borrow theirs. I'd forgotten mine, too, and they were fine with letting me use it, but when he asked them, they were all mean to him and told him off. Melinda was like, 'No, you can just burn!'" She did a pretty accurate impression of Melinda's snobby, clipped manner of speaking. "I went along with it, but I felt bad for him."

I remembered this, though I hadn't thought about it for a long time. It hadn't seemed like a big deal to me back then, nor had it surprised me that Helen and Melinda had acted like that. Elizabeth was usually nice enough, but I never cared for her two friends, who had always been mean, and not just to me. Jay was one of the group of geeky misfits in our class, someone whom most people didn't like, and it wasn't unusual for people to snub him or his small group of friends. My feelings toward them fluctuated from contempt to indifference, but on this occasion, I wasn't cruel enough to withhold my sunscreen.

"So anyway," Elizabeth continued, "I happened to think of this when... Well, the other Ray was going on with me and the other vampires about our abilities, what we could do and couldn't do, like not being able to be out in the sun, or it would kill us. He was being very, I don't know, matter of fact about it… Actually, that's not the right word. Just very cold, or bossy… That was it. Just like, 'this and this and this…'"

I tried to picture it, my double rattling off the rules and regulations of what it was to be a vampire, much like Susanna had done when we were younger. I nodded, and she continued her story.

"It was just really dull. It was informative, sure, but I felt like I was in some classroom. So when the thing about sunlight came up, I remembered the swimming party thing, then just kind of couldn't help myself and blurted out: 'What if we use your sunscreen?' I expected a laugh or at least some kind of recognition, but he just looked at me, completely baffled."

"He did?"

"Yeah. So… and I guess I shouldn't have done this, but I pushed it, wanting to make the joke clear, so I said, 'Like that time at that party when you let Jay use your sunscreen. You were generous enough with it then!' It wasn't going over well, and the others were looking at me like I was crazy. But it was his response that was the weirdest part: 'That wasn't me.' And then he just looked away, all dismissive, and kept on with his class on the finer points of vampire etiquette or whatever. I think that was the first time I started to get fed up with him."

"That's interesting. He really said that? 'That wasn't me?'"

"Yep. I understood a bit more when he and I talked alone a little later; he wasn't being quite as annoying and all Army-general-ish then. He explained how he wasn't actually you, but someone separate. And for some reason, he genuinely did not remember that thing at the swimming party. I thought that was weird."

"It is. I mean, I remember it, so why wouldn't he? I thought we had the same memories."

"I think you do. Maybe just not all of them."

"I wonder why," I said. "Maybe he's… Hmm."

"What?"

"Like, not just my vampire self, but my evil self? Only my evil parts, not the rest of me. I don't know. It sounds stupid."

"Not necessarily. It wouldn't be that much weirder than everything else we've been talking about."

"Fair enough." There was an awkward silence, and I found myself at a loss as to how to continue the conversation. "So…" I managed to say, but I couldn't think of how to follow that.

"So."

"Was that enough of an explanation for you?"

We talked for a while longer, but then I realized that I needed to get back inside soon. For one thing, I had no idea how long we had been talking or what time it was, and I began to get nervous. Even though things had finally changed enough between us to where I felt like I could actually talk to her, it still felt strange, and the entire situation was so bizarre that I was still trying to get used to it. I needed to be alone with my thoughts.

I also remembered that I hadn't locked my bedroom door, which made me fear that at any moment, I might see a light come on through my window across the street, my parents having discovered my sneaking out. That didn't happen, but in the future, I made myself remember to lock the door whenever I did leave. Tonight would turn out to be the first of many nights spent sneaking out, both to talk to Elizabeth and for other reasons.

In fact, the following night would prove to be very interesting indeed.

CHAPTER THREE

Sunday was a strange day. I was exhausted by the time Carolyn took me to the cemetery in the afternoon, something I had initially tried to get out of, but she insisted that I go through with it. This was something we had agreed to a couple of days before, that once she got back into town after visiting a friend in Athens, she would take me there so I could say my proper goodbyes to Elizabeth. Of course, those were plans we had made before I knew that she had come back as a vampire.

As for how I felt about that, it was a weird mixture of emotions, and they tended to fluctuate. On the one hand, I was glad that she wasn't truly dead and that I could see her and talk to her, but I also hated the fact that she had been turned into a bloodthirsty killer. But even that wasn't the whole story.

She had explained to me the night before that yes, she had killed, but she didn't always do that. Sometimes, she just wounded people and flew away; it wasn't necessary to drain a person's entire blood supply in order for her to satisfy her hunger. This was something she had learned early on and even passed along to the rest of my clone's group of vampires.

In the past, my friends and I had almost always killed, drinking as much blood as we could get, then leaving the bodies to be found later. That always made it obvious where we had been, so we were constantly trying to vary the locations of our attacks in order to outmaneuver the authorities. Since their emergence, the clones seemed to be doing the same thing, and I'd tried to figure out some pattern to their movements according to the nightly news reports of where bodies had been found. This had only proven barely successful.

But Elizabeth had demonstrated to the group that it was in fact preferable to wound and take small amounts of blood. That way, there wouldn't be as much physical evidence to go on, and they would be harder to find. I was intrigued by how intelligent this was of her, to say nothing of sneaky, but even that bugged me, too.

I had always known that she was smarter than she let on back at school, and while that made her interesting, it also made her dangerous, at least now. I still didn't fully trust her, and I'd decided to continue to bring my wooden stake with me whenever we met up. I wouldn't threaten her with it, but I wasn't ready to let my guard down. For all I knew, she might suddenly turn on me and bite me, or maybe once she had learned all she needed to about my past and how it was relevant to her current situation, I wouldn't be useful to her anymore. Thoughts like this didn't usually run through my head when we were together, but once we were apart again, I became more suspicious.

I wasn't even sure if she was telling me the truth about not killing or if that was just to placate me. It had taken a while, but she had eventually grasped the concept of just how much I hated having been a vampire and the fact that she was one, too. She even sounded intrigued by the notion that there might be a way to "cure" her, an idea that came to mind not long before we'd said goodbye the night before. I had no idea if it would work, but I wondered if I could somehow get my hands on the antidote for our old vampire potion, then maybe it might change her back to human, just as it could do with us back in the day.

And yet, I didn't want to ask Susanna to whip up another batch of the antidote for this purpose. For some reason, I didn't want to tell her or anyone else about Elizabeth, which was part of why I'd hoped to come up with a lie to get out of going to visit her grave with Carolyn. As I had thought about it while trying to fall asleep Saturday night, I concluded that I wanted to understand the situation more, to gather more facts before sharing them with anyone else. But it was deeper than that, and it took me a while to realize what the problem actually was: I felt guilty.

Elizabeth was a vampire. I had vowed to eliminate all the vampires, yet here I was making an exception for her. And why? Because she was pretty? Because I loved her so much? She hadn't threatened me yet, and it sounded like she wasn't exactly evil, but I just wasn't sure. I didn't know what to think. I wasn't even sure if I could bring myself to kill her or any other vampire; I hadn't killed anyone for years.

For the moment, it seemed that Elizabeth and I had called a truce. She wouldn't bite me, and I would allow her to continue to live and to feed, though I tried to be in denial about that last detail. And I had no idea how stable this arrangement was or how long it might last.

So on Sunday, I found myself riding along in Carolyn's car on the way to the cemetery, trying to work through all of the possibilities. I didn't talk much, which Carolyn probably assumed was because I was thinking about what to say to Elizabeth at the grave, which was more or less the case, just not in the way she thought.

"You sure you don't want me to come with you?" she asked me after parking the car. There were narrow, unmarked streets that wound throughout the cemetery, and she had parked not too far from Elizabeth's tombstone. I'd had to act like I didn't know exactly where it was at first, pretending I was going on some directions I'd heard from someone at school a while back.

"No, it's fine," I said, reaching for the door handle but then hesitating. Realizing that I was appearing too eager and not sullen enough, I acted like I was reluctant to continue.

"It's okay, Ray," Carolyn said, briefly reminding me of our mother. Often, particularly in recent years, she and I didn't get along at all and were likely to snipe at each other. But this was — as far as she knew — a tender and vulnerable moment for me, so she was being uncharacteristically nice and supportive. "You need to do this. To say goodbye."

"You're right," I said, faking sincerity. As I made my way out of the car and up the slight incline of the hill, I added under my breath, "You have no idea what happened the last time I tried to say goodbye to her." I smiled at this, realizing that it was kind of fun to be keeping this secret from my sister.

I approached the gravestone, which looked completely different in the daytime. The whole place looked different, everything seeming smaller and less intimidating than it had at night. I stopped a few feet short of the grave, occupying more or less the same spot from two nights ago.

"So, here we are again," I said quietly, smiling. My back was to Carolyn, so I was free to indulge in the playful mood I was suddenly in, but I still had to keep my voice down.

"Bear with me while I go through the motions to satisfy my sister. I don't know if you can hear me, but... Now, there's a thought." I clammed up, pondering the implications. It already felt weird enough to know that she was in fact just a few feet below the ground beneath me, though not a lifeless corpse like the ones in all the other graves. But what if she could actually hear me? What if I woke her up, and then she rose to the surface, only to be caught by the sunlight?

I shoved this notion aside when it began to lead to me imagining her bursting into flames; I couldn't bear envisioning that. So I just stood there, my left hand holding my right arm's wrist in front of me, a pose I sometimes saw people do at solemn occasions. I recalled some of the things I had said to her, or at least to the imaginary her, back before I knew that she was a vampire. And I thought about what had happened since then, the conversations we'd had.

Other things occurred to me, things I realized I wanted to ask her the next time I saw her. These weren't heartfelt and tender; I had questions for her. The past two nights had mostly consisted of answering her questions, so it felt fair to have my turn to put some to her. I started to head back to the car, but then I felt that I hadn't stayed for long enough. Again, this was a performance mostly for Carolyn's benefit, so it wouldn't be good to just stand there for a minute and then leave.

The fear over Elizabeth being caught by the sun reminded me of the sunscreen story she'd relayed to me the night before, which led me to think back to that swimming party in more detail. She had looked so damn sexy in her bathing suit, as had plenty of the other girls there, though I was still relatively young and new to thinking such things. In a sense, a lot of what I was thinking and feeling in those days was more like an imitation of how I'd known older kids to act and what they would say, but that didn't make the feelings any less real to me at the time.

So it was a pleasant memory, her in her one-piece red bathing suit. It was also interesting to see the rest of her appearance change from having been in the water, her normally perfectly styled hair going limp and her make-up being partly washed off. Some of the other girls, like Annie and the rest of the cheerleaders, never even went fully into the water because they didn't want to mess up their massively sprayed and sculptured hairstyles.

This began to remind me of a conversation with a friend from shortly before the party, but then my thoughts jumped back to the vision of Elizabeth getting out of the pool, toweling herself off and looking so different from what I was used to, yet still undeniably beautiful. And then something clicked in my head, something I realized I should have noticed before. I made a mental note of it, adding it to the list of things to talk to Elizabeth about when I saw her later that night.

I returned to Carolyn's car to find her fussing with her hair in the rearview mirror, then readjusting that into place. She had, incidentally, more or less the same color hair as Elizabeth, mostly blonde but with some traces of brown.

"You on your way to a hot date?" I asked her.

She rolled her eyes. "No. Just had something in my eye. A stray hair, I think. Feeling any better now?"

It took me half a second to realize what she meant. "Yes. Thanks. You were right. It felt good to get some things off my chest. Maybe now she can rest in peace." I stopped, realizing that I was spouting too many clichés to sound genuine.

"Any tears?" she asked, her tone slightly goading.

"No, just a few sniffles. Similar to tears, but they don't float."

She laughed, as did I. This was one of our long-running private jokes, things that no one but us found funny because they didn't know the context. It was based on an incident that happened several years earlier during one of our family's trips to the beach.

We had been staying at one of my father's friend's beach house, though the friend wasn't with us at the time. He had also let us borrow his boat, which the previous day we had taken out into the ocean, but my mother hadn't liked the roughness of the waves. So the following day, we instead journeyed along the inland rivers and inlets of coastal South Carolina, which were much more calm.

At one point when the water was shallow, my mother spotted something beneath the surface, which she pointed to after getting mine and Carolyn's attention. There was a handful of dark, rounded objects, and they seemed to be moving slowly. "Are those ducks?" my mother asked, seeming excited. "I think they are!"

As the boat drifted closer, Carolyn and I noticed around the same time that the supposed ducks weren't moving at all; it was just the ripples on the water making them appear to. "No, Mom," Carolyn said. "Those are rocks. Similar to ducks, but they don't float," she added sarcastically.

My mother was annoyed and embarrassed by this, but we found it hilarious. We'd gotten Susanna and my father in on the joke, too, but Carolyn and I were the ones who kept it going over the years, bringing it up whenever two things were compared. The second thing would always be described as similar to the first, "but they don't float." This, and our getting along and joking around in general, tapered off the older we got, just as our family trips did. But every now and then, we could still make each other laugh with these obscure references, like how we would refer to something annoying as a "panda butt," which came from slurring the phrase "pain in the butt."

As before, I had to wait until my parents had gone to bed before it was safe to sneak out through my window to see Elizabeth. She had shown up around the time we had agreed to, 10:00, but it took a little longer than that for my father to finally make it to bed.

Our plans were further compromised by the fact that Dr. Meng's house, unlike the night before, was lit up by several floodlights along its front. Elizabeth speculated that this was to discourage burglars or trespassers. "Maybe someone spotted us here last night," she said.

"I guess," I said. "Good thing they didn't call the police."

"Or there could be…" She broke off, stepping closer to the house and bending down, trying to look into one of the windows. I couldn't help but steal a glance at her ass. For a teenage boy, that was almost instinctual.

"I can't tell," she said, turning back and almost catching me in the act.

"Tell what?"

"I was thinking there might be a security system. Anyway, it doesn't matter. Can we go somewhere else, please? All this light is hurting my eyes."

At first I thought that this might be another vampire thing, a sensitivity to light, until I happened to look one of the floodlights dead on and was temporarily blinded. I winced, shielding my eyes. "Yeah, you're right." I walked a few paces to my right, turning so that the light was behind me. This was the most clearly illuminated that I had seen Elizabeth since she'd become a vampire, and it confirmed the suspicion I'd developed earlier in the day.

"So," I said, "not wearing make-up anymore?"

"What?" she asked quickly, looking surprised.

"I'd been wondering why you looked so different now. It's because…" I stopped because she'd suddenly clamped her palms over her face, then turned to one side.

"I know, I know," she said through her hands, sounding tense and upset.

"What?" I asked, stepping forward and grabbing one of her wrists, almost without thinking. I withdrew immediately, unsure of what I was doing.

She took her hands away, then glanced at me sideways, avoiding eye contact. She seemed genuinely upset, but I had no idea why. When I had imagined how this conversation would go earlier, I'd anticipated that she might applaud me or maybe even laugh at me for taking so long to notice the change. I was a little mad at myself for not realizing that her lack of cosmetics was why she had looked so different to me all along, but at the same time, I was proud of myself for finally figuring it out.

"You just had to point that out," she said angrily. "Goh…" she began, but then choked. She coughed a few times, clearing her throat.

"Are you okay?" Again, I drew closer to her, holding my hand up to her but stopping short of touching.

"Give me a second. Yeah." She shook her head, blinking a few times. "That's weird," she whispered, then added in her normal voice, "That's the second time that's happened."

"What's happened?" I was concerned for her, but I was also bewildered.

"Let me see," she said, looking thoughtful. "G--..." Her voice broke off again, this time less violently, and her eyes darted up for a split second. She seemed to be concentrating, then said, "Oh my G--..." The same thing happened. "Shit, really? I can't even say..." She stopped, looking frustrated.

"Can't say what?"

"That's just it. I can't. Let me see... Jee--..." She choked again, seeming to gag a little, then cleared her throat, looking more angry. "That's just bizarre."

"Wait..." I was beginning to understand. "You can't say the word 'God?' Or 'Jesus?'"

"Apparently not!" She looked at me directly, her expression beginning to soften, moving from anger to an almost baffled amusement. "I... I guess it's something to do with being a vampire."

"I've never seen anything like that before," I said, slightly relieved that she seemed less angry. "I mean, certainly not when we were vampires. Hell, you should have met my friend Carl. He was always cussing up and down, all 'God damn shit fuck' all the time."

She smiled weakly; apparently my brief spew of profanity had amused her. "Well I think I can still say some of those. Shit. Fuck. Cock."

I couldn't help but laugh. "Very ladylike of you," I said with a smile.

"Fuck off," she said, but she was also smiling. "Look, can we just get out of here? I'm still really not liking the spotlights out here."

"Where do you want to go?" I asked, but she had already headed toward the street. I caught up with her, and we paused at the end of the driveway. "We could walk down to the school, I guess," I offered, pointing to our right. "Bryant Elementary. It's a few blocks down that way."

"Works for me," she said resignedly, and we began walking along the side of the road.

We walked in silence for a while, and I tried to figure out what to say. I wanted to apologize for upsetting her, but I wasn't even sure why she had gotten so mad. I was just pointing something out that I'd noticed about her. Back when I knew her at school, she had always been exquisitely made up, so much that it was a little unnerving. Ever since I'd met her at the age of thirteen, she almost always looked perfect, unlike most of the other girls, who were still going through those early awkward stages and not knowing what did and didn't look good on them. But Elizabeth looked more like she had her own professional stylist. It was simultaneously intriguing and off-putting, she and the other girls often doing each other up during lulls in class and going on about what products they liked to use. But then, I had grown up with two older sisters, so I was used to the phenomenon even though I never really understood it.

"Look," I began, but she cut me off, holding up her hand. "No, listen!" I insisted. "I didn't mean to make you mad. I was just wondering why you quit wearing make-up, that's all."

She stopped walking and turned to face me, giving me a withering look. "Have you ever tried putting on make-up without a reflection?"

Finally, I understood. She hadn't chosen to stop wearing it; she wasn't able to. That had never occurred to me. Still, the way she'd worded things caused me to break into a smile. "Okay, think really hard about the logic of that question," I said to her. Her angry look softened again, her eyes narrowing as the smirk she was fighting back shifted to one side. I couldn't resist driving the point home: "I've never tried putting it on *with* a reflection, either."

"Okay, smart-ass," she said.

"It's just… I don't know. I've never really understood the point of putting colored gunk all over your… over one's face. I mean, I know it's to look pretty and all, but sometimes… You remember that nasty looking pink lipstick that Tammy used to wear in eighth grade?"

She laughed and nodded, then rolled her eyes. "Oh, poor little Tammy."

"Yeah! And I remember thinking, if you think you're going to attract a boy with that…"

"And there it is," she interrupted. "Typical male."

"What?"

"You all think that it's all about you." She turned and began walking again.

Catching up to her, I asked, "What do you mean? 'All about you?' Girls make themselves pretty so they can attract a mate."

"Right, because we all live in an episode of *Wild Kingdom.*"

"Okay…" I managed to say, recovering from the admittedly good comeback.

"Has it ever occurred to you that maybe we do it just because we like it?"

"I… No, not really. But I guess I can see that. I remember you and Helen and Melinda always doing each other up in class and all…" I said this with a condescending tone, miming the way they would hold their various cosmetics close to their faces, usually hunched over small mirrors.

She sighed. "It's just one of our things. Girls do it, whether you understand it or not."

Her tone was becoming more bitter, so I tried to salvage things. "Well, you always looked better than the others. I mean, how you did it and all. Kind of made you look older, more mature."

"Hmm," she said. "Probably because I got an earlier start on it than them." After a short pause, she added, "I suppose you could thank my sister for that."

This surprised me. "Your sister? I didn't know you had one. Older or younger?"

"Older," she said. "She died."

I stopped in my tracks. "Oh, crap. I'm sorry. I didn't know." Seeing that she hadn't stopped walking, I hurried to catch up to her again. "Really, I'm sorry."

"It's okay," she said, the pitch of her voice going up briefly. "Most people don't know. I usually don't talk about it."

I didn't know what to say. I had known her for over two years, but not once had this come up, and I began to realize just how little I knew about her and her family. I'd admired her for so long, wanting so desperately to get close to her, but when it all came down to it, I barely knew her.

I was just about to say something along these lines and to apologize yet again, but all of a sudden, I heard a car coming up the road behind us. Its headlights cast our shadows along the street, veering off to the right as the car got closer, and it was moving pretty quickly.

Just as the car zoomed past us, I caught a brief glimpse of some guy leaning out of the passenger side window and shouting something excitedly, but I couldn't make out the words. It sounded something like *"Hi thirty-six!"* followed by an extended *"woo!"* The sound of it was distorted by the Doppler effect as the car went on, just as a car horn or siren would have been. The whole display was obnoxious, not to mention a mood killer.

After a few seconds, I heard more noises farther up the road, a loud bang followed by the sound of breaking glass. I realized what had happened: The guy had thrown something, probably a beer bottle, at a street sign. I had heard stories of some of the more badly behaved boys at school, particularly upperclassmen who were the older brothers of some of my classmates, doing things like this.

"Rednecks," Elizabeth said with contempt.

"Yeah," I added, but I stopped short of what I was about to say next. I was going to mention our classmate Kirby, his friends, and their older brothers from our school, but given what she and I had just been talking about, I wasn't sure if bringing up siblings was a good idea. And I was angered by the interruption, how our conversation had been derailed. Still, I felt a small satisfaction when I heard a police siren in the distance, and I hoped that whoever those jerks were, they were just about to get pulled over for speeding.

We eventually made it to the school, though the walk had been longer than I'd anticipated. By car, it would have been just a few minutes, but I was bad at judging the difference between driving speed versus walking speed. Still, Elizabeth and I had plenty of other things to talk about, including one of the main things I'd been meaning to ask her: where my clone was hiding.

"I really don't know if I should tell you that," she said in a low voice.

"Why not?"

"It's… It's not safe."

"What isn't safe?" This was beginning to make me suspicious. "Elizabeth, you know what I have to do. I can't let him keep going on killing people. What, are you trying to protect him or something?"

Once again, she stopped briefly to turn and glare at me. Then she rolled her eyes and let out an aggravated sound, then kept walking.

"Well?" I pressed.

"I'm not trying to protect him," she said angrily. Then she added more softly, "Just… trying to protect *you,* I guess."

"Me? From what?"

"Oh, I don't know," she said sarcastically. "Getting killed?"

This touched me at first, but then I saw it as misguided. "Elizabeth, I told you. My clone can't kill me. If I die, so does he."

"But there are other vampires besides him! What are you going to do, bust in there like Rambo and wipe them all out on your own?"

I didn't want to admit that I had in fact had fantasies along those lines, particularly just after my clone had killed her. Rather than a machine gun, my weapons would be things like those used by the vampire hunter Van Helsing. Hearing her disdainful tone made me question the plausibility of such an idea.

Still, with a little more prying, I finally got her to reveal the location of the hideout. I didn't recognize the name Sibley Mill, but once she described the place, I knew where she meant. It was this very old, very large brick building not far from downtown, one that I had seen many times from the outside when I happened to be driven by it. It looked almost like a castle, with these small, rectangular turrets on top, and one tall tower that was the remains of an old chimney.

According to my father, the place used to be some kind of Confederate building, apparently something to do with the Civil War. American history wasn't a strength of mine, so I barely listened to his explanation, but I did retain the knowledge that it was now a factory used for making jeans, or maybe just the material for making jeans. For all I knew, the jacket I was currently wearing had come from there.

I mentioned this to Elizabeth, and she told me that yes, part of the building was still used for that, but there were other parts that were disused, including one far wing where my clone and his minions hid. Picturing the place in my mind, I realized that choosing that location made sense. One feature that had always caught my eye was that one could see where there used to be windows all around it, but they had been bricked up, the outlines of the frames still visible in the way that the newer bricks, while the same brownish-orange color, didn't quite match up to the rest of the walls. The interior was probably perfectly shielded from any sunlight.

"It's what I would have done," I said.

"You can't get there on foot anyway," Elizabeth said. "There's a fence, and they lock it up at night. We could only get in and out through a broken door on the roof."

"Damn," I said, regretting for the first time not being able to turn myself into a bat anymore. "There's got to be another way in."

"Not that I know of," she said resignedly, and I wondered if she was telling the truth. Suddenly, her face lit up. "Oh. Oh!"

"What?" I hoped she had remembered another entrance.

"I just remembered…" She broke off, gathering her thoughts. "So that's what that meant. Well, that's interesting."

After she didn't say anything for a few seconds, I asked impatiently, "Care to share it with the rest of the class?"

She smirked at me. "I was just thinking about what we were saying last night, about how maybe he's not really you, or all of you. Just certain parts. Like the part of you that remembered that mill and needed a place to hide. But he's missing certain… I don't know… aspects. And I remember now something he said one night, back when we were still talking. He said that he couldn't 'sense' you."

"What? He couldn't? I figured he had more psychic powers than I did! That's how it was when I was… you know, when I took the potion."

"But don't you see? He doesn't! That's what he meant that night. I just thought he was being melodramatic, talking about trying to figure out what you were doing. But no…" She paused again, and another revelation seemed to come to her. "'I can't sense him, or *anyone.*' That's what he said. I remember now. So he doesn't have any psychic powers!"

This was an interesting development. I had assumed all this time that he had at least the same level of psychic ability that I did, or perhaps more ominously, his powers were as strong as mine had become during those last few weeks that I was a vampire. In retrospect, that had been a scary time, how powerful, dangerous, and sadistic I had gotten.

As this sunk in, I began to feel even more confident. This was an unexpected advantage over my clone, just as discovering that he couldn't kill me had been. I started to come up with a plan to attack the vampires at the factory, hopefully with Elizabeth's help. If he couldn't sense us coming, we might have the element of surprise on our side.

By this point, Elizabeth and I had reached the school, and I was distracted by her asking me where we should go. We were in a parking lot between the main building and the street, and there were lots of floodlights around. It felt too conspicuous, too visible from the road, which I mentioned.

"It's getting cold, too," she said, hugging her arms with her hands. "Maybe we could sneak inside?"

She'd indicated the school building with a tilt of her head, but I'd become distracted once again, this time by how incredibly beautiful she was. As it had been back at the house, the bright lights illuminated her perfectly, and now that I knew what was different about her appearance, I wanted to take it all in. Just as I was figuring out that the reason her eyes looked smaller was the lack of eyeliner, she scowled at me and said, "Stop it."

Realizing that I had been staring, I looked away, embarrassed. Then I looked back.

She sighed, almost growled, then repeated her move from before, covering her face with her hands as she turned away. "Will you please just... I'm really not happy about the fact that I have to be ugly for the rest of my life."

"You're not!" I almost shouted, stepping closer to her, again afraid to touch her. "Really! You've never been ugly!"

"Well, I am now," she continued, her voice still muffled. I feared that she might start crying.

"Elizabeth, you are not ugly," I said firmly. "I even kinda think you look better like this." It was true, though I hadn't realized it until the words came out.

One index finger poked away from her face, enough to expose her left eye. Peeking at me, she said, "You're just saying that."

"No!" I stepped forward again.

The finger clamped back into place. "Oh, you just mean that I look better with my face covered up."

Crap, I thought to myself. "That's not what I mean. Will you stop doing that, please?"

"No." The finger poked out again, and before I knew it, I was reaching up for it, cautiously touching it with my right hand. She didn't pull away, though I expected her to. Next, I found myself with both of my hands over hers. I pulled at them, which she resisted a little, but not much. As her hands came away, I expected to see tears on her face, but there weren't any. Instead, she was smiling at me, that familiar, wicked look in her eyes that I'd come to love all those years ago.

After a brief, almost subconscious glance downward, I leaned in, and after a few seconds of anticipation combined with panic, I was experiencing my first kiss. It felt amazing, and to this day, I am grateful for a memory that ran through my head right then, that of a celebrity on TV talking in an interview about how he screwed up his first kiss by moving his head around too much and trying to imitate the kisses he had seen in the movies when he was younger. Instead, ours was more simple, gentle, and sincere.

Naturally, I had fantasized about doing this with Elizabeth countless times, but those thoughts had always been more passionate, even animalistic, like we would embrace while breathing deeply and begin tearing off each other's clothes. But that wasn't how it happened. This was infinitely better. Our tongues touched, and I felt hers lightly rolling against mine. There was a strange taste to her, something that for some reason reminded me of the smell of the coffee my parents drank in the morning.

We disengaged after a few seconds, our foreheads still touching as we both exhaled. I couldn't help but smile, and she did the same back at me. Without realizing it, I had put my arms around her, and hers were behind my back, resting near the base of it. We leaned backwards from each other, taking in the moment.

"Was that okay?" I asked her.

"Not bad," she said, still grinning.

I mocked offense at this half-hearted praise, and she giggled, then leaned toward me again to let me have another go.

Not long after, the two of us were running away from the school and up the street, but Elizabeth cautioned me to slow down once we had gotten far enough away. Otherwise, we might look conspicuous. We had attempted to explore the school through an unlocked door, hoping to find somewhere more private. The last thing I wanted was for our intimate moment to be interrupted by more rednecks speeding down the road and throwing things.

Instead, we had only made it a few feet inside before I noticed an infrared sensor, a small rectangular object near the top of a wall with a smaller white square on it. Without warning, a red light appeared at the top at the same time that a piercing, electronic shriek began to sound, and the two of us bolted out the door within seconds. Neither of us had been expecting there to be an alarm, but then, this public school was probably better funded than the crappy private one she and I had gone to the past few years.

Once things had calmed down, we continued walking back toward my house, which we knew would take about half an hour. That left us with plenty of time to talk, plus I was basking in all of the warm feelings I had inside. I held her hand as we walked, this time more slowly, noticing how soft the palm of her hand felt against mine. For the moment, I didn't care that she was a vampire. She was just Elizabeth Morgan, the girl I had loved and wanted for so many years, and that girl was holding my hand. I was nervous but happy; I'd never had a girlfriend before. I knew that she'd had at least one boyfriend when we were younger, that jerk Kirby from school. Remembering that made me feel jealous, so I pushed that memory aside, just trying to enjoy things.

Talking about the alarm at the school led us to talking about our own school, Bethlehem Baptist, which we both hated. She didn't have to attend it anymore now that everyone thought she was dead, and of course, technically, she was. But she still had plenty of memories of her time there, including how she sometimes got in trouble for defying authority.

One of these incidents was one I hadn't known about until she told me this night, but I had been nearby when it had happened. Apparently, she had been reprimanded by Mrs. Manning at that swimming party for initially wearing a bikini, which the girls had been instructed not to wear. She would have been sent home if Melinda hadn't seen this coming, having brought a spare bathing suit for Elizabeth to wear.

"So I wore that instead, and the uptight old bat had to let me stay." She sounded more amused than bitter. "Too bad, though; it was a cute bikini. But maybe it's just as well that I didn't wear it and make you stare at me even more than usual."

My hand involuntarily gripped hers more tightly as I flinched, and she giggled, grabbing back and gently yanking my arm towards her, throwing me off balance for a second. We looked at each other, and her mischievous smile was the same as it had always been. She liked to make me squirm.

"Was I really always that obvious?" I asked.

"Mmm, let's see. On a scale of one to ten, I'd say... *Hell yes.*"

I laughed, a little miffed at her but not really. It felt good to finally be honest with her, but it was still taking some getting used to. "Well, that was what finally got me to realize the whole no make-up thing," I said, "remembering that party. And I... You remember Ken?"

"Ray, I've only been gone from school for a week."

"Right, sorry. Feels like longer than that for some reason. Anyway, I ended up riding with him and Jay in the back of Aaron's mom's station wagon to the party..."

"Bet that was a lot of fun," she interrupted.

"Yeah, I know. But at least out of the three of them, Ken's the least annoying. But... and I don't even remember how we got to talking about this, but one of us mentioned Lita Ford and her video for that song 'Kiss Me Deadly.' That's right... He hadn't seen it, and I was telling him how stupid it was, how she was all sliding around the floor with her guitar and spreading her legs, trying to be all sexy. And he was like, 'That sounds cool!' So I was trying to explain to him how her being all trashy like that was a turn-off. He didn't get it."

"I liked her," Elizabeth said pointedly. "And the song."

"Oh," I said, feeling awkward. "Well, I mean… I don't know, I guess I just didn't like her image. All…" I was going to use the term Carolyn had used when we'd watched the video together back then, but given how the conversation was going, I realized that describing a singer she liked as "super slut-tastic" probably wasn't going to win any points with her.

Instead, I tried to question just what the phrase "kiss me deadly" even meant, and she said that the song was talking about frustration and passion. I figured this was something I could actually relate to; I'd been passionate for her and frustrated over my lack of being able to approach her for years. "Well, I guess I can admit now that there were times at school when I just wanted to grab you and kiss you."

"Yeah, and if you'd done that, I'd have slapped the crap out of you." That wasn't the response I was hoping for.

"But… I thought that…" I tried to pick my words carefully. At least when I had been too shy to talk to her, I'd had less opportunities to put my foot in my mouth. "So, what *does* do it for girls, then?"

"Not getting mauled in the hallway at school, that's for sure." She was starting to sound more annoyed.

"Okay, fine. So what does work?"

"Trial and error," she said with a slight smile in her voice.

"Can't you just tell me what you want and keep it simple?"

"Nope. Trial and error," she repeated.

The conversation continued along similarly frustrating lines for another few minutes, things taking a positive turn when we found that despite our differences of opinion on more current things, we had some obscure similar interests as children. This included a couple of science fiction shows that aired in the early 1980s, and it surprised me to hear that she had been into them at all, which I told her. She scoffed at my saying that it was unusual for a girl to be interested in such things, and I could see myself being talked into another corner.

I changed the subject by checking to see what time it was on my digital watch, which I had finally remembered to bring with me while sneaking out at night. I couldn't be out too late; I had school the next day. When Elizabeth said that she'd always thought my watch was cool, I figured out that she was just baiting me.

"No, you didn't," I said.

"What, you don't believe me?" she said through a tight grin.

"No." I was beginning to get the hang of dealing with her manipulative sense of humor. "But you have to admit, the fact that it plays music is pretty bad-ass." I pressed a button on the side of the watch, causing a bleeping version of the theme from *The Twilight Zone* to play for a few seconds.

"Nope, not girly enough for me," she said slyly. "Now, if it was pink and played the theme from *My Little Pony,* that would totally rock."

It was my turn to stop walking and look at her despairingly. I rolled my eyes, unable to come up with a witty reply to top hers. She was clearly better at this than me.

"So what's the scar from?" she asked me out of the blue, pointing up toward my face.

"What? Oh, that." She was referring to the small, crescent-shaped scar on my left cheek, one that had mostly healed over time and was barely discernible except from up close. She must have noticed it earlier back at the school. Reaching up to touch it, I explained, "It was from a cat one of my sisters had when I was little. Hurt like hell when it happened. I remember swearing at the time that I would never like cats again, but that changed. We had another one when I got older."

"Did it bleed?" she asked me.

"Yeah, it did."

"A lot?" The sudden eagerness in her eyes unnerved me.

"I... Yeah, I think so. I was only five."

"Aw," she said, then leaned forward rather quickly and kissed me on the cheek. I expected it to just be a little peck, the kind a relative and I might give to each other when I was that little, but instead, she lingered there for longer than I expected. After a few seconds, she let out a low "mmm" sound as she began licking the exact spot where the scar was.

I pushed back from her, suddenly feeling scared. The expression on her face was familiar, another triumphant and wide grin, punctuated by her biting her lower lip. In the dim light, I wasn't sure if it was my imagination whether or not her fangs had grown slightly.

"Okay," I said nervously, "that wasn't…"

"Yes it was," she said quickly.

"Elizabeth…" I began, unsure how to continue.

"You are so easy to play with!" she said, putting her arms behind her back and squatting a little, her cheeky grin never fading. She then let out a little squeal and began running up the street, and I hesitated before pursuing her.

I caught her hand, and she spun around quickly, her shoulder-length hair spinning slightly out of sync with the rest of her in a way that reminded me of some cheesy shampoo commercial. She skipped a little as she stopped, her trademark, lip-biting grin punctuated by her tongue sticking out slightly in a silly way. She was infuriating, frightening, and adorable all at the same time. I loved her more than anything.

"So?" she asked in a leading way. Then her mood seemed to change, becoming more serious. She closed her eyes and looked down at the pavement briefly, then back up at me, holding my right hand in both of hers. "Actually, no. Time to go. It's a school night, right?"

She said this with her eyebrows raised as she turned back around, leading me with one hand farther up the road, still in the direction of my house.

I hadn't even meant to do it, but I ended up leading us to the other side of the street right at the spot where those guys in the car had smashed that beer bottle on the road sign. This weird, uneasy feeling had begun to grow inside of me for some reason, and I'd gotten the urge to lead Elizabeth over to the other side from where we were. She didn't protest, though I inwardly questioned what I thought I was trying to accomplish. After all, going along this side would lead us to Dr. Meng's house; staying on our previous course would have taken us right to my front yard.

Dodging the broken glass on the pavement, we continued along a bit more, and then I heard a noise. A quick rustling sound came from a shrubbery along the opposite side of the road just a few yards up from where we'd been walking. Two figures rose from the bushes, and Elizabeth gasped as they began walking quickly towards us. It was Carl, or rather his vampire clone, and another vampire that I didn't recognize.

CHAPTER FOUR

"Well, this is going to be fun," Carl said, stopping in the middle of the road. I dropped Elizabeth's hand from mine, unsure what to do next. I was still recovering from the shock.

As Carl paused, he held out his arm, indicating to the other vampire to wait as well. He was a boy who looked to be about our age, maybe a year or two younger, and almost as tall as Carl. Even when we were growing up, Carl had always towered over me, but now he looked even bigger and more menacing. The boy, who had tousled dark hair and narrow eyes — not unlike Carl, actually — stood with his arms slightly apart from his sides, almost like a gunfighter in an old western.

"What do you want?" I asked, trying to hide my fear.

"Ray…" Elizabeth began, sounding scared.

"Oh, the little bitch answered your question for me!" Carl said, followed by a goofy laugh. It was the same one he'd always had, though deeper than when we were kids, but this wasn't really my old friend. It was a copy of him, his vampire self incarnate. "Who's she? Some slut from that piece of shit school you go to?"

Despite how scared I was, his insults angered me, and I reached into my jacket for my wooden stake. I pulled it out and held it up in what I hoped was a menacing way. Elizabeth made another frightened sound, but I didn't take my eyes off of Carl and his companion.

"Back off," I said.

"Ooh, tough guy," Carl said mockingly. "Just like always."

Carl and I had been friends as children, but there had been some rough patches, and we had occasionally gotten into fights at school. Usually, those were just intimidation matches, each of us staring at each other until things simmered down to nothing. I recalled this and realized that this encounter would have to end a lot differently. I began to wish that the real Carl were here, holding his father's crossbow or some similar weapon. Even though it was two against two, I only had the one stake, and I had no reason to think that Elizabeth might be similarly armed.

As I tried to think of something tough to say back to Carl, I saw both his and the other vampire's expressions change, their eyes going wide simultaneously with surprise. At the same time, I heard a fluttering sound in my ear, and when I looked to my left, Elizabeth was gone. It only took me a second to realize what had happened.

"What the fuck?" Carl exclaimed. "She was…?"

"Yes," I said angrily, turning back to face him.

"Where did she go?" the other vampire asked rather stupidly.

"Doesn't matter," Carl said impatiently. "We'll just have to share."

He stepped forward, and I turned and ran, not knowing where I was going. I was in somebody's front yard, and as I barreled along, I narrowly missed tripping over a sprinkler head. I stopped, looking around to try to figure out where the control knob for the sprinklers might be. Hearing the two vampires thundering up behind me, I broke off running again in a random direction, immediately cursing myself for heading away from the house when I should have gone toward it.

If this property was like my own, the knob would be next to the house; ours was right by the front door. While running water was a lesser known vampire deterrent than garlic or crosses, my friends and

I had successfully used it against vampires in the past. If I could just get to that knob or even to a hose, I might stand a chance.

No sooner than I'd thought that, I stumbled upon a hose lying on the ground near a small flower garden, the only reason I spotted it being that the metal sprayer attachment happened to catch a reflection from the nearby streetlights. I picked it up and spun around, hoping to catch Carl or his new friend in the face with a lethal spray of water.

Carl struggled to slow down as he ran toward me, panic on his face as he realized what I was holding. But as I squeezed the trigger on the sprayer, the pressure I expected to feel gave way immediately, and only a small trickle of water came out. In order for a sprayer to work, the water had to be turned on. He laughed quietly, and the other vampire caught up behind him and stopped.

Unable to think of anything better, I slid the hose through my hand a few feet and then swung it like a whip, clocking Carl in the face with the metal attachment, which caused him to fall backwards awkwardly and gave me a chance to run. Carl swore at the injury, and as I fled, I heard his friend pursuing me as I headed back toward the street.

Suddenly, I heard a scream from behind me, and I stopped running to turn back and see the anonymous vampire struggling, flailing at his face in agony at a small, furry, light-colored object that seemed to have attached itself to his cheek. After a few more swats, the thing fell to one side, growing and changing into Elizabeth's tumbling form before settling on the ground as she steadied herself on all fours.

The vampire frantically wiped at his face as he let out various swear words, blood streaming from his wound. "You stupid little…!" he shouted at Elizabeth, not finishing his sentence. "You're supposed to be on our side!"

"Whatever," she said defiantly, out of breath but starting to get to her feet.

Taking advantage of the distraction, I lunged at the vampire with my wooden stake, shoving it as hard as I could into his chest. I was only partly successful; my momentum knocked him onto his back, and the stake managed to penetrate, but not all the way. He screamed and tried to reach up with both hands to pull the weapon out, but I matched his move and clamped both of my hands over his.

At the same time, Carl came running up and screamed, "No!"

Knowing I'd won the moment, I plunged down with all my strength, pushing the stake all the way into the boy's chest and piercing the heart. There was something sickening about the way the stake felt going in, how the bone and flesh resisted. It reminded me of a time when I was much younger and had tried to help my father carve a jack-o'-lantern for Halloween, how the pumpkin was much harder and tougher to penetrate with a knife than I'd expected.

Even worse was the vampire's scream, which quickly went from an almost pitiful, boyish wail to a muffled gurgle. Blood began to pour out from his mouth, and I leaned back to avoid it. I glanced over at Carl, who was still standing and staring as he panted, a combination of anger and fear in his eyes. Elizabeth, meanwhile, was still squatting on the ground and was also looking on in horror, her hand over her mouth.

Not surprisingly, all of this commotion did not go unnoticed, and all three of us looked toward the house as the lights on the front porch came on. I could hear movement inside, and I knew that any second now, we would be confronted by the residents.

"You son of a bitch," Carl hissed at me, and with that, he turned into a bat and flew away.

"Come on!" Elizabeth whispered harshly, jumping up from the ground and reaching for me.

"Just go!" I said, immediately regretting making so much noise. She seemed surprised by this, so I added, "Run! I'll catch up!"

She still looked confused, but she did as I said and ran across the lawn toward the street. As I heard the front door being unlocked, I quickly grabbed the stake from the chest of the dead vampire and wrenched it out, again trying to avoid the splattering blood. In retrospect, I probably shouldn't have bothered, but in my panic, I found myself remembering the various crime shows I'd seen on TV throughout my life, how the murder weapon always seemed to lead straight back to the killer.

Elizabeth and I met up about halfway to my house, once we had both stopped running, that is. When I'd first sped away from the neighbors' yard, I'd heard a woman screaming followed by a man's voice, and I had no idea if the man might have a gun or if he might be pursuing me. I hoped that the sight of a dead vampire on their front lawn would be enough to distract them, and once I had gotten far enough along, I realized that this must have been the case.

As I ran, the couple of minutes I had alone with my thoughts made me question other things. Had Elizabeth led me into a trap? Had all of her sweetness and everything been a ploy to lull me into a false sense of security? I wondered if I had been a fool all along, if this was just some big game to her. Then again, she had saved me from that other vampire. It just really bugged me the way she had suddenly disappeared and flown away when he and Carl had arrived.

Once I caught up to her, though, my feelings softened, particularly when she threw her arms around me and held tight. "I'm so glad you're okay," she almost whispered. "Oh, thank G— " Again, she choked on the word, apparently forbidden for her to say.

"Shh," I said, some kind of comforting instinct kicking in. She seemed genuinely shaken up, and I rocked her back and forth as we hugged. "It's okay now." Still embracing, we leaned back and looked at each other, and I could see tears in her eyes.

She said in a broken voice, "I'm sorry I panicked. I just... I didn't know what else to do. I got scared."

"Yeah, but you came back!" I said in an encouraging tone. My suspicion and even anger at her had immediately melted away, and all I wanted was for her to feel better.

She sniffled and looked down at her chest, still breathing heavily from all of the running. "I just... I don't know. I got scared," she repeated. Then she looked up at me, swallowing hard as she tried to regain control. "But I couldn't let them get you."

"And they didn't," I said firmly. "Thank you." There was silence, and my mind was still racing. "So," I then said meaningfully, "it looks like my clone isn't the only one who's making his own group of vampires. Carl's doing it, too."

Elizabeth and I dropped our arms and stood apart, and she seemed to be getting her composure back. She blinked back tears and then wiped at them quickly as she turned away, almost as if she were ashamed of being so emotional. "Yeah," she said, her breathing almost back to normal.

"Actually, that kind of makes sense," I said, remembering that Carl and I had spent a large portion of fifth grade forming two rival clubs, groups of friends who opposed each other for no real reason other than to be exclusionary. As Elizabeth and I walked back to my house, I told her more about my past.

The following week was unusual for several reasons. For one, I only went to school for two days. Because I had been up so late Sunday night thinking about everything that had happened, getting to sleep at a reasonable hour had been impossible. I'd ended up faking being sick in order to get out of school on Monday, and fooling my mother into letting me stay home hadn't been hard.

That had given me a chance to get acquainted with the washing machine. My mother had always done the laundry in our household, but I couldn't very well explain to her why I needed to get bloodstains out of my jean jacket and the other clothes I'd worn the night before. Fortunately, I'd seen enough TV commercials about detergents and stain removers to get the concept, and following the directions on the bottles wasn't difficult. By the time my parents had gotten home from work that evening, my clothes were safely clean and evidence-free.

I was out of school on Thursday and Friday that week because of the Thanksgiving holiday, one that I had never been all that into.

Every year, my family went out to Appling to eat dinner with my cousins and extended family, but I never had much to say to them beyond polite conversation. And this year, I was even more distracted because of everything that was going on. While on previous visits I would quickly be itching to return to Augusta just to get back to my comfort zone of cable TV and a city with a population of more than a couple thousand people, this time I had more pressing reasons.

While I was eager to see Elizabeth again, we had agreed to wait a few nights before meeting up. She said she had some things to look into, which made me a little suspicious. I still couldn't be sure just how honest she was being with me, and I would go back and forth between that feeling and telling myself to just calm down and do my best to trust her. I had grown up being a rather deceptive person my entire life, and she had always been an enigma to me even before she'd become a vampire, so it was a difficult struggle.

The main thing she said she wanted to do was some research at the downtown library. She and I had both grown up in the suburbs, so she felt confident that no one she knew would show up there. After all, as far as her family and everyone else was concerned, she was supposed to be dead, and being spotted would not be a good thing.

Even though she was a vampire now, it had never been something she had known or cared much about before it had been thrust upon her unexpectedly. So she wanted to learn more about the whole thing, including finding out if there might be a cure, a way for her to become human again. I'd wondered if the antidote to the vampire potion we had used might work, but after we discussed it further, we became doubtful of that. As far as we could figure out, that antidote had only worked on me, my sisters, and my friends because the potion was what turned us into vampires in the first place, but Elizabeth's case was different.

So it made sense for me to give her a few nights to go do that, but I hated it just the same. I loved her, and I ached for her like any teenage boy would. The nights I spent lying awake thinking about her and trying to fall asleep alternated between longing for her, wondering what she might be doing, rerunning conversations we'd had through my head, fantasizing about ones we might have, and sometimes fantasizing about her sexually.

But what if there wasn't a cure? What if this was just what she was now, an undead creature who, even if she didn't kill every single night, still did occasionally? Was I just as guilty and responsible as she was for those deaths for letting them continue? Was it my duty, I who had sworn to eliminate all the other vampires, to destroy her as well? Would that stake I used to kill that other vampire on Sunday night one day have to be used against her? I couldn't bear that thought. I hoped so much that her research would prove fruitful.

Fortunately, I had something else to think about. The day after my encounter with Carl's clone, I had contacted the real Carl by phone and told him what had happened. I completely left out any mention of Elizabeth, though. For now at least, she was still a secret.

Our conversation eventually led us to meet up with Tim on Friday night near Sibley Mill, the plan being to attack my clone and wipe him and his own new vampire group out. Of course, because I wasn't telling either of them about Elizabeth, I'd had to lie about how I knew they were there.

"So I guess your powers must have come back stronger than mine," Tim said, sounding slightly sad.

"Yeah, I guess," I said lamely, dancing around the lie. Since I couldn't tell them — or Dennis, had he bothered to return my calls — about Elizabeth, I had made up a story about how Carolyn and I had driven past the mill over the weekend, and I had sensed psychically that my clone was there. I later added that I had seen some bats flying into it, but I changed the subject whenever I was pressed for any details.

"Never mind about that," I said harshly after one of Tim's questions got too close to the truth. "We just need to get in there and take care of it." The three of us weren't nearly as close friends as we once had been, but it felt oddly comforting to fall back into the role of being the one in charge.

"At least we have an advantage," Carl said hopefully, "the other you not being psychic and all. He won't see us coming then."

"Right," I said. Again, I couldn't tell them just how I knew that my clone didn't have the same powers I did, but it helped in terms of convincing him and Tim to come along on this mission.

We had parked a couple of blocks away from the mill, Carl having stealthily procured his older sister's car while both she and their parents were out of town, something he did occasionally. When he had picked me up from my house, I had pretended — as Tim did shortly afterwards to his parents — that he was old enough to drive and that this was just a regular night of us guys hanging out and driving around, possibly going to the mall.

"Well, you know, 'mall,' 'mill,'" Tim had joked once we were safely on our way, "not that much of a difference." Carl had laughed politely, but I was too focused to bother doing the same.

As we walked toward our objective, our backpacks loaded with weapons and other equipment, we talked about what had happened recently.

"Too bad you didn't manage to kill Carl's clone," Tim said to me.

"Yeah, I know. I just had the one stake."

"And that vampire, the other one, he just died?" Carl asked.

"Yes?" I wasn't sure where he was coming from.

"Just that…" He paused. "Well, Nick, you know?"

"What about him?" I asked, noticing the unexpected bitterness in my voice.

"Didn't he say that when he killed his clone, it kind of, I don't know… evaporated?"

"Hmm," I said thoughtfully, "that's true. I guess…"

"The clones must be different from the vampires they make," Tim said, finishing my thought. He always was the smart one of the group, but he was also psychic like me.

"Oh," Carl said. "So, they're real vampires, not fake ones. And I guess, well, our clones are kind of fakes, too?"

"More like ghosts, I'd say," Tim clarified. "Apparitions."

"But solid ones," I added. "Until they get killed, and then they just, you know, fade away. Makes sense, I suppose." As we continued walking, I thought about how all of this pertained to Elizabeth. It also occurred to me how weird it felt to be talking pleasantly with Carl given how an almost exact copy of him had tried to murder me just a few nights ago.

Still hiding the fact that I had already talked to someone else about this, I continued the conversation with more speculation about the nature of our clones, how they weren't exactly like us but were instead the distillation of our evil sides, all of the bad traits and none of the good ones.

"Which could maybe be why they don't have your powers!" Carl said. "And you could… I don't know… sense that somehow?"

"Sense what? Oh, that mine didn't have them. Yeah." I was still lying, and I was becoming more and more uncomfortable with that. I was used to getting away with things and running circles around the other people in my life, but these guys were my old friends, ones with whom I'd shared a dark secret for many years. Adding another layer of deception to that bothered me a bit.

"I can't sense my clone at all," Tim said. "Maybe if he had some powers of his own, that would make it easier. Like a connection, somehow."

"Maybe," I said.

"Now, hang on a minute," Carl said in a tone that made me nervous. He also stopped walking and had turned toward me.

"What?" I asked.

"What about Damon?"

"Damon?"

"He said that when he killed that vampire, it didn't dissolve away or anything… Oh, wait." He let out a short laugh, then rolled his eyes and looked a little embarrassed. "Never mind. He was lying. Making up a story for that news show." He turned, and we continued walking. "Good thing he did, too," Carl added.

"How do you mean?" Tim asked.

"That was when he established that bullshit story for everyone that the vampires can disguise themselves as other people."

Carl and I had already talked about this on the phone the other day, how Damon's interview on TV had effectively gotten us off the hook in case anyone who happened to know us ever encountered one of our clones. That had proven useful for Carl, as he had recently run into just that scenario. He recounted the story again for Tim.

"Wow," Tim said. "So this person saw your clone killing someone, and they thought it was you."

"Right," I said. "But because of the story about them being able to supernaturally transform into other people, Carl could just mention that and say, 'It wasn't me!'"

"And it wasn't, of course, but it still kinda weirded me out," Carl said with a dramatic shudder.

"I can imagine," Tim said. "Even if you didn't see it, it probably bugged you even picturing it. I get that way whenever I think about what kinds of horrible stuff my own clone might be doing out there."

"Me too," I said gravely.

"You remember how freaked out Dennis got when we encountered his clone," Tim said. "At least I haven't actually seen mine yet. I mean, not since that first night."

"Yeah, and that was bad enough," Carl added.

"And even if that happens to me, you know, like if someone tells me that they've seen him and I can just be all 'that was a vampire pretending to be me,' well, I'm still going to feel guilty." There was silence, none of us wanting to add to that. "I know he isn't really me, but deep down, we're all still responsible, aren't we?"

There was more silence, and I wanted to change the subject. Carl did it for me.

"I wonder who the guy was that my clone turned into a vampire," he said quietly.

"No idea," I said. "I didn't recognize him. Seemed to be about our age. Maybe someone from another school?"

"Could be," Tim said. "Or just some random guy. Something's bugging me, though…" He trailed off.

"What?" I asked.

"Just the…" He scratched his chin, thinking. "Well, actually, there's something else, too. You said that Carl's clone got all upset when you killed his vampire? I mean, the other vampire that attacked you?"

"Yeah," I said. "He was all, 'No!!!'" I did my best impression of the way he had reacted.

"Seems kind of emotional for something that's supposed to just be an evil, hollow kind of being. Wouldn't someone like that just be all cruel and uncaring?"

"Maybe," I said, seeing his point. "You're right, though, now that I think about it. He did seem genuinely, I don't know, hurt. Or at least angry."

"Maybe they care about other vampires, but not other people," Tim surmised.

"Fuck, does it really matter?" Carl said, his voice a little higher than usual. "Anyway, look, we're almost there." He pointed at the chain-link fence that surrounded Sibley Mill.

As I'd remembered from previous visits to the place — which really just consisted of occasionally passing it in the car whenever my parents or sisters happened to drive by it over the years — there was barbed wire along the top of the fence, so climbing over it wasn't an option. Until our arrival, I hadn't even been sure if that memory had been correct; it wasn't like I came here often. The mill was along the Augusta Canal, the border that separated downtown Augusta from the westerly section of town, and most of my life had been spent in that more affluent part of the city.

Still, I was glad that as I'd been planning this expedition all week, I had correctly remembered that it would be necessary for us to cut our way through the fence in order to make it through. As instructed, Carl had brought along some wire cutters, as had I.

"Well, that only took a good slice of forever," Tim said as we made our way across the grass almost twenty minutes later. "We're lucky the police or someone didn't come by and catch us."

"Sorry," I said, surprised at his bitter tone. Tim was usually the more upbeat one, the guy who wanted everyone to get along. "I didn't think it would take that long." I shook both of my hands to try to wring out the soreness from them as we walked.

"So now that we're in here," Carl said, his voice lowering to a whisper, "any idea on just where we need to look?" As he said this, he gestured grandly at the huge four-story building before us. From far away, which was the only way I'd ever seen it before, it looked impressive and ancient, like an orange-colored brickwork castle. Up close, it was even more colossal, almost impossibly big, the size of at least two or three city blocks.

"Let me see," I said pensively, though truth be told, I had no idea where to begin. There was no main entrance to the place as far as I could see. Looking around some more and seeing where the ground sloped down in a small hill to meet the building, I spotted a red, wooden door. "That might be a way in," I said, pointing. "There."

"It's probably locked," Tim said.

Surprisingly, it wasn't, as Carl found when he tried the door. "I guess they forgot to lock it," he said. "Or they think the fence is enough to keep people out."

"There might still be people here," I said, remembering a couple of cars I had seen in the nearby parking lot.

"This time of night?" Carl asked.

"I don't know!" I said, frustrated. "Let's just go in and see what we can find."

We did, and the interior of the place looked nothing like I had expected. The notion that this place was a factory had put the picture in my mind that the interior would be huge, a vast inner space that stretched from floor to ceiling as large as it looked from the outside. I imagined that there might be big machines inside pumping away like in a steel mill, an assembly line cranking out finished pairs of Levi's jeans from bales of cotton in some long, drawn-out process.

Instead, the ground floor where we entered led straight to a poorly lit wooden stairwell that went upward, so we followed it carefully. This led out onto a large, open space, though the ceiling was more or less a normal height, not stretching to the top of the structure like I'd pictured.

The place was dingy and lit by banks of fluorescent lights, not all of them working, and the entire floor was punctuated by evenly spaced rectangular columns. Other than that, it was completely unoccupied by either personnel or equipment. A faint thumping sound not unlike that of my mother's clothes dryer seemed to be coming from somewhere nearby.

"Think that's the machinery?" Tim whispered, again echoing my thoughts.

"Probably," I said. "El…" I caught myself before saying Elizabeth's name. "Uh, from what I've been told, some parts of this place are still in operation."

"So then where are, you know…" Carl trailed off, and I knew who he meant.

Remembering what Elizabeth had told me, I tried to think just where my clone and his group might have set up camp. Logically, if there were still some manufacturing being done in the place, they would be far from it. In a building this large, that wouldn't be too difficult. What frustrated me was that I was completely unfamiliar with my surroundings, and I wished that I had asked Elizabeth for more details.

I had in fact initially wanted her to be the one to accompany me here to confront and hopefully kill my clone, but she didn't want to have anything to do with that plan. She'd said that the place creeped her out, which I found odd considering that she was a girl who slept every night in a cemetery. But now that I was actually here, I could see her point. It was a weird place, somewhere that had obviously seen better days, and the vast emptiness and almost palpable sense of abandonment gave me an eerie feeling.

"No idea," I said, answering Carl's unfinished question.

"Well, can't you like, you know… *woo-wooooo…*" As he made this weird sound effect, he put his fingers to his temples.

"Worth a try," Tim said. "Remember how we did it before, combining our powers? That kind of worked."

"Yeah, but that time, we had Dennis," I said. "I don't know if it will work with just us."

"Just because that dork-head isn't here…" Carl began, but Tim cut him off, holding up his hand.

"Let's give it a try." He closed his eyes, and I did the same. I reached out to him with my mind, and I could feel something there: a presence, a vaguely tingling sensation running across my scalp and forehead. I could tell that he was probably feeling the same thing.

"Okay," I said firmly. "Now reach out. Try to find someone else nearby." Carl coughed, and I added, "Besides him."

It seemed to work; aside from Carl's obvious presence right next to us, I got the feeling that there were other people nearby. Focusing, I tried to narrow down their direction. "You feel that?" I asked Tim.

"Yeah," he said. "Behind me." He was right. We were facing each other, Carl to my left, and the people we were seeking seemed to be ahead of me and off slightly to the right. I opened my eyes, and Tim did the same, inhaling deeply.

"Okay," he said with a dramatic exhale. "Let's go see." As he turned around, he held up a wooden stake, and from behind, I saw him reach into his left jacket pocket to pull out something else. It was a container of garlic powder.

I got my own stake ready as well, and Carl held up his crossbow meaningfully. Then we headed for an open doorway at the far end of the room.

The confrontation was a bit of a mess, and it didn't go at all like I'd imagined. It did in the beginning, us sneaking up on the room where my clone and his vampires were, hearing their voices as we approached along a darkened corridor. I had initially pictured myself like a guy in a cop show, making silent gestures to my companions to indicate just how we would attack. But there wasn't anything for me to say when the moment came, no coded movements to tell everyone just what to do.

"So what now?" Tim whispered harshly as we peered in through the doorway.

The room we looked out on was another dimly lit one like the one we had been in before, just as dull and dingy. Papers and other various bits of trash were scattered in places along the concrete floor, and in the far corner, I could see a few mattresses. Near one wall to our left, there appeared to be a prone body, possibly the vampires' latest victim, someone they had brought home to feed on.

In the center of the room, there stood my clone, talking quietly with two other vampires, one male and one female. They were both a little taller than my double, but from what I could tell, they were probably about my age. The boy had dark hair and was wearing a black leather jacket, and the girl, who had thick, curly red hair, had on a long, flowing dress that looked like it was made out of green velvet.

This was the first time I had seen my clone in weeks, and immediately, a rage built up inside of me. Whatever apprehension I had been feeling up to that point disappeared, and all I could think of was how much I wanted to kill him. He represented everything I despised, and I hated him for what he had done to Elizabeth. What's more, I hated the pain he had made me go through, the loss I had felt when she died.

Before I knew what I was doing, I began running towards him and the other vampires, my stake held high. A scream began pouring out of me that built to a higher pitch as I ran, and I was aware of Tim and Carl stomping along behind me. Our approach didn't go unnoticed, and my clone and his vampires looked up at us in surprise.

"It's payback time, motherfuckers!" Carl yelled from behind me.

"Yeah!" Tim added, but that was all he had to say. By then, the vampires had taken on defensive positions, their arms held out and their fingers sprawled. Their looks of fear had quickly hardened into determination, and they bared their fangs angrily. I tried to pretend that it didn't intimidate me.

Several yards before we reached them, though, all three vampires shrunk into bats and fluttered upwards, and I heard a small, tinny laughing sound as they did so. The bats began to circle just beneath a rectangular fluorescent light fixture.

"Well, I'm impressed!" I heard my own voice say from above. "You found me! Well done."

"Get your ass back down here and fight!" I said, surprised by the words. It felt like I wasn't entirely in control, that things were just happening and I was taking part. The whole situation felt surreal.

"Or what?" one of the other vampire bats said, the male one.

"Come up and get us…" the female sang.

"Or I could just…" Carl said, pointing his crossbow at them.

"Don't!" Tim said, catching his arm. "You won't hit them. Don't waste an arrow."

"Smart boy," the bat version of me said. "Just like always. *Tiiiiimm knooooows!"* he sang, repeating an old joke from elementary school. The other two bats laughed tauntingly, which struck me as odd given that whoever they were, they hadn't been a part of that particular in-joke from our past.

One bat stopped circling and hovered in place, and the other two followed its lead, forming a triangle beneath the light.

"Go on!" my clone's voice called down. *"Hit me with your best shot!"* he sang, citing the title of a popular song from my — from our — childhood.

That caught me off guard, as it reminded me of something Carolyn had told me about when I was in first grade. Back then, when she was about twelve years old, she and some of the kids in her P.E. class had beaten another team in some competition, and they were angry about it. To taunt them, one of the girls had starting singing the chorus of that song, and Carolyn and her friends had joined in. She later told me about this, and for years afterwards, I would think of that incident whenever I heard the song on the radio.

This showed that my clone did in fact have some of my memories, but like Elizabeth had speculated, he must only have had the bad ones, or more accurately, the evil or cruel ones. More than likely, he wouldn't remember the time I vacuumed the entire house for my mother as a birthday present for her when I was seven. I may have done a crappy job of it, and it had worn me out, but it had been a nice gesture. She appreciated it, and it was one of my nicer memories of her from back then.

Carl started to aim, but like Tim, I warned him not to. My clone's bat form was still too small of a target, even if they had stopped circling. Still, I had something that might work, and I pulled the small plastic bottle of garlic powder from my jacket. I quickly unscrewed the lid, dumped out a big handful, and tossed it up into the air.

The bats scattered, but the powder caught one of them, causing it to transform into its vampire self and tumble clumsily onto the concrete.

It was the red-haired girl, and she cried out as she rolled over on the floor. Carl sprinted towards her, crossbow aimed, and she held up her hand in a futile gesture.

"Rosemary!" I heard an unfamiliar voice call out, and I turned to see one of the bats, apparently not my clone, circling back to the aid of the vampire about to be killed.

As the bat neared, I reached into my jacket and pulled out a large wooden cross, which I managed to smack into the bat as it neared us. It flew backwards, falling onto the floor as it changed into the boy I'd seen before, skidding as he tried to break his fall with his hands.

"Get him!" I shouted at Tim, who had already moved to take out the vampire with his stake.

Without warning, and without my seeing his bat form approach in the dim light, my clone appeared standing right next to Tim, grabbing him and throwing him roughly to the floor. I ran up behind my clone and attempted a similar movement, but he resisted, and we struggled for a few moments.

A girl's scream rang out from nearby, and I looked over to see Carl standing over the vampire girl as she writhed and grabbed at the wooden arrow that had gone through her heart. Her scream devolved into bubbling gurgles as she slowly stopped moving. Carl's back was to me, and he stood with his legs spread over the dead girl as I watched, temporarily distracted from the struggle with my clone.

He had also stopped fighting briefly, transfixed by what had happened. We turned to face each other, and he swore as he pushed against me and toppled me onto my back. It hurt as I hit the floor, and I looked up to see my clone starting to run away. Ignoring the pain I felt in my backside, I forced myself up and ran after him.

I caught up after just a few seconds, grabbing him from behind but uncertain what to do next. I needed to somehow force him onto the ground so I could ram my stake through his heart, but it was all I could do to control him now.

"Here," I heard Tim's voice say from my left, and before I knew it, he had kicked my clone's leg and made him fall over, and I managed to pin him down by his wrists. That didn't leave a hand free for putting a stake through his heart, though.

"Oh, great," he hissed at me, and I tried not to be unnerved by how weird it felt to be looking into his hateful face, *my* face. "Sure, get little Tim here to do it for you. That'd be great."

"Shut up," I said. "Just shut the hell up. You don't deserve to live. You don't deserve to *exist!*"

"And you do?" he asked, his eyes brightening. Then he laughed, and I hated it. Growing up, it had always hurt when my sisters laughed at me. This was like having a psychotic twin brother doing the same thing, but it was ten times worse. "Do you have any idea how much these guys really despise you because of everything? And the others?"

"Just get rid of him!" Tim said from my side. "I'll hold him, and you can…" He showed me the stake he was holding, and I knew that he was right. It was time to end this.

"Tim, look out!" Carl yelled from outside my field of vision.

"Ow!!!" Tim shouted, and his stake clattered to the floor.

Taking advantage of the distraction, my clone thrust hard at me with his arms, rocking his body forward like he was doing a sit-up. My arms gave way and I was forced to stand up clumsily, then found myself skidding backwards across the concrete.

By the time I had recovered, my clone was nowhere to be seen. I looked over at Tim and saw that he was clutching the back of his left hand, which was bleeding. Nearby, a girl I didn't recognize had suddenly appeared on the ground. She had very long, straight black hair and narrow eyes, which looked even smaller due to the fact that she was scowling at Tim angrily, her fangs bared.

Carl ran up with a cross and held it out at the girl, who recoiled and held up one hand to shield her vision. I reached into my jacket for my stake, but before I could do anything with it, I heard the voice of the boy vampire calling out from somewhere close by.

"Come on, Kay, let's get out of here!" he called. "Ray's already bailed." For a second, I thought he was referring to me; it was an odd feeling to remember that there had been someone else there with the same name as me.

Kay quickly changed into a bat and flew away, and I tried to still my breathing as I looked around the room, listening for any more fluttering sounds. There were none. My friends and I were alone apart from the corpse of the red-haired girl near the center of the room. Then I realized something.

"Wait, where did…?" I began to ask, but I figured out the answer halfway through my sentence. What I'd mistaken for a body near the edge of the room had in fact been that girl Kay, who for some reason had been lying still on her back away from the others when we first arrived. I had no idea why, nor would I get a chance to ask her.

"What?" Tim asked, and I explained what I'd figured out.

"Hmm, a Chink vampire," Carl said. "That's new."

"She wasn't a 'Chink,' Carl," I said. "She was Korean. At least I'm pretty sure she was. She looked a lot like Natalie, this Korean girl who used to live across the street from me."

"Yeah, whatever," he said.

"And this one," Tim said thoughtfully, turning to look at the dead vampire. "Her name was Rosemary. Pretty name."

"Oh, don't get all stupid and sappy, Tim!" Carl barked. "What, do you want to do it with her or something? I mean, she's right there. I doubt she'd…"

"That's disgusting, Carl!" Tim shouted back. He looked over at the body again, then let out a weird sound as he crouched down slightly. He clamped a hand over his mouth, spun away, and staggered a couple of paces before collapsing to the floor. Soon after, he threw up.

"God, what a pussy," Carl said, turning to look at the girl. "Oh… Oh shit. I see what you…"

Finally, I saw it, too. From where I'd been standing, I couldn't see her face at first; the rest of her body had blocked that from view. Her chest, still impaled by the wooden arrow, had risen as her back arched upward. The green velvet dress she wore, with its long skirt and long sleeves, hid most of her flesh. But upon closer inspection, we each in turn saw the way her skin had turned almost completely black in some places, all veiny and blotchy. The face looked more like some kind of Halloween horror mask than that of a human being. I tried not to notice where some of the girl's auburn ringlets had detached from her head and settled onto the floor, but it was too late.

"Okay, let's get the fuck out of here," Carl said firmly.

"Sorry I was such a prick to you in there, Tim," Carl said, exhaling from a cigarette as we walked quickly back towards the car. It was odd seeing him smoke, particularly given how he used to be so athletic when we were growing up. For some reason, he'd given that up and had taken up the unhealthy habit instead.

"It's okay," Tim said, but he didn't sound like he meant it.

"That was really, really horrible," I added. "Maybe even worse than those vampires we killed a few years ago. Remember?"

"Yeah, I remember," Carl said gravely. "But I guess… I mean I guess what happens is that when you kill a vampire, then it looks like how the person would have looked if they'd died normally. All decayed and stuff, after all that time."

"Right," I said. "And the longer they've been dead, the more they don't even look like a body anymore. That's how it was for those two back when…"

"Can we *please* talk about something else?" Tim almost shouted. The rest of us clammed up.

After a few seconds of walking, Carl asked, "How's your hand?"

"It's okay, I think," Tim said. "Stopped bleeding, anyway."

"Why did she bite your hand?" I asked.

"She was going for my neck," Tim said, his tone still bitter. "Flew straight at me, and I reached up at the last second. I was lucky. If Carl hadn't warned me, I'd probably be…" He didn't finish his thought. He didn't have to.

We walked for another minute or two. Things hadn't gone very well. We had managed to kill one vampire, but the rest of them, most importantly my clone, had gotten away. I wondered how or when I might find him again. I also wondered just what he meant about the others hating me.

My thoughts were interrupted by Carl talking about how strange it was encountering these new vampires, the ones made by my clone, plus there must be countless others made by the rest of the clones, too.

"I'm not so sure about that," Tim said, sounding pensive.

"About what?" I asked. "Our clones' victims come back as vampires. We know that. We've seen it."

"Yeah, but I don't think that all of them do."

"What do you mean?" Carl asked.

"Well, think about the math of it all. There's, what…" He quietly rattled off the names of those of us whose clones were still out there, counting on his fingers as he went. "So yeah, six of them. And so they kill six people every night. Then another six. Then another. Considering how long it's been since the emergence…"

"And then what about the vampires those victims make?" I broke in, getting his point. "Those vampires then kill, so the number doubles…"

"Not even doubles," Tim said. "It's exponential. By now, there'd be something like, well, hundreds!"

"This city is totally fucked," Carl said in almost a whisper, throwing down his cigarette and putting it out with his shoe.

"But that's just it, Carl," I said. "It must not be like that. Otherwise we'd already be overrun by tons of vampires. It must not be automatic."

He gave me a confused look, but then his expression changed. "Oh! So it must be like, sometimes they just kill people, and sometimes they bring them back as vampires, but only when they want to?"

"It's got to be," Tim said.

"And maybe they're not killing all of the time, but just wounding," I offered, not wanting to reveal that Elizabeth had already told me that this was the case.

"Hmm," Tim said. "Probably. Well, yeah. Definitely." He held up his injured hand to me, a stern look in his eyes.

"Still," Carl said, "this is all looking pretty grim."

"We just have to keep trying," I said, immediately thinking that the words sounded trite.

"But did you…?" Carl began, then stopped. "Um… Okay, I don't really want to admit this, but…" He went quiet again.

"What?" I asked.

"Killing that girl tonight. The vampire. It kind of tripped my shit a little, if you know what I mean."

"No?" Tim said with a leading tone.

"I mean, yeah, okay. I did it. I killed a vampire. Go, me. But… I didn't like it. It was hard. I didn't like seeing it. And especially after the fact, when she was all…" He shuddered.

"I know," I said. "It weirded me out too when I killed that one the other night."

"Funny how things change, huh?" Tim said pointedly. "We used to kill people all the time. God forgive us." He added that last bit under his breath.

CHAPTER FIVE

"Oh, it's beautiful!" Elizabeth said, holding up the gold necklace with one hand, the other holding the small box I'd packaged it in. "Thank you!" She gazed at the necklace as it dangled, glinting in the faint blue glow of a nearby streetlight. Then she looked at me, her expression changing from a sweet smile to a pout. "I feel bad, though."

"Why?" I asked.

"I didn't get you anything. Didn't even think about it, really. Not into the whole Chr… well, holiday spirit thing this year, you know." She shrugged, letting her hands plop down into her lap. "I'm sorry." Her tone, coupled with the look in her eyes, seemed to be pleading for forgiveness.

"It doesn't matter," I said, leaning toward her. Truthfully, I was a little disappointed that she hadn't thought to get me anything, but her explanation made sense. "I'm just glad you like it."

"I do!" she said, holding it up again and catching the other end of it with her left hand. "Let me…" she began, then said, "Here." She handed me the necklace, then scooted around on her knees as she maneuvered her back to me, lifting her hair with her hands.

Realizing what she wanted me to do, I positioned myself and went up on my knees, reaching around her to take the necklace in my fingers. I fumbled with the tiny latch and the small loop it was supposed to attach to, but I couldn't get them to connect.

Sensing what was going on behind her neck, Elizabeth giggled and said, "Here, I'll do it." She tossed her golden hair over one shoulder, then reached back with her hands and took the two parts from me, maneuvering them into place within seconds. She then flipped her hair back, and it briefly smacked me in the face. I didn't mind.

She shuffled around again, facing me, my gift to her now circling her neck and coming to rest on the front of the black sweater she was wearing. She smiled and glanced to one side, seeming self-conscious. Her eyes then locked onto mine, and she asked sweetly, "Pretty?"

"Of course!" I said. "Always." My heart raced as I reached up and cupped her face with my hands, and we leaned in and kissed. I was used to this by now, the kissing and the intimate moments, but it wasn't always like this with us. Our relationship, if it could even be called that, was problematic.

Over the past month, we had continued to meet up at night, usually once or twice a week. Sometimes, we talked about serious things, like my attack on the mill or what she had found out in her vampire research, and other times, we just talked and joked around, enjoying each other's company. And yes, there was quite a bit of flirting and occasional physical affection, but what was frustrating was that we didn't see ourselves as an actual couple. That had been how I'd thought things were at the start, but the longer time went on, the more we realized that it wasn't that simple.

I had always grown up thinking that I would eventually get a girlfriend, we'd be in love, later get married, have children, and all that. That was what was normal, even expected. Elizabeth was the first girl who had even approached that fantasy, but we knew from the start that as long as she was still a vampire, things were never going to be like they should.

"Anything turn up in your research?" I asked her the night after our battle at Sibley Mill a few weeks earlier.

She sighed, then began twiddling the collar of her blue denim jacket absently. This was a slightly different look for her than I was used to, particularly the fact that her hair was combed back and in a ponytail. It was still taking me time to get used to this less glamorous, toned down version of her, but that didn't make her any less beautiful.

"Yes and no," she said, sounding frustrated.

"Meaning?"

"Meaning," she said pointedly and with a mocking tone, "that I have found some stuff out, just not what I wanted to. The only 'cures' I've been able to find so far are things like chopping my head off and running a stake through my heart."

"No!" I said, instinctively reaching for her hand. She flinched but didn't pull away.

"Or setting me on fire," she said bitterly, nodding and looking down at the ground where we were sitting. "That's another favorite."

"Elizabeth, I'm sure there's got to be a way."

"If there is, nothing I've found so far seems to show that anyone cares. It's all about 'how to eliminate the terrible creatures of the undead.'" She said this in a hokey, dramatic way.

"Maybe you just haven't found the right books yet," I offered.

She sighed again, looking up at the sky. "Maybe. There have been some useful things, or at least interesting, but still, I have to be careful."

"Careful how?"

"Like the other night. When I was leaving the library, there was this guy named Mr. Cooke who showed up. He was a friend of the family, someone my dad knew through the Army. 'Mr. Cooke with an *e*,' he'd always say to me with this big goofy grin, so I used to joke that he was really 'Mr. Cookie.' Kind of looked like a younger version of Santa Claus." She paused, looking thoughtful. "He used to do repair work around the house, like fixing our washing machine, which was always breaking down. No idea what he was doing at the library, but there he was, him on his way in, me on my way out, and we saw each other."

"Oh, shit," I said. "What happened?"

"I tried to pretend like I didn't see him, just kept my head down and walked out. But he insisted on following me, calling after me, all that. He caught up and grabbed me by my arm, and, well. I had to." She stopped, looked down at her lap, then back up again, still avoiding eye contact with me. Angrily, she added, "Stupid old fat man didn't even taste good."

"Elizabeth, I didn't need to hear that."

She turned sharply and looked at me, and for the first time in a long time, I wished that she hadn't. "Look," she hissed, "don't forget that I am what I am and survive how I have to because you made it this way. However indirectly, you made me. Don't get all *hck*— 'olier than thou…" She broke off, the word "holier" having gotten stuck in her throat. "Damn."

"Hick-olier than thou?" I asked, smiling. Her sudden defensiveness had caught me off guard, and I found comfort in the fact that she'd stumbled in her tirade. Humor seemed like a safe refuge.

"You know what I mean," she said, trying to fight back a smile. "Sorry."

"I'll try not to be so 'hick-olier' from now on."

She smacked at me and said with a combination of frustration and playfulness, "You are such an ass!"

"Yeah, but you love me anyway." I hadn't meant to say that.

She froze, looking shocked, but then her face softened. After a smirk, she nodded, looked down, and then her eyes met mine. "Yes, I do."

It surprised me how well I handled this; it was the first time "the L word" had come up between us. Although I could just as easily have ruined the moment by stammering nervously or saying something stupid, I instead moved closer to her, then put my hand on the back of her head, the base of her ponytail between my index and middle finger. Her eyes darted downward briefly, then met mine again, and I kissed her. We breathed each other in, and I loved how everything felt.

After a few seconds, we stopped, our foreheads still touching, and she let out a small laugh, which I followed up on. "As much as I try to disapprove of you," I said, "I can't help but love you, too."

She sighed again, but she was still smiling, her features out of focus because we were so close. "I know," she said.

It may have been a back-handed compliment on my part, or at the very least a judgmental thing to say, but it was true. When I was alone and thinking about her, I would come to the conclusion that it was wrong for me to keep things going and let her live; she was a vampire, and I was a vampire hunter, or at least, that was what I should be. I hated the vampires, hated having been one in my past, and I wanted to put an end to them. But then, once I was in Elizabeth's presence, I couldn't resist her, and I'd find myself coming up with all sorts of excuses as to why I shouldn't kill her.

Some of that was probably just lust, my teenage hormones having the greatest say in the decisions I made at the time. But there was also a strategic reason to keep her around: She told me things about the vampires that I otherwise would have no way of knowing. It wasn't often that this was tactical information that I could use against the clones or their offspring, but there were times when she described other things to me, including this night, which we spent on the far corner of my parents' property, well away from the house.

"Did he really taste bad?" I asked her, referring to the family friend she'd been forced to kill. The only reason I asked was that there had been a lull in the conversation after we'd stopped making out.

"What? Oh, Mr. Cooke? Yeah, he did. Fat people usually do. I guess it's all that cholesterol and stuff…" She then gave me a baffled look, though she was still smiling. "Why are you asking me this? And besides, you should already know. You were a vampire once."

"I know. Don't remind me." I thought for a second. "Actually, no, now that you mention it, I don't remember noticing a difference. Fat people, skinny people, nothing like that. Even white people and black people didn't taste different. Or if they did, maybe I was too young to notice."

"Different races don't taste any different," she said. "That much I've noticed. It's more to do with their health. I can even sort of smell on someone if they've got a blood disease, like AIDS or herpes. I stay away from those."

"Oh…" I said.

"What?"

"Just… something from a long time ago. We had that, that sense. We noticed it when we raided a hospital one time."

"A hospital?" she asked, surprised. "And you call *me* evil?"

"It was a long time ago!" I said. "I'm not proud of it. Any of it." She started to say something, then stopped. "And I never called you evil."

"I know; I'm sorry." Almost a minute of awkward silence passed before she asked me, "Did you like the taste? Of blood?"

"Did I…? No!" A few seconds later, I added, "Okay, no, that's a lie. I did. But back then. And no, I don't miss it, if that's what you were going to ask me."

"I wasn't," she said simply. "I was just going to say that I didn't like it, not at first. But it's something you get used to."

"Maybe," I said quietly.

"Like turning into a bat. I have to say, changing my body that… I don't know… drastically, it really freaked me out at first. Not to mention I was scared of heights. But I got over it pretty quickly."

I held back from what I started to say, which was that I had really enjoyed the whole being a bat and flying thing. Maybe I even missed it. If that were true, I certainly didn't want to admit it. It was definitely outweighed by the guilt I felt over the rest of the things I'd done.

We would have these conversations on the nights we'd meet, the topics jumping all over the place. Sometimes, I gained useful information from them, and other times, I just liked being with Elizabeth and getting close to her physically. My qualms about the ethics and morality of everything plagued me, but not to the point where I would ever have had the strength or good sense to just call things off with her.

One night, this time on the back porch of a house in my neighborhood that was up for sale and uninhabited, we found ourselves talking about Bethlehem, the school where we'd met and that I still attended. I hated it there, as had she, because the place was so constraining and full of rules, many of them based on the uptight beliefs of the Southern Baptists who ran it. They claimed to be doing God's work and that they were trying to teach us sinful young people the right way to live, but more often than not, it seemed more like they were just trying to outlaw anything that was fun or enjoyable.

A particular quirk of this was that they forbade any kind of dancing. The rationale was that dancing "leads to other things," that is, sex. Elizabeth brought this up after I happened to mention one of the things that had occurred during ninth grade in the spring, a school-wide talent show. Students were encouraged to participate and demonstrate their various creative skills, like singing, playing instruments, acting out sketches, and such. It had been a dismal affair; they made the entire student body sit through it in the gym one afternoon, and the audience was so apathetic that I even felt bad for the people on stage.

What I hadn't known at the time was that Elizabeth had tried to take part, but the teachers had forbidden her to do so because of the type of act she had proposed.

"What?" I asked, genuinely surprised. "Were you going to juggle or something?"

She laughed and smiled, pushing against my leg playfully. "I was going to dance. I used to be a dancer when I was little."

"Are you serious?"

"Yes, I'm serious!" she said, looking a little hurt but still being charming. "Back in Kansas, I actually won a couple of dance competitions."

My mind immediately went to an unexpected place, remembering the TV show *Star Search,* where various unknowns would perform acts like stand-up comedy, singing, and dancing. I always thought the show was stupid, particularly the little kids who would ham it up for the audience in an excruciatingly cheesy way while squealing out their renditions of the latest pop songs. I also remembered the dance teams that would perform what I saw as ridiculous, choreographed displays of idiocy, and the idea of Elizabeth doing the same thing seemed extremely laughable to me. She had always been so quiet and reserved.

But something else from what she said caught my attention: "Wait, Kansas?"

"That's where I'm from. My family moved here in '84."

"I didn't know that! Wow. I just always assumed you were from here. But now that I think about it, you have always had a little bit of a weird accent."

"I do not have an accent!" she said, though she over-annunciated each word.

"*'Iyy doo noht hahv an ahk-sehnt?'*" I asked, mocking her.

She tilted her head to one side and smirked, giving me a withering look. "Yeah," she said, then put on her best over-the-top southern accent: *"Ah giss I ain't frum araound heah."*

"Oh, God, that was horrible," I said, laughing.

She pursed her lips at me. "So, *anyway,*" she said meaningfully, "I tried to get them to let me do one of my routines in the stupid talent show. Put on a song, I dance to it, no big deal. To be honest, I kinda wanted to show up Annie and Sandra and the other cheerleaders, you know, show them how real dancing is done. Not like those stupid pep rallies we had to sit through."

I laughed. "Yeah, they still have those. Boring as crap, and the cheerleaders are all like, 'Woo!' and everything, but don't let it be too sexy!"

"Yeah," Elizabeth said, remembering the ones she'd been forced to endure as well. "But Mrs. Nesbit, Mrs. Carlton, the others… They were all like, 'We don't think that this would be appropriate…'" She said that in a lower, mockingly authoritative tone.

"Oh, man," I said, laughing, trying to picture how it might have gone had she succeeded. She'd always been gorgeous, but the idea of her all decked out and bopping around in some dumb, sequined outfit like one of those *Star Search* kids, spotlights shining all around her, seemed hilarious. "What song would you have done if they'd let you?"

"I don't know," she said, sounding disappointed. "I didn't get that far."

"I just can't picture you doing that. Like Debbie Gibson or something, all…" I started bouncing around in my sitting position, arms extended, doing my best impression of a corny 1980s dance video.

"It actually kind of hurt," Elizabeth said, suddenly quiet.

"Oh, come on…" I said, still joking around and grinning. My expression melted when I saw the stern look in her eyes.

"I'm serious," she said, her voice a lot deeper than usual. "You don't need to make fun of it."

I realized my mistake, and I reached out to her with my hand, but she drew back sharply. "Don't," she said firmly.

"Elizabeth, I'm sorry," I said, meaning it. She just stared at me, her expression blank. Several seconds went by, then more. She wasn't moving; she just kept staring at me.

"Look, stop," I said. "I didn't mean it. I'm sure that was very important to you." Still, she said nothing. She blinked once, but that was it. Clearly, I had hurt her feelings. But there was something else.

"Look," I repeated nervously. "I'm really, really sorry. I didn't mean to… I just… I didn't mean to, okay?" I hoped for some recognition on her face, but there was nothing. Just that empty look.

I suddenly became aware of a faint noise, but it wasn't really that. It was a pulsing sensation in my ears. My heart was beginning to race. I suddenly remembered that the girl I was sitting here talking to wasn't an ordinary girl. She was a vampire, and if she wanted to, she could lunge at me and rip out my throat. Worse still, she could bite me, drain my blood from me in as many swallows as it would take, and then bring me back to life as a vampire if she chose to. I would be damned forever.

"I think I'd better go," I said, and I moved to get up.

Her hand was suddenly touching my forearm gently. "No," she said quietly and with a smile, shaking her head slowly, eyes locked onto mine. It wasn't a warm or friendly look; it was the coldest expression I had ever seen on her face.

I didn't know what to do. I'd apologized as many times as I could, but that hadn't seemed to have worked. I didn't want to have to fight her, or worse, nor did I want her to kill me.

Finally, she laughed loudly as she gripped my arm, which she shook back and forth as she comically stomped her feet several times. "I got you!"

Confused, I pulled back from her. She let my arm go, covering her mouth with both hands as she caught her breath. "You…" I started to say.

"Oh, your face!" she said through her fingers, looking over at me with tears welling up in her eyes. Once she pulled her hands away and settled them on either side of her, I could tell that she was genuinely smiling, that she'd been joking all along. "That was priceless."

I felt a strange combination of relief and anger, but the latter didn't last long. She was just entirely too adorable when she was enjoying herself. Or, pretty much all of the time.

"Your heart was pounding," she said, calming down but still having a good laugh at my expense. "I could hear it. That was actually kind of a turn-on!"

"It was?"

"Of course it was," she said in a sexy manner, scooting closer to me.

"I really thought…" I began, but she cut me off, putting a finger over my lips.

"Shh," she said seductively. "It's okay. I could never do that to you." This led to more kissing, which did away with any feelings of hurt or fear I might have left.

Once we stopped, something occurred to me, and I laughed.

"What?" she asked.

"You should have done 'Like a Prayer.'"

She burst out laughing, and we spent the next few minutes joking about how the straight-laced staff at Bethlehem might have reacted to her performing to Madonna's infamous, controversial song.

My fear of her never fully went away, but it became buried over time the more I got to know her and trust her. I knew full well that if she'd wanted to turn me into a vampire like her, she could. That had been the case since our first night together. But she made it clear to me that she had no interest in doing that.

She knew how much I hated the idea of being a vampire, and she assured me several times that she would never force that on me. "You'd hate me for it," she'd said one time, "and I couldn't bear that." I had to hope that she was telling the truth. Even so, I never went out at night without that stake on me.

Early on, I had even been afraid to kiss her, fearful that one of her fangs might accidentally scrape my tongue. Would that count as a bite? Like Tim had mentioned to me after his wounding at the mill, there was a fear that once bitten, the vampirism could be like an infection, and maybe even if we weren't killed and brought back deliberately, could it be possible that years later, dying a natural death, we might then come back?

Elizabeth assured me that this wasn't the case. For one thing, her fangs only came out when she meant for them to, when she was ready to feed. And she hadn't found anything in her research so far that supported the theory that someone could be bitten and then come back to life as a vampire years or even decades later. I tried to convince Tim of this, but again, I couldn't tell him that it was Elizabeth who had told me. Instead, I had to reason with him, much like he had done with citing the math of the situation, why Augusta wasn't already overrun with hundreds of bloodthirsty beasts.

"Was it a nice funeral?" Elizabeth asked me one night in mid-December. This was the first night we had met inside the framework of a house that was being constructed around the corner from mine, and it would become a frequent meeting place for us. It was nice in that it helped shelter us from the increasingly cold weather, plus we both liked the feeling of it in general. There was something vacant and spooky, yet the newness was inspiring, too. I found that I actually liked the smell of sawdust and lumber, though that may have just been because I came to associate that with being with Elizabeth.

The site of the new house stood on what used to be a large overgrown lot that Carolyn and I had explored once when I was much younger. Our parents didn't like for us to go there because it was technically still someone else's property, but the dilapidated house that remained hadn't been lived in for years. I never got the full story, but it had something to do with an elderly couple who had lived there until they died sometime in the 1970s, and for many years after that, their adult children had refused to do anything with the house other than let it fall apart. For some reason, that had changed over the past year, and the entire lot had been bulldozed and would soon have a few smaller houses built on it.

I was sad to see the woods go; I had gotten used to how they looked from my backyard. I was also annoyed at how Scout constantly barked at the construction workers through the fence, sometimes even after we put him in his pen. My parents, though, saw this new development as a good thing. They were very progressive and liberal, and my mother encouraged me to embrace change, not rail against it. I mostly just rolled my eyes at this and acted like I didn't care.

Still, since I'd begun sneaking out at night to meet up with Elizabeth, I was grateful for a new place to go. There was something neat about seeing the way the construction of this house progressed each time we came back: New walls would be put in, carpentry equipment would have been moved around, and once it was ready, we could go up to the second floor, guided by my flashlight and from the outside streetlights that shone in through the open window frames.

"Your funeral?" I asked Elizabeth. This was a topic I had hoped to avoid.

"No, Queen Victoria's," she said sarcastically, her head nestled in my lap as I sat with my back to one of the walls. "Yes, my funeral. It's not like I was there... Well, okay, I guess I was. But not really, you know."

I hadn't thought of that. Her death had been traumatic for me, not least because I knew I had been indirectly responsible for it, but since she had come back, it was easy for me to forget that she had, in fact, been truly dead for a time.

"I... um... Yes, it was nice." I had been stroking her hair, running my fingers through it and occasionally getting them caught, having to pull up long sections of it to gently untangle my fingers. At this point, I stopped.

"That's it?" she asked.

"Well, that's what I heard." I flinched as I said this.

Elizabeth immediately sat up, then spun around to face me. "You didn't go to my funeral?"

"No, I didn't. I'm sorry." Her mouth gaped open indignantly. "I couldn't! I was too upset. But…" I tried to find the right words to say. "It was a nice service, from what I was told."

"I can't believe you couldn't even be bothered to go to my own funeral," she said, pouting.

"It wasn't that I couldn't be bothered!" I said defensively. "I just… I couldn't! I knew what had happened to you. Everyone else didn't. And, okay, yeah. I felt guilty."

She looked at me sternly, but then she softened, though still perturbed. "I guess I can understand that. So… What did you *hear* about it, then?"

I sighed. "Plenty of good things, I guess. Lots of people there."

"Well, that's something," she said, looking down and stroking absently at the wooden floor.

"Oh, and there was the song. Helen told me that some woman sang 'His Eye Is on the Sparrow' for you."

She rolled her eyes and threw her head back. "Oh, Goh—" She choked, then caught herself. Clearing her throat, she recovered. "That stupid old thing?" she said with a disbelieving look, but there was something else underneath.

This surprised me. "Stupid? They said it was your favorite song. Like, when you were little."

She laughed, but she seemed more annoyed than amused. "Good old Mom…" she said quietly, looking off to the side. She then brushed her hair over her left ear and said, "Just because one time, *one time!* She never would let that go."

"What do you mean?"

She sighed again, shrugging her shoulders while putting her hands in her lap. Her expression shifted again, this time from anger to a resigned smile, and she rolled her eyes again. "One time," she repeated, "when I was a little girl, like six I think… No. Seven. Eight?" She seemed to have forgotten that I was there, lost in thought. Then she nodded quickly. "Right. Seven."

"Okay," I said, trying to prompt her to get on with it.

"A bunch of us little kids had to sing that song in this... I don't know... performance thing in front of the churr... ch..." She raised her eyebrows as she looked down briefly. "Hmm... I can almost say that one. *Chirr-ch...* Hmm. Okay." She shook her head, closing her eyes for a couple of seconds. "Sorry. So, yes, it was just some little thing, all of us up there, singing for the congregation."

I got it immediately; I had seen similar performances from children at my previous school, plus I'd been forced to take part in a couple of them when I was little. It had also been a private Christian school but was Episcopalian and more laid back than the extremely strict Baptist one I currently attended. Still, there were times when religious services or school plays would occur, and these sometimes included brief recitals of songs and hymns. Most of the children were shy, not wanting to be there as they frowned at the audience and nervously sang off-key. The older I got, the more cynical I became about having to sit through this kind of thing, wondering why the adults who ran things insisted on putting their precious little darlings through it.

I told Elizabeth some of this, and she laughed. "It wasn't that bad! Well, maybe it was. I didn't really mind it. Performing just kind of came naturally to me." Again, it surprised me to hear this, but I knew better than to scoff at this given our earlier encounter when she'd mentioned her dancing.

"And I remember, leading up to that day, singing it on my own around the house. We'd been rehearsing it the week before." She breathed in, then looked up towards the boards of the unfinished ceiling, putting her arms out to her sides and clutching the cuffs of her sweater.

"I sing because I'm happy...

"I sing because... I'm freeeee..."

The hair on my arms stood up; I was stunned at how beautiful her singing voice was. It wasn't the sound of a little kid honking out some lyrics she didn't understand in front of a bunch of smiling but pained grown-ups; it was operatic, almost angelic. Something on my face must have betrayed my surprise.

She blushed, her chin plunging downward as she pulled her arms back in. "Okay, stop that," she said playfully.

"Stop what…" I started to say.

"You know what," she said, fighting back another of her sweet smiles. She shook her hands nervously, then went back to her story: "So, sure, we did that song, and for years after that, whenever it would come up, Mom would be like, 'You like that song! That's your favorite song!'" She rolled her eyes and shook her head again. "I just kind of went along with it. I mean, I didn't hate it, but I did get kind of annoyed at how much of a big deal she made over it. And she'd do that a lot, telling me what I liked. 'You like it…!' No, Mom, not really. She kind of didn't have a clue." She sighed, looking a little sad.

"Yeah, I get that," I said. "My own mother's always been pretty clueless, too. I don't hate her or anything, but it's just… I don't know… kind of like I've always had to be hidden from her. The real me." I laughed resignedly. "Hell, if my dad and her had known even half the things my sisters and I had gotten up to, they'd have to lock us up and throw away the key."

Our vampire activity aside, that had pretty much been consistent throughout my life. It was like our parents, who were never all that hands-on anyway, knew their children in one way, but we had completely separate identities that they knew nothing about. I was used to running circles around them when it came to keeping secrets, and I suppose I learned some of that from my sisters.

But the more I got to know Elizabeth, her childhood trickling out to me in bits of conversation here and there, the more confused I became. Back at Bethlehem, she had always been so quiet, yet at the same time, she was a billion times more attractive than any other girl at that school. All this talk of her being a dancer — and apparently a pretty damn good singer — made me wonder why she'd never joined the cheerleading squad or been part of the more popular crowd. I tried to ask her about this, but she changed the subject, talking about how much she liked our current meeting place, the house that was under construction.

So we continued to meet there, though we knew that someday, the house would be fully built, and some family would move in. We'd have to find another place. But for now, it was ours, this half-constructed shell that was constantly changing.

This led to the night of December 25th, which was when I gave her the necklace. When she asked me how my holiday had gone, I said, "Oh, the usual, I guess. Presents in the morning, going out to Appling to see the rest of the family in the afternoon, all that."

"Hmm," she said simply.

"Had to wait until everyone went to bed before coming out here tonight," I continued. "Like I told you."

"Yes, I know. That's why I'm here." She held out her hands in a falsely dramatic gesture.

Things seemed to be going flat, so the only thing I could think to do was lean forward and kiss her again. She reciprocated, but there was something missing. I told her a little bit more about my Christmas, including how my father had gotten me a VHS camcorder, though it wasn't something I had asked for. I didn't have much use for it, but apparently, he had heard that one of his friends had gotten one for his children, so he thought that it would be a cool gift for me as well. I appreciated the gesture, but I wasn't sure just what I could use it for. Eventually, after I'd gotten bored of shooting footage around the house — including one time the following January when I did a mock nature documentary of Scout in which I pretended to be "stalking the mysterious wild beagle" — my father would end up getting more use out of it than I did, apparently using it for recording events at the library he managed.

"Susanna was there, too," I said, "even though she didn't come home for Thanksgiving last month. She claimed she had some school stuff to work on."

"You think she was lying?"

"I don't know. Maybe. It's just hard to tell with her. The older we've gotten, the more we've drifted apart. I mean, things were kind of like that before when I was little, but then through all the vampire stuff, we seemed to get closer. And then she got more distant again."

"Yeah, that happens, I guess," she said quietly. After a long pause, she said with more emotion than I was expecting: "Ray, I miss my mom and dad." She was looking down at the floor, her eyes seemingly focused on the outspread hand that was supporting her.

I immediately felt like an asshole. I scooted over to her and put my arms around her, and she leaned her head onto my chest, sniffling. "I am so, so sorry, Elizabeth," I said to her, my voice low. "I've been yapping all about my family, and I didn't even think about what this Christmas must have been like for you."

"Yeah, it's been pretty shitty!" She said this like she was joking, but I could hear the tears in her voice. "I mean, sometimes I'm okay with it all. It's not like I was all that happy with my life before. Maybe you noticed that." I hadn't really, but it explained things a little more. "Usually I don't let it bother me. But, you know, with all this 'holiday cheer' crap and everyone talking about being close with family..." Her voice was becoming more shaky and high-pitched.

"I know, I know," I said, squeezing her and then kissing the top of her head. "Shh. It's okay." Those last two words echoed in my head several times, and I again felt stupid. How was it okay?

"Have you ever gone by your old house and looked in on them?" I asked after a couple of minutes.

"No," she said firmly, and I felt her grip on my arm tighten, then relax. "I think that would just make things worse."

And I felt like I was making things worse with every word I said, so I clammed up. We held each other in the dark for at least half an hour, saying nothing. Her limbs occasionally made these strange, quick movements, which I didn't know at the time were indications that she'd fallen asleep and was dreaming. Soon enough, I ended up falling asleep as well.

"Did you know that you snore?" she asked me after we'd woken up.

"Well, no, not exactly."

"Not exactly?" She seemed amused.

"Carolyn used to say that I did, but I didn't believe her. Our father snores, pretty damn loud sometimes in fact, but I've never heard myself do it."

"That's because you're asleep," she said slowly and deliberately. I laughed, as did she. Our nap seemed to have lightened her mood.

We had stood up and were stretching, working out the kinks from having been in the same position for so long. Elizabeth then reached up and tugged at the necklace I'd given her, peering downward to try to get a look at it.

"You like it?" I asked.

"Yes," she said a little impatiently. "I told you I did. Where did you get it, anyway?"

"Hmm? Oh, that store across from the mall, Service Merchandise. I was there with my mom getting presents for my sisters, and I saw it and thought, 'Hey, why not?'"

She grinned, still holding the necklace between her fingers. "What did you tell your mom?" I wasn't sure what she meant, so she clarified: "About who you were getting it for."

"Oh," I said, suddenly feeling guilty. "I, um…"

She dropped her hand, and her expression changed. "Oh my… Ha! You stole this, didn't you?" Her look was one of both mock indignation and delight.

"Mmmaybe?" I said. She was right; I had grabbed the necklace from the rack and pocketed it when no one was looking, nervous as hell when my mother and I walked out of the store. But no alarms went off, and I felt a little thrill in getting away with something criminal. I hadn't planned on telling Elizabeth this, though.

"It's okay," she said, still grinning. She then grabbed the sides of her jacket and held them out in a pose, saying, "Where do you think I got this? Or this." She indicated her sweater, then her jeans. "Or these. They only buried me in the one dress, you know. And it's not like I can just go shopping like everyone else."

This was something I hadn't even thought of, but it made perfect sense. "So you just steal all your clothes?"

"Kinda have to! And I have to admit that it's kind of fun." She sounded pleased with herself.

"Quite the little klepto," I said, amused, and I stepped forward and held her. It wasn't a full embrace, just my hands touching her elbows as she playfully rested her hands on my chest. She flashed me a smile, her eyes slightly squinting.

"Well, I don't think that Macy's is going to go bankrupt because one girl sneaks in in the middle of the night and takes a few outfits."

"Is that where you go?"

"Yes. And some of the other stores in the mall. Have to avoid the rent-a-cops, though."

I misunderstood her. "The rental cars?"

"Rent-a-cops!" she said more clearly, then laughed. "The security guards? Don't tell me you've never heard that term before."

I hadn't, so she explained the reference to me further. Truth be told, I had no real reason to know anything about rental cars, either; I'd only heard of them from comedians I'd seen on TV. Like a lot of kids of my generation, the majority of what I knew about the outside world, particularly the adult world, came through television.

I pictured her sneaking through the darkened mall at night, slipping unseen among the racks of clothes, but then another thought flashed through my mind. If she ever did get caught by one of these security guards, she'd have to kill them. I wondered if this had happened, but because I didn't want to know the answer, I didn't ask.

"You know what sucks, though?" she said. "Getting home and finding out that the clothes sometimes have those ink tag thingies on them. And then I can't get them off without breaking them and ruining the clothes, so I have to just throw them away."

"Home?"

"Well, you know, the graveyard." She had begun to look a little sad as she said this, so I quickly changed the subject.

"Look, I need to get going. It's almost…" I pulled back from her and checked my watch, surprised to find that it was after 3:00. "Whoa. Yeah. It's late."

"Sorry."

"No, don't be sorry!" I said reassuringly. "I wouldn't be out here if I didn't want to. You know that."

"Yeah, I know," she said, slightly flirty. "You know what else?"

"What?"

"We've slept together."

My heart leapt. "What? When?"

She giggled. "Just now!" she said, pointing at the spot on the floor where we had fallen asleep.

"That's not…" I began, feeling nervous. "That's not what that means."

"Yes it is," she said in a clipped, comical manner, a look of mock sincerity on her face as she nodded.

It wasn't like I hadn't thought about having sex with her, but it was a topic that had not yet come up between us. It was certainly something that I wanted to do, something I'd wanted for years. But when she began joking about it at this particular moment, I found myself feeling inexplicably afraid.

"Look…" I began, stepping forward.

"No, no!" she said quickly, holding up a hand. "We can talk about it later!" I wasn't sure if she was annoyed with me again or was just playing. "See you again before the New Year?"

"What? Oh, yeah. I guess so. Yes. Definitely." I was still thrown, which she seemed to be enjoying.

"1990," she said wistfully, but then her tone hardened. "New decade and all that. Whoopty doo."

Grateful for the new topic, I said, "You know, I've seen some people on TV going on about how it's not really 'the new decade' until 1991. Because of the way the calendar started, birth of Jesus and all that, so there wasn't a Year 0, but it really started with 1, so the first decade ended in 10… All that."

She looked pensive, biting her lower lip as she looked to one side. Then she nodded. "That's really fucking stupid."

I laughed. "I know! It's not like anyone's going to say that 1980 was part of the '70s. It was 1980. So it's part of the '80s."

"Yeah," she said, still looking thoughtful. "1930 wasn't part of The Roaring Twenties." I got the reference; I remembered learning about it in History class. I also remembered that she'd sat in the row next to mine at school that year. We'd had our share of nervous, fragmented conversations then, though the nervousness had been mostly on my part, not hers. I liked how she was so much easier to talk to now.

"Glad to see that we're on the same page," I said, then winced at how clichéd that sounded. She just smirked at me smartly, the same as always.

As we said our goodbyes outside the doorway of the unfinished house and made plans to meet up next time, we talked a little more about the fact that a new year was coming.

"It's just a turning of the calendar, really," she said, clutching her clothes to herself against the cold. "Not a big deal."

"I suppose," I said. "But I kinda like the idea of a new start, that maybe things can be better."

"Maybe," she said. "You'd think that they'd have to be."

It was impossible to predict, really. The following year would indeed be filled with lots of new things, some of them good, and some of them more terrible than I could have expected.

CHAPTER SIX

It wasn't like the only thing I did with my time was to have occasional nocturnal meet-ups with my pseudo-girlfriend. The rest of my life continued on as usual, an odd balance of the supernatural and the mundane. I still had to get through school, for instance.

That was difficult for several reasons. For one, I hated Bethlehem Baptist. The longer I was there, the more it seemed like a joke. It barely even felt like a real school, especially compared to what I knew of others like the ones my old friends were currently attending. Even St. Joseph's Elementary, where I'd been before, seemed much better. I hadn't realized it at the time, though.

Growing up, I'd always been a smart-ass, so it was only natural for me to clash with the teachers there. Adding in the fact that I had this dark secret that none of them could ever know about, I'd often felt this sense of superiority despite the fact that they were in charge. The way I saw it, I was smart, and they were stupid, even if they were much older than me.

I had hoped that my new school would be better, that things would be cooler and more grown up, but in fact, the opposite had happened. Aside from the staff's preoccupation with shoving as many close-minded Christian ideas down our throats as they could on a daily basis, there was the fact that the curriculum was substandard, as were some of the teachers. Not all, but most. On my more cynical days, I would ask myself how any of them felt they had any business standing in front of a classroom.

St. Joseph's had also been well-funded, unlike Bethlehem, which seemed to be barely scraping by. It took me a while, but eventually, I began to retroactively appreciate many of the teachers I'd had at my old school, even Mrs. Warren, my seventh grade English teacher. I'd hated her at the time, thinking she was just some mean old woman, but she knew her stuff. Her classes on diagramming sentences and composition seemed brilliant in comparison to the ones in which my ninth grade biology teacher, Mrs. Manning, insisted that believing in evolution was a sin that would send you straight to hell.

My social life wasn't much better. I didn't have any close friends at Bethlehem, and the friendships left over from my former school were tenuous at best. After that encounter with my clone at Sibley Mill, Carl and Tim had been hard to keep in touch with; things had become uncomfortable between us. We had all been pretty freaked out by what we'd seen, and while we agreed that the vampire threat should be dealt with, neither of them seemed willing to step up and take any further action. I still hadn't been able to get Dennis to call me back, and Nick was a lost cause.

I wanted to do more, but it just didn't seem possible. Maybe by the next summer when I turned sixteen and was old enough to drive, I could have more autonomy and be proactive, I thought. Until then, all I could do was watch the news and hear about the latest vampire attacks. They had begun to spread out more widely, mostly concentrated in downtown but occasionally springing up in unexpected parts of the city. Whether these were kills perpetrated by our clones or the vampires they had made was never clear, but maybe that distinction didn't matter. One way or another, I felt responsible.

Sometimes, I was crushed with despair, fearing that everything had gotten too far out of control, that there was no way to contain it. Other times, I'd get this burst of determination, feeling that I needed to do something. That would come to nothing, though; there were a few nights when I would sneak out of my house armed with my stake, garlic powder, and a cross, walking around my neighborhood and feeling ready to do battle with any vampire that might cross my path. And then nothing would happen. I wanted to kill my clone, but unless he came to me, I wouldn't get the chance. And he knew that.

There was one night when I saw some bats fly overhead, and I thought I might have a fight on my hands. But they just flew by, and even though I tried to run after them, there was no way I could catch up. Defeated, I began walking back home. Not long after, I heard what I was pretty sure were screams in the distance, and I knew what had happened. Sure enough, there was a news report the following day of two victims of "alleged vampire attacks" a block away from where I'd been. I hated that the news media still insisted on calling them that; everyone knew what was really happening.

"In lieu of any official statements by authorities on the specific causes of these attacks," a typically coiffed female news anchor said on one of the nightly broadcasts, "police still urge residents to use caution and stay indoors as much as possible after dark."

"Why won't you just admit it?" I shouted at the TV, then hoped that I hadn't been overheard by my parents.

The camera cut to the woman's co-anchor, a serene looking black man with a neat, thin moustache. "Some residents of the Augusta area have looked to themselves for a solution to this ongoing problem," he began.

"Again?" I asked quietly. Two and a half years ago, a bunch of self-made vampire hunters calling themselves Life Force had tried to bring us down, and they'd come pretty close to succeeding. The police saw them as vigilantes, and eventually, they were rounded up and taken in. When our clones emerged and began wreaking havoc on the city again more recently, I'd wondered if that group might return.

The reporter went on to explain that while there was no official movement this time, various individuals and groups of people had been trying to fight back. What I found interesting, though, was the way the story sort of danced around the topic, never giving any specific details on just who was doing the fighting or how one might get in touch with them.

"That makes sense, I suppose," Susanna said over the phone, sounding only partly interested.

"Right," I said. "Whoever's doing it, they don't want the police to come after them again. But it seems kind of weird how they did a news story on it but then left out any real details."

"But did they show any places, like churches or schools or anything like that?"

"Yeah," I said, recalling the broadcast. "There was that one on Walton Way, not too far from here."

"One what?"

"Church. You know, the one with the loud bells."

"Well, I think what was happening there was that someone at the station was either a part of a group or at the very least supports the idea, so they sort of slipped the story on the air to try to get the word out. But like you said, they couldn't tell too much, or that might make the police angry."

I pondered this for a moment. "So that church might be a meeting place?"

"That would be my guess. Why?"

"Just… I don't know. I want to do something about all this. And I can't get Carolyn or any of my friends to help, not anymore."

"Ray, listen to me," she said firmly. "Do not get mixed up with those other people. You have no idea who they are or what they're up to. For all you know, they could find out the truth about you. About all of us. I mean it. Stay away from them."

Normally, I would feel defiant whenever Susanna got so authoritarian with me, but I had to admit that she had a point. "You're right," I said with a sigh. "I just can't seem to get anything done on my own."

"Then let the other people deal with it if they think they can. And the police."

"Yeah, because they were always so good at stopping us back in the day," I said sarcastically.

"It's better than you going out and getting yourself killed!" she shot back. "Besides, they managed to kill my clone, right?" That was true, as far as we knew.

"I guess." It struck me as odd that she was advocating so much caution. I would have expected advice like this from Carolyn, who had been too scared to take action ever since the clones had emerged. And while this out of character attitude of Susanna's confused me, it was better than the indifference with which she'd reacted over the past several months.

"Did you decide about my room?" she asked, changing the subject.

"What? Oh, that. Nah, I don't think I'm going to bother with that. But thanks anyway."

Back when she'd visited for Christmas, we hadn't talked about anything vampire-related, and she had avoided the topic the handful of times I tried to bring it up. One thing she had told me, though, was that if I wanted to move into the upstairs bedroom that used to be hers, I could. "I don't plan on moving back here," she'd said, "so it's yours if you want it."

The offer appealed to me at first; the room certainly would have given me more privacy. For a teenage boy, that's an important thing, and I liked picturing Elizabeth flying to that bedroom window and maybe even coming into the room with me some nights. But it was impractical in terms of sneaking out. It was much easier to climb out of my ground-floor bedroom window than it would have been to make my way onto the roof, then somehow to the ground below without breaking my neck. I couldn't tell Susanna any of this, naturally; I just said that it seemed like too much trouble.

"Well, if you change your mind…" she said, not finishing her sentence. "It doesn't really matter to me either way."

"Oh!" I said, remembering something. "There was one more thing at the end of that news story that I wanted to tell you about."

"What's that," she asked flatly.

"It was just kind of a throwaway thing at the very end, nothing the guy went into any detail about. But apparently, according to him, there have been recent sightings of vampires in other cities. Like, around the country."

"That's… interesting," she said thoughtfully. "Did he say where?"

"Yes," I said, trying to recall all of the places named. "I think he said somewhere in Arizona… Flagstaff. That was it. And a place in Texas I've never heard of, somewhere called Del Rio. And one or two others… Oh yeah, Boston. And Los Angeles."

"Hmm," Susanna said. "I wonder if any of that's true."

"It might be," I said. "From what I've been able to find out about the vampires and the clones, they don't all get along."

"Yes, you mentioned that. So you think these other places are where they've gone? They've left town?"

"That was my thought, yes."

"Well, I don't see you going all around the country and tracking them down, Ray."

"I know, I know," I said.

"Maybe they'll all leave town, go somewhere else. Then you'd be safe."

"I don't think that's going to happen, Susanna."

It was an intriguing notion, but I found it hard to believe. I figured that if anything would make the vampires leave Augusta, it would be because they had drained the entire city and needed somewhere else to feed. I hoped that things would never get that bad, but I hated the fact that I felt nearly powerless to stop them if they did.

The next major development came from an unexpected source: Carolyn. One Saturday near the end of January, she had as usual come by the house to do laundry; her apartment didn't have its own washer and dryer. Quite unexpectedly, she asked me if I would like to come back to her place after she was done and spend the night, "just for old time's sake."

When we were much younger, she, Susanna, and I had spent nights out at our aunt and uncle's house in Appling, sleeping in the living room but staying awake late, making each other laugh in the dark. A little later on at our own house, Carolyn had all but begged me to spend the night sleeping on her bedroom floor after a scary movie she'd seen with her friends had left her not wanting to be alone. She alluded to this, and I knew that something was up. It wasn't like she was a scared little teenager anymore, but something was obviously bothering her, and she didn't feel comfortable talking about it at our parents' house where they might overhear.

The drive from my house to her apartment was only about ten minutes, and once we were alone in the car, I asked her, "Okay, so what's really going on?"

She exhaled sharply, not taking her eyes off the road. "Some really serious stuff went on last night," she said, her voice shaking, "and I really don't want to be on my own. The only reason I was able to sleep last night was that I was so damn exhausted, and I had nothing but nightmares the whole time."

"And you couldn't get… What's his name again?"

"You mean Andy? We're not together anymore." She said this with a scowl, again not looking over at me. This didn't really surprise me; she had dated a few different guys since she and Damon had split up a year ago, but none of the relationships had lasted more than a few weeks, if that. "And even if we were, it's not like I could talk to him about this. You're pretty much the only one."

I had suspected this; it was something to do with the vampires. She had a story to tell me, which she prefaced with mentioning her first apartment, where she'd lived just after high school. I remembered it, a neat place that was half of the upstairs of a large, old house downtown. The other three quarters of the house were uninhabited and were instead used as storage space by the old man who owned it; the rooms were filled with tons of old furniture and boxes. The ceilings were very high, and the huge, spacious rooms had hardwood floors. There was even a fireplace, something that had made Carolyn fall in love with the apartment and decide to rent it. Technically, it was our father who was paying the rent, not her, just as he continued to pay for Susanna's apartment in Columbia.

Unfortunately, one thing Carolyn had failed to notice until after she'd moved in was that the house stood right next to some train tracks. During her first attempt at sleeping there, a train rolled through at two separate times in the middle of the night, sirens blaring. The vibration of the train, which she could feel even though she was on the second floor, had been frightening enough, but the insanely loud horn had "nearly made me poop myself," as she put it when she told me about it back then.

"So yeah," she said as we drove, "that place. You remember. And then I got my friend Catherine to take over the lease so I could move out and into a different place."

"And she was okay with the train?" I asked, never having been clear on the details of her move.

"Yeah, that girl could sleep through anything," she said. She then looked sad.

"What?" I asked.

"Give me a second," she said quietly.

"Okay," I said, unsure.

Eventually, she continued, "I hadn't heard from her for a while. We were supposed to hang out after Christmas, but she didn't call. And she didn't call me back. I didn't know why she was standing me up, so I went by her apartment the other night to see what was up."

She stopped talking, and I wasn't sure what was coming next. "So…?" I asked.

She closed her eyes for a moment, breathing out. Blinking rapidly, she still kept her eyes on the road. "I'm really damn lucky the way the timing worked out," she said finally. "I went along 6th Street and came to that 4-way stop… You remember, the one next to the place?"

"Yeah." I could see it in my head; the house was on a corner.

"So I'm at the stop sign, waiting for my turn to go through. I could see the apartment upstairs, and there was a light on, so I figured she must be home. If I'd gotten there just a minute or two earlier…" She shuddered, then suddenly gasped and slammed on the brakes. I looked up to see that we'd almost driven straight through a red light. I held out my hands, bracing myself on the dashboard as the car lurched and stopped. Another car coming the other way sped through the intersection.

"Sorry," Carolyn said, recovering. "Got distracted."

Breathing heavily and with my heart pounding, I said, "Maybe we should just wait until we get to your place. We're almost there."

"Yeah, I think you're right."

Eventually, we made our way into her apartment. Like the one she had been talking about, this too was an old house that had been divided into apartments, though this one was a lot smaller. Half of the downstairs was hers, while the other three-fourths of the house was rented by a married couple with whom Carolyn had minimal contact. She'd had another apartment between this one and the downtown one, a small cottage behind someone's house, but I had never been over there.

I had lain out my sleeping bag on the floor of her bedroom while she did various stuff in the bathroom, getting ready for bed. It was an oddly nostalgic feeling, simultaneously nice and unnerving. While it was pleasant remembering the times I had slept in that sleeping bag while camping out with Susanna and Carolyn as a child, the last time I had actually used it had been when we were vampires. I didn't like being reminded of that.

After a while, we had settled down for the night, a white pillar candle burning in one corner of the room. Carolyn was finally ready to continue with her story.

"So, like I said, I was pretty damn lucky that I saw what I did."

"Saw what?" I asked.

"When I was at that stop sign, I looked up and saw that the lights in the house were on. Then one of the windows opened, and out flew four or five bats, just like that." She was sitting up in bed and had made a sweeping gesture with her hands, sliding them against each other with a light clap.

I gasped, taking this in and beginning to put the pieces together. "So Catherine…?"

"She…" Carolyn clammed up for second. "I didn't know at the time. But I was pretty sure she was dead."

"Oh my God," I whispered. "Damn. I'm… I'm really sorry, Carolyn."

"Oh, it gets a lot, lot worse, let me tell you," she said bitterly. "I just sat there at the intersection, frozen, until some asshole behind me slammed on his horn for me to go. So I just sped up and then pulled over in that big parking lot across the street. I was shaking, trying to figure out what to do."

She went quiet again, so I had to prompt her after a bit. "So what did you do?"

She sighed heavily. "I don't know what possessed me," she said. "I should have just gotten the hell out of there. But I needed to know. So I just stayed in that parking lot, my car doors locked, hoping I'd be safe. I'd moved my car around to where I could see the apartment, and I waited for them to come back.

"And after a while, they did. I saw them walking along the street, all laughing and in a great mood. It was me — the other me — and Damon, you know, the other him. And there were three other people — vampires — with them, too. They didn't look that different, but… I could just tell. The fact that they were there and getting along with the clones of me and Damon… Suffice it to say it freaked me out."

"I can imagine," I said.

"They looked around, and thinking no one was looking, they all turned into bats and flew back in through that open window."

"Was Catherine one of the…"

"No," she said, cutting me off. "I think they just killed her." She said this last sentence very softly, her voice shaking.

"Man," I almost whispered. "I'm really sorry." I felt kind of stupid repeating the same platitude, but I couldn't think of anything else to say.

"Like I said, it gets worse. I was scared, but I was also really, really mad. Something about seeing them just set me off. I think I was still in shock about Catherine. I drove home, but I barely remember it. I'm surprised I didn't get into a wreck. And then when I did get home, I did something I didn't think I'd ever do."

"What was that?"

"I picked up the phone, and I started to call Damon."

"What?" I almost shouted. This was a surprise, to say the least. I knew that she hated him and wanted nothing to do with him. They had dated for a couple of years, and unlike some of the guys she had been with, Damon was a cool, really nice guy, at least in the beginning. He was this happy-go-lucky rock star type who played guitar and sang in a local band, and he was nice to me, plus he kissed up to our parents, so they liked him, too.

We had roped him into the vampire situation in 1987, and he'd gone along with it, sticking by Carolyn throughout even when things had gotten as bad as they did. But eventually, they'd had a really bad break-up due to the fact that he'd cheated on her. Once I found this out, I hated him almost as much as she did, feeling sort of betrayed by proxy. Carolyn had severed all contact with him, so to hear that she'd gone back on this caught me off guard.

"Why did you do that?" I asked.

"It seemed like a smart thing to do," she said sternly. "Remember the whole thing about how our clones can't kill us because then they'll die."

"Right…" I said, still feeling thrown.

"I was so mad about what they'd done to Catherine. My friend was dead. I know it's not exactly the same thing, but it's kind of like how you felt when that girl you liked got killed by your clone."

"Elizabeth," I clarified, suddenly feeling defensive. Carolyn had sometimes talked as if the feelings I had for girls were a joke because I was so much younger than she was, like they weren't real.

"And…" She sighed angrily. "It's that advantage thing you talked about before. How we should go after our clones since they can't kill us. And I never wanted to because I was so scared. But not anymore." I understood. I'd been through the same thing.

"So… Anyway, by the time I started to call Damon, I realized that it was like one o'clock in the morning, and that wouldn't have looked good. So I had to try to just go to sleep and wait till the next day. Let me tell you, it wasn't easy. I didn't even go to class all day Friday."

I waited for the rest of her tale. I could see where this was going, and it reminded me of something that I'd been regretting for a while. When I had decided that we needed to take on the clones, what I'd pictured had been a lot different from how things had turned out so far. I saw myself as a vampire hunter, leading my old friends into big, epic battles against the evil vampires. We would heroically defeat them and save our city, and finally, we would be redeemed for all the wrong we had done in the past.

I also tried to imagine all kinds of clever uses of weaponry, like a special crossbow that fired full-sized wooden stakes instead of arrows, hidden banks of sprinklers and hoses that I'd use to ambush a flock of vampire bats and take them down all at once, and even tripwire-triggered springboards full of wooden spikes that would swing up from the ground and impale a vampire, maybe even multiple ones.

But I could barely get the guys together, Susanna was hiding out in Columbia, and Carolyn had refused to take part in the hunt. I had plenty of great ideas, just not the ability to make them actually happen. I didn't even bother to ask Carolyn for her help building these things, even though I knew that, unlike me, she actually had the skill to do so. She may not have done so in a long time, but when we were younger, she and my dad used to build all kinds of things.

So the fact that she was telling me that she had decided to take the fight to them surprised me, much more so because she was involving Damon. I told her as much.

"I know," she said, a groan in her voice, "and I regretted it as soon as I saw him face to face. I tried to be all practical about it on the phone once I got him, but still, seeing him in person brought back a ton of bad memories. But like I said, I had to try to be practical about it. He really was the best person for the job."

"You could have called me!" I said. "I've already killed one of the vampires!"

"You have? When?"

"A couple of months ago. Not too far from our house. It was one of the ones that Carl's clone made."

"Really," she said. "I didn't know that."

"And Carl and Tim and I killed some at that old Confederate mill!" That was a slight exaggeration.

"Well, good for you," she said sarcastically. "Okay, that was mean. Sorry."

It felt like things were heading in a bad direction, plus I was beginning to feel defensive again. So I steered the conversation back to her story, asking her what it had been like calling up Damon after so long.

She sighed. "It was weird. I just tried to lay everything out as best I could, all diplomatic and official. And it seemed to go pretty well at first. For one thing, he'd seen his clone downtown, too. So he already had some idea that he might be around there. Once I told him that he and my clone were staying in Catherine's apartment, he came to the same conclusion I did, that we should attack them there."

"Yeah, that's how it was for me. It'd taken me so long to actually find my clone, so once I knew where his group was, I had to go after him."

"Did you get him?"

I shook my head. "No. He got away."

"Hmm. Too bad. Well, anyway, so we meet up, and keep in mind that I still haven't ever told him where *this* apartment is, so we meet up at this gas station not too far from the downtown place. And as soon as I get out of the car and he sees me, he moves like he wants to give me a hug."

"Are you kidding me?"

"Right! I backed away real quick, and I think he got the message. I gotta say, it took all I had not to just reach back and kick him in the balls." I couldn't help but laugh at picturing that, and she let out a small laugh, too.

"And then he's all like, 'I just hope we can smooth things over, and…' And I'm like, there's nothing to 'smooth over!' You cheat on me, you put your hands on me… No. Just, no."

"Put his hands on you?" I wondered if this might be a reference to something sexual.

"He hit me, Ray. When we were fighting the night we broke up. I said some pretty nasty things to him, which he deserved, by the way, and… You remember how, after that, I didn't come by the house for a couple of weeks?"

I hadn't thought about that for a while, and it hadn't seemed like a big deal to me at the time. She just hadn't come over and done laundry for longer than usual; that was the way I'd seen it.

"Well, that was because I had a black eye. And I didn't want Dad to see it and then get all John Wayne on Damon, you know, go after him with his gun or something stupid."

That wasn't something I could picture. "Wait… Dad has a gun?"

"You didn't know that? He did grow up on a farm, Ray. Just like Mom. Oh, I know they're all 'tolerance and liberalness and do the right thing' and all that now, but that's not how they grew up. They may have moved to the city once they were old enough to get away from 'the country folk,' but there's still some of that in them."

"Hmm. I didn't know that." Honestly, I didn't know a whole lot about my family's history; I'd never bothered to care. I knew bits and pieces, little facts here and there, but not many details. And at this point, I was far too distracted by Carolyn's other revelation. "He hit you."

"Yes. It's one of the reasons why I dumped his ass. You know, as if cheating on me with at least three other girls wasn't enough. It was Catherine who tipped me off to that, by the way."

I seethed for a bit, hating Damon more than ever. "You know, if I ever see him, *I'm* going to kick him in the balls."

She laughed, more heartily than I'd heard her do in a long time. It was the same wide-mouthed cackle that she would snidely direct at me when we were children and she felt she'd gotten the better of me, the kind only a big sister can give. But then another thought occurred to me, and I suddenly felt concerned. "Wait, is he okay?"

"Who, Damon?" Carolyn asked, still recovering from her laughter. Then her voice went more stern. "Yes, he's okay. We both made it out alive. Or else I wouldn't be here telling you this. I have to admit, I didn't think we were going to make it. But the fact that we did, or actually, *why* we did, that's one of the main things I want to tell you about."

"What do you mean?"

"Just let me tell the story. It will all make sense, I hope."

The way it went was that Carolyn and Damon had waited, this time in his car, in the same parking lot across the street from the house where Carolyn's — or Catherine's — old apartment was. They got there just before sunset, even though they had planned to arrive a lot earlier just to be safe. Carolyn had been late getting to the gas station, which she told me was because she kept procrastinating before leaving to go meet up.

"So that meant that we didn't have long to wait. And I was grateful. Sitting in that car felt weird as hell, just one more reminder of things I didn't want to think about. I made it clear to him that this wasn't some kind of reunion or reconciliation; we were there to get the job done. He finally shut up and agreed.

"And so we — or really, he — saw the bats fly out that same window. 'There, I see them!' he says, all whispering.

"I told him, 'You don't really need to whisper. I don't think they can hear us in the car.'

"He goes, 'Just trying to keep things stealthy,' giving me that stupid shit-eating grin of his. I just rolled my eyes, then asked him if he'd got the weapons. And he did; there were two backpacks in the back seat, all loaded up with stakes and garlic and crosses, the usual stuff. At least he'd managed to get that right.

"So then we made our way over the street and into the house. The door to the main house was locked, but one of the things I never liked about it — you know, besides the world's loudest train being right there — was that it always seemed like it'd be real easy for someone to break in; all you'd have to do was just bust out one of the small windows in the door, then reach in and turn the deadbolt. So that's what Damon did, plain and simple."

I remembered visiting this place with her when she was first moving in, so I was able to picture everything she was describing.

Even though I hadn't been there at night, the interior of the house was dark even during the day, since three quarters of it was uninhabited, giving everything a creepy atmosphere, but also kind of cool. The door she was describing was on the back of the house next to a small alleyway; that's where she had parked her car when she lived there. Once inside, a stairwell that had two right turns led to the top floor, leading to a long hallway that ran to the opposite side of the building. At the end of it, on the left, was the doorway to the only habitable apartment.

"This was where we had to gamble," Carolyn said. "Either we'd have to break the door down, or, as I'd hoped, Damon — the clone, you know — was hopefully being as slack about locking doors as he'd always been. And sure enough, I tried the doorknob, and it was open; we were able to walk right in.

"The living room didn't look all that different from when Catherine lived there, but it looked like they'd thrown some of her stuff out. They still had the TV, the bean bag, the sofa, all that, and there were a couple of new mattresses laid out in the kitchen. The windows in there were blacked out with trash bags, the same way we used to do it in our house. That must have been where the new vampires slept, you know, the ones that Damon and the other me made.

"Anyway, that's not important. After I put my flashlight away, I went through the kitchen and to the back bedroom. It was… I'll just say… kinda disturbing. I was already icked out enough over the idea of my double and Damon being together, but apparently they were. But seeing all of those…" She stopped.

"What?" I asked, having kept quiet for a while.

She cleared her throat. "Let's just say that I'm not comfortable talking about whips and chains with my little brother."

"What?" I repeated. "I don't understand."

"Never mind," she said quickly. "It doesn't matter. It's just… I never was into any of that, but if this other me and other Damon were some kind of darker, evil versions of us, then I guess…" She paused, then shuddered visibly, almost comically. "Doesn't matter, doesn't matter. I don't want to think about it."

"Carolyn…" I said impatiently. If she were going to tell me this story, she needed to get on with it.

"All right, all right!" she said, throwing up her hands. "The point is that what we were doing was waiting for them to come back. That's when we'd attack them. Now that we knew that, well, they had their own private room, hopefully that meant that we could get them by surprise when they were away from the other three. No idea who they were; I guess just some random victims they decided to turn into vampires, too.

"So anyway, we waited, stakes and weapons all ready, waiting for them to come back. And they did, and like, my heart was pounding once I heard their voices. I was like, 'I'm not ready for this.' But once those other versions of me and him came strolling into the room, I just jumped up, screaming, and I went right for Damon's heart.

"They were surprised, enough to throw them off guard I guess, but Damon — the one I was attacking — managed to hold me off at the last second. I had my stake up like this," she said, holding up her right hand in a fist in the dim light of the room, "and this big clove of garlic in the other, so I just smacked him in the face with it. He fell against the wall by the door, yelling and all, like it had burned him or something. That gave me enough time to jump forward with my stake, and I nailed him, right in the heart." She pointed at her own heart.

"I heard a scream to my right, and I looked over, seeing the other three vampires running in through the door. That was when I started to panic. I had some more stakes in my pack, but it began to dawn on me that there was no way I would be able to get them out before any of these other three pounced on me. I remembered how it had been when we were vampires, how quick we were. How easily we killed. And I knew that it was my time, that I was going to find out what that felt like." As she spoke, she absently stroked the side of her neck.

"I looked back and saw that Damon, the one in front of me, was trying to grab at the stake I'd put in him, apparently not all the way. He looked, I don't know, kind of sad, like he knew it was over for him. Just for a tiny second, I started to feel sorry for him, but some kind of instinct took over. I was breathing really heavy, like *'hhhuhh, hhhuhh, hhhuh...'* without even meaning to. I think that's what they call hyperventilating. I'd heard of it, like on TV or whatever, but I'd never experienced it.

"So I pushed harder on the stake, and it went all the way in... It felt so... gross. The way it sort of..." She flailed her hands quickly, shaking her head back and forth and letting out a small gagging sound.

"I know," I said reassuringly.

"Yeah. So it goes in, and he screams, then just... *poof.* He disappeared like a ghost, with this kind of shimmering effect. Like on TV when someone's having a flashback and says, 'It's a looong story...' and the picture gets all wobbly." She began swaying back and forth herself.

"That's how Nick described it," I said, recalling the time he told me about killing his own clone.

"Yeah, and I knew that and knew to expect it, but it still freaked me out. Not that I had much time to think about it. Right after that, two of the vampires, a boy and a girl, grabbed me from either side, and I could feel my head being pushed down, turned to one side. I almost thought they were going to break my neck instead of biting me.

"But that meant that I could see Damon, who had just flipped the vampire me onto her back like a rag doll, screaming, *'Bitch!'* at her as he did so. That was disturbing, and it wasn't something I wanted in terms of the last thing I'd ever see."

"But wait a second!" I interrupted. "If they'd killed you..." I felt a shudder of my own. Obviously, she'd survived, but the thought of things having turned out differently scared the hell out of me. "Didn't they know that if you died, your clone would, too?"

Carolyn paused, thinking this over. "I guess not. Maybe they never told them? Hmm. That's... You know, I didn't really think about that till just now, but... Right..."

"What?"

She seemed to gather her thoughts. "That might be what I heard the other me saying. She kept screaming stuff like 'no!' and 'stop!' and maybe 'wait!' Which of course was also disturbing to hear. I assumed she was saying it to Damon, but now that I think about it..."

"She was warning the other vampires not to kill you," I said, completing her thought.

"Maybe. You know, I think that could have been it. In fact..." She gasped, more memories surfacing. "It wasn't just 'bitch' that he said to her; it was 'Shut up, bitch!' So maybe he knew what she was trying to do, and I just couldn't tell in all the confusion."

I started to suggest that she could ask him about this, but I still needed to hear the rest of the story, how they'd managed to get out of the situation alive. "So, what happened? Sounds like you were outnumbered pretty bad."

"Yeah. I really thought I was going to die. But like I said, the way they had me pinned, I could see Damon throwing the vampire me down on the floor. He ran his stake through her just as the other vampire, some trashy looking blonde, jumped onto his back. I could feel the breath of the one who was about to bite me on my neck... I swear I felt her fangs touch, too, but maybe I just imagined that.

"And then, when the clone me died and disappeared, the weirdest thing happened. I nearly went deaf from the screaming in my ears — from both sides since both of the vampires who'd got me were doing it — and they let go of me and fell back. I wound up on the floor, and when I looked up, all three of the other vampires were screaming, clutching at their heads like they had massive migraines or something. Then they grabbed at their chests, like maybe they were having a heart attack, and they looked like they were gasping. Like they couldn't breathe."

"What was wrong with them?"

"They were dying," she said simply. "It took about ten seconds, maybe longer, but then there they were, falling on the ground and… Well, I wish they'd disappeared like the clone ones did. But they didn't. They went all…"

"Yeah, I know," I said gravely. "All decayed and stuff. I've seen it."

"Right. I jumped right up and ran out of there, but I tripped over one of the mattresses in the kitchen and fell down. Damon came running out after me, catching up just in time to see me puke all over the place. It was one of the worst things I'd ever…" She gasped suddenly, throwing her hands against her face. I thought for a second that she might be about to throw up again, but instead, she started crying, sobbing uncontrollably.

I'd heard of a maternal instinct, but I realized as I jumped out of my sleeping bag and onto the bed that there must be some male equivalent of that, though I'd never actually heard the term "paternal instinct." But that's pretty much what it was: I was seeing someone I cared about in pain and felt an intense need to comfort her. I sat on my knees in the bed, pulling her crying form to me, hugging her tightly the same way I would have done for Elizabeth if she'd needed it.

"It's okay, it's okay…" I said several times. "You're okay now."

"I know…" she said through tears, gasping for air with a sharp shriek that broke my heart. My mind immediately went back to a time several years ago when the situation had been reversed, how she had comforted me at a time when I was overcome with so much grief.

This went on for several minutes, mostly silent comforting on my part while her sobbing slowly died down. At first, my only thought was to get her to that point, to try to help her calm down. But I was distracted by something else, something much bigger.

"So that's what you wanted to tell me, huh?" I asked, still keeping a comforting, encouraging tone in my voice. "About the other vampires dying when you killed your clones?"

"Yes," she sniffled. "I mean, aside from just telling you what happened. I think it helped to get it all out. Not like I could talk to anyone else about it." She pulled away from me, straightening up on the bed and wiping the tears from her face.

"You could have always called Susanna," I offered.

"Pshhht..." she exclaimed. "Right. Like she's always been a wealth of comfort and understanding."

"I know, I know," I said. "But what about Damon?"

"What about him?" she asked coldly, clearing her throat and brushing back her hair with her hands.

"I don't know, I... Did he have anything to say about what all happened?"

"Oh, he tried to," she said, sounding angry again. "I think he wanted it to be some big tearful moment of relief or something, but I just wanted to get the hell away from there as soon as possible. We got back down to the car, and he tried to talk to me one more time, but I just told him that this was it: I never wanted to see him again, and I wanted this whole thing behind us. Something like that." As she spoke, she seemed to have regained some of her usual confidence, but she was still pretty shaky. "Thank you, by the way," she added.

"For what?"

"For just... you know..." She waved her hand back and forth between us, then did a quick gesture indicating a hug. She sat back against the headboard, her legs extending. I edged over slightly to give her room. "You're actually pretty good at this," she said with a slight smile. "I think you'll probably make a good boyfriend someday." That was uncharacteristically sweet of her, and while I knew she meant it as a compliment, it made me uncomfortable because of the secret I had to keep from her. "Anything going on in that department, by the way?"

"What? No. Just…" Of course, there was, but it was way more complicated than I could begin to tell. "So, what's all this about Dad having a gun?"

She laughed. "Changing the subject, huh? They teach us that kind of thing in Psychology, you know. Paying attention to what's not being said."

"What?" I asked again, feeling nervous.

"Nothing," she said, still smiling. "It's okay. So, what else don't you know about our family?"

"I don't know," I said. "If I knew, I wouldn't, well, know." I was beginning to feel stupid.

Carolyn went on to reveal to me many things about our parents and even our grandparents that I had never known, things that had either been told to her by our mother or our older sister over the years, but almost never by our father for some reason. After reiterating the notion of our parents growing up on farms in the country — my mother in Appling, my father somewhere in South Augusta — she told me that both sets of grandparents had been very strict and old-fashioned, which was what led my mother and father to seek new lives in the city, wanting to raise their kids in a more relaxed and progressive fashion.

She also told me that before I was born, my father had been quite the drinker, but she was reluctant to use the term alcoholic, "even though that's probably what he was. But he cleaned up once they started having kids, which apparently they waited to do for a few years after they got married in their 20s."

I nodded and gave the appropriate "mm-hmm"s and prompting questions throughout all of this, but mostly I was just faking interest. The conversation, or really narrative, was informative, but I got bored early on, though I was glad to see that Carolyn had moved on from being upset about the previous night's events to just wanting to talk and tell me stuff that she knew. In a way, it was the closest I'd ever felt to her as a brother in my entire life, and I might have enjoyed her confiding in me in this much detail had I not been distracted by something more immediate and important to me.

Her story of what had happened with her and Damon's clones had been a useful one, and it changed the game in terms of what needed to be done in order to deal with the vampire threat. For one thing, two more clones were gone, which was good. That only left four more to go. I'd been thinking up until this point that such a figure had become meaningless given that the clones had been creating their own vampires, so the number of them must have been more than any of us could have imagined.

But now I'd learned something new, that killing a vampire meant that once it died, the vampires it had made would also die. It was some sort of mystical connection, much like the one that bound our clones to us. If I were to die, so would my clone. We'd figured that out a long time ago. But apparently, if my clone died, so would the vampires he had created, including Elizabeth.

CHAPTER SEVEN

I wasn't sure how to reveal this latest development to Elizabeth. My first instinct was to tell her as soon as I saw her again, but the more I pictured this, the more reluctant I became. For months, I had been determined to kill my clone, to kill all of the vampires, but I'd faltered when it came to Elizabeth. I didn't want her to die, and the thought of losing her twice was more than I could bear.

The analytical side of me wondered about the mechanics of the situation, this mystical chain that apparently connected me to my clone and him to the vampires he'd made. Did it go even farther than that? Supposing for example that Kay, that Korean vampire girl I'd briefly encountered at the mill, had killed someone and then brought him back to life as a vampire as well.

I found myself picturing another one of my imaginary vampire-killing scenarios with high-tech or improvised weapons, in this case using a can of hairspray (or some other aerosol) and a lighter as a flamethrower, something I'd seen demonstrated before. I imagined myself in a confrontation with Kay, spraying her with lethal fire as she screamed and withered to death. This hypothetical other vampire that she'd created was standing nearby, but then he died, too, the source of his life extinguished.

Did the chain work like that? I didn't know. If it did, it would make the whole problem of eliminating the vampires from Augusta — and wherever else they may have gotten to — much easier. Just find the original clones, wipe them out, and then every other one down the line would vanish or crumble into a decaying corpse. And that's where the idea of doing this screeched to a halt in my brain, because that would also include Elizabeth.

Or would it? I wondered if maybe the thread might only work by one degree of separation, that is, in the example with Kay, if I killed my clone, she would die, but not the vampire she'd made. If I killed her, only then would that one die. Did that even make sense? Even if it did, I realized, it still wouldn't help Elizabeth. She was directly connected to my clone, though the thought of that sickened me.

I considered putting this question to Tim or Susanna, figuring that they would have the most scientific knowledge or at the very least good speculative skills, but I couldn't. As before, I didn't want to tell anyone about Elizabeth, and she was the entire reason why I wanted there to be some kind of limitation to this connection. This also reinforced my wish to find some way of curing her, to somehow turn her back into a normal human again, if that were even possible.

I would still need to pass on to the other former vampires what Carolyn had told me, but I couldn't think of a way to introduce my other question without giving too much away. At the end of it all, I knew that there was only one person I could talk to about this.

"I said I'll look into it," Elizabeth said firmly, pushing me away and turning her head from me.

"I know," I said, my voice becoming whiny, which I tried to keep in check. "Can't we at least... I don't know..."

"The sooner I get started, the better," she said, her body now fully turned away. "We need to figure this out."

And with that, her normally gorgeous form shrunk down into a bat and flew out the nearest open window frame, leaving me alone in the half-constructed house. I still didn't like seeing her do that, but I knew that I had to accept it. That was part of who she was, maybe forever.

It was a crappy end to what had started out as a promising night. I'd brought my sleeping bag with me to the house so that we could get into it together, keeping each other warm in the increasingly cold winter. That had gone rather well, but I quickly regretted not also bringing a pillow. Still, it was wonderful to get this close to her, to feel her body and her limbs, fully clothed though they were, tangled up with mine as we made out.

As passionate as all of this was, Elizabeth still couldn't help being her. As things were becoming more heated between us, she suddenly stopped and looked me square in the eye. "You're poking me," she said sternly.

It took me a second to realize what she meant, but a quick glance downward followed by a cheeky, eyebrow-raised look back up at me cleared things up. This wasn't the first time I had gotten an erection in her presence — or alone and thinking about her, for that matter — but it was the closest we had gotten so far. As I mentioned, we were still fully clothed, but that didn't stop my arousal from showing through, or in this case, being felt by her.

I felt embarrassment, panic, and worry all within the span of about two seconds. "Sorry," I said nervously.

She just smiled mischievously as she nodded, saying, "It's okay." She then reached up a hand and pulled my head down to hers, and we kissed some more. I was on top of her; this was the first time we'd taken on such a sexual position. It felt perfect.

"Do you want to… you know…" I asked, glancing downward and back up at her.

"No, it's too cold!" she said, laughing. That hurt more than I expected, and something in my face must have betrayed me. Her expression softened, and she looked to one side. "Well, maybe."

My heart leapt. I hadn't really thought before that I might lose my virginity in a dark, sawdust-ridden house on a wooden floor in the middle of winter, but if that's how it was going to happen, I'd take it. I had fantasized about having sex with her more times than I could count, both before and after she'd died.

"Have you... you know... before?" I asked.

Her movement beneath me suddenly stopped, and she looked annoyed. "What?"

"You know, done it."

She sighed, rolling her eyes. "Does that really matter?"

"I don't know!" I said, suddenly feeling defensive. Her lack of a frank response made me realize the answer to my question, and I felt disappointed. But honestly, once she'd asked me what she had, I wasn't sure why it mattered, why a girl being a virgin was such a big deal. It was just something that I knew was important to people, whether or not someone was "your first." There were even mentions of it in the Bible, I knew from my overly religious education, how sacred and vital virginity was. But why?

I tried to convey some of this confusion to Elizabeth, but it didn't seem to help. I wanted to explain to her where I was coming from, but the more I spoke, the more I realized that I didn't even know. She, meanwhile, seemed increasingly irritated, and things between us quickly went from romantic to uncomfortable. She'd grown hostile, and I was feeling desperate, just wanting to get things back on track. It didn't work.

As time went on, it became apparent that we weren't going to go all the way that night, so I just talked to her about other things. I had it in the back of my mind for a while that if I could somehow steer things back in the right direction, I might get lucky after all, but really, there were other things we needed to discuss.

I told her about Carolyn and Damon's encounter with their clones, but not all of the details at first. I also mentioned what I'd seen on the news about other people in the city rising up to fight back against the vampires, and I warned her to be careful of them. She seemed to appreciate my concern, but there was still something cold to me in her tone. It was more like we were talking shop than anything else; we had by then worked our way out of the sleeping bag and were sitting on it as we talked.

Things took on a nicer bent when we got sidetracked into talking about more obscure things from our past that we had in common. We had already talked about *The Tomorrow People* before, a British science fiction children's program that we'd both watched as little kids. It came up again because we had gotten to talking about my psychic powers, which the kids on that show also had.

"But my powers, even when they were really strong when I was a vampire, weren't really like on TV," I said.

"But you could read people's minds?" she asked.

"Kinda. Actually, yes, sometimes. But other times, it was like my thoughts would project outwards and into other people, sometimes without me meaning for them to. Like I was some big satellite dish or something."

"Hmm," she said. "Maybe that's why all those other people, and even your sister and that guy…" She trailed off, glancing to one side as she stroked the fabric of the sleeping bag absently.

"Why they what?"

"You know, went all vigilante and decided to go killing all the vampires they could. It was your desire to do that sort of… beaming out." She sounded bitter as she said this, and I started to protest, but then I realized that she might be right.

"Maybe. I don't know if my powers are all that strong anymore. I still see some things happen that I think are them, but I'm not always sure."

"So you don't just teleport to another planet whenever you feel like it?" she asked, a hint of a smile returning.

"No, it was never like that. And I didn't have telekinesis, or the ability to create illusions, nothing like that."

"Hmm. Too bad. I remember watching as a little girl and being like, 'I want to be a Tomorrow Person! I want to be telepathic!'" She pitched her voice higher as she said this.

"Yeah, me too."

"And you got your wish! Well, kind of." She was smiling again, and I could tell that she was thinking back to specific moments in the series. So I prompted her with certain examples, bits and pieces that I could recall from the show even though it hadn't been on the air for several years. We traded memories, both of that and of other things we'd liked to watch.

I was taken aback when she mentioned that she'd enjoyed *The Young Ones,* another British show that aired on cable TV. Nick had gotten me interested in that one, and I thought it was hilarious, but the humor was pretty raunchy. It didn't strike me as something that a girl like Elizabeth would be into at all, but she scoffed at this when I told her.

"Yeah, sure, but I thought the guys on it were funny. They were so… I don't know… over the top. And I liked the music." Each show included a musical performance from some band, usually one I hadn't heard of.

"Now, wait a minute," I said. "I remember mentioning that show at school one time when a bunch of us were talking, even quoting one of the bits. Yeah, the one where Neil spilled the soup on the floor and then was like, 'There's some dinner on the floor!' And you acted like you didn't know what I was talking about." Quoting funny lines from TV shows and comedians was a habit of mine, one which occasionally got me positive attention from classmates, though less frequently the older I got.

She looked sheepish, then said simply, "Yeah, well."

"'Yeah well' what?" I felt like I had caught her out in something. "How come you didn't say you recognized that? You did, didn't you?"

"Sure I did," she said, "but I didn't want to let Helen and Melinda know. They'd have thought I was stupid for liking something like that."

"So?"

"So…" she said pointedly, but then she stopped. "I don't know. Maybe you can't understand. I guess…" She paused. "Having the support of my friends was really important to me."

"I get that," I said, but I still didn't fully understand.

"It's a girl thing," she said, sounding more authoritative. "What they think of you really matters. When you're a girl…"

"I don't plan on being a girl, but okay," I interrupted, smiling slyly.

She glared at me, giving me a sarcastic sneer. "No. So maybe I shouldn't bother trying to explain."

I tried to salvage things, apologizing even though part of me enjoyed tripping her up. But at the same time, I didn't want to make her too mad. The conversation steered to a related topic, her questioning why it was that boys hated anything that was considered girly, or they hated boys who liked anything like that. I couldn't give her much of an explanation; it was just the way I'd grown up. That led to her having the upper hand in the argument, if that's even what it was.

Eventually, we changed the subject, and I told her the rest of the story about Carolyn and Damon, a topic I'd been avoiding all night. It led to the inevitable conclusion, the fact that killing a vampire would result in the death of the vampires it had made. If things had been chilly between us before, that was nothing compared to how things got once I dropped that bomb.

"I see," she said in a low tone, staring past me when I first told her. She held her hands to her shoulders, then stood up and walked to one of the window frames. By this point, the construction workers still hadn't put in any glass.

I stood up and joined her, gently turning her around as I spoke. "I know," I said somberly. "It's a pretty big deal."

"You're not kidding," she almost whispered, avoiding my eyes. "So... So if you kill him, the other you, then I just... go away?"

I started to correct her, but I caught myself at the last second. To be more precise, the clones would disappear into nothing when killed, but the vampires they'd made would die more normally, collapsing in agony.

"Or worse," she said, worry creeping into her voice. I pulled her to me, hugging her. She didn't fight it.

"I think so," I said. "But I'm still not sure about all of it." I told her my hypothesis about the thread, how maybe it didn't extend beyond more than one generation, so to speak.

"That doesn't help me, though!" she cried, pushing back from me. Then she regained her composure, but she still avoided looking directly at me.

"I wonder if there's some way to test it," I said, remembering something I'd thought of earlier. "Like if we could somehow find one of these second-generation vampires and..." I broke off, realizing how impractical that was.

"You couldn't, but maybe I could," Elizabeth said, looking pensive. I noticed the tears welling up in her eyes.

"What do you mean?"

She pondered for a moment, then looked at me, blinking. "Just let me look into it," she said, reaching up and quickly wiping at her eyes, almost like she thought I wouldn't notice.

"There could be another way," I said, trying to sound encouraging. "If we can find a way to cure you..."

"Oh, right, like that's ever going to work," she said angrily, looking away again.

"Has anything in your research..."

"No it hasn't!" she almost screamed, then caught herself, holding up her hands as she tried to calm down. She let out a few controlled breaths. "Sorry."

"I'll try to see what I can find out from Susanna. Or maybe Tim has some ideas." I wanted nothing more than to hold her and kiss her, as if somehow that would make everything better.

After she stormed out on me, I walked back to my house alone in the cold, angry about so many things. It wasn't fair. I loved her so much, and I didn't want anything to happen to her, certainly not more than already had. I just wanted to somehow fix everything, have her back to being human, and to get rid of my clone and all the other vampires. As I hurried along the sidewalk, the wind picked up, making things even colder and more miserable. That just made me angrier, but deep down, what I was most mad at was me.

I barely even tried to be quiet as I made my way back in through my window, so pissed off that part of me even wanted to get caught. But I knew that was stupid. I'd gotten to the point where I could expertly maneuver the screen on its hinges without it coming off, and while I started to slam the fasteners in place out of anger, I thought better of it and pushed them down slowly like I usually did. The room was still cold from the brief time that the window had been open, but I knew that it would heat back up soon enough. If only I had Elizabeth there with me to make things warmer.

It took forever to fall asleep, and I continued to berate myself for how badly I'd handled things. I hadn't known that asking Elizabeth if she were a virgin would offend her, but apparently it had. It's not like I was an authority on these things. As much as I, like any boy my age, thought about sex and imagined what it would be like, I'd never even seen a porno movie, though I'd heard about them from some of the boys at school. I would of course act like I knew what they were talking about in order to seem cool, but honestly, the closest I'd ever come to seeing a girl naked were the times I'd seen breasts in a few R-rated movies on TV, plus there was the time in seventh grade when Dennis brought a dirty magazine to school and showed it to me and some of the boys. We'd barely known what we were looking at.

I was in a bad mood at school for most of the following week. I kept thinking about Elizabeth, which wasn't unusual, but my thoughts were more bitter because of how we'd left things. What I didn't know at the time was that it would be a full week before I would hear from her again, by the end of which I was extremely anxious. That was a slow progression, starting with being angry that she hadn't contacted me for a few days, worrying that I had pissed her off more than I realized and that she just didn't want to see me, then being afraid that something bad had happened to her.

It was important for me to keep my thoughts in check, I remembered, because if I were mad at somebody, bad things might happen to them. It was another part of my psychic powers that I couldn't always control, though sometimes, it was amusing. That was when it applied to people I didn't like, such as Kirby, whom I was pretty sure was the one Elizabeth had slept with before.

He wound up getting into a small accident on the way to school that Tuesday morning: He had collided with the corner of a parked car while driving through a neighborhood where the sun was in his eyes. He wasn't seriously injured, but he did have to deal with his friends ridiculing him afterwards with taunts, like when Chris said to him, "Hey man, you gotta watch out for them parked cars. They'll jump right out at ya!"

I took some guilty pleasure in that, but for the most part, I was still moody and angry most of the time. Things that annoyed me seemed that much worse, and I was cold and indifferent to anybody who tried to talk to me, my parents included. I hadn't felt this belligerent since before my clone had emerged from me the previous year, but that was because I had a vampire inside of me that was clawing to get out, at least in a psychic sense.

That emergence had been a pretty frightening experience, but it was also one of many things that bugged me when I thought about it in too much detail. I had learned in Physical Science class that matter couldn't just be created, only changed. So how was it that these clones had been able to magically spring out from us and take on physical form? Similarly, there was the issue of a vampire's ability to change into a bat, clothes and all, those rematerializing with them when they went back to their person form.

I'd tried to put questions like this to Susanna before, and Tim had asked ones along the same lines. There was even one time when I'd started to ask her about the bat thing when we were still vampires, and something weird happened to me where I felt disoriented and strange, like I was no longer where I'd been and had trouble remembering who I was. It only lasted briefly, but when I recalled it later, it reminded me of that weird feeling one gets when they're dreaming and then start to wake up.

But overall, even in our post-vampire era, Susanna had been evasive whenever I questioned her too much on the details, presumably out of guilt or fear. This was frustrating, and I couldn't understand why she wouldn't just tell me what she knew, but maybe that was the problem. Maybe she just didn't know, and being the oldest of us, she felt like this was a failure: She *should* know. Other times, I figured she was just being difficult on purpose, not telling me things because she liked to lord that over me. But that was all speculation on my part since she would rarely if ever let me in on her private thoughts.

At school, I began to feel that there was a similar problem with my teachers, whom I had very little respect for. Sure, they were adults, but the older I got, the more I realized that they were just people, flawed and lost and confused, maybe as much as we teenagers were. Rather than feel sympathy, I felt annoyance because they would insist on being right even when I knew they weren't. But if I or anyone else openly defied them or tried to call them on this, we were punished, discouraged from having any original or progressive ideas.

I had often balked at the religious aspect of their teachings, not outright disbelieving in God, but increasingly questioning their interpretation of things. I learned that some people were more lenient about this than others; my parents, for example, were fairly open-minded. My current teachers, meanwhile, seemed to revel in their close-mindedness, wearing it like a badge of honor.

Our homeroom class with Dr. Phillips — who doubled as our teacher and the principal in tenth grade due to the school's staffing shortage — was called "Bible," which I found particularly pretentious given that the same class back at my previous school, St. Joseph's, had been called "Religion." There, they had taught us mostly Christian stuff, but things about other religions were included in a less judgmental manner. Judaism, Islam, and even other varieties of Christianity like Catholicism were presented in a manner that basically said, *This is what these other people believe.* At Bethlehem, those same topics were presented as: *This is what these other people believe, and this is why they are wrong and are all going to hell.*

One morning the previous year, not long before Elizabeth was killed, Dr. Phillips was talking about the supposed conflict between science and religion — or really, his narrow interpretation of Christianity — and he said that just because there were some things in the Bible that science couldn't explain, that didn't mean that they weren't true. "After all," he said haughtily, "at one point, the best scientists in the world thought that the world was flat, and we all know that turned out not to be true."

"Those people weren't scientists," a familiar voice almost whispered from behind me. I turned around almost involuntarily, spotting Elizabeth looking down at her desk and doodling absently.

As the meaning of Elizabeth's words sank in, I laughed as I turned back around, my face falling as I met the teacher's glare. "Ray?" he asked sternly. "Is there something you find funny?"

"No!" I said, feeling caught off guard. Nervously, I turned back around to look at Elizabeth and my other classmates, blushing as I felt so many eyes upon me. Elizabeth looked at me sharply, but there was something in her eyes that seemed to plead, *Don't tell on me.* I knew what she meant, and she was right. It was the scientists of the time who disproved such ignorant ideas of the common man that the Earth was flat or that the sun revolved around it, while it was the church who condemned them for saying so.

"Nothing, nothing," I said, turning back around. "Someone just said something about not liking scientists. Sorry."

Sadly, this was typical of the way things were hammered into us at this school. Opinions were taught as fact, and disagreement was met with hostility and punishment. Later on, I would look back on these people who tried to keep us confined to such small-minded beliefs with pity, both for them and for those whom they successfully subdued.

"Does he still have his obsession with abortion?" Elizabeth had asked me with a laugh one night when we'd met up and found ourselves talking about him.

"Oh, of course," I said, also laughing. "He can't go one week without working it into the lesson somehow."

"That guy," she said, rolling her eyes but still grinning. "You've got to wonder what his hang-up is about that."

"I know. I mean, I don't know how I feel about that. Sure, killing babies is wrong, okay. But I'm at least willing to admit that there could be some situations in which a woman would be better off doing that. Like if the baby would end up being born deformed, or the family was just too poor to take care of it. It'd have a shitty life."

"You're going to hell!" she joked, pointing at me accusingly. Then she looked sad and sighed. "Probably shouldn't joke about that, I know. He was probably just doing it to justify expelling Sandra."

"What?"

"You didn't know about that?"

I knew that Sandra, one of the girls in the grade above me, had left Bethlehem unexpectedly, but I'd just assumed that it had been for some reason like her parents moving away or something like that.

"No," Elizabeth said knowingly. "It was because they found out that she'd had an abortion a year or two ago. Some guy… Actually, no, I don't know the whole story. But yeah, she admitted to having done that, so they kicked her out, saying she'd be a… *bad influence.*" She said this last bit with a stern tone and her hands held up, making the "air quotes" gesture. "Way to not shame the girls in your school for telling the truth, asshole," she added bitterly. "There's something I don't miss."

These criticisms of Dr. Phillips, his school, and the way things were taught there were all valid. I hated the place, and I hated their stupid ways of thinking that in my mind bordered on criminal negligence when it came to the education of children. Even so, I sometimes found myself thinking in the opposite way, maybe not that far off from what the teachers there were trying to push.

Science had its rules, and it clarified both the existence and the impossibility of certain things. So what would it have to say about the existence of vampires or the fact that my friends and I had been able to take a potion that turned us into them? Would a scientist dismiss that as impossible? Even if they did, I would know that they were wrong; I'd seen all of these things, experienced them, and they were real, explainable by science or not. So maybe, at least in that sense, Dr. Phillips was right.

Regardless, I was miserable at that school. One thing in particular that annoyed me this week happened when I noticed the graffiti drawn on the back of the desk in front of me. There, scrawled in ballpoint pen, was a pair of initials separated by a large plus sign: *AC + NB.* I was pretty sure that represented Annie and her current upperclassman boyfriend; she tended to only date the boys in the higher grades. There were other similar pairings scribbled elsewhere along the back of the desk, and it was pretty easy to tell which ones were written by girls as opposed to boys. The girls' ones were always neater, the boys' more crude-looking and also less frequent.

I'd seen these things before, but because of my mood, they grated on me more than usual. As much as I wanted to, I couldn't write *RY + EM* on there. Anyone who saw it would know that it was me; no one else in that tiny school had the same initials as mine. And it wouldn't be too hard for them to figure out who the other initials belonged to, someone who for all intents and purposes was dead. Even more obvious would have been to write out our full initials like I'd seen people do: *RAY + EPM.*

Then, in what may have been another case of my thoughts echoing outwards, Kirby and Chris started picking on me the following day for not having a girlfriend. Kirby had begun dating a girl named Amy, and for whatever reason, he decided not only to brag about this but also to point out the fact that I didn't have anyone.

"Yeah, well, at least I don't run into parked cars," I said, repeating Chris's joke.

I expected Chris to laugh along with me, but he just said, "That's 'cause you don't have a car!"

"Fuck you," I said, stinging from the comeback. "And I do too have a girlfriend. She just doesn't go to this school."

"Really?" Kirby asked, surprised. "Where's she go?"

"Westlake," I said angrily. It was the first school that popped into my head, the one that Carolyn and Susanna had gone to. "And it's a lot better of a school than this piece of shit place." I didn't know that for a fact, but I figured it must be true.

"What's her name?"

I faltered, not wanting to say that it was Elizabeth. If I'd had time to think it over, I might have realized that I still could have used that name; it was common enough. Another name flashed across my mind for some reason: Elaine. But then I realized that if I were to tell someone the name of a girlfriend — even if Elizabeth wasn't *really* that — I wanted to use her middle name. But I didn't know it; I only knew that it began with a *P.*

Instead, all I could think to say was: "None of your damn business!" I quickly walked off, feeling stupid, making a mental note to ask Elizabeth what her middle name was the next time I saw her.

By the end of the week, I was worried about Elizabeth, and I had hoped that she might come to my window on Friday night, but she didn't. I was still plagued by the notion that killing my clone would mean killing her as well, and at the same time, there were still the almost nightly reports of vampire attacks on the news. I was supposed to be doing something to stop all of that, but I didn't know how. Things had gotten so complicated.

At times, I tried to tell myself that I really should just do what was right. Then I'd turn around and feel helpless, angry that I didn't have the means to properly go after the vampires anyway. That would hopefully change over the summer when I got my own car, but my sixteenth birthday was still months away. And there was a part of me, though I didn't want to admit it, that was glad that I was incapable of actually pursuing my clone.

As I drifted off to sleep that night, I began to think along different lines. Elizabeth was a vampire, but she wasn't purely evil, right? I'd known her for a long time, and she wasn't some brutal, mindless monster who killed people left and right. She drank blood to survive. Were some of the other ones like that? Maybe they didn't all need to be wiped out. But then, even if there were some "good" ones here or there, there probably were plenty that were just as bad as I imagined, if not worse.

The following day, I initially didn't even remember that I'd begun to think that way, but when I did, it angered me. All I was doing was trying to twist things, to justify my own inaction. Of course the vampires should die. And I needed to make it happen. I just had to find some way to do it without also killing the girl I loved, to somehow make her human again. Then we could truly be together.

Even so, I was frustrated over not hearing from her for so long. In order to distract myself from that, I did something I'd been meaning to do for over a week, which was to call and let Tim and Carl know about the new development, that killing the clones would kill the "subset" vampires, which was what Tim called them once I'd told him about this.

I had to be careful not to let on about my frustration over this, how it made me worry for Elizabeth's safety. What's more, I had to hide my annoyance when both of them talked like this was a good thing, that, as I'd concluded earlier, it meant that if we — or maybe even one of those eager wannabe vampire hunters in town — managed to take one of the clones down, that would eliminate a lot of the subset vampires all at once. They were intrigued by this possibility; I was terrified by it. For all I knew, it had already come to pass, and my beloved was already gone. I felt a little better, though, after hearing what Susanna had to say about the topic.

"Well, remember, if that happens, you'll feel it," she said, referring to what happened when some unknown person had killed her clone a few months before. "There will be that strange impression of a thread detaching from you, drifting away into the distance."

"That's true," I said. "And I haven't felt that yet, so…" I wasn't sure how to finish the sentence. I was also trying to hide the relief in my voice, knowing that it would be difficult to explain to her if she asked.

As the day went on, I managed to get some things done, including calling these various people and letting them know about the chain and the subset vampires. Part of me hated doing it, but I knew I had to. The others had a right to know. I tried calling Dennis to tell him as well, but as usual, he didn't answer the phone, nor did he call me back.

This made me angry, too. I really hated the way he had distanced himself from us throughout all of this. He was just as responsible as we were for everything that was happening, but ever since he had seen his clone kill someone a few months ago, he'd refused to take part in the hunt for the rest of vampires. Obviously he'd been freaked out, but that shouldn't have been an excuse. He tried to pass himself off as this aloof, tough kind of guy, but the fact that he was being such a coward bothered me.

Winding down and trying to get to sleep that night was difficult; I again kept hoping that Elizabeth would show up and allay my fear that something had happened to her. At one point, well after 1:00 in the morning, I thought I heard something at my window. But when I got up to check, there was no one there.

Sunday morning, I woke up pretty late, but things seemed more or less the same as usual. It wasn't until I opened my drapes that I spotted the folded piece of paper tucked under the screen on my window.

I practically threw the window frame upward as I opened it, eager to get to the note that had been left there. As I had hoped, it was from Elizabeth, an intricately folded up sheet of notebook paper formed into a perfect square.

Hi there, the unfolded message read, and I couldn't help but notice how neat the handwriting was. *Sorry I've been out of touch for so long. I had a lot to do, and I still need to look into a few more things tonight before seeing you again. If things go okay tonight, I should be able to meet up with you at the usual place on Sunday. Deal?* I noticed how she'd left out the word "night" after "Sunday." One trick to writing notes in high school was to keep things vague in case the note were intercepted.

I think some of the stuff I've found out will be interesting to you, the note continued. *And I'll probably be stroking your ego too much to admit this, but I miss you. Talking to you, anyway. I was going to say I miss seeing you, but to be honest, I've checked in on you a couple of times this week just to make sure you're okay. So I've been seeing you when you didn't know it, hee-hee. Take care, and we'll talk soon. Love, me.*

That one word, "Love," immediately wiped out any resentment I'd felt towards her the previous week, plus I was very relieved to find out that she was safe. The idea of her sort of spying on me without my knowing it was admittedly a little disturbing, but I was just so happy to finally hear from her that it didn't really matter. I would finally get to see her again that night.

There was one other thing that ended up happening first, though, which was unexpected and interesting to say the least.

CHAPTER EIGHT

"Should've known I'd run into you," Dennis said nonchalantly. "I had a dream last night that you were in." He turned away from me with this last sentence, his gaze turning back to look absently at the interior of the mall. He leaned forward on the railing, peering downward at the shoppers on the lower level.

"Looking for someone?" I asked him.

"No, just people-watching. There's something about seeing the mindless masses just wandering through their lives, not a clue about what's really going on in the world. Or when it might be their turn."

"Turn?"

"To die," he said firmly.

This was a darker conversation than I was used to having with him, but then again, I hadn't actually talked to him for months. And while I knew that he'd been avoiding me all this time, he didn't seem particularly unhappy to see me or hostile. We were standing outside of one of the mall's music stores; Carolyn had just gone inside and left me there to talk to my old friend.

"So, do you hang out with your big sister at the mall often?" he asked, turning back to me with a slight sneer.

"No, no. We're here looking for a present for our dad."

My father's birthday was on February 14th, which he told us always bothered him because it coincided with Valentine's Day. It wasn't exactly that he despised the holiday or the spirit of it, but as a child, he resented the fact that everyone's attention was always focused on that rather than his birthday.

"When I was growing up," he told us one time, "I had this friend named Jerry who had it worse than me. His birthday was on New Year's Eve."

"So?" Carolyn asked. "Seems like that would be pretty cool. All fireworks and everything, everyone going all like, 'Woo! Happy Birthday, Jerry!'" She waved her arms around and made silly faces as she said this. I also didn't see the problem, but at the time, I was still pretty young. What I knew of New Year's at this point was that there was a cool sounding countdown to midnight on the radio that my sisters and I stayed up to listen to, and when I got a little older, I saw the footage of people cheering and partying in Times Square as the famous lighted ball dropped.

"But that's just it, you see," my father said. "They were all concerned with it being New Year's Eve, not Jerry's birthday. So he couldn't just have a regular birthday party like most people. It wasn't a problem when we were younger, but the older we got, the more people were interested in their own New Year's Eve parties than they were with him."

"Right," Susanna said, looking thoughtful. "It would be like if your birthday was on Christmas. I've got a friend whose birthday is in January, and her mom is always gypping her on it. She'll say something like, 'Okay, Colleen, since I got you this present, it's part of your birthday. So you won't get as much stuff then.'" I'd heard similar stories from friends of mine at school whose birthdays fell too close to Christmas, either before or after it. Once I understood this, I realized how lucky Susanna and I were to both have our birthdays in

July; it meant that they were sufficiently spaced far enough ahead for us not to be affected.

"But couldn't he have just, I don't know, taken it on?" Carolyn asked. "Like, pretend that the reason everyone was celebrating was because of him?"

My father laughed. "I think he tried to do that. But he knew it wasn't really true. So after a while, he got to where he just hated New Year's. And his birthday. Shame, really."

"Which is why I kept getting short-changed on Valentine's Day for the first few years we were married," my mother called out from the kitchen, apparently having been listening to our conversation. She didn't sound terribly angry, but I noticed that the loudness of the utensils striking the cookware as she prepared that night's meal had been steadily increasing.

"And you taught me a lesson on that," Dad said, his playful tone suggesting that this was an old argument that he'd long since lost. My mother responded with a laugh, and the clanking from the kitchen died down.

So after that, my sisters and I made it a point to make sure that any presents we got him for his birthday had absolutely nothing to do with Valentine's Day, hearts and flowers, or anything like that. Carolyn, with whom Dad had worked many times on projects like building cages for our pets or other work around the house, usually wanted to get him tools. Susanna appealed to his librarian side by trying to get him books she thought he'd like, and our mother paid for these accordingly until we were old enough to do so ourselves.

As the youngest of three, I went along with this as best I could, usually partnered with either of my sisters on what they were doing. But I couldn't help but feel a sting of embarrassment over the gifts I'd made for my father as a young child, ones that showed my ignorance of his disdain for the coinciding holiday. It bothered me to find out that he must have faked his appreciation for things like a glued together construction paper monstrosity that included a poorly cut-out heart with *I love you, Daddy* scrawled on it.

Once I'd told Dennis why Carolyn and I were at the mall, he said sarcastically, "How nice." But then he seemed to catch himself. "How old's he gonna be?"

"55," I said simply, and Dennis's eyes went wide. He'd started wearing these round-framed glasses that, combined with his long, reddish-brown hair, made him look quite a bit like John Lennon, but a little more heavyset.

"Really?" he asked, laughing. "Damn! I didn't know your dad was that old!"

I laughed nervously in response, though part of me felt offended. "Yeah, I know. Carolyn and I were talking about it on the way here. Apparently, he and my mom waited a while after they got married to start having kids."

"Hmm," he said. "Mine didn't."

"Your dad doing okay?" I remembered him from the times I used to go over to Dennis's house when I was younger, but I hadn't seen him for years. He'd always been nice, if a little goofy.

"He's better now," Dennis said, "but things have been kind of shitty lately."

"How?"

He went on to explain how his older sister, Joanna, had run away from home and was missing for a while. She'd always been a bit strange and was prone to getting into trouble, but then, so was Dennis. Apparently, she'd ended up living with their mother instead, which their father wasn't happy about but had accepted grudgingly. Dennis was fuzzy on the details, though.

After an awkward silence, I looked at the plastic bag he was carrying, one that came from the music store. I pointed and asked, "What did you get?"

"Oh, a few things," he said, holding up the bag but not opening it. "The latest Grateful Dead CD, the one that came out last year. I just now got around to getting it. Have you heard it?" I shook my head. "And a couple of Dylan tapes."

"Dylan?"

"Bob Dylan," he said impatiently.

"Oh." This wasn't the kind of music I was into. I couldn't even name a Bob Dylan song if someone had asked me to, and I was only vaguely aware of him as some old, hippie kind of guitar playing guy with a weird, whiny voice that comedians liked to make fun of. As for the Grateful Dead, I knew that they'd been a big deal twenty years ago or so, plus they'd recently made a comeback. I thought it was weird to see these old grey-haired guys on MTV, but really, it wasn't all that different from seeing The Monkees, whom I did like, also showing up on the otherwise youth-centered music channel.

"Well, you always kind of had…" I stopped, remembering another old friend who had strange taste in music. "That reminds me. You ever see Nick?"

"At school, you mean? Yeah, sometimes," he said, rolling his eyes. "We never really talk, though. We don't have any classes together, and besides, he's kind of a dick."

I laughed. "Is he still all, 'You guys are all posers! I'm so much cooler because I listen to punk!'"

"Yep, pretty much." He'd been mostly deadpan up to this point, but then he laughed unexpectedly. "Oh, you know what I found out? His middle name is Preston. *Preston,*" he repeated with a nasally tone.

I couldn't help but laugh again, picking up on what he thought was funny about that. Continuing my impression of Nick, I spoke in a low, condescending tone: "'Yeah, I'm a bad-ass punk rock guy and my name is… *Preston.*'" I repeated Dennis's pinched way of saying the name, and he laughed again.

"So, you don't have any classes with him at all? That's kind of weird."

"Not really," he said, returning to his previous demeanor. "It's a big school. Not like the one you go to." This last bit was said with noticeable condescension.

"Don't get me started," I said, though my anger wasn't towards him. "I'm just about sick of that place."

We talked a little more, but the fact that it was just small talk was getting on my nerves. Things felt uncomfortable enough as it was, and neither of us was talking about what we both knew we should.

"So," Dennis said, "you heard about Mrs. Warren?" He said this almost rhetorically, his tone suggesting that he expected me to say yes.

"What about her?" I asked, picturing our former English teacher.

"She's dead," he said simply.

"Oh no…" I suddenly felt cold. "What happened?"

"What do you think?" Dennis said bitterly.

He didn't have to explain. She, like so many other people in this seemingly doomed town, had been killed by a vampire. This was the first time since Elizabeth's death that someone I'd known personally had died this way, and like before, what I felt was a combination of shock and guilt. "When did it happen?" I asked.

"Couple of days ago. I read about it in the paper. I mean, they didn't just say 'died of a vampire attack,' just the usual bullshit 'acute blood loss' or 'severe blood loss' or something like that." The news media, both in print and on TV, tended to use this euphemism. I couldn't understand why they refused to just say "vampire" when everyone knew that was what was really going on, and it angered me.

"Pretty sure it was my clone who did it, too," Dennis added.

"How do you know?"

"Oh, I know," he said, then flicked his eyebrows up and down a couple of times meaningfully. This gesture was a code he and I had come up with when we were kids and our psychic powers were first coming about, one we would use to indicate that something telepathic had occurred. It was a secret we'd kept from almost everyone for a long time.

Mrs. Warren had always been mean, this loud, wizened, grey-haired woman who often took to ranting at the class about how lazy and irresponsible we all were. At the time, she seemed horrible, but what she was really doing was trying to prepare us for life after elementary school, being cruel to be kind, as my mother put it.

Certain members of the class, mostly boys, were occasionally singled out by her and — so it seemed to me then, anyway — unfairly ridiculed. In hindsight, she was probably just trying to get it through their heads that they needed to work harder in order to succeed, but finding one's self on the receiving end of one of her tirades was a very unpleasant, sometimes humiliating experience. I had gone through this a handful of times during the two years she'd taught me, but other boys, including Dennis, seemed to get yelled at by her on an almost daily basis.

"Let me guess," I said more quietly. "You were thinking about all the times she picked on you."

"Yep," Dennis said. "And I'll bet you anything that those thoughts zoomed on out." He made a gesture with both index fingers thrusting out from his forehead, then brought them down in a tight arch. "And then right into the other me, and he goes off and… Well, then that's that."

"Man, that sucks," I said. "Something kind of like that happened to me a few months ago. This girl I really liked…" I stopped myself. I'd started to think that I could tell him about my clone killing Elizabeth, but I was afraid that I might reveal too much. "Well, anyway, I'm sorry."

"Sorry?" He seemed surprised. "What for?"

"I mean, you must be feeling…"

"Don't tell me what I'm feeling!" he shouted. I looked around to see if anyone had noticed, and sure enough, an older couple sitting on a nearby bench had looked over at us. I glared back, and they turned away, the woman taking a drag off of a cigarette. The man with her looked away a moment later.

"Wish they'd blow some more of that over this way," Dennis added, his voice low again. "I'm dying for a cigarette." I knew that he smoked, but it had been a while since I'd seen him do it. I turned back to look at him, and he shrugged. "Look, yeah, it's too bad that she died. But she was a bitch anyway."

"That's really harsh, Dennis," I said.

"So's everything else," he said, then looked away again. "I just don't want to be all weepy and stupid about it. Not like Tim."

"Tim? What do you mean?"

"You know, all hiding in the locker room at his preppy little school and crying. You didn't know about that?" I indicated as such.

Dennis went on to explain that he'd heard from a friend who went to Tim's school that on more than one occasion, Tim had been found hiding away from the rest of the students, apparently hysterical with tears over something he refused to explain. All he would say was that it was something between him and God and that no one else could do anything to help. This mutual friend, whom Dennis never named, just thought that Tim was a weird, emotional guy with some kind of problem. Nobody knew just what was wrong with him, but we figured it out.

"And he needs to quit with that shit," Dennis said. "He's drawing attention to himself."

"That's so weird," I said. "I didn't know anything about that. He was always so smart and together, it seemed like."

"Yeah, well, sometimes those are the ones you have to wonder about," he said, but I didn't quite know what he meant. "And it's not like he didn't keep things from us before."

"That's true." As hidden as our entire group had always been from the rest of the world, sometimes we were just as secretive with each other. That had been true in the past, and it still was. "Plus he tends to think of himself as the one who started this whole thing, you know, the one who suggested we take that damn potion in the first place."

"I'd forgotten about that," Dennis said, a faraway look coming into his eyes. "Yeah, you're right."

I glanced around again, making sure that no one was listening in. In the din of the mall, it wasn't likely that anyone would pick up on what we were saying, but I'd realized that it wasn't entirely safe for us to be talking about this here. But I'd been waiting to talk to Dennis again for so long, and I worried that if I let him go now, I might not get the chance to tell him what I needed to.

I edged closer to him. "Look, I've got to tell you some things."

"Like what," he said flatly.

I proceeded to run down the latest information that I'd been passing along to the other former vampires: Carolyn's and Damon's clones were dead, the feeling one got of a thread detaching from them when their clone was killed, and how killing a vampire meant that the ones it had created died as well. Dennis tried to look bored and uncaring as I rattled these things off, but I could tell that he was becoming more intrigued as I went on.

"Well, I haven't felt any psychic thread disconnecting or anything," he said, "so I guess that means I was right about my clone." He thought for a moment. "I just wish I could stop being so…"

"Hey guys," Carolyn said from behind us. She held up a bag from the music store and said to me sarcastically, "No, really, Ray, thanks for all your help." The idea had been that we would pick out tapes for our father together, but I'd spent the whole time outside talking to Dennis instead. "I got him a Statler Brothers tape, but I couldn't find anything by that Mark Russell guy he likes. The guy behind the counter said that he might have a videotape out, or maybe a book instead, since he's always joking about politics. We'll have to check those stores next."

"Yeah, okay," I said.

"And you," she said, turning to Dennis, "you've got to stop getting so tall. It's freaking me out." She was right; Dennis had grown from a pudgy, goofy kid into a much more imposing figure, almost as tall as Carl.

"Yeah, I'll get right on that."

"You doing okay?" she asked him. "With, you know, everything?"

"I guess," he said simply. "Trying to stay out of trouble. And trying to avoid the whole, you know, vampire crap that's been going down." There was an odd look to him; I noticed that his eyes seemed to be moving up and down as he looked at Carolyn.

She looked nervous and hissed *"Shh!"* at him, but I'd already realized that we weren't in any danger unless we called attention to ourselves.

"Calm down, Carolyn," I said. "No one's going to notice."

"You don't know that," she said angrily.

"We've been talking about it the whole time!" I said. "And no one's…"

"I can't believe you two would be so stupid as to talk about this stuff in public," she shot back. "Come on, Ray, we've got to get going." She began to walk off.

"We should talk more," I said to Dennis, hoping that this conversation wasn't a one-off. Maybe if I could keep in touch with him, I might actually convince him to help with tracking down the vampires.

"Sure, I'll give you a call," he said, but I could tell that he wasn't serious. "And I'll give you a call, too, Carolyn!" he shouted as she got farther away. "Pick you up at 7:30?" Dennis had always had a crush on her, which was kind of cute and laughable when we were kids, but for some reason, it suddenly seemed creepy. A few people had noticed us by this point, and I realized that what he was really trying to do was embarrass her.

Carolyn stopped, then took a few steps back in our direction. "Sorry," she said loudly enough for the onlookers to hear, "but I only date guys who are old enough to drink." With that, she stormed off.

Dennis looked angry, but all I could do was shrug my shoulders, slightly apologetic. I caught up to Carolyn as she stomped away, secretly admiring her for her clever comeback but not wanting to show it. As she reached towards her purse for something, all of a sudden, one of the buckles on the strap came loose, and the purse clattered to the tiled floor.

"Damn it!" she said, kneeling down to pick it up.

I started to help her, but then I looked back at Dennis, who had seen the incident. He stood there with his arms folded, then wiggled his eyebrows at me. In the past, that gesture was usually accompanied by a smile, but like earlier during our conversation, this time he looked more resigned.

"Hold this," Carolyn said, thrusting her purse at me as she fumbled with the plastic bag with her other hand.

I started to protest, but the angry look in her eyes quelled that immediately. I hated whenever she made me do that in public; it always made me feel so self-conscious. After she set the bag down by her feet, she fumbled with the end of the strap that had broken and set about making a quick fix to it, trying to adjust a buckle so that it could attach to the hook on the main part of the purse. I looked around nervously, trying to avoid the eyes of the curious people passing by.

The fix seemed to work, but then Carolyn insisted on zipping open the purse while I still stood there holding it, prolonging my discomfort. Inspecting the contents, she pulled out a round make-up compact, opened it, then closed it quickly. "Fucking great," she said sternly.

"What?"

"The mirror broke. So that's ruined. I knew the strap on this thing was getting old, but..." She sighed angrily, then shoved the compact back inside and zipped the purse closed, snatching it from my palms.

Throwing the strap back over her shoulder, she looked at the main part and then pushed down on it gently, testing her repair job.

I looked back to Dennis, who by this point was walking away from where we'd left him and was heading for the stairs to the lower level. I quickly shut my eyes and envisioned a dark-colored rectangular cube materializing around me, a technique he and I had settled on as kids for creating shields around our minds. If I hadn't done that, I knew from experience, my powers might shoot out from me and cause him to go tumbling down the stairs.

"And I'll bet that you were just mortified for those two or three seconds that you had to hold it for her," Elizabeth said to me that night.

"It was longer than that!" I protested. "All those people in the mall, walking by, looking at me and…"

"And what? Probably thinking, 'Oh, look at that nice guy holding that girl's purse for her.'" She sighed and rolled her eyes. "I swear. Boys get so damn scared that anyone might think there's anything remotely girly about you, even for a second."

I started to protest again, but then I remembered something from a few years back and laughed. I told her about a time, also in the mall, when I'd been there with Carolyn and Damon back when they were still together. For whatever reason, she'd made him hold her purse, but instead of making a big deal and complaining about it like she said he would, he immediately started prancing around in an overly effeminate way. He swung his arms as he walked and made his wrists go limp, grinning ridiculously and acting like he was gay. Annoyed, Carolyn had snatched her purse back from him, at which point he returned to normal. I, meanwhile, had been laughing my head off.

"Well, that's one way of handling it," Elizabeth said. "But then, homophobia isn't that far off from misogyny." I wasn't even sure what those words meant, but before I could ask, she went on, "Do you even know anyone who's gay?"

"No!"

"That you know of," she said meaningfully. "It's different when you know someone who is. They're not all 'queers' and 'fags' or whatever." She then stopped and changed her tone. "Sorry. Feeling a little preachy tonight, I guess. Just, well... I had a gay uncle, you know."

"Really?" This was the second revelation about her extended family so far this night. Earlier, when I'd asked her what her middle name was, she'd told me that it came from another relative, her aunt Pamela.

"Or, as we liked to call her because of how she talked, 'Aint Payum.'" Seeing my confused look, she added, "She was from Texas."

I snickered. "Oh, I get it. 'Hah! Ah'm Aint Payum! *Poo-kwah!*'" That last bit was a reference to Mrs. Birch, the French teacher Elizabeth and I had endured the previous year at Bethlehem. The woman had such a thick southern accent that that her French words tended to be pronounced in a hilariously bad way. The sentence "Où est la bibliothèque?" became mangled into what sounded like *"Oh ay lah beebleotaak??"* Similarly, the question "Pourquoi?" became *"Poo-kwah?"* via Mrs. Birch's strong drawl.

Throughout the night, our conversation had taken its usual twists and turns, moods occasionally getting volatile, but for the most part, we were glad to see each other. When she'd first arrived at the house, I'd kissed her for a good two or three minutes before we'd even started talking.

And she had a lot that she wanted to tell me. As I expected, she'd been doing more research, but instead of risking being spotted at the public library downtown again, she'd started looking through books at a local college library. There had been a few books on vampires there, and she'd read and learned a lot, though how useful it was, neither of us could be sure. Much of what she found raised more questions rather than providing the one big answer I kept hoping for: a way to cure her and turn her back to human again.

"It's all so complicated," she said with a sigh, "much more than I ever thought it would be. I mean, before when I was reading up on stuff, it was mostly what I expected, all eastern European kind of stuff, traditions, Dracula, all that. Coffins and garlic and sunlight… Oh my…"

I snorted, and she giggled, her speech having accidentally derailed into misquoting *The Wizard of Oz*.

"Anyway," she said firmly, trying to stay on topic, "what's been such a pain is how I keep reading things that conflict. Like there was this Hungarian woman named Elizabeth Bathory about four hundred years ago, and she was a vampire. She killed something like four or five hundred young girls and drank their blood — or bathed in it, depending who you read — in order to stay young."

"Wow," I said, simultaneously disgusted and intrigued.

"But then, other books say that that didn't even really happen, like maybe, yes, she killed those people, but not because she was a real vampire; she just did it because she liked to and was a psycho. Then you turn around and there's other speculation that it was just a conspiracy, something made up by other noblemen of the time to try and take her down."

I thought for a bit. "Hmm. Well, seeing as how her name was Elizabeth, she probably must have been a psycho."

She rolled her eyes and sneered at me, then flatly said, "Funny."

"Thank you," I said, continuing to smile.

"But that's just a small part of it," she went on, ignoring my attempt at humor. "There are all kinds of vampire legends out there, and they all vary in huge, huge ways. Some of them are way older than any of the European stuff. There are even ones from China that go back thousands of years. They didn't use the word 'vampire,' but it was the same thing, a person who came back from the dead and drank the blood of the living. And other places, like Russia. Or Spain. Or Sweden. Just all over the place, all through history.

"And with all these different legends, where things start to get strange is when it comes to what can kill a vampire, or what makes someone become one in the first place. We think of it like: A person gets bitten by a vampire and their blood gets drained, they die, and come back to life as a vampire. The only way to kill it is with the traditional stake through the heart, sunlight, et cetera. But you know what's really weird?"

"The fact that you're starting to sound like a schoolteacher?" I quipped.

She looked angry. "Will you stop..." Then she looked surprised. "Really?"

"Kinda, yeah," I said. I knew that she was being serious, but I think because I was so excited to see her again, I couldn't help but be in a good mood and want to joke around.

"Hmm," she said, looking thoughtful and slumping her shoulders briefly. "Never really thought of that. I am kind of lecturing here, aren't I? 'The habits of the Hungarian vampire...'" she said in a mock authoritarian voice, holding out her hand towards an imaginary chalkboard. "I guess so. But this stuff is interesting to me, and I think it's important. And I think you should listen."

"Yes, ma'am," I said, sitting up straight and folding my hands in my lap.

She rolled her eyes again, but then she went on talking, and I could tell that she was trying to keep things less formal. "Okay, so let me ask you something. Tell me what you know about Jewish people."

"What about them?"

"What do they believe? Think about what they used to tell us at Bethlehem, why they're different and all that."

I tried to recall the things I'd been taught. "They don't believe in Jesus. Or they do believe that he existed, but not that he was the son of God, just some prophet."

"Right," Elizabeth said in a leading manner, "and what else?"

I was beginning to feel frustrated, knowing that she was getting at something but not telling me just what. "They… um… I don't know. They wear those funny-looking hats?" I indicated the back of my head as I said this.

"Do they wear crosses?" she asked quickly, reaching up to touch her necklace.

"Well, no, of course not. That's a Christian symbol. Some of them wear those little six-pointed stars, though."

"Okay, so, tell me this," she said, folding her arms. "Supposing a Jewish guy gets killed by a vampire. And then he comes back to life as a vampire. If you held up a cross in front of him, would he shrink back from it?" She mimed doing so herself.

"Sure, why not? If he's a vampire now, that's going to kill him."

"Not necessarily. What I've found is that the different kinds of vampires around the world are repelled by all kinds of different things, some of them so arbitrary and silly that I couldn't believe what I was reading half the time. Like for some, it's the usual stake through the heart or burning or whatever. That's the European kind. For others, you're supposed to cut the head off, and some cultures say you then have to boil the head in oil or vinegar or something. Others, you put poppy seeds on the grave. Or a bunch of rocks. Or you cut off their toes, or —and this was my favorite one — stick a nail in its belly button."

I laughed at the mental image. "You're making this shit up."

"Nope, not a bit," she said, smiling smartly. "It's all over the place like that. And it makes for some pretty weird questions, like, if you find yourself faced with a Greek vampire, what do you do, chop off its head or stick a gold coin in their mouth?"

"Or a wild rose…" I said thoughtfully, remembering something from my past. Suddenly, what she was saying started to make a weird sort of sense. Even though I'd been a vampire myself, I hadn't known all of the limitations and defenses against them. At times, Susanna had revealed ones I had never heard of, like running water.

"You know about that?" Elizabeth asked me, surprised. "Well, yeah, that's another one, too. Can't even remember which one that applied to."

"So you think that if there was this Jewish vampire guy you're talking about, he wouldn't be afraid of a cross because he wasn't Christian? But maybe he'd be afraid if I held up one of those stars to him instead?"

"Maybe," she said. "I'm not even sure. But it seems to me like belief and faith is a big factor. I mean, okay, what about me?" She spread out her arms in an open gesture. "I'm an atheist. So what does that mean?"

"You don't believe in God," I said simply. "There used to be all these rumors going around school about you and that, by the way."

"Yeah, I know," she said, rolling her eyes again. "Totally going to burn in hell and all that. Well, not if I don't believe in it I'm not."

I thought about this. "That's an interesting way of looking at it. So... You really just don't believe that there's a God?"

"Do you?"

I sighed. "I don't know. Kinda. Given everything that I went through before, well... I guess that's when I first started doubting. Like why, if he was really there, would he let us get away with such terrible things? Or allow vampires to exist in the first place? But then I know what someone like Dr. Phillips would say to that. 'He's testing your faith,' or something."

"Catch-all answer to everything..." Elizabeth muttered bitterly.

"Yeah. But I think what really killed it for me was how much they kept shoving it down our throats at Bethlehem, you know? No room for doubt, don't question. After a while, that just seemed pretty insecure to me."

"No kidding."

"But it's not like science can explain everything, either. I was thinking about that a while back, like the whole, 'matter can be either...'" I blanked for a second, then asked myself aloud, "How's it go again?"

"Matter can neither be created nor destroyed, only changed," Elizabeth rattled off. I looked at her, surprised, but she just smiled back, her eyebrows raised. "The law of conservation of mass. I do know things, Ray."

"I never said you... Yeah, okay. Fine." Thrown, I forgot the point I was about to make. Trying to pick up somewhere, I told her how our science teacher, Mrs. Manning, had a problem with this law of nature and with teaching it to her class because of her belief in the Creation. "But I still think that the whole 'religion versus science' conflict is... I don't know... overdone, maybe? I don't think it's impossible that there could be a God that could create things, but I also don't think that if that's true, then science should just be ignored, either."

"Room for both, you think."

"Yeah."

She looked somewhat resigned. "Who knows."

I smiled. "You know, this is the first time I've really thought about all this, at least while talking to someone."

"Yeah, me too," she said, and there was something sad in her voice.

Wanting to keep things light, I laughed and said, "It's not like I could really talk to anyone about this at school."

"They'd burn you at the stake, probably," she said, her smile coming back.

"And I guess another way I've come to think of it is, well, if there is a God, then I just don't want to mess with him. And it bugs me, the idea of some invisible person watching over everything I do, or having control over things. Deciding my fate, or judging me at the end. Or maybe..." An old memory flashed through my head. "Wow, there's something I haven't thought about for a while."

"What?"

I told her a story from my childhood, back when I was still at my previous school along with Carl, and he'd asked our Religion teacher an interesting question. The lesson centered around the Bible verse John 3:16, which Father Merchant said was the core belief of Christianity, a guarantee of salvation.

"So as long as you believe in that," Carl asked him, "no matter what you've done, you're still forgiven and going to Heaven?"

"That's right," Father Merchant said. That struck a chord with me, and looking back on it, I realized why. My young mind had interpreted this exchange as a sort of "Get out of Jail Free" card, so it followed that someone who had sinned as much as I had would cling to such a notion.

I told Elizabeth this, and while she seemed to get what I was saying, she didn't seem particularly taken with the idea.

"But that's kind of, I don't know..." She drifted off, looking thoughtful. "It still comes back to the same thing. If there actually is no God, then what do all the rules even mean? What defines..." She suddenly stopped, gaping, and then she gasped and put a hand to her mouth.

Startled, I sat up again, leaning toward her with an outstretched hand. "What's wrong?"

"Oh my God," she hissed, looking around. "Did you hear that?" My head turned quickly, and my eyes darted around the room as I wondered what she'd heard. "No!" she said, tugging on my arm, and I looked back at her. Her expression was hard to read; I expected her to look scared, but there was something different there.

"Is someone here?" I whispered. "Or maybe it's nothing again." A couple of months before, we had been startled by what sounded like someone sneaking up on us in the house, but it had turned out to just be a stray possum, one that we wasted almost fifteen minutes tracking down before we found out what it was.

"No," she repeated, "not that. You didn't even notice, did you? Did you hear what I just said there?"

"About what?"

"About God. *God,*" she emphasized, a smile broadening on her face. She laughed slightly. "Jesus. Holy."

The penny dropped. "Ohhh…" I said. "You… You couldn't do that before."

"And now I can say it. God Jesus holy church Christianity," she said, bouncing a little as she spoke, her voice almost musical. *"Eeeaster* Bunny." She giggled. "It doesn't affect me anymore. I guess I've… changed."

This was an interesting development, though we weren't exactly sure what to make of it. Our conversation continued well into the night, occasionally coming back to the topic of Christianity and other religions, even Satanism. How would someone like that, if also a vampire, be affected by a cross? Would it repel him twice as much, or would the two beliefs cancel each other out? This led me to mention to her that I had in fact once met a Satanist, but it had been a really unpleasant experience for me. I didn't tell her the details, just that he was in fact a vampire who had tried to turn my sisters, my friends, and me into truly undead vampires. We had barely escaped from that, and it wasn't something I liked thinking about, so I steered the conversation elsewhere.

"That kind of reminds me," I said, "we've got more book reports coming up in Mrs. Cartwright's class at school."

"Same kind of thing?"

"Yeah. Pick from a list of these books, and no you can't come up with one of your own because God forbid we actually let you think for yourselves."

She laughed. "So what's it going to be?"

"I'm not sure yet. Some of them are really long, and I don't want to deal with that. But the shorter ones are kind of weird, too. They've had this list since the beginning of the year, so I'm thinking that maybe if I pick one of the ones that someone else read last month, maybe I can just get them to tell me about it, and I can fake it and write my report that way."

"Anything to avoid actually reading, huh?" she said with a sneer. By this point, we had reclined on the sleeping bag and pillow I'd brought to the house, our talking occasionally interrupted by brief making out sessions. We had also changed our usual habit of hanging around in the outer parts of the house and were in an interior room away from the open windows, better sheltered from the cold. We guessed that it might end up becoming one of the bathrooms once the place was complete.

"Yeah, whatever," I said, knowing that she was right. Despite the fact that my father was a librarian, or maybe even because of that, I'd never been too keen on reading. "But one of the books is called *The Satan Seller,* and I've been thinking about doing that one."

"What's Satan doing in a cellar?" she asked.

"What?" Then I laughed. "No, no. Seller. With an *S.* Someone who sells things."

"Oh." She pursed her lips, which I could barely see in the dim glow of my nearby flashlight, propped up against one of the walls. "What's Satan doing in a 7-Eleven?"

I laughed again, as did she. "Not that either," I said. "No devil in a convenience store, as far as I know. No, it's supposedly this really creepy true story about a guy who gets involved in the Church of Satan, then gets out of it somehow. Melinda was telling me about it; she read it last month."

She sighed. "Melinda. How's she doing?"

I often felt weird around her, both because I knew what had really happened to Elizabeth and because, since her death, both Melinda and their other friend Helen had been nicer to me. Before, they'd always been really snobby and mean.

"Fine, I guess," I said, and then I told her my thoughts on how my treatment from the two girls had been different.

"That's just them being them," she said.

"You miss them?"

"Not really." This surprised me, and my expression must have shown it. "No, don't get me wrong. They were good friends to me back in the day and all. But it was kind of by default. We just sort of fell in together. I didn't fit in with the popular cheerleader girls, and I — *we* — definitely weren't like the pious, smart Christian girls, either."

"Yeah, I picked up on that."

"Sure. But we fought sometimes. Plus there was the fact that Melinda..." She paused, then shook her head. "I shouldn't be telling you all this."

"All what?" I asked, intrigued.

She sat up, so I did, too. "Nothing. Just... We've been talking all night, and I still haven't told you the rest of what I've been up to this week."

Something in her tone troubled me, the way she suddenly sounded more serious. "What?"

She recounted how things had ended between us the previous weekend, her being upset once I'd told her about the thread connection. She then told me that when her research hadn't led her to any new information about that, she had taken another tack.

"So I started hanging out with the other vampires around town," she said. "Just to feel them out. It ended up being pretty interesting."

"What?" I repeated. The thought of this scared me, but I wasn't quite sure why.

"They're not really all that... cohesive, I guess you could say. Like, not all one big thing, like you told me you were when you and your friends were doing it. Really spread out, as it turns out." She waved her hands around as she said this, like someone floating in water.

"So... What, there are a bunch of different groups?"

"Not even groups, sometimes. I mean, yeah, there are, but a lot of times, they're just on their own, trying to figure themselves out. And they're not all evil and terrible," she said, suddenly firm and fixing me with a stare.

"I'm… not really sure what to say to that." I really wasn't; there was something accusatory in her tone.

"No, you're not," she said meaningfully. "But what I really wanted to tell you was that, when I went around talking to them, I made sure to tell them about the thread thing, asking them if they knew about it, stuff like that."

"What do you mean?" I had folded my arms and was sort of hugging myself, not even realizing I'd done it at first. Carolyn had told me once that doing so was an unconscious defense mechanism, something that people did when feeling threatened. I forced myself to relax and stop doing it.

"That if they knew whether or not if their host died, they'd die, too."

This bugged me further. It felt like she was betraying my secrets. She put a hand on my arm, and I realized that my breathing had started to increase. "It's okay; calm down," she said. "It ended up doing just what I'd intended. Well, okay, so maybe that wasn't true at first. But I realized it as time went on. It ensured your safety."

That last word relaxed me a little, but for the most part, I was still uncertain. "How do you mean?" I asked her.

"Think about it," she said, the corners of her mouth turning up. "I go around and mingle with the rest of the vampires, just being one of them. Most of them don't even know who I am. Though I did encounter that girl Kay at one point… It doesn't matter. The point is that I told them about all this, and so then they tell the others, and it spreads throughout the vampire community. If you kill the source of what you came from, then you'll die, too. So that means that they'll be more careful, and none of them are going to kill you. Or your friends. Because if they do, they'll get wiped out, too."

Finally, I got it. The tension I'd been feeling as she spoke suddenly went away, and she smiled broadly as it did, her eyes squinting. "That's… kind of brilliant," I said, exhaling sharply.

"Isn't it, though." She bit her lower lip as she smiled, and I pulled her to me and hugged her tightly.

CHAPTER NINE

Elizabeth was drinking from my neck, the sound of each swallow of blood filling my ear. This had been inevitable; I'd always known that it would eventually happen. I couldn't fight her off, and even though I'd tried to resist, part of me knew that deep down, I didn't want to. I owed her this.

Something had happened to her earlier that night, something that was my fault, and she needed me to feed her. I could no longer recall what it was, but it didn't matter anymore. When she'd first lunged at me with fangs bared, it felt like it wasn't really happening to me. It was like I could see myself from the outside, like I was an actor on TV. Finally, I was giving myself to her, my body beginning to go limp as she held me roughly, one hand on my left shoulder, the other on the right side of my head. Between every few gulps, she paused to breathe through her nose, the air tickling the back of my neck. Then she would resume drinking. It hurt, but only in the beginning.

Her pace increased, her grip on me tightening. She was no longer pausing to come up for air. The swallows became faster and rhythmic, and somehow, my head had drooped at an angle where my eyes were partly covered by her long, blonde hair. The strands tickled my eyelids as they brushed against them. All I could see, feel, hear, and smell was her, and it was enough.

As I grew more delirious, the sound of her grew louder, a pulsating *gulp, gulp, gulp, gulp...* The tugging sensation from her mouth on my neck increased, and any second now, she would drain the very last drop from my body...

I woke with a start as the orgasm kicked in, and it took me less than a second to realize what was happening. This wasn't the first wet dream I'd ever had; those had begun a couple of years earlier, so I was familiar with the sensation and the odd emotional state they put me in once I was fully awake.

I swore in a half-whisper, my voice box not yet functional, and I pushed the bed sheets off and set about cleaning up. As usual, everything had been contained in my underwear, but I still felt strange. I had no idea if the same were true for girls, but for teenage boys, orgasms usually resulted in fumbled cleaning up coupled with a sense of shame or embarrassment. Although I couldn't know for sure, I assumed that this must be different when having actual sex with another person, but all alone, there was only myself and my own psyche to answer to. At least when one masturbated and had some semblance of control, they could be prepared, but nocturnal emissions left me feeling much more vulnerable. It was like my brain had decided to pop one off all on its own whether I liked it or not. It almost felt violating.

The dreams weren't even usually about sex. It wasn't like I dreamed about doing it with some hot girl and then came in my sleep. If they had been like that, I probably would have enjoyed them rather than feeling put upon by my bizarrely aroused subconscious. One of the earliest ones I'd had involved something vague about helping two people I didn't know try to move this big sheet of metal, but then it fell on us. As we tried to lift it off, it kept falling back down, first once, then twice, then over and over in a regular pattern, that same familiar pulsating sensation… And that was all it took. It wasn't even an erotic dream; it just left me feeling very weird when I woke up.

At least I knew I wasn't alone in this. Dennis had in fact told me on the phone back in eighth grade about his first one, the content of which was also strange and not worth repeating. I wondered if girls also had orgasms in their sleep, and because Dennis didn't know either, I asked Carl about it one time, and he said that they did. I assumed that he must have known this because his father was a health teacher and a coach, a guy who had some kind of medical background but wasn't actually a doctor. And of course, I couldn't help but be curious as to whether or not he'd had any, since by this point I was beginning to feel left out, not having had one of my own yet. Carl had, practically bragging to me about a wet dream he'd had which involved oral sex, but he refused to tell me from whom.

"It's someone you know, and that would just be weird," was all he would say. That drove me crazy, and I spent a good day or two wondering if it might have been either of my sisters, or maybe it was just one of the girls from our old school. Then I realized that I was spending way too much time contemplating one of my male friend's sexual dreams, which creeped me out.

This had been my first wet dream about Elizabeth, which I might have been fine with if not for the fact that she had been killing me in it. Plus there was the fact that it was vampiric in nature, which bothered me quite a bit. I would never admit it to anyone else and didn't even like acknowledging it myself, but there had been times when I had, while awake, sometimes had sexual fantasies that included vampires. That had only been prior to the emergence of my clone, so I chalked it up to the strange build-up of hostile emotions I'd felt during that time.

But the thoughts had been there, and I tried to shake them from my head whenever they'd come back to me. Sometimes I would fantasize that I was a vampire again, and I would force myself on girls I liked at the time, including Elizabeth. In some of those daydreams, I would still have the intense mind-controlling powers that I'd had as a vampire, and I could seduce people with those as well. If these fantasies culminated in my having an orgasm, the disgust I felt for myself inside seemed mirrored by the grossness of having to clean up after an ejaculation.

Since Elizabeth and I had gotten together, my thoughts on sex had changed in ways I didn't fully understand at the time. I would say that they mellowed, but that wasn't really true. They just shifted, moving from lonely imaginings to something that actually involved including another person in a more realistic sense.

I'd once heard Carolyn disdainfully describe some scenes in an old movie she'd seen as "rape-tastic," and although I didn't really get it at the time, I later realized that some of my sexual fantasies had been the same thing. And it was all over the place in pop culture, even in old-time movies or the joking bits in shows as innocent as *The Monkees* when guys would lasciviously — and sometimes literally — chase girls around even though they didn't want it. Even pop music wasn't immune: The majority of love songs seemed to be centered around the idea that as long as the singer were persistent enough, the object of their affection would eventually have to give in.

None of this had ever worked out in that manner in real life, including with Elizabeth. For one thing, I had been terrified of the idea of honestly expressing my feelings to her back when she'd been human. Now that she was a vampire, there was no way I could force anything on her even if I'd wanted to. But was that because I was really a nice guy who wouldn't do such a thing, or because I knew I couldn't take her? Given my violent past, I found that when these questions bubbled up in my mind, I shoved them aside. I liked to think that now that she and I were on more open terms, I stood a chance of having a decent, normal relationship. And then I would try to ignore how laughable that idea seemed given the mechanics of the situation, who and what she really was.

This particular dream, though, opened up one important door for me, making me realize something I hadn't before. Throughout the next day, I kept thinking about it, feeling a mixture of emotions. The fact that I'd had an orgasm over the thought of her draining my blood bothered me, but I tried to write it off as equally as non-sexual as some of the other wet dreams I'd had. I also tried to ignore the tingling feeling I got down below whenever I replayed the sequence in my head.

But there was also fear. What if the dream had in fact been a premonition? What if she really did bite me — maybe even soon — either out of anger or lust? She'd joked about it from time to time, but she'd always assured me that she would never really do it. She wasn't evil. She didn't want to kill me. She didn't want to turn me into a vampire like her. But what if she changed her mind one day?

I dropped my pencil and put a hand to my mouth in shock as the revelation hit me in the middle of class. A few of the other students looked at me strangely, but I just tried to play it off as I bent down under my desk and picked the pencil back up. The few seconds down there gave me enough time to smile briefly, which I then suppressed as I straightened back up in my chair, pretending to resume paying attention to Mrs. Cartwright's latest lesson.

Elizabeth couldn't kill me. Well, she could, but only if she had a death wish. It was the thread, something that had been troubling me for weeks, but only now had I managed to put the pieces together. If she were to bite me and drain me like she had in my dream, I would die. But then, so would my clone. That would in turn kill her.

Did she know this already? Probably. She'd spent the past week spreading the information to the other vampires that if any of them killed me or the other "originals," they'd wind up dying, too. Still, as a point of self-preservation, I told myself to be sure to find a way to work this latest conclusion of mine into the next conversation I had with her, just to be safe.

I hoped that I was right, that I was more or less safe, but that depended on how well Elizabeth's information spread. I figured it probably would, just as her suggestion of the practice of vampires wounding people rather than fully draining and killing them seemed to have. I'd noticed over the past few months that the news reports had mentioned several cases of people being attacked by vampire bats but surviving instead of dying, though actual killings did still occur. Over time, these injuries appeared to get so frequent that the news often glossed over them and only emphasized the cases where people actually died.

My monitoring of the vampires' activities around town had up until recently been confined to the TV news, but after my encounter with Dennis at the mall, I decided to start reading the obituary section of the newspaper each day. It bugged me the way that his revelation about Mrs. Warren had surprised me, so I reasoned that if I could find out about such personal, hard-hitting things first, that would be better than being caught off guard in conversation with someone else. It didn't take long for me to regret doing so.

It was Wednesday evening when I spotted Gary Bertram's name. I hadn't seen him for years, nor had I wanted to, as we weren't friends. I hated the guy most of the time when I was younger. But it still hurt to see him listed there among the rest of the dead, and it was a very odd feeling knowing that someone I'd grown up with, someone my age, was gone.

Back in 1985, he had almost discovered the fact that my friends and I were vampires, but we'd managed to fool him and his mother into thinking that it was just an elaborate game we were playing. And back then, we had sometimes seen it that way, not realizing the magnitude of it all, what the far-reaching consequences would be. Gary's name printed on the page in front of me was the latest one.

I couldn't help but wonder if it had in fact been my clone who had killed him, and the more I thought about it, the more likely that seemed. With everything that had been happening the past few months, it was entirely possible that Gary might have remembered those days and begun to suspect something, and if so, he might have exposed us. Certainly my clone had no love for me, but because of the thread, he did have a vested interest in keeping me from winding up with the death penalty.

Also, since it was probably Dennis's clone who had killed Mrs. Warren the week before, it could have been that my clone was trying to one-up him. The real Dennis and I had been friends in our younger days, but it was a tenuous relationship, sort of on-again, off-again. He and I would sometimes try to top each other, so it followed that this competition might be darkly mirrored in our clones' activities. Or, for all I knew, they might have become friends again, and this was something they had coordinated. It frustrated me that all I could do was speculate, not know for certain.

Of course, I felt tremendously guilty over Gary's death. Even if my clone hadn't actually been the one who'd killed him, I was still responsible in at least an indirect way. I tried a couple of times to stop myself from being upset by thinking about how much I'd disliked him as a child, all the mean things he'd done to me and my friends, but that didn't help. The fact that he'd been an asshole wasn't the point; no one deserved to die that young. I wondered, as I had after our conversation on Sunday, if Dennis had felt more guilty than he let on about Mrs. Warren's death, his tough guy act notwithstanding.

The following day would be the last time I would read through the obituaries. It was just too nerve-wracking; I'd find myself feeling tremendous anxiety whenever I started to read them. Even if I didn't recognize any of the other names, it bugged me to see each of the victims listed one by one. Every entry felt like a finger pointing at me saying, *You made this happen.*

That Wednesday was, by the way, Valentine's Day, which I had hoped before might be a good night for me and Elizabeth, and maybe

I could get her something special. But as it turned out, she wasn't very keen on the holiday, though for different reasons than my father.

"I boycott it, and I usually wear black in protest," she'd told me the last time I'd seen her, the night we talked about all of that religious stuff. "Or at the very least, black underwear."

That made me laugh, but I didn't quite understand why she was so opposed to it.

"It's just… When you're single, it's all up in your face. And sure, I chose to be single, but whatever. Just never liked it, not since… Well, anyway." She was being evasive, and something told me that I shouldn't pry. The whole night, I'd kept hoping that we would end up having sex, so I'd been trying to keep things from steering into any territory where I might say the wrong thing and make her mad.

"I'm surprised they even let us mention it at school anyway," I said. "Surely if those fine upstanding Baptists let us acknowledge a holiday about romance, that will lead to horrible things! Like everyone having premarital sex!"

She laughed. "Everyone slow dancing in the hallways, leading to uncontrollable fucking," she said with mock seriousness, and we laughed again, leaning into each other, our foreheads touching. Then we kissed, and I couldn't help but picture the two of us doing what she'd just said.

When we pulled back from each other, she said with a curious look, "You know what I've been thinking?"

"Sometimes, but my psychic powers kind of come and go," I quipped.

She looked at me sideways. "Shut up. I meant that, well, how about next time we meet, we get a hotel room?"

This surprised me. I didn't like hotels; the last time I'd been in one was when our entire group got together and the clones emerged from us. Prior to that had been back when we were vampires and had to confront the famous vampire hunter Van Helsing, something that had also not gone well.

There had only been one other time in my life, an incident I barely remembered from one of my family's vacations when I was little. We were on our way to a place in Florida called Sanibel Island, but because the weather had been so bad during the ten-hour drive, we had to make an unexpected stop at a Holiday Inn halfway through. It wasn't very pleasant, our family of five trying to cram ourselves into a single room.

"What?" I asked Elizabeth. "Why?"

"It would be a nice change," she said, sounding slightly miffed. "You know, from this freezing house." I couldn't argue with that. I also noticed how the flashlight propped against the wall was growing dim, the light from it a dull yellow as its batteries began to run out.

Not wanting to recount my more recent hotel visits, I told her what little I could recall of my family's Florida experience, including how Carolyn slept on the floor on two seat cushions, and Susanna had to endure a makeshift bed made from the chairs those cushions had come from. I'd slept in the bed with my parents, and I was just old enough at the time to realize how weird and unfamiliar that felt.

"Your parents couldn't afford a bigger room?" she asked.

"I have no idea," I said. "Give me a break; I was only four or five. From what I remember, it was this last minute thing." I tried to recall the few fragments that I could. "There was this huge rainstorm, and something about the station wagon breaking down and my dad trying to fix it in the rain. I can even… wow… There's something I haven't thought about for a long time."

"What?"

"Just this image of the… I guess it was the hazard light thing on the dashboard. These two green triangles flashing, and this *clunk-cluck, clunk-cluck* sound going along with it. And I was in the front seat with my mom. She was holding me in her lap."

"Aw," she said, smiling, which I could barely make out in the dim light. "Little bitty Ray in his mother's arms."

I grimaced; one thing teenage boys hate the most is being thought of as lesser or emasculated, particularly by girls they're trying to impress. But at the same time, I couldn't help but feel a little nostalgic. I'd forgotten what it was like to be that small.

"The only other thing I can remember is… I guess it must have been later, where I was being carried along by someone, either Mom or Dad, rushing through the parking lot in the pouring rain. I guess they were trying to get me from the car to the door of the hotel room."

"In the middle of a huge thunderstorm?" She shuddered. "I don't envy you there."

"Yeah, I know." I could recall flashes of other things from the trip, later parts on the beach both in the day and at night, enjoying the ocean and being simultaneously awed and scared by the Fourth of July fireworks. "I miss that stuff," I said, feeling a little sad, "our family going to the beach like that. We used to do it a lot, but the past few years, the trips have become a lot less frequent. Not really sure why that is."

"Hmm. Money?"

"Could be. I don't really know. My mom inherited a lot from her parents after they died, but I'm not sure about my dad. Things are a little fuzzy on that side of the family history. Carolyn and I have talked about it a few times. She knows more of it than I do." Then I caught myself. "Sorry, I'm doing it again. Talking all about my family, and I know that makes you uncomfortable."

"No, it's okay," she said. "I shouldn't be so…" She shrugged. "I don't know." She shook her head quickly as she frowned, like trying to erase a thought. "But anyway," she continued, brightening again, "this won't be like that. I can get the room, and you can meet me there. We'll hang out like we usually do here, but hey, it will be warmer."

"Can't argue with that," I said. "Sure, why not?"

I spent the week after that looking forward to our next meeting, especially once I realized that being in a hotel room might mean that we'd finally have sex. It frustrated me that we kept doing nothing but talking. It wasn't that I didn't enjoy that plus the occasional making out, but I wanted more.

It was similarly frustrating to me the way that so much was happening around me, but all I could do was hear about it secondhand or read about it in the paper. I wanted to get out there, to be a part of things and take action. Instead, I was stuck at home, my existence feeling boring and constrained when I knew that it could be so much more. Other people, including Elizabeth, were able to be out in the real world doing things, and it was unfair that I couldn't do the same.

The reason I didn't see her at all until the following weekend was because, like the week before, she wanted to mingle with the other vampires around town and find out more. The thought of that bothered me for some reason, but I tried not to let it. She also said that she wanted to try doing more research at a different college library, one in South Augusta.

Although the possibility that we might make love hadn't clicked in my head immediately when she'd first mentioned the hotel, I'd gotten it later on in the night, but I didn't actually say so. Instead, I'd suggested that we meet again sooner, but she said no, citing her reasons. If I hadn't angered her, I might have been able to talk her into doing it that very night, cold though it was in the house. But no, I had to screw things up by suggesting to her that she could act like a double agent, manipulating the vampires she talked to and maneuvering them into situations where the two of us could kill them.

"That's not what I'm after," she'd said bitterly, and the more I tried to backpedal and talk my way out, the worse I made it. Things didn't end on as bitter of a note as the previous time, but I still regretted pissing her off.

She was in a better mood by the time I saw her next, while I was pretty nervous. I wanted so much for things to go right this night, plus the notion of being in a hotel felt so alien to me. The one I was headed to was just up the road from where we had fought Van Helsing three years ago, and remembering that encounter made me uneasy.

Elizabeth had left me a note on my window again, this time telling me the name of the hotel and which room number to come to. She had also suggested that I take a cab there instead of stealing my mother's car again, and I had it pick me up from the Mengs' house across the street. That probably didn't make any difference since it was already late and my parents were in bed, but it felt safer to do it that way.

I had never ridden in a cab before, so this was another unfamiliar experience that did nothing to help calm my nerves. I had expected the driver to be all chatty like the ones I'd seen on TV and had even prepared a cover story for him had he asked me what I was up to, but he barely said a word. This left me alone with my thoughts, but honestly, I would have preferred to have passed the time lying to a stranger.

Just what was going to happen tonight? Would Elizabeth answer the door clad in lingerie, acting all sexy like that woman in the movie *Ghostbusters?* What was the protocol here? Should I have directed the cab driver to stop off somewhere so I could buy some flowers? And what about birth control? I remembered seeing on a sitcom where a teenage boy was told by his girlfriend to get some condoms before their big night, but I didn't even know where to get those. The closer we got to the hotel, the more uncertain I became, and I had half a mind to chicken out and tell the man behind the wheel to just turn around and take me back home.

But I didn't; I had to see this through. What's more, I just plain missed Elizabeth, and I needed to see her again. If I could calm down and manage not to screw things up, it could wind up being a very good night.

As it turned out, things were much less ceremonial than I'd feared. Elizabeth was dressed more or less the same as usual when she opened the door to Room 212, wearing blue jeans and a pink, long-sleeved shirt that buttoned up the front. Even so, she looked more beautiful than ever. She smiled broadly as she said hi and invited me in, waving her hand theatrically as she did so. "You made it!"

"Yes, I did," I said, unable to think of anything more witty, though I tried to at least sound clever.

As she closed the door and locked it, I took in my surroundings. The place was a weird mixture of being decorated and spartan. The room was neat and clean, and there were a couple of rather bland framed pictures hanging above the bed's headboard. There was a desk against one wall, and next to it was a TV set into a large, wooden cabinet. Near the bed, which was much bigger than the ones I was used to seeing, was a small, dark green recliner, which I put my jacket onto. It wasn't all that different from the one my friends and sisters and I had met in the previous year, just smaller, like one big room with what I assumed must be a bathroom behind the door at the far end.

"You like?" Elizabeth asked cutely, gesturing outward with her arms and looking a bit like a game show hostess. For a second, I thought she was referring to what she was wearing, but as she glanced from side to side, I realized that she was talking about the room.

"Yeah, it's fine," I said rather noncommittally. Her face fell, so I tried to recover. "I mean… Sorry. I thought you meant you, not the room."

Her arms fell to her sides as she pouted, but then a seductive smile returned to her face as she cocked her head to the left. "Oh," she said. "Well then…" She sauntered up to me and rested her arms on my shoulders, pulling me closer to her. "You like?" she repeated in a purring voice.

"Of course," I said slyly, putting my arms around the back of her waist and kissing her tightly. It felt so good to hold her again, and the nervousness I'd felt earlier started to fade.

After we'd kissed, we continued to hold each other, and she smiled at me. There was something about her that seemed different, which prompted me to ask, "How come you look so beautiful?"

She bowed her head, like she was trying to hide her open-mouthed smile. Then she looked back up at me, crinkling her nose as she said, "Sweet talker."

"No, I mean it! There's something…" I looked around the room, noticing the many lamps it had. "Maybe it's the lighting. I guess I'm not used to seeing you in something other than dim streetlights."

She pulled away from me gently and said, "Could be. Actually, I think you're right. You look kind of different, too." She then stretched out her arms again, spinning around slowly and looking at the room. "Amazing how being in a fully built place makes a difference, huh?"

I laughed nervously, then reacted with surprise as she jumped onto the bed, turning back around to face me with a single bounce on the mattress. I half expected her to caress the bedspread and invite me to join her, but she didn't. Instead, she just looked at me, grinning. "It's been so long since I sat on a real bed. I missed it!" She then reclined, rubbing her face on the comforter, her expression filled with something that looked like longing, but it wasn't for me. I suddenly realized that, given everything she'd been through the past few months, this really was a luxury to her. I'd taken for granted the ability to sleep in a bed night after night.

I sat down next to her, watching with amusement as she slid her way up to the headboard, then began smashing her face into one of the pillows as she let out little moaning sounds. She smiled as she did so, and she was making quite a show of it. It wasn't so much sexy as it was cute, though really, she'd always managed to blend those two things. This was just an entirely new venue.

"Would you like to be left alone?" I joked, pointing at her and the pillow she was holding to her face.

She opened her eyes and practically leered at me, like this pillow was her new lover and I was the one intruding. Then she giggled and straightened up, her clothes hissing against the fabric of the bedspread as she did so. The bed had what I considered an obnoxious amount of pillows, way more than anyone would normally need, but apparently that was what they did in hotels.

"Wait a minute," I said in a conspiratorial tone.

"What?" she asked, but the way she smiled as she said it made it sound more like *"Mmwhat."*

"How long have you been here? In this room, I mean."

"A little while," she said innocently.

"You totally did all this writhing around on the bed thing before I got here, didn't you."

She giggled through clenched teeth. "Yes, I totally did."

"Well, fair enough, I guess. This really is a luxury you haven't had in a long time, huh?"

"No kidding," she said with wide eyes, then proceeded to cuddle the pillow beneath her again.

"So we probably should do this kind of thing more often, is what you're saying." I had to admit that it was a lot nicer than the near-frigid construction site we'd been frequenting.

"When we can, yes."

I settled down onto the pillow next to hers, relaxing and loving the moment. "So, do you want to…" I drew out the last word expectantly.

She glanced downward, then back up at me. "Maybeeeee…"

I laughed again, my nervousness returning. "I'm a little worried, though… I mean… I didn't bring any condoms or anything."

Her smile deadened briefly, but then she became more warm. "It doesn't matter," she said, sliding up closer to me.

"You sure? I don't want to get you pregnant or anything."

"You won't," she said, more sternly than I liked. "I can't have children." This surprised me, and it bothered me for a reason I couldn't quite place. I just knew that whenever a woman said that, it was usually a sad thing. Not having the ability to produce children was looked upon as something pitiable by society, and I had to admit that I had occasionally imagined a future in which Elizabeth and I would be married and living happily ever after, and that included having children.

"You can't?" I asked. "Is that because you're a vampire, or…?"

"Yes. I haven't had a single period since I came back to life." That much at least I understood, how all women eventually got to a point when they stopped producing eggs and having periods. It seemed unfair for it to have happened to her so early. She didn't seem terribly upset, though. "So, no, I can't have children." She squinted and grinned as she added, "Except as an appetizer."

My mouth hung open, and she pulled back from me, laughing. "Oh, come on!" she said. "I was just kidding! I don't kill children, Ray. And you know that one was funny."

"It…" I sighed. "Yeah, maybe. But you know I don't like hearing you talk like that."

"Still a vampire here, y'know," she said, holding up a hand and gesturing to herself. "That hasn't changed and you know it."

I sighed again. "I know. Did you find anything in your reading this week that might lead to a cure?"

"No," she said with a frown. "Not yet. Turns out the Augusta Tech library didn't have much in the way of literature and folklore. It's more of a… well, technical school, so most of their stuff is geared towards practical things, mechanics, stuff like that."

"Actually, there was something I wanted to ask you about," I said, suddenly realizing that I had stopped trying to push things forward in terms of having sex. Usually I was the one to accidentally kill the mood, but her little quip about killing children had instead derailed things for me.

"Hmm?"

"There was this thing I read about a while ago, and I thought about it this past week. In *Dracula,* they had this deal where a vampire couldn't come into someone's house unless they were invited first. But that seemed really stupid to me, and it wasn't something that affected us when we were vampires. We went wherever we wanted. You ever run across anything like that?"

"Sure, I've seen it," she said, "but it's like I was telling you before. It's in some of the legends, then not in some of the others. Lots of variation, sometimes even contradiction. So maybe you were a kind of vampire who could go in somewhere uninvited, but a Transylvanian vampire would be the kind who couldn't." She delivered this last sentence with a gentle finger pressed to my chest.

"Have you ever heard of vampires who can make these big tunnels underground? Ones that lead to people's houses?"

She gave me a confused look. "No, that's a new one on me. Did you guys do that, too?"

"No, not us, but some other vampires we encountered. In fact, they were the ones who first… Well, no, not both of them. But one of them, this guy named Robert that Susanna knew in high school, he was the one who first developed the vampire potion, or part of it, anyway. Susanna helped him perfect it. And then, a couple of years later, we ran into him after he'd died and come back as a real vampire, and we barely made it out of that alive. Remember how I told you I met a Satanist before? Same guy." I thought back to our earlier conversation. "So yeah, I guess I did know a Satanist vampire. I wonder if a cross would have worked on him."

"That's… interesting," she said thoughtfully.

"Or maybe it wasn't because he was a vampire that he could make those tunnels. Maybe it was some black magic thing. We never really found out." I told her a little more about the tunnels, how they would crumble when they came into contact with human skin, which was how we had eventually collapsed them to keep them from being used again. "That was after we'd burned down Robert's house, though. Not on purpose, but yeah, it happened."

"Interesting," she repeated quietly. "I'll have to look into that, see if I can find any mention of vampires making underground tunnels."

"We also encountered his uncle in that house, well, you know, before we burned it down. He was a pretty creepy guy, too. He injected us with another potion that turned us all into werewolves for a little while."

"Seriously?"

"Yeah. Not something I'd want to go through again."

"That's — I know I keep saying this, but — interesting, too, when you consider the fact that werewolves and vampires originally came from the same legend."

"They did?" I'd never heard that before; I'd always assumed they were two separate things.

"Yep," she said. "In Europe, initially it was the same creature… I wish I could remember the name. Something like *wulpir* or something… Can't remember. But yeah, it was an undead monster who could look like a man or change shape into a wolf, and it drank people's blood. Later on, over the years, the two legends kind of branched off into two different things."

"You're right, that is interesting. If I'm remembering it right, Robert's uncle and the other guy he was working with were going from Robert's notes for the vampire potion, so yeah, I guess if they made the potion a little differently, it wouldn't be too much of a stretch to make it into a werewolf one, if what you're saying is true. Then again, I don't know shit about chemistry, or how somebody could ever make a potion and build in certain traits and not others, but whatever. That's way out of my league."

"Mine too," she said simply.

We continued to talk for a while, and eventually, the conversation drifted away from vampires and werewolves and the like. She told me about her plans to soon try visiting a couple of college libraries in Aiken, South Carolina, but I wasn't even sure where that was. It sounded like a long way for her to fly, but she told me that it wasn't all that far, and she hoped that the libraries there might have more interesting things to read.

As it turned out, she didn't exclusively read about vampires but had occasionally gotten sidetracked onto other topics. These included history, philosophy, and even feminism, which she assured me wasn't strictly male-bashing vitriol even though TV tried to depict it that way. It was an odd notion to me, the idea of reading all of this stuff when she didn't have to. The vampire research I could understand because it was relevant to our current situation. But the other things? I hated being assigned to read boring crap at school enough as it was, so for her to do this on her own seemed bizarre to me.

"But it's not boring!" she insisted. "You'd be surprised how many really cool things there are out there to read, especially when you're not being quizzed and graded on them. Not that they'd let you be exposed to half the stuff I read at Bethlehem. Too much free thought for their liking, I'm sure. But reading can be fun, Ray. You should try it sometime."

"Elizabeth, I can read," I said grumpily.

"But do you ever do it just for fun?"

"Well, no."

She laughed, biting her tongue and looking triumphant. "And you said your father is a librarian?" she asked with surprise. "Not looking to follow in his footsteps, huh?"

"Haven't really thought about it, to be honest. I don't know what I want to be when I grow up."

"Me neither," she said. "Oh, right. Not an option for me." I could tell she'd meant that as a joke, but during the awkward silence that followed, it seemed to sink in that we both had uncertain, possibly bleak futures.

As we lay there, it occurred to me that given her penchant for what she later described as "pleasure reading," my father probably would have liked her. But it wasn't like I could just bring her over to the house one night and introduce her to my parents as my undead girlfriend. Well, maybe I could have — minus the "undead" part — and they might have been happy to think that I was dating this nice, well read girl. But I knew that this was just a fantasy.

Trying to keep things light — and hopefully steer things around to where we might actually have sex — I asked her, "Hey, you know what I saw on MTV the other day?"

"What?"

"An old Lita Ford video. That made me think of you."

She laughed. By this point, we had each rolled over and were lying side by side on our backs, looking up at the stucco ceiling and occasionally glancing over at each other. "Not the 'Kiss Me Deadly' one, but that other one she had. 'Close My Eyes Forever,' the duet she did with that guy Ozzy Osbourne."

"Aw, I remember that one." Our arms were both bent at the elbows, and we'd started holding hands.

I laughed a little. "It always cracked me up how he was doing this song with her about closing your eyes, but then he's got those big bug eyes of his." I then rolled over to face her, letting go of her hand as I used my fingers to pull my eyes open wide, doing my best impression of him singing his part of the song. "And I'm like, 'No, you close *your* eyes! And go bite the head off a bat or something.'"

I expected her to laugh, but she just let out a little *"pfft"* sound and rolled her eyes.

"Well, *I* thought it was funny," I said, slumping back down onto the bed. I let out a *"pfft"* of my own and then added, "Speaking of Satanists."

"Ozzy Osbourne wasn't a Satanist!" she spat. "He actually made some pretty good music!"

Shocked and hurt, I said, "Sorry!"

She turned toward me and softened, saying, "No, I'm sorry I snapped at you. Just that I always get sick of people saying that crap about him."

"Oh, so he was someone you liked, too? Like Lita Ford?"

"Kinda, yeah." She smiled weakly, then added more quietly, "Actually, it was my sister who was really into him."

"Oh," I said. "The one who died?" She nodded. "You want to talk about it?"

She shook her head quickly, looking downward and biting her lower lip. "No, not really. It's not something I like to think about."

"Aw, I'm sorry," I said, edging closer to her. She leaned her head into mine. *Crap,* I thought to myself. *If this keeps up, there's no way I'm getting laid tonight.*

After another lull in the conversation, I decided to ask her how the rest of her week had gone, if she'd found out anything interesting from the other vampires. I also wanted to know if she'd run into my clone, if anything had happened with him.

"Just for a little bit," she said, sounding annoyed. "I refused to talk to him. He, of course, wasn't too happy about that."

"I'll bet," I said. This gave me a sense of relief, but I wasn't sure why. "Did you see Kay again?"

"Yeah, but all she wanted to do was give me the hairy eyeball."

I laughed. "The what?"

"Hairy eyeball!" she repeated. "You know, like stink eye. A dirty look. You've never heard of that before?"

"Nope."

"Well, it's just a phrase I grew up hearing. My… Well, anyway, yeah, she was all pissy at me, though I didn't really know why."

"You think maybe she was jealous?"

"Of what?" she asked indignantly. "Oh, I see what you mean. But no, I didn't get the impression from their body language that she and Ray — the other Ray — were any kind of an item. In fact, I wonder if he's even capable of that kind of thing."

I remembered what she'd said about him not being a whole person. "Well, maybe he isn't, but she is? Who knows."

"It's probably more like they're pissed that I won't be part of their stupid little group."

"I could see it being that," I said. "I was always big on that kind of thing growing up."

"So, tell me more about that," she said, "about what you guys did as vampires. You've only told me bits and pieces."

This made me uncomfortable; I suddenly felt like I was being interviewed. "I… That's something I don't like thinking about," I said, echoing her earlier sentiment.

"I know," she said, pouting, "but I feel like… I share the stuff with you that I've been finding out. It's kind of this need of mine. So it's only fair that you do the same. It might help me figure things out." She'd started holding my hand again, and then she pulled it to her lips, kissing it gently.

A tingle ran through me, and I decided to give in. "What do you want to know?"

"I don't know; lots of things. Like, okay, tell me more about these tunnels you were talking about. Where did they come from again?"

"I never really understood it," I admitted. "It was just something that other vampire guy could do, I guess either because he was a vampire, or, like I said, some black magic thing. I sometimes pictured it as some kind of spell, like he could just make the tunnels appear and go wherever he wanted."

"Like where?"

As I explained that the main one led from the basement in our house to another house several miles away in a town called Evans, she changed position again and turned on her side to face me, listening intently. "Really, it was a trap. He and this other girl — another vampire, I mean — had been spying on us for weeks, maybe longer than that. The tunnel led us to them, and then they tried to take us over, to make us like them. Undead, real vampires. It was pretty damn scary."

"If things were so scary, then why did you do it?"

"You mean, in general?" She nodded. "Well, they weren't always that bad. Sometimes they were even… fun." I didn't like admitting that. "But we were young, and stupid, and we didn't know what we were doing. Or if we did, we didn't know that it was wrong."

"You didn't know that flying around and killing people was wrong," she said with a hint of sarcasm.

"No, fine…" I paused. "We did know; you're right. But it wasn't all about that. It was more like the main fun was in all of us being together, staying up all night, doing stuff we weren't supposed to do. That sort of thing. To be honest, the older I get, the more I wonder if that whole 'we were too young to know better' excuse really even applies. I mean, Susanna was older than we are now when we first started out."

"But you did enjoy being a vampire sometimes," she said pointedly. "Even the killing."

"No!" She fixed me with a firm look, her lips pursed. "Okay, so yeah, sometimes. Maybe. We just… I guess you're right. But that's something I really hate about remembering the whole thing. Once it was all over, I struggled with guilt over that for years. I still do."

"Do you ever miss it?"

"Absolutely not," I said firmly. A thought flashed through my head, one that immediately filled me with even more guilt. Prior to the emergence of our clones, there had been a few times when I had recalled the very last kill I made before the final time we had all changed back to humans, this beautiful, dark-haired girl. I could still picture her face whenever I allowed myself to, right down the little dimple in her left cheek. On some of my darker days, I would sometimes imagine killing her again, feeling aroused as I did so. And then I would hate myself for that.

To counter this memory, I dug up another one, and I told Elizabeth about one of my earlier victims, this very young blonde-haired girl. Carolyn, not entirely in her right mind, had gone on a killing spree one night, disappearing from the rest of our group. I had managed to track her down on my own, and by the time I did, I found her in the middle of killing three young people in the front yard of a house not far from our own.

By the time I'd arrived, she'd already killed one teenage girl and was in the middle of drinking from a boy about the same age. She had also fatally wounded the little girl, who wasn't much more than a toddler. In a twisted act of generosity, Carolyn encouraged me to finish her off, telling me, "I saved her for you." Ultimately, I drained her until she was gone, but it was a mercy killing, not something I enjoyed in the least. In fact, it had upset me to the point of breaking down in tears. I genuinely felt sorry for her, and I despised what I'd done.

"But you did it to help her," Elizabeth said with a soothing tone. Recounting the tale to her was almost as painful as the memory itself, maybe more so. I had never told any of the others about this; Carolyn had been the only one who'd known about it. "Killing isn't always wrong. Some people even deserve to die. Those are the ones I try to concentrate on when I have to kill. Bad people."

"Who are you to decide that?" I shot back, but her expression made me regret lashing out at her.

"Who am I to decide anything?" she asked. "If I'm walking along a sidewalk, and someone gets in my way, do I step out of their way or keep going and make them move instead? Does everything have to be a big philosophical decision with cosmic consequences, or do things just happen? Does it even matter?"

I wasn't sure what to say to that. This was probably related to some of the high-minded literature she'd told me about reading, and given that I wasn't versed in any of that, I couldn't come up with a counterargument. Maybe she had a point.

"I don't know, Elizabeth," I said, closing my eyes and pressing my forehead to hers. With shame, I noticed that I'd built up some tears. Then something occurred to me, and I said with a weak smile, "You ever notice how much we keep saying that? 'I don't know. I don't know.'"

She let out a little giggle. "That's the human condition, I think."

"I'm not sure I'm going to be able to keep up with you if you keep being all philosophical like this."

We continued to talk, the conversation shifting to her telling me more about some of the non-vampire literature that she'd been reading. After a little while, though, we got back onto the topic of the vampire summers. While it seemed initially that she was more interested in the bad things we had done, which I didn't like talking about, she also began to express interest in the more mundane aspects.

Despite all the killing and the brutality, sometimes we really were just like normal kids, watching TV or playing games. And there had been occasional rifts in the group over the years, like the time that Dennis and Tim defected from the group because they didn't want to be in it with Carl.

"So they stopped?" Elizabeth asked me. "Just went back to being human?"

"No, not at first," I said. "They thought they could just go off on their own. And then they ended up getting changed back to human a day or two later because they didn't know where to hide from the sun." I laughed; something about that had always seemed funny to me.

"Amateurs," Elizabeth joked, but then she let out a sigh. "Still, it sounds like you had fun. I kind of wish I could have something like that with the other vampires, but it just doesn't work."

"What do you mean?" I wasn't sure how I felt about this.

"I just don't like them, I guess is the best way to put it. It's like they're trying too hard. Like, really, really hard to be evil. And bad. And wrong. 'Let's kill, kill, kill, *moo-hoo-ha-ha-haa.*'"

"Really?"

She nodded, the look on her face showing her disdain as much as her tone did. "Oh, and I should tell you about this. You know how I got it to where it didn't screw me up and make me choke to say words like 'God' or 'Christian' or whatever? I told some of the others about that, and it caught on. Boy, did it. I swear it wasn't five minutes before some of them were running around going, 'Yeah, fuck God! The Bible sucks!' And I'm like, really? Don't get me wrong; I have my own opinions against Christianity and the way people have abused it all through history. All this controlling people and making them feel shame, or even entire countries going to war and killing everyone who didn't believe the exact same thing they did.

"But you don't have to be a dick about it," she continued. "It was just really immature. If the only thing that defines you is that you're *not Christian,* and that's all you want to talk about, well, that's kind of boring. That's what a lot of these people were like. It was like, 'We're vampires now! We're so, so evil! Look at us!' Stupid."

"So they just all decided to become Satanists?" I asked.

"Not really," she said, "but I say that because Satanists aren't really into hating God and worshipping the Devil."

"They're not? I thought, you know, *Satan*-ists…"

"That's a common misconception. And yeah, to be fair, one that I had until recently. But that was something else I found out when doing my research, just this past week in fact. Satanists are more about being free from Christianity and its restrictions, just kind of doing whatever you want, and not harming anyone unless they deserve it. I can get behind that, to be honest, but I still don't like how structured it is. It's kind of like me being an atheist, or maybe more of an agnostic, really." I wanted to ask her what that meant, but she was on a roll, not leaving me time to interject. "But it's not like I believe strictly in the absence of God. Or any religion. So I feel like if I say, 'I'm an atheist,' well, it sounds like I have some firm, strong belief. An 'ist.' And I don't, really."

"Hmm. That kinda reminds me of someone my sister used to know, this girl who was apparently a witch, but she wasn't into devil worship. I didn't really get it until Carolyn explained it. Or maybe it was Dennis. I can't remember. But… Now there's something…"

"What?"

"What you're saying about… Hmm. I don't remember Robert actually saying he was a Satanist, just that he worshipped the Devil. So maybe there was a difference. And you remember what you told me about the different vampire legends? How they're all different, like what affects them and all? Does that apply to how someone gets turned into a vampire?"

"Sure it does," she said. She went on to authoritatively cite — in addition to the traditional biting and draining of blood — other causes, like being excommunicated from the church, committing suicide, or being of illegitimate birth. "All over the place, really. Like everything else."

"But that was the thing about Robert and Jennifer," I said.

"Who?"

"What? Oh. Jennifer. That was the name of the girl he was with." It occurred to me that I hadn't said her name the entire night, and I suddenly realized why. As frightening as the two of them had been, I had also been very taken with her. She was simultaneously gorgeous and terrifying, this sultry, spooky seductress who looked like something straight out of an old Hammer horror movie. The attraction that I felt to her, especially at such a young age, had made me very uncomfortable. She was, in fact, the first girl I had ever felt a sexual attraction to, but I didn't even realize that's what it was at the time. As a result, the memory of her made me squirm, so I tended to avoid thinking about her.

I continued, "I specifically remember him saying that it was this Satanic — or devil-worshipping, I don't know — ritual that they did. They couldn't recreate the potion, so they did that, and that's what killed them and turned them into vampires."

"Really…" Elizabeth almost whispered. "That's…" She didn't finish.

"Yeah. They were pretty horrible. If Dennis and Tim hadn't shown up when they did, we'd have been dead. They were *this* close to killing us…"

"But you got out okay," she said simply. "How? Actually, no, hold on. There's something else I want to know. What were they like? Like, how did they dress, or act."

I thought for a moment. "Pretty weird, now that you mention it. Robert was really tall, as I recall, but then, I was shorter back then. But yeah, he was kind of your typical 'tall dark and handsome…' Though I don't know if handsome would be the right word. More like tall, dark, and creepy. And Jennifer, she was…" I blew out quickly, like a cross between a whisper and a whistle.

We were both looking up at the ceiling by this point, and I pictured Jennifer more clearly than I had in years, the memories coming back to me. "They both dressed all in black, elegant clothes and all that. Like you'd see in a movie. It was kind of hokey, now that I look back on it. They had this hypnotic hold over us, and we couldn't move. We just had to stand there and let them gloat, talking about what they were going to do to us… Though really, Robert did most of the talking. Jennifer just stood there a lot of the time being gorgeous." I bit my tongue, worried that saying that might make Elizabeth jealous. But she didn't say anything. "Well, no, she did chime in occasionally. Had this really musical way of talking, kind of high-pitched. And she had some really dark colored red hair, sort of unnatural." I remembered how Susanna and Carolyn had later commented on her appearance, and I was trying to recall what they'd said.

"But in the end, we managed to kill them and get away," I said. "But even that was horrific, the way that they died and crumbled into decaying corpses." I shuddered at the memory, then was reminded of what I had seen more recently when my friends and I had killed that vampire back at Sibley Mill. "Sorry. That's probably not something I should…"

"I know what happens to vampires when they die," Elizabeth said firmly.

I flinched. Obviously, I never wanted the same thing to happen to her. I looked over at her, but she just kept staring up at the ceiling. "So that was the house…" she began.

"Yes," I said. "The one that we went back to two years later. Apparently, Robert's uncle inherited it… He'd killed his parents. Robert, I mean. Back when he and Jennifer became vampires. So then, once they were dead, the uncle moved in and I guess at some point found his notes, and they wound up making that werewolf potion, which they tried on us when we showed up. We barely made it out of that one, too."

"Ray?" Elizabeth asked, her voice suddenly very sharp. "Can you just stop talking for a minute?"

That rubbed me the wrong way. Here I was, finally talking about all of this stuff that I had kept hidden for so long, and I'd suddenly realized that it felt good to let it out, difficult though it was. "What? I thought you wanted to know about my past."

"Please, just stop for a little…" she said, turning over in the bed and facing away from me. Clearly, something I'd said had upset her.

"Elizabeth?" I asked, leaning in.

"I said be quiet," she whispered harshly, and her tone didn't leave any more room for debate.

I lay there in silence for a good thirty seconds or so, confused. Had all of this honest talk about what had happened to me as a vampire struck some kind of nerve? Was she feeling more guilty about her own activities than she'd previously let on?

"Jennifer was my sister," she said.

CHAPTER TEN

I was stunned. Lying there on the bed, my first instinct was to pull Elizabeth to me and hug her, but there was another part of me that told me I'd better get the hell out of there before she turned on me and ripped my throat out. I had, after all, essentially just told her that I'd killed her sister. Though, technically, I hadn't been the one who'd done that.

I had gotten up from my reclined position and was propped up on my left elbow, peering over at her as she kept her back to me. She was breathing quickly, and I could almost feel the anger wafting off of her like waves of heat. I reached up a hand to comfort her, but I wasn't sure if that was the right thing to do.

"Elizabeth," I almost whispered, "I'm so, so sorry."

"Just give me a minute," she said quietly, her voice quavering. I wondered whether she was just taking time to process everything or if she was plotting her next move, one that would be very painful for me indeed. I also thought that this might be a good time for me to make sure that she knew that killing me would result in her own death, but there was no way for me to bring that up without sounding like even more of an asshole.

From my vantage point, I couldn't see most of her face, but I could make out that she'd started clutching one of the pillows to her front, her chin probably buried in it. She began to shudder, then went into a quick, rocking motion, and while she barely made a sound, I knew she was crying.

I couldn't help it; I had to hold her. I couldn't stand for her to be in this much pain. I'd always wondered what had happened to her sister and why she never wanted to talk about it, and now that I knew, I wished I didn't. "Shh," I said to her.

Instead, she responded with a deep inhalation and a little shriek, and her sobs became more pronounced. The sound of it broke my heart. I kissed the back of her head gently, hoping that it might give her some comfort but also feeling completely useless.

Her crying died down surprisingly quickly, and she pulled away from me, though not particularly harshly. I feared that she might lash out at me, but instead, she sat up as she turned back towards me, but not all the way. She pushed herself and a couple of the other pillows up against the headboard, then wiped at the tears on her face.

"Elizabeth, please don't hate me," I pleaded, sitting up to match her move.

She looked over at me, obviously still upset, but not nearly as angry as I felt she had a right to be. "I don't hate you, Ray," she said, her voice still slightly distorted. She swallowed hard, clearing her throat. Looking away and keeping her lips pursed, she breathed deeply through her nose, sniffling as she did so. She then let out another deep breath through her mouth.

"It's actually…" she began, then stopped, blinking back more tears and looking up at the ceiling briefly. She frowned, looking pensive. "It's a relief. To know what really happened to her. I had *no* idea it would be something like that, but… I guess it's good to finally know the truth. Not the official version, or what our parents tried to keep from me."

"How do you mean?" I asked, reaching for her, but she flinched, clutching the pillow to her front again. I backed down.

She looked thoughtful again. Then, in a voice that more closely matched her regular one, she said to me, "Look. What I need from you right now is for you to tell me everything. Every little thing you know about what happened to her. Things are starting to make a lot more sense to me, but only if I can fully understand and know all the facts." She sighed and looked up again, then back down at the pillow. "I should have guessed as soon as you said 'Robert,' but I figured, 'No, that's just a common name.' But the more you talked, the more the pieces fell into place."

"Elizabeth…" I began, but she cut me off.

"Tell me what you know," she said slowly and firmly.

As it turned out, this was helpful for both of us. I recounted everything I could about the confrontation with Jennifer and Robert, plus all of the details that they'd revealed to us about their past, which weren't many. This led Elizabeth to tell me more about her sister and who she was before I met her, and between the two of us, we managed to construct a more coherent narrative than either of us had been aware of before.

The story unfolded more or less in reverse, beginning with my telling her about the summer of 1985, when our victims' bodies kept mysteriously disappearing. This was, we found out, because Robert and Jennifer had been sneaking around behind us and harvesting them, resurrecting them and turning them into vampires themselves. After being lured to Robert's house via the tunnel, we had been forced to fight these new vampires. We managed to defeat them despite being hopelessly outnumbered, but that was partly because they were more like zombies, slow and easily outwitted. Once Robert and Jennifer revealed themselves, they were going to kill us and resurrect us as well, but then Dennis and Tim, who had splintered from our group already, showed up and staked the two vampires, saving us and changing us back to human.

"Who killed Jennifer?" Elizabeth asked me. "Specifically."

"What? Oh. It was Dennis." Her eyes narrowed, and my pulse quickened. "Elizabeth, no. Don't go after him. He was just doing what he…"

"I know," she said calmly, reaching out and gently touching my arm. "I just wanted to know. Details, like I said. This matters to me."

Uneasy, I continued my story, including the detail that Tim had been the one to drive a stake through Robert. Who had done what hadn't mattered to me all that much at the time, but given that I'd been angry at Dennis for initiating their secession in the first place, it had been a bit poignant that he had in turn been the one to save me from Jennifer.

I jumped ahead to two years later when we revisited the house, were captured by Robert's uncle, and eventually ended up burning the house down, but this didn't interest Elizabeth as much. Instead, she made me backtrack and tell her more about what Robert had revealed to us about their activities prior to our final confrontation with them.

So I told her what I knew, how Robert had tried for years to develop the vampire potion without Susanna's help. They'd created it together in 1983, but after they left high school, she'd taken the only copy of the formula. He had in fact insisted on this because its effects in their initial trials frightened him. Somewhere along the way, he'd had a change of heart, but Susanna refused contact with him, and in the meantime, she'd used the potion on herself, her siblings, and my friends.

That was how Robert wound up interested in black magic, which allowed him to, according to his own story, get turned into a vampire by the Devil himself along with Jennifer. They in turn killed his parents, took over their house, and then set about stalking my family. Where Jennifer had come from, I'd never known until now.

As I relayed my tale to her, Elizabeth occasionally interrupted, either to comment on something or to express an opinion about Jennifer specifically. "Oh, Jennifer," she would say resignedly, and one time, she even muttered, "Stupid, stupid, stupid." This surprised me, as I'd assumed that she'd admired her big sister and was sad that she had been killed. But it was more complicated than that, especially in retrospect.

"Make no mistake," she said when I expressed confusion over this, "I loved my sister. I looked up to her, thought she was the coolest thing in the world when I was little. But the older I got, the more I realized that she made some really bad choices. Truth be told, and I hate saying this now, but she was probably kind of a slut."

I started to laugh at this, mostly from the tone she'd used, but I clammed up immediately when she glared back. "Sorry," I said.

"No, it's okay," she said sadly. "Looking back, it seems like she was with a different sleazy guy every other week. And when I was little, I thought that was pretty cool, like, she must have been really popular or something if so many guys liked her. Deep down, I think she was just really easy. But I didn't figure that out until later."

I tried to relate to this, wondering what it might have been like to have had a big brother who got all the girls. But the closest thing I'd ever had to a brother was Carolyn, who was a tomboy when she was young, and I did look up to her and think she was great. The older she got, though, the more girly she became, and the less we had in common.

"I remember the night before she ran away," Elizabeth said with a faraway look. "She'd gotten fed up with our parents, who were admittedly pretty strict and controlling. They let up on that a lot after Jennifer died, I think because they were afraid of me winding up like her. But she was so excited that night; I can still see it.

"I was sad that she was going away, but at the same time, I was happy for her. She made it sound so thrilling, sitting next to me on my bed in the dark, her red duffle bag right next to her, assuring me that everything would be okay. 'Robert's such a neat guy,' she whispered to me."

It unnerved me that the way she imitated her sister's voice sounded remarkably like my own memory of it. Earlier, she had mentioned how Jennifer went by the name Jenny up until the age of twelve. Then, all of a sudden, she insisted that she be called Jennifer. "'It's Jen-ni-fer,' she would emphasize," Elizabeth said in the sort of musical, purring way that her sister spoke. It was one of the things that was simultaneously so alluring but so scary about her.

"'You be the prettiest and the best girl you can be,' she said before she left. 'Make all those boys out there line up around the block waiting for you, because that's your right as a woman. And if Mama and Daddy wind up treating you the same way they did me, punishing you just for being who you are and not their perfect little angel, then you get out of this house as soon as you can. Go out in the real world and live your life.'

"I didn't really understand what she was telling me, and I'm sure she probably knew that, but it stuck with me, especially once I found out that she'd died. I felt like I had to… I don't know… kind of honor her memory, or something."

She took a break from her story, and after a few seconds, I asked her, "How did you find out?"

She sighed deeply. "That was… complicated. Once the police found the bodies, they let my parents know, and they told me as gently as they could. But of course, it still tore me up. I was only eleven at the time. So they tried to sanitize it and leave out the details, but I kept asking questions. They tried to quell that, but still…"

We talked a little more, piecing together that it must have been Robert's uncle who alerted the police, probably discovering the bodies on his own, or at least knowing that the family had disappeared and getting the authorities involved. Not long after her family had been informed, Elizabeth had secretly overheard her parents talking about everything, including some gruesome details about how the corpses they'd found were too decayed to determine a cause of death. Remembering how Robert's and Jennifer's remains had looked after we'd killed them, I could easily believe this. There was also talk of discovering some occult paraphernalia at the crime scene, which naturally made Elizabeth's parents uneasy.

"So that's actually how I ended up at Bethlehem," Elizabeth said, her tone a little brighter. "Mama and Daddy might not have known everything, but they knew that Jennifer had gotten involved with someone really bad, and I think they were embarrassed about that. So they moved me to a school where I didn't know anyone, so then no one would ask me about my sister. And…" She laughed slightly, but it was a sad laugh. "Yeah, that makes sense now. They told me not to tell anyone about Jennifer, saying it would 'raise hard-to-answer questions,' or something like that. And yeah, now that I think about it, they probably sent me to good old Bethlehem Baptist thinking that I'd get taught all that wonderful biblical crap, and then I wouldn't be like…" She broke off, then let out an angry sigh and shook her head.

I could see where she was going with this, but I wasn't sure how to articulate it. I also understood why I had never known that she'd had a sister. But had anyone known?

"Helen and Melinda did," she clarified. "And Mrs. Carlton, since she was the guidance counselor. Maybe Dr. Phillips, too. I was never clear on that."

She then told me about one afternoon when she and her mother happened to drive by Robert's burned down house. The parents had known which house the police had told them about, so her mother was surprised to see it in ruins. They didn't drive by it on purpose; it had been on their way to something else.

Elizabeth didn't understand what the big deal was, but she got it once her mother clammed up halfway through her sentence: "That's where the police found… Never mind."

Elizabeth looked at her pointedly and asked, "Where they found Jennifer's body and that other guy?" She thought she was being clever about it, dropping a bombshell that let her mother know that she wasn't as naive and in the dark as they might have believed. However, this only served to upset her mother a great deal, particularly because it brought up such painful memories. Elizabeth ended up apologizing to her profusely and trying to comfort her after the car had pulled over to the side of the road.

I felt bad for both of them, imagining the memory as she described it. I then asked her specifically how she had dealt with losing her sister at such a young age. She said that she'd coped as best as she could, which hadn't always worked out.

"For one, I think I took some of her advice to heart that I shouldn't have. That's how I wound up having sex way, way too young."

I bristled at this, but I kept my mouth shut. It didn't matter. She fixed me with a stern look.

"Yes, Ray, I fucked Kirby when I was in seventh grade, long before I met you." Her tone was bitter and accusatory, but then her face softened. "Sorry. That was crass. It's just... It wasn't a good time for me. He was all insistent, and I was thinking that I should give myself up to him, that it would make me feel all grown up and stuff. Like Jennifer, to be honest. And it didn't. It hurt, it felt weird and gross, and I've gotta say, he really, really sucked at it."

I laughed despite myself. I didn't like hearing about or imagining her having sex with this guy whom I despised, but her last bit of narration struck me as funny.

She smiled, too, going on to describe how clumsily he went about everything, trying to be cool but utterly failing. "He kept sliding down and slipping out, I think getting hurt when his dick would poke into the bed instead of me. And here I was trying not to laugh at him, but overall just weirded out at what was happening."

I laughed again nervously, recalling an old Eddie Murphy routine in which he talked about young guys having sex and not knowing what they were doing. I'd barely known what he was talking about when I'd first heard the bit, but the crowd laughed, so I knew that what he was saying was funny. Hearing Elizabeth recount a similar story, particularly about a guy I hated, made me smile inside. I hoped that once I got the chance to make love to her, I would do a better job.

"I broke up with him pretty soon after that," she concluded.

I ended up leaving the hotel room that night disappointed, though I also felt really sorry for Elizabeth. My fear that she might hold me responsible for Jennifer's death was allayed by her insistence that she didn't blame me, or even Dennis. Instead, she blamed Robert, plus she had to admit that Jennifer's own reckless choices had led her to be with him. What's more, it was Robert who had developed the potion in the first place, not me, so there was that.

Still, I felt put out by the way that she insisted that I leave and let her have the rest of the night to herself to think through everything. It had been a night of unexpected revelations, and I knew that she had a lot on her mind, but I couldn't help but be mad that I had once again missed out on an opportunity to consummate our relationship, such as it was.

She had called me a cab from the hotel room's phone, then bade me goodnight, wanting to be on her own. I felt stupid standing outside the hotel entrance waiting for the cab to arrive, but there was nothing else for me to do. I thought through everything that had been said, and I realized that in a lot of ways, I understood Elizabeth more than I ever had.

She'd always been gorgeous, even incongruously so, but she'd also been very quiet and withdrawn. Having lost a sister at so young an age must have affected her greatly, and while she'd stated emphatically that she didn't hate me and that I wasn't to blame, I still felt that I was, at least in some way. It also seemed unfair that, even though she had come back to life as a vampire after being killed, she was stuck in a body that had no reflection, unable to do herself up all pretty like she had in the past, which now struck me as a sort of tribute to her long-dead sister. I still thought she looked wonderful, but I'd already learned how not being able to see herself in the mirror really bothered her, and I understood that a lot better now.

It was late at night, well after 2:00, and the city alternated between being quiet and occasionally noisy. The hotel was located on a side street off of Washington Road, one of the main streets in town. During the lulls between cars zooming by, I suddenly began to feel uneasy. I feared that any minute now, I would hear a woman's voice crying out in pain, a victim of another vampire attack. And then I would be left to wonder whose sister she might have been.

"Have you spoken to Tim recently?" my mother asked me one day before school.

"Why?" I asked, surprised but also irritated. I wasn't a morning person, not least because I often stayed up late sneaking out to meet Elizabeth. My mother, meanwhile, would become a chatterbox once she had coffee in her and pelt me with all sorts of annoying questions. This one, though, caught me off guard.

"I ran into his mother at the grocery store last night," she said. "She and Jack are worried about him. Apparently, he's been doing poorly in school lately, and he seems very withdrawn. Just not himself. Something's clearly bothering him, but he won't talk about it. I just wondered if you might know what it was."

"No," I lied. "We don't talk much these days."

"Well, maybe you should. If there's something wrong, then maybe he'd be more willing to talk to one of his old friends than to his parents. You think you could give him a call sometime soon?"

"Sure," I said, then went back to scowling into my cereal. Most mornings, I would say whatever I could to shut her up, my brain not fully awake or ready to take on her latest verbal barrage. And while I knew what was probably going on with Tim, the fact that his parents were concerned began to bother me.

So I did call him, and he assured me that there wasn't anything to worry about. "I'm not going to tell anyone about us," he said to me.

"I know, Tim," I said. "It's not that."

"Then what is it?"

I drew a blank. Maybe I really was afraid that he might crack and rat us out to the police or whoever. "Well, just kind of worried about you, I guess. Plus I get pretty bummed out about it myself sometimes, too. I know this girl who…" I stopped, not wanting to reveal too much.

"Who what? Oh, somebody who knows someone we killed?"

I was shocked by his insight, but he went on to explain that he'd been in that situation as well. Like me, he felt especially guilty about it, more profoundly than the somewhat abstract guilt we'd experienced over the anonymous deaths on our hands.

"Yeah, but this was even worse," I said. "You remember those two vampires we fought back in 1985? Robert and Jennifer?"

He was quiet for a bit. "Oh, right. I'd forgotten their names. The ones at the house at the end of the tunnel."

"Turns out I know that girl's sister. She's our age, and she was really young when we… you know."

"Man, that's sad. How did you know it was her?"

I blanched, again realizing that I was talking too much. "Just things she said. Sister died under mysterious circumstances, found at a house that burned down a couple of years later…"

"But you can't be sure," Tim said. "Could just be a coincidence."

"Maybe," I said, knowing he was wrong but unable to tell him why. "Anyway, it doesn't matter. I guess what I mean is that I know what you're going through. We all do."

"I know," he said simply.

He then asked me about school, and after I told him my usual disdainful views on the place, he suggested that if I hated it there so much, maybe I should leave and go to a different school.

"Yeah, Dennis said the same thing," I said, then told him about running into him at the mall recently.

When the subject changed again to Tim talking about his plans for the future — a subject I'd given very little thought to, I admitted to him — my mind began to wander. He was saying something about hoping to grow up to become a public defender, which was some kind of lawyer like his father, but different. I wasn't paying attention because I'd started to worry that I'd let on too much about Elizabeth to him, that if he were to ask around, he might figure something out. But that didn't seem too likely. It was probably just paranoia on my part, coupled with the fact that I had omitted telling him that Dennis relayed to me the story about Tim crying at school, presumably over the same guilt we'd been talking about earlier.

And really, Tim probably didn't even know any of the people at my school. I didn't know why exactly, but everyone at Bethlehem seemed somehow isolated from the rest of the people in my life. Carolyn had once described to me the way that people in Augusta all tended to be interconnected in weird ways, where you could find out that some friend of yours was in fact the cousin of someone else that you had known for years, for example. Susanna had told me similar things, saying that Augusta was "the biggest small town in Georgia." It was in fact the second largest city in the state besides Atlanta.

I'd experienced that phenomenon myself upon finding out that Elizabeth was Jennifer's sister, and it unnerved me. Maybe Bethlehem wasn't immune after all. There might have been several people there who, if I cared to dig deep enough, would reveal that they knew some of our former victims. But then again, talking about vampires was forbidden at that school, another example of their strict rules and insistence on obscuring the truth.

"That's not what he told me!" Carl said, referring to Tim. I had called him a few days after talking to Tim, wondering if he might have any news.

He did, having fought and killed two vampires over the past month, which he sounded rather proud about, if a little shaken. I wanted to know more details, but he got sidetracked telling me that Tim had also killed a vampire recently, and he'd reacted very weirdly when the two of them had talked about it.

"He didn't even mention that when I talked to him," I said.

"I'm not surprised. He was all kinda fucked up about it. It was some kind of chance encounter — I forget where — but yeah, he got attacked by not one, but two vampires… I think they jumped him or something. And he managed to fight them off with some garlic powder he had on him, and one got away, but then he happened to spot this big pointed stick nearby. So he got to it, and he managed to plunge it straight into that bitch's heart. She crumbled down into… Well, you know how they do."

"Yeah," I said, feeling disgusted.

"But then he's all, 'That felt like murder, too. Just like we used to do. I really didn't like it.' Blah, blah, blah." His tone was unsympathetic, and unfairly so, I thought.

"Where did you two even talk about this?" I asked.

"It was at the Smile gas station. The one on Davis Road. They had some kind of special going on where the gas prices were really low, so there was a long line inside when both our parents went in to pay for it. So I went over and talked to him in their car, and he told me what happened."

"I wonder why he didn't say anything to me," I said. "Did he mention anything about school?"

"Of course. He's Tim. What else is a nerdy guy like that going to talk about?" He laughed, but I didn't respond. "No, well, actually, all he said was that it was fine."

"My mom said that she heard he'd been doing bad in school," I said, recalling that I hadn't remembered to ask him about his grades when we'd talked.

Carl let out a short huff, and I could picture him rolling his eyes. "Well, for Tim, that probably means that he started getting a few Bs instead of all As."

"Hmm, maybe. That's a good point. But he told you he was doing fine?"

"Yeah. He didn't give me any sign that something was wrong there."

"Weird," I said, unsure why Tim was being so inconsistent. But then I realized that it wasn't all that unusual for him, nor was it for the rest of us, come to think of it. We all lived double lives, hiding our dark past from the people around us. Maybe there were even some cases of triple lives, if there were such a thing.

Something unrelated occurred to me. "So anyway, you're turning sixteen pretty soon, right?"

"What?   Oh,   yeah."
"Guess that means you'll be able to drive legally now. You know, without stealing your sister's car anymore."

"Oh, shut up," he said. "I'll be getting my own soon enough."

"That's what I was hoping! Maybe once you do, we can start hanging out again."

"Sure," he said. "We could do that, I guess." He didn't sound terribly excited by the idea.

"And we could finally start going after the vampires. Once we have that kind of freedom."

"Yeah, maybe."

I didn't know then that he would never follow through on this.

CHAPTER ELEVEN

Bethlehem had gotten on my nerves almost as soon as I started attending the school in eighth grade, but once I had the seed in my head that leaving it might be a good thing for me, it didn't take long for me to become even more sick of the place than before. Aside from all the things that I'd always hated, it felt like everything that happened to me from that point on was just one big neon sign after another flashing in front of my eyes: *THIS IS WHY YOU NEED TO LEAVE.*

First of all, I hated Kirby's guts. I always had, but knowing that Elizabeth had lost her virginity to him had made things even worse. I told myself that I shouldn't be jealous, and I did find some cruel comfort in the mean things she'd said about how bad he was in bed, but I couldn't help but want to knock his teeth down his throat almost every time I saw him. I tried to restrain that emotion for fear of something truly bad happening to him because of my powers, especially once I realized that if he were to end up getting killed or something, then I would feel sorry for him. I didn't want that; hating him was easier.

Another thing that bothered me was when Elizabeth's name would come up, which wasn't often. But whenever it did, it made me cringe.

Everyone else thought of her as this sweet girl who had been killed, and even though they knew how, no one was allowed to talk about that. I knew that she wasn't truly dead, but a vampire, though of course I couldn't tell anyone. Keeping that secret had been a little bit fun at first, but over time, it just wore on me. What's more, sometimes people would describe her in ways that I knew were totally inaccurate, even Helen and Melinda. I knew her better than any of these losers did.

The final nail in the coffin, so to speak, came a couple of months before the end of tenth grade. Mrs. Cartwright had assigned us term papers to do, which was a daunting task, but not impossible. Most of the students had never tackled such a thing before, but because the English teachers at St. Joseph's had been as good as they were, I had in fact learned how to do this back in seventh grade. Then, Mrs. Warren had assigned our topics to us, but at Bethlehem, the teacher made us pick our own.

The brief was that we should choose something that we knew a little bit about already but wanted to learn more, and the first thing that sprang into my head was vampires. Without meaning to, Elizabeth had inspired me by doing her own research, and I thought that this might be a chance for me to learn more about the things that she had only mentioned to me so far. She'd also said that because of what happened to her at the downtown library and her reluctance to return there, she hadn't gotten to go through all of the books that she'd meant to. So this could be a way to kill two birds with one stone, getting an assignment done for school while also learning more about something important to me in real life. Maybe I could even find a cure for Elizabeth.

The notion intrigued me, but then I realized the problem: All talk of vampires was forbidden at Bethlehem. The entire topic was considered Satanic, which was a convenient blanket term the faculty liked to use for anything that they didn't like or thought was against God. Rock music, long hair on boys, short skirts on girls, or questioning whatever the latest idiotic thing that flew out of a teacher's mouth was evil, against the rules, and even grounds for discipline.

Knowing that I might be treading on thin ice, I chose another possibly forbidden topic close to my heart: psychic powers. I knew about my own experiences with them, which — like my vampire knowledge — I had to keep secret. But I also knew that a lot of people had researched and written about them over the years, and I definitely wanted to know more.

The study of this phenomenon fell under the topic of parapsychology, something I had picked up from *Ghostbusters*. I used to like that movie a lot when I was younger, as had my sisters. But after everything that we went through as vampires, I found that I no longer liked movies or TV shows that dealt with supernatural horrors and such. *Ghostbusters* had been a comedy, so it wasn't quite as off-putting for me, but anything that was straight up monsters and gore, especially vampires, was anathema to me. I wondered sometimes if Dennis felt the same way given that he had been such a big fan of the *Friday the 13th* movies when we were younger.

So I chose to do my term paper on parapsychology, and I was surprised when Mrs. Cartwright didn't object to my choice. The encyclopedias in the school's limited library provided me with some information, most of which I already knew. There was nothing in terms of actual books on the subject, so I wound up getting my father to take me both to his library branch and to the one downtown so I could find out more.

While it was interesting to fill in some of the gaps in my knowledge, there wasn't a whole lot that I found that was truly useful to me, at least outside of fulfilling the needs of the assignment. My paper talked about the history of psychical research, and while I could have thrown in some anecdotal evidence of the reality of the phenomenon based on my own experiences, I knew better than that. Like Elizabeth had joked before, the teachers probably would have burned me at the stake.

The D grade I ended up getting on the paper was, I suppose, the academic equivalent of that. I was stunned when I got the assignment back and saw that letter on the front page, large as life and surrounded by a sloppy circle. I angrily flipped through the pages at my desk, glancing over the occasional notes that had been made. There were a handful of grammatical errors here and there, but for the most part, I knew I had written a good paper, that I was capable of that. Back in seventh grade, my paper on the life of President Jimmy Carter had gotten an A, and I was only twelve at the time.

Mrs. Cartwright's other scribbles and criticisms throughout the paper were vague; they looked like hurriedly scratched notes that might have been made by a right-handed person trying out writing with their left hand. Phrases like "unclear here" and "already known??" made repeated appearances, and her notes on the last page were barely legible. I managed to make out something along the lines of "should have chosen a more appropriate topic" before I became too disgusted and didn't bother to read more.

I was so angry, though I wondered if maybe while grading my paper, she had been having one of her trademark headaches and had been feeling particularly bitchy at the time. We often came to class to find her squinting and complaining about having a headache, something that seemed to happen more often as the school year had gone on. Early on, I'd felt sympathy for her, but the more this kept happening, it just seemed repetitive, something else to find annoying about her and about the school in general.

And I knew what was happening here. My paper wasn't bad; it was the fact that I had chosen to do one on something that she, like the rest of the supposed teachers at that school, was afraid of and believed was occult and evil. I hadn't written a manifesto on why evil psychic people should oppose God and worship Satan; I had written, to the best of my ability, an objective paper on a branch of science that I found interesting.

I probably could have challenged her on this, but instead, I decided I was just done. Bethlehem and I were over, and my parents had better let me go to a different school the following year, I thought. On the way out of class, while most of the students carried their graded papers out with them along with the rest of their books, I tossed mine into the trash can near the door, wondering if Mrs. Cartwright even noticed.

"You know what it probably was?" Elizabeth asked me. "I'm betting that she didn't even know what parapsychology is."

I considered this, leaning back against one of the walls of the newly completed but still vacant house. "Oh…" I said. "So she… Yeah, I could see that. I kept wondering why she didn't shut me down in the first place." I laughed. "You know, you're probably right. She's like, 'Sure, parapsychology. Great.' And then once she reads the paper, she realizes that I'm talkin' 'bout some *eeevil* Satanic stuff."

Mrs. Cartwright, unlike many of the teachers and students at Bethlehem, didn't actually have much of a southern accent, but it was typical for those of us who didn't to adopt one when talking about people being stupid and close-minded. Actually, I had always thought of her as one of the more intelligent staff members, but this latest display of hers had just been too much.

"So I told my parents I was done with that piece of shit school and that I wanted to go to Westlake. Sure, it's a public school, and I've always heard that private schools give you a better education, but I just couldn't stand being there another year. I thought we might fight about it, or that there'd be some big, sit-down discussion we'd have to have, but they were surprisingly cooperative. 'If you think that's for the best,' my mother said. And my dad seemed to take my point about how the education I thought I was getting there was substandard."

I looked over at Elizabeth, who was sitting beside me. She merely continued to stare ahead, nodding.

"So, I'll be going to Westlake in the fall!" I said with an upbeat tone. Part of me was nervous about changing schools again, but I was also hopeful that it would be a new beginning for me. What worried me, though, was that I had come to Bethlehem with the same hopes after graduating from St. Joseph's, also tired of the people in my life at the time. And I had wound up being miserable there, too. At least at Westlake, some of the people I'd grown up with were there, so maybe I could reconnect with them. I told Elizabeth some of this, including the fact that Carl would be there, though I wondered why I hadn't heard from him since before his recent birthday.

"Well, that sounds like it will be good for you," Elizabeth said, but there was something odd in her tone. It was almost condescending, the way Susanna sometimes spoke to me, particularly when I was younger.

Trying to ignore that, I jumped back to the topic of my parents, how they had agreed so easily to let me change to a different school. "Don't get me wrong; I'm glad they did. But I kinda started wondering, was that because of my powers? Like, was I influencing them and making them do what I wanted?"

"Could be," Elizabeth said quietly.

"Or maybe I'm not giving them enough credit. I guess it's not out of the question that they really did listen to me and understand. They're not stupid, not really."

"Hmm," she said.

"Elizabeth, is something wrong?"

"As a matter of fact, yes. How kind of you to bother to ask."

I realized that I'd repeated a *faux pas* that I had been guilty of more than once in the past. When we would first meet up, I had this bad habit of rattling on and on about whatever it was I wanted to tell her, not even asking her how she was or allowing her to tell me something first. She'd pointed this out to me before, and I tried to keep from doing it. Sometimes, I failed.

I apologized profusely, and she grudgingly accepted, but I could tell that she was in a bad mood, and I'd been so caught up in my latest news that I hadn't even noticed until now. Since she'd finally been given a chance to talk, she told me that she'd discovered that her parents had moved away.

"Moved?" I asked. "Where to?"

"That's just it. I don't know. I went by my old house a couple of nights ago, which I hadn't done since…" She paused.

"I know." It wasn't like her to mince words; I was the one more likely to avoid speaking directly about the reality of her situation.

"And I shouldn't have kept putting it off," she said, sounding frustrated, "but it seemed like it would be too upsetting. Seeing them, seeing the old house… And I kept trying to say to myself, 'That life's not mine anymore. It doesn't matter.' But then… I guess with all that I found out from you about what happened to Jennifer, and thinking about that over the next couple of weeks… I don't know. I just got it in my head that I wanted to see them, maybe one last time.

"And now, they've gone somewhere else, and I have no idea where. I looked in the mailbox, thinking maybe there'd be something in there like a forwarding address, but no. Nothing but a 'For Sale' sign in the front yard. And an empty house."

"Damn, that sucks," was all I could think to say.

"Yeah," she said bitterly.

I leaned forward and tried to hug her, but she pulled away, saying that she wasn't in the mood to be hugged right now. She was angry, and for whatever reason, she seemed to want to stay that way.

This frustrated me, and I said so. "It just hurts me to see my… Well, I guess I can't say 'girlfriend' since you're all against that." That came out more angrily than I meant for it to.

"Well, Ray, I'm not," she said emphatically. "We've been through this before. I love you — you *know* I do — but it's not fair to you to think of us like that. I can't be some regular, normal girl that you can go out on dates with."

"I know!" I said, catching myself when I realized how whiny I suddenly sounded. "But if we could just find some way to turn you back to…" The glare she shot me stopped me dead in my tracks.

"To what? Normal? That's what I am now? Something abnormal, something that needs to be fixed?" She practically spat out that last word, and I cringed. "Sorry," she said, backing down. "Maybe that was unfair. But, you know, it frustrates me too sometimes. I know you love me, Ray. And I… I'm fine with that. But it's not like the two of us can go get married and live happily ever after."

That stung, but it wasn't the first time she'd said stuff like this. She had even scoffed at the very idea of marriage, saying that it was something she'd never wanted to do anyway, vampire or not. Deep down, I hoped that I could wear her down on this, to someday change her mind, especially if we could find some way to change her back to human.

The conversation continued along similarly upsetting lines, including when she told me that I was free to date some other girl if one came along and I wanted to. I hated even contemplating that; I loved her completely and with all of my being, and for her to say something like that made me wonder if she did not in fact feel the same way towards me.

Trying to hide the hurt in my voice, I asked her, "So if I can't say you're my girlfriend, then what do I call you? 'Friend?' 'Female friend?'"

"Call me Elizabeth," she said. "Or… call me Ishmael," she said with a slight smile. Then she wrinkled her nose and said, "No. Don't call me that."

I got the reference, though I'd never actually read *Moby Dick*. And while I wasn't in the mood for jokes, I couldn't help but smile back.

Our conversations often went like this, fluctuating in mood and jumping from topic to topic. Where this one ended up going, and what stopped us from sniping at each other, was to devise a scheme to try to find out where her parents had moved to.

For all she knew, they could have just moved to a smaller house somewhere else in town. They hadn't done that when Jennifer had died, but maybe now that both daughters were gone, two empty bedrooms might have been too much to bear. On the other hand, her father might have gotten reassigned by the military and gone somewhere else entirely, and it seriously bothered her not to know where that was. She'd tried to be detached about her former life before, but now that the decision had been taken out of her hands, she wanted at the very least to know where her mother and father had gone.

I thought of asking someone at school if they knew anything, but that was problematic. I couldn't just walk up to them and ask, "Do you know where Elizabeth's parents moved to?" Obviously, the next question out of their mouths would be something like, "Why do you want to know? or "How did you know they moved?" And of course, I couldn't tell them that.

We agreed that Helen or Melinda would be the most likely to know, given that they had been friends and that their parents knew each other, too. But the problem was still there: I couldn't ask either of them without raising some kind of suspicion.

What I came up with was that I could make up a story to tell to either (or both) of them that I saw a woman in the grocery store recently who looked a lot like an older version of Elizabeth, and I wondered if that might have been her mother. Elizabeth pointed out that she in fact more closely resembled her father in terms of facial features and hair color, while Jennifer took after their mother. But this didn't matter; I would be making up this pretend woman and would be intentionally mistaken about her. I hoped that mentioning her would be enough to prompt one of the girls to say something about how they'd moved away and where.

Elizabeth refined the plan by saying that I should say that it was a couple I saw, not just the mother, and that the man called her by name. Then I could ask them if her mother's name was Mary.

"That's your mother's name?" I asked.

"No. Her name is Joann." At first I thought she'd said "Joanna," which struck me as an interesting coincidence given Dennis's sister's name. But it wasn't like there weren't people in the world with the same names, or in this case, similar names, which I understood once I asked Elizabeth for clarification. She continued, "What I mean is that you can say something like, 'Did you know Elizabeth's mom's name? Was it Mary?' And they're like, 'No, it was Joann.' 'Oh. I saw this woman at the grocery store named Mary who looked like she might have been her mother.' Something like that."

"Sneaky," I said admiringly. "Hopefully then I can casually ask them if they're still around or not."

The plan worked more or less like we'd hoped, with Melinda revealing to me that Elizabeth's parents had moved back to Kansas, "some place called Leavenworth," she said. "I think that's where they came from."

She didn't know all the details, but when I passed this on to Elizabeth, she clarified that her mother had some family in the area, plus her father had been stationed there before. So it was probable that he'd gotten transferred back, though we had no idea if that had been by choice or not. While she knew more than I did since she'd grown up as an Army brat (a term I hadn't known until she explained it to me), neither of us were clear on the procedures for how such reassignments happened. Augusta had its own Army base, Fort Gordon, which was why their family had moved here in the first place.

"Well, at least I know now," she said, her tone a combination of sadness and relief. We were walking down the same street towards the elementary school where we'd first kissed, no longer able to go to the house next to my own. The last time we'd met, the house had been locked, and we'd only been able to get into it because she'd done that weird, creepy zooming effect that allowed her to slip under the door and unlock it from the inside. In the week since then, a family had moved in, and the house was no longer ours to sneak into.

We talked about various things as we went along, including how she'd thought about trying to fly to Kansas and actually find her parents, but she didn't feel like there was much point to that. She'd gotten the answer to her question and found out where they were, and she said resignedly that that was good enough.

Once we arrived at the school, we were reminded of what happened there, and there was a sweet moment where we playfully recreated that first kiss, the way she hid her face from me in order to maneuver me into getting close to her. From there, we went around to the back of the building, ending up on the playground.

Sometimes Elizabeth could be profoundly moody and serious, and other times, she was extremely cute and playful. She'd been the former a lot more often recently, but she surprised me by insisting that we play on the swing set for a little while, though I protested. It seemed too juvenile. But I had to admit that as we swung back and forth, occasionally kicking up dust and sand as we did so, it really was fun and reminded me of a much younger, more innocent time in my life. And here I was, reliving it with this gorgeous, grown-up girl, someone I loved more than anything.

We used to have a swing in my backyard when I was little, one that my father had rigged up on one of the larger, taller trees. My sisters and I each had to take turns on it, and occasionally, minor fights broke out about whose turn it was.

While the initial design of it was more than adequate, one afternoon, Carolyn had managed to rig up these ropes onto it that, when pulled by someone on either side, made the saddle jerk back and forth. This made the swinging more fun, and for reasons unknown to me to this day, somehow managed to make the swing go faster and higher. It was much more exciting — and probably less safe — than the properly constructed swings at my elementary school. And it meant that when one child was in the swing, the other two had a chance to take part in the experience rather than just standing there bored while they waited their turn.

One time when I was swinging and my sisters were manning the ropes to make me go higher and higher, Susanna suddenly called out to me, "Jump!" I had jumped out of swings at school plenty of times, and it had always felt fun and daring to do so, flying through the air a few feet and landing on the ground below. Unfortunately, doing this on our modified swing at home resulted in me zooming down in an arc for several yards, and I landed flat on my butt. Within seconds, I was crying in pain.

My sisters rushed up to me, concerned but also laughing at the same time, and they did their best to comfort me. It was a miracle that I hadn't broken my tailbone, and I hated the fact that they were laughing while I was hurting so much. Carolyn had thought it especially funny that when I jumped out and sailed to the ground below, I was still in a sitting position, looking almost like I was still in the swing.

I managed to escape without serious injury, and even though I walked strangely for a day or two, I quickly healed. When our parents asked us about what had happened, my sisters just played it down and said that I'd gotten hurt jumping out of the swing. I probably could have told on them for what they'd done, but they'd urged me not to, and I went along with it. It was one of our first instances of collectively keeping things from our mother and father in order to keep from getting into trouble.

This story would come up from time to time over the next few years, and I was able to laugh about it along with my sisters whenever it was retold. Even so, I always resented them a little for it, particularly Susanna for telling me to jump.

"I didn't think you'd actually do it!" she'd protested once, still chuckling at the memory.

I told Elizabeth this story shortly after finding myself plopped on my ass again, this time having backed up and accidentally fallen into a sandbox. I wasn't hurt, just embarrassed, and she found it hilarious. I played things up by dangling my feet up in a silly way, then patted the sand next to me. "Come on in!" I joked, "the sand's fine!"

She giggled and — much more gracefully than I — maneuvered into a sitting position next to me. I told her about the incident with the swing, and she said, "Sounds like your sister had it in for you!"

"No, I'm pretty sure she felt bad about it. At least, she better have." Then I checked myself. "Sorry, I'm doing it again. I shouldn't go on and on about family to you."

"It's okay," she said in a way that sounded resigned but not angry.

I pulled her to me and kissed her, but after a short time, she drew back and started brushing at her shoulders with her hands, looking annoyed. "You're getting sand all over me."

"That's the danger of sitting in a sandbox, I guess."

She shot me a look, then stood up, continuing to brush herself off. Apparently, I'd also gotten some sand in her hair, as she started batting at that. I drew back, feeling a few grains hit me in the face. She fussed for a while longer, and something occurred to me that never had before.

Once she'd settled down, I asked her playfully, "Done primping?" She scowled at me but then relaxed and said yes. "So, answer me this. How is it that you know when you're done? I mean, how do you know that you look all right? For someone who can't see herself in a mirror, you look pretty damn good."

She smiled knowingly, then asked, "You really want to know?"

"I asked, didn't I?"

"It's a combination of things," she said, sitting back down, this time on the wooden edge of the sandbox that I'd tripped over earlier. "For one, I can feel where things are, like my hair, if it's out of place or not. But there's other stuff, like other people's perceptions. Some of it's body language, how they look at me and act, but there's also this other sense I have, something I didn't before I was a vampire."

I knew what she meant about being able to feel one's head and know if something wasn't right. I could do that, and back when I was a vampire and didn't have a reflection either, that was the only way I could ensure that I looked okay. I didn't really care much about it back then, though, as most boys that age didn't. But sometimes, one of my friends or sisters might point out: "Your hair is sticking up," and I'd instinctively fix it by touch as best as I could.

Elizabeth went on to explain that she'd learned to psychically peer into the minds of people around her, to use them as a sort of mirror. It wasn't the same as having a real reflection, but it helped. I regretted asking her if this included her occasional victims, which it did. Even so, it was an interesting thing to find out.

As we parted at my house later on in the night, she happened to mention that she had a longer flight to get home than usual, which confused me. As it turned out, she no longer slept in her grave every night and hadn't for a couple of months, though I'd assumed all this time that she had been. It just hadn't occurred to me to ask otherwise.

As early as the end of 1989, she'd started to accumulate more clothes for herself, and she'd found that staying in her grave was too confining. She didn't need to breathe when she slept, so the lack of air underground wasn't a problem, but the idea of it started to make her feel claustrophobic. She had already begun to use the mausoleum at the cemetery to store her new clothes; there were several empty crypts inside, so she used one like a storage locker. In time, she decided to take over another one as her resting place during the day, which was still cramped, but the simple fact that it was above ground made her more comfortable.

That came to an end when she woke up one night and found that her clothes had been replaced with a dead body, which didn't scare her nearly as much as it made her mad. She then realized that it was entirely possible that someone might open her own tomb during the day, thinking it wasn't occupied since it shouldn't have been, and that wouldn't be good.

Since then and up to the present day, she'd been squatting in various people's attics or basements, ones that she felt safely hidden in. Sometimes she would stay in these places for several nights in a row, and other times, she'd rotate among them. It mostly depended on how concealed she felt.

This sounded dangerous, but she assured me that everything was fine and that she was very good at it. It occurred to me that since her parents' old house was now vacant, she could sleep there, but that might wind up upsetting her too much. Then another idea came to mind: Why not stay in my own basement?

She dismissed the idea immediately, giving another one of her characteristic head shakes. "That wouldn't be a good idea, Ray."

"Why not?"

"Because," she said gravely, "sometimes the people who live in these places actually do find me."

I felt a chill as I realized precisely what she meant. If she were discovered, her only recourse was to kill the people who found her.

The summer passed slowly that year. My parents didn't go to the American Library Association conference in June like they normally did, my father citing financial issues as the reason. I didn't pry, but I had heard other mentions in the news about the economy doing badly, but I didn't understand exactly what that meant.

One thing I was able to comprehend was that Augusta itself wasn't doing too well. Attendance at the yearly Masters golf tournament, the city's main tourist attraction, had been down earlier in the year, and my father mentioned to Susanna during her visit in July that the construction of a new high-rise condominium downtown had been abandoned after some foreign investors had pulled out. It was supposed to help revitalize downtown Augusta along with some other reconstruction that had been going on the past couple of years, but given how dangerous that area of town had become recently, people no longer felt confident putting any more money into it.

This of course was due to the rise in vampire activity, though I suppose there could have been other factors I wasn't aware of. I tried to engage Susanna in a private discussion about this during her visit, but as usual, she changed the subject. Another time, not long before she left town, I asked her if she thought it might be possible to cure a vampire victim, that is, one who had been turned into a vampire that way.

"I don't see how," she said dismissively.

She acted as if the situation were out of her hands, like it didn't matter anymore. I still felt some responsibility for what was going on, and I wanted to find a way to stop it, or at the very least to minimize the damage. And Susanna had always been the authority figure to me, the one who knew the most about the vampire potion and its consequences. So it was very frustrating the way she kept avoiding the topic.

Elizabeth, meanwhile, wound up changing her mind and left town for a few weeks to go to Kansas and try to find her parents. She couldn't really explain why other than with vague statements like "It's just something I need to do." I knew I would miss her terribly, but I also knew that I couldn't stop her from doing what she wanted. She'd left in late June, and it would be more than a month before I saw her again.

She called me a few times from the road, which was always nice, though I hadn't been home the first time. My mother had taken the message, which confused me at first because Elizabeth had lied about who she was and claimed to be someone named Pam. I quickly figured it out when my mother quoted "the girl, who had this cute little accent and said, 'Naw, just tell 'im that *Payum* called, and I'll call 'im back later!'"

Thinking on my feet, I also lied and explained that she was someone from my old school who still had a book I'd let her borrow. I ran the risk of getting caught when my mother offered to take me by this fictional girl's house, but I faked my way out of it as usual.

Fortunately, I managed to be home most of the other times Elizabeth called. She'd been flying not by plane but as a bat, which meant that the journey took a long time, and she told me some about the various states and towns she'd travelled through. Selfishly, I only feigned interest in these stories, much more concerned with asking her when she would be back. Over time, the calls became less frequent.

Susanna's July visit had been about halfway between our respective birthdays, which were just over a week apart. Because of this, our parents opted to have a joint celebration and a shared birthday cake, which I bristled at a little inside but tried not to.

Like both of my older sisters on or within a few days of their birthdays, I got my driver's license and was given a car. But while they had taken special trips to the car dealership with my father to pick one out, I instead was presented with a used 1989 Ford Mustang, a white hatchback with red interior that Dad had bought from one of his friends. This was meant to be a surprise, and it was, but not a pleasant one. I was disappointed that I didn't get the same treatment as my sisters, which I later realized was a spoiled way to think. Once I got to Westlake, I learned that not every kid who turned sixteen was lucky enough to even get a car. I had grown up attending private schools my whole life, and it wasn't until I began attending public school that I got a broader sense of how other people lived.

And it was a nice car. It just took me a while to get used to it and to get over the resentment I felt over it being forced on me. Having it also meant that I had a lot more freedom, the kind that any boy prior to the age of sixteen dreams about. But unlike nearly all of them, I had an agenda that extended far beyond just going to the mall or taking friends around town on joyrides. Having this car also meant that I finally had more opportunities to go out on my own and hunt down the vampires that had been plaguing my city.

Those ventures proved only marginally successful, but some of that was my own fault. Angry that Carl hadn't returned my calls for months, I didn't invite him out with me. I tried calling Dennis once, but I wasn't the least bit surprised when I didn't hear back from him.

Tim, meanwhile, had also turned sixteen a little over a month before, and he hadn't bothered to call me up and tell me about whatever fancy new car I was sure his extremely rich parents had gotten him.

So I went out a few times on my own, and I did have one successful encounter in which I managed to confront and kill a vampire, but only because he had been too busy killing his victim to notice me sneaking up behind him and staking him through his back. As the vampire struggled and died, I noticed that I didn't recognize him or have any idea who he might have been: maybe one of the ones made by my clone or any of the other surviving clones, or one of the other ones further down the chain.

My heart wasn't really in it, and when I realized this, I felt angry at myself. All of that time spent with Elizabeth had made me slack off, to try to justify not going after the vampires because I also didn't want anyone to go after her. Furthermore, I was glad that I never ran into my clone, but I felt guilty about that, too. I couldn't bring myself to kill him because that would result in Elizabeth dying, but at the same time, I worried about the possibility that somehow, sooner or later, someone else more dedicated than I might find him and do the job.

I wondered if —maybe hoped that — my clone had left town as well. The news had mentioned vampire attacks in other cities around the country, so it was perfectly plausible that my clone had emigrated to somewhere else, maybe to avoid me. He might have even taken his entire group with him, determined to wreak havoc in some other town. I tried to think that this took some burden off of me, but deep down, it just made me feel worse.

It was also true that the number of fatalities around Augusta had begun to decline, but whether that was due to the vampires leaving or just killing less frequently, I couldn't be sure. And really, it didn't matter. I still should have been more proactive.

That summer was hotter than usual, and there were also more thunderstorms. Apparently, these two things were related. I didn't know much about meteorology, but my mother, whose parents had been farmers out in the country, mentioned something about how they'd said that the weather had changed and become more volatile over the course of their lives, making their crops less reliable.

I didn't really care about this, but it did occur to me that it was just as well that Elizabeth had been out of town during all of this. Running water, including in the form of rain, had been something we had always had to avoid back when we had been vampires. It wasn't as well known of a "vampire killer," but it was definitely on the list. I had also noticed that the news reported fewer vampire attacks on nights when there had been heavy rain.

And of course, Elizabeth and I never met up on nights when it was raining, particularly when the weather forecast predicted it. I had no idea what conditions might have been like wherever she was travelling from one place to another during this time, but I did recall that she joked before she left that the weather in Kansas was usually "tornado weather." Presumably, she was staying out of it. She was a smart girl, and I trusted her to take care of herself, but I still missed her a lot.

By the time she showed up in Augusta again, I'd almost gotten used to her being gone. I was a little pissed off at her for leaving me for so long, but I couldn't fault her for going off on her quest. She'd seen her parents in their new life and had made peace with that, then made her way back. If I asked her any details, she'd dodge them.

It was fun to make out with her in the back seat of my car, like the time we parked it at Lake Olmstead and went at it like two typical teenagers, but at the same time, there was something missing. I had hoped for us to pick up where we'd left off, maybe even eventually having sex, but she kept being distant from me. If I moved my hands under her shirt, she'd seem okay with it at first, but if I tried to go up under her bra, she'd shove my hands down again. I knew better than to try to force anything past that point.

Conversation also seemed more stilted than usual, but I tried to ignore that, hoping that she'd loosen up. Maybe she was still processing everything that had happened on her trip, especially seeing her parents again. Had she actually talked to them? I wondered about this and pictured it, but I shied away from actually asking her. If she wanted to tell me what had happened, she would in her own time.

As had been the case before, I felt guilty when talking to her about certain things, like my father getting me my car and how much I liked having it. She'd also gotten a car just a couple of months before she died, and when she told me that she missed it, that's when I started to feel bad. Things only got worse when she once described what had happened to her as being "yanked out of my former life, everything being taken from me."

In a later discussion, this time outside of yet another vacant house but also in my newly acquired car, I told her how I'd tried to put the question to Susanna about how I found it confusing that while she and I were vampires, our victims didn't come back to life, but our clones could somehow resurrect theirs. As usual, she'd just given me a vague "I have no idea" and dismissed the topic.

"Well, did you ever try?" Elizabeth asked me.

"No! We just killed and that was it."

"I know. But did you ever actually *try*. Or did you just assume that you never could?"

I thought about this, and really, it had never occurred to us to do so. Susanna had told us in the beginning that our victims didn't come back, and that was that.

"Maybe she was wrong," Elizabeth said, her eyes narrowed. "Remember what we talked about before with belief and faith being a factor? As in what vampires can and can't do?"

"Yeah…" I said, suddenly feeling uncomfortable for some reason.

"So maybe if you'd believed that you could resurrect them, you could have." She gave me a sort of smirk, but it was more humorless than I was used to, almost condescending.

"Could be, I guess." Wanting to talk about something else, I pointed to the necklace I'd given her, which she was still wearing. "When did you get the thingy?"

"The thingy?" she asked with a sneer, but she knew what I meant: a pendant that now hung from it. "I got it on the way back from Kansas. And yes, before you ask, of course I stole it. Diamonds are expensive, you know."

"How much did it cost?"

"Nothing. It was free." She laughed a little, but again, her tone was rather gloomy. "I just thought it looked nice, and I wanted it. And you know what they say, diamonds are forever." She sighed, then added as she shrugged her shoulders: "Like me, I guess."

I leaned forward and hugged her, and she turned around in my arms, moving so that her back was to me. We then reclined on the folded down back seats of my car; the neat thing about it being a hatchback was that we had plenty of room.

After lying there for a while and thinking about what had been said, something else occurred to me. "That stuff about belief and all," I began.

"What about it?"

"Well, if that's all true, I wonder if you could… I don't know… If you believed it hard enough, you could turn yourself back to human."

Her response disturbed me, and I didn't push the point any further or bring it up again that night. "Maybe I don't want to," she said quietly.

CHAPTER TWELVE

Westlake High School may not have been everything I'd hoped, but it was certainly bigger and better than Bethlehem Baptist ever was. There were so many people, more kids than I'd ever seen in one place. Each of the four grades was split up into several homerooms, and even the various subjects had to be divided among multiple classes in order to accommodate everyone. It was a little overwhelming, but I was so thrilled to finally be in what I considered a real school that I welcomed the challenge.

Susanna and Carolyn had both attended this school, so they were able to tell me some things to look forward to and also things to look out for. Carolyn had pointed out that I was lucky to be starting there in eleventh grade, not ninth, as the freshmen routinely got picked on by the upperclassmen. Once I got there, I saw this firsthand. I felt a little bad for them, but mostly I was just grateful that I wasn't in their shoes.

It turned out that my new English teacher, Mrs. Hammil, had also taught Susanna, and during my first few days there, she mentioned her several times, including how I looked so much like her. This rubbed me the wrong way, almost like she was saying, "You look like a girl!" But I knew what she really meant, the fact that with our similar facial features, brown eyes, and brown hair, we looked alike, and we'd always known that we both resembled our father. Even so, it was kind of embarrassing to have it repeatedly pointed out, particularly when I was the new kid, trying to establish myself as someone cool.

That had its ups and downs, and it took me a while to settle in. It was a little disorienting to be around so many black people, both students and teachers, but I got used to it soon enough. My parents had always taught me to be tolerant of other races, but at the same time, I didn't have much actual exposure to them apart from what I saw on TV. Both of my previous schools had been almost completely full of white people, which a classmate later told me was because they were private schools.

"My parents always said that private schools were better because you could get a better education," I told Mike, a boy in my new homeroom.

"Doesn't sound like it, from what you told me about where you just came from." He was a pretty cool guy from what I could tell, rather laid back and with dark brown, unkempt hair. He tended to squint a lot for some reason, too.

"Yeah, I know. Good point. But, yeah, I'd just always heard that."

"You know what that is, don't you?"

"What what is?"

"That whole 'better education' thing."

I tried to see what he was getting at. "Well, the schools are more expensive, so I guess…" I broke off, then shrugged.

"'Better education' was something rich white people came up with during desegregation as a code for 'away from scary black people,'" he said pointedly. I knew a little about forced desegregation during the Civil Rights Movement, but not a lot. My father had once mentioned that while he and my mother had been in favor of it at the time, the rest of her family was not, which had caused some friction.

Mike went on to explain further, but I quickly grew bored with the conversation. Politics wasn't something I was interested in; I just wanted to make it through day to day and get on with my life. I also didn't like the insinuation that my family was rich, snobby, or secretly racist, which I knew wasn't the case.

My father had said, though, that he was glad to no longer have to be paying for me to attend Bethlehem, which I told him was a waste of money anyway. I suspected — and I was right — that I would get a better education at Westlake not because of how much the school cost, but because it was more part of the real world and populated by a diverse range of people.

Another unexpected unburdening of my family's finances came when Carolyn decided to take a break from college. She hadn't done well during her last quarter and was feeling stressed out because of that, so she felt like taking a little time off would do her good. She wouldn't elaborate much when I asked her about this, which bothered me because she tended to adopt the same dismissive tone that Susanna would when I tried to ask her anything about vampires.

As far as that topic went at my new school, I'd been curious all summer as to how that might play out. I wondered how students and teachers, not bound by strict and sometimes arbitrary rules that forbade so much, would handle such a thing. As it turned out, some of what I predicted was true: They were a lot more relaxed about it.

It wasn't discussed on a daily basis in class or anything that blatant, but it did come up sometimes. People were pragmatic, citing it as an unfortunate reality, not unlike the gang violence that we heard about happening in larger cities like Los Angeles, New York, or even Atlanta, which wasn't that far away. There had been some fear that Atlanta's gangs might spread to Augusta at some point, but Derek, a particularly funny black guy in my History class, quipped, "They'd better not if they don't want to get bit!"

That phrase — or the more grammatically correct "get bitten" — was one that I quickly picked up on, something the students said when referring to vampire attacks. Considering the fact that non-fatal wounds from vampires were becoming equally as common as actual deaths, the term was a fitting one. There was a lot of fear and speculation, too, including the possibility of the spread of AIDS or other diseases, and I put forth in more than one conversation that I'd heard that vampires were immune, so the diseases weren't likely to be spread that way. Some people would accept this possibility, but others challenged me on how I could know this, so I'd clam up. It wasn't like I could tell them how much I knew or how I knew it.

I had to be careful, just like at my previous school. And while I still felt the same guilt as always, I couldn't let on about that, either. Carl, who also attended Westlake, even pulled me aside in the hall one time and warned me that I'd better keep my mouth shut if I knew what was good for me.

That bugged me. I had hoped that when I started going to the same school as him, he and I might become better friends again. But we didn't have any classes together at all; it was that big of a school. So we rarely saw each other, and he seemed to resent my presence, which I didn't get. Maybe it all came back to that same feeling of guilt, or maybe it was the fear of being discovered.

As before, my insight into the vampires' activities, apart from what I saw on the news, was supplemented by what Elizabeth told me. But that relationship, such as it was, had continued to go downhill for reasons I couldn't understand. We still met up about once a week, sometimes less. And we still made out occasionally, but there would be other nights when that wouldn't happen at all, though we would still at the very least sit very close to each other and seem at least marginally intimate.

But it wasn't like it had been before, and while this sometimes made me sad, it also made me angry. If I tried to ask her what was wrong, she'd just say, "Nothing." If I tried to push things and insist that it didn't seem like nothing, she'd just get mad and more distant. Then I would feel hurt, and I'd avoid pressing the matter further.

Even when we weren't "talking shop," our small talk sometimes fell flat, but not always. She could still be charming and funny, outwitting me and making me remember why I loved her so much, but other times, she'd get all sullen and morose. We didn't even see each other on her birthday in late September. I'd wanted to get her a present, but she told me ahead of time that she didn't feel like celebrating her birthday anymore. That was her old life. And when I tried to talk to her about my experiences at my new school, I realized eventually that she probably felt jealous.

Here I was going on about all these new things that were happening, new people in my life, both good ones and bad ones. Occasionally, she'd have something to say, but she often went quiet, probably resenting me for having a normal, high school existence, something she could never have. She seemed to have given up on the idea of becoming human again, accepting her fate, which I didn't like at all. I still hoped that somehow, someday, we might find a way to change her back.

And it wasn't like I had a completely normal life, either. I was still me, the boy with the dark past, trying to keep that hidden and just wanting to fit in among my peers. I'd initially tried to reconnect with some of the people whom I'd known as a child at St. Joseph's Elementary, but that hadn't really worked. They remembered me, and they would be polite enough, but any attempt at truly becoming friends usually petered out quickly. Then I would remember that we hadn't been all that close as children, either, and I'd get bitter. One good thing about the size of the school was that there were still plenty more people to choose from, new friends I could make.

So that's where I found myself, still harboring my secrets and still occasionally sneaking out at night to indulge in them. I had grown and changed, some for the better and some for the worst, drifting apart from people from my past. I hated that Elizabeth seemed to be falling into that category as well, and I would continue to fight against it. One time, when I tried to pry too deeply into what she was thinking, she hurt my feelings by saying bitterly, "Ray, I don't tell you everything." I wanted to scream back: *Why not?* But I didn't. There wasn't any point.

I didn't want to just write her off, and it wasn't like we ever got into any actual fights or wound up screaming at each other. And I still needed her for information about the vampires at the very least. But I was entering a new chapter in my life, and how much of that she wanted to be a part of would have to be up to her.

"What's so funny about that apple?" I asked the girl in the lunchroom. I was on my way out when she happened to catch my eye, partly because of her bright red hair. I'd never understood why that hair color was called "red" when it was clearly orange, and in the case of this girl, it certainly was. As I walked by her table, I noticed that she'd begun to bite into an apple, then stopped short and started laughing quietly to herself, her eyes almost closing and her nose wrinkling.

She looked up at me, startled and confused at first, then looked back at the apple in her hand and said, "Oh." She laughed nervously. "I just thought of something funny for a second there."

That reminded me of a quote from a movie called *Arthur,* which I'd seen parts of but never the entire thing. It had come out several years ago, and both Carolyn and Susanna liked it. It was apparently quite funny, and they would occasionally quote lines from it, including one in which the drunken lead character bursts out laughing for no reason, then claims that it's because he sometimes thinks of funny things. I'd picked up on some of these quotes from them as a child, and they became part of my repertoire, even though I hadn't actually heard the actors speak them in some cases.

I probably should have recited the appropriate line to the girl at the table to make her laugh, but I thought of that just a few seconds too late. Instead, the best I could come up with was, "Well, don't choke and die or anything!"

She still laughed, then took an almost vicious bite from the apple. I laughed in response, but then, not being able to come up with anything else, I just said, "See ya," and walked away.

That might have been the end of it, but the following day, I happened to encounter her in the library when my class had been sent there by our History teacher to work on a report. She hadn't been at the same table at lunch that day; I'd looked. So it was a pleasant surprise to run into her again.

She smiled when she recognized me, so I asked her, "Been eating any more hilarious apples lately?"

She giggled and tilted her head slightly, saying, "No, I survived. Didn't choke." Her skin was very pale, which was something else that had caught my attention the day before. Both her face and her arms were covered with light-colored freckles, and her thick, wavy hair was pulled back into a ponytail, just as it had been the day before. I started to wonder what it looked like when she wore it down.

Again, our conversation was brief, and she seemed to be in a hurry. She said she needed to get to the band room and nodded her head down towards the stack of books she was carrying. Apparently, someone there needed them. I might have asked her more, but I was distracted by the fact that she'd started blushing, which on a girl with skin that white was very noticeable. In turn, my face also got hot, so I let her get on her way. When was the last time I'd blushed while talking to a girl? It didn't happen with Elizabeth; I was far too comfortable with her for that. And overall, I was more confident around girls in general by this point in my life, my time with Elizabeth having helped with that.

It was frustrating that I still didn't know this girl's name, and I kicked myself for not bothering to ask her. It also struck me as odd that I was as attracted to her as I was. As a little kid, I'd actually found the natural redhead, pale, and freckled look rather repulsive. The first time I'd met a girl who looked like that was in kindergarten, and she'd looked so strange to me that I'd thought she was some kind of alien or monster or something.

But adolescence had made many of the things I found "icky" about girls intriguing instead, and this new, attractive little mystery was no exception. I was determined to fight down my nervousness and really talk to her the next time I saw her, but I'd have to find her again first.

As it turned out, it was Mike who told me who she was. His girlfriend, Mary Dunn, was in Band, and I'd already met her a couple of times when she'd stopped by homeroom to see Mike. She was also in one of my classes, but we hadn't started talking in that context, not until we got to know each other through Mike. She was a nice enough person, though for whatever reason, she was known by most people not simply as "Mary" but as "Mary Dunn." It was rare that anyone other than Mike called her only by her first name, I think because there was something musical about saying both together, a nice rhythmic quality.

Once I remembered that his girlfriend was in the high school band — as presumably this mysterious girl was, too — I began to describe her to Mike, hoping he could tell me something useful. He started laughing, holding up a hand to cut me off.

"Don't worry, man," he said with a grin. "She's been asking about you, too."

My heart leapt, but I tried to play it cool. "What's her name?"

"Eileen."

"Oh!" I said, relieved to finally know. It was a beautiful name, I thought. I was reminded of the old popular song "Come on Eileen," and I sang the first few words of the chorus, almost as a reflex.

"Yeah, and *don't* do that the next time you see her, or you're likely to get hit. She hates that song."

"Why?" I asked, but then I got it. What I'd just done was probably the first thing to come out of anyone's mouth upon meeting her and learning her name. Back at Bethlehem, there had been a cheerleader in the grade above me who was named Veronica, though I didn't know her very well; it was more like I knew her through Annie and the other cheerleaders in my grade.

A year ago, a song had come out called "Veronica," and I liked it. Veronica herself, meanwhile, quickly grew to hate it, because instead of people just referring to her normally, they would instead sing the name to her, usually in a poor impression of Elvis Costello's distinctive vocals. Sandra, another cheerleader whom I was sort of friends with, also told me that the song actually upset Veronica. It told the story of an old woman suffering from senility, and Veronica had to deal not only with her grandmother's real-life struggle with Alzheimer's disease but also the fear that she might develop it herself once she reached old age.

Eileen's annoyance with her own accidentally eponymous song probably wasn't as traumatic, but I took Mike's advice to heart. The song — and her hatred of it — would eventually come up after we'd started dating, but I did my best to stay on her good side about the entire thing.

And that's what happened: I finally got myself a genuine, normal, officially-called-that girlfriend. It all happened so quickly, a couple of rushed, nervous encounters during the last week of September leading to me hanging out with Eileen, her best friend Mary Dunn, and Mike that Friday night. The four of us spent time together at Mary Dunn's house in Martinez, a suburb of Augusta where a lot of Westlake's students lived.

Eileen was adorable, funny, and very sweet, and we got along really well. We weren't a couple just yet, but everything that happened that first night inevitably led to that. We were nervous around each other early on, afraid to admit just how interested we were, but deep down, everyone knew what was going to happen. I'd heard the term "magnetism" used before when describing couples' attraction, but I didn't fully get just how appropriate that word was until this night.

As we rode in the back seat of Mike's car to a nearby Dairy Queen, we nervously started holding hands. But then when Mike rounded a corner a little too quickly, inertia landed me right in Eileen's lap, which we laughed about. I started to straighten myself up, but a warm look from Eileen as the passing streetlights illuminated her face, and then a hand placed gently on my forehead, told me to stay put.

Each couple ordered Blizzard ice cream treats, which we shared in turn. After we left the drive-through and sat in the parking lot eating them, Mike warned us not to drip anything onto the seats of his precious Ford Escort, which might have happened had I not been so eager to accept the spoonfuls that Eileen maneuvered into my mouth. It was the most fun I could remember having in a long time, and my affection for this new girl in my life was almost more than I could bear.

The evening ended with me and her saying goodnight next to the door of my car. Mike and Mary were back inside the house, no doubt waiting for Eileen to return and tell them the details of what was just about to happen. We'd had a great time, and before I knew it, I was kissing her. Part of me wanted to pull her tight to me and totally stick my tongue down her throat, but I restrained myself. That didn't seem like the right way to kiss this girl. So I kept it more gentle, and the little "mmm" she let out told me that I'd done it right.

She pulled back from me, smiling as she blinked and looked up at me through eyelashes that seemed to be blonde. I'd noticed that about her for the first time earlier that night, how her eyebrows and eyelashes weren't black or brown like most people's, and they looked even weirder beneath the purplish streetlight from nearby. It was one more thing about her to find fascinating, intriguing, and new.

We laughed nervously, and then she asked me rather coyly, "So, want a girlfriend?"

As nice as it was to at last be with someone officially, part of me felt weird about it. I still loved Elizabeth. While she'd told me before that it was okay if I chose to date somebody else, I kind of didn't want to. But there was another part of me that felt defiant, thinking that if she was going to be as cold to me as she had been lately, then maybe I deserved something better. Even so, being with Eileen gave me a nervous tingle deep down, like it was something I shouldn't be doing.

But it turned out that Elizabeth was incredibly gracious about it, so much that it threw me off. The night I told her, she got quiet at first, but then she smiled and said that it was good, and she was happy that I'd found someone so nice. Either she was a really good actress, or she just didn't give a shit. Frankly, I'd have liked for her to have put up more of a fight.

When I first told her Eileen's name, she predictably starting singing the chorus of "Come on Eileen." Like Mike had before me, I corrected her on this, telling her that it was an old joke. She just laughed and started singing again, but I cut her off.

"It's funny," I said, "given how common a name Elizabeth is, I can't think of a single song with your name in it. Otherwise I'd bust out with one of those just to annoy you."

She flashed one of her typical smirks, then said, "No 'Ray' or 'Young' songs are springing to mind, either."

I went on to tell her how, because both my first and last names were also regular words, they did pop up occasionally in song lyrics or just in regular conversation. Sometimes it would feel weird, but other times, I'd barely notice.

"Besides," I said, "what about that Rod Stewart song? 'Forever Young?'"

"Oh," she said, closing her eyes and nodding quickly. "Can't believe I forgot about that one." She began singing the end of the chorus, sauntering up to me as she did, like she was taunting me with it. I didn't really mind, especially because she had such a beautiful voice. But then she broke off, laughing.

She got me to tell her a little more about Eileen, which felt weird, but I did it anyway. And then the rest of the night went more or less the same as usual, though there was no touching or kissing. Again, I felt disappointed that she didn't seem more upset about my having a girlfriend, but it was also a relief.

At the end of the night, we hugged before parting, and then she gently patted me on my chest over my heart. "I wish you the best, Ray," she said, and I thought I saw a glimmer of pain in her eyes, or maybe I just wanted to. She turned into a bat and flew away, leaving me standing by my car.

Driving home that night, I thought a lot about her reaction, how it had surprised me. It even upset me a little, but I kept telling myself that I needed to be grown up about this, that being with Eileen was better for me. Elizabeth was a vampire, and as much as I kept wishing for it, nothing had turned up over the past year that indicated that she could ever be human again. What's more, I was supposed to be someone who hunted down and killed vampires, not someone who periodically made out with one just because she was hot.

The finality of her last words to me bugged me, too. It almost sounded like she was saying goodbye, and I began to worry that I might not see her again. Because she was so nomadic, there was no regular way for me to get in touch with her; our encounters were always initiated by her or planned in advance by the two of us. This particular night, we hadn't said anything before parting about when we'd meet again, and once I realized that, it bothered me.

But I would see her again in a couple of weeks, though it would be under less than ideal circumstances.

"See, that's the thing," Eileen said to me one night at her house. "Everyone always gets the oboe and the clarinet confused."

"They do?" It certainly wasn't anything I'd ever wondered about, but then, I didn't know much about musical instruments.

"Yeah! They're always like, 'Oh, you play the clarinet?' And I'm all, 'No, it's not a clarinet. It's an oboe.' 'Well, what's the difference?'"

I thought for a moment. Unable to come up with anything else, I asked, "Well, what's the difference?"

She rolled her eyes and sighed exasperatedly, but she wasn't really angry. "Cost, for one thing. Oboes are a lot more expensive. My parents still aren't happy with me for choosing it. And it's harder to play."

"Hmm," was all I could think to say.

"Plus I think the oboe has a lot prettier sound. Clarinets are all... *whuhhh oooh whuhhh...*" She did her best impression of the instrument.

I laughed, still not much the wiser. "I guess it's not something that non-Band people think about," I said.

"Well, then you should come by the practice room sometime," she said, somewhat conspiratorially. "That's where we normally hang out at lunch. Maybe Mary will play some, and you can find out how much she sucks on the sousaphone. And don't tell her I said that."

"She sucks on the sousaphone?" I asked playfully. I'd meant to follow that up with something about how she should be blowing into it instead, but Eileen mistook my joke for a sexual one.

"Not like *that.*" She smacked my arm lightly. "Don't be gross."

"I'm not!"

"Uh-huh," she said, annoyed but not terribly.

She was a sweet girl, but sometimes my jokes seemed to go over her head, which was frustrating. Elizabeth and I were right on the same wavelength as far as our senses of humor went, and it bothered me the way that Eileen and I sometimes didn't connect. But I liked her a lot, and I knew she liked me.

There was also the fact that she was so much more normal, just a regular girl. I didn't have to keep her a secret, and I liked the fact that I could hold her hand as we walked the halls of the school. Everyone who saw us knew not only that she was my girlfriend but that I was a guy who was worthy of having one. It wasn't something I'd experienced before.

The fact that she was a Christian was interesting, too, but she wasn't over the top or obnoxious about it. I'd gotten so fed up with uptight Christians at my old school the past few years, so it was nice to finally meet one who wasn't all strict and afraid of everything, condemning everyone to hell if they happened to disagree with her beliefs. She even invited me to go to church with her family sometime, but I wasn't sure if I wanted to do that.

"Don't worry; we won't bite," she assured me. "You might actually get something out of it."

"Yeah, maybe," I said noncommittally, still hoping to avoid going.

The lights flickered for a second, and then we heard a rumble of thunder.

"Come on," she said with a smile as she grabbed my hand. "Let's go watch."

There had been a thunderstorm in the forecast that night, and Eileen had told me that one of her favorite things to do was to watch them. We'd been in the living room for the first part of the night, sitting on the couch and talking while her parents watched TV in a nearby den. They were nice people, and I liked them just fine, though I did feel a little uneasy around her father. Eileen was an only child, and she'd mentioned more than once how protective of her he was.

Once the storm started, we went to the other side of the living room and pulled back the curtains, then turned off all the lights in the room. We sat together, very close, resting our arms and chins on the window sill. Flashes of lightning would dance across the sky, illuminating the clouds, followed a few seconds later by thunder. Sometimes it was so strong that we could feel it. The intervals between the lightning and the thunder varied, and it was fun guessing how long each would be.

Eileen taught me how to count these seconds in-between to calculate how far away the lightning actually was, which was fun, too. It also occurred to me that this was something I could never do with Elizabeth, as I knew that she hated thunderstorms. I'd never been keen on them, either, especially since my vampire days when rain was always the enemy, but this felt different.

After the storm had passed, we watched the movie *Arthur* on VHS; I'd picked it up from the video store on the way to her house. I'd already told her how the very first thing she'd said to me reminded me of the film, plus how I knew it was funny but had never seen all of it.

"Then how do you know it's good?"

"My sisters really like it," I assured her. "And like I said, I've seen part of it. Just the first part, a couple of years ago. Carolyn got me to tape it for her off the TV, and I cut out the commercials as it went along. At least, until my dad made me stop watching it."

"He did? Why?"

"He thought it wasn't something I should be watching at that age, and apparently he had a problem with the idea of a funny movie about this drunk guy. It was like he thought that if I watched it, I'd think drinking was funny and then get into it myself, or something. Didn't make a lot of sense to me at the time." It was also unusual for my father to censor my viewing like that; usually if anyone were to, it would be my mother, and even she was usually pretty laid back about such things.

"Well," she said slowly, "maybe we shouldn't watch it tonight, or else we'll both wind up becoming raging alcoholics." She narrowed her eyes and smiled conspiratorially, which made me melt. She had a way of pursing her lips that made her mouth look very small; there was something cat-like about the expression.

I laughed, and then she asked me, "Do you ever drink?"

"No. I'm not terribly opposed to it or anything, but it's just not something that's ever interested me. The people I have known who were into it always seemed kind of lame to me."

"Like they're doing it just to be cool?" she offered.

I nodded. "And to impress other people. Just seems kind of dumb. I mean, I know that my sisters drink sometimes, but… I don't know. Maybe I'll get into it when I'm older or something, but whatever."

She agreed, saying that she didn't have much interest in it, either. "Same with sex," she whispered, "at least for now. Not until I'm ready."

I'd already known that she was rather virtuous, but this was the first time this topic had come up. Apparently, being virgins was something we had in common. "Me too," I said, blushing slightly. I hoped that this scored some points with her, but deep down, I was already wondering how I might manage to break down that wall and get her into bed.

We liked the movie; even though it was almost ten years old, it didn't seem too out of date or cheesy. It managed to strike a good balance between being funny and sad, and it got me thinking about my father's objections to it years earlier. If he had, as Carolyn had indicated, struggled with alcoholism in the past, I could see how this movie might make him uncomfortable. But it wasn't like I'd been in and out of rehab, so I could have watched it when I was younger and been just fine.

One fun thing about the movie was the difference between the version we were watching and the one I remembered from before. Almost all swear words were forbidden on network TV, so they were censored, but there was one method of this which my sisters and I found particularly strange and unintentionally hilarious. Instead of simply bleeping the words, somehow they would edit the sound so that the offensive words were replaced with innocuous ones, though almost every time, it was very obvious that the replacement word was spoken by someone other than the original actor. It sounded out of place and unnatural, and it was something that Carolyn and I used to joke about a lot.

In fact, some of the lines she and I quoted to each other over the years were these censored ones from *Arthur*. One in particular was when the butler sarcastically offered to wash his master's dick for him, indicating how spoiled and unreasonable the lead character could be. He wasn't just a drunk; he was a millionaire, and because he'd had everything handed to him, he had no self control. It was one of the main themes of the movie. In the censored version, the line had been changed to "wash your *neck* for you," and Carolyn and I often tossed that one at each other, always emphasizing the word *"neck"* in a deeper voice to make it sound artificial.

As Eileen and I watched the film with all of its original swear words intact, I told her about the censored versions of the lines. She didn't seem to think that it was a big deal, and she pointed out that it probably made the overall experience less intrusive than just replacing everything with loud bleeps. She may have been right, but it annoyed me that she didn't think that my story about the replacement words was as funny as I always had. Still, I managed to turn one of the phrases into a recurring joke between us: When either one would say something that rubbed the other the wrong way, we'd say, "Go *stuff* yourself."

It was also neat to be doing yet another normal, everyday thing with my new girlfriend, renting a movie on a Saturday night and watching it on the couch together. We were just a regular couple watching a romantic comedy, and when there were tender moments in the film, we'd squeeze each other or let out little "aw"s or something similar.

I did get uncomfortable during one point that was meant to be funny, but I didn't think it was. In the scene, Arthur had a confrontation with the father of his future bride, the joke being that the father was this intimidating character. He told Arthur that he killed a man when he was only eleven years old, a man who had broken into his house, so he had to stab him. Eileen laughed at Arthur's nervous reaction, but I kept quiet, remembering how many people I had ruthlessly murdered as a child, and not in self defense.

I also felt uneasy in a more general sense with all the talk of marriage, my thoughts drifting back to how Elizabeth had scoffed at the idea of ever doing that when, deep down, I'd always hoped that somehow we could turn her back to human and get married someday. It didn't help that the bride to be looked kind of like Elizabeth, the same wide blue eyes and long, blonde hair.

Not long after I'd noticed this, there was a scene in a hospital in which Arthur was tending to his ailing butler, who was nearing death. During the comical scenes, his character was obnoxious, but when he was being serious, he was more endearing. "You look like him," Eileen said to me suddenly, meaning Dudley Moore, the actor playing the title role.

"Really?" We both had brown hair and brown eyes, and we were on the short side, my height only reaching 5 feet 6 inches by this point in my life. Elizabeth was the same height, while Eileen was a few inches shorter. But I didn't think I particularly looked like him, and I said so.

"Not exactly," she said, "but more like you make the same facial expressions. It's cute."

"Hang on," I said, starting to sit up. "I thought you didn't like the word 'cute.'" This had been a source of friction between us early on. When I'd called her that, she bristled, saying that she didn't like the term because it was something you would call a baby. She'd probably run into the word many times throughout her life; apparently it was a pet peeve of hers.

She insisted that I use the word "pretty" instead, which certainly did apply to her, but I thought it sounded sort of generic and bland. And I'd come to believe that being cute was actually an important component of being sexy. What little pornography I'd seen in print — and in a broader sense, graphic depictions of women in regular advertisements in magazines or on billboards — often showed women trying to be sexy either by looking vacant and stupid, or they'd be making what I called "fart faces," looking like they were straining to squeeze one out. The few models I'd seen that actually did look attractive to me had a different expression, a sly, knowing look to them. A woman's naked body could be hot as hell, but if she looked like an idiot, it wasn't a turn-on.

Elizabeth had always managed to hit all the right points, which was one of the many reasons I was so crazy about her all those years. And while she didn't wear make-up anymore because she was a vampire, Eileen also didn't. When I asked her why one time, she'd said something about not having the right features for it, and she'd never cared enough to learn how to do it right. There was even something a little boyish about her looks, but not in an unattractive way.

"Girls can call boys cute if they want to," she said, continuing our latest playful argument.

"Isn't that a double standard?"

"No." She knew she was being unreasonable, but she wouldn't admit that she was wrong.

"Whatever you say, baby," I joked, knowing from another previous conversation that she hated that term of endearment as well.

She let out a little *"psshht"* sound as she rolled her eyes, then picked up the remote, complaining about having missed what was said. The footage sped backwards silently, and then we resumed watching.

We kissed goodnight as I left her house, but I was distracted. I kept thinking about the bigger picture, including how I found myself comparing Eileen to Elizabeth so much. I wasn't meaning to, but it was hard to get used to being with somebody new after having been in love with someone else for so long. I shouldn't have been thinking about her so much while with my new girlfriend. I even thought I saw her standing across the street when Eileen and I had first walked outside, but when I blinked and looked again, I realized it was just my imagination.

On the way home, I thought about my relationship with Eileen and where it might go. I loved her; it wasn't hard for a boy my age to fall in love. Mike had warned me, though, not to spring that word on her too soon, as apparently she had some kind of problem with that as well. The timing had to be just right, or she'd get scared and run away. I didn't like this feeling of walking on eggshells around her, but I liked her enough to want to make things work.

So I wondered: What if things really did work out long-term? What if, like the happy couple in the movie, we overcame our obstacles and wound up at the altar? Maybe we'd have kids, and I'd be the proud father of a little boy who looked like me and a pretty little red-haired girl who had round freckled cheeks, small eyes, and a little button nose just like her mother's.

Picturing that made me smile, but it also worried me. What if the vampire situation continued to get worse? It seemed to have plateaued somewhat in recent months, but that could always change. Was this really a world I'd want to bring kids into? My mother had told me over the summer that Tim's mother was pregnant, which she of course saw as happy news. I faked it and pretended that I felt the same way, but I also found it troubling, though I didn't fully understand why.

As for my own possible future, I felt uncertain. Even if I managed to wipe out all of the vampires and get things back to normal —a prospect which seemed ridiculous to me at times, to say nothing of difficult given the fact that I was still so in love with one of them — what then? Could I ever tell Eileen about my past? Most likely, I'd still have to keep it a secret. If she ever found out, she'd probably think I was a monster, and rightly so.

Or maybe she would understand. If I somehow wound up being a hero, saving the town and making everyone safe like I sometimes daydreamed I could, maybe she could forgive my previous transgressions. Perhaps she wouldn't see me for the horrible person I knew I was deep down.

Unfortunately, I'd never get to find that out.

CHAPTER THIRTEEN

I stood in the cemetery, waiting by Elizabeth's grave. Even though it wasn't possible for me to call her up on the phone when I wanted to see her, I had remembered something she'd once told me from her research on vampires. According to more than one source, if somebody disturbed a vampire's grave while they were away from it, they would feel compelled to return to defend it. We'd theorized that this might be a way for me to contact her in case of emergency, but we'd never gotten around to testing it.

So I took it upon myself to try it out, using my stake to dig up some of the ground in front of her tombstone. I was glad that the weather was getting cool enough for me to start wearing my jacket at night again; carrying a concealed stake on me was hard to do in summer clothes. Apart from using it as an impromptu shovel, I wondered if I would be using it for its more traditional purpose soon enough.

The day before, Monday, Eileen hadn't been at school. Mary Dunn, who was in my Chemistry class, told me that this was because she was sick. It was weird being in that classroom, by the way, because unless the lab had moved since the days when Susanna attended Westlake, this was the exact same room in which she and Robert had first developed the vampire potion back during her senior year. I found myself wishing one time as I looked around the room that I could somehow travel back in time to 1983 and interfere with that, to prevent this whole mess from ever starting. But that was of course impossible.

I'd also wondered, as had Susanna, if her old Chemistry teacher was still at the school, but he wasn't. As it turned out, he'd been killed in a vampire attack nearly a year ago, a fact that my own teacher somberly conveyed to me when I asked her about him after my first class with her a month ago. It hurt to hear that, and I wondered which one of our clones had done it.

After school, I called Eileen to check up on her, and she said she was okay, but she didn't sound all that great. She said she was just really tired, but she didn't have any other recognizable symptoms like a sore throat or headache. When she was out for a second day, I called her again, and she sounded even more run down. She'd been sleeping a lot, and she even sounded like I'd woken her up when I called her, but she clarified that she'd been up for a while.

So I went to see her, the first time I'd been to her house in the middle of the week. I would have brought her some flowers, figuring that was something you were supposed to do for someone when they were sick, but she'd already told me in conversation before that she didn't like flowers. She thought that they stunk. I'd mentioned this to Carolyn once when I was telling her about my new girlfriend, and she'd joked, "Hey, cheap date!"

Eileen looked pitiful as I sat beside her on her bed, her back against the headboard. She was already pale enough at the best of times, but she seemed even whiter, her freckles looking more pronounced. "Maybe you should go to a doctor," I offered.

"If I'm not better by tomorrow, I'm going to," she said. "Daddy was thinking of going ahead and prescribing some antibiotics, but Mama jumped in and said no." Her father was a dentist, and she explained to me that sometimes he preferred to forego a doctor's visit and just prescribe medication for her or her mother when they got sick. Although not a regular doctor, he could do this, but apparently this had resulted in the mother having an allergic reaction to a drug called tetracycline a few months earlier. As a result, she insisted that Eileen see a general practitioner instead if they deemed it necessary.

We talked for a little while, but my visit had to be brief since it was a school night. I felt sorry for her, and I told her that I hoped that she'd be better soon. Then the conversation took a bizarre turn.

"Me too," she said, breathing in deeply and sliding down to lie flat on the bed. She stretched out her arms and turned her head as if to yawn, but no yawn actually came, only a small whimper. She then sat up again and fixed me with a strange look, her strength seeming to have returned. "The sooner I get to feeling better, the sooner we can get back to… other things."

I didn't know what she meant, and she glanced downward, then back up at me meaningfully. I followed where her eyes had gone, noticing that she'd positioned herself in a way that, while still under the covers, her crotch was very close to mine. Realizing what she meant, I felt myself blushing, the blood running to my face. Her eyes went wide and seemed to scan my entire face wildly for a second or two, and then she breathed in deeply, grabbing my head and kissing me.

Her tongue snaked over mine rapidly, and she was breathing heavily while I held on and tried to comprehend what was happening. This wasn't like her at all, and while part of me enjoyed this sudden assault, the fact that it was so out of character for her was unnerving. I also began to worry that one of her parents might catch us in the act; the bedroom door had been left open at her mother's insistence.

I pushed back from her, and she flopped back down onto the bed, out of breath. For an instant, she looked up at me with the most lustful, predatory look I'd ever seen her give, but then she closed her eyes suddenly, like she'd fallen asleep. While I was still trying to understand what was going on, she appeared to wake again, looking as tired and worn out as she had just a minute before. She looked confused, and she pushed a lock of hair from out of her eyes. When she did, I spotted some marks on her lower right arm that I hadn't noticed before.

"Are you drooling?" she asked me with a small laugh, her eyes squinting at me curiously.

"What?" Instinctively, I reached up to my mouth, wiping away the saliva that had resulted from our strange kiss. "No. I'm all right. Are you?"

"Not if I don't shake this weird whatever-it-is," she said, twisting in the sheets clumsily. Her seductiveness had disappeared as quickly as it had come. "Mama thinks it might be mono, which if it is could be bad news for you and me."

"What?" I repeated, still confused.

"They call it the kissing disease," she said. "Something you can get that makes you real tired, and you can pass it along just by kissing. So if it turns out to be that, then no kissing for me and you for a long time." She'd lifted a hand from under the sheets as she said this, wagging her finger at me as if she were an old-fashioned schoolteacher.

"Then why did you just… you know…"

"Just what?" she asked, genuinely perplexed. "Ray, you're acting weird. I'm the one who's supposed to be sick here."

She didn't remember what had just happened. And the way she'd gone at me a few moments ago was totally unlike her. Even though our first kiss had involved a gentle rolling around of tongues, which I liked, she'd since told me that she didn't like doing it that way. Most of the kisses we'd had since then had been more tender, sometimes prolonged pecks, which I'd struggled to get used to as she'd taught me what she preferred. Elizabeth and I had almost always been more tongue-intensive.

"Sorry," I said, collecting my thoughts, an unpleasant idea forming in my head. "But what's this?" I asked, grabbing her right arm and turning it so I could see the underside.

"Ow," she said. She then saw what I was referring to, a series of small marks. "Hmm. That's weird. I don't remember getting that." There were four small, round bruises that were red at the center. Two of them were only about a centimeter apart and close to her wrist. The other two, which were larger, were farther up and about an inch and a half apart. "Maybe I bumped into something and forgot it. You ever do that? Find a bruise on yourself and have no idea where it came from?"

"Yeah, sometimes," I said quietly. As I reached for them with my other hand, I asked, "Do they hurt?" But I didn't hear her reply.

Instead, as my finger touched the smaller wound, I suddenly got a vision in my head. I saw a small, golden colored bat fastened onto a pale arm and feeding from it. It was just a flash, but it was vivid. When my finger slid up to the larger wounds, I got a series of further rapid flashes, visions of Elizabeth. These were from the times when I thought I'd seen her lurking around recently, but I'd always dismissed it as my imagination. Now I knew differently.

It took all of my self control to make as polite and normal of an exit from that house as possible. Once in my car, I began repeatedly slamming my fist onto the steering wheel. It was the angriest I could remember being in a very long time.

So I went to the cemetery and, at least in theory, summoned Elizabeth back to her grave. I was still fuming, composing what I wanted to say to her in my head. It didn't take her long to arrive, and as I watched her bat form fly up to me and transform into her regular self, I briefly considered punching her in the face and knocking her to the ground.

Whether she psychically picked up on that or just saw something in the expression on my face, I couldn't be sure, but she visibly flinched from me. She'd been smiling the same way she always did when we first saw each other, but her face fell, and she drew backwards.

"What's wrong?" she asked.

I just stared at her. I'd come up with a few different opening lines, among them *Give me one good reason why I shouldn't stake your sorry ass right now* and *Who the fuck do you think you are,* but once faced with her, I lost some of my nerve. I was still mad as hell, but she was still Elizabeth, and having this much hatred for her was a very unfamiliar feeling.

I restrained my voice as I asked her, slowly and deliberately, why she was feeding on my girlfriend. If I hadn't forced myself to hold back, I would have screamed at her. Part of me hoped that she would deny it, that maybe I was wrong. I hadn't had such a specific, detailed premonition — or in this case, a sort of after-the-fact premonition — since my vampire days, but my psychic powers had slowly been coming back and improving over the years. But sometimes, I wasn't sure if the things I saw or felt were just my imagination.

She seemed shocked for a moment, then looked down and said with a strange expression, "Damn, you guessed." She was smiling, but not in a happy way. It was more like she felt embarrassed at having been caught.

"Elizabeth!" I shouted.

"Oh, come on!" she said, keeping her inappropriately glib tone. "It's not like I'm actually killing her. Besides," she added with a lascivious leer, "she tastes so *good.*"

I almost slapped her. I even pictured myself doing it, then held back, and she again flinched. Apparently, she'd picked up on that thought. Her own psychic powers were more developed than I'd realized.

"Fine," she said, the humor gone from her face. "I'll stop. Is there anything else?" She held her arms out by her sides.

"Why did you do it?" I demanded, stepping closer to her. She didn't back away. Instead, she had taken on a defiant, almost dismissive attitude.

"I don't know," she said uncaringly.

"What do you mean you don't know? How can you even say that?" I suddenly felt like an adult. I remembered my friends and I getting into trouble as kids, and when a teacher would ask us why we did something, we'd say we didn't know. *Yes you do,* they'd say, and they were right. We just didn't want to admit the truth, and we knew that *because I felt like it* wasn't an appropriate response.

Elizabeth just folded her arms and shrugged at me, looking off to one side. "Was it to get back at me?" I asked her.

"Get back at you for what, Ray?" she asked, flatly and with contempt. "Maybe I just did it because I could. Because of what I am."

"I know what…" I began, but I broke off. The look she gave me was so full of spite that I wanted to die. "Okay, look," I said, stepping closer again and putting a hand on one of her arms. She avoided my eyes. "Never mind about why. What about how? She never said anything about getting bitten."

"No, she wouldn't," Elizabeth said, a hint of cleverness in her voice.

"What do you mean?" She didn't answer but only turned to face me with an evil, crooked grin. "You were able to feed on her without her knowing it? How does that even happen?"

"Are you going to stop attacking me and actually listen?" she asked snidely, her eyebrows raised.

"Sorry," I said, letting go of her. She unfolded her arms and sat down on the grass, and I joined her.

She went on to tell me how she was learning how to hypnotize her victims, to make them go into a trance so she could feed on them less violently. She'd lost her necklace, the one with the diamond pendant, a few days earlier when someone she attacked had fought back.

"I didn't even notice that it was gone until well after the fact," she explained. "By the time I realized it and went back, it was gone. Pissed me off."

"So you can just make people stand there and get bitten? And not even remember it?"

"Sometimes," she said thoughtfully. "Doesn't always work." I didn't like talking about this, and she knew that, but she seemed to be enjoying my discomfort. It was more cruel of her than I was used to. But at the same time, I was fascinated with the mechanics of what she was telling me. Back when my psychic powers had been at their peak, I'd used them to control my victims more brutally, sometimes humiliating them before going in for the final kill.

When I asked her how she'd learned how to do it, she said that it was something she'd picked up on from some of the other vampires in town. "It's not always been just me teaching them how to swear and use Christian words," she said. "There's an exchange of information in the community." Her words disturbed me; it sounded like she belonged to a group I previously thought she'd shunned.

She explained how she'd fed on Eileen one night after I'd left her house, luring her outside with the power of her mind. She'd even gotten it to where she could come into her bedroom while she was sleeping and drink from her arm, forcing her to stay asleep through the entire thing.

She then sighed dramatically, saying, "But I'll stop it if that's what you want." It was almost like she expected me to say that it was okay and that I'd let her continue.

"It is," I said firmly.

She gave me an odd look, then glanced down. "And maybe you're right."

"About what?"

"Getting back at you."

"You were jealous?"

"A little," she whispered. That felt like a victory, but at the same time, I felt guilty. "I really should just back off and let you be happy with her. She's cute, by the way."

I laughed. "Don't let her hear you say that."

"She doesn't even know I exist. Not really."

"I know," I said. "Keep it that way."

"I will." She sighed again, then relaxed, putting her arms behind her and stretching out her legs. Then she turned to me. "Friends?"

"Friends," I agreed. Deep down, though, something about that word hurt.

Eileen recovered soon enough. The doctor believed that her condition was caused by anemia, and a blood transfusion returned her to normal health. He did seem confused by her saying that she hadn't been attacked by a vampire, saying that he had treated several other patients for that very reason.

"But, you know, I think I'd remember getting bitten," Eileen said sarcastically as she told me her story.

I had to restrain myself; there was no way I could tell her what I knew, and that killed me. But when she said that she wasn't even sure if she believed in vampires, I had to speak up.

"Eileen, they're real. Trust me. I know people who have died because of them. And people whose family members have died." I couldn't say the rest of what was in my head: *And it's my fault.*

"Really?" she asked, reaching out to touch my hand. "Ray, I'm sorry. I didn't know."

"Could you...?" I began, but I stopped talking and instead reached for the large vanity mirror on her dresser. Around the edge of the glass, there were tucked various photographs, including several with Mary Dunn, some with Mike, some not. She was quite young in a couple of the photos, even more impossibly cute than she was now. I wondered if I should give her one of the wallet-sized versions of my last yearbook picture to put up there as well.

For the moment, I was concerned with a necklace that I'd seen hanging from a pin stuck into the side of the mirror. Other bits of jewelry hung here and there, but this one caught my eye because of the pendant hanging from it: a small, gold cross. I reached for it and picked it up gently.

"Oh, wow," she said, "I haven't worn that in years."

"How come?" I asked, dangling it from one hand and looking at it curiously. It felt like an odd thing for me to do, given my history.

"I didn't want people to think I was too much of a Jesus freak," she said with a grin. "You know, like the people at your old school."

"Do you think maybe you could start wearing it again?" I asked her.

"Seriously?" She seemed almost shocked, but then she mellowed. "If you think I should, then okay. If it'll make you feel better."

Over the past week, she hadn't had a recurrence of her odd, lustful behavior, at least as far as I knew. But the fact that it happened at all intrigued me. For a while, I thought that it might have been something else Elizabeth had done to her, like intentionally planting something in her psychically to make her act that way. But she assured me that she hadn't; she was just as surprised as I was when I described it to her.

I then wondered if this was something that happened to everyone who got fed on but not killed, if their behavior altered, even briefly. Or maybe what happened to Eileen was a side effect not only of getting bitten but also Elizabeth's psychic influence on her to keep her subdued. Maybe this didn't happen to other people, or maybe only to some. There wasn't enough data to go on. The only other person I'd known who had been wounded by a vampire and survived was Tim, and that had been almost a year ago. He'd never mentioned anything about feeling compelled to act strangely.

Eileen's wearing that necklace, even though it had been my suggestion, did feel weird for me. In a way, just that one little detail did remind me of some of the girls at Bethlehem, or maybe it was something else. Crosses didn't bother me in the same way they had when I was a vampire, but they still made Elizabeth uncomfortable, I knew. She'd mentioned in the cemetery that one of the reasons she'd stopped staying there was that all of the crosses bothered her. It wasn't until then that I noticed just how many of the gravestones were shaped like crosses, or they had the symbol carved into them. Elizabeth's, I noticed, did not.

Elizabeth happened to catch me just in time on a Friday night, coming to my window shortly before I was about to leave for Eileen's house. She said that she had something important to tell me, so I called Eileen and made up an excuse as to why I couldn't see her that night. I claimed that I wasn't feeling well, and while I hated lying to her, I did want to find out what Elizabeth had to tell me.

Pretending to my parents that I was still headed for my girlfriend's house, I instead drove to the Daniel Village shopping center, where Elizabeth and I had agreed to meet. It felt weird being in that place, particularly at night, since I could remember killing there as a vampire all those years ago.

Once Elizabeth arrived and knocked on my window, I got out of the car. On the way there, I'd thought that we'd sit in my car and talk like before, but something about that idea felt too intimate. It already felt weird enough meeting up with her in secret like this and lying to my girlfriend about it, but then again, what if someone she knew spotted us in the parking lot? I figured that if that happened, I could always pull the other convenient lie about how the vampires in town could supposedly disguise themselves to look like anyone they wanted. Deception came to me easily, and it was a long-standing survival tactic given everything I'd been through in my life.

There were some people around but no one I recognized, and Elizabeth and I leaned on the driver's side door of my car as we talked. "Damn," she began, "I forgot to bring it."

"Bring what?"

"I'd gotten you a copy of that INXS tape you mentioned the other night."

She was referring to *Kick,* an album by the Australian pop band that I'd borrowed from a guy at Bethlehem a few years back to make a copy. Since then, my cassette of it had gotten chewed up by my stereo, and I'd been meaning to replace it but never had. I just happened to mention this to Elizabeth in the cemetery the last time I'd seen her, though I'd already forgotten how it came up or why we'd talked about it.

"What?" I asked, surprised. "You mean, like, from the store?"

"Yeah," she said with a sweet smile.

"You didn't pay for it, did you," I put to her.

"What do you think," she said with a grin, but then she rolled her eyes and threw up a hand. "But it doesn't matter I guess, since I had to go and be a dumb-ass and forget to bring it to you. It was meant to be a peace offering. You know, for… what I did."

The idea that giving me a present — a twelve-dollar cassette that she'd stolen, no less — to make up for the fact that she'd been preying on the girl I loved should have seemed ludicrous to me, even offensive. But instead, I couldn't help but see it as a nice gesture. "Well, it's the thought that counts, I guess," I said.

She rolled her eyes again, seeming embarrassed.

"Is that what you brought me out here tonight for?" I asked, suddenly annoyed that I'd skipped out on a night with my girlfriend just for this.

"No, no," she assured me. "It was something else. Something I thought you'd want to know."

"Well, what then?"

She began to tell me how she'd found out that, contrary to my suspicions — or hope — my clone was in fact still in town. She hadn't encountered him directly, but she'd asked around and learned that he was, but she didn't know precisely where yet. I'd already told her that I suspected that he'd been hiding from me, and while I intended to expand on this to her, we were interrupted by an unexpected but familiar voice nearby.

"Well, look who it is!" Tim called out. He was several yards away, approaching us accompanied by a girl I didn't know. I hadn't seen him for several months, but he looked exactly the same as the last time I'd seen him, the same short curly brown hair and small, blue eyes. I'd always felt, particularly when he smiled as he was doing now, that he looked kind of rat-like, but not in an ugly way. He was more likely to be thought of as cute, I figured, and the girl he was with must have thought the same thing given that he had his arm around her shoulder.

"Hi, Tim," I said, feeling nervous. It had always been my intention to keep Elizabeth a secret, but apparently that was out.

"How's it going?" he asked me cheerfully, and the girl nodded to us in a friendly manner, though she seemed a little uncomfortable. She was pretty, too, with wide brown eyes and shoulder length blonde hair that was brighter than Elizabeth's.

"Good," I said, still caught off guard.

"And who's this?" he asked, gesturing towards Elizabeth.

"Elizabeth," she answered, but there was something icy in her tone.

"Very nice to meet you," Tim said. It slowly occurred to me that he was acting pretty weird, but maybe he was just trying to impress the girl. Growing up, I'd seen how my sisters would act a lot more fake and social around their friends than they normally would around me, so maybe this was a similar phenomenon. "And this is…" He paused, gesturing towards her.

"…Nicole," the girl said, and I flinched, knowing that this was Eileen's middle name. It was an odd coincidence. I also noticed that this Nicole was rather preppy and made up, not unlike some of the rich girls at Westlake. Maybe this was someone from Tim's private school. Tim had never struck me as a ladies' man, but it looked like he'd been doing well for himself.

"So how long have you two been going out?" I asked, trying to make conversation.

"Ray…" Elizabeth said to me, something tense in her voice. Was she jealous of this other girl's presence?

"Oh, we just met," Tim said with a smile, moving his hand up from the girl's shoulder and to the side of her head.

Nicole's eyes drifted over towards Tim, and she seemed a little testy. "Yeah, like two minutes…" she began, but her words were cut off with a quick choking sound when Tim grabbed both sides of her head and fiercely spun it to one side, breaking her neck. Before I could react, he had sunk his fangs into her neck and taken a few gulps of blood.

Tim — or rather, his clone — then threw the girl's body at me and Elizabeth, causing us to topple against the car. I tried to hold the girl up as her remains crumpled to the pavement, but she just fell dead at our feet. I called out to Tim, but he was already on the other side of the parking lot, talking to two policemen that I hadn't noticed earlier. It hadn't even occurred to me that Elizabeth and I meeting up at this place might have been a bad idea given that there was a police substation within the shopping center, a recent development that I'd forgotten about.

"Those two!" he shouted, pointing in our direction. "Over there! They're vampires! I just saw them kill that girl!" The taller of the officers said something to Tim's clone, and then the two began rushing towards us, guns drawn.

"Elizabeth, get out of here," I said.

"Not on your life," she said sternly. I'd never actually heard someone use that phrase in real life; it was more like something someone would say in a dramatic scene on TV.

I found myself breathing heavily, terrified as the two policemen cornered us with their guns, shouting at us. It wasn't the first time a weapon had been pointed at me, but back then, I'd been immortal, or so I thought. I backed away from the dead body on the ground, still in shock from having witnessed a murder right in front of my eyes.

"It wasn't us!" I pleaded. My hands had been raised in an expression of surrender, but then I began to point. "It was him! That guy you just…" My words died as I saw that Tim's clone had already vanished from the spot where the policeman had left him.

"You shut the hell up right now," the shorter cop said, coming to a halt just a few yards away from us, his gun pointed straight at my face. He was sweaty and angry, a dark-haired man close to my own height. I began to wonder if he'd had any previous experience with real vampires, or maybe he knew somebody who had been killed by one.

The taller officer leaned down, keeping his eyes on us but also reaching for the dead girl. He touched the side of her neck, presumably feeling for a pulse, but it was far too late for that.

"We didn't do it," Elizabeth said, sounding much more calm than I felt.

"We didn't! We really didn't! We're not vampires!" I had a distinct feeling that any second now, a bullet would go through my face. I relaxed a little when the man stood up and holstered his gun, but I was still scared.

"You sure?" he said to me, then suddenly shoved a big silver cross into my face. I flinched at the proximity of it, but once I realized what he was doing, I forced myself to relax further. It also struck me as odd that metal crosses had somehow become standard issue police equipment, but for a town like this, that wasn't unreasonable.

"Yes," I said as calmly as I could, looking straight at the cross determinedly. I began to worry what would happen if he turned the cross on Elizabeth, but then something else happened. A low, almost inaudible humming filled my ears. I didn't hear it so much as felt it, and it had a strange effect on me.

"This isn't necessary," Elizabeth said in a very firm tone. Her words seemed to mix with the hum, and I realized what was happening. With an effort, I shielded my mind from the psychic field she was projecting, and I felt normal again.

"You don't need that," Elizabeth said, her voice more gentle. "Please put it away." The two officers lowered their arms, their expressions becoming less hostile. The officer put the cross back into his jacket, and I either felt or just imagined Elizabeth's relief.

The psychic hum dissipated, and I hoped that the officers would be more reasonable. "We're not vampires, I promise," I said reassuringly. "See, let me show you…" I started to reach into my jacket, thinking that showing them that I carried a wooden stake would be proof enough.

The taller man suddenly lunged at me, pinning me against the car with surprising force. With an expert move, he shoved my arms apart, fixing my eyes with a powerful gaze. "Never reach into your pockets when a police officer confronts you, young man," he said menacingly. Slowly, he reached into my denim jacket's inner pocket and felt around, then pulled out the stake. He backed away and examined it, but he wasn't about to let me off the hook.

"Could be a trick," the other cop said, once again pointing his gun at me.

"Maybe," the other guy said. "This isn't technically a weapon," he continued, his eyes boring into mine. "But I could still get you for…"

Without warning, a scream rang out from the other side of the parking lot. More screams followed, and I could see people running away from what appeared to be a vampire feeding on someone on the sidewalk outside of the record store. I couldn't tell if it was Tim's clone or not.

"Stay here," the cop said firmly, pointing at me with my own stake. He then ran off with it, heading for the scene of the crime. The other policeman remained, uncertain what to do.

I felt a burst of psychic energy come from Elizabeth, a little nudge that almost sounded like a short *whoomph*. But it wasn't directed at me. With an angry look, the shorter man said to us, "Don't even think about leaving." He ran to catch up with his partner.

"Not bloody likely," I said quietly, quoting one of the British comedy shows I used to watch. It seemed like an absurd thing to think of at the time, but I was still in panic mode.

I reached for my car's door handle as Elizabeth raced around to the other side, and once we were both safely inside, I started up the car and sped away.

The abandoned site of the now-demolished Veteran's Administration hospital wasn't far from the shopping center, and I found myself heading there almost out of instinct. Somehow, it had popped into my head as a safe place to hide, an isolated, out-of-the-way spot that no one ever went to.

"Did you see the nightstick that one guy had?" Elizabeth asked me, obviously shaken as well. "It was sharpened, like a stake. If he'd pulled that thing out…"

"Elizabeth, please!" I shouted, my eyes focused on the road. Then I felt extremely guilty. "I'm sorry. I'm sorry. I didn't mean to yell at you. I just really need to concentrate here, okay? Give me a second." My arms and legs were shaking from all of the adrenaline, my mind racing. I couldn't get the image out of my head of Tim breaking that girl's neck, her eyes bugging out in surprise, and the weird, quick "*ghlkk*" sound that came from her throat as she died instantly. It just kept running over and over on a loop in my mind.

I parked the car in what had once been the hospital's parking lot, cutting the engine and killing the lights immediately. I was still breathing heavily, shaking. Elizabeth, who seemed pretty worked up as well, put her hand on my arm as a comforting gesture, but for reasons I couldn't understand, that made things worse.

I didn't want to calm down; I wanted to freak out. I really had, for a moment there, thought I was going to die. I'd faced death before and caused it many times more than that, but for some reason, this incident had really rattled me. Unable to stay sitting down, I jerked open the car door and jumped out, slamming it behind me. Elizabeth followed, and I wondered if anybody might have seen us.

"Close it, close it!" I whispered harshly, afraid that the car's internal light might attract attention. She did, then walked quickly around the car to where I was, putting her arms around my shoulders and pulling me close to her.

"Shh," she said. "It's okay. It's okay."

"No it's not okay!" I shouted, then cursed myself for being so loud. "We could have died back there," I said. "And why didn't I pick up on the fact that that was Tim's clone, not the real him? I'm supposed to be a fucking psychic."

"It all happened so fast," Elizabeth said. "I knew it immediately, but there wasn't time to warn you."

My entire body felt numb, and Elizabeth's arms felt strange on my back. "If that guy had shot me… And then my clone would have died. And then you would have died! If anything happened…" My voice was cracking, and I felt the tears building up.

"But it didn't," she insisted reassuringly, pulling back from me, then firmly gripped my upper arms. "We got away." I could just barely make out her features in the moonlight, but I knew that her expression was a tender one.

Before I knew what I was doing, I grabbed the sides of her head and kissed her, breathing in sharply as I did. She seemed to resist at first, but then she returned the kiss, our bodies melting into each other. I could feel the dampness of her shirt under my fingers as they ran across her back, and I realized that both of us were sweating, still recovering from our ordeal.

We disengaged from the kiss, still gasping. Our foreheads, also damp with perspiration, seemed to stick together. She whispered my name, and there was something of a reprimand in her voice. "We shouldn't…" she began.

"I can't help it," was all I could say, and I kissed her again, this time for a lot longer.

I broke up with Eileen the following day.

CHAPTER FOURTEEN

We had only been together for about three weeks, but my relationship with Eileen had felt like a lot longer than that. It wasn't that it seemed long and drawn out; instead it was more like what she and I had experienced together had existed even before I'd known her. What Elizabeth and I had wasn't a normal, traditional relationship, and while some elements of it had been like what I'd always imagined having a girlfriend would be like, a great deal of it wasn't.

My time with Eileen, on the other hand, had been. She was someone I met at school, this pretty, funny, interesting girl who liked me, and I liked her. We'd even gotten to the point where it was safe for us to say "I love you" to each other without it seeming premature or, as I'd heard could happen at the other end of the spectrum, a phrase that got parroted by couples who had been together so long that it lost its impact and meaning.

I really did care about her, which was why I had to break up with her. I knew that I needed to the moment I kissed Elizabeth, though I started to backpedal on the idea while going to bed that night. I didn't want to hurt her, but if we stayed together, I'd just keep cheating on her. That wasn't fair, not to either of us.

The phone conversation was a difficult one, and while I tried to avoid the clichéd "it's not you, it's me" phrase, I still ended up saying some things along those lines. I lied when she asked if there was someone else, and the more we talked, the worse I felt. I felt like a different kind of monster than the one I was used to being, one that hurt someone emotionally rather than physically.

She didn't cry, but I could hear in her voice that she was about to. While I'd worried that she might plead with me to stay with her — or worse, that I'd give in and wind up hurting her again further down the line — things never came to that. She did say one thing in particular that really hurt: "I thought you were different."

But that was part of the problem. I was different, but not in the way that she meant. She was, as I'd said from the beginning, a sweet girl. I'd hoped that being with her might be a way for me to overcome the darkness within me, but that just wasn't going to happen. She deserved someone better than an evil, worthless mess like me. And I didn't deserve someone as nice and normal as her.

The fact that we didn't have any classes together was good, but I knew I'd probably still see her in the halls occasionally. Both she and Mary Dunn were in the grade below me, so that helped. But I also knew that I would probably have to endure a grilling or at the very least some dirty looks from Mary Dunn in Chemistry. Some classes had students from mixed grades; others did not.

Mike, meanwhile, surprised me by being as laid back about everything as he was. "Sorry to hear it didn't work out, man," he said to me when I saw him in homeroom the following Monday.

"Is she okay?"

"She'll be all right," he said. "She's been through it enough times."

"Really?" This surprised me. She and I had talked a little about her previous boyfriend, some guy I'd never met named Alan, but we'd never discussed just how many people she'd dated before.

"Yeah, it's kinda this recurring thing with her. Guys get with her, find out that she won't put out, then move on."

"That's not why I broke up with her," I said, suddenly angry.

"No, it's okay, man! I understand. Mary's the same way. I love her and all, but she just keeps being all 'saving it for marriage.' So, at least until she changes her mind, well…" He lowered his voice and leaned in, and his face broke out in a wide grin. "That's what the other girl's for. The one she doesn't know about. So with Mary, if it happens, it happens. If it doesn't…" He shrugged.

At first, I was impressed. He'd certainly had me fooled; I had no idea that Mike was the kind of guy who would run around on his girlfriend. When Eileen and I had hung out with them, they both seemed very much in love, the kind of couple one could look up to and aspire to be like. But apparently, Mary Dunn didn't have a clue.

The more I thought about it, though, the more it bothered me. I didn't like the kind of guy I'd just found out that Mike was. I'd always hated guys like that. What's more, I hated the fact that I too had become a cheater, that I'd broken Eileen's heart the way I had. Even if she didn't know, I knew.

My nightly meetings with Elizabeth became more frequent again, which I was grateful for. It wasn't like my breaking up with Eileen meant that we could become a real couple, but it was nice to have things at least partly back to where they were before.

We decided to try something new, which was to have Elizabeth sneak into my bedroom at night rather than us meeting up somewhere else. I'd heard that teenagers sometimes did stuff like this, and I liked the idea of seeing if we could pull it off. If not, well, it certainly would be an interesting way to introduce Elizabeth to my parents.

So after they'd gone to bed and I'd pretended to, I would let Elizabeth in through my window, and we'd spend time together, whispering and being sure not to make any noise. This was spread out over three separate nights, though only the first two were consecutive.

Initially, we'd just sat on the bed with nothing more than a flashlight for illumination, but in time, things escalated to where we ended up under the covers, snuggling and occasionally making out.

Our conversations were, like before, all over the place in terms of tone and topic, sometimes light and other times dark. One time, we found ourselves talking about the rivalry between the United States and The Soviet Union that had recently ended. Our generation had grown up in the Cold War with the fear that a nuclear attack might happen, and while those fears were beginning to be allayed due to changing global politics, some of them still lingered.

"It could still happen," Elizabeth whispered. "Those bombs still exist."

"I know," I said, shuddering slightly. I had seen clips of the devastation of Hiroshima and of nuclear bomb tests, and I'd even had a nightmare in the mid-'80s in which missiles had struck Augusta, and all these tall buildings were turning into fiery, rectangular pillars that let out a horrible screeching sound as they began to melt away. "What do you think would happen to you if they dropped the bomb?"

"I don't know," she said after a few seconds of thought. "That's a good question."

The worst case scenario in a nuclear holocaust, as we understood it, was that tons of people would be wiped out at once, and after that, those who survived would probably die of radiation poisoning. What would that mean for all the vampires? Nuclear fallout wasn't on the list of things that could kill a vampire, so presumably, they'd survive. Elizabeth speculated that the initial blast might be bright enough to simulate the sun and kill them that way, but if not, then if all the people died, there would be nothing left for the vampires to eat.

"So, would you... would they all starve to death? Is that even possible for a vampire?"

"Only the good die, Young," she whispered, but even in the dark, I could hear the smile in her voice. I got the reference; she was making a play on words based on the name of an old Billy Joel song. "Can we change the subject?"

We did, moving on to talking about music and the various performers we did or didn't like. Because of the way her life was now, it wasn't really practical for her to collect albums and tapes like she once had. I had some and had also made copies of ones belonging to my friends and my sisters, but the primary source of my recordings was the radio. I'd been taping songs from that for years, and our conversation led us to talk about music that we'd liked when we were younger but had since grown out of.

She mentioned a song called "Automatic" by The Pointer Sisters, which I remembered but wasn't all that keen on. "The funny thing is," she continued, "I totally thought it was sung by a man for the longest time." I played the song back in my head, and sure enough, the female singer's husky voice did sound an awful lot like some of the male black singers of the era. I could see how she could make the mistake, but it was still funny, and I had to stifle a laugh.

"That's okay," I whispered. "When I was little, like maybe seven or eight or whenever the song came out… You remember that Hall and Oates song 'Maneater?'" I quietly sang the chorus to her, which talked about a woman who would, at least figuratively, eat people up.

"Yes," she said.

"The first time I heard it was when I was riding in the car with Susanna. So I asked her, and I was being completely serious, 'Is this song about Ms. Pac-Man?'"

Elizabeth burst out laughing, quickly covering her mouth. She recovered, then said through forced down chuckling, "Sorry, but that's just so damn cute."

"Well, we were on our way to the arcade at the time," I said, trying to justify my younger self's mistake. "So it was on my…" I stopped when I heard something.

Footsteps were coming up the hall. "Shit," I whispered harshly, and we both became deathly still. I hoped that the steps wouldn't stop outside my door, but they did. I'd remembered to lock my door, but when I heard someone try to turn the doorknob, my heart almost stopped.

"Ray?" my father's voice called out. I didn't answer.

Elizabeth, who was on the side of the bed closer to the door, slid out from under the covers. The creak the bed made as she stood seemed like the loudest sound in the world, and her back was to me.

"Elizabeth, don't!" I whispered.

"Trust me," she whispered back, her words barely more than a breath.

As she stepped slowly and deliberately towards the door, I began to sit up, but then my head felt weird. I was dizzy, not unlike the feeling one gets when standing up too quickly.

My father repeated my name, this time more firmly. I could feel that familiar weird vibration coming from Elizabeth, the one I'd felt the night of the confrontation with the police. *Go back to bed,* a voice seemed to say, but it wasn't even a voice, more like a vague impulse. I could picture myself lying back down on my pillow. *You didn't hear anything,* the thought floated in the ether. I had trouble remembering what had just happened, why Elizabeth was standing in the middle of my room. I heard the sound of my father's footsteps going down the hall, but they were slower than usual.

I was startled awake by Elizabeth, whom I was surprised to find next to me in my bed. Then, just after a second or two, my thoughts came back to me, and I remembered what had happened.

"You're really getting good at that," I whispered to her.

That close call had led me to think that maybe meeting up in my room wasn't such a good idea. Sure, Elizabeth could telepathically subdue my parents and even make them sleep through her visits, but something about that made me uncomfortable. This led me to explore the idea of us getting a hotel room again, maybe even regularly, which would be more private and less risky.

My hope was that I could surprise Elizabeth by getting one without telling her ahead of time, so I went by a hotel a couple of nights later, hoping that it wouldn't be too expensive. I wasn't even sure how much it would cost, and it wasn't like I was rolling in money at this point in my life.

My parents gave me an allowance of fifteen dollars a week, which up until I'd gotten my car had only been five dollars. When my sisters and I were younger, we'd each been given allowances and were assigned certain chores around the house. But as we'd gotten older and they'd gone off on their own, my allowance had become more of an arbitrary thing, an old tradition that kept going. The only real chores left to me were to feed Scout every night and occasionally take out the garbage, but it's not like those took a whole lot of effort. The extra ten bucks I had begun to get this year were to pay for gas, but because I didn't have to fill up my car every week, I was able to build up a modest amount of savings.

The plan I had was ruined, though, when the man in the hotel office asked for my driver's license and then told me that one had to be eighteen years old in order to rent a room. This didn't seem right; I knew that Elizabeth had rented that room for us before, and she didn't even have an ID. But the man was firm, even rude, and he sent me on my way.

I told Elizabeth about this the next time I saw her, again with us whispering under the covers in my bed. She thought it was a nice gesture, but she understood why I hadn't been able to make it happen.

"Then how come you were able to get a room? Did you get a fake ID?"

"No. But I have my ways," she whispered slyly. I wasn't sure how I felt about that.

As before, we talked about all sorts of things, most of them flippant and nothing to do with the bigger picture. I still felt this underlying guilt over what was happening, how she was a vampire and I was letting her continue to go around and feed on people. I tried to believe that she always did so in a non-lethal way, but deep down, I knew that I was probably kidding myself about that. But whenever I let my thoughts drift in that direction, it would spoil the mood, so I avoided doing so.

Our conversation meandered towards music again, this time in regards to being able to play an instrument. I'd told her some about Eileen and how she was in the high school band; we'd had an uncomfortable encounter in the halls that day where we'd spotted each other and then avoided eye contact. Elizabeth said that she regretted never learning how to play the piano, an instrument that had always been a favorite of hers.

"Well, you always could," I offered.

"Yeah, right," she said, her bitterness showing through even in a whisper. "I don't think most piano instructors would welcome a student who could only meet them after dark."

I sighed. She was right. "Elizabeth, I don't know if I've said this to you enough before, but I'm really sorry."

"For what?"

"For taking all that from you. A normal life. Being able to take piano lessons. Just… I don't know. Growing up and living."

"And growing old? And dying? Look, if I play my cards right, I can live forever. That's not a bad thing as far as I'm concerned." She nudged forward, touching her forehead to mine as we lay there on my pillow. "It's not the worst thing in the world."

Things were quiet for a while. I thought about Susanna, memories from way in my past, being a little boy and sitting in the living room admiring how well she could play the piano. She'd never had any formal training, but somehow, she could still play rather well, just remembering songs she'd heard and being able to figure out which keys to use to recreate them. I could do this, too, but only rudimentarily, able to recall a basic melody and picking out the right keys to play a Christmas carol or two. Susanna, meanwhile, could recreate full pieces, chords and all. She was nine years older than me, so a lot of what she did seemed almost exotic, strange but intriguing.

That was when she'd been in high school, long before the vampire potion came along and wrecked our lives. I could even vaguely remember a boyfriend she'd had before Robert, some guy who was also a pianist, and maybe that's where she'd learned her skills from. My favorite thing for her to play was the theme from the horror movie *Halloween.*

The song was so pulsating and rhythmic, and even though I'd never seen the movie because I was far too young at the time, I could still appreciate how scary the music sounded. I would get a little bit frightened listening to it, but it was a good scare, the kind that little kids like. Susanna knew this, too, and one year, she decided that it would be fun to play the song on the piano every time trick-or-treaters came to our front door, which was right next to the living room. Kids would come on Halloween night begging for candy, and my big sister would play the song, taunting them with the eerie atmosphere it created.

A few years later when Susanna was home from college, I brought my tape recorder into the room while she was tooling around on the piano. I asked her to play the *Halloween* theme again, and she tried to, but she kept forgetting how to do it right. She'd get the rhythm and tumble along through the tune for a few bars, but then she'd taper off into something else. It was disappointing for me; she'd lost something along the way.

Elizabeth got us a hotel room that weekend, which I felt a little nervous about. It wasn't like we hadn't done this before, but because of a bad dream I'd had recently, I was apprehensive. I didn't even want to tell Elizabeth about the dream because it had been about her, but I eventually would.

Like before, she'd gotten the room and left a note on my window telling me the hotel name and room number, and I'd met her there once it was late enough for me to sneak out. My car, by the way, was bigger and heavier than my mother's Toyota, so it was harder to push it down the driveway and out to the street where it was safely far enough from the house to start up without raising suspicion. But I got used to it. Scout had also grown accustomed to the routine: To keep him from barking at me and alerting my parents, I'd give him a piece of cheese through the fence, then whisper my gratitude to him for keeping quiet.

When Elizabeth let me into the room, she greeted me with her usual warmth and sexiness. We hadn't seen each other all week apart from briefly at my window a couple of nights earlier, making plans for this night. So it was good to see her again, and we kissed deeply.

Not long after that, she put her hands up to my face, right up to my nose. "Smell," she commanded, and I did, but I recoiled, not liking the scent. She'd been using some kind of hand lotion, but it smelled too strong and floral for my liking. I didn't like strong scents and perfumes; they'd always annoyed me.

"You don't like it?" she asked, pouting.

"No," I said, breathing out strongly through my nose and grimacing, trying to rid my nasal passages of the stench. "Sorry."

She looked at me, her head tilted to one side. "Too bad," she said. "Get used to it."

"Do I have to?" I asked.

Her expression had grown angry, but then it changed, more like she was disappointed in me. She shook her head as she turned and walked away, then sat down on the bed, leaving me standing by the door. "Ray, when a girl gets something new that she likes, and she asks you if you like it too, you're supposed to say yes."

"Even if I don't? You want me to lie?"

"Wouldn't be the first time," she said. That stung. "Sorry. That was mean."

"Yeah, it was. But true, I guess." I walked over and cautiously joined her on the bed.

"I was just trying to make myself less stinky," she said. It hadn't really occurred to me before, but her options for self grooming may have been rather limited, and this was an attempt to counter that. It wasn't like she could take a shower like a normal person, what with the whole running water thing, though she probably could still take baths. Regardless, I'd never found her or her usual scent repulsive, even if I did object to other things about her lifestyle.

"You're fine just the way you are," I said to her, turning as I sat to face her more directly. "You don't need stinky perfumy stuff."

She rolled her eyes and sighed. "You really don't know how to talk to girls, do you?"

That rubbed me the wrong way. I thought that I'd gotten a lot better about talking to girls over the past year even though I'd been terribly shy about it up until then. My experiences with Elizabeth — after she'd died, that is — had made me more confident, and I'd had positive results with Eileen once I'd gotten over my initial nervousness with her. In fact, one of the things that was bugging me now was that Elizabeth seemed to be being kind of petty, not unlike Eileen could sometimes be, insisting on arbitrary rules that I didn't agree with. "Don't call me 'baby,'" she'd insist, or "Don't say I'm cute."

I said something along these lines, then added, "Or maybe I just don't know how to talk to dead girls."

I'd meant it as a joke, but her face hardened. "Dead girls," she repeated, clearly not amused. "Do I look dead to you?"

My heart raced. "No! No, I'm sorry. I didn't mean…" I reached out and touched her hand, and she started to pull away but then didn't. Her eyes were fixed on mine, her jaw set. "I was just… you know. Like how all those books and movies call vampires dead. Or undead. I didn't mean it as an insult. Really. But I guess they say it because, you know, the person died, and so…" I wasn't sure how to finish the sentence, and my voice had taken on a pleading tone. I couldn't stand for her to be mad at me.

"So," she said, looking down at our hands, which were still touching. "Answer me this. Say there's some guy in a hospital, and he's in really bad shape and close to dying. Like of a gunshot wound or something. And the doctors are fighting to save him, all rushing around."

"Okay," I said, picturing the scenario.

"The man's heart stops, and he dies. But they keep fighting it, you know, *'Clear!'*" She mimicked the motion of paramedics trying to bring the patient back to life with defibrillators. "And then, boom, his eyes open and he comes back. He's okay again. *Beep... beep... beep...* Heart's beating again. And he lives for another twenty, maybe thirty years." She looked at me meaningfully.

"Sure," was all I could think to say in response.

"Would you call that man dead? All the rest of those years?"

Finally, I got it. "No," I said.

"But he died," she said, nudging my leg with her knee.

"Okay," I said, feeling embarrassed but enlightened. "I get it."

"I died, Ray. But I came back. I'm alive now." She leaned towards me, her eyes glancing down at my lips for a fraction of a second.

We kissed, breathing each other in. The smell of her hand lotion still lingered, but it didn't annoy me as much as before. When we stopped, she pulled away from me, but only a little. "Maybe even more than before," she added.

She then sprawled back onto the bed, much like she'd done when we'd last been in a hotel room. I matched her move, reclining next to her. "It's kind of like the Death card in the tarot deck," she said.

"The what?" I asked.

"Tarot cards," she said, though at the time, I pictured the unfamiliar word in my head as *tarrow*.

"You know what I'm talking about," she said impatiently. "I know you've seen them. Those cards fortune tellers use, cool looking, spooky pictures on them, and they place them on the table all meaningfully... 'This card represents your past... This card is your future...'"

"Right, right," I said, the images falling into place in my mind. I'd seen this kind of thing on TV, but never in real life. Then I remembered one TV movie in particular where a woman was getting a tarot reading, and I told Elizabeth about it. In the scene, the Death card came up, and it was a really ominous thing. The woman thought that it meant she was going to die.

"But that's just it," she said. "The Death card doesn't mean actual death, but change. Something ends, and something new begins. That's kind of how I see myself. I didn't just die; I changed."

"Okay," I said, "I can get behind that."

She smirked at me, the same way she always did.

The rest of the night went okay, though as before, it didn't culminate in us having sex like I kept hoping it might. We talked, we kissed, and we felt each other up, but things never went as far as I wanted. She was the one calling the shots, and I could only go as far with her as she allowed. Part of me was okay with that, but I couldn't help but feel frustrated. When would we actually get to, as the parlance went, do it?

I mentioned to her the dream I'd had about her recently, but I was very reluctant to tell her the details. She insisted, and I couldn't resist her.

"I guess it was about tonight," I said. "You know, leading up to it. We'd gotten the room, and we were just hanging out and talking, no big deal. But then I heard a noise coming from the bathroom, this muffled sorta moaning. You tried to act like nothing was wrong, and then you tried to stop me from going in the bathroom. But I did, and there was a girl in there, tied up and gagged in the bathtub. Apparently, this had been her hotel room to begin with, and you'd somehow gotten in and tied her up before I came over."

"Interesting…" she said. "Not really something I'd do, but okay."

"I know. Carolyn got me into the habit a while back about trying to figure out what my dreams mean, or really, why I dream them. Usually, it's something symbolic, something representing some other thing in my real life that's bothering me. Or it can be trivial, like a conversation I had a day or two ago, and it ends up being represented in a dream."

"And what does me tying up girls and putting them in the bathtub represent?" she asked, smiling.

"Probably me wondering how you're able to check into hotel rooms without ID. The thought had crossed my mind that maybe you… well." I didn't want to say it, but I'd already let too much out, and the look on her face told me that she wasn't going to let me off the hook. "That you killed someone in order to get their room."

I was afraid she might get mad, but she surprised me by tossing her head back and laughing. She then fixed me with a sly grin and shook her head slowly. "No," she said simply.

"Then how do you do it?"

She opened her mouth to speak, then stopped. "Tell me the rest of your dream, and I'll tell you."

I sighed, then continued reluctantly. "I forget how it happened exactly, but somehow we went from the bathroom to the main part out here, and you'd brought the girl out and had her on the floor. She was struggling and pleading, and you said something about how you were going to kill her. I guess she wasn't gagged anymore at this point. And I begged and pleaded for you to let her go, but you said we couldn't, or else she'd talk. Like, tell people about us.

"And then I remembered that the last time we'd gotten a room, some guy had burst in on us, like maybe it was his room to begin with, and we were just squatting there. So you killed him."

"I don't remember that," she said innocently.

"I know! I'm just saying, it's one of those things when a dream makes you think you remember something that happened before, but it didn't really."

"I know; I'm just messing with you. So what happened?"

"You said something about how you were going to kill her and you wanted me to watch. And I really didn't want to. The girl was crying and saying, 'Please, please let me go! I swear I won't tell anyone!'"

"What did she look like?" She seemed really intrigued by the story.

"Hmm? I don't know, kind of... Nothing too out of the ordinary. Brown hair, I think, short. Pulled back in a ponytail. Why?"

"Just asking."

"Well, anyway, I couldn't take it anymore. I knew you were going to kill her, and I couldn't stop you, so I just ran out of the room. I knew that any second now, I was going to hear her scream when you bit her, and I ran as fast as I could, hoping to be out of earshot when it happened. But I couldn't get away in time, and I heard the scream and tried not to picture you biting into her neck." I heard a noise. "Was that your stomach rumbling?"

"No," she lied, trying to hide her smile. "It was my shoe. You know, sliding on the bedspread." She moved her foot back and forth a few times, but it only made a swishing sound. "Damn. Can't make it do it again. Like that time you farted in class."

"I can't believe you remember that," I said, recalling the embarrassing incident from eighth grade. "And it really was my shoe scraping the floor. Even if you don't believe me."

"Sure," she said playfully.

As promised, she told me that the way she was able to get rooms wasn't nearly as brutal as I'd imagined. She simply used her psychic powers to confuse the desk clerk, making him think that she'd shown him a valid driver's license.

"And you can really do that?" I asked her. We were sitting on the bed at this point, cross-legged.

"Yeah! You'd be surprised how easy it can be. I can make people do things without them even realizing they're doing it."

"Like what?"

"Like why are you holding your arm up over your head?" She pointed with her finger, and I looked up. I was surprised to see that I had indeed raised my arm, which was lazily bent at the elbow so that my forearm was slightly drooping. It looked kind of like a pose I'd seen ballet dancers make.

I quickly brought my arm back down. It didn't take any special effort; it wasn't like she was forcing me to hold it up. She'd just somehow — subconsciously, I supposed — made me do it. I gave her an indignant look, but she just raised her eyebrows at me and grinned mischievously.

"So, no killing people for their rooms, then," I said.

"No." I wondered if she might be lying, but there was no real reason to think that she was. "Why? Do you want me to?"

"No! You know that." I paused. "And the money to pay for the room?" I immediately regretted the words even before I heard her answer.

"Oh, that totally comes from killing," she said flippantly.

As for her reaction to the story in my dream, it did bug me the way that she seemed to have fun with it. I'd found the dream very disturbing, and it pained me to recount it to her. But at the same time, her making light of it did seem to alleviate things for me. With nightmares, one particularly frightening aspect of them was the fear that they would return. I did have recurring nightmares from time to time, but this turned out not to be one of them.

When I thought about it later, I had to admit that Elizabeth wasn't being entirely unreasonable. Her life as a vampire wasn't something she'd chosen, and I, however indirectly, had forced that upon her. So could I really blame her for occasionally trying to have a little fun?

However tolerant I found myself being on this occasion, nothing could have prepared me for what was to come the following night.

Even though nothing sexual happened between us in the hotel room on Friday night, Elizabeth surprised me by saying that she wanted to get another room on Saturday. "I like this," she said with a slight purr in her voice, gesturing around the room with her hand. "Let's do it again tomorrow. Earlier this time. Just tell your parents you're going out with friends."

So I did, again referring to the note she left on my window to find out just where to go. I had in fact heard her leave it, which was around 7:45, much earlier than I'd expected. For all I knew, she always left her notes for me that early, but this had been the first time I'd actually heard her tucking the paper under my window screen. By the time I'd gotten to the drapes and pulled them back, she'd already gone.

The fact that I was telling my parents I was going out meant that I wouldn't be able to stay out very late; my curfew was 10:00. As I drove to the hotel, I thought that maybe I could go home at the appointed time as planned, then sneak back out after Mom and Dad went to bed. I figured it would depend on how things went.

"Hi," Elizabeth said as she let me into the room. There was something strange about the way she was able to draw that one syllable out and make it sound so arousing. I moved to kiss her, but she held up a finger, telling me to wait.

"Why?" I asked, feeling a little offended.

"Just a second," she said, sauntering into the room as the door swung closed behind me. She then spun around, fixing me with a strange look. "Okay," she said, holding her arms out to me.

I walked up to her and put my arms around her, but something felt weird. My forehead touched hers, and I immediately noticed how different it felt. I pulled back, surprised.

"God, you're cold," I said. "Were you just outside?" I reached up and touched her face with my hands, and it was like she'd just come in on a cold winter's night. But it was only in the 60s tonight, so I was confused.

"No," she said, still smiling at me strangely. "See, this is what I'm like when I haven't fed." She waited for me to fully comprehend her words.

"Oh," I said. "Oh. So… that means…" I wasn't sure what to say.

"Every night that you and I've met," she said with measured patience, "I've always made it a point to feed first. Curbs the temptation to bite you. So that's why I always feel warm to you, like a regular human."

"So…" I said again, still unsure.

"I'm not going to bite you now, either," she said. "Promise." She pulled herself close to me, and I could tell that her body felt different. It wasn't exactly cold, just sort of room temperature. It felt unfamiliar, unnatural. "I just thought that it was time you experienced this part of me," she added, her voice almost a whisper.

She kissed me, and it was a very bizarre experience. I was used to the way it normally felt, warm and inviting, but this was completely different. It felt more like a large, tepid earthworm was squirming its way around my tongue, and once I thought of that, I wanted to gag. I pushed back from her, panting.

I started to say something, but she just said to me very firmly, "No. *No.* Don't you turn away from me, Ray. Or else I really will bite you." Her clammy hand gripped the base of the back of my head, and she forced me into another kiss. I tried to pull back from her, but her hold on me was unbreakable. Not since the first night I'd encountered her as a vampire had I tried to pit my strength against hers, and I'd forgotten just how powerful she could be.

I fought down the urge to resist, trying to go with the flow. Clearly, if I fought her too much, she'd get even more angry. And once I got used to it, the kissing wasn't so bad. It was just different, not what I was used to. Her grip lessened as she could tell that I was relaxing, and things became a little less scary.

The kiss ended, and she exhaled strongly. Even her breath was cool; it felt like an autumn breeze on my face. She continued to breathe heavily, then asked me meaningfully, "Do you love me, Ray?" I then noticed her fangs.

"I… Yes, of course I love you. You know I do."

"Don't worry about those," she said, obviously having seen where my eyes had gone. I forced them back up to hers. "I told you. This is who I am. I'm this person too, every night before I feed. I want you to know all of me, not just what you consider the good part of me."

"Okay," I said stupidly. My heart was pounding.

"Mmm…" she said, closing her eyes and turning her head to one side. "I can hear it. Such a beautiful sound. Even musical. All that blood, just pumping away inside of you." She fixed her eyes on mine again. "Are you afraid?"

I was terrified. I tried to believe that she wouldn't hurt me, but I couldn't be sure. "A little," I lied.

"Keep being afraid," she purred. "I won't hurt you, but damn it, this is just so… so…"

I suddenly felt myself being lifted by my arms and tossed onto the bed. It wasn't forceful enough to injure me, but it still freaked me out. Within seconds, Elizabeth was crawling on top of me as I turned to settle on my back, my knees raised.

"Be brave," she said to me in a weird combination of seduction and condescension, one of her hands stroking through my hair. "You'll be all right."

She then stopped her approach, seeming to calm down. She'd started to straddle me, but I was surprised when she repositioned herself on the bed, sitting with her knees pointing towards my prone body.

"You going to take that jacket off?" she asked me simply.

Uneasy, I sat up, pulling my jean jacket off almost as if I'd been commanded to, without thinking. I started to drop it onto the floor by the bed, but Elizabeth pointed and said, "Wait. The stake in the pocket."

"What?" I asked.

"I know you've got it in there," she said. "Take it out." I did, uncertain what was coming next.

"Put it on the night table," she said, pointing behind me.

"Why?"

"Do it," she ordered. As I turned around and found a spot for it, she added, "Not that you'll need it. But I think having it nearby will help you feel better. I'm all about playing fair."

I turned back around, startled to find that she'd somehow silently moved to where her face was right up against mine. "Now," she said, "a little more."

She then grabbed at the base of my shirt, and before I knew it, she'd pulled it over my head and tossed it onto the floor. I sat there, bare-chested and amazed, watching as she repeated the move on herself, pulling her own shirt off. Her eyes were once again locked on mine as she reached behind her back and unhooked her bra, which slid off her shoulders and onto the bed. For the first time, I was seeing a girl's naked breasts in real life.

"Come here," she commanded, and I was pulled towards her, our chests touching. Her breasts were softer and more lightweight than I'd imagined; I'd always thought that girls' boobs were more firm than that. I'd touched hers before, but only when she'd still been wearing a bra, so my mind assumed that their natural texture was similar to that.

She breathed in deeply, her cold arms rubbing up and down my back, and I did the same to her, following her lead. Her whole body felt strange and cool, like she was some kind of animated mannequin. But I loved the softness of her skin, the way it felt against mine. Holding hands, kissing, stroking her hair, and occasionally getting my hand up her shirt all this time had been one thing, but it was nothing compared to this quantity of skin-to-skin contact. My fear of her melted away under the weight of sheer bliss.

We kissed again, and I began to get used to the clamminess of her mouth. It was strange, but it was becoming more pleasant. When we stopped, we were both breathing heavily again. "G--..." she began to say, but she choked, then recovered quickly. "God, your tongue is so warm. It's like it's on fire." It hadn't even occurred to me how all of this must have felt for her, that she was experiencing the same contrasts in temperature. *"All* of you is..." she continued, her hands still rubbing up and down my flesh passionately. "Just... so... warm..."

She pushed me backwards, and I again found myself on my back. She lay on top of me, writhing as she kissed my face, my neck, and my shoulders, letting out little moans of pleasure. I got nervous whenever she kissed my neck, still picturing those deadly fangs of hers. But at the same time, I couldn't help but get an erection. She had never been this passionate with me before, and any fantasies I'd had in the past paled in comparison to all of this. I'd never been more turned on in my life.

"Good boy..." she hissed in my ear, and I didn't know what she meant until she started rubbing my crotch with her hand. "That's it."

She slid back from me, and I instinctively reached for her, letting out a little whine that I felt embarrassed by. She just smiled at me knowingly, then positioned herself sideways so she could take off her jeans. Her panties went along with them onto the floor, and I could feel my eyes wanting to pop out of my head as I saw her completely naked for the first time. She was the most beautiful thing I had ever seen in the entire world.

Whether she was actually reading my thoughts or just interpreting my actions, I couldn't be sure, but she seemed quite pleased with herself, giggling gently as she slid back around and began undoing my pants. I helped her along, and soon enough, I was naked as well. My dick stood erect, and all I could think about was how it would feel inside of her.

She didn't waste any time, maneuvering herself on top of me, taking on that same straddling position. I wasn't entirely sure how to move myself into her, but things literally slid into place. It happened faster than I expected, and we both gasped.

As I've said before, I was marginally familiar with pornography, and I knew that one of the clichés about that type of magazine was that men would falsely claim or just joke that they "read it for the articles." Somehow, that was supposed to distract from the fact that the magazine was filled with full-color photographs of naked, horny looking women.

But I had in fact read some of the articles and letter columns in that "porno mag" of Dennis's, which he'd let me borrow for a night. I liked reading them, even the dirty stories from readers that, I figured out later on, were probably fake. One thing that was often mentioned — and I'd heard guys in real life describe this as well — was how warm, even hot, a girl's vagina was. But Elizabeth's wasn't like that.

Like her mouth, it was cold, clammy, and slippery. It wasn't an entirely unpleasant sensation, just not what I'd expected. I had also always thought that my first time having sex would be in the missionary position, as I knew it was called. But if she wanted to be on top, I wasn't going to argue.

We thrust at each other, gasping and moaning as we went, and I wasn't even sure how much of my doing that was because I felt physically compelled to do so; it also felt like I was expected to make those noises. She was making them, so it seemed like I should, too. It was almost like a duet. And it did feel good, plus I was so glad to finally be losing my virginity to the girl I loved.

This went on for a few minutes, and I just held on for the ride and hoped I didn't screw anything up. She appeared to be enjoying it, so I figured I must be doing something right. Her entire body bobbed up and down, her back straight but sometimes curving backwards while she sat on top of me. Sometimes her hands were touching my chest or my shoulders, and other times, they touched the bed instead. I was fascinated with the way her breasts flopped up and down, though I did feel embarrassed when she caught me staring. For a lot of the time, her eyes were closed as she kicked her head back or moved it from side to side, but other times, she'd lean forward and bore her eyes into me with a hungry, animalistic look.

"So do you like it?" she asked me, her voice halting and punctuated with slight grunts that matched our rhythm.

"Yes…" was all I could think to say. "I do… I do like it. I love…"

"Do you like how it feels, Ray?" she interrupted. Her thrusting became faster and more forceful.

"Yes… Yes… Elizabeth…" It was getting harder to breathe.

For some reason, she laughed, just a short cackle. Her fangs were clearly visible in the lamplight. When she closed her mouth, the tips of them still protruded over her bottom lip, and her smile seemed to wrap around them. I couldn't be sure, but it looked for a moment like one of the fangs had pierced her lip, and there was a drop of blood. When I blinked and looked again, there was nothing.

She gave me another one of those piercing stares. "Do you like fucking your dead girl?"

That shocked me, and I stopped pushing into her.

"Oh, no you don't," she hissed, then pushed even harder onto me, not losing her ever-increasing rhythm. I resumed, trying to keep up. "Tell me you like it. Keep fucking. Harder. Harder! This is what you wanted, isn't it?" She was screaming by this point, and I shouted something positive in response, really just a wail.

But this hadn't been what I wanted. From the moment she'd brought up the "dead girl" thing, all I could think of was how different she felt, all cold and gross. I'd heard of necrophilia, specifically of the bizarre practice of some funeral home workers having sex with dead bodies. The thought of that had always disgusted me; who could ever possibly enjoy fucking a corpse? But then, how different was that from what I was doing now?

Elizabeth was grunting even harder, and I was doing the same, still gasping for air. I felt like I might pass out, and there was a weird choking sensation that began to build up in the back of my throat, like I might gag. Her movements began to slow down, almost imperceptibly at first, and she gripped my shoulders tightly. When I looked into her eyes, I saw something I'd never seen before. The blueness of her irises seemed to glow, looking like a bright summer sky. I felt pulled into those eyes: They were like mirrors, my entire soul reflected in them. She grinned widely, and her fangs looked more menacing than I'd ever seen.

There was a flash, and I could see her rushing down and burying her teeth into the side of my neck, but it wasn't something that actually happened. It was more like a vision, something I vividly imagined, but she was in fact still hovering above me, a strange look on her face.

Before I could ponder this further, Elizabeth suddenly pulled herself away from me, sitting back on the bed as she panted wildly. My penis felt colder than ever, now damp from her but exposed to the air in the room. The rest of me also felt cooler without her on top of me, even if she hadn't been much of a source of body heat. She, meanwhile, was holding her arms to her sides, her hands gripping her own shoulders now, and she continued to look at me bewilderedly.

She screwed her eyes shut and fiercely shook her head. "I'm sorry, Ray," she said, still out of breath. "I have to go." She then slid off the bed, picking her clothes up from the floor and struggling to get them on as quickly as possible, seeming upset.

"What? Why?" I sat up, then began crawling forward, reaching out to touch her.

She flailed back with one arm to make me stop, a clumsy maneuver given that she hadn't quite gotten her hand through the sleeve yet. "I just… I just have to." She hadn't even put her bra back on; instead she crumpled it up and stuffed it into one of the front pockets of her jeans. As she fumbled with her tennis shoes, I noticed that she was shaking.

"Elizabeth, what's wrong?" I pleaded. "Are you okay?"

"I'm fine… I'm fine…" she said, her voice quavering, "I just really need to get out of here." She kept avoiding looking at me. When she finally did, I suddenly felt stupid, standing on my hands and knees, completely naked and vulnerable. "I'm sorry," she repeated, and before I knew it, she'd run out of the room, the door slamming behind her.

I just lay there for a few minutes, trying to figure out what had just happened. I thought I'd done something wrong, offended her in some way, but once I was on my own for long enough, I figured it out. For a moment there, I really did think that she was going to bite me. And there was something so hypnotic about the way her eyes looked that, had she lunged forward, I wouldn't have resisted. Just for a second, I would have completely given myself to her.

I wanted to enjoy the fact that I'd finally had sex, that I'd just got done fucking the most beautiful girl I'd ever known. That's how the typical teenage boy in me should have felt. But the truth of the matter was that I'd almost died. She'd left abruptly in order to prevent that.

It was weird to see her snap so quickly, to go from being so powerful and in control to so frightened. And it wasn't me she was afraid of; it was herself, what she might have done. I was glad that she'd managed to regain her self control at the last second, but at the same time, I was still very disappointed that things hadn't gone better.

After cleaning myself up, I wondered if she might come back once she'd calmed down. But because I knew that the only way she could do that was to kill, to satiate her bloodlust on someone other than me, I didn't want to wait around for that. Besides, I needed to get home.

I was worried about the whole process of returning the room key to the hotel's front office; it wasn't something I'd ever done before. Elizabeth was the one who was experienced in these things, not me. I was afraid that the person behind the counter might ask to see my ID, but as it turned out, the woman only briefly looked up when I slid the key into a little indentation beneath the drop-off window. Apparently, the check-out process was a lot less complicated than I'd thought.

The drive home was strange, my head filled with so many conflicting emotions. Part of me was glad to have lost my virginity;

it felt like a milestone had been passed. *Now you're a man,* someone might congratulate me if I told them about it. But I wasn't going to tell anyone. Elizabeth was still a secret, and on this night, she felt like an even darker one.

I dreaded the notion of seeing my parents once I got back home. I just didn't want to talk to them. I felt kind of dirty, like I was a different person. Fortunately, the path from the back door to my bedroom was clear, and I made sure to make enough noise to let them know I'd gotten home without actually having to speak to them.

After I changed clothes and went to bed, I had a hard time getting to sleep, the night's events running through my head over and over. I'd felt such a weird combination of horror, arousal, and disgust during my encounter with Elizabeth, but now that I was safely home and in bed, I wasn't sure what to think. I even worried that Elizabeth might avoid me because of what happened, but that fear went away when I heard a familiar tapping at my window shortly after midnight.

I maneuvered myself under the closed drapes, then slid up the window frame. I started to reach for the clasps at the base of the window screen, but Elizabeth told me to stop. "Let's just talk through here," she whispered.

I started to ask why, but then I decided to just go along with it. "Are you okay?" I whispered back.

"Yeah," she said, glancing down. "You?"

"Pretty much," I said. "Just a little freaked out."

"I know. I'm sorry. I really thought I could handle that, but I… well… When that orgasm hit, I just couldn't… I almost…" She looked down again and sighed loudly, and I worried that my parents might overhear us. I started to reprimand her, but I changed my mind.

"Elizabeth, it's okay."

"No it isn't! I could have killed you. That's not cool." She looked to one side, scrunching up her eyebrows. "'Not cool?' That's an understatement and a half."

I laughed nervously, then stifled that, again trying to keep from getting too loud. "Don't worry about it," I whispered. "I'm fine."

"You're sure," she asked, her words a combination of a question and a statement.

"Yeah. Maybe we can try it again sometime. You know, when you've already fed. When things aren't so crazy." I'd put my hand up against the screen, the wire mesh pressing into my fingers.

"I..." She looked down once more, then back up at me. "I'm not sure that's a good idea."

"Why?"

"I'm sorry, Ray. I have to go." She turned away, quickly sliding past the shrubbery outside my window and out of sight. I heard a flapping sound, and I knew that she was gone.

CHAPTER FIFTEEN

High school is a difficult thing for any teenager to endure, but for me, it was even more so given the fact that I couldn't really let on to anyone around me just what I knew or who I'd been in my past. The vampire attacks around the city, which fortunately seemed to be mostly confined to downtown and to the south of Augusta, were a topic of discussion from time to time, but I always had to play dumb. I had to act like I didn't know as much as I did, often finding myself in the middle of conversations in which I had to just go along with whatever was being said, however ignorant the people around me were.

Because we were all nearing the end of our time in high school, there was a lot of pressure in terms of what everyone wanted to be when we grew up, what careers we might want to go into. The expectation that we would all go on to college and train for careers that we would eventually have as adults was prevalent, but this was a concept that terrified me. I had no idea what I wanted to do, and I dodged the topic for as long as I could.

The older I got, the more self aware I became, and it occurred to me that maybe the right profession for me was to become an actor. I had grown up lying to people and pretending to be something I wasn't, a regular high school kid and not the murderous monster that I'd been in my past. The idea of becoming some famous movie star appealed to me until I began to feel guilty, thinking that I didn't deserve such a glamorous lifestyle, a happy ending like that.

Even so, I considered it from time to time. Maybe I could be someone who worked behind the scenes instead of being some big star, like a cameraman or a director. My life as far as other people were concerned was a fabrication, I felt, so maybe that was the route I could take.

But some part of me knew deep down that this would never come to pass, and it frustrated me. My role in the world as it stood now was to be a vampire hunter. That was what really mattered, even if I never could tell anyone about it. I needed to make up for my sins in the past and get rid of all of those horrible monsters that were terrorizing the town I grew up in, but it was so damn complicated. Every now and then, I'd get a burst of inspiration to do something about the problem, but then I'd crumble once I realized how difficult it would actually be.

This made me a very bitter person. I could fake being normal and even upbeat around people, and maybe sometimes I genuinely felt that way. But beneath the surface, I was a very dark and angry boy, someone who raged against the world around him and hated everything. Even so, I made some friends, but I never felt all that close to any of them.

That was the case with Melody, a girl who sat behind me in History class. She was fun, even though she wasn't traditionally beautiful like Elizabeth. She had an odd look to her, sort of a big nose and short hair that was cut in a strange style. I wouldn't exactly have classified her as a punk, but she did seem to have some leanings in that direction. She preferred to describe her style as "alternative."

I could make her laugh pretty often, but really, I wasn't as much of a cut-up as the other kids in that class were. For some reason, the class had a disproportionate amount of delinquents in it, and it was an almost daily occurrence that someone got sent to the vice-principal's office for misbehaving or being excessively rude to our teacher, Mrs. Eldridge. Nearly all of us disliked her and thought she was rather stupid, so it was not uncommon for the more badly behaved among us to come up with new ways to be mean to her.

Derek had this really cool move he could do where, when Mrs. Eldridge was writing on the board and had her back to the class, he could hop up in his desk, sling a piece of chalk — which he'd pilfered earlier at the beginning of class — very quickly at the board, then slip back into his chair. Mrs. Eldridge, startled by the impact from the chalk, would have no idea where it had come from, and by the time she turned around, Derek was looking innocent like he had no idea what was going on. We all thought it was funny, and no one pointed a finger to give him away.

The same solidarity was displayed when Brad, another delinquent with shaggy blond hair, brought a small spray bottle to class and began squirting it at the board from his desk on the front row. Somehow, he managed to keep it concealed from the teacher, but he made sure that the rest of us could see it so he'd get all the laughs. Yet another prank, one that played out over the course of a few weeks, involved a guy named Mitch secretly trying to poison and kill the fern she had hanging by the window.

I wasn't really into trying any of these physical jokes myself, but I did appreciate the humor in them. My defiance was more verbal, and like everyone else, I wasn't afraid to smart off to Mrs. Eldridge if I felt she deserved it. She didn't take kindly to my rudely correcting her on the pronunciation of the name "Trafalgar," which she said as *"traffle-gar."* And when she tried to deter the class from their various pranks and warned, "I'm keeping my eye on you," I stole an old joke from Dennis when we'd been at school together, jumping up and brushing at my clothing as if she'd meant that she'd actually put an eyeball on me. That had gotten some laughs, too, including from Melody, who later joked by acting like she'd taken out her own eyeball and was putting it on my sleeve.

I had to ramp things up a notch on a Tuesday morning when we were forced to sit through a horrible musical about the signing of the Declaration of Independence. We'd started the movie the day before, and it was excruciating. Usually, when a teacher had a TV and VCR set up in front of the class, that was a good thing, and everyone looked forward to a day or two of not doing any real work.

But this musical, *1776,* was the corniest, dumbest, most obnoxious thing any of us had ever seen. I'd never been keen on musicals anyway, though I had liked *The Wizard of Oz* when I was little. But that was part of the problem: This film seemed so juvenile and goofy, not the kind of thing you'd show to a room full of sarcastic teenagers. It felt like torture; we were way too cool for this.

However, it just so happened that the VCR on the cart was the same brand as one of the ones we had at home. So on Tuesday, I brought the remote control for it with me to try to bring some relief to my suffering classmates. A couple of minutes in, I surreptitiously pulled out the remote and, keeping it hidden from view, used it to turn off the player. The harsh sound of TV static that followed was only slightly less jarring than the cheesy song the actors had begun to belt out.

Mrs. Eldridge got up from her desk and walked to the front of the classroom, confused but undeterred. She turned the VCR back on, then started playing the tape again. A minute or two later, I repeated my move, forcing her to get up again. The class was loving it, but I wasn't letting on to any of them that I was the one responsible. Melody knew, though, as I'd told her before class that I was going to do something about what she called "so much cheese that I just might die from a heart attack." This second time, I felt a little poke in my back from her pencil's eraser, her way of letting me know that she was on to me.

The third time, I timed things so that when Mrs. Eldridge approached the VCR and was about to turn it on again, I ejected the tape, which spat out at her and startled her. Other people gasped, too, but then started cracking up.

"Ohhh, shit! That thing's haunted!" Derek declared, prompting more laughs.

One more attempt was made to resume the movie, and just to draw things out, I allowed it to play for a few more minutes before ejecting the tape again. Melody poked me with her pencil again, giggling.

Outside the classroom, Melody stopped me, laughing about what had happened. "I about peed myself when the tape popped out the first time!" she said. "How did you...?"

I slung my backpack around, still keeping its strap on my arm, and I unzipped it. She leaned in, and I pulled back the flap, showing her the remote. She giggled again, shaking her head. "Oh my God," she said. "You're evil, Ray!"

I wasn't sure how I felt about that. I knew she meant it as a cool thing, but something about that word bothered me.

"Evil, I'm telling you, evil!" she called out as she walked away, off to her next class.

To make matters worse, Eileen happened to be walking by at that moment, hearing what Melody had said. She stood still and looked at me blankly, then kept going. I just stared at her, the mere sight of her making me feel guilty. I also noticed that she wasn't wearing her necklace with the cross on it anymore.

The following morning before class, Melody invited me to hang out with her and some of her friends at a club I'd never been to before. It was simply called The Joint, and it had recently moved from its previous location downtown to somewhere west of the city, probably because that was a safer location. Local bands played there on the weekends, and Melody was planning on going there this Friday night.

"Sure, I guess," I said. "You'll have to give me directions, though. You want me to meet you there?"

"No, you can pick me up," she said. "I'll even let you pay for me to get in," she added with a twinkle in her eye. It was only then that I realized that she was asking me out. I was also slowly realizing how attractive she was, which I hadn't thought of before. But she was, just in a weird way. She was definitely a lot prettier when she smiled, which she was doing now.

"Oh, okay," I said, trying to play it cool. "Well, in that case, I'll need directions to your house, too."

She let out a short *"hee"* sound as she gave me a sweet look, then took out a piece of paper and began drawing crude maps.

Part of me was excited, but an even bigger part was uncertain. I hadn't heard from Elizabeth for a few days, but I was still pining for her, especially because of what had happened between us. I'd also been sore for a couple of days after that encounter, my body not used to the physical rigors of sex. Still, it wasn't an entirely unwelcome sensation, as the pain served to remind me of what I'd done. Even though it had been weird, I still missed it and hoped to do it again, hopefully under better circumstances.

Mike had even noticed on Monday morning that I let out a slight groan when I sat down at my desk, and he asked me what was wrong. When I said I was just sore, he got a big grin on his face and asked knowingly, "From what?" I didn't answer and just shot him a look, but apparently, that was enough for him. "Ah, I thought so. Good for you, man."

"Thanks," I said weakly, not really meaning it.

"I got some this weekend, too," he said more softly. "And no, Mary's still playing the virgin card. Don't say anything."

"I won't," I said, feeling contempt for him. And then later that day in Chemistry, Mary Dunn tried to give me some crap over something I'd said earlier to our teacher, and I had to hold back from saying something along the lines of, *Well, you're the one who has no idea that your boyfriend is screwing around on you.* But I didn't; I just ignored her. As much as I disapproved of Mike's actions, his secret wasn't mine to tell.

But as far as Melody was concerned, I wasn't sure if I really wanted to go out with her or even how serious of a date this might be. It was nice that this interesting girl had apparently taken a liking to me, but at the same time, I was still hung up on Elizabeth, and I didn't know where we stood. When we'd had sex, I thought that might have meant that she'd changed her mind on whether or not we could be "boyfriend/girlfriend," as some people put it, but the way she acted when we talked at my window made me second guess that. For all I knew, she might wind up avoiding me after all, a thought I hated. It also made me resent her a little.

The conclusion I came to was that I might as well go out with Melody at least this once, seeing where it went, if anywhere. She wasn't exactly my type of girl, but I liked her well enough. And if Elizabeth was going to shun me, well, why not?

I tried not to be nervous about our date, but I still was to some extent. The fact that I wasn't all that into her helped, but at the same time, I did kind of want to impress her. I wasn't used to her lifestyle, her weird clothes and all, but I did find it intriguing. She always wore strange clothes at school, but this night, she was even more decked out, her long, cut-off denim shorts covering tights with a funky, swirling pattern on them, leading down to big, black boots that she'd told me were called Doc Martens. It occurred to me more than once that she might be a better fit for someone like Nick, or maybe Dennis, who was more into the hippie side of things than the punk one.

We found our way to The Joint, and even from the outside, the place seemed intimidating. It was a large warehouse somewhere on the outskirts of town, and I could hear loud music thumping away, muffled by the walls but not entirely. There were lots of people around, some my age and some older, probably college students, and I started to feel somewhat small and uncomfortable. I didn't want to let that on to Melody, so I just pretended that I was okay with everything.

We passed by a couple of guys who were smoking cigarettes as we approached the entrance, and when I gave one of them a friendly nod, he just glared at me. I was surprised when a man at the door asked to see our IDs, but I went along with it, acting like I was used to such a thing. Once inside, the sound was deafening, and I had to shout to ask Melody, "What's that all about?"

She turned and put her mouth close to my ear, shouting back, "They don't let anyone under sixteen in. There's no drinking allowed officially, but they're not really strict about it. You can get a beer from one of the guys around back if you want. They sell them out of their car."

I pulled back, giving her a surprised look.

"You want one?" she asked me, though I barely heard her; I was mostly reading her lips.

I shook my head, saying, "Nah. I'm all right."

"Well, I do," she said, but then she was interrupted by someone who ran up and almost collided with her, a girl with very long black hair.

She laughed as she said "Heyyyy" to her, also shouting over the din of the music, if you could call it that. Glancing over at the stage at the far end of the club, I saw the band, whom the large, handwritten signs at the door had announced was called The Futile System. Guitars and drums thrashed chaotically as the singer shouted and grunted unintelligible lyrics into his microphone, and while the majority of the crowd simply milled around or stood still facing the stage, I could see that closer to it, there was this frenzy of activity as twenty or so young people scampered around, bumping into each other violently.

"This is Jade," Melody shouted to me, holding the new girl's hand as she pulled her closer to us. "One of the people I told you about."

"Hey!" she repeated, waving at me with her free hand. She seemed rather out of it, but I couldn't help but notice that she was extremely beautiful. She had a similar style of dress to Melody's, but her face and hair were much prettier, even with the black lipstick she was wearing, something I'd never been that fond of. Still, like Melody, she was interesting. While Melody had short, cropped hair that was dyed black, Jade's was long and straight, almost down to her butt, and there were blonde streaks dyed into it on either side of her face.

She pulled Melody by the hand as she began walking, so I followed, and we were led past a makeshift partition that spanned most of the width of the warehouse. In the middle of it was a large gap, and beyond it, there were several chairs, tables, and even couches scattered about. Jade, who was walking kind of strangely, plopped herself and Melody down onto a couch just around the corner from the gap, and I immediately noticed the change in sound. The roar from the amps was blocked by the wall, so it was finally possible to have an actual conversation.

Sitting down next to them, I tried to keep up as Jade rambled to Melody about all the things she'd been dying to tell her, as she put it. Melody interrupted her early on, though, by putting up a hand and indicating to her that she needed to stop. "This is Ray, by the way," she said to her, nodding towards me.

"Oh," Jade said, seeming to remember her surroundings. "Hi, Ray!" She held her hand out to me, expecting a handshake, so I obliged. The skin on her fingers felt so soft.

"He's in the same homeroom as Mike," Melody added, and there was something meaningful in her tone.

"Oh!" Jade said as she pulled back her hand and leaned backwards onto the couch. "Really?"

"Yeah. You know him?"

"Well, we fuck sometimes, but that's about it."

I tried to hide my shock, realizing who she was. It was one thing to know that Mike had a "mistress," but actually meeting her wasn't something I expected to happen. Still, Augusta always had that weird way of interconnecting people. "Do you go to Westlake?" I asked her. "I haven't seen you around."

"No, I'm at Copeland." That was another school in town, apparently Westlake's main rival in football games, but I didn't care much about that. I had tried to take some interest in it initially, particularly when one of the cheerleaders in my Computer class sold me what she called a spirit ribbon. I thought she and I might become friends, but things never went beyond anything superficial, and I quickly lost interest in her.

At first, though, I was reminded of how Susanna had been a cheerleader, and I wondered if she'd also gone around selling these things, which apparently helped fund the cheerleading squad. I hadn't understood much of what cheerleading was all about back then, but as I got to know some of these girls at Westlake, I found a lot of them to be kind of vacant and stupid, plus some had reputations for being promiscuous. But not all; a few of them seemed genuinely nice.

Melody, meanwhile, had a great deal of contempt for all of them, plus she disliked the jocks whom they tended to hang around with. She called them conformists, usually almost spitting out the word as she said it.

"So," I asked Jade, "do you know a guy at your school named Nick Davies?"

"Nick?" she asked, sounding surprised. "Yeah. He's a prick." I laughed, surprised by her brutal assessment of him, which wasn't entirely wrong. "He's here, somewhere," she said, leaning forward and looking around.

That made me uneasy; I wasn't sure if I wanted to run into him. I started to ask her if she also knew Dennis, but we were interrupted by a big guy with short, almost shaved hair.

"There you are!" he almost shouted, speaking to Jade. He was holding two red plastic cups, one of which was sloshing its contents onto his hand. "Got this for you." As he handed her the cup, he sat down on a small ottoman that was positioned in front of the couch.

"Thanks," she said, then drank. She made a face, exhaling sharply and shaking her head rapidly. As she did, her long, dark hair flowed back and forth, almost hypnotic in the way the light shone on it. "What's in this?" she asked.

"Just drink," the guy said.

"Hey, I want to have some!" Melody chimed in, leaning over onto Jade and grabbing the cup. She sipped from it, then made a similar face. "Whew! That *is* strong. Vodka?"

"Yeah, but not straight," the guy said.

Melody turned to me. "You wanna try?"

"Nah, that's okay. Not really my thing."

I worried that she might think badly of me, but she just shrugged and said, "Nothing wrong with that. Either do it or you don't, and not because someone else tells you to."

I liked that; it seemed in line with her desire to be a nonconformist. Growing up, I'd been forced to sit through countless lectures and presentations about peer pressure and the dangers of people pushing drugs and alcohol onto innocent children. But I'd never experienced that, not once. No one had ever forced me to drink, and it wasn't like Dennis or anyone else had ever shoved a cigarette into my mouth and lit it, insisting that I get addicted to their habit. People were a lot more laid back than teachers and the media tried to lead us to believe.

Often, I'd hear stories from people at school about the wild parties they'd been to over the weekend. Mondays tended to be a time for these partiers to trade tales of their drunkenness, which they were quite proud of. I didn't object to it on moral grounds exactly, but I did find it kind of stupid the way that some of them would go on and on about it, sometimes even bragging about how they'd gotten so trashed that they couldn't even remember what they'd done. Several of the boys and girls in my History class would say things like that, probably thinking it was impressive. And maybe it was to them, but my take on it was that it seemed pretty pointless to supposedly have such a good time but then not be able to remember it.

Melody had been enlisted by Jade to help her finish her drink; it was too much for her to handle on her own. After that, the guy — whose name I was never told, by the way — led us back to the noisy section of the club and to the front of the crowd, where "the pit" was, the area where all the kids were doing their slam dancing. It looked kind of fun but mostly dangerous, the way everyone was sort of running in a big, rotating mass, bumping into each other roughly.

Jade and the guy, who may or may not have been her boyfriend, joined the crowd, but Melody refused. There happened to be a break in songs at that point, so I was able to actually hear what she was saying as she shouted into my ear about how she'd gotten hurt in the pit one time over the summer, so she preferred to just watch. As she spoke, her lips grazed my ear a few times, and I really liked the sensation. Since she'd had that drink, she'd become more physical with me, often grabbing onto the sleeves of my jacket as we interacted. I didn't mind.

As the music went on, we watched the spinning teenagers as they went, and occasionally, I caught a glimpse of Jade and the other guy. The whole process looked exhausting, but I could also imagine myself in the middle of it, slamming up against everyone. In time, I could see the appeal, a way to let out lots of pent up rage and hostility. But given my much more violent past, this kind of seemed manufactured to me, even trite.

Not long before Melody suggested going outside for some fresh air, I caught sight of Jade again, fumbling her way through the mass. There was something about her, and not just the fact that she was pretty. I kept thinking that she reminded me of someone, and it had been bugging me all night. Finally, it clicked, but I was disturbed by the revelation.

Her long dark hair, even the shape of her face, made her look an awful lot like the very last girl that I'd killed back in 1987, the one with the dimple in her cheek. I'd never forgotten her, and I would even dream about her sometimes. In a sense, she represented every person I'd ever killed, the final one, and I always felt guilty whenever I remembered her. I sometimes wondered who she might have been, what she was like, whose life I'd extinguished. That could have applied to any of my countless victims over the years, but for some reason, my mind tended to fixate on her. I hated it when that happened.

It felt a lot better out back; inside had been stuffy and hot. While some people had been smoking inside, there were more of them out here, and I tried not to stare once I realized I'd been doing it. It just wasn't something I was used to seeing people my age do, even though I knew it went on.

My ears were ringing, and as Melody and I talked, I found myself shouting, not knowing I was doing it at first. She asked if I was having a good time, and I said I was, but honestly, I felt out of my element. It was more like the evening was interesting rather than it actually being fun.

I did like the smiles I kept getting from Melody, drunken though they were. She tended to sway back and forth a lot, rotating her body, like she was trying to shake something off. When she said that she needed to get something to drink, I thought she meant more alcohol, but she instead led me back inside to the bar, which only served soft drinks.

There, she talked briefly to yet another girl with dyed black hair, this time pulled back into a ponytail. Like Jade, she had that gothic, pale look to her, and she seemed nice enough, though she and I never spoke to each other. When Melody and I began heading for the back door, I asked her who the girl was, and I thought she said her name was Nicholas. That sounded like a strange name for a girl, and then I wondered if maybe she was actually one of those gay guys who liked to dress up as women. She certainly didn't look like a guy, though.

Back outside, we drank our Cokes from plastic cups like the ones Jade and that guy's drinks had been in, and that helped me feel a lot better. I hadn't even realized how thirsty I was until that point.

"Ooh, wait," Melody said suddenly after quickly forcing down a swallow. "I want to show you a trick I learned."

"What?"

"Just go with it." She appeared to drink from her cup again, but then I saw that she'd taken one of the ice cubes into her mouth. Setting the cup onto a chair that was against the warehouse's outer wall, she began chewing the ice. Once she was done, she swallowed. "Come here."

Surprised, I dropped my cup onto the grass as she grabbed my head and pulled me to her, kissing me. For a split second, I was glad that this had happened, but then I felt the coldness of her tongue as it pushed into my mouth and worked its way around. It felt almost exactly the way Elizabeth's tongue had felt when she kissed me without having fed, a cold, dead vampire forcing herself onto me.

Shocked, I pushed back from her, breaking the embrace. I immediately regretted doing so, afraid that I might have offended her. But instead, she just laughed.

"Feels kinda creepy, doesn't it?" she said.

"Yeah, it does," I said, out of breath.

"Here, you try." She turned and reached into her cup, pulling out another ice cube. She then placed it into my mouth, and I chewed it while she looked on expectantly.

I'd barely swallowed it before she zoomed in and frenched me again. This time, her tongue felt warm like it was supposed to, and mine felt slightly numb. When we stopped, she shuddered comically, letting out one of her high-pitched giggles. "Bleh!" she exclaimed, seeming disgusted.

"That's not something a guy likes to hear after he's just kissed a girl!" I said, faking offense.

Melody turned back to me, feigning concern. "Aw, did I hurt your feelings?" She took both of my hands in hers and lifted them away from my sides.

"Yes. I'm heartbroken."

She grinned, then began kissing me again. Our mouths' temperatures had gone back to normal, and we were finally free to make out normally. This went on for close to a minute, and then some guy walked past us and said, "Jeez, Kubiak, let the poor guy up for air sometime!"

He was addressing Melody by her last name, something she apparently didn't appreciate. With her lips still pressed to mine, I opened my eyes and saw that she'd taken her right arm away from my back to flash her middle finger at the passing boy, whom I didn't recognize. I let out a small laugh, which was a weird feeling given that I was basically laughing into another person's mouth. She didn't let up, though, and I thought that if I wound up suffocating, at least it would be a good way to go.

Although we hadn't officially designated ourselves as a couple, we still had fun hanging out together. The following night, we rode out to Clarks Hill Lake with some other friends of hers, some of whom were beyond high school age. While some of them had moved on, the connection they'd all had at one point had been that they worked at Dairy Queen, the same one that Eileen and I went to the night of our first date. For all I knew, some of them may have been there that night, but if so, I didn't remember any of them.

It was revealed during the long drive out of the city that Melody had a huge love for fireworks, which were illegal in Georgia but easily obtainable just across the Savannah River, which marked the border between our state and South Carolina. She'd gotten Pat, one of the guys who still worked at Dairy Queen, to pick some up for us before we'd met up.

It felt strange to be going to the lake on a November night; traditionally, it was a place that people went to in the summer. But that, I discovered, was mostly the point. The site we went to was in fact supposed to be closed for the season, but it was simple enough to bypass the gate on foot and walk to the campground. There, we would hang around and joke, having a good time. Even though what we were doing was forbidden and in some ways illegal — including the fact that some of the guys brought beer to drink — to me it felt almost quaint in comparison to the horrible things my friends and I had done in the past.

I did feel kind of outclassed by these older friends of Melody's, though, particularly when I learned that she'd dated at least one of them. Ryan, a senior from Copeland whom she'd met through Jade, even called her a "serial dater," and I was annoyed when his girlfriend referred to me as Melody's "latest victim." They were an interesting bunch, but I found that I enjoyed myself a lot more when Melody and I broke off from the group and went for a walk along the shore of the lake. Watching her combination of delight and terror as she lit fireworks, then went running for shelter in case something went wrong, was particularly fun.

Being with her made me see Eileen as pretty boring by comparison. I didn't have that many bad feelings towards her, but I found that it was easier for me to realize just which things about her I hadn't liked, even though I wouldn't have admitted them at the time. It also helped to focus on those things rather than the guilt I felt over cheating on her and leaving her. And since she probably believed that the reason I'd left her was because she didn't want to have sex, well, maybe that helped her hate me and get over me, too.

Monday morning, I'd been looking forward to telling Mike that I'd met Jade, thinking that it might surprise him. But he reacted with his usual relaxed attitude.

"Yeah, I know. She said you were kinda rude to her that night."

I didn't know what he was talking about; I thought we'd gotten along rather well. In fact, I'd wanted to say bye to her and her friend from the pit before Melody and I had taken off that night, but for some reason, she'd wanted to leave without saying goodbye. Maybe that's what Jade was referring to. I was also disappointed when Melody didn't invite her to join us out at the lake the following night, but I tried not to show it, also not wanting to let on to the fact that I actually found Jade more attractive than her, at least physically.

After I expressed my confusion over what Jade had said, Mike told me not to worry about it. "She was pretty blitzed that night anyway, from what I heard. By the time I talked to her, she might have gotten you mixed up with someone else. She gets like that a lot." He paused, looking thoughtful. "Reminds me," he said more quietly, "I need to remember to get some more weed from her before this weekend."

Finding out that she was a drug dealer probably should have been a turn-off, but it wasn't really. The more I was getting to know these juvenile delinquents, the more normal my life felt. These were kids who were doing things they weren't supposed to do, but in a much more mundane way when compared to my dark past. This was how teenagers were supposed to misbehave, being stupid and getting drunk, not going around murdering people. Maybe if I delved more into this lifestyle and learned how to have fun with it, I could have a more regular life. But of course, that wasn't what fate had in store for me.

CHAPTER SIXTEEN

"Well, aren't you just the little stud," Elizabeth said, smiling at me smartly.

"Oh, shut up," I said, feeling a weird mixture of embarrassment and pride. In a sense, she was right. I'd gone from being a shy kid who was too scared to talk to the girl I liked to someone who, in less than three months at my new school, had managed to rack up two girlfriends, three if I counted Elizabeth. She may not have been on board with that idea, but sometimes I thought of it like that anyway.

"And don't feed on her," I added pointedly. "I mean it."

"I won't," she said, sounding impatient. Then she nodded her head quickly, seeing how serious I was. "Really, I won't. I promise. It was wrong of me to do that before, and it would be wrong now, too."

"Thank you," I said, suddenly feeling like a parent scolding a misbehaving child.

"But maybe you shouldn't be going around kissing other girls when you've got a girlfriend," she said, raising her eyebrows at me.

That had happened when I'd greeted her earlier this night, overjoyed that she'd shown up at my window and invited me out to join her. I'd been so glad to see her again, knowing that she hadn't decided to cut me out of her life like I'd feared.

"I know," I said guiltily. "But… I don't even know if Melody and I are really… what do they call it… exclusive. She gets kinda vague when the topic comes up. And my parents haven't even met her; she gets all weird about the idea of that, too."

I was more uncomfortable with this than I wanted to reveal, not so much due to anything to do with Elizabeth but because of my own insecurity. I liked knowing where I stood with a girl, official statuses and such. On TV, even if a boy and a girl had been fighting for the first ninety percent of an episode, once they kissed, that meant they were together. If things changed later to where they were "seeing other people," that just meant that they'd broken up. I'd wanted life to be that simple, that black and white, not with these nebulous pseudo-relationships I kept finding myself in.

It seemed like half the songs on Top 40 radio were all about winning someone's heart or loving them forever. Or if you'd just broken up with someone and were miserable, there were plenty of songs that could be a soundtrack for that, too. There weren't any songs that said, *I love you but can't really date you because you're a vampire,* nor had I heard any with lyrics like *We had sex last weekend but haven't said "I love you" to each other yet, and I'm still not sure if this is an exclusive thing or how seriously I should be taking all of this.*

That was where Melody and I stood at the moment, though I decided not to share that particular detail with Elizabeth. We'd had sex at her house while her parents were away, and I liked it, particularly the difference in warmth from how Elizabeth had felt. It was also nice to have a girl climax and not immediately run out of the room, but I knew that thinking like that was unfair. Elizabeth hadn't done that out of anything other than trying to keep me safe. Then again, it was also nice to be intimate with a girl who wasn't one feeding away from threatening to kill me.

One thing I did feel weird about and wouldn't admit to anyone was how my own orgasm had come about that night. As we'd been getting to know each other, Melody had mentioned being interested in sadomasochism, which I had only vaguely heard about. She'd even said she liked to be tied up during sex, but I didn't like that idea because it reminded me of that dream I'd had about Elizabeth tying up a girl and killing her. I also couldn't see what the turn-on could be, being restrained like that; it would just make me feel vulnerable and unsafe.

When we were going at it, though, Melody instructed me between gasps to hold her wrists down, pinning her to the bed. She seemed to like it and became more animated, so I played along. It was then that I began to see the appeal; there was something powerful in the notion that she was at my mercy, even if it was mostly pretend. Not long after she'd come, I was beginning to feel exhausted from all the effort, and my head was drooping onto her shoulder. Her neck was right there, slick with salty sweat, and I kissed it, running my tongue over her flesh.

Just for a moment, I imagined what it would be like to bite into her neck, to taste her blood the same way I'd done with my victims in the past. I had no wish to actually harm her, but the image flashed through my head, coupled with wondering if her blood would be as salty as her sweat. That, in addition to all of the physical sensations that were overwhelming me, pushed me over the edge. When I thought about it after the fact, I felt disgusted with myself.

Tim wasn't thrilled with life, either. I'd been meaning to call him ever since my encounter with his clone, but the rest of my life had gotten so busy. By the time I had decided to set aside an evening to call him, he wound up calling me instead.

He really didn't like hearing about what his clone had done, and I kicked myself almost as soon as the words came out of my mouth, describing the way he'd brutally murdered that girl right in front of me. I left out the fact that Elizabeth had been with me, but the story made almost as much sense without her. But while I had been thinking about how shocking and scary that had been for me, it hadn't occurred to me how much the story would upset Tim.

"Sorry," I said to him over the phone. I changed the subject slightly by telling him about the cops and how they'd taken my stake, how that had left me worried.

"Why? You made another one, didn't you?"

"Sure, of course I did. The very next day. But that's not the point. They had my stake. With my fingerprints on it! What if they traced them or something, then showed up at my house? I mean, it's been long enough now that I figure they aren't going to, but…"

"That wouldn't happen," he said. "They'd only have your fingerprints if you'd committed a crime before and they had them on file."

That was reassuring, but then something else occurred to me. "But I have committed a crime," I said gloomily, "many times over."

He sighed. "You and me both. They didn't take down your license plate number, did they?"

"No. There wasn't time. Not before… Well, not before they ran off."

"Then you're safe. We're all safe. No one's going to catch us. Just like always." He sounded exceedingly bitter, more than I'd ever heard him be.

"Yeah," was all I could think to say. I listened to him breathe, trying to come up with something else. "Don't suppose you've gotten a girlfriend or anything, have you?"

"A girlfriend? No. I don't have time for crap like that. I don't think I really deserve one, either."

"Oh, come on, Tim," I said. "Don't talk like that. Maybe it would be a good thing for you, you know, have someone to take your mind off things. There's this girl in my Chemistry class named Kirsten who I think kinda might be your type." I started to regret my words, realizing that if he were to ask why, I'd have to say that it was because she was extremely nerdy, all pale and with glasses, and not very popular. She wasn't exactly ugly, though, and it had occurred to me as I'd gotten to know her that maybe Tim would like a girl like her, someone as smart and studious as him.

"No thanks," he said.

"Fine," I said, then repeated the word less harshly. Trying to salvage the conversation, I brought up another topic: "So, Mom tells me that your mom's pregnant?"

"Hmm? Yeah. She is. That's going to be weird, having a little brother or sister who's so much younger than me. I might as well be a third parent to it."

I laughed nervously, but I was glad to hear that his tone had started to brighten. "When's she due?"

"When does she do what?"

"When is she *due,*" I repeated more clearly. "To give birth."

"I know," he said, laughing slightly. "Just messing with you. Next month. Pretty close to Christmas, actually."

"Ah," I said knowingly. "Poor kid. Probably going to have his birthday mashed up with Christmas every year."

"Yeah, probably. Glad we never had to deal with that." His birthday was a little over a month before mine. "Look, I should probably get going."

"Oh. Okay. But look, you wanna hang out sometime? Maybe this weekend? I haven't seen you in forever. And maybe we could, you know, go do some vampire hunting again. Like, try to do something about all the... Well, you know."

"I don't know about that," he said. "But maybe you're right. I do feel sometimes like I should be doing more than just sitting around feeling guilty about everything. But it's just so frustrating. I keep wanting to do the right thing, but then I don't even know where to start. And I get... well, scared."

I sighed sympathetically. "I know the feeling, man. Well, even if we don't go out and do all that, maybe you could at least hang out and meet my new girlfriend."

"You've got a girlfriend?"

"Yeah! You don't have to sound so surprised."

He laughed. "Well, aren't you a stud." It weirded me out to hear him echo Elizabeth's recent words so closely, but then, he was psychic like me, so maybe he'd just picked up my thoughts. "Sure, maybe."

I told him I'd give him a call in a day or two; I needed to check with Melody to find out what, if anything, she had planned for the coming weekend. I also began to wonder if inviting him out with us was a good idea or not. She might not like him, given that he was kind of geeky. Or maybe her alternative, nonconformist nature also dictated that it was okay to hang out with nerds, too. They certainly weren't as mainstream as the popular people were.

When I asked Melody about it, she did have some plans, but those were for Friday, and she wasn't sure about the rest of the weekend. I'd thought she meant Friday night, but she was actually talking about during the day. I'd known about her cutting school in the past, and this particular time, she and Jade were planning to go to the mall to do some shopping.

"Maybe even some shop*lifting,*" she added in a sly whisper. She let out a giggle when she saw my reaction. Her laugh was a little on the obnoxious side, just a bit too loud. I had no idea how long she and I might last as a couple (or even a pseudo-couple), but I sometimes wondered if there would come a time when that laugh would get on my nerves too much.

And really, the thought of things ending with her didn't upset me terribly. Part of me almost expected it. Breaking up with Eileen had been heartbreaking for me, and I hated hurting her the way I had. But if things didn't work out with Melody, I told myself that I probably wouldn't lose too much sleep over it. She was fun, and I liked the affection between us, but I still wasn't sure how good of a fit we were.

Her overtly contrarian manner of dressing, for one thing, struck me as kind of pretentious. While she claimed to despise all the preppy, well accepted kids who were obsessed with fashion and the latest trends, it also seemed like she was just as bad, only with a different kind of fashion. And she had plenty of friends — even if they were scattered among various schools — who tended to dress the same way, so didn't that make them their own little clique?

Nevertheless, when she invited me to skip school with her and join them on Friday, I agreed. "Maybe your friend Tim would like to come, too? You think Jade would like him?"

I laughed. "No, I don't really think they're the same type. He's… well, kind of a goody-goody. He sometimes goes off on these God-related tangents. Feels all guilty." Then I hurriedly added, "About things."

"You don't seem to be able to get away from people like that, do you?" she asked, recalling my horror stories about my previous school. I later thought that she might have been making a dig at Eileen as well, but if she had been, I missed it at the time. "Is his family Catholic?"

"Hmm? No, no. He told me once that they used to be, but then they became Episcopalian."

"Oh, 'Catholic Lite,'" she said with a smile. Seeing my confused look, she explained how Episcopalians were a lot like Catholics, but less rigid.

"Oh. And what are you?"

"Catholic!" She laughed again. "Well, not exactly. My parents are a lot more into it than I am. My mom especially tries to make me feel all guilty for not being all… you know. But that's a big thing with Catholics: guilt. That's why I don't like it."

I then repeated a joke I'd heard a comedian tell in which he lampooned the Catholic practice of confession, saying that it didn't matter what bad thing you did as long as you told somebody about it.

"Yeah, yeah, yeah," she said. "I'm not all that big on bashing Christianity, either. Not like you do."

"I'm not bashing it! You try being tortured by holy rollers for three years and see how you like it!" We were fighting, but playfully, like we often did. Sometimes we would go too far, but this wasn't one of those times.

"Uh oh!" a voice called out from across the room. "Some trouble in paradise!"

"Fuck off and die, Derek!" Melody said, mimicking his tone.

He just laughed in response. "Man, that girl's got some balls, I tell ya. Girl got balls." She gave him a pretend angry look, and I laughed, too.

The plan had been that I would meet up with Melody in the parking lot of a shopping center that was not far from our school, so I was annoyed when she didn't arrive. It wasn't the first time she'd stood me up, either.

There had been a night the previous weekend when she was supposed to come over to my house, but she didn't show up when she said she would. I called her about an hour later, and her father answered the phone, telling me she'd fallen asleep. I started to ask him if he could wake her up for me, but the impatience in his voice made me think better of it. I still hadn't met him, just as Melody had never met my parents, but she'd told me stories about how much of an asshole he was, how he was usually pretty quiet but could fly off the handle at a moment's notice. Apparently, this had something to do with him being a Vietnam veteran.

She did call me back about an hour after that, groggy and apologetic, offering to come over then. But it was already too late for me to go out. I was ticked off at her, but I tried not to be too mean about it.

She had mentioned at school on Thursday that something could end up going wrong, that maybe Jade wouldn't be able to make it. Their escapades didn't always go as planned. I wasn't clear on the details and just hoped that things would be okay. But at the same time, I was a little nervous and started to hope that maybe plans would fall through after all. I'd never cut school before or even skipped a class, and while the idea of being bad like that appealed to me, there was another part of me that squirmed a bit.

Also, I wasn't above hanging out at the mall and looking around at stuff, but the notion of premeditated stealing did feel a little weird to me. I had shoplifted before myself, but that had been a spur of the moment thing. Would I be able to pull it off if I went in there with the intention of doing it? Maybe I could just keep an eye out for any security while my two lovely accomplices pulled off their scheme. But what if we got caught, even arrested? Would the police somehow end up connecting me to my past crimes?

But all of this became a moot point, Melody's failure to show up striking me as another example of her being flaky and unreliable. In a lot of ways, I liked her being something of a misfit and a troublemaker, but when I found myself on the receiving end of that, it wasn't nearly as much fun. Defeated, I went into class late, having to accept a tardy.

"Come on," Melody said to me, her voice pleading for forgiveness. "I said I was sorry. I promise I'll make it up to you."

We were standing outside by the curb in front of my house that night, her black 1985 Camaro parked and still warm on the hood from being recently driven. I had my arms folded, still angry with her. But it was hard to keep that up when she looked so alluring, the pale blue glow from the nearby streetlight catching her face.

"I had to get bitched at by Mrs. Eldridge for coming in late," I said.

"Oh, I'm sure you survived," she said dismissively, but she was still her usual playful self. There was something in that smile of hers and the way her somewhat slender eyes matched it that always got me.

"So Jade couldn't make it?" I asked, reiterating what she'd already told me.

"No, something came up," she said vaguely.

"*What* something came up?"

She grinned at me conspiratorially. "Come out with me and I'll tell you. Go on, tell your parents you're going out. I'll wait."

I'd noticed something strange over the past few months, which I'd mentioned to Melody. I didn't go out with friends all that often until the eleventh grade, but once I'd started attending Westlake, it had become a more regular thing. Something happened, which I didn't notice at first, where it had gone from my asking my mother if I could go out with my friends — and saying where we were going, even though sometimes that was a lie — to simply telling her. "Can I go out to…" became "I'm going out to…" almost imperceptibly, maybe because I got used to her always saying yes. She never objected, only said at the end of each exchange: "Be careful." I had no idea how concerned she was about the vampire threat in Augusta; we'd never talked about it, and I certainly wasn't going to bring it up.

So I rode along in Melody's car, not for the first time. It struck me as a little odd that someone who was so insistent on being nonconformist drove the same model car that a lot of the guys I knew saw as really cool and bad-ass, especially the rednecky guys back at Bethlehem. But then again, I'd found myself involuntarily put into a 1989 Mustang by my father, so maybe the same thing had happened to her. I'd never asked, maybe because I also liked the car and thought it looked cooler than mine.

"So where are we going?" I asked.

"To Jade's," she said, not looking away from the road, her left hand resting lazily on the gearshift.

"Oh. So… She couldn't make it out for a day of shoplifting, but now we're going over to her house?" Melody nodded, again not looking over at me. I felt an urge to reach over and hold her hand, but then she gripped the gearshift, shoving it around and making the car go faster. The engine revved impressively, and I felt myself being pushed back into the passenger seat.

"Where's she live?" I asked once the noise of the engine died down.

"Not too far," she said, a lilting, comforting tone in her voice. "It's maybe halfway between your house and Copeland."

"Okay then," I said.

"So Ray," she said, slightly pointedly, "you ever been in a three-way?"

"A what?"

"You. Sexually. With two girls at once. I'm going to go ahead and guess not."

My heart skipped a beat, and I tried not to let on how surprised I was. "No! No. Not that I haven't…" I caught myself, not wanting to say too much. In that old porno magazine I'd borrowed from Dennis, the most erotic section of it for me had been this part where these two overly made-up women, in carefully posed photos, acted out a scenario in which their cars had run into each other, and then they started making out. It was all very staged and fake, the two models feigning indignity but then going at it. Even though the story was told in still pictures, I could tell that it was badly acted, but I also couldn't help but get aroused when I thumbed through those pages. At my young age, I thought that I'd come up with an original fantasy that no one else ever had: *I'd love to get in the middle of that.*

I didn't relate any of this to Melody, but she just giggled, her usual high pitched laugh seeming more subdued and controlled this time. "It's okay," she said, glancing over at me and looking more sexy than I'd ever seen. "All guys want that."

"Maybe," I said stupidly, knowing that she was right. "So…" I cleared my throat. "Any reason why you're asking me that?" We'd stopped at a traffic light, and the clicking of the turn signal seemed deafening. I knew that she was in control, and I had a good idea where this conversation was going.

"You know why," she said slyly. "Like I said, we're going to see Jade. Her parents are out of town, and she's waiting for us."

"Us?" My mind began to fill with images.

The light turned green, and she shifted the car into gear, lurching us around the turn. I knew that Melody was into some kinky things, but what she was implying was beyond anything I'd expected.

"Yes, us," she said, again focusing on the road as we rounded another corner. "Don't think I didn't notice how you looked at her."

I felt hot, probably blushing. "I… What do you mean?" Lying to her seemed kind of futile by this point, but some part of me still wanted to pretend to be innocent.

"She likes you. And so do I." She sped up again, the car pulling us along a straight stretch of road. "Just shut up and go with it, Ray."

I swallowed again. "Okay," was all I could think to say. We drove in silence after that, my mind racing with fantasies of what it would be like to do what she was hinting at. Whatever reservations I might have had about her before, they were beginning to dissolve.

We pulled up and parked in the driveway by a house that was in a neighborhood I wasn't familiar with. As near as I could tell, it was a little nicer than my own, maybe having been built more recently. While a lot of the houses had lights on both inside and out, this one was completely dark, which surprised me.

"You sure she's home?" I asked, feeling excited but nervous. "There's no lights on."

"Yeah, she's here," Melody said, though she sounded pissed off for some reason. "Should've remembered to…" she began, then opened her car door. "Doesn't matter. Come on."

I got out of the car, almost forgetting to undo my seatbelt first. I looked at the large front window, which had translucent white drapes. I wondered if I might see the light from a TV flickering inside, but there was nothing. As we approached the front door, I heard a small click as a pair of floodlights came on. I recognized the fixture as a sensor light; our house also had one by the carport, and I often had to unplug it when sneaking out in order to avoid alerting my parents.

"There you go," Melody said, pointing up. "Lights." She was walking several steps in front of me, shielding her eyes. When she reached the top of the small set of stairs that led to the front door, she simply opened it. Again, I was surprised, this time for two reasons. It seemed strange that a house in a neighborhood like this wouldn't have its front door locked, but it was also odd that she would just walk right up and let herself in, not stopping to knock or ring the doorbell.

I stopped walking at the base of the steps, trying to figure out what was nagging at me. Something just felt wrong. There was an eerie stillness to that house, and it made me uncomfortable. But there was something else.

Noticing that I'd stopped, Melody turned back to me. "What's wrong?" she asked with a smile. "You scared? We'll go easy on you, I promise." When I didn't move, she started back down the stairs, leaving the door open. "Ray, come on," she said impatiently. "Don't be such a chickenshit."

When she was right up to me, I drew back, feeling genuinely frightened for reasons I couldn't explain. Finally, I understood when she grabbed me by the hand, insisting again that I come inside. Her hand was cold and lifeless, not as much as Elizabeth's had been the night she hadn't fed, but close enough. I snapped mine back from her, quickly realizing what had happened.

"Oh, God, Melody…" I said, a lump rising in my throat.

"Damn it!" she said, her face screwing up in anger as she stomped her feet. "You just had to go and mess it up, didn't you?" She was scowling at me now, fangs clearly visible in the floodlight. "Always have to be so damn smart!"

"Melody…" I repeated, backing farther away from her. Afraid I might bump into something, I looked around, but I didn't want to take my eyes off her. She seemed more interested in ranting than pursuing me, though, at least for the moment.

"I had this whole damn thing planned out! You were supposed to come inside, where I've got pretty little Miss Jade propped up on the couch. And then we'd start making out with her, and I'd see how many seconds it took for you to realize she was dead. It would have been hilarious!"

"That's sick," I said, horrified that this creature that had once been my girlfriend could come up with such a thing. I was also shocked to hear that Jade was dead.

"The other you wouldn't think so," she said, her anger giving way to a menacing amusement. "I was really looking forward to telling him about it once I was done with you here." She began slinking towards me, her footsteps matching my own, the distance between us remaining constant.

"When you were… Melody, no."

"Why not?" she asked, almost seductively, fangs bared as she spoke. "I'm sure you'll taste really, really good."

"The other me did this to you?" I asked, already knowing the answer. On some level, I was relieved when she'd mentioned him, because my first thought had been that Elizabeth had turned her into a vampire.

She nodded, her eyes brightening with delight as she smiled. "And I'm so glad he did. Also really glad that I met him, I mean, he's a lot more fun than you. Much more evil."

That bothered me, but there wasn't time for jealousy. I needed to get to my stake, which was inside my jacket, but I feared that if I went for it, she'd be on me in a second. If her reflexes were anything like Elizabeth's, there would be no way I could be quick enough. As I continued to back up, my right foot bumped into something, and I glanced down to see that it was a sprinkler head. I might just get out of this after all.

"Surely he told you about the thread," I said to her, trying to stall, maybe even to reason with her. "The one that attaches him to me, and him to you."

"Oh, I've heard all about that," she said dismissively, still walking steadily toward me as I backed away, beginning to lead us in a curve.

More than likely, the sprinkler control was by the front of the house, so I needed to get us back over there. But could I get to it and turn it on before she was on top of me?

"Then you know that if you kill me, he'll die, and then so will you." As I spoke, I realized another consequence, that Elizabeth would die. I couldn't let that happen. More selfishly, I didn't want to die myself.

"See, that's the theory," she said thoughtfully, creeping forward, "but I think it's wrong."

"Wrong?"

"Yeah. See, Ray — the other Ray, I mean — made me like this to torture you. He's way into torture." She let out one of her giggles, which now sounded thoroughly evil and twisted. "He's got these plans, wanting to set up this big place where he keeps human beings like cattle, in cages and everything. He and me and all the other vampires can just feed on them whenever we want, sometimes for food, sometimes just for fun. I love that idea."

It sickened me. What was worse was picturing him doing it, him looking exactly like me but doing something so brutal and depraved. Things only got worse when Melody continued to describe how the long-term idea was to make some of the people breed. "Again, like cattle," she went on. "And then we'll have little babies to drink from, too. Have you ever eaten a baby, Ray?"

"Stop it," I said. "I don't need to hear any more."

"Have you? Or was that little blonde girl young enough to count." She laughed again when she saw the pained expression I must have made. "Oh yeah, he told me all about that. It's the one memory you regret the most, but see, he's just the opposite. His only regret was that he didn't enjoy it more, drinking the life out of someone so young and innocent. He even said that if he had it to do all over again, he'd have left the little bitch's body hanging on the front of the house like a door knocker."

"God damn it," I said, screwing my eyes shut as I looked away from her, trying to shut the images out that she was putting into my head.

She giggled again, that same sick, despicable trill. "This is so much fun! I love doing this! And I'm obviously a hell of a lot better at it than that little whore you run around with. She was supposed to do this to you, you see. But no, she had to go and think she was all better than my Ray, the real Ray."

"I'm the real Ray," I said through clenched teeth, stopping in my tracks.

Surprised, she stopped as well, her raised eyebrows seeming to challenge me. "Is that what you think? Because, see, I've got another theory. That thread you mentioned? I think that if you were to die right now, then my Ray would come back to where he came from, to the source. That's his body you're squatting in, mister. And I'm here to get it back."

"That doesn't make sense, Melody. You don't know what you're talking about. I'm the source, where he comes from. If that source gets cut off, then he's gone. Then so are you."

"But not…" she said, raising a finger meaningfully, "…if someone on the other side of the thread from him drinks in that source." She began tracing her finger in the air, illustrating her point. "It's not a straight line, here to here to here, but a circle. I read something like it in a book once."

"That doesn't make it real," I insisted, but I had to admit that I was curious as to whether or not she was right. "And the other me is okay with this?"

"Oh, he doesn't know. I went rogue. It's meant to be my big surprise for him. I kill you, and then he winds up here, back in his original body. Or, hey, who knows? Maybe if I'm really lucky, I'll end up with two vampire Rays."

"Melody, stop it," I said. "You're endangering all of us."

"No, I'm not," she said childishly. She began to creep closer. I reached for my jacket, and then she paused, holding up a hand. "Ah-ah," she cautioned, "don't even try it."

We both stood there, frozen, each one daring the other to make a move. I wondered if there might be a way to influence her psychically, the same way that I'd seen Elizabeth affect people. But I wasn't sure if my powers were strong enough for that. I concentrated, feeling my scalp and temples tingle, a sensation I'd felt when my powers were stronger, back when I was younger. I pictured a force pressing back on her, holding her back, slowing her down.

Whether that gave me the extra split second I needed or was simply my imagination, I never knew. But in a flash, she zoomed forward as I jerked the stake out from my jacket, pointing it toward her as she fell onto me. The dull side of it hit me in the chest, hurting me as I fell backwards, Melody on top of me. I'd felt the stake go into her as she ran into it, and then once we were on the ground, I rolled us over, still gripping the weapon as I held it firmly in her heart.

I expected her to scream, but it came out as more of a whine, her eyes pained and filling with tears. "Damn it," she half-whispered, and I began to feel sorry for her. I'd felt the same way the moment I realized she'd been changed, but her subsequent taunting of me had quashed that. Now I was back to feeling regret, knowing what I had to do.

She was still alive, and her arms began to reach up toward me weakly, one last attempt to embrace and destroy me. Her face was contorted in pain, but there was something pitiful about it as well. I used both hands to plunge the stake all the way into her heart, loathing every bit of myself as I did so.

I walked all the way home that night, exhausted and overwhelmed with guilt. I hadn't loved Melody the same way I did Elizabeth or Eileen, but I hated what had happened to her, how I'd had to kill her. When I'd left the house, I'd been in survival mode, trying to decide what to do. I thought of taking Melody's car and using that to get home, but that would just end up leading the police to me. And because it was such a long walk, I considered trying to find a pay phone to call a cab, but it would be pretty stupid to have someone drive me to my house while I had blood all over my shirt.

The long walk left me time to think, but that wasn't necessarily a good thing. I kept running the scenario over and over in my mind, wishing it had gone differently. I would picture things as they had played out, but with tangents at various points. Maybe I could have telepathically summoned Elizabeth to me if I'd tried hard enough, and she could have saved me. Or maybe if I'd been able to make it to the sprinkler control, I could have killed Melody in a more hands-off way, the running water doing the dirty work and sparing me the memory of her body going still and dead beneath me. At least she hadn't decomposed as horribly as some of the other slain vampires I'd seen; after all, she must have only been dead since the night before.

I even imagined someone else entirely, somebody I didn't know, happening by during the confrontation and helping out, like maybe the police or even a former member of Life Force, the vigilante anti-vampire group. Why couldn't one of them have shown up and killed Melody for me? Would I have felt less horrible then? Maybe they could have at least given me a ride home.

And how was it that my clone had found out about Melody in the first place? I got what she'd said about how he'd turned her into a vampire in order to get at me, and his doing that to Elizabeth a year ago was finally more clear to me. I'd wondered if he'd done that to punish her for not loving him — or me, prior to his emergence. But he wasn't a whole being, just all of my negative traits, so love probably didn't even factor into it. Still, did the fact that he knew about Melody mean that he'd been spying on me all this time? And if that were true, why hadn't he gone after Eileen earlier?

Finally, I figured it out, remembering our night at The Joint. Jade wasn't stoned or out of it when she thought that I'd been rude to her.

She had in fact met my clone, who must have been there that same night, either because he followed me or just by coincidence, maybe one of those maddening interconnections Augusta was so full of. So sometime after meeting me, she must have run into him, and he acted like he didn't know her because, well, he didn't. And that may have led him to discover me and Melody, or maybe he already knew about her. I'd never know for sure. But this notion did at least help me believe that Eileen was probably safe, that he didn't know about her.

When Elizabeth had died, I felt terrible, knowing that my clone had done it. I may not have murdered her myself, but I was at the very least indirectly responsible, I knew from the start. And at least she'd come back, after a fashion. But this time, with Melody, my clone had killed her and brought her back, and then I'd killed the vampire version of her. So in a way, it felt like we'd both murdered her, sort of like a sick and twisted team effort. It made us feel more like one person, and I didn't like that idea at all.

Worse still, it made me wonder: What if Melody was right? If she'd managed to bite and drain me, could my clone have somehow been absorbed back into me, making us one horrific, murderous person again? Maybe the whole idea of the originals dying and eliminating their clones was a false notion, and if so, that would change the game considerably.

CHAPTER SEVENTEEN

Being back at school the following Monday was hard, and I'd considered playing sick in order to get out of it, but I decided against that. Melody's death would no doubt soon be known, and once I'd gotten over the initial shock of it and everything that had happened that night, I'd begun to worry if I might become implicated.

I'd cried myself to sleep Friday night, then done my best to avoid my parents the rest of the weekend. Even so, my mother had picked up on the fact that something was wrong, and she even asked me if I wanted to talk about it at one point. She'd known that I was dating Melody even though she'd never met her, so once I'd gone from seeming happy to extremely gloomy, she inferred that the two of us must have broken up. I admitted that we weren't together anymore, but I didn't dare tell her the details and just said I didn't want to talk about it.

I was pretty sure that I hadn't left any evidence at Jade's house that could be traced back to me, but I also hated to think about Melody's body just lying there in the front yard. Presumably, the police or some neighbors discovered it — along with Jade's body inside the house — the day after our confrontation. There wasn't anything about it on the news, but that didn't surprise me after I talked to Carolyn about the incident.

I needed someone to talk to, and while I'd hoped to tell Elizabeth about it the next time I saw her, I didn't know when that might be. So when Carolyn came over to the house to do laundry on Saturday, I spilled my guts to her. It was cathartic, and she wasn't judgmental of me like I feared she might be. At least I was able to be honest with her about everything this time.

She also reassured me that it was unlikely that the police would come find me. They hadn't questioned her after Catherine's disappearance, nor had the bodies of the vampires that she and Damon killed led back to them. Her take on it was that the police, even now, were kind of hush-hush about vampire killings, maybe trying to sweep things under the rug, hoping they'd go away. I didn't know if she was right, but I could see where she was coming from.

It broke my heart to walk into Mrs. Eldridge's classroom and see Melody's empty desk behind mine, and I almost turned around and walked out of the room. But I didn't want to make a scene, plus I was already dreading anyone asking me where she was. I knew that when the teacher called roll, the silence that would follow her calling out Melody's last name would feel like a knife going into my heart.

Or so I thought, but then I was surprised when she skipped straight over her name. That was even more shocking to me, and I heard a few gasps from some of the other students when it happened. When Mrs. Eldridge got to the end of the roll, one of the girls in the class whose desk was near hers leaned in and asked quietly, "What happened to Melody? Did she… um…"

The teacher just nodded her head solemnly, and I slowly became aware of heads turning away from her and towards me. Avoiding their gazes, I slumped down in my desk, arms folded.

"Oh, man..." I heard Derek whisper, and there were similar sentiments throughout the room. I suddenly began to think that coming to school had been a mistake after all.

Mrs. Eldridge's chair made a scraping sound as she got up from her desk, but instead of heading for her usual spot in front of the chalkboard, she walked to the classroom door and stopped there. "Ray?" she called. "Can I see you for a moment?"

Had this been any other day, my smart-ass nature would have kicked in, and I would have said something like: *You can see me now, can't you? What am I, invisible?* And then Melody would have let out one of her high-pitched giggles, probably fighting to keep it down. The thought of this, and especially the knowledge that it would never happen again, cut deep into me.

Hating the feeling of everybody watching me, I walked across the room, wishing that I'd chosen to sit closer to the door at the beginning of the school year. I didn't know what was in store for me, but I feared that I was about to get that interrogation I'd been fearing. How much did Mrs. Eldridge know, and how did she know anything in the first place?

Outside the room, I avoided eye contact as she spoke to me, her eyes trying to fix on mine. "Ray, I know you and Melody were... were close. I know this must be a really difficult time for you."

"Yeah," I managed to say angrily.

"When the office told me to take her off the roll this morning, I was really... Well, I wish I could say that this was an unusual thing, but it isn't. It happens more often than... well, than it should. Are you okay?"

I looked back at her, suddenly unable to speak. Inside I was screaming: *DO I LOOK OKAY?* Normally, I hated this woman, so it felt unsettling for her to be acting so nice to me. I felt like I didn't deserve it.

"I know," she said more quietly. "We've all lost people. Myself included."

"Sorry," I said.

"Look, clearly you're upset. I don't think my class is the best place for you today."

"You want me to go to Mr. Anderson?" I asked, referring to our vice-principal.

She laughed gently and said, "No, I don't think that will be necessary. Not today, anyway." She said this with a slight smile, and I involuntarily returned it, angry at myself for doing so.

She had intended for me to go see the guidance counselor instead, which I agreed to, grateful to get away from her class. It wasn't somewhere I enjoyed being even at the best of times, and this was certainly far from that. But instead of going to the office, I left the building, sneaking around to a corner where I knew some kids, including Carl, sometimes went to smoke. I almost hoped that he would be there so I could talk to him, but I was on my own, which was probably for the best. I leaned against the building and looked up at the passing clouds, tears welling up in my eyes.

I managed to slip back inside just before the bell rang, then made my way back to the classroom to pick up my books. When I got there, most of the other students had already left, and I saw that Mrs. Eldridge was busy at her desk, bending down to get something out of a drawer. Derek was nearby, talking to another guy from our class about something, but when he saw me, he broke off and walked over.

"Hey, man," he said to me, his voice uncharacteristically soft. "I'm sorry about what happened to your girl."

"Thanks," I said, unsure what else to say.

"She was cool. Real, real cool. She didn't deserve to get bit."

"I know," I said, trying to cover up my sadness with toughness. Derek, while usually funny, was also a pretty tough guy, so I'd learned to try to match that whenever I spoke to him. Really, it was that way with most of the people in that class.

"This town is so effed up, I'm tellin' ya. Seems like everybody I know knows at least one person who's gotten bit. Like my aunt." I noticed that he pronounced that last word differently than most people I knew; the way he said it, it rhymed with "font." "She passed the same way."

"Sorry to hear that," I said simply.

"Yeah, well, I gotta get to class. You take care, ya hear me?" He gave my upper arm a slight punch, sort of a sideways tap with his fist. It was meant to be a comforting gesture, so I took it as such, but part of me still felt like dying inside. Who had his aunt been? Had she died within the past year, a victim of our clones, or was she someone my friends and I had killed years ago? The more I thought about it, the more I realized that I didn't want to know the answer.

Elizabeth was of course similarly sympathetic, and it made me feel better to confide in her. "You did what you had to do," she told me as I lay my head on her lap, hanging out with her in the back of my car behind the elementary school. "Sounds like she really was a danger, and not just to you."

"I know," I said bitterly. "I just wish she... I mean, why did she have to turn out so evil? You didn't."

After a few seconds of thought, she said, "I guess we're just two different people."

"I guess."

"I will say one thing for her, though: I like how she stood up to him. The other you, I mean. Apparently he wasn't able to make an obedient slave out of her, either." That brought me some comfort, too; at least my clone's plans had failed him again.

Elizabeth also said that she regretted not being around to help me when I needed it, but she'd had no way of knowing that I'd been in danger. To that end, we tried some experiments in which I attempted to call out to her telepathically, but they never really went anywhere. There would be a lot of "Did you hear that?" and "Maybe," but it was never clear whether or not any of the supposed successes were real or imagined.

We tried getting out of the car and sitting on opposite sides of it, the idea being that she wouldn't come around to me until I sent my thoughts out to her. But that didn't work either, which frustrated me. My psychic powers had improved over the years, and hers had certainly progressed quite a bit, but it was pretty clear that mine would never be as strong as they were before. Apparently, being a vampire was part of that.

It wasn't unusual for Augusta to experience heavy thunderstorms in the summer, sometimes for two or three days in a row. But for us to have such a strong one during the last week of November was definitely unusual, and I realized that it must have been connected to the unseasonably warm weather we'd been having over the past couple of days. I had no idea why it was happening, but it bothered me nevertheless.

I hated nights like this because they always made me worry about Elizabeth, and ironically, my clone as well. I knew that they were probably fine and well versed in avoiding rainy weather, but still, whenever these storms occurred, I knew I wouldn't get to see Elizabeth.

What pissed me off more was the fact that this particular storm hadn't been in the forecast, not really. There was a twenty percent chance of rain, which usually meant next to none, but in this case, I guess nature had won out over probability. It always bugged me that there was all this technology to predict the weather, even a 24-hour weather channel that the local cable company ran. But when the forecasts were wrong, the weathermen could always claim that meteorology wasn't an exact science, which to me sounded like a cop-out. Cynically, I thought that maybe I should grow up to become a weatherman myself since I'd always been such a good liar.

Storms this strong tended to remind me of one night back in 1982, when Susanna came home from her summer job and dramatically slammed the door behind her, exclaiming to everyone in the den, "It's like daytime outside!" I didn't realize what she meant until she brought me over to a window and pointed out how the nearly constant lightning was illuminating everything outdoors in a way that seemed unnatural at night.

This night, the lightning wasn't quite as intense, or at least it didn't seem like it was. Or maybe I was just remembering that storm from my childhood as bigger and more frightening than it truly was. Things always seem bigger when you're younger. I tended to remember that one as full of what I'd recently started to refer to as "Hollywood lightning." In the movies and on TV, whenever there was a thunderstorm, the lightning and thunder were always simultaneous, especially in cheesy horror films. But after what I'd experienced with Eileen, I realized that those depictions were largely inaccurate. It was very unusual for thunder and lightning to occur at the same time, and if they did, that meant that the storm was right on top of you and that you shouldn't just be sitting around casually talking about spooky things.

Tonight's storm wasn't that terrible, but it was enough to evoke certain memories, both distant and recent. It started around 10:00, and about an hour later, I went to bed wondering if the noise and flashes would die down enough for me to be able to get to sleep. The heavy rain was somewhat hypnotic and soothing, and I'd almost drifted off when a sharp rapping at my window started me awake.

I'd heard this sound before, or one very much like it, and it usually meant that Elizabeth was at my window, trying to get my attention. But she couldn't be out in this weather, surely. Cautiously, I pulled back the drapes and peered out, straining to see through the rain-soaked window and the screen beyond it.

A figure drew closer, and I almost screamed, but honestly, I was too scared even for that. The lightning flashed again, and I saw Elizabeth's face, though her hair was wet and slicked back, raindrops pelting her as she smiled at me. As I stood up and undid the latch on my window, the thunder roared again, and I sat back down on the edge of my bed, shoving up the window frame. Wetness made its way through the screen in tiny bits, hitting my hands and my face.

"Know a place where a girl can dry off?" Elizabeth asked, nearly laughing.

My heart was pounding, more so as I put two and two together, realizing what must have happened. I started to go out the window to join her, but I realized that if I did, I would get soaked. I told her to meet me at the front door, which was just a few feet to her left.

I quickly shut the window, ducked back under the drapes, and rolled over on my bed, my feet hitting the floor as I leapt up from the bed. I then caught myself, realizing that I needed to be quiet. Looking at the clock, I saw that it was just after midnight, and while my parents were definitely in bed by now, I still needed to be careful not to wake them. Given the storm, they might very well still be awake, but I hoped not. I would have to slowly unlock my bedroom door and then creep around to the front door to meet Elizabeth, all the while hoping that the rain and thunder would help mask whatever sounds I might make.

It wasn't like I hadn't snuck through my house plenty of times before, but this time, I was almost frantic to get to the door. Elizabeth was out there, soaked in rainwater. That could only mean one thing: Somehow, she was human again.

I quietly picked up the front door key from the small iron table in the foyer and slid it shakily into the lock, turned it, and opened the door quickly, slipping out to find my Elizabeth, soaked and standing beneath the small overhang above our front door, her arms folded around her.

"Oh, God," I whispered, then realized that the sound of the rain had drowned out my words. I pulled her to me, not caring how wet she was and how that would soak me, too. I had thrown my arms around her shoulders, nearly crying. I'd almost given up hope that this could be possible. "You're here… you're here… and you're…"

"…fucking drenched!" she exclaimed, but I thought I heard playfulness in her voice. I pulled back from her, still holding her arms with my hands, looking at her in disbelief. The rain continued to pour down just to the side of us off the edge of the roof, dispersing the streetlight and making it easier to see her than on other nights. Lightning illuminated her further at brief, random intervals.

"I'm sorry," I said, still dumbfounded.

She bowed her head for a second, then tossed it back, the water flying out of her hair and reminding me briefly of that swimming party at Chris's house all those years ago. I hadn't seen her with her hair wet since then, and I hadn't seen her as a human being for over a year.

"Yeah, me too," she said, half-smiling. "I pretty much walked here all the way from Walton Way. I ran at first when the storm hit, then just kind of said 'forget it' and resigned myself to being wet. And I figured I could come here and maybe wait the storm out, or at least dry off for a little bit if you didn't mind."

"Um, sure, but…" I was at a loss. Why was she acting so normal? Did she not realize what had happened? "Are you… um… Are you okay?"

She glared at me, but comically. "Well, aside from being really tired and wet and actually kind of freezing…! Sure, I'm great!" She laughed a little, but she was beginning to get a confused look. It was probably in response to my own. Our faces were only inches from each other; we had to talk quietly enough not to be overheard inside, but the rain meant that we had to be close enough to hear one another.

"And," she continued, just slightly more subdued, "there's the taste of this guy I drank from on the way to try to warm up a bit, and that didn't even work." She continued a bit more confidently, "I think he was drunk. I really wish I could get that taste out of my mouth, but I'm sure you don't want to hear about that."

"Wait, what? How could you have…? You're…" The pieces began to fall into place. "You're not."

"Not what?" she asked with an increasingly aggravated tone.

I sighed. Now I didn't even want to say it. "I just… I thought that with all the rain and everything, you'd…" I sighed again, looking away from her, feeling like crying again but for a completely different reason. My hopes had been impossibly raised and then brought down in the span of just a couple of minutes.

"Okay, what's going on?" she demanded, her smile completely gone.

"I thought that the rain had changed you back into a human," I said, defeated. "Running water, and all…" I trailed off, wondering if I should say the rest of what was on my mind. "I thought that's why you'd come here tonight, to show me."

"I told you why I came here, Ray," she said, now genuinely annoyed. "And no, I haven't been magically transformed back into a perfect little human."

"But…"

"We've talked about this before. The rules that applied to you under the influence of the potion aren't the same as they are for me and the other vampires." She said this quickly and impatiently, like I was an idiot for believing otherwise. Then she began backing away and into the rain.

"No! Wait!" I started to edge toward her, then held back to avoid the rain. She kept going. Water briefly splashed the sleeve of my shirt, and I backed up under the porch.

"Just never mind, Ray," she said, the rain pouring over her again. She acted like it didn't bother her at all, even though I knew it did, because that was why she'd come here. I felt guilty over the lust I began to feel, noticing the way her black T-shirt clung to her chest, how her hair held tight to her head from the wetness, looking more brown than blonde. But I knew that she wouldn't let me touch her then, and I made out what details I could in the dim light. I had no idea when I would get to see her like this again, if ever.

She began to run towards the street, and part of me wanted to go after her, but I didn't have any shoes on. And it was pretty clear that she didn't want me to follow her.

Back inside, I went to the bathroom and dried off, angry at myself but also rather ticked at her. We could have talked more if she hadn't gotten so mad. And was it really so wrong of me to have wished and mistakenly believed that she'd become human again? She was right, though, in a way. The "vampire killers" that changed us back to normal didn't do the same for her. But how come the rain hadn't killed her? Had the rules changed yet again? If so, how?

I got my answer, or the prelude to it, in the form of a key left jammed under my window screen the following night. Attached to the key were two plastic fobs, one of which indicated that it was a hotel room key. The other, which didn't match and was held on by a second ring, had the number *139* written on it in black permanent marker. Clearly, this was from Elizabeth, her way of telling me to meet her at the hotel named on the other fob and which room to go to.

I wasn't sure why she hadn't left me a note instead like she usually did, and the fact that she'd chosen to be cryptic this time got on my nerves. It was almost like she was telling me she wanted to see me but at the same time was giving me the silent treatment. But as I wiped the residual rainwater off the key, I figured it out. A note probably would have gotten soaked and ruined in the day's thunderstorm, which had mostly died down but continued to come back in short bursts. It was still unclear how mad at me she was, but I hoped that the fact that she wanted to see me was a good sign.

Once it was late enough for me to sneak out, the rain had ended, but the wind had picked up. That made things colder, and because it had been so warm the past few days, I didn't dress quite as warmly as I should have. Still, I put up with the discomfort, eager to see Elizabeth again.

I was nervous knocking on the door of the hotel room, but the look on Elizabeth's face when she let me in dispelled a lot of that. She looked sad, even pitiful, and I couldn't help but step forward and hug her. Pulling me inside the room but not letting go of me, she let the door slam behind us, nuzzling my shoulder with her head.

"I'm sorry about last night," I said to her, my words slightly distorted by the way my chin was pressed onto her shoulder.

"Me too," she said, then pulled back from me, still holding on. "Guess I did overreact a little. I was just having a bad night, and I thought seeing you would make things better, but…" She looked off to the side, then back at me, sort of pained. "What you said pissed me off more. It wasn't what I expected."

"I know," I said, though I did feel deep down that she'd been unreasonable. But I was so glad to see her again, to know that she didn't hate me, that I just went along with what she was saying. "I was kind of shocked to see you, I mean, I thought that the rain…"

"I know," she said pointedly. Turning away, she went and sat at the foot of the bed, then looked up at me. "I got it. But seriously, rain? You thought that counted as running water?"

"It was one of the 'vampire killers' back then for us," I said, trying not to sound defensive.

"Seriously?" she repeated. "Rain changed you back."

"Well, no, not exactly," I said, reaching for a chair that was under the nearby desk, spinning it around, and sitting down in front of her. "Running water did. So, by extension, rain could have if we'd ever been caught in it. So we just never went out. I remember one night when it *poured,* and we were trapped inside for a long time, really wanting to go out. Though to be honest, that only happened once. Or was it twice? I can't remember. I do remember noticing how lucky we were, how — for the most part — all three summers, the rain came just before and just after our time as vampires."

"Rain doesn't hurt me, Ray," she said, doubt in her voice. "Are you sure it would have hurt you?"

"Well, no, it wouldn't have hurt, just changed us back to human. Actually, now that I think about it, I used to have this fear that maybe we could have gotten killed, like if we were out flying around, you know, way high up in the air, and then a single drop of rain might plop down unexpectedly on my wing and then, *poof!* There I am, a hundred feet up or whatever, but a regular person. Then I'd plummet to my death. I once had a nightmare about that, in fact."

She still looked doubtful, her forehead creased. "I'm not so sure about that. If I get caught by rain, yeah, it bothers me, but it's not painful. Not like some of the other things we've talked about. Like garlic, that will totally burn. And a cross, well, maybe. I know they hurt other vampires. Not sure where I am on that spectrum. But even then, they wouldn't actually kill me. Sunlight, fire, and of course the old stake through the heart..." She glanced down at the side of my jacket where I kept my stake. "Yeah, that'd probably do it. But I think you're kind of confused on just which of those things kill as opposed to just really annoy a vampire."

"But we did get changed back by them! I used hoses and sprinklers on the others, and I remember Dennis turning me back using a cross one time."

"Again," she said, sounding more impatient, "things were different for you than they are for me. And for the others. You weren't real vampires."

I didn't want this to turn into another argument. I was starting to feel angry, but not necessarily at her. I'd begun to wonder if she were right, and it was very frustrating for me to keep thinking that I knew where I stood, how things worked, only to have some twist like this come along and prove me wrong. I felt more in control when I understood the boundaries because then I could act accordingly.

Elizabeth stood up from the bed. "Let me show you something." I followed her into the bathroom, unsure what she was up to. When I got there, she was kneeling down by the bathtub, looking back at me. "Now, watch."

After putting the stopper in place, she turned on the water, letting it rush into the tub. She then faced me, and there was something odd in her expression that I couldn't quite place. "Okay," she said, almost shouting over the rush of the water. "Running water, right?"

I got where she was going with this; Susanna had demonstrated it to the rest of us back in 1983 using the kitchen sink and a bowl of water. The point was that as long as the water was flowing, it was dangerous, but once that stopped, she was able to dip her hand into the bowl of still water with no ill effects.

I waited for a few moments, as did Elizabeth, wondering when she'd get to the point. I thought I knew what the punch line was going to be, but she surprised me by rolling back her sleeve and turning back around, having screwed her eyes shut just before doing so. Feeling protective, I almost screamed as she plunged her forearm under the faucet, letting the torrent flow over it. She held it there, seemingly unharmed, but after just a few seconds, I could see her body starting to shake. I started to reach out for her, but then she jerked her arm back, spinning back around to face me, sitting back against the edge of the tub and shaking the drops off of her arm, holding it with her other hand.

She was panting, and I thought she was in pain, but she held up her hand to me as I started to draw closer. "I'm okay, I'm okay," she insisted. She then looked at her dripping arm, almost like she was forcing herself to do so. In a fast motion, she halfway stood up and snatched one of the white towels from the rack above the toilet, then sat down again, quickly drying her arm off.

Once she was done, she looked more relaxed, and I felt relieved as well. She shook her left hand quickly, a shudder going through the rest of her body as she closed her eyes. She then sighed heavily. "See?" she said to me.

"I guess…" I said, still uncertain. She'd successfully demonstrated that running water wasn't fatal to her, but she still looked like it had hurt her.

She got a weird look in her eyes, peering behind her, where the bathtub was still filling up. She rose on her knees, her face hardening, then turned her back to me again. I sidled in closer, also on my knees, wanting to get a better look. She sat there with her hands propped up on the edge, and I wondered what would happen next.

She reached towards the rushing water once more, then paused, uncertain. Then she reached up and quickly turned the knob to stop the flow. A heavy sigh went out from her, and she bowed her head dramatically. "Okay, no," she said. "Once was enough. And yet…" She lowered her right hand again, this time into the now calm bathwater, swirling it around very slowly. "That's no problem at all."

"Yeah, but you still seemed really freaked out by the whole thing," I said, glad to see her feeling better.

She slid back and up onto the toilet seat, looking down at me. "But that's just it," she said, her breathing mostly normal again. "It bothered me, but it didn't kill me. That's what some of those 'vampire killers' do."

Memories flashed across my mind, her reaction suddenly reminding me of the way that my mother and my sisters reacted to roaches, which we sometimes had in our house. There wasn't much a roach could do to you aside from crawl over your foot or wherever else it happened to land, but the way the women in our family acted, one would think that the gross little things were armed with submachine guns. It wasn't unlike the stereotypical image of the women I'd seen in old movies and cartoons jumping up on tables and chairs, terrified of a little mouse and screeching for a man (or, in the case of the *Tom and Jerry* cartoons, a cat) to save them from it. That had been mine and my father's duty in our house whenever this situation arose, the designated bug-squishers.

Thinking of this made more sense of everything. Elizabeth couldn't actually be harmed by this seemingly terrifying rushing water, but it still wasn't something she liked to touch. As I conveyed my analogy and understanding to her, she confirmed it, adding, "It's just something innate in me. I don't care if it's not rational. It just is. That's why I — really, most vampires — don't go out on rainy nights. You know those little rivers of water the rain sometimes makes in the street when it's really heavy? Like along the curb?"

"Sure." I'd always found them kind of neat.

"Don't like those, either. In fact, it takes a lot of effort to even bring myself to step over them. And as far as a real river goes, forget it."

"What do you mean?"

"Remember when I was going around doing research at those other libraries? The ones at the colleges around town?" I nodded. "Things got a little hard when it came time for me to try to go to the ones in Aiken."

"Why?"

"Aiken, South Carolina," she said, looking at me meaningfully. "Across the Savannah River."

"Oh…" I said. "You couldn't?"

"Nope. I'd start to fly over it, then just suddenly get terrified and say, 'I don't think so!' and turn right back around. I'd try one or two more times, then give up. Then I remembered the trick from *Dracula.*" I gave her a confused look, unsure of what she meant. "Ray, you told me you read the book."

"I did! Well… okay, just the Cliff Notes."

She rolled her eyes and sighed. "Ray, one of these days, you're going to have to read an actual book." I just sneered at her. "Well anyway, the way he got to England in the story was to hitch a ride on a boat, hiding in a coffin. Like it was okay for him to be carried over water, but he couldn't do it himself. So I did my own take on that and just snuck my way over the bridge, hiding out as a bat in the back of someone's truck. And even then, it felt really weird as we passed over. Didn't like it at all." She got a slightly queasy look.

"So," I said, a wicked idea forming in my mind, "if I were to reach up like this and flush the toilet while you're sitting on it…"

"Don't you dare!" She scowled at me, pointing.

We talked a little more, and it became clear to me that I had once again assumed things about her based on my own experiences as a vampire, never bothering to ask her and consequently getting them wrong. Back then, we'd had to cut the water supply to our house off each summer to avoid accidentally changing ourselves back, which meant that we couldn't take baths or showers the entire time, not without going through a complex procedure. As a young boy not well versed in the importance of personal hygiene, this didn't bother me much, and if we all stank, I barely noticed or cared. Carolyn and Susanna, though, insisted on cleaning themselves with baby wipes. Elizabeth found this simultaneously gross and funny, then clarified for me that she could in fact take baths and wash her hair, but she never took showers because she was too scared of them.

She was also amused and surprised to find out that I had never heard of holy water, which apparently was something that Catholic people used. But I had no reason to know about it; the first person I'd ever really known who was a Catholic was Melody, and it wasn't like we'd talked about her family's religion all that much. But the reason Elizabeth brought it up was because it was apparently a well known vampire deterrent, another one that could harm a vampire but not actually kill it.

"What, you never saw *The Lost Boys?*" she asked me. "They used it in that." I shook my head. "I thought everyone had seen that movie!"

"Not me," I said. "I remember it came out just after our last stint as vampires. I had no interest in seeing it. Not really big on any kind of horror stuff these days, you know, having lived it."

She gave me a sympathetic smile. "I can understand that."

"So, regular water doesn't burn you, but holy water does?"

"As far as I know. I haven't been unlucky enough to find out firsthand. So far, anyway. But I have heard that some of those people going around Augusta trying to kill vampires have been using it. But then again, you've got to wonder…"

"What?"

"What we talked about before. People of different religions and all that. Maybe it wouldn't even bother me." She shrugged.

"That's a good point," I said, shifting to relieve the cramped feeling I was getting. The bathroom floor was getting uncomfortable, so I stood up, wiping at the back of my jeans. "You mind taking this conversation out of the bathroom?"

She laughed a little and agreed, then stood up and followed me out. Most of the hotel rooms I'd been in before had separate bathrooms altogether, but this one had the toilet and shower in its own little partition with a door, while outside it was a sink, counter, and large mirror that was open to the rest of the room. I had no idea why it was designed like that, but I didn't think much about it when I'd noticed it earlier.

As Elizabeth and I were exiting the small bathroom, I glanced to my left, almost instinctively checking my reflection. I may not have cared much about my appearance when I'd been a little boy, but these days, it mattered to me. What shocked me, though, was the fact that I could see not only myself, but the mirror image of Elizabeth right next to mine.

I stopped in my tracks, and she bumped into me, protesting at my apparent clumsiness but laughing about it. "Elizabeth," I said, pointing at the mirror, my hand almost shaking. "Look."

"Look at what?" she said, facing the mirror. "Oh, damn it, Ray, don't remind me. You know how I feel about that."

"But you have a reflection!" My heart was beginning to race, much as it had the night before when she'd shown up in the rain and I'd thought she was human again. As my words came out, I realized that this must have been a similar mistake, and I tried to curb my enthusiasm, afraid that it might piss her off yet again. Apparently, she had a reflection after all, even though I never had one as a vampire. But what she said next confused me even more.

"What are you talking about?" she asked. "No I don't!"

Baffled, I said, "Yes, you do! Look! Right there! I can see you!"

In the mirror, she looked irritated and perplexed. "Ray, I don't see anyone in that mirror except you, pointing at nothing and gaping like an idiot."

"I'm not… Wait. Really? You don't see yourself at all. Just me. Are you sure?"

She sighed angrily. "Sure as I've ever been for the past year! You're there in the mirror because you're human. I'm not because I'm a vampire. We know this part of the story already."

"Elizabeth, I'm being totally serious. I can see you in the mirror, plain as day." I winced, wondering if that had been a poor choice of words.

Her mounting anger began to give way to wonderment, and she asked in a whisper, "Really?" I could tell from the way her eyes moved that she seemed to be searching the mirror, and it became clear to me that she truly couldn't see herself. Her eyes would meet mine occasionally, and to me, it just looked like we were two ordinary people reflected in the glass.

I moved to stand behind her, then put my arms on both of her shoulders. "Okay, now. What do you see?"

"Just you," she said, sounding frustrated. "Like you're holding… nothing." She reached up with her right hand and touched mine. "I can feel you right there, but as far as I'm concerned, you're the only one in the mirror. That's really weird. I don't like it." She spun around quickly, hugging me and burying her face in my chest.

"Oh, Elizabeth," I said, "I'm sorry. I didn't…" I wasn't sure what to say. "Let's just move away from here for right now, okay?"

It took a little coaxing to calm her down, but eventually, we settled onto the bed together. Apparently, I wasn't the only one who didn't understand the mechanics of this entire thing. I'd always understood it, as had she, that vampires just didn't have reflections at all. I could remember multiple examples of movies or TV shows in which other people had discovered that someone was a vampire by spotting the fact that they didn't have a reflection. It was part of the folklore. But as Elizabeth had pointed out to me before, sometimes that folklore was inconsistent.

As we talked through it, we realized that it actually made more sense in terms of physics that it wasn't that vampires didn't cast reflections at all, only that they couldn't see their own. Standing right next to her, I had clearly seen her in the mirror. She was there. So there must have been something within her that left her unable to perceive herself, a limitation of hers along the same lines as not being able to go out in the sun or tolerate holy water. It surprised us both.

Still unnerved by this, Elizabeth also got me to question something from my past, but I couldn't give her a satisfactory answer. She wondered if even though vampires couldn't see their own individual reflections, maybe they could still see another vampire in a mirror, like if they were standing next to each other the same way we'd been doing earlier. What frustrated me was that I could not remember a single time during the vampire summers if I'd been in front of a mirror — or, as she put forth, another surface like a window or something else reflective — with one of my friends or siblings.

I tried to think back, to picture some time that any of us had been in the bathroom at the same time. But as far as I could remember, that just never happened. The closest I could recall was when Carl first learned that we didn't have reflections, and I'd watched him from the doorway as he stood in front of the mirror, amazed. If I had just stepped in there with him, I might have seen him but not myself, or maybe neither of us. But it was too late; I'd never know the answer now.

Thinking about my past also made something else click in my head that I'd never realized, but it was related to the earlier revelations she'd given me about the less intense vampire deterrents not being lethal but only irritating. In fact, I'd actually already known this, but I'd never put the pieces together until tonight. I'd used garlic powder against vampires already, wounding them but not killing them. Nick had done the same thing to his clone; it was in fact his telling me this that inspired me to adopt it as a weapon. Presumably, if I'd ever managed to successfully use those sprinkler systems against the vampires I'd battled over the past several months, the same thing would have happened: It might have disoriented and hurt them, but it wouldn't have killed them.

But then I remembered something else. "Okay, wait, wait, wait," I said, simultaneously confused but also strangely excited.

"'Wait wait wait' what?" she asked.

"Those vampires… The ones that were made by Robert and… your sister." I flinched, uncomfortable over bringing her up.

"What about them?"

She didn't seem angry, so I continued: "We killed them with running water. Remember?"

She shrugged. "No, not really. You just said you killed them, how they were all stupid and zombie-ish, so they were easy to defeat." I remembered our earlier conversation differently, but I accepted that she might be right. That night, she'd been more interested in what I could tell her about Robert and Jennifer, so it was entirely possible that I'd glossed over that particular detail.

"Well, we did! Using a hose. They just withered away. So how does that fit in with what you showed me earlier?"

"I don't know," she said, seeming intrigued. "Different kinds of vampires; different things. You know, that kill them. Different belief systems and all." She pondered this briefly. "Maybe they believed they would be killed by it, so…" After another pause, she shrugged again.

"Well, they were kind of… vacant. I'm not sure if they were even complex enough to *have* belief systems." I thought a little more. "Or maybe it was because *we…*"

Something weird happened in my head. I felt dizzy, disoriented, a strong sense of déjà vu running through me. For a few seconds, I completely forgot where I was. The feeling passed, and then I was back on the bed with Elizabeth again, my mind having cleared.

"What were we talking about again?" I asked her.

She looked a little perturbed. "You know, I can't remember." Then she laughed. "Don't you hate that? You're talking to someone, and then your mind wanders, and they lose their train of thought, too. Then they're like, 'What was I saying?' And you don't want to admit that you weren't listening…" She chuckled, but then frowned with a sigh and added, "Sorry."

"It doesn't matter," I said forgivingly. "I think it was something about the whole rain versus running water thing. And again, I'm sorry about making you mad last night, and about making you walk all the way home in the pouring rain."

"Actually, I didn't," she said, another smile creeping in.

"What? You flew?"

"Oh, hell no," she said, breaking out in a laugh. "Are you kidding? Flying as a bat with rain pelting all over your face is damn near impossible. We don't have windshield wipers, you know."

I laughed at the image that brought to mind, a little bat wearing goggles with miniature wipers on them. "So what did you do?"

She squirmed on the bed, averting her eyes. "If you must know… I went back to your house."

"You what?"

"Yep," she said. "Then settled down in your basement. It was the nearest place I knew that would be dry. And comfortable. But dirty as hell, Ray, are you kidding me? Don't you or your family ever clean up that place?"

I propped myself up on one arm, looking at her with surprise. "Are you serious? You were in my basement that whole time? After I went to bed, the next day…?"

"Calm down," she said, reaching her hand up and gently pulling me back down onto the bed to face her. "I was mad at you after we talked. And yes, I had to storm off… no pun intended…"

I fought back a laugh. "Oh, shut up."

She grinned at me. "It was what I had to do. And so I hid in there, waiting out the rain, and then it just made sense for me to hang out there and sleep the rest of the day. I left once the sun went down, then came here."

"Elizabeth, you could have just come inside and been with me."

"Not the way I was feeling, I couldn't," she said, pursing her lips.

I sighed. "Fair enough, I guess. Still, it kinda weirds me out to think that you were sleeping that close to me and I never even knew it."

"Doesn't it, though," she purred, then leaned forth from her pillow to mine, kissing me gently. I didn't resist.

December began with the weather mostly back to normal, and I remembered to dress warmly when I went out to meet up with Elizabeth Saturday night. Once again, we spent part of the night in a hotel room, a different one than on Thursday night. I noticed as soon as I walked in that this one was more like the others I was used to, not having the large mirror that was visible from the main room. She probably preferred it that way.

We started off with some brief making out, then took a break to talk shop, including what she'd found out about my clone the night before. Unfortunately, there wasn't much to tell. I'd hoped that she might be able to find out where this torture chamber of his that Melody had mentioned was, but when she asked around to some of the other vampires in town, no one knew what she was talking about.

Later, we made love, which she'd suggested we do properly this time, that is, with her having fed earlier and not being so brutal with me. It certainly was different, and it felt great physically, but my heart wasn't really in it. For one thing, the fact that she was her more normal self — the reason this time contrasted so much with the previous one — was just one more reminder of what she was, that she'd fed on someone before meeting up with me. Had she killed them or just wounded them? I didn't like thinking about it either way.

The other problem was that because she felt like a regular human, that just served to remind me of Melody, how she'd felt. I found myself comparing the two of them, noticing the differences in the ways they moved or the sounds they made. Elizabeth was more smooth and flowing in her rhythms, almost gentle, not only in comparison to our previous encounter but also to how Melody liked to do it.

And really, I was still grieving over Melody's death, but I didn't realize how much until tonight. Whether Elizabeth picked up on that psychically or just knew that I wasn't as into it as I should have been, I wasn't sure. But eventually, we stopped at her prompting: "You're just not feeling it, are you?"

Lying next to her, I apologized more than once, and while she kept saying that it was okay, I could tell that she was disappointed. I was too, and frustrated with myself. It felt like there was something wrong with me: What kind of teenage boy didn't like having sex with a beautiful girl?

We held each other for a while, not speaking, but it wasn't like we were mad or anything. Eventually, we started talking again about various things, but it felt kind of empty, like we were making small talk to get our minds off of how let down we both felt. Things looped back around to talking about the vampires, and I brought up something that maybe I shouldn't have.

I told her about my frustration over not being able to get more done, to go after the vampires myself and kill them. I felt like it was my responsibility. But it was so hard to do anything on my own. Even if I could find a vampire or two, there was always the danger of my winding up dead if I wasn't successful in my attempt. I stood a much better chance with help, but I hadn't heard from any of my old friends for a long time.

"I mean, you could help me," I said to her. "We could get stuff done together. You've got all of the powers and abilities that a vampire does…"

"Because I *am* a vampire, Ray," she said.

"Right! So imagine how much you could help me in tracking down and getting rid of the other ones!" I stopped for second, realizing how crass that had sounded. But I didn't want to back down; I needed to make my point. "They're evil. They're not like you. You don't just kill all the time like…"

"You know, Ray, it kind of seems to me like you're the one who's more obsessed with killing. It's like you want this to be some big action-adventure story, with you as the hero. But have you ever thought about thinking outside of that box and seeing a bigger picture?"

"What do you mean?" I asked, feeling defensive.

"How do you know that all of those other vampires are horrible and evil? Or that they aren't being more careful, like I've been? Better yet, how do you know that I've even been telling you the truth?"

"Have you?" I managed to shoot back before the implications of that notion hit me. It gave me a chill.

"Of course I have," she said, rolling her eyes and shaking her head slightly. "Maybe." Her eyes suddenly locked onto mine, but I knew this game, even though the context of it was usually more playful. She wanted to gauge my reaction. Normally, she'd go from a cold stare to a mischievous giggle, but not this time. "Okay, fine, so I have. But what if I wasn't? Would you kill me then, too?"

That was too painful to think about. "No, I…"

"Where's the line, Ray? What's the standard? And is your judgment really that perfect and flawless? I mean, sure, thanks so much for not staking me through the heart yet, but why don't you ask yourself why you're so eager to go out and eliminate all those other vampires, vampires that you helped create, by the way, and you're not all gung-ho to do the same thing to me?"

I didn't know what to say. And then she pierced me with those deep blue eyes of hers again, never giving me the option to look away.

"Or *are* you?" she added.

"Of course not!" I almost shouted, more out of feeling hurt than angry. How could she even think that?

She started to say something else, but then I saw her draw back. I hated it when we argued, which wasn't that often, but this was clearly something that had been bugging her. She wasn't exactly wrong, but it also felt like she was being unfair. She sighed angrily, then turned and lay on her back, looking up at the ceiling and clutching the bed sheet close to her chest.

"Elizabeth, I love you," I pleaded.

"I love you, too," she said, but the resignation in her voice wasn't very comforting. She sighed again, then rolled over, still holding the sheet close. Then she moved forward, closer to me, and she leaned her forehead against mine.

Once the fight died down, we kissed some more, but there was a forcefulness to how we did it, even bitterness. The way we looked at each other between the kisses was harsh, not tender like most of the time. I got the feeling that both of us were mentally daring the other to say something else, something that might spark off another debate. We did apologize for hurting each other's feelings, but there was that undercurrent of resentment. The "I love you"s we exchanged sounded more like *I love you even though I'm still pretty pissed off at you right now.*

There were still issues between us, things that needed to be resolved. But not tonight. There had been enough fighting. Instead, we resigned ourselves to the simpler task of indulging our physical desires rather than ironing out our personal differences. In time, it became easier.

CHAPTER EIGHTEEN

"The funeral's on Sunday," my mother said to me. "You should make sure your church clothes still fit, or else we'll have to go and get you some new ones."

"Okay," I said, feeling numb. "I'll... um... I'll go check."

I all but staggered back to my bedroom, my mind racing with a thousand thoughts, still stunned by what I'd been told: Both of Tim's parents had been killed. And even though everyone was stupidly dancing around the topic, I had a pretty good idea what had happened to them.

As I made my way across the den, I tried not to hear my father's words, him talking about how he hadn't wanted until now to believe in "all of this vampire business," and my mother sadly saying something about how it couldn't have happened to a nicer couple. They were shocked and upset, as was I, but I knew more than they did. I just couldn't say so.

I pulled out the blue suit and white oxford shirt from my closet, hating myself and everything about this stupid world as I threw them down onto my bed. Somewhere in one of my dresser drawers was a beige colored tie, which I'd look for later. What I couldn't shake from my mind was the idea that I would soon have to face Tim, to tell him how sorry I was, and he'd probably feel even more guilty about what had happened than I already did.

I didn't know just who had killed Tim's parents or exactly how; it could have been his clone, any of the others, or some random vampires around town. Maybe it didn't matter. But one of the most horrible aspects of all of this was that Tim's mother had still been pregnant when she died, taking the unborn baby with her. What would have been Tim's little brother never even got a chance to live.

Having discovered that my formal clothes did in fact not fit anymore, I went to tell my mother this, but I stopped short of her bedroom door when I heard her crying. My father was in there with her, saying comforting things, and I didn't want to intrude. I already felt filled with shame and guilt, so I didn't want to interrupt them to say that we needed to go shopping and feel like even more of an asshole.

Giving her time to calm down, I went out into the backyard and played fetch with Scout. It wasn't something I did very often anymore, and he was eager for the attention, oblivious to the pain of the world around him. He just loved bounding back and forth across the yard, chasing the tennis ball down like it was the most important thing in his life. I envied him for being so simple. He didn't have friends whose parents had gotten killed. He didn't have girlfriends who got fed upon and turned into monsters. And his conscience wasn't burdened with having started off all of these horrible events years ago by stupidly taking a vampire potion just because we thought it would be fun. Sure, Tim had been the one to suggest it, but in one way or another, we were all to blame.

While Scout and I played, I was struck by how ordinary what we were doing felt, and there was a small comfort in that. I even managed to get a laugh out of my old trick of pretending to throw the ball, then watching as he ran off into the yard, looking around and then back at me as he tried to figure out what had happened. But as he padded back towards me, his head held low, I just felt like a jerk. He trusted me to do my part, and I'd tricked him simply because I could. I'd been getting away with things my entire life, and sometimes, I wondered why that was.

I thought about what my life might have been, if I could have just been a regular boy with his dog. Things wouldn't have been as exciting, but they sure as hell would have been a lot safer. Countless people had died, and even more lives had been shaken, the people who were left behind. A deeply cynical notion flashed across my mind that maybe Tim's unborn baby brother was luckier than all of us, never having had to face any of this.

Before we went out to buy me some new clothes, my mother gave me Tim's grandmother's phone number. He was staying with her, and my mother suggested that I give him a call and offer my condolences. I dreaded the idea.

"Can't I just wait until tomorrow night at the… What did you call it again? At the funeral home?"

"The viewing," she said, giving me a withering look. "Ray, your friend needs some support right now. I really think you should call him."

I gave in, taking the piece of paper from her with the number on it. I went back to my bedroom and called, and while the line was ringing, a chill ran through me as I suddenly remembered something. Tim and I were supposed to hang out a few weeks ago, but that had been the weekend that Melody died. Because of that, it had completely slipped my mind to call him back to cancel our plans. But then, he'd never called me back, either, so he must not have been too keen on going out in the first place.

An old woman answered the phone; she sounded tired. I'd only met Tim's grandmother once before, and that had been when I was a kid. She was a tall, friendly lady with big glasses and white curly hair that, when the light caught it just right, looked sort of blue. Whenever

Tim happened to mention her to me over the years, I would joke, "Oh, the blue-haired lady?"

I asked to speak to Tim, and when she asked who was calling, I told her. I was surprised that she remembered me, but then I realized that she must have been confusing me with Carl. She mentioned something about my mother having worked for her son, Jack, but that was Carl's mother, not mine. When I heard the pain in the old woman's voice as she said her dead son's name, I didn't have the heart to correct her.

Once Tim was on the phone, the conversation was stilted and brief. I told him I was sorry, but all he said was, "Yeah." I could tell he'd been crying.

"Mom said there's going to be a bunch of people over at the funeral home tomorrow. So I guess I'll see you then."

"Sure."

"Carolyn might come too, if that's all right."

"If she wants to."

I didn't know what else to say. "Do you... um... Do you know what actually happened? Who did it?"

He let out what sounded like a laugh, but it was more harsh than that, more like an expression of disbelief. "Are you...?" He let out a sigh, the breath distorting the phone's speaker. *"We* did it, Ray. All of us."

"Tim, I'm sorry, I didn't mean..."

"I can't talk right now," he said firmly. "Bye." He hung up the phone.

When I saw him at the viewing the following night, things weren't much better between us. He just gave me an angry, deadpan look, and apart from our initial greeting when I arrived with my family, we never spoke. I hated being there, feeling uncomfortable around so many strangers. I figured that Carl might be there, but I didn't see him.

Leaving my parents to socialize with the other adults, and losing track of Carolyn early on, I wandered around, trying to kill time. I found myself examining the decor of the funeral home, acting like it interested me. What caught my eye in particular were the many framed pictures of Tim's parents throughout the place, some on tables and a few on the mantelpiece above an unlit fireplace. Tim was in a few of the pictures, always as a younger boy, the one I remembered from my childhood. This brought back memories, some good, some bad.

What struck me as wrong was how everyone in the pictures was smiling, looking so happy. But this wasn't a happy occasion. My friend was inconsolable, and the cheerful looking man and woman in these photographs were both dead, lying still in a room at the far end of the building. I only caught a glimpse of them, having made a quick exit once I realized what I was seeing. I hadn't even recognized the caskets at first; they looked like big, polished pieces of wooden furniture with decorative plants around them, like something you'd see in some rich person's living room. Even that brief encounter made me uncomfortable.

Tim's grandmother, whose name my mother had mentioned earlier that night was Beatrice, was there as well, but I never actually talked to her. I noticed how much older she looked than I remembered, thinner and more wrinkled, with strange spots on the flesh that seemed to hang from her elbows and forearms. She was talking with some man I didn't recognize and with Tim, who was doing his best to keep up appearances and be polite. He seemed very much unlike his usual self, being very formal and nodding his head a lot, sometimes giving fake, weak smiles.

I could only overhear bits of the conversation, and I considered walking over and taking part, but then I thought better of it. I caught Beatrice saying something like "Are you sure?" and Tim saying something about how "this" — whatever that was — was important to him and that he needed to do it. The man put a comforting hand on Tim's shoulder and said something to Beatrice about "getting him there," and the matter seemed to be settled. I wondered what they were talking about; maybe it had something to do with the funeral the following day.

I couldn't sleep that night, and I was dreading going to the funeral. The only one I'd ever been to was my grandmother's, and I barely remembered that, having been a toddler at the time. It seemed so pointless to me, all of this formal grieving and ceremony, but I knew that it was important to other people, so I had to show up and take part. I guess the biggest thing that was bothering me was having to be around Tim again, knowing the guilt he felt inside and having it mirrored within myself. A big part of me wanted to try to comfort him, but he'd made it clear that he didn't want that from me, maybe not from anyone.

Tired of tossing and turning in my bed for over an hour, I decided to sneak out through my window and take a walk, bringing my anti-vampire weapons with me as usual. I did this from time to time on sleepless nights, knowing from experience that I probably wouldn't encounter anyone. But I had a lot on my mind and hoped that walking for a while might help me wind down.

I was also feeling bitter and defiant, almost hoping that, unlike other nights, I might actually find a vampire and have to kill it. It wouldn't bring Tim's parents back, but it might give me some kind of satisfaction, a way to vent my anger. But mostly, I wanted to work through my thoughts about Tim and the tragedy that had come upon his family.

There was a feeling I sometimes got of being watched, as if someone were viewing me like a character in a TV show. I'd felt it my entire life occasionally, and when it happened, I'd alter my behavior, walking more upright to avoid slouching or making odd expressions when something occurred to me, almost as if I were looking into a camera. Once I'd realized this about myself, I put it down to some residual effects from watching cartoons as a child, in which characters would often make a funny or thoughtful expression towards the audience, usually accompanied by a music cue that matched it.

I wound up doing something along those lines as I thought more about Tim, how his reluctance to speak to me actually kind of pissed me off. If not me, then who could he talk to about what had really happened? Maybe he was too busy talking to God, I figured, but I tried to restrain myself from thinking that was stupid or feeling resentful. I may not have been into Christianity anymore myself, but that didn't give me the right to begrudge Tim his beliefs, especially if they gave him what he needed, and I had to remind myself that not all Christians were as backwards and controlling as some of the ones I'd known. When this occurred to me, I stopped walking briefly, giving a small, crooked smile and looking to one side. It was a pensive look, one an actor might give to indicate having had a deep thought.

As I continued walking, I began to feel even more intensely that eyes were upon me, and sure enough, there was a couple walking along the road in the opposite direction, headed my way. I just wanted to pass them by and avoid eye contact, but then I realized how late at night it was and how unusual it was for me to run into anyone. My heart began to race as I began to wonder if I had managed to find some vampires after all. Once the couple came into view, I froze.

"Well, hello there," Tim almost sang, and this time, I knew right away that it was his clone I was seeing, not the real Tim. The girl who was with him was pretty and pale, with straight, darkly dyed red hair, her outfit reminiscent of a Catholic schoolgirl's uniform. There was the red and black plaid skirt and white turtleneck shirt, but the black tights and Converse high top shoes made the look seem slightly off, but in a deliberate way. I'd have found her beautiful if I weren't already terrified.

"Tim…" I said, and just for a second, my gut instinct was to tell him how sorry I was about his parents. But then I remembered who I was talking to. Toughening up, I asked, "Did you kill them?"

"Kill who?" he asked, stopping a few feet in front of me. The girl whose hand he was holding did the same, smiling at me smugly. "I do that a lot, you know."

"Hard to keep track," his companion added.

"Your parents," I said angrily.

I couldn't quite read his expression: He was either surprised or just acting like he was. "Really? How terrible for them!" he said sarcastically.

"Your mother was pregnant!" I shouted.

He maintained his detached demeanor, raising his eyebrows and wearing the same leering grin. "Not my mother, really," he said, shrugging his shoulders. "Not anymore."

"You sick bastard," I said, reaching into my jacket pocket and pulling out my stake. Half a second too late, I realized that I should instead have taken out the garlic powder I had on me, as I could have flung that at both of them at once. But the stake felt more powerful, like I was a cop drawing his gun. It was a stupid move.

I expected them to at least flinch, but instead, the girl seemed to get excited. "Ooh!" she said, stepping forward and poking her chest out at me. I tried not to stare at her breasts. "Me me me!"

"Careful, Nadine," Tim said, gently placing a hand on her shoulder but still maintaining his sarcastic air. "This is the famous Raymond Young, the vampire hunter. One wrong move, and he'll wipe out all the guilt he's felt all his life with one lethal blow!"

I tried to stare him down. "Shut up," was all I could think to say.

He glanced at the stake in my raised hand, then back at my face. "You got two of those things? Come on," he said, gesturing towards my jacket. "Surely you've got more in there."

"At least, you'd sure better hope you do," Nadine said with a triumphant smile. The implications of their words had already occurred to me, and I told myself that if I managed to survive this night, I might make a habit of carrying more than one stake on me at a time. Not that I could use them both at once, though. As the thoughts played out in my head, it occurred to me how doomed I probably was. But I wasn't ready to give up just yet.

"All right, look," I said, quickly reaching into my jacket's other internal pocket with my left hand and pulling out the bottle of garlic powder. "You want to play with this, then?" The plastic lid made a small *pop* as I flicked it open with my thumb. I liked to think that the noise would be as threatening as a gun cocking in an action movie, but Tim and Nadine didn't even blink.

"That could be a problem," Tim said. "Except for..."

Without warning, something slammed down onto my left forearm, causing me to drop the bottle of garlic powder. I almost dropped my stake, too, but I managed to hold onto it as I jumped to one side, turning to see what had struck me. It was a girl, another vampire, this one a short brunette with long, dark hair. She, as well as my other foes, had backed up a few feet from where the garlic powder had spilled, but I knew I was still in trouble.

"Got you," the new girl cooed with a fanged smile, and it was then that I recognized her.

"Laura?" I asked in disbelief. Normally, when I ran into someone I hadn't seen since the seventh grade, I'd be surprised and ask them how they'd been, wanting to catch up. That had happened a few times since I'd started attending Westlake, but even then, the reunions never seemed all that happy. This, of course, was much worse.

"Surprise!" Laura said to me, holding her hands out. While her face looked more or less the same as I remembered, her body had matured. She was quite curvy and a bit on the heavy side, but not unattractive, well, apart from having been changed into a bloodthirsty killer.

"Just thought you'd be happy to see a familiar face," Tim said. "So I decided to bring her along for the ride."

"And I'm so glad you did," Laura said, sidling over to Tim but being careful to avoid the spice container on the ground. When she reached him, she leaned up on her toes and kissed his cheek, then looked over at me. Nadine didn't show any signs of being jealous; she just stared at me hungrily along with the other two.

"So," she said smartly, turning briefly to look at Tim and Laura. "One, two, three…" she said as she pointed to each of them, then turned back to me and pointed again. "One."

"Not very good odds, Ray," Tim said. His normally mousy features now seemed positively menacing; gone was the quirky, nerdy boy from my youth.

"No," Laura purred, leaning forward. All three of them had their eyes fixed on me, and I began to step backwards.

"Should we let him run?" Nadine asked.

"That would be more fair," Laura said, "and fun."

"Sure," Tim said. "And we can give him a head start. How about it, Ray? Ready to run for your life?" His face took on a comical expression, fists held up and bent at the elbows.

I took off, leaping across the street and into someone's front yard. We were in more or less the same area where Elizabeth and I had confronted Carl's clone and the vampire he'd made several months earlier, and this time, I was determined to find my way to the sprinkler control. It even occurred to me that, if I survived, maybe I could make a project of finding out precisely where those controls were for all of the houses in my neighborhood. But there wasn't time to figure out how I might pull that off.

I sped across the yard, and it wasn't long before I heard the footsteps of Tim and his lovely but deadly minions hurrying along behind me. I tried to mentally call out to Elizabeth to help me, but I knew it probably wouldn't do any good. Her words from our recent fight ran through my head, the accusation that I kept wanting things to be like an action-adventure. One thing that hurt was that she was right, though I hadn't really thought of it that way. And this was more action than I'd bargained for.

Arriving at the door of the house, I frantically looked around for a knob at ground level by the wall, similar to the one at my own home. There was nothing. If I couldn't find it in time, I'd be dead.

All of a sudden, Laura appeared out of nowhere and quietly said, "Boo," just inches from my face. It scared me, and I turned to run, but then I tripped over a hose. Falling to the ground and then tumbling over, I tried to crawl backwards as she walked towards me, a gloating, haughty look on her face.

A memory flashed across my mind, one from second grade. Our teacher had us line up outside the door to our classroom one morning, and she insisted that everyone be quiet. "I don't want to hear a peep out of any of you!" she said. Even at that age, I was a smart-ass, so I let out a small "*peep*" to be funny, trying to be stealthy about it. "Who said 'peep?'" Mrs. Stewart angrily demanded, and Laura wasted no time in pointing straight at me, that same arrogant look on her face. I got in trouble, and it was on that day that I decided I hated this bratty little tattler with the squinty eyes and big nose.

My attitude towards her mellowed over the years, but I still never really liked her. Seeing that she'd been killed and turned into a vampire had made me sad, but now that it looked like I might meet my end because of her, I felt a keen sense of disappointment. After all I'd been through, all I'd gotten away with and survived so far, was I finally going to be beaten by this little snob from my childhood?

I rolled over, trying to get to my feet, but someone shoved me to one side, causing me to tumble over the grass and onto my back again. The force of the blow was painful, and I winced as I looked up to see Tim, Laura, and Nadine surrounding me. They moved in slowly, the girls raising their hands menacingly like something out of an old horror movie, smiles wide and fangs ready.

Tim approached, looking triumphant as his feet reached my own. I began to panic as I realized that there was no way out of this. I tried pushing outwards with my mind, thinking that I could somehow make them stop, then wishing that I could telekinetically repel them. But it was no use. This really was the end.

But then, for no apparent reason, Tim straightened up, his hands snapping up to his face as if some invisible person had struck him. He gasped, a strange look on his face, and all of a sudden, he vanished, his entire image shimmering away like a ghost. A second later, Nadine and Laura started shrieking, falling to their knees as they reached up to their heads, looking terrified and bewildered.

I jumped up, trying to get away from them, but I couldn't help but watch as the process continued. After a few more seconds of agony, both girls fell still and silent. Laura, who apparently hadn't been a vampire for long, just lay there. But I had to turn away in disgust as I saw Nadine's flesh start to turn black, her long-dead body decomposing.

I ran from the house, wondering if, like before, the occupants might have heard all of the commotion and come outside. I couldn't be caught by them; there would be too many awkward questions. A day or two later, I would find myself wondering if this had in fact been the same house where I'd fought Carl, and if so, if the owners might be wondering why dead vampires kept turning up on their lawn.

But this night, there wasn't time for thoughts like that. I was in flight mode, tearing along the street as I ran back towards home. I couldn't believe my luck, how I'd escaped from such an impossible situation, but when the reality of it hit me, I practically crumbled onto the grass of yet another lawn as I dove away from the pavement, my legs having suddenly given out beneath me.

There was only one thing that could have made Tim's clone vanish like that, disappearing into nothingness as the vampires he'd made subsequently perished. Tim Donnelly, my friend since the second grade, was dead.

Getting to sleep that night had been impossible, but I must have passed out at some point, because I was woken up by my father knocking on my door. I groggily stumbled to it and unlocked it to let him in, making my way back to my bed and noticing how late in the morning it was, almost noon. I usually slept in on the weekends, but not this late. I half expected my father to say something about this or how I needed to get ready for the funeral, but instead he just sat down on the bed next to me.

"Ray, I have some… some really terrible news," he said to me. My head began to clear as I recalled the events of the night before. "Tim, your friend…" He sighed, looking up at the ceiling. "God, there's no easy way to say this, is there?"

I already knew that Tim was dead, but I didn't know quite how. I figured that some other vampire must have killed him, and while I was grateful for the timing that had saved my life, I felt ashamed for thinking that. But I couldn't let on that I knew what had happened yet.

"What, Dad?"

He bowed his head, eyes closed. "Tim took his life last night, Ray. I'm really sorry to have to tell you that."

At least I didn't have to pretend to be surprised. "What?" I whispered. "Are you… Are you sure?"

"Yes. He, um… Apparently, instead of staying with his grandmother last night, he got Dan, a friend of the family, to take him back to his house to spend the night. He's the one who just now called and told me. He sounded so angry with himself for leaving Tim there…" He swallowed hard. I wasn't used to seeing my father this upset, and it wasn't helping me keep my own tears at bay. He looked up at the ceiling again. "Tim shot himself. That's what happened. I'm really sorry." He put his hand on mine, an uncharacteristic gesture of comfort for him.

I had no idea what to say. Something practical? "When's the funeral?" I asked.

Dad sighed again. "Well, that's the thing. They've rescheduled the one that was supposed to be this afternoon. Going to bury all three of them together. But it's going to be a private ceremony, just close family. Less of a fuss that way, I guess." A small part of me felt relieved not to have to go, but then I hated myself for that. I also was still stunned over what Tim had done.

"I always told Jack that having a gun in the house was a dangerous thing," my father said in a low voice.

"You have one," I said, causing him to pull his hand back and look at me, apparently caught off guard.

"How did you…" He didn't finish his sentence.

"Sorry," I said. "Carolyn told me a while ago. I didn't know it was supposed to be a secret."

"It's not…" He looked down again. "I mean, not really. Though I suppose all families have their secrets."

You have no idea, I thought to myself. I fought back tears, not wanting to break down into a blubbering mess in front of him. But then a memory flashed through my mind, that of me as a much younger child, crying on his chest over the death of my first pet, a small lizard I'd had for only a few days. It seemed stupid to compare that to what had happened, but the thought was enough to push me over the edge.

He held his arm around me as I leaned into him, sobbing as quietly as I could, still not wanting to fully let loose. Moments like this between us were extremely rare, and I noticed how different the proportions were compared to that old memory, how small my body was back then and how much bigger he seemed to me at the time. Now, we were practically the same size, and I felt more equal to him, the two of us grieving over the same thing.

The conversation ended with him offering to let me be on my own, and I later wondered if this father-son encounter had made him as uncomfortable as it did me. We just weren't usually like this with each other, and while I appreciated the effort, it didn't change anything between us long-term. He did tell me that if I ever needed to talk to him about anything, I could, but I knew that it wasn't really true. He'd probably said that hoping to prevent my ending up the same way as Tim, maybe afraid that I could have dark things I was keeping to myself that would lead me down the same path.

And maybe I did, or at least I had. I'd already courted the idea of suicide before, not long after Elizabeth was killed. I'd figured it was the only way to get rid of my clone. Once I remembered this, I realized that Tim must have come to the same conclusion, probably coupled with all of the guilt he'd felt all these years. Once I recovered from the initial shock of his death, though, I had more questions.

I put these to Elizabeth when I saw her that night. She was of course very sympathetic and sorry that I'd lost such an old friend, and as usual, I found more comfort confiding in her than in anyone else. Our fight from the last time we'd seen each other was all but forgotten.

"I wish I could say that I can't understand why he did it," I whispered. Not wanting to bother with the complexities of sneaking out, I'd convinced her to join me in my bedroom this night. "But in a way, I can."

"Ray, don't talk like that," she said in a strange combination of gentleness and firmness.

"I know, I know. But I guess what's bugging me is… Well, I'm kind of confused."

"About what?"

"When I was little, maybe six or so, I was told that when people die, they go to Heaven. And it's supposed to be this great place. So I asked Carolyn one time, 'If it's so great, then why don't people just kill themselves so they can go there?'"

"You asked a question like that at six?"

I laughed a little, probably for the first time in days. "Yeah."

"Seems a pretty…" She broke off, then asked, "How did you even know what suicide *was* that young?"

"Because of the song. 'Suicide Is Painless.' It was the theme song to that show *M*A*S*H.* You remember it?"

"Yeah, but…"

"We had a book of sheet music on the piano in the living room, and that song was in it. When I realized it had something to do with the TV show, I asked Susanna what the word 'suicide' meant, and she explained it. So then later, I asked Carolyn about it. She said that people who died normally went to Heaven, but if they committed suicide, they went to Hell. Only she didn't actually say 'Hell;' she called it 'the hot place' and pointed down. I still remember that."

Elizabeth let out a quick breath, sort of like a whispered laugh in the dark. "Pretty heavy conversation for a six-year-old."

"I may have been older; I don't know. But that's the thing about Tim, I mean… He must have known that he'd end up there if he, you know…"

"You still believe in all that?"

"I don't know. Maybe. But the point is, I know he did."

She sighed. "That's true. And sad."

"So I guess it was his clone that killed them, his parents I mean."

"Not necessarily."

"What, do you know something?"

"No, I'm just saying that it could have been someone else. Just a coincidence."

"Do you think you could find out for sure? You know, ask around?"

She paused, and I wondered what expression she was making in the darkness. "I'm not sure what good that would do."

"If I knew who it was, if it wasn't Tim's clone, I mean, I'd really like to go after them."

"Revenge."

"Yes," I said firmly, starting to feel defiant. "Maybe you could help."

"Ray, don't," she said, a pleading tone in her whisper. She then surprised me by nudging her head closer to mine on the pillow and kissing me gently, just a peck. "Let's please not fight about this again." There was another quick kiss. "Not now."

The seduction worked, at least long enough for me to start kissing her more deeply. Our bodies drew in closer, the physical comfort distracting me momentarily. The silence, however, began to let other thoughts creep in, and my grief resurfaced after a very short time.

When I broke away from her and began crying, she drew back and just let me do it, my head burying itself in my pillow. As she pulled me closer again, her arms guided me to roll over in the bed, and she held me from behind as I cried myself to sleep. Occasionally, she kissed the back of my head or just nuzzled me to express sympathy and comfort, sometimes squeezing me gently with her arms. It helped a little, but mostly, my head was filled with memories of Tim, of all the things we'd been through, and it hurt so much that he was gone.

Surprisingly, I didn't dream about him that night, or if I did, I didn't remember doing so when I woke up the next morning. The sun was up, and Elizabeth was gone.

CHAPTER NINETEEN

I had not been looking forward to Christmas at all. Because of all the horrible things that had happened that year, I had half a mind to go all Scrooge on the holiday and try to opt out of it, but I couldn't really do that. When I tried running that by my mother, she insisted that it was important for me to stick with tradition, that I'd feel even worse if I didn't. Maybe she was right.

But all of the "good cheer" crap still got on my nerves. Anything I did to try to go along with that just felt like faking it. I enjoyed the almost two weeks off from school, or rather, I was grateful for them, even if I wasn't actually happy.

In the days leading up to that, I'd done my best to recover from Tim's death, and it wasn't easy. I practically sleepwalked through school, doing the bare minimum I needed to get by, hardly studying for my exams. I knew that I'd probably passed all of them, but the cynic in me was nonchalant about the consequences if I hadn't.

Carl had pissed me off, too, by still refusing to have a meaningful conversation when I tried to talk to him about Tim. I'd known him for almost as long, and even if we weren't as close as we once had been, it seemed like he should at least have the decency to give a shit about our old friend. And even though I could tell that he really did care deep down and was just playing the tough guy, he had increasingly pissed me off over the months by withdrawing from me almost every bit as much as Dennis had. As for Dennis, I'd also tried to call him to let him know what happened, but not surprisingly, I never heard from him. But he probably already knew, given how well known Tim's father had been around town.

I didn't even begrudge Elizabeth's decision to not see me on Christmas, though it did disappoint me. But because I was already feeling so gloomy myself, I understood. Unlike me, she did have the option of hiding out from other people throughout all of this enforced merriment. "Take what comfort you can in your family," she told me. "At least you have one."

So I did my best, and it wasn't terrible the entire time. Melody had said to me more than once that how happy or how miserable one was depended entirely on one's self, which I tried to take to heart. If I sat around moping and feeling sorry for myself, then I would continue to feel that way, and no one could change that but me. Of course, thinking of her made me sad as well, but eventually, I decided to try to take her advice and be strong.

It was weird being around my entire family at once, how all five of us knew that Tim and his parents had died, but only three of us knew the entire story. It wasn't like keeping secrets from our parents was anything new, but it made us squirm whenever the topic came up and we had to pretend that we knew no more than they did. No one ever brought up the term "vampire," which was a relief.

As for Christmas Day itself, despite the occasional lapses into sadness, it was a decent enough time. Presents were exchanged in the morning by the tree, just as they had been for as long as I could remember. I found myself caring a lot less about the gifts I received than in previous years, but I faked enthusiasm and gave thanks as needed. I actually found more joy in the reactions I got based on the gifts I gave, like the tripod that Carolyn and I went halves on to give to our father to use with the camcorder. He appreciated it, having mentioned to me a few weeks earlier that the one they had at the library was old and falling apart.

Carolyn and I rode with Susanna in her car out to Appling to see our cousins in the afternoon while our parents drove in theirs, and it didn't surprise me that we didn't talk about Tim. I didn't really want to talk much by then anyway, partly because it would have been depressing but also because I was pretty exhausted, having been up late the night before. I'd had a hard time getting to sleep, fantasies running through my head of getting too upset at some point and lashing out at someone, angry at them for trying to have such a happy occasion when things really weren't okay. I would imagine myself flying off the handle suddenly, giving some big speech about how bad things really were, even yelling at my parents for not having a clue as if that were somehow their fault.

Dinner was polite and decent enough, and more gifts were exchanged among the extended family. In time, I allowed myself to give in to the pleasantries of the holiday, to just do this ordinary, normal thing like everybody else. At least for a while, I could pretend to forget my real life troubles and act like — maybe even briefly believe — that everything was okay and at peace, even if just for one day.

All of that flew out the window when we got home that night, and I found Scout lying dead next to his doghouse.

"Must have been whatever everyone keeps blaming those vampires on," I heard Susanna say. My bedroom door was locked, but it was still close enough to the den for me to hear most of what was being said. My father agreed, saying that it was a shame.

I had stomped back into the house and slammed the back door angrily, and to the surprise of the rest of my family, I announced, "Christmas can officially fuck off as far I'm concerned!" It was perhaps overly dramatic of me, but I was so livid that I didn't care. I'd been faking my way through happiness the entire day, but finding my dog dead — with two small puncture wounds on the side of his neck, no less — was the last straw.

"Ray, what…?" Carolyn began to ask while the rest of my family stared at me, open-mouthed. I may have sworn plenty of times around my sisters, but this was the first time I'd done so in front of my parents.

"Go out there and see for yourself!" I shouted, pointing towards the backyard. "Scout's dead. And I'll give you three guesses what killed him. Merry stupid goddamn Christmas, everyone." With that, I stormed away and locked myself in my room.

I felt a bit stupid about the outburst once I was alone, face down on the bed and too angry to cry. I gripped my pillow beneath me, breathing heavily into it, almost hyperventilating. I listened as the others made their way outside, and there was silence for a while, followed by their coming back in. That was when Susanna made her declaration about vampires, but the way she'd done it was a clever dodge.

I knew why she'd done it, to further put our parents off the scent and cast doubt on the reality of the situation, but all that did for me was add to my anger. They'd probably buy it, maybe even think that there weren't any real vampires, just wild bats or whatever other bullshit excuse the city had come up with all these years.

Carolyn said something about burying Scout, and the thought of that brought me closer to tears. But when I made out a few words from my father saying something about going to the pound or the pet store, I slammed my hands down onto the bed and forced myself up, marching angrily to my door. I forgot that I'd locked it, so my hand scraped against the doorknob, making an odd sound. This just added to my fury, and I all but yanked the knob off as I twisted it to unlock it.

I stomped back into the den, interrupting my family's conversation as I pointed accusingly at my father. "If you're thinking about going and buying another puppy to replace him, don't you dare." I flinched inwardly, realizing that I'd never spoken to him this way.

Still, one thing I had initially resented about Scout was how he had been forced upon me. I hadn't asked for him; my father had just insisted on getting him to make up for the loss of the family's previous pet, a cat named Crowley. Carolyn, Susanna, and I had cared a great deal for him, but he had barely been gone before Dad just plopped another furry responsibility into my lap, whether I wanted it or not.

"Ray, you may feel that…"

"Don't tell me how I feel!" I shouted. "How would you even know?" He looked shocked, even wounded.

"Ray, please," my mother said.

I looked over at her. "And if you're about to say that every cloud has a silver lining, or some other useless crap like that, don't even bother."

My father then stepped forward and said very firmly, "That's enough." My mother reached up and put a hand on his shoulder, as if she were gently holding him back. There was something in her eyes, a vulnerability that I wasn't used to seeing. For some reason, she reminded me a lot more of Carolyn than herself.

"Okay," Carolyn said, her voice more high-pitched than usual as she stood up from the wicker chair. She stepped forward, subtly positioning herself between me and my parents. "I think it's time everyone calmed down. We're all upset here."

"I agree," Susanna said. She'd been standing off to the side of the room with her arms folded this whole time, but now she walked over to me and put her hand on my back, turning me with her other one to guide me out of the den. I complied, letting her walk me back to my bedroom. "I think you need to go to bed," she said quietly, "before you blurt out anything worse."

My anger flared again, this time towards her, but I kept it in check. There wasn't any point in making a further scene, and I was already starting to feel bad about what I'd done.

It hadn't been fair for me to lash out at my parents like that. And it wasn't even them I was really mad at. Scout's death had just been my breaking point, and all sorts of past resentments had come to the surface at once. I knew that I'd have to apologize, but I decided to wait until morning once I'd calmed down.

It was a little after midnight when I heard the singing. I'd been lying in bed for hours, unable to sleep from all the anger and the adrenaline. It had taken at least an hour for my heart to stop pounding so fiercely. I was angry on many levels, and my mind kept running in circles. Who had killed Scout? Had it just been a random attack by a vampire bat? I didn't know if attacks on animals were a common thing or not; if they were, the news didn't report them as far as I knew. Maybe my clone had done it, or maybe Carl's or Dennis's for some reason? I even briefly wondered if Elizabeth might have been the culprit, but I knew that was ridiculous.

When I first heard the music from outside, I was confused. Someone was humming the tune to "We Wish You a Merry Christmas," and then it was more like singing but without the actual words: *"Bump BUMP bump ba-da-da BUMP bump…"*

I was reminded of the way that the Mengs had decked out their house one year at Christmas several years ago, back when they still lived across the street. It was an impressive but obnoxiously huge display, and there was even some sort of sound system installed that played holiday tunes well into the night. Most of the neighbors loved it, but my father had grumbled that it was just Dr. Meng trying to show off how wealthy he was. I'd thought it was cool, at least until I went to bed and noticed how the lights were so bright that I could still see some of the illumination through my drapes. I then began to be afraid that if the display was as garish as my father seemed to think it was, it might scare Santa Claus away and make him skip over both their house and mine.

I hadn't believed in Santa Claus for a long time, and because of all of the bad things that had been happening for years, I'd begun to doubt the existence of God as well. But by this point, I also felt that my belief or disbelief in him didn't really determine whether or not he was out there, no more than the people at Bethlehem Baptist choosing not to believe in science made it untrue.

The music I was hearing couldn't have been coming from the house across the street. Aside from the fact that it was still uninhabited, even if there had been a display like the Mengs' from years ago, I wouldn't have been able to hear this voice so clearly. It sounded more like it was coming from my front yard. As I remembered the words to the song, I became annoyed. I'd had anything but a merry Christmas.

I pulled back the drapes but couldn't see anyone, though the singing continued. A suspicion began to build up in me that Elizabeth had decided to pay me a visit tonight after all, her playful attempt at caroling meant to cheer me up. But I definitely wasn't in the mood for it.

I was already halfway out the window when I realized a major flaw in my reasoning: The voice didn't sound like Elizabeth's at all. I wasn't sure if it was male or female, but it certainly wasn't like the angelic singing voice I'd heard her demonstrate in the past. The smart thing to do would have been to go back inside and try to ignore it, but I was already too curious to find the source.

Looking around the yard, I still didn't see anyone, and I couldn't figure out where the sound was coming from. I was confused to find that the tune grew more quiet as I stepped farther away from the house; I'd expected the mysterious singer to be somewhere out in the yard. I was just starting to figure things out when the singing stopped, replaced by a familiar laugh. The small, tinny voice starting singing to the tune of "Happy Birthday:" *"Merry Christmas to me, Merry Christmas to me! Merry Christmas to Ra-ay..."*

It then broke off and laughed again just as I spotted the source: a bat perched on the rain gutter above my bedroom window. The laughter continued as the bat suddenly leapt from its position and flew right over my head, heading across the street to the unoccupied house. I chased after it, patting my jacket's inner pocket to make sure my stake was still there, then cursing myself for not remembering to get some new garlic powder.

The bat's form was too dark to follow, and I lost it by the time I reached the street. Once in the neighbors' yard, I looked around desperately, hoping to spot it again. Then the bat started singing again, and I followed the sound, realizing that it had landed on the roof above the house's front door. I stepped closer, and the bat's body grew and changed, resolving itself into its person form. In the dim glow from the nearby streetlight sat my clone, grinning down at me.

"You piece of shit," I spat. "Get your ass down here."

"Why don't you fly up here and come get me?" he asked, and as before, it felt very weird hearing my own voice taunt me. "Oh, right. You can't."

That was frustrating; I wanted nothing more than to be able to be eye level with him, to knock that stupid smile right off his face. "Coward," I said bitterly.

"I thought you'd be glad to see me!" he lied. "Didn't you like the present I left you?" My anger grew as I realized what he meant. "Isn't a dead dog what every little boy wants for Christmas? How's the song go… *I want a dead beagle for Christmas…*"

"Shut the fuck up!" I shouted, but then I looked around, afraid that someone might overhear.

"Shh…" my clone cautioned me sarcastically, putting a finger to his lips. "Gotta keep everything secret, you know. Just like always. Actually, you should be grateful. At least I let you have a decent Christmas. My original plan was to kill that stupid little dog on Christmas Eve. Then you could have had all the joy of waking up the next morning to find him."

"Why?" I demanded, my voice again getting too loud. "Why the hell did you do it?"

He let out a "*pfft*" sound as he rolled his eyes. "Please. It's not like you ever wanted him anyway."

"That's not true!" And it wasn't. I had resented Scout's presence in my life at the very beginning, but in time, I'd grown to love him just like any other pet.

"Oh, come on. It's me here." He put a finger to his chest as he spoke. "You don't have to lie to me."

"I'm not lying," I said through clenched teeth.

"Whatever you say."

"What the hell are you doing here?" I asked firmly.

"Just wanted to say hi." He shrugged. "It's been a while."

"Bullshit," I said.

"What, didn't you miss me?" he asked, spreading his arms out like he wanted to give me a hug. He then slipped a little on the roof and quickly steadied himself. The small blunder brought me a brief sense of satisfaction. "Surely you like seeing the embodiment of everything you used to be."

It was my turn to roll my eyes. "Whatever," I said, wanting to come up with something more profound but unable to.

"Shame about Tim, huh?" he asked with that same sick grin. "Didn't see that coming." A wave of sadness went through me, but I tried not to show it. "I mean, I knew killing his parents would upset him and all, but…"

"You killed them?" I nearly shouted.

"I had to!" he said, almost indignant. "Dumb little shit was feeling *oh so* guilty… just like all you stupid little humans do. And it was getting to the point where his parents were beginning to suspect."

My mounting anger subsided, giving way to curiosity. "Suspect?"

"His involvement in everything."

"How do you know that?"

He smirked at me, and it occurred to me that I'd never seen myself do that in a mirror, so it was odd to see what that looked like. "You'd be surprised how easy it is to spy on people when you can turn into a bat. Or don't you remember?"

I toughened myself up again, not wanting to give him any satisfaction. "Not really."

He leered at me, probably knowing that I was lying. "Didn't think he'd go and kill himself, though. Little pussy just couldn't take the guilt, I guess."

"Shut up," I said.

"You should be glad! He might have gone on to expose us, gone to the police, gotten you a nice little seat in the electric chair. Is that what you would have wanted?"

I couldn't think of anything to say back. I turned away from the roof, looking down at the porch. I still wanted to be defiant, but all this talk of Tim was beginning to depress me.

"Oh, and by the way," he continued, "you don't have to worry about Dennis going around and killing people anymore. I got rid of him, too, the big stupid hippie."

I jerked my head back up to him, hating his leering expression even more. "You killed his clone?"

"Clone?" he asked with amusement. "Is that what you call us? We're 'clones?'" He laughed condescendingly. "How very sci-fi of you."

"It was Tim's idea," I said sadly, then regretted showing any vulnerability.

"Yeah, well," he said nonchalantly. "Sure. I killed his vampire *clone*. The dickhead was getting too full of himself. And I didn't like the competition."

The implications of this began to sink in. If Dennis's clone was gone, plus all the vampires he had made, that would mean that there were even fewer vampires in Augusta. I'd had a similar thought earlier in the month in the wake of Tim's death and that of his clone, but the optimism that had brought to me was tinged with guilt and sadness. Even though I knew it was true, I didn't like to acknowledge that something good had actually come out of Tim's suicide.

"Oh, and then I killed the human Dennis, too," my clone said flippantly. "I just couldn't resist. Sure, it would have been more efficient to just kill him first and wipe out the other him — the *clone* — that way, but this was more fun, like killing him twice."

I nearly collapsed from this news, gripping the handrail separating the porch from the shrubbery beside it, and I found myself involuntarily sitting down on the steps. It wasn't a good move on my part; turning my back on a vampire never was. But I couldn't help it. I'd always heard people talk about warning people to sit down before hearing shocking news: *I hope you're sitting down.* Now I fully understood the phenomenon.

"Dennis is dead?" I asked, my voice cracking.

A shuffling noise came from somewhere above, and I heard my clone land on the brick surface behind me. "Yes, he is," my own voice practically whispered, his tone triumphant. "No need to worry about him anymore."

I was broken. Part of me wanted to stand up and spin around, plunging my stake into the heart of the monster standing behind me. But I could barely breathe, and I hated the fact that I was feeling so helpless.

"That's right," my clone said, apparently having knelt down to speak into my ear. "Go on and cry, little baby. I killed your friend. And you know what separates me from you? I'm not going to shed a single tear because of it. You're the one with the conscience, the guilt, all that stupid crap. I don't have any of that. That's what makes me better than you."

"It does not!" I hissed, trying to be right.

"Good job on Melody, by the way," he continued. "That went pretty much like I'd planned."

"What?" I asked, finally facing him, hating the fact that he could probably see my tears streaming down.

"That girl," he said wistfully as he straightened up. "She really thought she was something else. So I let her go off and do her dumb little scheme and all, but really, the plan all along was for you to kill her. I knew you'd be all moral upright guy and have to do the right thing, killing her and being oh so sad about it after the fact. She didn't even know that I followed her, spying on her the whole time. I figured you'd get the best of her, as inexperienced as she was. But I couldn't take the chance that she might actually succeed."

He loved to gloat, apparently. Was I really this arrogant and full of myself? I had a hard time accepting that this creature was truly a mirror of my evil side; I didn't want to believe that I was quite this bad, that everything he was came from within me. And I hated the fact that I felt so emotionally crippled in front of him, but then, I saw a way to get back at him.

"Is that what you tried to do with Elizabeth last year?" I asked angrily.

He briefly looked shocked, then returned to his condescending attitude. "Pretty much, yeah. Too bad she thought she was too good for all that."

"Too good for you, you mean." He flinched, his smile fading. "You couldn't handle her, keep her in check. And I'm sure you couldn't stand that."

He backed up, and I stood, straightening up as I kept my eyes on him. "So, what now?" I asked. "I know you're not here to kill me; you can't. Did you just come by to show off how big and bad and evil you are? Well, congratulations. I'm really impressed." He had begun to look more uncomfortable as he slowly backed away, my renewed confidence apparently making him uneasy. If he could be cruel, so could I. "Why don't you go run along and hide again, like you've been doing all this time. Back to your little medieval torture chamber or whatever it is."

He looked down, disappointed. "Oh yeah, Melody told you about that." He shrugged, then looked back up at me. "Actually, that never really got off the ground."

I couldn't help but laugh at how sad he looked. "It didn't?"

"No. It got too hard to kidnap people for it like I thought I would. They'd struggle, and then I'd just have to kill them. After a while it just seemed like too much trouble." Something on my face must have betrayed my disgust, and his expression began to brighten. "But maybe I should try a little harder. It was a really good idea, you know!"

I'd had enough. "Okay, you've had your fun," I said, reaching into my jacket and pulling out my stake, which I held up threateningly. "Time for you to go."

He looked frightened for a second, but then he just sneered at me. "Oh, right," he said. "Like you're going to do anything with that. We both know you won't, because of her." He was right, and I despised him for it. He began to look more triumphant. "Another thing that makes me better than you. If you had any balls whatsoever, you'd end this here and now and kill me with that thing."

Defeated, I lowered the stake and put it back into my jacket, but then a flash of inspiration — a bluff — came to me. "But I bet this garlic powder will fuck you up instead," I said, pretending to shuffle around inside the pocket.

Immediately, my clone's form shrank into a bat, and he zoomed up into the air. I couldn't see him, but he must have remained close by for a moment. I heard him say to me sarcastically, "We must do this again soon," and then I heard the sound of fluttering wings, which faded into the night in a matter of seconds.

I wasn't sure which one of us had won the fight. Really, it was a draw, at least in a physical sense, but we'd been locked in that pattern for months. He couldn't kill me because then he would die, and I couldn't kill him because that would eliminate Elizabeth. As for the psychological aspect of it, I'd managed to get some good punches in here and there, but even though I hated to admit it, he'd caused more damage to me than I had to him.

Tim was dead, Scout was dead, and now Dennis was dead, too. I didn't even know how far back that had happened, and I didn't want to call Dennis's father to find out. I just accepted it as fact, and I cried more that night as I went to bed. He and I hadn't been on the best of terms the past few years, but we'd been through a lot when we were younger.

We'd even hated each other when we first met, and I'd picked on him for being the new kid at school, this pudgy, dumpy kid with a lisp who wore what I thought were stupid looking clothes. In time, circumstances had forced us into becoming friends, and he'd gotten caught up in the vampire situation once I brought him into it. I remembered the slumber party at his house when we'd watched cheesy horror movies, and more importantly, how he'd introduced me to the psychic powers that we found we both had. We'd had our secrets, our fun, and our darker times. Knowing that he was gone broke my heart, and Elizabeth patiently listened to me as I told her all of this, knowing how much pain I was in.

She comforted me as best as she could, the two of us cuddling in the backseat of my car, the engine still running to keep the heater going. We were parked at the former site of the VA hospital again, trying to ignore the unpleasant memories of the last time we'd been there.

One thing that came up in that conversation surprised me, something that hadn't occurred to me during the confrontation with my clone.

"Really?" Elizabeth asked me. "He sang?"

"What? Well, yeah, sort of."

She looked confused, maybe intrigued. "That seems kinda... I don't know. More upbeat than I remember him."

I then got what she was saying. The way she'd described my clone to me over a year ago, he'd been this dull, sort of lifeless figure, someone with no personality. We'd concluded that this was because he wasn't really a whole person, just my evil traits compiled into one being, not having any of my more human aspects. I told her my thoughts on this.

"Right," she said. "So it sounds like maybe he's grown, become more of a real person."

"You know, I didn't even think about that when I met Tim. His clone, I mean. He was pretty jokey and taunting and all that, too. And there was the time…" I broke off, shuddering as the memory of him killing that girl in front of us played itself in my head again.

"Yeah, I know," Elizabeth said, putting a comforting hand on mine. There was a pause, and she breathed in deeply, then exhaled slowly. "Ray?"

"Hmm?"

"About your clone."

"What about him?"

"You really should have killed him last night when you had the chance."

CHAPTER TWENTY

The plan Elizabeth and I came up with was not one that I was happy with. In fact, I'd had to talk her out of her original one and come up with a compromise, and even then, we had no idea if it would work.

After all of the horrible things my clone had done near the end of the year, Elizabeth's conclusion was that we needed to get rid of him, even though that would mean that she would die as well. I objected immediately, but she slowly tried to convince me that there was no other way. He had become more bold and daring, causing the death of two of my oldest friends, a girlfriend, and — presumably just for kicks — my dog as well. Apparently, he had made it his mission to torment me in the worst ways he could get away with, only without actually killing me. And there was no reason to think that he would stop.

"He might go after your family next," Elizabeth said to me. "Your sisters. Your parents. Anyone else you try to get close to."

I knew she was right, but I couldn't stand the thought of her dying as well. "I'm not too thrilled about it either," she quipped, "but maybe it's time. Past time, even."

This was all very stoic and brave of her, but I hated it just the same. Initially, the idea was for her to kill him, maybe getting close enough by pretending to have changed her mind about being with him instead of me. I wasn't sure if he'd fall for that, plus the idea of her being seductive in order to convince him disgusted me.

Instead, it was decided that she would try to find some way to imprison him, perhaps indefinitely. I'd heard of this being done with vampires before, as had she, in stories where instead of a vampire being killed, a way was found to keep it locked away in a tomb. Neither of us were certain just how to pull it off, but once we settled on this, she decided that she should resume her research into vampire folklore and see what she could come up with.

What I really hated, though, was that in order for the overall plan to work, she and I would have to break contact for a long time. Essentially, she would be acting like a double agent, having to convince my clone that she and I were no longer speaking and that she'd decided to be a part of his vampire group instead. Because of what he'd said to me the night before about spying on people as a bat, I realized that there was no way to be sure that he wouldn't see us together; he may in fact have been peering in on us plenty of times over the past year.

I couldn't sense him psychically, at least not without help, and now that Tim and Dennis were gone, that was no longer a possibility. Elizabeth, meanwhile, had learned to sense his presence. Once our conversation made its way to this point, she quickly got quiet, closing her eyes and shushing me when I asked her what she was doing. I then figured it out, and I waited, noticing how beautiful and peaceful she looked with her eyes closed, almost as still as if she were sleeping. I also started trying to absorb and remember every aspect of her, realizing the more we talked that I might not see her for a very long time.

He wasn't around, she concluded, so this night's conversation was safe at least. We worked out a few more details, including the unfortunate fact that she couldn't even leave me notes to let me know what she'd found in her research or how the scheme was going. It was too big of a risk; if she left a note on my window, my clone might find it. We really did have to maintain the proverbial radio silence, which was frustrating to say the least.

It was decided that at the start of the new year, she and I would break contact, and hopefully, our plan would work. We did manage to work in one more lovemaking session in a hotel room before she left, which was nice. And finally, it was perfect. I didn't screw things up by saying something stupid to derail it, nor did she do anything to scare me or put me off. It was bittersweet in the sense that I had no idea when we would see each other again, but I was still very grateful that we got to have this night. I just hoped that the kiss I gave her as I left wasn't the very last one.

The first couple of months of 1991 were hard at first, but in some ways, life seemed to get better and return to normal, or as normal as my life ever got. I missed Elizabeth terribly, and I worried about her, but I tried my best to believe that our plan would succeed. Sooner or later, I hoped, she'd contact me again and tell me that all had gone well.

I was able to concentrate on schoolwork again, doing what was necessary to get by, but not in any danger of failing any of my classes. Carolyn, meanwhile, had returned to college, but for whatever reason, she lost interest after a while and dropped out again. My parents weren't happy about that, but rather than pressure her to go back, they instead encouraged her to get a job. She did so, working in a retail store for a short time before later landing a waitressing job at one of the local restaurants. She wasn't thrilled with it, but occasionally, she relayed to me funny stories about some of the customers she had to deal with.

My clone, meanwhile, seemed to have backed off on his personal vendetta against me; nothing else bad happened to anyone I knew. Because the only two active clones remaining were him and Carl's clone, wherever he might be, the number of attacks in the city had declined.

Having gotten used to my relatively new freedom as a licensed driver, I occasionally patrolled the city on Friday and Saturday nights, my backpack of anti-vampire weapons in the passenger seat. But I never found a reason to use them, even on the more daring weekends when I ventured downtown or into South Augusta, where the vampires were most prevalent.

And really, I was glad that I didn't run into any of them. That wasn't cowardice as much as it was thinking of Elizabeth, hoping that our scheme was playing itself out. By the end of February, I hoped that she'd managed to successfully infiltrate my clone's group and earned his trust, waiting for the right moment to take him down. Still, the more time passed, the more anxious I became.

It was exasperating not being able to contact her; even if I did the trick of summoning her to her grave, that could jeopardize the plan. I was also angry with myself for not telling her something I'd meant to, but I'd kept forgetting until it was too late. It had occurred to me after we'd parted the night we came up with the plan, and while I'd wanted to tell her when I saw her that last time, it completely slipped my mind.

The fact of the matter was that I knew of a way to imprison a vampire, but I hadn't thought about it for ages. Even though I'd told Elizabeth quite a bit about the summers when we'd been vampires, I'd left out some of the details, particularly the more frightening and traumatic ones. One of those was how we had battled and eventually defeated the famous vampire Dracula, but that had been such a terrifying ordeal that I didn't like to think about it.

When he'd first shown up, he spoke of how he had been held in his coffin for nearly a century, one of the methods being used to trap him being a wild rose. Van Helsing had used this and other techniques to keep him imprisoned, and in the end, we wound up doing the same once we'd defeated him. Prior to that, I'd never heard of a rose being used against a vampire, but then, it wasn't any more obscure or strange than any of the other esoteric "vampire killers" that Elizabeth had turned up in her research.

I probably forgot to tell her that final night because I was so caught up in how much I was going to miss her, plus there was the whole sex thing. Despite all of our pseudo-military planning, this talk of spies and double agents and such, at the end of the day, I was still a horny teenager, easily distracted by sex. But it wasn't cheap and tawdry; I genuinely loved her. And in the months that followed, I eventually remembered that the wild rose had come up during one of our conversations, but I couldn't recall just what we had said. Maybe she already knew about the method for using it, or if not, she might very well find it on her own in time.

But something else began to bug me, particularly as the weeks went by and I didn't hear from her. What if she actually did change her mind? Would spending all of that time with my clone and the other vampires make her, as the term went, "go native?" Maybe, now that my clone had apparently developed more of a personality, she might find him appealing after all, more so than me. They might have more in common now.

A distraction from this paranoia came to me unexpectedly in March, when I ran into Carl's clone again. I'd been having another one of my insomniac nights, wandering the streets of my neighborhood only halfway hoping to actually encounter any vampires to fight. He caught me off guard by flying right in front of me and then landing in his person form, and while my first instinct was to stake him on sight, he surprised me by putting his hands up in a surrendering pose.

"Hold on, dork-head," he said, almost affectionately. That had been his signature insult when we were younger, or at least, it had been the real Carl's. Seeing this imitation version of him use it seemed like a mockery. "I just want to talk to you about something."

"You think so?" I asked defiantly, my weapon held high.

"I'm serious," he said, pointing his still raised hand at the stake. "You won't need that."

"I'll be the judge of that," I said, then winced when I realized that it sounded like some kind of tough guy cliché from a TV show.

Carl seemed unimpressed, and he just gave me a weak smile. Then he backed up, hands still in the air. "Look, I'm just going to sit down over here on the curb. I'm not going to bite you. I just want to talk to you about, well, the other you."

As he carefully maneuvered himself down, briefly using his hands to steady himself but then putting them back up again, I began to believe him. I was still suspicious, but I was curious about what he had to say.

A couple of months earlier, I'd become worried about the real Carl, given what my own clone had been up to. I'd taken what Elizabeth had said to heart, how people close to me might be in danger from him. Carl just avoided me at school, and when I tried to call him on the phone, he didn't return the call, not surprisingly. So I just showed up at his house, which he wasn't happy about. But when I explained everything to him, he seemed to genuinely understand and appreciate the warning, though he still tried to cloak it in his usual macho way. "I can take care of myself," he said, but he wasn't quite as cold to me by the end of the conversation as he had been when it started off.

Speaking to his clone now was odd, given how he too was being more accommodating. "Okay, fine," I said. "Go."

"He's been up to a lot of insane shit lately," he said.

"Like what?"

"Like killing everyone. I don't mean regular people; I mean vampires. First I thought he was just killing mine because… well, because he's an asshole, I guess."

This was a surprise. "Yours? You mean the ones you've made."

He nodded, lowering his hands to his lap but never taking his eyes off of me. "Right. And I thought, 'That sucks,' but then I come to find out that he's killing some of his own, too."

"What? Why?"

"Because he's an insane little prick?" he joked. Like my clone and Tim's, he seemed to have a sense of humor and was no longer some empty shadow of the person he'd come from. "Seriously, though, I think it's because he wants to be in control of everything. He couldn't stand it before when we all didn't want to be together and let him be in charge, and I guess he was okay with that for a while, making his own group of vampires to do whatever he said. But I guess that didn't work out for him, either, because now he's being all crazy and killing whoever he doesn't like."

I considered this, and it made some weird sort of sense. I'd always liked to have control over things and felt uncomfortable when I didn't, and because my clone was an extreme version of my darkest traits, maybe this was the result. But where did Elizabeth fit into all of this? Had he killed her as well? I wasn't sure if I should ask.

"So why are you telling me this?" I asked.

"Because..." He paused, then looked at me curiously. "How much do you know?"

"About what?"

"About the other you. And the army he's trying to build."

"Bits and pieces," I admitted. "That word 'army' sounds kind of..." I stopped short of saying "ominous," not wanting to let on how much the notion disturbed me.

"Okay, okay," Carl said, relaxing more and stretching his legs out from beneath him. "Let me tell you."

He went on to explain in more detail, reiterating how my clone had tried to keep the entire group of clones together shortly after the emergence, just as they had been before as vampires, but none of them were interested in that. I'd figured that out already based on what Elizabeth and Carolyn had told me, but hearing this firsthand confirmed it. The truth was that they all simply didn't like each other.

"So now," he continued, "he's trying to just wipe everyone out. It'll be just him, just him in charge of everything. And then he's going to start over, make a new vampire army. One that will do what he says. A new vampire army, all under his control." He shuddered dramatically.

Something about this seemed wrong, but I couldn't put my finger on it. "He even tried to kill me tonight!" Carl exclaimed. "I just barely got away. Barely. So that's why I came to you. I was hoping you could help me defeat him."

"Help you…?" The idea of cooperating with him seemed ridiculous. Scheming along with Elizabeth was one thing; I trusted her. But this vampire had already tried to kill me once, and I didn't even want to think about all the other people he'd killed.

"I mean it!" he said, almost pleading. "I figured you and me could work together. Then we could defeat him. You and me, together."

Finally, it clicked in my head what was bugging me, but I decided not to mention it yet and continued the conversation. "Maybe," I said. "But how do you know all this? Like, how is he going to control his new army when he couldn't do it before?"

"With his psychic powers! He's got some new… you know, some kind of method. Some new method with his psychic powers and stuff. Going to make him be all in control of them."

"And he told you this?"

"Yeah, just before he tried to kill me tonight."

That part I could believe, given how much of a braggart my clone had shown himself to be the last time I saw him. But even before the major flaw in Carl's story had come up — my clone didn't have any psychic powers — I'd already figured out that he was lying to me.

Back in elementary school, Carl had gotten in trouble with Mrs. Warren over an incident that involved another boy named Owen, a goofy kid in our class whom almost nobody liked. The teacher had handed out assignment sheets and, because some of the less responsible students had been losing theirs lately, she had harshly decreed that anyone who lost this particular assignment would not be given a replacement and would automatically receive a failing grade.

As soon as the following day, Carl had managed to lose his, and when he begged Mrs. Warren for leniency, she refused. So he decided to steal Owen's sheet, which I saw him do but chose not to say anything. He then told Mrs. Warren that everything was okay and that he'd found his, but things got complicated when Owen reported his sheet missing, swearing up and down that it had been on his desk just moments before.

A few other students, in a rare show of support, stood up for Owen. When Laura said that she thought Carl had taken it, a sort of trial ensued, with Mrs. Warren asking everyone what they had seen or might know. It went on for the entire class, people testifying, lying, pointing fingers, and Carl insisting on his innocence. It seemed like a ridiculous waste of time to me, and I even said so when called upon, insisting that I thought we were supposed to be having class, not *The People's Court.* That of course didn't go over well with Mrs. Warren, who had a short temper even at the best of times.

In the end, Carl confessed, but not without a fight. He first insisted that he'd been at his desk the entire time, saying so several times. Laura contradicted this, and it was pointed out that Carl had gotten up to go to the pencil sharpener around the same time that Owen's paper had disappeared. He then changed his story, saying that he'd just gone straight to the chalkboard — the sharpener was mounted on the side of it — and back. This lie was disproven as well.

I noticed that Carl kept saying the same things over and over: "It wasn't me! It wasn't me!" "I've just been sitting here the whole time. The whole time." "She's just trying to get me in trouble. She always does that. Trying to get me in trouble." And I knew the entire time that he was guilty, so I found it interesting to note that when he was lying, he tended to repeat himself.

Even after this incident was past, I would pick up on this nervous habit of his whenever he felt the need to lie about something. On most occasions, he managed to squeak by, and even though I could have, I never mentioned this flaw to him or anyone else. It was a neat little personal secret to have, to know that if he ever tried to get something past me, I'd be able to see through it.

All throughout the following years, this had never come up between me and the real Carl. There hadn't been any reason for him to lie to me and repeat himself, so I never got to spring my trap on him. At least, not until now.

"So," I said to the clone, "you think we should work together to defeat him."

"Yeah! We could, I don't know, maybe lure him out somehow. Like I could, you know, somehow lead him somewhere, and then you could get him."

"Maybe," I said, playing along. "And you say that he's killed all the vampires he made before?"

"Yeah. Well, not all of them. I think some of them got away."

"There's this one," I said, trying to choose my words carefully and not tip my hand. "A blonde girl named Elizabeth. Have you seen her?"

"Not recently," he said, getting a strange look on his face.

I wanted to know more, like if he knew whether or not she was alive, but I couldn't think of a way to ask without giving too much away. I decided to change my tactic, again testing his honesty.

"What about a redhead named Rosemary?"

"Hmm," he said. "Yeah, I think so." Another lie.

"Do you know anything about where his torture chamber is? He — the other me — has this place where he kidnaps and does all this horrible stuff to people before killing them."

"Are you serious?" he shouted, suddenly becoming angry. He stood up, which caused me to step back, still gripping my stake. He glanced at it, then said more calmly, "No, man, I'm not mad at you. Just at him. He totally stole that idea from me. I was the one who came up with that." Anger began to creep back into his voice. "And he said, 'No, Carl, that wouldn't work…' Fucking liar. Like he has any idea how to do any real torture, that son of a bitch. I'll bet he's never tied a man up and used a scalpel to filet his…" He'd been looking away from me as he ranted, lost for a moment. Then he caught himself and looked back at me, looking pained. "Oh. Yeah, I guess that's not going to win you over, is it?"

"Too late for that," I said, lifting my stake slowly. I'd learned all I could from him, and it was time to end this.

"Come on, Ray," he said, a strange smile creeping onto his face. Not for the first time that night, his eyes darted briefly to the left, pinpointing my neck. There had never been a real plan in his mind for us to cooperate. "Surely we can work something out."

"Such as…?"

"Such as," he said, his already naturally wide grin becoming menacingly large as he showed his fangs, "me killing you and getting rid of that other piece of shit you at the same time." His voice had started to become a whisper; he was obviously quite pleased with himself.

"Why didn't you just do that in the first place?" I asked.

"More fun this way," he practically purred, leaning in. He was nearly a foot taller than me, and when I raised my stake again to threaten him, he let out a small laugh. "You're not going to be fast enough." His eyes bore into mine, and I feared that he was right.

"Carl, no," I said. "Hang on. Maybe you're right." He looked surprised as I lowered the stake, pointing it downward as I reached for it with my other hand. He stopped his approach, buying me the few seconds I needed.

The thing about being away from Elizabeth for so long was that it had given me a lot of time to myself, which I used to expand on some of the ideas that I'd had for a while but never been able to realize. I had done that survey of the houses in my neighborhood to figure out where all of the sprinkler controls were, occasionally risking being caught as a prowler even though my intentions were innocent. And while I'd never managed to figure out how to rig up some big springboard full of stakes to catch a fleet of flying vampires or anything else that grand, I had learned how to use a knife to whittle a sizable chamber into the base of my stake, fitting it with a plastic lid that held a potent supply of garlic powder inside.

In a quick motion that I had practiced numerous times, I popped off the lid and slung the stake in an arc, flinging the garlic powder right into Carl's face. He howled in pain and anger, clutching at his eyes, and that gave me the advantage I needed.

"MOTHERFUCK...!" he began to swear, but before he could finish, I plunged the wooden stake right into his heart. *"...errr..."* his voice gurgled, and the damage was done. His hands moved from his face to his chest, but then in just a few seconds, his body faded into nothingness, his voice disappearing along with it. It was a very strange thing to see, and it also felt weird to find myself suddenly alone, still holding my stake in place where it had gone into him. There wasn't even any blood on it.

I was surprised when Carl called me the next day. I'd already thought of calling him, but I was reluctant to. Although I was glad, even proud of myself, for managing to best his clone and destroy him, it also felt weird plunging that stake into his chest. I knew that he wasn't really Carl, but he was so much like him that some part of me felt like I'd just murdered my friend. And given that I'd already lost two childhood friends not too long ago, the idea of the same thing happening to Carl upset me. In a way, hearing his voice on the phone was a relief, maybe even a redemption.

"Just wanted to let you know that my clone's dead," he said, trying to sound aloof. "I felt that thread detaching thing you'd told me about. Last night, in fact."

I don't know why I decided to lie. "Oh, really? Well, that's good news." For some reason, I didn't want to tell him that I'd been the one to kill his clone. "Did it, I don't know, hurt or anything?"

"Nope. I'd always wondered if it would. But yeah, I'd gotten up to pee in the middle of the night, and on my way back to bed, all of a sudden, there it was, clear as day. It was like something was quickly peeled off my chest, right over the heart really, and I got this sort of vision, like a big cord floating away from me, kind of like when you see that footage of those astronauts floating in space on those big… I don't know what you call them… air hoses maybe?"

"Yeah, maybe. I know what you mean."

"Yeah. Kinda like that. Just sort of… *zhwoooop*… floating away."

"Well, that's good to know."

"It's definitely a relief. Anyway, that's really all I wanted to tell you."

"Carl, wait. There's something else. I don't want you to get all complacent and think that everything's okay now."

"What?" He began to sound angry.

"No, listen! My clone has been up to some really bad shit again. Apparently he's going around killing lots of vampires."

"So? Maybe he's the one who killed my clone last night. I don't see how that's a bad thing."

"But it's not just that," I said. "He's gone all power trippy or something. You remember how he killed Dennis's clone, then Dennis too."

"Oh," he said. "Oh. Right."

"Just be careful. Keep a stake on you."

"I already do," he said impatiently. After a pause, he added, "Better not show up at my house unexpectedly again, Ray, or else I might, you know…"

I pictured what he was thinking, my approaching him innocently but being mistaken for my clone, then staked by him. "I get it."

"How do you know he's going around killing other vampires?"

"What?" I froze, again not wanting to reveal the fact that it was his clone who told me, just before I'd killed him. "I… I've got someone on the inside. A vampire who's telling me things. Kind of like a spy."

"Are you serious? That sounds pretty damn dangerous to me. How do you know they won't kill you?"

"We… have a deal. I really shouldn't talk about it." This was making me increasingly uncomfortable; I didn't want to tell anyone about Elizabeth. What's more, I'd been worrying about her since the night before, wondering how much of what Carl's clone had told me was true. Had it all been made up, a ruse to lure me into a false sense of security so he could get close enough to kill me? Or had my clone really been killing all of the vampires he'd made? And if so, had he managed to kill Elizabeth, too? I couldn't bear the thought of that.

"Well," Carl said, "whoever he is, just watch your back. I know we're not as good of friends as we used to be, but I still don't want you winding up dead. There's been too damn much of that shit already."

"Yeah, I know." This was uncharacteristically caring of him, but I knew that even though we were two guys trying to be all tough and unsentimental with each other, there was an underlying sense of concern between us. I wasn't sure if I'd be pushing my luck or not, but I wanted to continue the conversation by asking him why he'd been such a dick to me lately, why we hadn't been better friends, especially since I'd started attending Westlake. But then something else happened.

There was a weird sensation in my chest, a mild sort of pop. It reminded me a little of when I'd been a kid and was losing my baby teeth, the way a tooth would feel as it was pulled out, having been only attached by a small thread. In my mind, I could see a long, thick cord floating away from me and disappearing into nothingness.

"Carl, I have to go," I said suddenly.

"Um, okay," he said. "You take care of yourself."

"I… Thanks. Bye."

After all this time of having it described to me, I'd finally felt it. The thread had detached, and my clone was dead.

It was a good thing that my parents weren't home, nor had Carolyn come over to do laundry that day. I cried so loudly and uncontrollably once I realized the implications of what had happened, sometimes screaming into my pillow as I gripped it, rocking back and forth. I should have been glad that my clone was gone. It was a good thing. But his death, however it had happened, also meant that Elizabeth was dead. I didn't know if she'd killed him, perhaps in self defense, or maybe somebody else entirely had done it. Either way, he was gone, and so was she.

Once the sobbing settled down, I was numb. I couldn't bear the fact that I would never see Elizabeth again. Losing her once had been painful enough, but back then, I'd barely known her. This was so much worse, having had all that time to be with her and fall in love, and every time I pictured her beautiful face or thought about her, I broke down. Her cute little laugh, the way she would smirk when she was being clever or when she was playfully annoyed by something I said, the way her body felt when we made love, and how warm her kisses were…

It was too much to bear. In the days that followed, I barely spoke to my family, and I felt so horrible that I couldn't even eat. I claimed that it was because I was sick with something, and I missed school for two days. I did consider committing suicide, but I couldn't bring myself to do it, especially not after what had happened to Tim. It almost felt like a betrayal of his memory, or maybe it was more like a betrayal of my own, how I'd felt after he died. I'd been sad, but I'd also felt angry, mad at him for leaving the rest of us behind. I knew that if I took my own life, my family would feel the same way, and it wouldn't be fair to do that to them. And because of that, I found myself resenting them, too.

I guess what kept me afloat was the knowledge that, despite my personal pain, the nightmare was for all intents and purposes over. With my clone gone, and all of the vampires he'd ever made, that meant that Augusta was finally free of the threat. It was a victory, but one with such a high cost. Never again would I get to hold my beautiful Elizabeth, to feel the touch of her skin, the softness of her gorgeous blonde hair. And really, I deserved this grief. I'd been responsible for so much suffering all these years, so this was payback served in full.

I felt empty, not wanting to do anything, and even when I did go back to school, I couldn't bring myself to care. My grades went down again, and I got in trouble more than once for my bad attitude and tendency to lash out at people, both students and teachers. In time, this mellowed out, and I realized that all I could do was keep going, to try to stop being so miserable and just live my life, pointless though it was. I hated everyone and everything, and while I did what was necessary in order to scrape by, I didn't care about a single bit of it. I was just existing, going through one bullshit day after another. All of the excitement, all of the fear, all of the longing to make things right for so many years was over, and nothing mattered to me anymore.

I made it to the end of the school year, my misery having waned enough by then to where I was able to get my grades back up and not fail out. Part of that was due to a renewed sense of purpose, or maybe mystery. If all of the vampires were dead, then how come there were still occasional reports of people being killed or wounded?

The number of attacks had declined late last year, coinciding with Tim's and Dennis's deaths. That made sense. I had no idea how many vampires each of their clones had made, but once they were gone, the numbers went down. Once Carl's clone and mine had been killed back in March, the result should have been for the reports of attacks to have dropped off completely.

But there were still a few, and I began checking the news more often once I realized this. Were they hoaxes? Did people claim to be attacked in some twisted attempt to get attention? Or maybe these were regular, human-made homicides or assaults, but they were incorrectly attributed to vampires. The city had certainly lived with that phenomenon long enough, so it was possible that people might be seeing vampiric activity where there really wasn't any.

Another idea formed in my head, revisiting an earlier theory of mine. What if the chain that bound each vampire to the one that had made it didn't extend all the way down? If Kay, that Korean girl whom my clone had turned into a vampire, had made some vampires herself, could those have survived even if my clone's death had wiped her out? And if they had in turn made their own, would they be okay, too? Elizabeth and I had speculated about this, but we'd never been able to test it.

If that were true, then maybe there still was a threat after all. I told myself that if I ever encountered any of these leftovers, I'd kill them on sight. Aside from feeling obligated to do so out of a sense of duty, it might give me some satisfaction, a way to vent my anger. But then again, for all I knew, these reports were false, and there really weren't any more vampires in town.

For a brief moment, this supposition gave me hope that maybe Elizabeth was still alive after all. Since her death — her second death, as I'd come to think of it — I had of course fantasized that somehow she'd survived, that I might see her again. But that was impossible, I soon realized. Even if this notion of "subset-subset vampires" surviving might be true, it wouldn't apply to her anyway. My clone had died, and she was directly linked to him, so she was dead, too.

My heart almost stopped when I saw the note tucked under my window screen one morning in early June, having just opened my drapes. It felt like I came close to breaking the glass in the frame as I shoved the window open, and because I was in such a rush to practically tear my screen open to get to the folded up piece of paper, I accidentally let it fall to the ground.

Swearing as I made my way out of the window as quickly as possible, I retrieved the note and then got back inside, my pulse pounding the entire time. As I sat down on the bed, I could feel the veins in my neck throbbing as I unfolded the note, expecting to somehow, miraculously, be getting a message from Elizabeth that she was okay.

But what I saw on the page wasn't what I'd expected. It was a crudely drawn map, a diagram indicating some street names along with a small cartoon drawing of a house. There was some text written at the bottom, and it read: *Playtime is over. It's time for the end game.*

I recognized the handwriting. It was mine.

CHAPTER TWENTY-ONE

The house was small, one story, and falling apart. There were plenty of houses like it on this side of town, the part of Augusta that probably had once been home to the wealthy and well-off families thirty or forty years earlier, but it had since been abandoned as the city grew to the west. The rich families had moved and expanded out into Columbia County and Evans, leaving downtown and the east boundary to decay.

I sometimes wondered if our time as vampires, and the subsequent activities of the clones and their vampires, had contributed to this. It certainly could have, prompting the well-off to migrate away from this part of town, leaving the poor to make their homes in these dilapidated relics. Maybe that shift would have happened anyway, but I couldn't help but feel guilty as I drove down Broad Street past downtown. Maybe I was even being egocentric in thinking that I had anything to do with it at all.

I had also begun to think about how my father had briefly talked about moving our family elsewhere after Scout had been killed, but those plans never went anywhere. By then, though, I'd run out of time to reminisce. I had arrived, following the directions the note had given me, the note that was in my own handwriting. Somehow, my clone was still alive, but that should have been impossible given that

I'd felt the thread detach months earlier. I wanted to know how he'd survived, and it made me wonder if maybe Elizabeth had as well. That hope was dashed once I thought it through far enough: If she had been alive, I would have heard from her by now. As for my clone's pretentious claim that it was "time for the end game," I fully agreed. With Elizabeth gone, there was no reason for me not to kill him. I was going to win this time; he would not be allowed to wear my face and continue to hurt people any longer.

Initially, I'd put the car into neutral as I'd coasted down the dirt road, hoping to cut the engine and coast in quietly, but the roughness of the road killed the car's momentum. So that plan was out, and sneaking up on him wasn't an option. Did he know that? Had he thought of that because he knew how I'd think, and was that why he'd chosen this house?

Giving up on a stealthy approach, I pulled into the driveway, still cutting the lights and the engine as quickly as possible out of habit. Just before that, I caught sight of a truck parked in the driveway of the house next door, but with all of the overgrown weeds and the general state of decay, that one looked just as abandoned and unlivable as the one I'd come to.

I was still for a bit, listening with the window down to see if he might try a direct attack. There was nothing aside from the engine's ticking sounds and the ambience of a typical Georgia summer night, complete with croaking frogs, or possibly cicadas; I sometimes had trouble telling those two sounds apart. As my eyes adjusted to the absence of the headlights, I realized that the front windows of the house were glowing slightly orange, flickering with candlelight. That seemed overly dramatic, and it got on my nerves.

Okay, screw this, I thought, reaching for my backpack in the passenger seat. *It's time to get this over with.*

I opened the car door and stepped out, pulling the backpack with me. My stake had been sticking out of it in case I needed it in a hurry, so I grabbed it and held it in my left hand, ready to strike at the first sign of my clone. Seeing no immediate threat, I slid the backpack —

still partly unzipped — onto my right shoulder, and I proceeded to the house, determined and bold, ready for the confrontation.

The small porch was close to falling apart, and some of the boards seemed ready to give way under my feet, but since it was only a few inches off the ground, that didn't seem like a big deal. The overgrown grass, peeling paint, and broken windows might have struck me as sad if I wasn't already so pissed off and, admittedly, a bit frightened. I could tell that my clone was making me jump through hoops, and I hated that. And since he was partly me, he knew I hated that. Having to play along made it even worse.

I turned the doorknob and pushed the door, but it resisted. At first, I thought it was locked, but a quick kick to the base of the door forced it to slide unevenly on the floor and forward. Dirt and paint chips rained down on me as I went in, not helping my mood. Once inside, I saw that large, pillar-shaped candles had been placed all around the front room, flickering and half-way illuminating the mostly destroyed furniture and ruined carpet. The place had probably been abandoned for years, with stray animals, rain, and mold having had their way with it for a while. I imagined that most if not all of the rest of the houses on this street were in similar shape.

"All right, this is really impressive and pretty fucking disgusting as well," I said loudly, knowing that he could hear me but not quite sure from where. I stood there for a second, my hand still on the doorknob, waiting for a response. As I looked around what used to be this house's living room, I saw some more abandoned treasures, among them a mantelpiece littered with ugly ceramic knick-knacks, probably cute kittens or something equally banal. I thought cynically that whoever lived here before must have had just as much good taste as my clone.

"Do I really have to plow through all this garbage to hunt you down and kill you?" I asked defiantly.

"Oh, come on," my own voice said to me from not very far away, probably the next room. "Are you sure you're the one who's doing the hunting?"

I gripped the stake in my hand as he appeared in a doorway — which I noticed no longer had a door on it — to my left. The candlelight made him look more ominous, I hated to admit, but there he was, a smug smile on his face. Obviously he felt that he was in control, and he pretty much was. But any minute now, I'd change that.

"Are you ready?" he asked, still smiling, stopping just short of the doorway.

"For what?" Suddenly, something occurred to me: There was an overly fragrant scent to the entire place, but it was that kind of smell that comes from a perfume trying unsuccessfully to cover up a stench. Looking at the pillar candles situated around the room again, I had to stifle a laugh. "Oh my God. You got scented candles?"

His expression became angry. "It wasn't my choice. It's what they had at the store I hit." I knew what he meant, and my face must have indicated this, because he switched back to that same self-satisfied smile. "The girl closing up last night was really nice."

"You mean you..."

"Drank every drop of her." He then added in a mocking tone: "Just enough for a little boy!"

I got the reference: It was from my early childhood, when I was in kindergarten. One morning at breakfast, my mother had poured me some milk, emptying out the last of a half-gallon carton, which happened to be the right amount to fill the glass. "Just enough for a little boy!" she'd said playfully, and I laughed. The following morning, even though she hadn't emptied out a carton as she poured the milk, she still said the same thing, and I found the repetition funny. That had led her to say it on subsequent mornings, to the point where I grew tired of it.

"Don't say 'just enough for a little boy' again!" I shouted at her one morning, and she was taken aback.

"That hurt my feelings!" she said, almost like she was on the verge of tears. When I recalled this incident as I got older, I realized that she probably wasn't genuinely wounded by my words; more likely, she was trying to teach me that being mean and snapping at people like that was bad. But in my younger days, I still felt guilty whenever the memory resurfaced, which was pretty much whenever I poured something and happened to be emptying the last few drops of it into a glass.

I was annoyed that my clone had reminded me of this, but even more so, it bugged me that he had the same memory as I did, and he'd chosen to mock me with it. My irritation must have shown, and he laughed. I really hated seeing him laugh, especially when he'd gotten one up on me. Seeing my own face leering at me was not something I liked. The only defense I had was to throw sarcasm right back at him, knowing he hated it just as much.

"So, you cryptically invite me here to the house of mold and potpourri for… what? To show off your big mansion here in Downtown Crackville?"

He laughed again, which wasn't what I'd hoped for. He bowed and shook his head, then looked back up at me, for a second looking so much like my father that I felt a chill. "Yes, that's what our sister would call it."

"My sister," I insisted. "Carolyn is not…"

"…The one who held that little girl up to me eight years ago and said, 'I saved her for you?'" I fumed. It was all I could do. "It's my memory, too."

"Shut up!" I shouted. He enjoyed his victory, smiling as arrogantly as always. Did I really look like that when I was feeling superior?

I wanted to change the subject, and there was something more pressing on my mind anyway. "Carl's clone told me…"

"Before you killed him?" he asked brightly. "Thanks for that, by the way."

"He told me," I continued firmly, "that you killed all of his vampires. And all of yours as well. Is that true?"

"Mostly," he said. "A few of them got away." At least that part of Carl's story hadn't been a lie.

"And Elizabeth?"

He sneered. "What do you think?" I refused to answer, afraid to learn the truth. "Oh, she came to me all right. All, 'Let's be friends!' Did you two really think I was going to fall for that crap?"

My heart raced, but I tried to hide my anger, not wanting to give him the satisfaction.

"Okay," he said, suddenly gracious and holding his hands out to his sides. "Enough playing around. There's a reason why I brought you here."

"You didn't bring me anywhere. I came of my..."

"Oh, what the fuck ever," he interrupted. "You're here because I manipulated you, and the sooner you just fucking admit that and fucking deal with it, the better off you'll be."

He may have been right, but I couldn't resist the opportunity he'd given me: "So, since you're only about fifty percent of me, does that mean that I have a much better developed vocabulary than you?"

He had turned away from me after his last sentence, but then he glared back, no humor in his expression. "Come here, and show me just how developed you think you really are," he said, more coldly than could I remember either of us sounding in a long time.

He headed for another room, and I followed, stake still in hand. I probably could have disabled him with the stake's hidden garlic powder chamber and killed him right then, but something was keeping me from doing that, perhaps a morbid curiosity about what he was planning. Whatever he was up to, however manipulative he thought he might be, I was going to beat him. So why not let him play the role of the James Bond movie villain a little longer? I still wanted to know how it was that he was even alive.

I followed him into what used to be the kitchen; an open refrigerator covered in mold and a half-disassembled stove indicated this. There were a lot more candles in here, too, and I noticed that at least half of them were shorter — and therefore older — than the ones I'd seen in the living room. The perfumy smell was also less obnoxious in here.

Nearly every available surface had a candle, and the room seemed almost as bright as if the place still had electricity. What must have been the pantry was off to the far side of the room, and as he headed for it, I noticed several knives and other metallic instruments I didn't recognize on one of the counters. Were those meant for me?

"Here we go," he said, reaching for the pantry's door and opening it, revealing what he'd been waiting for me to see.

The first thing I saw was her face as she raised her head, looking out at me, wide-eyed. The amount of candles in the room allowed me to see plenty of detail, which was the point. Her blue eyes stared out, but they didn't even look like hers. They were devoid of any real thought, completely raw and animalistic. She had jerked up, squinting at first as if the candlelight was too much for her, and then she thrust her head back to one side, hiding her face. But I'd seen it. It was no longer the full, perfect vision of beauty that I'd fallen head over heels for all these years. It was tight and almost skeletal, narrow and angular. This wasn't my Elizabeth.

She was breathing heavily, gasping. It was then that I noticed the rest of her, the position she was in. She was tied up with a combination of white rope and other restraints; I couldn't quite make them out. Her arms were tied to either side of the small space, which was like a tall, narrow closet, and what was left of a shirt hung halfway off of her. I could see one of her breasts sagging far lower than it should have been.

As I took it all in, I realized that the cords tying her arms to either side of the inner walls were dog leashes. The clasps were doubled over and fastened to themselves, the white canvas rope twined around behind her neck and providing some kind of support, the way one might tie a piece of furniture into a truck to move it across town. These were supplemented with what must have been duct tape; the dull metallic sheen of it reflected some of the orange candlelight of the kitchen. Her lower half was restrained with some sort of canvas strap that, as far as I could make out, was fastened to the wall behind her, and her legs were crumpled beneath her in some fashion. She'd been forced to sit like this for who knows how long. Maybe her feet were also tied behind her; I couldn't tell. I didn't care. I dropped my backpack from my shoulder to the floor.

"You bastard!" I screamed as I lunged for my clone, stake in hand, ready to beat him to death and run his heart through with my weapon. But he'd been expecting this; after all, he'd set the whole thing up. He caught my move easily and held my arm in place, not even allowing my momentum to topple us over like the typical fight scene I was hoping for.

Our faces were inches apart, and it would have felt like looking into a mirror if I hadn't been so completely disgusted with him. I gasped as I struggled against him, and he was still smiling that arrogant, conceited grin that couldn't possibly be the same as mine.

"Go ahead," he said, still smiling. "Go on! Kill me! Kill her, too! You know the drill. Kill one vampire, and the vampires that he's made wither and die."

I stopped struggling with him. He was right.

"You can't win this," he said, relaxing as I had. Defiantly, I pushed away from him. We stood apart from each other, and while I tried to look as determined as possible, he just maintained his arrogance.

"*Ray...*" a harsh, guttural voice quietly called out from behind me. Every hair on my body stood up, and I didn't turn around.

The other me smiled more broadly. "Oh, go on."

"*Ray...*" the inhuman voice repeated more loudly. I turned around.

It was Elizabeth, or what was left of her. Even though I wished they could, my senses wouldn't shut off, and I took in more of what I saw. She didn't even look like her. What I'd thought before might have been some kind of rope or other material behind her wasn't that; it was her hair. Her blonde hair was now like straw, rough and torn and, as I could now see, all the way down her back and past her hips. She was sitting on it, possibly too weak to stand up. She looked so much older, but not exactly like a regular old woman. She wasn't wrinkled in the face, though her limbs and fingers still looked very skeletal, the skin drawn against them and barely leaving any room for muscle. Her face was skinny and unlike her, devoid of any expression. Her eyes bugged out, making her look more like a jack-o-lantern or a Halloween mask, not the slightest bit human. I knew that she was a vampire, but at least she'd looked like a human before, minus the fangs. Her mouth looked oddly the same, but that may have been because she was keeping it closed most of the time. What did her teeth look like now?

I didn't want to know, and it was just as well, because she managed to keep speaking without revealing them to me. She'd bowed her head again, but her voice continued to filter out in that same grating, scraping tone. She almost sounded like an old woman, but not quite. I could tell, somehow, that she was still as young as she'd ever been, but that so much had been taken from her.

"Whyyyyy." Her voice was like rocks being dragged across broken glass, more tired and worn than any I'd heard before. I wanted not to hear it, to never have heard it. But I also wanted to listen, to find out what she had to say, to know that she was still alive somehow. I needed to find out what had happened. *"Whyyy did you do this to me."*

"I... I didn't!" I shouted. "Elizabeth..." I walked toward her slowly, leaning forward, and I began to reach out to her. Was there any possible way I could comfort her in this state?

Suddenly her head shot up, her expression twisted and angry, even more horrible and inhuman than before. "You... hurt me." She took a few more labored breaths. *"You abandoned me!"* she shouted, her voice tearing through me. It was a monstrous shriek, more akin to an attacking cat's snarl than anything like a girl's voice.

I jumped back as she struggled against the restraints, giving up quickly but still glaring at me, her mouth now pursed shut as she continued to breathe heavily, angrily. I had seen her fangs when she'd snarled at me; they looked longer and more menacing than ever. In fact, all of her teeth and her mouth seemed larger, probably because the rest of her face had shrunk. I wasn't sure whether or not she could actually attack me; it seemed that if she'd been able to get out of those ropes, she'd have done it by now. That didn't make her any less terrifying.

My emotions were all over the place. I felt scared, and I felt sorry for her. I'd already thought she was dead for months now, and while I might have been relieved at finding that she wasn't, I couldn't bear seeing her like this. She wasn't the same. She was broken. I was fully absorbed in the surreality of the experience until a small laugh behind me reminded me of the situation. I looked back at my clone, and I started to express my contempt for him when Elizabeth began to speak again, this time in a more soft tone.

"No more fighting," she said, almost in a whimper, or like a song. I turned back to her and saw that she was gazing off to the side again, and she looked terribly sad. "No more competition." She shook her head, and she half-smiled. "That's what you said." She laughed briefly for no apparent reason. "Don't struggle; it won't do any good."

I'd never said that to her. I didn't know what she was talking about. "Elizabeth…" This was breaking my heart. "I never…"

"Yes you did!" she shrieked again just as loudly as before, this time not looking up. "I waited… waited so long… so long… so tired… so hungry… I couldn't feel anymore. You didn't have to put me in here." She began crying softly, and I felt like I was dying inside.

"It wasn't me!" I insisted, trying to fight back tears of my own. "It was him! The other… The vampire Ray! Remember? He was the one who did this to you, not me!"

She seemed to laugh again, but it was hard to tell the difference between that and her sobs. "No…" she said, her eyebrows raising. "No. You did it. I saw you. I was there."

"Elizabeth, no! It was my clone! See?" I pointed behind me. "Him! He isn't me! He did this to you!"

"Don't even bother," my clone said. I spun around to face him, wishing I could kill him merely by thinking it. "She doesn't see me anymore. In fact, it took me a while to figure out that she literally can't even see or hear me."

"What do you mean?"

"She stopped talking to me after the first few days of being conscious. Before that, she'd been out for weeks, five or six I think, starving away while the spell I'd gotten kept her dormant. It really did work like the guy said! I thought she was just being stubborn at first, not talking to me. And maybe she was, you know, before she went completely off the deep end. She really doesn't know I'm here." He never stopped smiling; he knew how much power he had over this moment. I despised him more than anything.

"You did *what* to her?" I raised the stake again, and he held up a hand as if he were telling a dog to stay still.

"You really better be more choosy about where you point that thing," he said.

I ignored his advice, continuing to hold it at the ready. "Tell me what you did," I said firmly.

"Well," he began, pacing back and forth slightly and holding his hands together, every bit the evil genius in the spy movie. "Let's see. Once I figured out your game of trying to have little Elizabeth here be some kind of double agent, I decided to come up with a plan of my own. I knew she couldn't kill me, otherwise she'd die herself. I wasn't even sure what the two of you thought you were planning, but I wasn't going to let you get away with it."

"It's so quiet now..." Elizabeth murmured from behind me. I looked back at her; she was still staring off into space. "Aren't you ever going to talk to me again? I miss you so much..." She wasn't making any sense.

The other Ray laughed slightly. "So I got a spell from a guy I'd heard about. Good stuff, apparently, just the thing you'd need to knock a vampire out and keep it unconscious for weeks. Vampires used to use it to make long trips overseas without having to be aware of the length of the journey. As time went on, they'd still be alive, but grow weaker and weaker from lack of blood, losing some of their powers, like being able to change form. Eventually, they'd wake up and have to feed a lot to rejuvenate. The blood isn't just what keeps us alive; it keeps us young."

This was intriguing, but I was becoming increasingly preoccupied with one particular detail. "Speaking of 'alive,' how come you're not dead? I felt you die."

"You thought you did," he corrected me, "when I severed the link between us."

"How?"

"Believe it or not, our wonderful big sister helped with that."

"What? Susanna? She helped you?" I couldn't bring myself to believe that.

He laughed. "Well, not on purpose, she didn't. I called her, pretending I was you, and she fell for it, the stupid arrogant bitch." I stepped forward angrily, feeling an instinctive need to stick up for my sister. He backed up a little, but then he stood his ground, again holding his hand up to me. "I almost messed it up, I'll admit. I didn't know that you two had already talked about trying to take the cure to the potion, and she of course was all condescending, like, 'Ray, I *told* you that I already tried that and it didn't work. *Why* do you keep bringing this *up*...'"

It was a pretty accurate impression of her, and it cleared something up for me that earlier in the year had confused me. When Susanna had come home for a brief visit near the end of February, she'd said something to me, just an aside from the rest of what she'd been saying, that seemed to indicate that we'd talked recently. But I hadn't seen or heard from her since Christmas. At the time, I'd been in a bad mood, still worrying about Elizabeth and what might have happened to her, so I just blew it off and assumed that she was mistaken, possibly confusing a conversation she'd had with Carolyn instead, maybe pertaining to our father's birthday.

But as my clone continued to gloat and explain, I learned that when he'd talked to her, he basically tricked her into revealing that while any of us taking the cure wouldn't automatically kill our clones like we'd hoped earlier, if a clone took it, it might sever the thread but leave them alive. She'd also theorized that had we taken the antidote as far back as 1987, our inner vampires never would have had the chance to grow and fester within us, so by the time we tried to take it, it was "like shaking up a Coke bottle and then popping the cap off, trying too late to pour something else inside."

Soon after their conversation, he'd flown all the way to Columbia to steal the formula for the cure from her apartment. Back in Augusta, he managed to create the antidote himself, then drank it.

So that was how he'd done it, why I'd felt the thread detach and thought all this time that he'd been dead. He knew this, too, which was why he'd lain low and let me wallow in misery. And while I resented him for that, as he continued to go on and on to show off how clever he was, I began to realize something.

I'd heard comedians joke about all those bad guy characters in the movies, how they would tell the hero — tied up and temporarily at the mercy of the villain — their entire plan. Then they'd leave the room for no good reason, allowing the hero time to escape from the pit of alligators or the laser beam slowly moving toward his crotch or whatever. Why bother explaining at all, when a simple bullet through the head would have been more efficient?

The truth of the matter is that smart people like to show off. And as much as I loathed my clone and found comfort in thinking of him as lesser than me, I knew that we were equally intelligent. Had Elizabeth and I succeeded in our plan and imprisoned him, I had to admit that if the opportunity presented itself, I might very well brag to him about every little detail before I closed the lid to his coffin, making sure that he knew just how cleverly I'd beaten him.

In a weird sort of way, I found myself almost admiring my clone, hearing about all of the things he'd done to outmaneuver me. I wouldn't tell him that, of course, but there was something oddly satisfying about being able to speak to someone whom I begrudgingly had to accept as an intellectual equal. I'd flown circles around so many people in my life, including my parents, who never had a clue what my friends, sisters, and I had been up to all these years. For a brief moment on Christmas night last year, I'd thought about letting loose and telling them everything, not so much because I felt confessional but because I was so angry at them that I wanted them to know how clueless they'd been all along.

So I let my clone talk, being tough and defiant but still hoping that I would be the one to come out on top this night. He was the villain, and I was the hero, and the more he rambled, the more I would learn. He revealed plenty, things that I otherwise wouldn't have known.

For one, I'd never even noticed that he and the other clones, even though they'd emerged from us a year and a half ago, had remained looking exactly the same as they had that night, right down to their clothes. They weren't real people; they were solid manifestations. I had in fact noticed when I confronted my clone last Christmas that the jacket he was wearing, my same blue jean jacket, still had the pins on it that I used to wear. I'd stopped wearing them shortly after I started attending Westlake, but he had remained locked in the same shape, at least until he took the cure and was fully separated from me.

From that point on, he'd become an individual, more like a real vampire, though those weren't the exact words he used. His way of conveying the tale was more boastful, meant to demoralize me and build himself up as this genius super villain who had beaten me. "Have you picked up on the difference yet?" he asked with dramatically outspread arms before explaining the clothing thing to me, displaying the same attitude he had each time he led up to another big revelation. And each time, I pretended not to be impressed, but deep down, I found the details fascinating.

Another of those was that he'd experimented with the concept of not feeding and how it aged a vampire, though not to the extreme he'd subjected Elizabeth to. He'd been stuck in the form of a 15-year-old boy ever since the emergence, but by abstaining from drinking blood for a few nights once he was separate from me, he'd managed to age himself to where he more closely matched my own age, nearly seventeen. And he was able to discard his old clothes and begin wearing new ones, like the black T-shirt he was now wearing. I noted to myself that it was in direct contrast to the white polo shirt I had on.

"Wow, dieting and fashion," I said sarcastically. "How utterly masculine of you." That earned me a satisfying flash of anger from him, but he recovered quickly enough.

All throughout this conversation, I still felt anger towards him over what had happened to Elizabeth, which was helped along by how she would occasionally pipe up with nonsensical phrases, just a few feet away and tied up in the pantry. Sometimes, I could kind of see where she was coming from, her shattered mind making a weird sort of sense. But mostly, she just seemed completely out of it, and I wondered if there was any hope for her even if I could get us both out of this situation alive.

Given what my clone had told me about how she'd somehow blocked him out, unable to perceive him, that meant that anything the two of us said sounded to her like half of a conversation, like overhearing a person talk on the phone. She'd remain silent for a time, but every now and then, she'd say something related to what I'd just said, crazy though it was.

Sometimes, she even sang song lyrics, which I thought were just random babblings, but then those too started to seem slightly relevant. When one of my sentences happened to end in the word "forever," she started cooing quietly, *"Diamonds are forever…"* Wasn't that the name of an old James Bond movie? I didn't recognize the tune, but then, I'd never been that big on Bond stuff. Carolyn and Susanna had occasionally rented the movies when we were younger, which was why I had a passing familiarity with them.

But I also remembered Elizabeth saying something about that before, back when she'd had that necklace with the diamond pendant. How much of her was still in there, this horrible, desiccated creature tied up in the closet? It hurt me inside whenever she spoke up, and each time, I found it hard to hide my emotions, which my clone enjoyed evilly.

I noticed too that the more she spoke — even if it was all nonsense — her voice stopped sounding as horrible and gravelly as it had been when she'd first been revealed to me. Whenever she sang in bits and pieces, it sounded almost as pretty as it had before. I wasn't sure if that gave me hope or just made me hurt more, afraid that she'd never be the same again.

This was reinforced a bit later when my clone was goading me over the topic of how I'd killed Carl's clone. He wasn't surprised to learn that he'd come to me and tried to enlist my help after my clone had failed to kill him, and despite that, he still felt proud of himself for wiping out Carl's vampires.

"It was kind of like the old days, you know?" he leered at me. "'The Club Wars' and all that."

This reference to our elementary school rivalry seemed so childish in comparison to what was happening now. "We didn't kill each other back then," I said angrily.

"No, but you wanted to sometimes." I refused to give him that one, but I could tell that he still thought he was right. "So it must have been very satisfying for you to get to kill Carl for real."

"No, actually, it hurt a lot to have to do that. Even if it wasn't the real Carl, it still felt like…"

"Oh, bullshit. You did it and you loved it."

"No," I repeated. "Maybe you would have loved that, but I still have a conscience. Like you pointed out before, that's one of the main differences between me and you. You're not a whole person. You're not real. That's why Elizabeth never wanted anything to do with you."

His smile finally faltered. Now I got to be right. His rhythm thrown off, he needed to regain his footing. "Whatever," he managed to say. "I was smart enough to lure you here, anyway. You want me to tell you why?"

"Fine," I said. I had hoped to follow that up with something more profound, but nothing came to me.

Elizabeth repeated the word, like an echo. Then she repeated it again, then again, to the point where she was just chattering it over and over. It reminded me of a conversation we'd once had about how saying a word repeatedly made it sound weird, to the point where it no longer seemed to mean anything. And she'd done this a few times earlier in the night, repeating the last word I said. After a while, I'd actually found her ravings distracting rather than simply pitiful.

"Elizabeth, please," I said, turning around.

"WHO THE HELL DO YOU THINK YOU ARE!!!???" she howled, lunging forward and struggling against the restraints again, so violently that I feared she might break free. She'd caught my eyes with her own this time, scaring me more than I ever thought she could, worse than that first night in the cemetery. Even in the orangeish-yellow candlelight, which I had grown accustomed to by now, her eyes seemed to glow bright blue. I again jumped back, this time bumping into my alter ego.

I turned and tried to right myself, finding that he'd caught me with his arms. In the process, I dropped the stake I'd been carrying all this time. It clattered to the dirty floor, rolling vaguely in the direction of the pantry where Elizabeth was tied up.

My clone grinned at me, triumphant as he had been almost the entire night. "You dropped your stick," he said. Could I reach it again somehow? "I could always let you get it. You'll need it, you know." He released his hold on me, allowing me to step back. Breathing heavily, I stared at him, wondering if I should make a play for the stake.

"Go on," he said. "You're not going to use it on me, after all."

Not bothering to stroke his ego by asking what he meant, I walked over and picked up the stake again, keeping my eyes on him the entire time. I was now positioned near the wall of the kitchen, Elizabeth to my left, my twin still facing me from the middle of the room.

"Like hell I'm not," I said, recovering my bravery.

"No," he said simply. He turned around and walked slowly to one of the drawers, pulling it open and brandishing a large knife from it. It looked shiny and new, not something that had been wasting away in this house over the years, and not part of the collection of sharp implements that were on the nearby counter. I knew now what he had likely used those for, but I couldn't stand the thought. The knife he held had probably been bought for tonight's occasion, or presumably, stolen. He fixed me with an eager stare, holding the weapon purposefully.

I was afraid, but then I remembered the way things worked between us. "You can't use that on me," I said. "You kill me, and you'll die, too. You know the drill." I liked throwing his own words back at him.

I expected him to wither, to be disappointed, but he maintained his composure. "Not anymore," he said gravely. "Aren't you forgetting something? No more thread." Balancing the knife between his thumb and finger, he wobbled the huge, serrated blade in the air in front of his chest, then gripped the handle tightly again. "That was always such a pain in my ass, you know. I could torment you all I wanted, but I could never actually kill you. So I settled for things like killing Elizabeth, bringing her back, killing other people from your past to make you feel guilty..."

"I know," I said impatiently. Was I beginning to sweat? It felt hotter all of a sudden.

"And I suppose just killing other people you'd never even heard of that you'd see reports of on the news..."

"That's enough!" I shouted. As angry as I was at the things he was saying, I was also trying to hide my growing fear. If what he said was true, then the playing field had suddenly changed significantly for the worse.

He laughed weakly, unimpressed. "So you see, I could run you through with this blade right now and walk away perfectly fine." He savored my reaction, even though I was trying to keep from giving him one. But I wasn't fooling him or myself anymore. "But I won't," he said. "Instead, I'm going to free her."

"What?"

"Elizabeth. I'm going to cut her loose."

"What?" I repeated, looking over at her prone form. For the moment, she seemed to have gone silent, possibly exhausted from her earlier outburst.

"A girl's got to eat," he said slyly. Before I had a chance to ask what he meant, he began walking toward her.

Barely even thinking, I stepped in his way. "Stop." I held up my stake again. He grinned, then glanced at the knife in his right hand.

"Stop," Elizabeth whispered. *"Stop, stop, stop…"* Her tone went from playful to pleading, like she was in pain. Deep in my mind, I knew that staking her might be the inevitable conclusion to this encounter. It might be better to end her misery anyway.

My clone smiled at me once again. "The thing is, she hates you. You may be able to see me as not really you, but her addled, fucked up brain can't see things that way. I'm not even here, as far as she's concerned. All of your arrogant, self-righteous claims that I'm not really a person are actually pretty relevant here, but not in the way you might think. You're the only person in the room to her, and once she's free, her survival instincts are going to make her go for the first source of food she can find."

I started to say something in defiance, but he suddenly slashed at me with the knife, catching me in the left wrist and making me cry out in pain. I dropped the stake again. Almost as quickly, he took advantage of my surprise and grabbed me, then hurled me to the side and onto the floor. As I skidded across it and into the far wall, I was aware of the filth and grime, my wound, and the realization that the talking part of this confrontation was over. I should have staked him as soon as he walked into the room, or maybe once he'd revealed the imprisoned Elizabeth to me, or whenever else I'd had the chance. Now I'd lost those opportunities, and I might have lost everything.

I rolled over as I tried to reorient myself. My wrist was bleeding and hurting terribly, and my backpack was too far away, but fortunately, he'd thrown me in the same direction as the stake I'd dropped. I picked it up and crawled forward, seeing him kneeling by the pantry and hastily cutting through Elizabeth's bonds.

Just as he'd said, she didn't even seem to know that he was there, and she just sort of nodded and smiled, murmuring or perhaps humming to herself as he quickly worked, freeing one of her hands and then the next. She smiled as her arm came loose, looking at it as it waved in front of her, almost as if she were underwater. A vague "*Ahh*" came from her lips as she grinned, toothy, fanged, and scarier than any vampire I'd ever seen. She looked delighted and also completely out of her mind.

"Yesss…" she hissed. "Finally…" She giggled, smiling almost sweetly, but it was entirely evil. This wasn't my Elizabeth. This Elizabeth was going to tear me to pieces as soon as she got free.

I tried not to panic, wanting to believe that I still had a chance. My arm was covered in blood, and I was struggling to clutch it and hold onto the stake at the same time. Dizziness began to set in, and I was trying my best not to go into shock and lose control. I had to keep myself together.

"Oh, and by the way," my evil twin said to me as he sliced away at the strap restraining Elizabeth's lower half, "once she's free, and while she's busy killing you, I'm going to get away. You know, just like I always do. And you're going to die knowing that I'm always going to be out there, terrorizing and killing everyone you couldn't manage to save." He paused from his work, looking back at me. "I love that thought." Smiling viciously, he went back to cutting the final restraint free.

I wanted to say something back, but I was too busy concentrating on not passing out. Either I had to get to him and stake him in time, or else I'd have to deal with staking what was left of the love of my life. Or worse, I might have to do both.

I stood up. Taking my hand off my wound, I was surprised to find that it wasn't as severe as I'd initially believed. I had thought that my clone had slashed my wrist and that I would bleed to death, but the actual cut was farther up my arm. It was a distraction, not something meant to be fatal, or maybe he'd simply missed. I had to focus on the moment, to do what I had to do, no matter how painful. I stumbled forward, raising my stake, hoping that I could stop him, but it was too late. The strap came free, and he tossed it aside, though it flopped back into place due to having been in that position for so long.

"There!" he said triumphantly. He got up, parading his arm up and down like a game show host. I had my stake in hand, but I was still unsure on my feet. Maybe, just maybe, I could manage to catch Elizabeth with it if she blindly lunged for me without thinking. That was my only strategy.

She stood up rather wobbly, grunting and wheezing, panting heavily. She was covered in filth, but she didn't seem to know or care. She was an undead beast now, nothing like the girl I'd fallen in love with. Her head swayed as she looked around the room crazily, but not at me yet. I knew that any second now, her eyes would meet mine, and that would be it.

"Are you ready?" my clone asked me, grinning more broadly than ever. He'd waited months for this, I knew. I didn't waste my strength replying, and I steadied the stake against my chest, the sharp end pointed outward.

"Are *you?*" Elizabeth said, also smiling, horrible and ugly in her current form. But instead of lunging towards me, she spun to her left, grabbing the other me by the head as he dropped his knife in shock. In less than a second, he was screaming as Elizabeth's head was buried in the side of his neck, her long, blonde, straw-like hair flopping back and forth along her half-naked back as she gnawed and fed on him.

He struggled, beating at her with his arms and then trying to kick, but his strength evaporated in seconds as I heard a loud slurping sound. She was drinking him, draining him more quickly than he could react, and he went limp in her grasp, which she shifted from his head to his body, supporting him as she continued to feed. He groaned, then just breathed loudly, eventually working his way down to faint gasps. Soon, there was nothing other than a faint chewing sound as Elizabeth sucked up the last of him. I could hear her swallowing the entire time, gulping him down like a huge drink of water.

It was over in less than a minute, maybe half. She kicked her head back, then let him drop to the floor like a sack. I hadn't been able to see him clearly as she'd drained him, but now I could, and what was left of his form was startling. He was even more emaciated than Elizabeth had looked while tied up in the pantry, almost a skeleton with clothes, skin, and hair still intact. And yet he was still moving, still trying to breathe, his eyes darting back and forth and his arms twitching.

"Give... it... baaaack..." the pitiful form managed to croak out. This confused me for a second, but I quickly realized that he meant his blood.

His hair was long and wavy, some of it grey, probably shoulder-length had he been standing up. But there was no chance of this drained, animated corpse standing; he was a pathetic, scrawny mess on the floor. The scourge of my existence, the evil double that I'd been trying to bring down for years, was now this: nothing, or next to nothing. He didn't even look like me anymore, and I stopped myself from speculating whether or not I could ever end up looking that disgusting several decades from now. I couldn't think about that anyway, because standing above him was my precious Elizabeth.

Except she still wasn't my Elizabeth, not before, and not now. She was completely different, both from the horrible, tortured creature I'd seen in that closet and from the girl I'd known before. The flesh on her body had filled out and was no longer as gaunt and thin as before, but she still looked tired and worn out, gasping from what she had just had to do. Despite her dirty, torn clothing, she was not entirely unattractive, but definitely older and out of the age range that would normally appeal to me. What's more, what was left of her ripped, pale shirt barely managed to cover her nether regions, and while under any other circumstances I might have been excited to be in the presence of a half-naked woman, I mostly felt uncomfortable.

She smiled at me, and just for a second, she seemed younger, more like the Elizabeth I had known. "Hell of a ride, wasn't it?" she said suddenly, breaking the silence. I just stood there, open-mouthed, and I almost flinched as she began to step closer. Reaching out to me, she said, "Give me that."

"What?" I managed to say, realizing that she was taking the stake out of my hand. I'd forgotten I was still holding it.

She knelt down, her incredibly long hair flowing over her back as she did so. It was no longer tangled and straw-like; now it was cascading and beautiful, honey-colored and pooling onto the floor behind her as it covered the backs of her legs. She was leaning over the helpless and worthless figure of my former twin, which was still twitching and quietly grunting, its eyes bugged out and seeming to plead for mercy. Its mouth was agape, opening and closing like a fish out of water, and its limbs were jerking about like a crab's. Elizabeth effortlessly tilted him over onto his back, raised the stake, and plunged it down into his chest.

"No, wait!" I managed to say, but it was too late.

There was a rippling effect accompanied by what sounded like my own voice crying out in pain, yet somehow muffled and echoing. The body that had been there vanished, though the clothes it had been wearing remained. I thought that Elizabeth might perish along with him, but to my surprise, she remained intact. She leaned back, sitting on her knees, then sighed. She looked up at me and laughed gently.

"Good," she said. "I wasn't entirely sure that would work."

"What...?" I asked, still stunned from what I'd seen.

She gently pried the stake out from the hole in the now empty T-shirt on the floor, but all of a sudden, she looked at the weapon fiercely and slung it across the room. "Oh, *Goh...*" she began, but she choked. Eyes watering, she sniffled as she said, "I didn't realize there was garlic in it." For a second, she glared at me and looked extremely angry, but then her expression abruptly changed, looking more tranquil.

I had no idea what to say. She stood up, and I didn't know whether or not to be afraid as she took both of my hands in hers. "Um…" was all I could manage to get out. I didn't know where to begin. "You look, um…"

"Older?" she asked, halfway smiling. It was a different smile than I was used to from her, pained and weary. And she had definitely aged: The puffiness under her eyes and the way the skin along her jaw seemed to sag slightly made her seem more like someone close to my mother's age. That felt really weird to see. "I suppose I am," she said, raising her eyebrows in a resigned way, causing a few horizontal wrinkles to appear on her forehead. "You have no idea." Her voice was a little huskier than it had been before.

"Are you… Are you okay?" It sounded like such a stupid thing to ask.

"Kind of," she said, looking down at the floor for a second, then back up at me. She flinched briefly. "Or I will be. I think. I wasn't quite as out of it as I let him believe."

"You…"

"…Fooled him," she said, finishing my sentence and nodding. She breathed in, looking pained, either emotionally or physically, maybe both. "I had to." Suddenly, she twitched.

Before I could ask her what was wrong, she screwed her eyes shut, and I heard a gurgling sound. As her head bowed again, I realized that the sound was coming from her stomach.

Looking up, she opened her eyes again, squinting. Then she pointed to my left and said through clenched teeth, "Okay. That arm."

"What?"

"It's still bleeding. I have to go." She turned away from me, looking around frantically all of a sudden. She may have been faking some of the way she'd been acting while tied up in the pantry, but now I wondered just how damaged she really was. It hadn't entirely been an act.

"Wait, don't," I pleaded. I didn't want her to leave; I had just gotten her back. "I don't understand what's happened. How come you didn't die?"

She looked around some more, her gaze darting about but seemingly looking at nothing. Her eyes fell briefly on my arm, but then it seemed like she had to force herself to look away from it and directly into my face.

"No more thread," she said meaningfully. "Like he said. When he took the…" She screwed her eyes shut, then put her thumb and forefinger to the bridge of her nose. "The thing. The cure. He didn't know that it worked both ways, separating him from me, too. I felt it. That's what kept me going, gave me some kind of… I knew that… Through all the…" She let out a sort of growl and sigh, sounding frustrated.

"Okay," I said, still confused but trying to understand.

She became more agitated, avoiding looking at me as she shook her head and began sort of flapping her hands like she was fanning herself. "I can't," she said, sounding on the verge of tears.

"Elizabeth…" I began, stepping closer to her. I just wanted to make everything be okay somehow.

Suddenly, she grabbed my shoulders, fixing me with a gaze that I wasn't sure I had missed or had never seen before. She looked quite different, but there was no denying that she was still beautiful, looking twice my age or not.

"I *have* to go," she said stubbornly.

"But…" I still didn't want to let her go. We'd been apart for so long, and I hadn't even gotten to kiss her yet, let alone hug her.

"Damn it," she whispered, rolling her eyes, looking almost like I remembered her from before. She looked up toward the ceiling, then pulled her head back down to face me. Without warning, she shoved me away from her, very hard. Before I knew it, I was skidding across the kitchen floor on my ass, landing painfully against one of the cabinets, a handle poking me uncomfortably in the back.

Dazed and with my legs spread out beneath me, I winced from the pain, leaning forward and massaging my bruised back. Plus there was still the wound in my arm, which I realized I should get bandaged up, maybe even stitched. Elizabeth was nowhere to be seen, and I knew that there was no point in trying to follow her.

CHAPTER TWENTY-TWO

The next few months were difficult for me, not least because it was a long time before I saw or heard from Elizabeth again. Our last encounter had left me with lots of unanswered questions, and I wanted more than anything to talk to her, to make sure she was okay. But then, given all of the torture that my clone had put her through, how could she be? Did she really, as he'd said, hate me? It had been my clone who had done those horrible things, not me, but maybe the whole experience had been too much for her, and she couldn't separate her resentment for him from her feelings for me, whatever those might be.

This was all speculation, and since she wouldn't contact me, that was all I had to go on. I was left alone with my thoughts, often replaying those last few short minutes we had together in my head. I understood why she had to force herself to leave after being tempted by my bleeding arm, but why was she still avoiding me? Was this going to be an indefinite thing?

It was very frustrating. I even dreamed more than once that she had left me a note at my window letting me know that she was okay, but once I woke up and found that it wasn't true, I became very angry. I didn't want to be mad at her, but part of me couldn't help it. During some of my more anxious moments, I began to wonder if maybe she had in fact died after all.

But when I was feeling more rational, I knew that this wasn't the case. I'd both seen and been told how quickly the subset vampires died when their source vampire was killed. And even though Elizabeth had seemed kind of freaked out once my clone was defeated, she didn't seem to be in any danger of keeling over or anything. She was hiding out, plain and simple.

I thought about doing that trick where I could disturb her gravesite to force her to come to me, but in a surprisingly mature decision for me, I opted to not do that, to just respect her wishes and let her work through whatever she needed to. I'd see her again, I was pretty sure. My patience would eventually be rewarded, but not until after the next school year began.

As for the rest of the city, the vampire menace had died down considerably, but it never fully went away. I had no idea how many of my clone's vampires had managed to escape his rampage and survive after he was gone, but presumably, they were lying low and playing it safe, not calling much attention to themselves. Reports of attacks were few and far between, and as before, I wondered if some of them might not even be true.

I wanted to feel some sort of vindication, but the underlying guilt was still there. Even if the threat was virtually over, that didn't make up for all of the pain and suffering we'd caused. I tried to take some comfort in a mission more or less accomplished, the elimination of all of our clones, but that only partly worked. And it still hurt that two of my oldest friends had died.

Scout's absence weighed on me as well, though there were times when I would actually forget that he was gone. It was standard practice after dinner to set aside any leftover scraps that weren't worth saving and mix them in with his dry dog food, and there were some foods that he preferred more than others. Corn was a running favorite, plus anything with meat in it. One night, I started asking myself whether or not he would like the green beans I was about to throw away, then became upset with myself when I realized that it didn't matter, not anymore.

But all I could do was keep going, to live my life. I still carried my wooden stake with me when I went out at night just in case I ran into any rogue vampires, but that ended up not happening, which was mostly a relief. It was an odd feeling; I was still on guard, but no real dangers presented themselves. Sometimes, I almost felt disappointed by this, but I knew that it was an irrational feeling. I should have been glad. Mostly, I was, but it still felt strange.

Twelfth grade began at Westlake, and while there was supposed to be a great thrill in finally being a senior, I didn't care all that much. I wasn't as miserable and melancholy as I had been in the years leading up to this one, but I couldn't bring myself to get as excited as a lot of my classmates were. I faked it, going along with what both students and teachers said about how great all this was, and from time to time, I almost believed it.

I even began going to some of the football games, which wasn't something that interested me before. But I'd somehow managed to get caught up with some of the guys in my Anatomy class, some of the more friendly jocks on the team who, for whatever reason, had taken a liking to me. It may have been because I was a bit of a prankster, resurrecting some of the jokes from my younger days like the one where one of us would start humming, then more and more of us, to the point where the teacher got fed up and yelled at everyone to stop.

Also, I was intrigued to find out from my new friends that Carl had joined the football team. He and I still didn't have much contact with each other, but he at least had gotten to where he'd give me a friendly nod in the halls if he happened to walk by me. He'd been really into athletics when we were younger, but something had happened after the vampire summers and throughout the subsequent events that led to the clones emerging and wreaking havoc.

Like Dennis, he had gotten into smoking and drinking, which I mildly disapproved of but didn't really begrudge any of the people I knew who were into it. I mostly just thought it was stupid, not my kind of thing. But for Carl, whom I'd known for so long, it struck me as sad that someone who had been so healthy as a kid had gone down that path, no longer caring about sports. Finding out that he'd taken them up again made me kind of happy for him; maybe he'd found some renewed hope in his life and decided to improve himself. And if he could do that, pick up the pieces and move on, then maybe I could, too.

It had been Marcus, Derek's cousin, who first told me about Carl joining the team, which he was also on. He was a fun guy, very gregarious and popular, but I never had the heart to tell him that his thin moustache looked kind of like he'd been drinking a glass of milk with Oreo sprinkles in it, which had subsequently stuck to his upper lip. I'd kept the thought to myself once I'd come up with it, but still, it made me laugh inwardly whenever we talked. Everyone seemed to like him, and he was voted "Best Dressed" in the Senior Superlatives section of the yearbook given the preppy clothes he always wore.

There were pep rallies in the gym, which I'd barely cared about during my junior year, but now that I actually knew some of the guys on the football team, I was a little more into it. The school band would usually play, and it hurt somewhat to see Eileen as she played along with them. I'd tried to talk to her not long after the school year had begun, running into her in the hall and saying that I hadn't seen her for a while, trying to be friendly to her.

"Yeah, it's been nice," she'd said sarcastically, then moved on. That stung, but I couldn't blame her, given that I'd broken up with her with little to no explanation. I later learned that she was dating another football player named Brett, whom I found myself hating out of a sort of default jealousy.

At least I was doing normal things. I was a senior in high school, I was going to pep rallies and football games, I had friends and got along with people… But even so, there was still that feeling that I was living a double life. I was still someone who had brought so much pain and destruction on my city, destroying countless lives. Sometimes I'd been directly responsible for that, other times not. I tried to tell myself that I had paid my dues, suffered in my own ways as well. But at the same time, I'd gotten away with it.

A harsh reminder of this came when I happened to run into Nick at the Westlake/Copeland game in October. We'd played Copeland at their field and lost, but I didn't really care about that. For the most part, I went to these games not because I felt invested in the competition; I just went to hang out with friends and wander around the bleachers, talking to people I knew. It was one more way for me to try to feel more normal, just a high school senior socializing and making small talk.

As the crowd was making its way through the parking lot to their cars after the game, I came across Nick, who was with a rather pretty girl with short, curly dark hair and wearing a band uniform, her tall, fuzzy white hat tucked under her arm. His arm was around her shoulder, and it struck me as odd that he would be dating someone like her given what I knew about his history. He was always into more rough, punk types, so for him to be dating a band girl seemed kind of weird to me.

I said hi to him, and he seemed caught off guard. The girl, who was fairly sweaty and looked pretty worn out, politely introduced herself to me as Emily before telling Nick that he could catch up with her at her car. He looked a little frustrated, but it had already been established that he and I were going to talk for a bit. It was a protocol that I'd learned from becoming more social lately, certain body language that required people to at the very least say a few words before moving on.

We were heading into adulthood at this point, and this was something we'd both learned.

"Girlfriend?" I asked him, pointing at Emily's departing figure.

"Yeah, for now," he said, rather aloof. His hair was cut short and somewhat spiky; the last time I'd seen him, it had been very long and past his shoulders. "Band chicks tend to put out."

I laughed. "Not in my experience. But hey, whatever works." He shrugged, then looked at me with an unreadable expression. Back when I'd first met him, he was into punk rock and other rebellious stuff, so I tried to continue the conversation along those lines. "I saw a Dead Milkmen video on MTV the other day." That was a lie. "You still into them?"

"Hmm? No, not really. They got pretty lame after a while. I'm more into the stuff they show on *120 Minutes* now. Blur, Ned's Atomic Dustbin, Smashing Pumpkins, stuff like that."

I'd heard of these bands and the show he was referring to, but I didn't really like them. I could see the appeal of the whole "alternative" movement that was starting to take off in music, but I still preferred stuff that was more accessible. The groups he was talking about were just a little too weird for me, almost like they were trying too hard to be strange.

I told him some of this, but I tried to phrase it as nonconfrontationally as possible, wanting to keep things friendly. That didn't stop him from giving me a condescending sneer when I mentioned that I liked the groups Midnight Oil and R.E.M., which he followed with, "Oh, *them.*"

Feeling defensive, I changed the subject. "I suppose you heard about Dennis and Tim," I said solemnly.

Again, his expression was hard to interpret. "Yeah."

"It really sucks what happened to them."

"And whose fault is that, do you think?" He glared at me, and when I couldn't think of anything to say, he walked past me without another word.

It was the following week when Elizabeth finally re-established contact with me, but things didn't go well in the beginning. It had been over four months since I'd seen her, so naturally, I was very excited when she knocked on my window late one night. As I opened the window and started to pull at the hinges at the bottom of the screen, she told me to wait.

"Let's just talk through the window first," she said quietly. She looked my age again, and her hair was back to its normal length, just past her shoulders.

"What? No! It's been so long!"

"Ray, don't," she said, but I ignored her. Whatever her reason for wanting to keep a barrier between us, I couldn't stand the thought of another night going by without touching her, especially not now that I'd seen her again. I pushed the screen forward and made my way through the window, out of practice from not having done it for so long. But by the time I made it out into the night, I heard the sound of fluttering wings, and she was gone.

I tried calling out to her in a harsh whisper, not wanting my parents to overhear if they happened to still be awake. But it was too late. "Well done, Ray," I muttered to myself. "Way to not screw that one up."

Having learned my lesson, I did as she asked when she came back to my window almost an hour later. She was very firm with me, insisting that if I tried to come outside again, she'd leave. "I'm just not ready for that yet, Ray."

"Why not? Elizabeth, I've missed you so much."

"I've missed you too," she said placatingly. "But I've been through a lot the past few months, and it's important to me to take things one step at a time. I don't want you to get hurt."

"This already hurts," I said, aching to hold her again.

She sighed. "I know. But I don't entirely trust myself at the moment. Please, just be patient with me."

She went on to explain how messed up she'd been, how it had taken her a long time to get back to herself, as she put it. I just thought she meant physically, how she'd restored her body to that of a teenage girl. But no, she really had been affected mentally by her ordeal. What she was most afraid of was that she might lose control of herself and bite me.

It was a little hard for me to follow, and I had to piece everything together on my own given that the overall conversation was spread out over a handful of nights. Our encounters were brief, her way of testing the waters and becoming okay with being around me again. Some of that was due to what my clone did to her, but it also had something to do with how, having tasted his blood — and, in a sense, mine — she'd found herself craving more of it. Essentially, what she needed to do was learn, in small bits, how to be in my company without harming me.

At first, I balked at this idea, at least to myself. Things seemed so fragile between us that I didn't want to argue with her, afraid that I might scare her off again. But for almost the entire time she'd been a vampire, she'd never threatened me or done anything to hurt me. She may have jokingly done that a few times, but I'd learned to trust her and not be afraid. Even that terrifying confrontation with her in that run-down house didn't seem to matter anymore; she was back, and I loved her, and I wanted more than anything to be with her physically.

And Elizabeth never could have killed me, not really. Well, she could have, but that would have eliminated my clone and then her. So that had always been a safety net. What I finally realized on the second night that we spoke through the window was that this was no longer the case. Elizabeth hadn't said so herself, but she must have known it, maybe even been afraid to articulate it.

The whole reason she was still alive, why my clone's death hadn't destroyed her, was because the thread between them had been broken when he took the antidote to the potion. It followed that if I were to die now, she'd still survive. Physically, at least, there was nothing stopping her from killing me. Once I fully understood this, I was grateful for the fact that she was being so cautious. I also realized that, if she chose to, she could even drain me and then bring me back to life as a vampire, which was the last thing I wanted.

On Saturday night, she finally let me join her outside. I had a wooden stake on me, but not the one with the garlic powder in it because I knew that the smell would bother her. Everything was very tentative and slow, and she warned me ahead of time that if she started to breathe heavily, that was a sign that she was losing control and that I should get away from her immediately, even hold her at bay with the stake if necessary. She seemed scared but also determined to give things a try.

I held her to me for a good five minutes straight, so happy to feel her body against mine again that I wanted to cry. Once it became clear to us that she wasn't going to go all crazy on me and do anything bad, we just savored the moment, breathing each other in. I'd missed her so much, and any fears that we'd had melted away.

We pulled back from each other, still holding on, and she looked very relieved. All the time we'd been talking before, she'd almost always been very stern-faced and serious, though she had managed to slip in a wry comment here or there. But this was the first time I'd seen her genuinely smile in months. She put her forehead up against mine, laughing. It was the most beautiful sound I'd ever heard.

When we kissed, I was in heaven, but as our tongues rolled over each other like they always had, I began to feel a little anxious. We were tasting each other, so was this going to be a problem? Despite our earlier victory, would she suddenly break off from me and shove me away?

The kiss became deeper, more passionate, and she began to grip me more tightly than I was comfortable with. I'd already started to get an erection, but that began to fade as I started to become afraid of her, the way she was breathing through her nose with increasing intensity. But it also felt so good that I didn't want to stop, even though I knew we should.

Forcefully, she pulled back from me, holding me at arm's length, a frightened look in her eyes. "Okay," she said, gasping, "I think that's enough for…" She paused, her mouth slightly open as her wide blue eyes quickly looked me up and down. Then she screwed them shut, turning her head away. "You have no idea how good you taste," she hissed, snatching her hands from mine.

I wanted to take a step back, but something was stopping me. Whether it was fear or passion, I couldn't be sure.

"Ray, get out your stake," she said, still not looking at me.

"What?"

"Do it," she practically growled.

"Elizabeth, I can't…" I began, but the piercing look she shot me forced me to obey. I held the stake unsteadily in my hand, knowing there was no way I could actually use it on her.

"Okay, that's good," she said, holding out her hand. "Just like that… You don't have to threaten me with it or anything. I just need to see it." She began backing away slowly, now with both hands held out, eyes on the stake. "I can't. I can't I can't I can't." She closed her eyes again and nodded as she said this, more like she was saying it to herself, not me. "Okay."

She seemed to relax as she let out a fierce breath, her cheeks puffing out as she did so. Then she looked at me again, giving me a half-smile. "This is going to take time."

I wasn't sure what to say. I didn't feel scared of her anymore; I felt sorry for her. She was suffering, and while all I wanted to do was hold her and kiss her, that wasn't what she needed. I felt sad, but I was determined to help her in any way I could. "I love you," I managed to say.

"I love you, too, Ray," she said. "Please know that. That hasn't changed. I just…"

"I know."

As Elizabeth had said, it took a while, but things eventually did improve between us, and our conversations began to return to normal. She told me that what she was having to do with me was a form of what was called immersion therapy, something she'd read about in some psychology books from the library. It was frustrating for me the way she kept limiting our contact, but if it was what she needed to do in order to be okay, to say nothing of sparing my own neck, I had no choice but to cooperate.

Over the summer, she'd established a new routine in terms of her living conditions. Rather than moving from house to house every few nights like she had before, she'd found a way to stay in hotel rooms long-term. I hadn't known this before, but it was possible for people to rent rooms for longer periods of time, not just for a night or two. What she would do was use her mental powers to trick the attendant into using their own credit card to pay, giving her a free place to stay. She'd have to pack up and move on shortly before the month was up, as the person she'd fooled would then get their credit card statement and find this unexpected charge on it. She just had to stay one step ahead of things, moving on to a new hotel month after month.

Room service was a bit of a problem, she told me. The cleaning ladies would try to let themselves in during the middle of the day, often ignoring the *Do Not Disturb* sign that hung on the doorknob. As the months went on, she found different ways to deal with this: ignoring them, letting them in but then running to hide under the bed sheets to avoid the sunlight, or leaving the door unlocked but racing to the bathroom to run the water and pretend she was taking a shower. It wasn't the most ideal way to live, but it allowed her life to be a bit more stable and a little less nomadic.

And yes, sometimes she would feed on these people, but not lethally. She could still do that hypnotic thing where they wouldn't even realize she'd bitten them, and while I didn't like hearing her talk about that, I knew I had to accept it. I also knew deep down that she probably still killed sometimes, that she had fully accepted the fact that she was a vampire, and there was no going back. If I tried expressing disapproval, she'd just get mad. Then I felt guilty on two fronts: that I was hurting her feelings and that I was letting her continue to exist at the expense of others.

Later, I would spend nights in these hotel rooms with her, but that didn't happen right away. Elizabeth still needed time to adjust, or really, we both did. As she became more emotionally grounded, we tried out the old method of having her sneak into my bedroom and talk with me under the covers in the dark. There was one time when things started to get too passionate between us again, too dangerous, and I had to be the one to tell her to stop. For safety reasons, she left immediately, and I wished she hadn't. But it wasn't something she got mad at me about; we both understood the situation.

There was another night when she really freaked me out, though, when I was woken up by her suddenly turning on my desk lamp. She was sitting in my chair, which tended to make squeaking sounds whenever I sat down or got up, but I hadn't heard any noise prior to her pulling on the lamp's chain. I cried out in surprise, sitting up in bed immediately, but she just smirked at me triumphantly, looking sexy but also extremely frightening, especially as the implications of what had happened quickly sank in.

My window was locked, as was the rest of the house, but she'd managed to get in anyway. I then remembered her ability to do things like this, to zoom through cracks in that weird and creepy way, and my heart continued to pound as I realized that she could have done this all along. Even back when she was insisting on talking through the window, she always could have gotten inside and preyed on me if she'd wanted to.

"Elizabeth…" I whispered, too scared to move.

She let out a long and soft *"Shh,"* smiling as she did so. "I won't hurt you," she whispered.

It was then that I heard my mother's footsteps coming up the hall, but before I could do anything else, I felt that familiar psychic hum emanating from Elizabeth. She gently turned in my chair to face the door, and the footsteps stopped, then went slowly back down the hall. It was a repeat of a similar episode from the year before, but something about this seemed more sinister to me.

Elizabeth slowly got up from the chair and glided silently over to the side of my bed, then knelt down, staring up at me in a strange manner. She still looked proud of herself, but there was also something pleading in her eyes. "I'm sorry I frightened you," she whispered. "I just needed to make a point."

What she'd done wasn't just to prove to me that she could get into my room whenever she wanted, nor was it to scare the shit out of me, which it had. Once we talked about it more, she assured me that the reason she'd done it was to show that she finally felt like she'd regained control. It was as much a test of her resolve as it was of my nerves.

This was the prelude to her allowing me to visit her in her hotel room, though I had to admit that I was nervous the first time. I was glad that she was feeling more like herself, but there was still something eerie about her that I didn't remember from before. Maybe it was just because I wasn't used to her; the previous year, we'd spent a lot more time together. She seemed a little more mysterious and careful in the way she spoke. There was something kind of intimidating about that, which reminded me of how I'd thought of her when we'd first met, this impossibly gorgeous, strange girl who had a lot more going on under the surface than she liked to let on.

I suppose all of this made her seem more mature, or maybe that was just my reaction to how she did in fact look just a little bit older than before. I mentioned that this first night in the hotel, and while she jokingly pretended to be offended at my saying that she looked "old," she went on to explain the details of what had happened to her earlier this year, some of which I'd already guessed.

Draining my clone's blood had pulled her back from the brink of being a shriveled, starving vampire, but as I'd seen, that had still left her with a body that looked maybe forty or fifty years old. Afterwards, she'd had to drink more blood than usual each night in order to make her body continue to age backwards; drinking the normal amount would just sustain her current age. I didn't like to think about just how many people she'd wounded or even killed in order to do this, and even though I didn't say so, she knew.

"That's why I didn't mention it earlier," she said to me, "back when we were still settling back in. I knew you wouldn't approve."

"Elizabeth, it's not about me approving of you."

"Isn't it?" she asked with a raised eyebrow. Something in her face seemed to be challenging me, like she was ready for an argument. Instead, I just kissed her. She reciprocated, but once we were done, she didn't let me off the hook immediately, saying cleverly: "Nice dodge."

"Wasn't it?" I smiled.

She pretended to be annoyed, but I could tell that she wasn't really. "So, yeah, that was a weird time. I went too far, even, maybe kinda getting addicted to the whole aging backwards thing. I wound up making myself too young, like, prepubescent even."

"Seriously?"

"Yeah. Got shorter and smaller and everything. Of course, I couldn't see myself in the mirror and all, but once it got to where my clothes were too big for me and I had to go out all like this…" She made gestures indicating having to struggle to keep her clothes from falling off of her shoulders. "Yeah, that was pretty strange. It's kind of a freaky feeling looking down and suddenly realizing that your boobs aren't there anymore."

I tried to picture this, and it occurred to me that I was glad I hadn't seen her during the period she was describing. While I could imagine that a younger, preteen Elizabeth might have been rather cute, the idea made me uncomfortable. It was more or less the opposite feeling of seeing her look like someone as old as my mother; seeing her as a little girl but still being in love with her might make me feel like some kind of pedophile.

"Yeah," she said, nodding nervously when I told her this. "So there was no way I was going to let you see me back then. I was pretty uncomfortable with it, too. So then I had to all but starve myself, forcing my body to age forward again so I'd get older. But not too much older... not too young..." Her voice raised in pitch as she said this and waved her hand back and forth. "Took me a while to get it right."

"How did you know when you had?"

"Just by feeling myself, really." A dirty joke shot through my head, and she either picked up on it psychically or just knew that I was still in many ways a typical seventeen-year-old boy. "Stop it," she said firmly, but still with a grin. "That's not what I mean. Like a blind person, you know? They can't see, but they learn how to feel faces and hair and all that kind of stuff. And yeah, I guess, these too." She cupped her breasts in her hands and jiggled them up and down lightly, looking down at them as she did. They weren't huge or anything, not like some porn magazine bimbo's, but they fascinated me nonetheless.

She cleared her throat meaningfully, and I jerked my eyes up from the mesmerizing display to find her staring at me, a stern and accusing look on her face. Then she laughed, and I did too. The playfulness reminded me of our older conversations.

We continued talking, occasionally touching each other affectionately as we did, and oddly enough, the topic of her breasts remained relevant. She asked me why guys were so fascinated with them, and I admitted that I honestly didn't know; maybe it was just because we didn't have them. She told me that when a girl first starts growing them, it feels weird, not just physically but psychologically.

"There's that whole, 'Hey, I'm growing up now!' thing; 'I'm becoming a woman!' But it kind of sucks, too, because you don't have any control over it. And then you've got boys starting to notice, staring at you and all, saying gross things behind your back. That's not fun. It feels… kinda violating. Like all these people are thinking about what they want to *do* to you. And you're just trying to come to terms with what the hell nature is doing to your body whether you want it to or not."

I'd never thought about it that way. I just liked pretty girls and all their curves, even if I couldn't really explain why. As I grew and changed as a boy, I felt kind of strange about it but accepted it, even found it exciting at times. But some of what she was saying reminded me of something my father had said to me when I'd first had to learn how to shave.

I was fourteen, and I'd been sporting that fuzzy pre-moustache that boys that age have for a few weeks or months before someone finally tells them that the chocolate-milk-upper-lip look isn't a good one. My father showed me how to use his electric razor, the idea being that he'd teach me how to use a proper razor and shaving cream sometime later when he had more time, but that never happened. He'd said that at my age, it was normal to feel kind of excited about the new development: *Hey, I'm shaving!* But then, very quickly, it would become: *Crap, I have to shave.* I took his word for it at the time, and after the novelty wore off as I got a little older, I saw his point. It was another bathroom chore like brushing one's teeth.

Elizabeth listened to my story, but she contended that extra body hair wasn't as traumatic of a thing to deal with as finding oneself involuntarily becoming all curvy and an object of desire. I tried to understand her argument, but I wasn't sure if I could accede to the notion that suddenly becoming beautiful was a worse fate than turning gangly and awkward, with a bigger nose and a prominent Adam's apple. She countered that the added danger of becoming pregnant was something that no boy would ever have to deal with, and I managed to stop myself just before blurting out something about how that didn't apply to her anymore since she was a vampire. That would have been a really shitty thing to say, I realized just in time.

Sensing that we were straying into genuine fighting territory, I found a way to defuse the moment. "By the way, speaking of all this boy/girl stuff, there's something funny I found out from my mother a few months ago. Well, maybe not funny, but an interesting little coincidence."

"And what was that?" She still seemed kind of worked up.

"Apparently, before I was born, the doctors kept thinking I was going to be born a girl."

She laughed. "Really? Why?"

"Something to do with my heart rate being faster, and so that made them think I'd be a girl for some reason. I guess that was some kind of indicator, like girl fetuses are smaller and have faster hearts."

"That's weird," she said. "They didn't do that thing, you know, where they take a picture of the baby and can see if it's male or female?"

"I guess they didn't have those back then."

"I thought they did," she said, looking pensive. "Or maybe they just weren't as common. Okay, wait, so how is that a coincidence?"

"I asked Mom what she would have named me if I had been a girl, and she said, 'Elizabeth.'"

She laughed again, then rolled her eyes. "Of course."

"Why 'of course?'"

"I don't know if you've ever noticed, Ray, but it's a really common name. *Really* common, like, obnoxiously so. I always thought my name was boring because of that."

"Well, I think it's pretty."

She gave me a crooked smile, grudgingly accepting the compliment. "Still," she added, her smile growing, "I'm glad you weren't born a girl."

I chuckled. "Me too. Otherwise you'd have to be a lesbian." That earned me a playful smack from her on my thigh.

She went on to ask me about my sisters, if either of them had been prenatally misdiagnosed in the same way. They hadn't, but after talking to my mother about my birth, I'd since come to the conclusion that I wasn't planned, that I was, as it's called, "an accident." My mother didn't tell me this, but certain clues around the house and what I knew about my family history had hinted at it.

For one, my parents waited for a few years after they were married to have children, which I'd learned was uncommon for their generation. Susanna hadn't been born until my mother was almost thirty, and I came along nine years later, quite possibly as an afterthought. I'd noticed things around the house, like more than one set of dual picture frames with photos of my young sisters in them, then with a separate photo of the young me off to one side. There was also the fact that the house originally only had three bedrooms, and Susanna's upstairs one was added on shortly after I came along.

"You never asked your parents about it?" Elizabeth asked me.

"No. I couldn't find a way to bring it up without it seeming too jerky, you know, 'Hey, Mom and Dad, you never wanted me in the first place, did you?' And I didn't feel comfortable telling either of them that the first thing that got me thinking along these lines, maybe the strongest evidence of it really, was how I'd noticed one day that my birthday was almost exactly nine months after my mother's."

Elizabeth understood, smiling knowingly. "So you were a birthday present. Or maybe I should say 'surprise.'"

I let out a small laugh. "Yeah." Then something occurred me, and I put my hand to my forehead, closing my eyes. "Shit, I'm doing it again, aren't I? Going on and on about family and all that, when I should know how much that upsets you."

"It's okay." She gently pulled my hand away from my face, then held it in her lap. "It doesn't bother me as much as it used to. That whole world: families, sisters, mothers and fathers... It's not mine anymore. That was taken away from me a long time ago."

"I'm sorry," I said.

"Don't be. I'm not. Not anymore." She looked sad, though, making me wonder how much she really believed what she was saying.

So this was our existence now, at least for the next several months anyway. We loved each other, but we still weren't a real couple, not "boyfriend and girlfriend." The term best describing us was one I'd learned recently from other people at school: "friends with benefits." There was physical affection, including having sex, but we weren't officially exclusive. As far as I knew, she didn't have another guy in her life, and I had no reason not to believe her when I asked her about it once.

She didn't have any contact with what few vampires still remained in the city, and getting romantically involved with someone was as alien to her now as the concept of family life. I was the closest thing she had to that, and she explained to me one night that the main reason she'd felt comfortable with me in the first place, opening up to me and getting to know me like she did, was that I could understand her, having once been a vampire myself. I wasn't sure if that comforted me or made me uneasy. But I loved her just the same.

I didn't have any interest in pursuing other girls at my school, either. There may no longer have been much danger of them getting preyed upon by vampires and turned against me like before — which had put me off of dating in the past — but even so, my heart really did belong to Elizabeth, problematic though our situation was. We only saw each other once a month, something that was established back when she was still carefully rationing our time together to keep from being exposed to me for too long. The pattern became a habit, and we stuck with it for a while.

Maybe I would eventually meet someone else who caught my eye, and I'd try dating her. But what would happen with me and Elizabeth then? Would we drift farther apart? Would she still be my little secret, something on the side to not tell my real girlfriend about? I didn't like that idea, which was another reason why trying to date normal girls barely interested me. If someone tempting enough came along, I might go for it, but I wasn't holding my breath.

When I did see Elizabeth during these monthly hotel room visits, it was nice, even if the overall circumstances were frustrating. Sometimes we'd have sex, or we'd just make out, and at other points in the night, we'd just hang out like two good friends and watch late-night cable TV. She'd been cut off from that luxury for a couple of years, but now that she had more stability in her life, at least that was something we could share, something more normal.

She also began collecting music, going to record stores some nights and exploring various artists and their material. Initially, she'd caught up on the more popular names, ones whose releases she'd missed during her first couple of years as a vampire, unable to have even these temporary homes. When that began to bore her, she started branching out, experimenting with bands she hadn't even heard of, snatching their tapes up and playing them on the presumably stolen boom box that she kept with her as she migrated from hotel to hotel, along with her collection. She'd play some of the more interesting ones for me at times, and whether or not I actually liked them, I enjoyed the time I spent with her.

I started to emulate this behavior, wanting to expand my own musical horizons as well. My encounter with Nick at that football game a couple of months earlier and his snobbish attitude towards more mainstream music was also an influence, but I wouldn't admit that at the time. So I explored the bins of records and cassettes at music shops, skipping over the CDs because I didn't yet have a CD player. That was a new and expensive format that I wasn't ready to delve into, though I would end up getting a player for Christmas later on.

One thing that surprised me was finding that at one particular store that sold both music and books, they also had large selections of comic books, something that hadn't interested me for a very long time. People flying around in tights and capes and bashing the crap out of each other was something for kids, I figured. Out of nostalgia, I picked up and thumbed through a few of them, initially confirming this stereotype.

All of the comics were lain flat along one wall of the store, the same as the regular magazines were, which I realized was different from the cylindrical, rotating metal racks I remembered from my youth. As young as age five, I'd seen those in convenience stores, which had led me to beg my father to buy me my first *The Incredible Hulk* comic book when I'd spotted it.

But something different was happening here. There was a section off to the right with a handmade sign above it designating it as *MATURE COMICS,* which struck me as odd, even an oxymoron. But once I looked through the first couple of them, I quickly realized that these weren't the same as the kind of comic books I'd grown up with.

The artwork in many of them was better than anything I'd seen in a comic before. They weren't like the cartoony drawings I was used to; they looked a lot more detailed. Some of them even depicted very violent and graphic stuff. There were still the dialogue bubbles with their bottoms pointing at who was supposed to be speaking, and the text looked like it was written by hand in all capitals. To me, that made things look kind of juvenile, but at the same time, it reminded me of some of the pictures and cartoons Tim had drawn when he was a kid.

Sometimes he would just doodle, but every now and then, he'd do a three- or four-page panel comic depicting something funny that happened at school. I'd drawn a few of these myself back in the day, usually to make fun of someone I didn't like: a teacher, a student, or both. But it wasn't something I stuck with or took very seriously, and my artistic skills weren't as good as Tim's.

The comic book that intrigued me the most, though, was completely unlike anything I'd seen. It still had the same dialogue bubbles and such, but the pictures were amazingly complex, looking more like paintings. This was a far cry from the comic strips I'd seen in the newspaper, just funny jokes where a talking cat would make a wry comment and then throw a dog into a ceiling fan. Something deep was trying to be said. Even more interestingly, there were vampires in this one.

I soon realized what I was looking through: a comic book version of the novel *Interview with the Vampire,* which I'd heard of a couple of years earlier, even before the emergence of the clones. Like most kids my age, I listened to Top 40 radio a lot, including the weekly countdown shows. During one, the DJ introduced a song whose name I'd already forgotten by this point, but what caught my attention was when he said that the song was inspired by this novel. At the time, I'd shunned this, not wanting to have anything at all to do with vampires.

But once I saw this comic adaptation, I recognized the title and couldn't help but be intrigued. It wasn't that expensive, just two bucks, so I bought it and took it home, then read it that night.

The issue was only the very first part of the story, and it simultaneously fascinated and repelled me. The protagonist — the vampire — was guilt-ridden, which I could certainly relate to, but he was also very matter-of-fact about what he had done. The plot was interesting, and because I knew that the novel the comic was based upon existed in its entirety already, I soon found it and bought it.

Although I knew that it was supposed to be fiction, I wondered if maybe it might have some basis in reality. After all, *Dracula* was a 94-year-old book, supposedly fiction as well, but then Dracula himself had shown up in Augusta five years ago and proven to be quite real.

So I read the entire book — neglecting schoolwork to do so — and for the most part, I found it very interesting. I wasn't sure if I could say that I liked it; parts of it made me feel very uncomfortable, hitting too close to home. The next time I saw Elizabeth, I asked her if she'd ever read it.

That was on a Friday night just after Christmas, and per my suggestion, we didn't just sit and talk in her hotel room but instead drove to Lake Olmstead in my car to hang out there. This time, I lit a fire in one of the grills, which reminded me of hanging out with Melody's friends at Clarks Hill, but this was a much smaller lake, one that was in town. The idea was that this could be a more romantic setting for us than the usual sterile hotel room, but as it turned out, it wasn't a very good time.

For one thing, she didn't like the fire. I hadn't even thought about it being an issue, but fire was one of the lethal variety of vampire deterrents, and while it was safely contained, Elizabeth made it very clear that its presence bothered her. I wanted to put it out, then realized that I had no way of doing so. We ended up just sitting far away from it, huddled close together against the cold. I was a little frustrated by this, knowing that we'd be warm if she could just stand to be close enough to the fire.

Still, we talked, and I told her about *Interview with the Vampire* and wanted to know if she'd read it. She hadn't, but she'd heard of it, or more specifically, seen it mentioned in the liner notes of some album that had a song based on it. I assumed she'd meant the same one that I'd heard on that Top 40 countdown show, but I would later find out that I was wrong. This night, though, I described the book to her, mentioning how the protagonist, Louis — which I'd read in my head as sounding like "Lewis" and wouldn't learn until later on was supposed to be "Louie," the French pronunciation — reminded me of myself. This surprised her, but then I clarified that it was his guilt, his revulsion at being a vampire, that I identified with.

"Sounds pretty depressing," she said flatly.

"Kind of," I said. "But it was still pretty good."

"Maybe I'll give it a read sometime." There was something in her voice that bothered me, but I wasn't sure quite what.

I was disappointed that she hadn't been more enthusiastic; after all, she'd always been encouraging me to read more. The topic exhausted, I shifted to asking her about the winter solstice, which had recently occurred. It was the longest night of the year, so I asked her if that was something that she or other vampires tended to get excited about, maybe even celebrate.

She laughed at the idea, but she conceded that she could understand why I might think that. "But no, it's not like Vampire Christmas or anything." She shrugged her shoulders and smiled slightly, adding, "Maybe it should be. I have to admit, winters are easier than summers, when the nights are shorter. Lots less rushing to make it to safety by sunrise, and being able to get up and about sooner. So yeah, I guess there is something to that."

"We were always vampires during the summer," I said, "so we never really got to tell the difference."

"Your loss," she said with a sly grin.

That made me uncomfortable, so I changed the subject slightly, mentioning something that had been bugging me for a while. We'd talked before about the inconsistencies in various vampire legends, how some of the rules applied to some vampires but not others. While I'd never read the full text of *Dracula,* I did know from the summary I'd read that he could in fact exist during the daylight hours, which was completely against everything else I'd ever read, seen, or heard about vampires.

"You can't be out during the day, right?" I asked her.

"Oh, no, definitely not. I mean, I can be awake, but sunlight? Hell, no. I don't go anywhere near it. But now that you mention it, there are some versions of the legend, not just that one I mean, where the sun isn't an issue."

"See, that just strikes me as… I don't know. Weird. And when we fought Dracula, it was always at night. If he'd been able to get to us during the day, we'd have been screwed."

"Wait, what?"

I thought back to our battles with him, which were probably the most horrifying part of our time as vampires. He'd almost beaten us and bent us to his will, and whenever I allowed myself to think about how things might have gone differently had he won, it terrified me.

"I never told you about that, did I?" I almost whispered.

"About what? You meeting a fictional character?"

"He wasn't fictional, Elizabeth," I said harshly, then caught myself. There was no reason to lash out at her. "He was real."

"Ray, Dracula isn't real. He was a character made up by Bram Stoker. And someone they later made into tons of cheesy movies. Trust me, I know. I've done my research."

Her condescending tone didn't help the mounting anger I was feeling. "Listen. I know what I saw. And yeah, I know that that Bram Stoker guy based him on someone else, some Vlad… Something-or-Other. Tim told me that. But then there was the time before that when we fought Van Helsing…"

She burst out laughing, which angered me further. "Now I know you're full of it. Van Helsing? Seriously? Another made up guy."

"No, he wasn't. He showed up in Augusta, tried to wipe us out."

The conversation continued to deteriorate. The more I talked, the more she became convinced that I was inventing things to make my past sound more dramatic. I couldn't argue her point that I'd never mentioned any of this to her before, despite all the time we'd known each other and what I'd told her about the vampire summers. But that was because those two conflicts — especially the things Dracula had done to my sisters and the mortal wound Van Helsing had managed to inflict — were some of my most unpleasant memories. Instead, I just glossed over the events as terrible things we'd survived, telling her instead about what followed and led to our downfall. Mostly, it was hubris.

I was used to Elizabeth being more understanding and accommodating; this snide attitude of hers was both unfamiliar and unwelcome. I became more defensive, and eventually, we agreed to disagree, but I still knew I was right and couldn't fathom why she refused to believe me. I knew full well what had happened to me was real, plus it was before I even met her, so in a way, it felt like she was some latecomer trying to stomp all over my past.

I drove her back to her hotel; we barely spoke the entire time. It only occurred to me on the drive home that she could have just flown back on her own, but for some reason, she hadn't. It was like she wanted to brood silently in the passenger seat despite me, arms folded and looking out the window. When I asked her what was wrong, she just angrily said, "Nothing." That got on my nerves even more, particularly when I realized that for her to be pouting and acting so angry was rather unfair; I was the one who had more of a right to be pissed off.

When I dropped her off, I tried to patch things up, telling her that I didn't want to say goodbye to her like this. She agreed and gave me a kiss, but it was one of those colder, angry ones. This wasn't the first time we had argued, and it wouldn't be the last, nor would it be the worst. That was still to come.

CHAPTER TWENTY-THREE

Dreams can be weird for anybody, but I always felt that they were more so for me. Being psychic, I'd had the occasional prophetic dream from time to time, though not nearly as many as I thought I should be able to. The problem with premonitions, even waking ones, was that I usually wouldn't realize they'd occurred until after the fact, that is, once the thing my powers had predicted came to pass.

My twelfth grade Psychology teacher, Ms. Perry, taught us about dream interpretation, including deciphering symbolism and the difference between manifest and latent meanings: how the things that happened in dreams reflected real life versus what they really represented on a subconscious level. There was also symbolism to examine, like how dreams in which one could fly were really, deep down, dreams about sex.

I found all of this fascinating, but when I brought it up to Carolyn, she scoffed at the idea. Ms. Perry was apparently a firm believer in Freudian psychology, but as more than one of Carolyn's professors had pointed out to her before she'd dropped out, many of Freud's ideas had since been discredited and were no longer considered valid. "Dreams are just a way for your mind to sort out the events of the day," she said to me. "They don't mean anything deeper than that."

I wasn't so sure. Her skeptical view just struck me as too boring. Cynically, I thought that my teacher probably knew more than my college drop-out sister did, but then, were her college professors smarter than my high school teacher? I couldn't be certain, so I had to come up with my own take on things, my interpretation of how significant my dreams were. I did occasionally have dreams in which I could fly, but was that because I was really thinking subconsciously about sex, or was it a memory from when I used to be a vampire? Or maybe both?

The vividness of my dreams varied from night to night; sometimes I wouldn't even dream at all, or so I thought. Ms. Perry said that everyone dreamed, even people who claimed not to, every single night. According to her, vivid dreams occurred when the mind was regenerating itself, and the more forgettable ones were on nights when the body was regenerating instead, like after a day of strenuous physical activity.

That more or less made sense to me, plus it fit in with the fact that most of the people I knew who claimed never to dream at all tended to be physically active people, like the jocks on the football team. I also noticed that I seemed to dream less on nights when I'd been out late with Elizabeth or on the prowl for vampires.

Ms. Perry had our class do a two-week-long assignment of keeping a dream journal, which was problematic for me, but I managed it okay. I had in fact kept a regular journal — or diary — on and off since I'd been a kid, but it wasn't something I ever stuck with for long. I never felt comfortable writing about truly private things in it lest it be discovered and read by my parents or sisters, plus there was the danger in writing anything truly incriminating with regards to vampires.

I had occasionally made cloaked references to that, usually with a euphemism. As far back as 1985, I'd hinted at our murderous activities as "it:" *We did "it" from July 5th to July 11th. It was scary sometimes, but fun.* When I read this years later, I was ashamed at my younger self for being so stupid and flippant. Worse still, Nick had once come up with his own twisted moniker for it, "the game," which I occasionally used in my writing as well.

When it came time to do this assignment, I ran into a similar difficulty. A good deal of my dreams were private, embarrassing, or even implicative, so I had to be very careful which dreams I talked about or left out, and I had to censor things quite a bit. I made it a point not to say anyone by name: Eileen became "an ex-girlfriend," and Tim was "a friend who died recently." Any mention of Elizabeth was strictly off-limits.

I got an A on the project, and some of Ms. Perry's comments in the margins were interesting and helpful. When I talked about a dream I had about trying to talk to Eileen by her locker and suddenly finding myself falling on my ass and unable to stand up again, my teacher wrote that this was due to my unsuccessfully being able to communicate with her. That was the latent meaning; the manifest meaning was that the dream had been inspired by the real-life episode of trying to talk to her in the hall that day and her telling me off.

Overall, the exercise got me to pay more attention to my dreams and to try to understand why I was having them, whether it was just understanding what actual events inspired them or what they might mean on a deeper level. As for whether or not they might be premonitions, that was still hard to say, nor was it an aspect of my life that I could share with my teacher or ask for guidance on.

Some of them were easy to interpret. A night or two after the time Elizabeth had shown up unexpectedly in my bedroom and scared me, then hypnotized my mother into going back down the hall, I wound up dreaming that she was standing by my parents' bed. I wasn't in the dream myself; it was like I was an invisible observer.

It was a dark, ominous scene, Elizabeth looking down at my sleeping parents with a sly grin on her face, proud of herself. I didn't know what was going to happen next, but then I began to think that I might. My pulse quickened as she began to step forward very slowly, her mouth widening and fangs extending. The fear of what I might see next shocked me awake, and I lay in bed for a while, afraid to go back to sleep and that the sequence might continue. I never told Elizabeth about the dream.

Others were even more weird and disconcerting, like the time I dreamed that I started making out with Carolyn. It only went on for a second or two, but like the dream about Elizabeth starting to prey on my parents, it forced me to wake up, leaving me feeling really gross about such an incestuous idea.

When thinking it over later, I decided that it must have really been a dream about Elizabeth; after all, Carolyn and Elizabeth both had blonde hair and blue eyes, and every now and then, Elizabeth's playful sense of humor reminded me of Carolyn's, particularly when she was younger and we'd gotten along better. More recently, Elizabeth had started being more difficult with me, so maybe my mind was connecting that with the times that Carolyn and I had fought with each other the whole time we'd grown up together, the way siblings do. While this analysis more or less satisfied me, it still made me feel almost violated the way my subconscious had made me dream such a strange thing.

Tim and Dennis both showed up in my dreams, though never at the same time for some reason. Almost always, they weren't the age they were when they'd died but were instead much younger, the boys I'd known growing up. It shouldn't have made sense, but in that weird way that dreams do, at the time I had no problem with the fact that they were alive and well but looked like they had in elementary school. When I'd wake up and remember that they were dead, I'd be very sad.

But sometimes, it was more twisted than that. There was one in which Dennis and I were at the mall together, looking around for something that had to do with our psychic powers, maybe some kind of talisman we could discover that would make us more powerful. He wasn't the grown-up, bitter teenager I'd had so much difficulty relating to; here was the younger, pudgy boy — still with a lisp and a bowl haircut — that I'd hated when we first met and later became such a close confidant to. We were conspiring together, us against the world.

We found the artifact hidden in a small door beneath something. That something then expanded in my mind to a row of CD bins in a record store, filling in the gaps in the narrative the way dreams have to do in order to make sense and keep going. Triumphant, Dennis pulled out a Bob Dylan CD, which was somehow made of stone, like an old relic. Bits of dirt fell off of it as he opened the case, and I suddenly felt afraid, wanting to tell him not to open it all the way. But it was too late.

The dust from the case shot up into his face along with a flash of greenish light, and he fell backwards, flailing around as he called out in his childhood lisp: "I can't thee! I can't thmell!" I wanted to help him, but I sat there, paralyzed and uncertain what to do.

All of a sudden, his form began to grow, becoming taller. His hair was long now, going down past his shoulders, and he began to tower over me. He looked down at me with his eyes glowing red, then began to reach forward menacingly. "Yooooou..." he said, but his voice was gravelly and strange, sounding exactly like the character Megatron from *The Transformers* cartoon we'd both watched as children.

Sometimes, nightmares this intense would scare me awake once they got to a certain threshold, but not always: Sometimes I would only think I had woken up only to find myself faced with a different but equally terrifying scenario.

Another thing that changed over time was that when my deceased friends appeared, I did in fact remember that they were supposed to be dead, but it wasn't a bad thing, at least not always. On my less troubling nights, they hadn't died at all; it had just been some mistake, a misunderstanding. It varied from dream to dream: Tim had faked his death and had been in hiding; my clone had actually lied to me about killing Dennis.

So I was glad that they were okay, and every now and then, events would progress normally. There were never any happy endings, or really any endings at all; things would just happen, and they'd either be interrupted by some new nonsensical plot or I'd wake up.

Often, things would feel like they were right on the verge of turning into nightmares, and I'd do my best to keep that from happening. But a lot of the time, whenever I realized I was dreaming, that's when I would wake up. That didn't just apply to these particular dreams, though, and it could be frustrating if I were having a very good dream, like one about being with Elizabeth.

Naturally, my dreams also involved vampires, and those were almost always bad ones. Some of the ones about an unexpectedly surviving Tim or Dennis could go that route, but they didn't always. There might also be generic vampires, or I might find myself in what started off as a pleasant encounter with Elizabeth, only to have her turn vicious on me.

Even more disturbing were the times when I wouldn't mind her feeding on me, at least while I was sleeping and my subconscious was in control. Upon waking, I'd hate myself for that, knowing full well that such a thing could never happen. Or at least, it shouldn't, and I really hoped that she'd never force that on me. I was pretty confident that she wouldn't; she'd made that clear.

She didn't want to turn me into a vampire, I knew, but that didn't stop me from also sometimes dreaming that I had become one again. That was probably helped along by the vampire fiction I'd started to read near the end of the year, like Anne Rice's *Interview with the Vampire* and the two sequels that followed it.

There was an incident in early January that probably contributed to the dream I had that night: I was watching a particularly tense scene on TV, nervously picking at the skin along the edge of my right index finger with the thumbnail from my other hand. I wasn't really paying attention to what I was doing, and then I felt a sharp pain as my nail dug too far into the skin. As a reflex, I put the finger to my mouth, thinking that sucking on it would alleviate the pain.

It did, but there was something else: a minute taste of blood. I pulled the finger from my lips and looked at it, and after a few seconds, a tiny amount of blood began to pool from the pinprick-sized wound. I sucked on it again, then immediately stopped when I realized what I was doing. It had been only been a small amount, but there I was, tasting blood again, something I hadn't done for years. I forced myself to refuse to contemplate whether or not the feeling made me nostalgic.

Was this something that vampires ever did, feeding on themselves? Maybe that was some sort of equivalent to masturbation for them. I thought of asking Elizabeth about that the next time I saw her, but the notion made me feel embarrassed. I also wondered briefly if maybe I could let her feed on me in this way, a non-lethal method that would allow her to have just a little taste. But I shoved that idea aside when I realized that it would probably just make things worse. It wouldn't satisfy a need; it would probably just make her feel more tempted to feed on me for real.

That night, I dreamed…

I'd woken up in my bed as a vampire, though how I knew that's what I was, I couldn't be sure. To test it, I reached up with my fingers and felt my teeth, my head still on the pillow. Sure enough, there were two fangs there.

My subconscious filled in the gaps, and I remembered how it had happened. There was some vampire I didn't know, a girl… It wasn't Elizabeth, but maybe some second- or third-generation vampire, one made by one of the clones, who were apparently still active. Dark hair, long and flowing… She'd zoomed in through the crack under my window, which I'd foolishly left open earlier.

I'd tried to fight against her, but she'd effortlessly drained me. Somehow, however it was that vampires actually did it — which I'd never been clear on — she'd made it so that I would become a vampire, too. She wasn't around when I woke, so there I was, alone in my bed, one of the undead, suddenly very afraid.

The sun was already up; I could see it through my drapes. If I pulled back the curtain, I'd be incinerated. Then the narrative shifted: It changed to where the sun hadn't actually come up yet; instead it was just about to, the sky already brightening. That's what I had seen through the drapes, not a harsh, killing sunrise. I had just seconds to figure out what to do.

Could I make it outside in time and find some safe place to hide? Maybe I could make it to the basement and shelter in there. It had been done before. But what if the sun caught me too quickly, reducing me to ashes?

Maybe I could shelter under my covers and just hide out until the day passed. But how could I do that with my parents home? What if one of them came into my bedroom to try to wake me, not knowing what I'd become? Would I feel an uncontrollable urge to lunge at them, tearing out their throat and drinking their blood?

The sunshine continued to intensify, and I began to become more panicked. Maybe my bed sheets wouldn't provide enough cover. The bathroom was just across the hall, and while there was a small window in there, too, at least it faced west. That could buy me some time.

But could I successfully sneak across the hall? Someone might hear me open my door. Or they might already be in the den and see me, then try to talk to me or ask me something, and I'd have to try to hide my fangs, which refused to go away. Would they ask me why I was covering my mouth with my hand?

To make matters worse, both Carolyn and Susanna were in the house, having spent the night. Maybe it was Christmas, or it was someone's birthday. I couldn't really hide out in the bathroom all day; surely they'd need to use it at some point. What if they came in there? I really hoped I wouldn't have to kill them; I couldn't live with myself if I did that.

Or maybe Carolyn would understand. This wasn't something I'd chosen; it had been forced upon me. I didn't want to be a vampire. But I was. Could she forgive me?

Susanna would probably be more harsh if she were the one to discover me, cowering in the bathtub, just trying to wait it all out until the sun went down. "It's your own fault," I heard her say with her usual superiority, and she slid back the shower door, its frosted glass blurring her image until it no longer separated us. I shrunk back, trying to hide from her. "Don't blame me," she said, looking down at me. "It's in your blood." Her eyes were glowing yellow.

That particular nightmare got mercifully derailed by my mother knocking on my door, urging me not to oversleep and to get up in time for school. It took me several seconds to recover and remember who I really was. Still, the dream haunted me the rest of the day.

About a month later, I had one that was equally if not more disturbing...

Elizabeth and I were in a hotel room, naked. She hadn't fed yet that night, but she wasn't cruel and threatening like she had been that time before. Apparently, she'd learned to control those urges. But she was still cold to the touch, and while it repulsed me a little, I didn't dare say so for fear of angering her and starting another fight.

She had a Coke bottle with her that was filled with blood; how she'd managed to fill it, I didn't even question — though it would occur to me once I was awake. Earlier, she'd talked about wanting me to try drinking some of her blood from a small tear she could make on her skin, but I refused. I was curious as to whether it might also be tepid like the rest of her, but I was way too scared to try even a drop of her blood. It might turn me into a vampire. All of this came to me as those false memories that dreams provide; the real narrative didn't begin until we started holding each other.

We began to have sex, and even though her body felt strange and cool, I still loved her, and I got more used to it the further we went. Things became more intense and passionate, and I remembered that the plan was that she would begin drinking the blood from the bottle as we went along, becoming warmer.

But just as I was nearing orgasm, Elizabeth took the plastic bag — which was no longer a bottle; I'd remembered incorrectly — and shoved it into my mouth, squeezing it hard and making it burst open. The blood flooded my mouth, and I choked, refusing to swallow it. As I pulled away from her violently, she just cackled wildly, the blood spilling all over both of our bodies, the bed sheets, everywhere.

I was horrified and also very angry with her; I couldn't believe she had done this and that she'd tried to force me to drink. I shouted at her, berating her, but my protests were short-lived. She'd leaned forward, smiling wickedly as she ignored my harsh words, then began licking the spilled blood off of my chest. Her tongue flicked about like a snake's, then began lapping more like a dog's. It was the most erotic thing I had ever experienced.

As she slurped away and swallowed the blood, her body grew warmer, more like it usually felt when we were together. That just added to the experience, and as our arms and legs entwined, her licking became more rhythmic. *Lick-lick lick-lick, lick-lick lick-lick...* faster, faster... Her body was becoming even hotter, almost as hot as the inside of her felt, and I needed to touch that again so much...

I was embarrassed when my orgasm woke me up, which wasn't uncommon. But I couldn't stop thinking about the dream. I didn't want to admit that I'd enjoyed it. I had, and I hated myself for that.

Thinking about the latent interpretation of the dream disturbed me, so I tended to avoid that. The manifest meaning, the events that inspired it, had been much more tame, having occurred in a hotel room two nights earlier. Nothing terribly out of the ordinary happened that night, but looking back on it, I realized that it was part of an ongoing trend between us, one that would lead to a very unwelcome change in my life.

CHAPTER TWENTY-FOUR

In the month since Elizabeth and I had last met and parted on not very pleasant terms, I'd become even more determined to read up on vampire literature, including *Dracula*. The Cliff's Notes had been good enough for me a couple of years ago, but now, I wanted to read the book for real and see if it gave me any more insight, maybe even ammunition.

I was still hurting from Elizabeth's dismissive attitude when I'd tried to tell her about my real-life encounter with Dracula, and I also didn't like being mad at her. I thought that if I read the book in its entirety, perhaps I could find some evidence that proved my hypothesis that Dracula wasn't just a reworking of some other real-life person. I'd also thought that maybe it was Bram Stoker who was made up, that the real author of the book was in fact Van Helsing, using Stoker as a pen name. After all, he'd used a false name when he'd come to Augusta to attack us all those years ago.

Getting through the book this time was easier for me; before, I'd had difficulty with the archaic language and the slow pace. I'd always tried to avoid actually reading books for school when I could, getting by on what the teacher said in class or what I could get classmates to tell me, just enough to pass the test or write the report. But Anne

Rice's first vampire book, which I'd enjoyed despite my reservations about the subject matter, had gotten me more used to really reading.

I had my suspicions about her as well. What she described in her writing was so vivid and true to life that I had a hard time believing that it didn't have some basis in reality. Was she a vampire herself, or did she know people who were? Maybe the interviewer in the first book was in fact her — despite the fact that the character was male — and the majority of the story had been relayed to her by a real vampire. Things got even more muddled in my mind with the next two books, which treated the first one as a separate work, one that existed within the context of the overall story, something the vampires in it commented on. It was a little confusing, but it certainly made things seem more real.

As far as *Dracula* was concerned, I didn't really get much more out of it, at least not in terms of anything I could say to Elizabeth the next time I saw her that would prove me right. But I did pick up on some things that I hadn't before. As I'd noticed in the Cliff's Notes, there were eerie similarities between the characters on the page and the ones we'd battled in 1987, right down to the way they talked and their physical appearances. That was what had led me to believe that the book chronicled real events.

However, I hadn't before made the connection to two specific things about the character Lucy that had in fact come into play in my own life since my initial reading of the book's summary. The first was the way that, shortly before dying but having been preyed upon by Dracula, Lucy suddenly went all wild-eyed and vicious on her lover, another character named Arthur. It was very uncharacteristic of her, a sign that she'd been infected by a vampire. It was also very similar to the way that Eileen had acted towards me when Elizabeth had been preying on her.

Also, Elizabeth's strange ability to make her body sort of zoom down into nothing in order to slip through cracks or into her grave was in fact something that Lucy — now a vampire herself in the story — could do, though the text of *Dracula* described it differently:

> *We all looked on in horrified amazement as we saw, when he stood back, the woman, with a corporeal body as real at that moment as our own, pass in through the interstice where scarce a knife-blade could have gone.*

This ability was referred to elsewhere in the book, and there were mentions of Dracula being able to slither up and down walls like a lizard. I'd seen lizards and also roaches do things like this, their bodies appearing to flatten and disappear through tiny cracks in stone walls or under baseboards.

I'd always referred to this — when I saw Elizabeth do it, that is — as "zooming," reminded of that special effect from *Star Trek* where that woman's body had gone from three-dimensional to two-dimensional, or 3-D to 2-D, as I sometimes thought of it. But a 19th-century writer wouldn't have used words like that, nor would he have had the same perception or frame of reference.

Back during my days at Bethlehem, I'd developed a similar idea, the notion that people from history just didn't have the words to describe things in the same way we did in modern times. The closed minded, anti-scientific teachers there would make broad claims of how anything that wasn't written about in the Bible couldn't be true, no matter how much current evidence to the contrary existed. I disagreed: The Bible may not have ever mentioned nuclear physics, but that didn't mean that power plants were a figment of someone's imagination or that Hiroshima hadn't been destroyed. Voicing thoughts like this, which I usually did rather sarcastically, got me into trouble.

I had corresponding views on things like Saint John's apocalyptic vision of the future in Revelation: Maybe he was actually a psychic, but he was just misunderstanding what he saw. What he described as a fire-breathing dragon that would end the world might have just been a 20th-century tank with a flamethrower. Or things could have been even more innocuous: Somebody from the Middle Ages might get a vision of what they would call "a roaring beast which sucked up all the earth before it," but what they were really seeing was nothing more than a modern day vacuum cleaner.

I related these ideas to Elizabeth when I met her in her hotel room at the end of January, pleased to find that she was in a more accepting mood. She was still skeptical about Dracula, but she had to admit that I might be right. According to her, there was a lot of history and documentation surrounding the creation of the book *Dracula,* but what if it wasn't true? If Van Helsing really was the author, had he gone through that much effort to cover his tracks?

"Maybe," Elizabeth said, sitting on the bed next to me. "Just seems like a lot of trouble. But if, like you said, he was keeping himself immortal in order to keep Dracula imprisoned, well…" She laughed, but it sounded more sarcastic than amused. "Talk about being a hypocrite," she added quietly, looking off to one side.

"What do you mean?" I asked.

She seemed to remember I was there suddenly. "Hmm? Oh, nothing. But, look, you've got to admit that some parts of your story are hard to believe. Like the vampires shooting red laser beams out of their eyes? That sounds like something out of a cartoon." She then looked thoughtful and began to continue, "Come to think of it…"

"It *happened,*" I said firmly. "I didn't say I could explain it."

She looked at me impatiently. "Fine." She then sighed and took my hand. "Ray, can we please not fight about this? I'm just surprised, that's all. You know how much I've read up on this subject. So when something comes along that I've never heard of, it strikes me as off, okay? I'm not saying you're a horrible person."

The warmth in her eyes and her pleading expression were enough to assuage my mounting anger. "Okay, okay," I said. "We really shouldn't waste the one day a month we have together anyway."

And so things were better between us that night, but we still talked a lot about vampires, more than usual, in fact. Not surprisingly, she'd done her own brushing up on vampire lore since I'd last seen her, and she pointed out that the vampires in Anne Rice's books weren't like any she'd encountered, though there were some similarities. The two things she found most unusual were that not only did Rice's vampires have reflections, they also became completely inert while the sun was up, almost like statues.

"That bugged me a little, too," I said. "But like you told me before, there's all kinds of inconsistencies in the legends, so maybe that's just another one. I remember how in the first book, Louis claimed that vampires being able to turn into smoke and go through keyholes wasn't true, but hey, we both know it is."

She grinned. "I don't smoke, though. I guess I could; it's not like it's going to kill me. I did try it one time, but I couldn't even get the thing lit. The flame from the lighter scared me too much."

I couldn't help but laugh at this, picturing her trying to be all tough and lighting up a cigarette, only to drop everything and run away screaming. I told her this, and she smacked my thigh playfully. "Come on, I wasn't that bad!" She looked away and then back at me sheepishly. "Maybe."

It was good to see her acting more like her usual self. We continued our conversation about vampires, the topic staying more or less on the mechanics of everything, just what was true and what wasn't. She got me to tell her more about my time as a vampire and the specifics of our abilities and limitations, occasionally countering with how that differed from herself or what else she'd read in the traditional folklore.

Clarifying what was real proved difficult; there were things that might have been so for me but weren't for her, or things in both of our reading that contradicted what we'd experienced. And there were still those grey areas, like people throughout history who may or may not have even been vampires but were touted as such, like Vlad Tepes and

Elizabeth Bathory. It was frustrating trying to pin anything down, but at the same time, it was a fascinating discussion. Maybe there really were other very different vampires out there, even ones with white skin that gleamed like marble, the way Rice had described hers.

As I was going home later, something bugged me about the way the night had progressed. I hadn't even realized it at the time, but once I was away from Elizabeth and alone with my thoughts, it suddenly occurred to me how I hadn't felt as much shame and revulsion about the topic of vampires as I normally did. Our discussion had been a more academic one, even scientific. Was I becoming more used to the idea, even numb to it?

Back when the clones — which Elizabeth playfully referred to this night as "ghost vampires," a term I had to accept was equally valid — were active, our talks like this had served a different purpose. We wanted to know as much as we could about vampires, she because she was learning about herself, and I because I wanted to find out a way to defeat them and possibly how to change her back to human.

I'd always hoped that if we could get rid of all the clones, I'd feel vindicated, having atoned for all the bad things I'd done. But that wasn't really the case. I was still guilty, not just of the deaths I'd helped cause but also the fact that Elizabeth was what she was. The fact that she was now okay with those circumstances also bothered me, but I'd learned not to tell her that if I could help it.

Although I didn't understand it right away, it was this night's events that led me to have that erotic but disturbing dream about her two nights later, the one with the bag of blood she poured into my mouth and all over us. I didn't like thinking about it afterwards, and it made me uncomfortable that sometimes when I did, I'd start to get aroused. That would just make me feel worse.

The fact that we only met up once a month had frustrated me early on, but it was a routine we'd established, one that I occasionally thought of trying to change. Since she no longer seemed to have trouble controlling herself around me, it seemed reasonable that maybe we could change things back to the way they were before her horrible ordeal at the hands of my clone, meeting up more often. But as 1992 rolled along, my attitude towards her began to alter slightly.

Maybe it was better that we kept things limited. I loved her so much, but at the same time, who and what she was still sometimes made me uncomfortable. This was amplified all the more in early March when she admitted that she wished I could join her in her immortality, that is, to become a vampire like her.

"But I know that can't ever happen," she added hastily, probably in reaction to my shocked expression. "I know how much you hate that idea. I couldn't put you through that."

"No," I agreed. "I would hate myself if I ever became a monster like that again." The pained look on her face made me feel bad. "No offense."

"None taken," she said softly, but I wasn't sure if she meant it.

I started to apologize further, but she abruptly switched gears and insisted on showing me the latest records and tapes she'd bought. I noticed that her collection didn't seem to be getting any larger as she continued to migrate from hotel to hotel, and she explained that she tended to only keep some of what she bought, trading in what she didn't like for other things.

Since I'd last seen her, she'd even taken a trip to Athens to visit the record stores there, which apparently had a lot more variety and interesting music than the ones in Augusta. Sometime soon, she hoped to visit Columbia, as she'd heard similar things about the stores in that town. I hoped that she wouldn't somehow run into Susanna, but then I figured that even if she did, it wouldn't matter since Susanna would have no idea who she was.

Some of the stuff she played for me I liked, but a lot of it was just too weird and out there for me. More than once, I just had to say to her, "Okay, next!" She'd give me a withering look, but it wasn't like she ever got truly mad at me.

She even surprised me by playing a song by a group called Concrete Blonde that was about vampires, which she sang along to during the chorus. Her gorgeous voice, as always, gave me chills, but I could tell that she got a little nervous when I began to stare at her too much, captivated. She tried to get me to sing along as well, but I was too insecure to do that. I felt like I was being put on the spot, plus I disliked the idea of singing lyrics supposedly being said by a vampire, fictional or not.

There weren't too many songs out there about vampires as far as I knew, and when I asked her about the one I'd heard of on that Top 40 countdown show a few years ago, she didn't know which one that was. I told her that it was based on the Anne Rice books, and we surmised that this Concrete Blonde song, "Bloodletting," was as well given that it mentioned New Orleans, where Rice's novels were set. As for the other song, I couldn't remember the name of it or the band, only that it was a rock song with lots of guitars, but Elizabeth said that she'd keep an eye out for it just the same.

After we parted that night, I was disturbed by what she'd said before about wishing I could be a vampire like her. I'd tried to bring it up again, but she just dodged the topic, saying that she was mostly kidding. But I didn't really believe that, especially not once I was on my own again. There was something sad in her eyes, and I wondered if maybe she had thought ahead, looking at the bigger picture.

I would continue to grow older and live my normal life, but as far as we knew, she could stay young forever. Surely it would be upsetting for her to see me grow old and eventually die. I'd read plenty of things along those lines in the novels, the way vampires felt about mortals, their lives so brief in comparison. And while I didn't want Elizabeth to be sad, I still could never become a vampire again. Aside from my own distaste, I couldn't do that to my family. As far as they'd be concerned, I'd be dead, or at the very least, I'd have to leave them behind without letting them know what had happened to me. There was no way I was going to cause my parents and sisters that much pain; I'd ruined enough people's lives already.

Once or twice over the course of the next month, I wondered if maybe I could take the vampire potion again, just for a little while, so Elizabeth could experience me that way. But I knew better than that; I'd probably lose control of myself again, maybe even turn out worse than before, or worse than my clone. The idea of that horrified me, and I didn't even bother to mention it to Elizabeth. If I did, she might encourage me. I didn't need that kind of pressure.

As usual, I was off from school the first full week of April. I hadn't known this until I was older, but while most schools around the country had Spring Break in March, Augusta's schools had coordinated ours to match up with Masters Week, when the famous golf tournament was held annually. Like many locals, I avoided anything to do with that tradition. The time out of school was nice, but it was common knowledge that it was a good idea to avoid Washington Road and the area around the Augusta National golf course, which was always overrun with tourists. Most of them were unfamiliar with the city and, as Derek had said at school one time, "drive like they been smacked upside the head with a golf club."

Elizabeth had her own take on the tourist season, which she jokingly referred to as "hunting season." As annoyed with the out-of-towners as I usually was, I didn't like the idea of them being preyed upon in a literal sense. I didn't object, though, to Derek's cousin Marcus's method: Because he lived in an apartment complex next to the golf course, he and some of his friends sometimes taunted the people who cut across their property with squirt guns, which they shot out of his upstairs window.

It was during this short vacation that I had another vivid dream one night about Elizabeth. In it, things were kind of blurred in terms of whether or not she was a vampire; it was more like she'd never died and we were just dating like a regular couple, but there was still some reason why we had to keep her hidden from everyone. Early on in the dream, she looked more like she had before she'd died, much more made up and stylish, which was how I knew that she was human, not a vampire.

We'd decided to go see a movie together, but because we had to avoid letting anyone see her and possibly recognize her, we went to a theater in South Augusta where we weren't likely to run into anyone we knew. That had always been a rougher area of town, so things felt a little uneasy. For whatever reason, I hadn't driven us there, and after leaving the theater, we had to wait for a cab to pick us up and take us wherever it was we were going to go next.

While waiting, we were suddenly approached by three tall black guys. The meanest looking one brandished a knife and demanded that I give him my wallet, but I objected, hands raised and pleading. There was something important in there that I didn't want to lose, but upon waking later, I couldn't remember what that was. It had to do with my past, something dear to me that I couldn't bear to have stolen from me.

I heard a scream from behind me, and I turned to see Elizabeth viciously feeding from the neck of one of the guys; presumably, he and the third man had surrounded us without my noticing it. She was practically gnawing on him as he struggled helplessly in her grip, and I was appalled by what I saw. As she drained the life from him, his skin went from dark brown to lighter, which made sense to me at the time. Somehow, the draining of his blood made him look more Caucasian.

I began to fear what the other two men might do, and as soon as that thought entered my head, I felt the one with the knife grab my shoulder from behind and shove the knife blade into my lower back, nailing me in the kidney. He then slipped my wallet from my pocket and began to run as I fell to my knees, trying to steady myself with my hands on the concrete.

Elizabeth, meanwhile, had dropped the corpse of her victim, which I now thought looked Korean. His dead eyes stared at me, and I turned away sharply, seeing Elizabeth quickly catching up with the two fleeing robbers. In a seemingly impossible move, she snatched one of them up by the legs and then swung him at the other one like a baseball bat, catching him in the head. There was a sickening crunch as the two skulls collided. Both men were killed instantly, and I saw both my wallet and the knife go flying off to one side.

While I was grateful to Elizabeth for eliminating our attackers, I was still very disturbed by seeing her be so vicious and deadly. I crawled forward to retrieve my wallet, the distance to it shorter than it should have been. Next to it on the ground was the dead man's knife, and I picked it up, feeling apprehensive. The wound in my back was apparently no longer a problem; maybe I hadn't been stabbed as deeply as I'd thought. But there was still Elizabeth, her face and arms smeared with blood, panting heavily from the exertion and looking like she wasn't done.

I worried that I might have to defend myself against her. All I had was the knife, but somehow, I knew that it would be enough. I wanted to say something to her, to beg her to stop and say that everything was okay now, but I couldn't bring myself to lie. As she leapt through the air at me, claws and fangs extended, I held out the blade toward her, knowing that she would impale herself on it.

"You know I would totally defend you if something like that happened," Elizabeth said to me when we met up a couple of nights later. I'd told her about the dream, but I'd left out some of the more brutal details, including the fact that I'd had to kill her.

"I know," I said, holding her close. "I just didn't like seeing it."

She breathed in deeply, then kissed me. "It was just a dream, Ray."

"I know," I repeated.

She drew back from me, sitting back on the bed. "How about we do that for real?" she offered.

"What?"

"Not the other stuff," she said with a smile. "The movie thing. You wanna do that? Obviously you must want to, since you dreamed about it. Let's go see a movie."

"Elizabeth…" I wasn't sure why I was objecting. "Dreams aren't always manifestations of…"

"Oh, don't get all psychological on me," she interrupted. "Come on. Let's look in the paper and see what's playing." She rolled over on the bed, then leaned over it to reach for the folded newspaper that was laying beside it. As usual, I couldn't help but steal a glance at her ass.

As in the dream, we opted to go to a theater in South Augusta, the same reasoning applying that she was unlikely to be spotted by anyone who might have known her when she was human. I was apprehensive about the idea of getting mugged in real life, but she assured me that we would be fine. I also didn't like the idea of the confrontation in my dream turning out to be real, but as it turned out, what came to pass was almost as bad, at least in terms of our relationship.

The movie itself was fine, and I enjoyed it well enough. It was a crime thriller called *Basic Instinct,* which I'd heard good things about from my friends at school. There were lots of twists and turns in it, the plot shifting in surprising ways to keep the viewer guessing as to who the killer was. There were also plenty of sex scenes, which were more graphic than either Elizabeth or I had been expecting, but I liked how they turned me on and made me think about the things she and I had done together or might do later on.

It was also nice to do something so normal with Elizabeth. I'd been to a few movies with friends before, and that had usually been fun. Even if the movie itself turned out to be a disappointment, there was still the camaraderie and shared experience, the popcorn, all that.

But for some reason, Elizabeth grew increasingly quiet as the movie went on.

I tried to ignore that at first, but it bothered me the more I noticed it. Initially, we'd held hands, and I even had my arm around her at one point, something I'd never done with a girl in a movie theater before. But I'd seen it done, so it seemed like the appropriate thing to do. She also seemed similarly worked up by the sex scenes, at least early on. But after a while, she grew more cold to me, barely responding to anything I whispered to her by the end of the movie.

When I asked her what was wrong as we were exiting the building, she just gave me a hushed "Nothing." I knew she was lying, so I pushed it, trying to get at what was bothering her. What she said next did nothing to assure me: "Just… This was a mistake." She folded her arms and walked quickly ahead of me, the two of us heading for my car.

I ran to catch up to her and reached for her arm, trying to make her slow down and talk to me. It annoyed me the way she spun around angrily, flinching like she didn't want me to touch her. "Elizabeth, what?" I demanded.

"That movie," she said. "It… bothered me."

"Why? I thought it was good."

"It was! I mean, mostly. But some of it rubbed me the wrong way."

I couldn't understand why. "Was it all the sex and… stuff?"

She halfway let out a laugh. "No. That was fine. And I could tell you definitely liked that." I smiled knowingly, but she didn't return it. "Parts of it made me… Like the scene where they're all in the dance club, being all seductive and everything…" She moved around a little, mimicking the actors' dance moves. "All those people, just doing the clubbing thing. I wish I could…" She sighed angrily.

"Elizabeth, I don't understand. What bugged you so much?"

"I don't know. I guess it was just how… I was seeing something I can't be a part of. And as for the rest of it, all the killing, well…"

There had been some graphic death scenes in the film, rather shocking ones, in fact. I wasn't used to seeing that much violence on-screen. Slasher films were one thing, but their depictions of killing were usually so over the top that I didn't take them seriously. The deaths in this movie were more realistically portrayed. "Remember how you said, 'Damn!' when she stabbed that guy in the beginning? Were you turned on by that, too?"

I felt myself flush with anger, perhaps shame. Sharon Stone's character in the film was admittedly quite sexy even if she was dangerous and evil, but then, that was the whole point of the movie. "No," I said.

Her expression was hard to read. Then it hardened, and she said pointedly, "I was." That bothered me, and something on my face must have shown that. "See?" she said, pointing at me. "See? That's what I'm talking about." She turned away from me again, stomping off. I hurried to catch up with her again.

Suddenly, she stopped and spun around once more, fixing me with another angry look. "Actually, that's not even what really bugged me," she continued. "Or maybe it was. I don't know. I just… Tonight felt like a whole 'date thing.' And I can't do the whole dating thing, Ray. I was nervous as hell the whole time that someone might see me…"

"I thought that's why we came out here!" I said, suddenly aware of the rest of the people in the parking lot, wondering if they'd taken any notice of the fight we were having. They hadn't appeared to, or they were pretending not to.

"It was," she said, seeming less angry for a moment. "But even then…" She sighed again, irritated, then threw her arms out in a wide gesture. "This isn't my world anymore. All this: the movie, the mall, the dating."

I felt hurt. The way she was acting confused and frustrated me, and I couldn't think of a way to make things right. "Elizabeth, you're the one who suggested we go out and see a movie together." That didn't help.

"I know!" she almost shouted, her voice cracking slightly. She was on the verge of tears.

I couldn't stand seeing her in so much pain, even if I didn't fully understand it. I stepped forward and hugged her, pulling her towards me. To my surprise, she didn't resist; I half expected her to push back. "Elizabeth," I began, whispering her name. But I didn't know what else to say.

She cried silently for a little bit, and I squeezed her, hoping to make her stop. "I can't be a girlfriend to you, Ray," she said, her voice distorted due to her chin poking into my shoulder. "You know that."

"No, I…" I wanted to tell her that what she was saying wasn't true. But it was.

The next time we saw each other wasn't any better. She'd worried me by skipping our monthly meeting at the beginning of May, but we did eventually meet up later on in the month. The extra few weeks left plenty of room for me to speculate. I'd always wondered just how she spent her time when we weren't together; she'd tell me bits and pieces whenever we met, but I knew that there must be a ton that she wasn't telling me. That wasn't so much paranoid suspicion as it was simply wonder: What did she do with her time?

I liked to think that she was just like any other girl, doing the things that she'd told me about over the years, like shopping for (or stealing) clothes, collecting music, all that kind of stuff. And I knew about some of the more unusual aspects of her life, like finding new hotel rooms to stay in month to month, sneaking around at night, and reading in libraries while also trying to avoid being spotted by anyone who might have known her before. I also had to accept the darker parts of her, the fact that she drank the blood of her various victims, hoping that she kept the actual killing to a minimum, but I could never be sure of that.

But there was still the fact that she wasn't an ordinary girl; she was a vampire. If I'd been true to my convictions, been the valiant hero that I should have been and eliminated all of the vampires in my town, I shouldn't have let her live or continue to feed. But I just couldn't go that far. I loved her, vampire or not. Even so, the fact that she was one kept driving an impossible wedge between us, no matter how much we tried to deny it.

What was upsetting me by this point was that she seemed to be realizing this more clearly than I was. I still had my life to lead, that of a supposedly normal high school senior. When we'd parted the month before, we had more or less reconciled and stopped our fight, but what she said about how I should just date a normal human girl — "because that's what you really want" — bothered me quite a bit.

But it also made me feel defiant. I didn't want to be mad at Elizabeth, but at the same time, part of me wanted to at least give dating a try. It didn't go well. I wound up going to my senior prom as more or less a "pity date" with this girl I barely knew or even liked, someone named Carmen. She was the friend of a girl in my homeroom class who all but begged me to take Carmen to the prom because her boyfriend had dumped her at the last minute, so I did, renting the tuxedo and going through the motions, pretending that I gave a shit.

It wasn't that my date was that bad of a person or even unattractive; I liked her okay. She was a little bit taller than me, at least in her high heels, and I did my best not to be annoyed by her overly sprayed up and stinky hair the night of the big dance. Normally, her light brown permed hair was chin-length, but the way she got it styled, it was like everything turned upside-down, making her look a bit like the Bride of Frankenstein. It wasn't a good look for her, but I didn't tell her that in order to avoid hurting her feelings. I just went along with the whole thing, trying to have a good time.

We barely spent any time at the prom itself; she and Antonella, the girl from my homeroom, insisted that it was kind of lame and not worth attending other than to make an official appearance. What's more, none of us actually knew how to dance, so being there felt rather pointless. Instead, the four of us (including Antonella's boyfriend Will) drove our cars out to a quiet, darkened street near a construction site and made out. I wasn't even planning on doing that with Carmen, but she and I felt almost obligated since that was what Will and Antonella were doing. She wasn't a bad kisser, but my heart just wasn't in it. Fortunately, I didn't see her much at school the rest of the year.

My insistence that Elizabeth could have a more normal life if she tried to didn't go over well. She'd been passing herself off as human when necessary for years, so I couldn't understand why she was suddenly making such a big deal about it. I didn't use those exact words with her, but my meaning probably shone through.

"I don't want a normal life, Ray," she said bitterly. "And even if I did, it wouldn't matter. That's for you to have, not me. Go to school, go out with your little friends, eat at Dairy Queen, whatever."

"So I did see you hovering around that night," I said, referring to a recent time when I thought I'd seen her spying on me and a couple of friends. She'd vanished before I could be sure.

"Yes. Congratulations." Her sarcastic reply didn't help the already deteriorating mood. The night had started off well, both of us happy to see each other and being physically affectionate, but once the real conversation started, things quickly went downhill.

"So, what?" I asked defiantly. "You say I'm free to live my life and all, but you still show up and hide in the shadows? What's the point of that?"

"It's just… something I do. Vampire, you know."

"Don't go after any of my friends," I said firmly.

"I won't," she spat. "And I'll leave you alone if that's what you want." I didn't like the finality in her tone.

"Elizabeth, it's not," I said, suddenly feeling afraid. I edged towards her on the foot of the bed, reaching for her hand. She didn't pull away, but she didn't respond to my touch. She didn't move at all at first. Then she shot me a hard glance.

"I just don't know if I can do this anymore," she said. "You have no idea how hard it is to keep from…" She stopped, then looked down.

"What?" I reached up and touched her chin with my finger, trying to be affectionate. But she just turned her head away quickly, eyes closed.

"Have you ever really thought about it?" she almost whispered. "Being with me like you know you… like you *could?*"

I shrank back from her when I realized what she meant. "Elizabeth, no. You know how I feel about that."

She let out a sharp breath. "Oh yeah. I know. Makes me feel all warm and fuzzy inside whenever I think about how much you despise what I am."

"I don't despise you!" I pleaded. "I love you!"

"Do you?" She glared at me. "Do you really?"

"Of course I do!" I leaned forward, starting to hug her, but she held up a hand to keep me at bay.

"Don't. Just don't. Because the way I'm feeling right now, as angry as I am, I just might give in to the urge I've been having to fight ever since this whole thing started."

My hair stood up as this sunk in. She'd always said that she wouldn't bite me, kill me, or worse, and for the most part, I'd believed her. "Elizabeth, please don't talk like that."

"Oh, stop worrying. You and I both know how much you'd hate me if I forced that on you. It would only really work for us if you wanted it. And you don't. You don't ever want to be a vampire again. You're so over that. It's in your past. You're so high and mighty and moral."

"Elizabeth, stop it," I said, feeling more wounded than defensive.

She didn't let up. "You know, sometimes I think you're a liar. Or maybe a hypocrite. I think that deep down, somewhere, you really do miss it."

Almost as a reflex, I stood up, suddenly very angry. I started to yell at her, but I wasn't sure what to say.

"Hit a nerve?" she asked, still sitting and looking up at me smugly. "Actually, maybe I didn't use the right words before. The word 'coward' is starting to spring to mind."

I was so mad that I was shaking, I realized. Part of me wanted to hit her, but then I felt ashamed at the idea. I did the only thing I could think to do: I stormed out of the hotel room, letting the door slam behind me.

Crying myself to sleep was something I'd done many times before, but this night, I was far too mad to do that. I just seethed, angry at Elizabeth and also at myself. I discovered how strange it is when you're angry at someone you're in love with: Things about them, like how beautiful they are, become twisted. You find yourself hating aspects of them that you thought you liked. That sweet, lilting voice of hers, her confidence and sharp tongue… They were all bitter memories to me now, her words from earlier in the night clattering in my head.

I should have handled things better and stood up for myself more. But everything I thought about having said or done differently during that climactic moment just made me feel worse. I even pictured myself whipping out my wooden stake and using it on her, bringing a stop to this once and for all. That too filled me with an enormous amount of shame.

Things between us could have ended much worse than they did, but at least the note she left me, which I found at my window the following morning, softened things a little.

Ray, I'm sorry for the things I said to you tonight. I wasn't being fair. I know that. But I wasn't entirely wrong, either. I'm just going through a lot right now, it's gotten so complicated and difficult that we need a break. I just need some time to myself to work things out. I don't know how long that will be. I hope it's not forever. I really do love you, and I know that you love me. Even if you are kind of an ass. I won't say goodbye here... I think instead I'll do the French thing and say "au revoir," you know, see you later. (At least I didn't say "poo-kwah.")

The joke at the end of the note made me smile, and it showed me that Elizabeth didn't hate me as much as I'd feared. It also made me feel less resentful toward her, even though the things she'd said back at the hotel had been hurtful. Her words about needing a possibly indefinite break still worried me, though. I really hoped that our relationship hadn't been damaged irreparably.

CHAPTER TWENTY-FIVE

My graduation from high school and subsequent attending of the local college were disappointing affairs, to say the least. So many of the people around me, parents and teachers alike, had gone on and on about how this was an exciting new chapter in everyone's life, but it didn't feel like that to me at all. Maybe it was that way for the friends I had who would be going away to college, some of them across the country, some of them as near as Athens to attend the University of Georgia. Their futures looked bright, full of exciting things like dorm rooms, fraternities and sororities, and wild parties.

For those of us who chose to stay in Augusta, there was little to none of that. Mike had jokingly referred to Augusta College as "Grade Thirteen," which he told me was what some of his friends who already went there called it. There was no on-campus housing; the college was located in a historical neighborhood, and the rich people who lived there didn't want it changed. So the majority of the students either still lived at home with their parents or just had apartments of their own around town.

The prospect of college did little to excite me, but I knew it was expected of me that I go. It just seemed like more school, and I still had no idea what kind of career I was supposed to be heading for. I honestly didn't care. I declared my major as undecided, and I took the core curriculum like any other freshman.

I could in fact have gone to other colleges out of town if I'd wanted to; I'd gotten literature from quite a few schools around the country throughout my senior year of high school. That had begun once I'd taken the SAT, and my scores were moderately impressive, I suppose. Colleges as far away as Boston, New York, and California had shown an interest in me, and while I briefly toyed with the idea of living somewhere new and far away, I just didn't want to. It wasn't so much that I was scared as much as it was that I had no interest in leaving Augusta, and while I couldn't admit it to anyone else, a lot of that had to do with Elizabeth.

I had no idea when or even if I would hear from her again, but the hope that I someday would was all that kept me going. I'd become terribly depressed after she'd broken contact with me, and nothing really mattered to me anymore. I missed her, and I sometimes dreamed about her, but day after day went by without a word from her. I fantasized about her, too, even sometimes that I allowed her to turn me into a vampire, but those thoughts just led me to feel angry at myself.

The idea of becoming a monstrous killer again wasn't just reprehensible to me; it also seemed kind of pointless. What good could possibly come of that? The vampire threat had all but disappeared from Augusta, and it was rare to hear of any attacks in the news. If I were to become a vampire, either through Elizabeth or by means of the potion, things would just start up all over again, becoming just as bad as before if not worse. The city had suffered enough. So had I.

I went about my daily life, slowly becoming less bitter as time went on but still mostly apathetic. The English, Psychology, and College Algebra classes I took my first quarter meant nothing to me, nor did the people around me. I recognized a few people from my past around campus, both ones I'd known at Westlake and others I hadn't seen since elementary school or Bethlehem, but I never reached out to them to try to rekindle old friendships.

I did briefly try dating this one girl in my Psychology class, an attractive but also extremely skinny girl named Monica. Like Elizabeth, she had long blonde hair with some brown mixed in, though I wasn't sure if the blonde part was natural. The brown was really dark, and she also had brown eyes. I probably took notice of her initially because she reminded me a little of Elizabeth, but she wasn't quite as pretty. Her features seemed too sharp in comparison, particularly her jaw line and pointier chin.

But she seemed interested in me. We'd started talking about various things before class in the hallway, waiting for the one before ours to let out. She'd gone to Tim's old school, but when I asked her if she'd known him, she said she hadn't. After a few days of getting to know each other, she invited me to meet up with her and some friends at The Ace, a local dance club.

I'd never been to a place like this before, and I felt out of my element. Monica herself hadn't seemed all that preppy when I'd talked to her at school, but once I saw her around her other friends, I began to see her for what she was. She wasn't a bad person or anything, but the snobby friends she had rubbed me the wrong way and didn't impress me at all.

The Ace was adjacent to a fancy hotel on the west side of town, and it was fairly new. Lots of places had sprung up in that area recently, and I noticed that nothing like that was happening downtown. The vampire menace might have been more or less over, but the damage had been done: Downtown Augusta was still considered an unsafe place.

Still, the club itself wasn't all that great. It wasn't cool looking and brightly lit like the one in *Basic Instinct,* and it wasn't like I'd been a huge fan of shows like *Club MTV* or *American Bandstand* before it. People dancing around just seemed kind of stupid to me, and I wasn't the slightest bit good at it myself, but I did my best to emulate Monica and her friends. It was actually pretty embarrassing, and I left there feeling like I'd made a fool of myself. Monica didn't talk to me as much after that night, either, nor did she ever invite me out again. It was just as well.

When I'd been there, I wondered if The Ace was somewhere that Elizabeth would have liked. She'd mentioned liking dancing, so for all I knew, she may have known about the place, even gone there. I had in fact looked around hoping to spot her that night, but I wasn't surprised when it didn't happen. And really, given my bad experience there, that only served to give me something else to resent about Elizabeth. The more time went on, as much as I loved her and missed her, I was mad at her for cutting me out of her life.

By the end of the quarter, I decided to, like Carolyn had, take a break from college. It just didn't feel like it was going anywhere for me, and I was still feeling depressed and aimless. My parents weren't thrilled with my decision, but they didn't deride me for it. My father did insist, though, that I get a job; he wasn't going to let me just sit around the house and do nothing.

He'd pissed me off, too, a few months earlier. When both Susanna and Carolyn had graduated from high school, he'd paid for them to move out and have their own apartments. As far as I knew, he was still paying for those. But for some reason, he hadn't done the same for me, and when I asked him about it, he just said that he didn't have that kind of money. That was part of his rationale for my getting a job: If I could save up enough, I could pay for my own apartment. Or he might pay for half of it. It was all very vague, and he never followed through on it.

I managed to get hired in January at a retail store that sold expensive furniture and home decorations, mostly overly fancy crap that I would never think of buying myself. Still, it was a job, and I was lucky to get it given that the Christmas season had just ended. Most places, including this one, hired extra help for the holidays, but once those were over, most if not all of those temporary workers would be let go. I was fortunate that they had one more opening than expected, so that left a place for me.

As it turned out, it was Marcus who put in a good word for me and helped me get hired. He and I weren't great friends, but we'd known each other in high school and had gotten along well enough. He was the one who explained to me what happened with the extra opening: One of the guys who used to work there had quit because he couldn't take the terrible music that played over the PA system.

I found this kind of funny, the idea that someone would quit a job over something like that. But the longer I was there, the more I began to see my predecessor's point. It wasn't so much that the music was bad; the problem was the repetition. The store had these special cassettes that were somehow four hours long, and they'd loop over and over. That wasn't so bad for the songs that I liked, but there were a few obnoxious ones that, over time, seriously grated on my nerves.

"Okay, I see what you were talking about with the music now," I said to Marcus one evening when we were restocking the rugs.

He chuckled. "Man, just be glad you weren't here at Christmas. That was the worst."

"Yeah, I heard it was really busy. Glad I missed that."

"No, I'm talking about the music. You think this is bad?" He pointed upward and moved his finger along as if to indicate the music floating by invisibly. "Imagine a two-hour — not four, *two*-hour — tape of some of the most god-awful Christmas music you've ever damn heard. And I'm not talking Christmas carols here, like normal stuff. I mean like cheesy Lawrence Welk, Dean Martin poppy kind of crap. Like, *'It's Chriiiiistmaaaaas!!! Yah-tah-dada-da-dada-daaaaa!'*" He snapped his fingers and danced around in as corny of a manner as he could.

"Oh, God," I said. "I know what kind you're talking about. There was this time a couple of years ago when I was Christmas shopping in the mall, and I walked into a store, and there was this…" I pitched my voice as high as it would go, screeching out a tuneless falsetto. "I had to turn around and walk right back out."

"Right. Now imagine being trapped in here on a six- or eight-hour shift, hearing those same damn songs over and over and over." He shuddered. "I'm telling you, man, it was torture. Pretty much ruined Christmas for me this year. I'd go home and go to bed at night, and all I can hear in my head is 'Baby, It's Cold Outside.' Or, as I like to call it, 'The Christmas Date Rape Song.'"

I wasn't familiar with the song, but he explained it to me, how it was actually pretty gross and creepy when you listened to the words and understood what was happening. The way he told the story was funny, but it was clear to me that he had been seriously aggravated by the holiday season, and I was glad that I hadn't had to go through the same thing. Christmas hadn't been very enjoyable for me anyway since Scout had died, and I surmised that had I been working here and subjected to all of that fake cheeriness, I might have had to quit as well.

I didn't enjoy my job, but I made it through day to day. Having more money was a good thing, but it would be a while before I saved up enough to be able to afford to move out on my own, if ever. What sucked was that I couldn't really spend any money, not on tapes or CDs, new clothes, anything. That, along with everything else in my dull and depressing life, made me a pretty miserable person.

Carolyn, meanwhile, saw her life take a surprising and dramatic turn for the better. I wasn't clear on exactly when it started, but she'd been dating this really nice guy named Luke for a while by the time I found out about him. I'd wondered why she hadn't been over to the house to do laundry as often, but then I found out that it was because she'd started staying at his place quite a bit. I eventually met him, and he seemed like a good person, very cordial and friendly, if a little on the fake side. I was somewhat suspicious of him when Carolyn told me that he was a devout Christian, but then I had to remind myself that being such didn't necessarily make him an uptight, intolerant person. Some Christians were like that, but not all.

But Carolyn was happy, and it wasn't like she needed my approval in order to love him. In just a few short months, they were engaged and then quickly married, which was surprising to the family, but not in an unwelcome way. The wedding was nice and all, though it was spoiled for me in the sense that I felt a little jealous. Seeing Carolyn and her groom at the altar made me wish that it could be me and Elizabeth up there instead, but by this point, I didn't know if I'd ever even see her again.

Susanna was kind of dark and cynical as well, though not to anyone's face but mine, as far as I knew. When I asked her why, she just said that she was annoyed by the extended family members who had been asking her when she was going to get married. Some had even gone so far as to rib her for not being the first to marry, despite being the older daughter. "I will if and when the time's right," she said to me.

When Carolyn announced just a couple of months later that she was pregnant during Susanna's visit to the house in June, Susanna grumbled to me privately that she wondered if that was why the marriage had come about so quickly. I felt that was pretty bitchy of her, but I didn't tell her that; I just ended the conversation and went off to do something else, not wanting to start a fight. And while part of me again felt envious that my sister was getting to experience something that Elizabeth and I never would, I couldn't begrudge her anything.

Whatever mine and Susanna's circumstances were at the moment, at least one of us was getting the chance to settle down and have a normal life. Did any of us deserve that, given all that we were guilty of in the past? Maybe it didn't matter. This was a new beginning for

Carolyn, and despite any jealousy I might feel, I nevertheless wished her the best.

I got a surprise of my own in the form of a cassette tape that I found sitting on my desk one morning later that month. I was getting ready to go to work when I spotted it, and I had no idea how it had gotten there. It was in a clear case with a cardboard label inside, a blank cassette that one could record music onto and fill out the label by hand.

My heart began to race when I recognized the handwriting: It was Elizabeth's. Some of the song titles and bands were ones that I recognized, but others were unfamiliar. I was so excited to finally receive some kind of communication from my long-lost love that I almost cracked the plastic case from gripping it so hard, and it wasn't until later on that I even thought about being creeped out by the fact that she must have snuck the tape into my room while I was sleeping. She'd been right here, and I hadn't even known it.

I opened the case, hoping that there might be a note to go with it, but there wasn't. There was just the tape, its contents written on the accompanying label. I was intrigued, and I wanted to pop it into my stereo and start playing it immediately. But then I remembered work, and I was already close to running late. I decided to listen to it as soon as I got home, resenting the fact that I had to go spend another pointless day at Fitzgerald's listening to their crappy music instead.

It wasn't until I was halfway to work that I realized that I could have brought the tape with me and listened to it in my car, but then I decided that it was better to wait and not do that. Whenever I bought a new tape or CD — which didn't happen much these days — I always made it a point to sit down and listen to it all the way through on my headphones, reading the accompanying liner notes and lyrics if there were any. Listening to the tape in the car would wind up detracting from the experience of hearing it for the first time, the road and the other cars demanding my attention. I would just have to wait.

But once at work, I couldn't stop thinking about the tape, or more specifically, about Elizabeth. It had been over a year since I'd heard from her at all, and sometimes, I'd worried about her and wondered if she was even still alive. I'd even hated her at times for leaving me, but a surprisingly mature part of myself told me that I needed to respect her decision, to let her come back to me on her own.

During some of my more lonely periods, I'd considered summoning her back to her grave like I knew I could, but that probably would have just made her angry. Whenever we had our reunion, it shouldn't be like that. I had to wait until she was ready to talk to me again, and now that I'd gotten this tape, I was almost vibrating with anticipation. Presumably, this was an olive branch, her way of letting me know that contact was something she was open to, and she must not hate me after all, something else I'd occasionally feared.

After only a couple of hours at work, I couldn't take it anymore. I'd been at the job long enough to resent it quite a bit, all of the frou-frou expensive crap, plus the snooty people who shopped at the store got on my nerves, too. Apart from Marcus, I wasn't too fond of most of my co-workers, either, some of whom thought they were way more important than they were just because they were good at arranging fancy displays of scented candles or being in charge of the stockroom. Marcus himself sometimes got kind of snide with me, too, particularly when he seemed to get caught up in the politics of the place.

He and I were two of the only three young men who worked there; the rest were either girls our age or much older women who had all sorts of hang-ups and neuroses that I didn't have time for. The place had an overall gossipy and back-stabbing atmosphere, and on this day in particular, I wasn't in the mood to put up with any of that. I had something much more important on my mind.

I faked being sick in order to go home early, saying I had some kind of stomach problem. I got home shortly before noon, not even bothering to eat lunch before locking myself in my bedroom and settling down on my bed to listen to the tape Elizabeth had left me.

It didn't disappoint. I liked nearly all of the songs, but what was interesting was the way that their meanings seemed to change because of the context. This wasn't just a bunch of songs thrown together arbitrarily; it was almost like a soundtrack for me and Elizabeth if our lives had been a movie. It took me a while to realize that, though. At first, it sounded like the tape was going to be full of vampire songs.

The first one was "Bloodletting," which she'd played for me before, followed by a Sting song called "Moon over Bourbon Street," one we'd talked about since then. I was pleasantly surprised to find that I recognized the third one even though I hadn't from its title on the label: It was "Forget Me Not" by a group called Bad English. This was the one I had described to her in the hotel that night, the hard rock ballad based on Anne Rice's books, just as the previous two songs were. I hadn't heard it in years, and the fact that she'd tracked it down for me and included it on the tape gave me a nice feeling inside.

But not everything on the tape was about vampires. A similarly sweet moment was when I discovered that she'd included the longer version of one of my favorite childhood songs, "Abracadabra" by the Steve Miller Band, on side two of the tape. Only once in my life, I'd heard this longer version on the radio, and I thought it was really cool but had never managed to catch it again and get it recorded. I'd even called the local radio station and specifically requested this version a few times, but it always angered me that they only played the short one. I happened to mention this to Elizabeth one night in conversation a couple of years ago, and when I realized that she'd somehow found this version and put it on the tape, it made me smile.

Another neat thing was that several of the songs, while not actually about vampires, could be taken that way with a little imagination. Sometimes it was the whole song; other times it would just be a line or two talking about being out at night, about death, or about eternal youth. I'd originally thought that this was accidental, but after a while,

I figured out that she'd been thinking the same thing when she put the mix tape together. Even the two Lita Ford songs seemed to fit, or at the very least, they served to remind me of conversations we'd had years before. She hadn't forgotten them, either.

I'd been confused when first looking at the label to find that there were what appeared to be three versions of the same song, "Forever Young." I'd already heard the Rod Stewart one, but I didn't mind it being on there any more than the Guns N Roses tune "November Rain," which I already had a copy of. The Rod Stewart track was presumably both a reference to one of our past conversations and also her making a dig at my last name. But as it turned out, the "Forever Young" songs by the other two artists, though they had the same title, weren't cover versions like I expected. One was by a group I'd never heard of named Alphaville, and the other was by Bob Dylan, whom I didn't really care for. I didn't like his singing voice, and his presence on the tape made me sad because it reminded me of Dennis. But at the same time, it had been clever of Elizabeth to put all three of those songs on there.

The best part was at the end, which came as yet another surprise to me because there had been nothing on the label to indicate that it was coming. It was Elizabeth, her beautiful voice coming through the headphones and right into my ears:

"Hi there, Ray, it's me. Guess who. I hope you liked the tape. I mean, you'd better like it; I put a lot of work into it! Anyway, I know it's been a long time, but like I said before, I had a bunch of stuff to work through. Things are better now. And I'd love to see you again, so...

"Well, I guess I should tell you where I'm living now. I'm not in Augusta; I finally realized that I just needed to get out of there. So I moved to Columbia. Sorry I didn't tell you. But yes, I'm here, and I'd really like it if you'd come and visit. We can talk and catch up, all that. I miss you. I know that things... well, maybe that was my fault, but... things left off on a kind of crappy note between us. So let's meet up...

I can show you where I'm living now, where I'm working, all that... Yes, I have an actual job now. More or less a normal life. You'd be surprised. I don't want to say on here just where it is, so... hang on."

There was a click from the tape as she stopped the recorder, followed by a short pause. Then the recording resumed:

"Okay. Had to decide where to put it. Go down in the basement, and look on the shelves on the left once you get down the stairs. I left you a note. Just like old times! Anyway. That's where the directions are to come meet me in Columbia. See you soon..."

I could hear the smile in her voice, particularly in that last sentence. She sounded almost conspiratorial, and I could picture the varying expressions on her face as she'd recorded what she'd said. It felt so great to hear her voice after so long, almost as wonderful as it would be to finally see her in person again, to hold her in my arms. I couldn't wait.

I listened to that tape almost non-stop over the next day and a half. I kept rewinding the last bit over and over just to hear Elizabeth's voice, so much that I worried I might wear the tape out and break it. By the time Thursday evening came around and I began the long drive to Columbia, I could practically recite the words along with her as the tape spoke them to me.

Memorizing the songs came about more or less accidentally as well; I even learned to anticipate what the next track coming up would be while hearing the final part of another. I also found that I picked up on certain nuances here and there that I'd missed on a previous listening, so there were still little surprises along the way. And a few of the songs that I hadn't liked so much during my first listen grew on me.

There was one called "Black" by a woman I'd never heard of named Sarah McLachlan, and while it was pretty cool, there were these strange sound effects throughout that I initially found distracting. Some were weird laughs or screams, telephone rings, and even a police or ambulance siren that, while listening to the tape in my car, once tricked me into thinking that there was an actual emergency vehicle somewhere nearby that I needed to look out for. But in time, I got used to the sounds, even found them endearing, just a part of the overall experience. It was Elizabeth's taste in obscure music manifesting itself again, another reminder of our past and the many things I'd loved about her all these years.

Two tracks by The Police on side one also bugged me because they were quite morbid, their lyrics talking about killing people in a blithe manner, which rubbed me the wrong way. But in time, I accepted them as part of the whole, and I could see them as another manifestation of Elizabeth's personality: her twisted sense of humor. I couldn't really fault her for that, not anymore. After all, I knew that my disdain for her darker side had been at least one of the things that had driven her away from me in the first place.

Maybe I should have still been repulsed by that, but I couldn't bring myself to be given how much I was looking forward to finally seeing her again. Regardless of my misgivings about that one part of the tape or, perhaps more importantly, what the overall theme of it seemed to be, all would be forgiven by the time the last few bars of The Escape Club's "I'll Be There" played, the final track leading into my beloved's sweet voice asking me to meet her in Columbia.

I wasn't expecting to be impressed by South Carolina's capital; what little I'd heard about it from Susanna and the few people I knew from high school who wound up going there for college were descriptions like "okay" or "not that great." But there was something neat about the way the city looked from afar. Its nighttime skyline loomed in the distance as I approached down a long hill, and while it wasn't as majestic as the larger cities I'd seen on TV, I found the effect intriguing.

Once in town, things seemed more ordinary, though its downtown area seemed more full of life than Augusta's. People and cars hurried along the streets well after dark; there wasn't the sense of hopelessness that had pervaded my hometown all these years. I'd heard talk of attempts to revitalize it recently, but so far, I'd seen no evidence of that. Columbia's vibrancy was in some ways even intimidating. I worried a bit that I might run into someone from high school or even Susanna, but I hoped that I could fly under the radar and not find myself in any awkward conversations.

The place Elizabeth's note had directed me to was a coffee shop called Recaffeinated. The name struck me as odd because Augusta had until a couple of years ago had its own coffee shop called Be Caffeinated, but that had closed down during the town's peak in vampire activity. I began to wonder if either place had ripped the name off from the other, but I later learned that Recaffeinated was in fact owned by the same people, opening up after the previous one had gone under. This new location was, the owners felt, a "sequel."

As I parked my car in the bumpy, uneven lot behind the place, I began to wonder just how I would find Elizabeth. She'd just said to meet her here at 9:00, but she hadn't clarified whether she'd be inside or outside, if I was supposed to just go in and try to find her or what. The uncertainty added to my nervousness, which had been increasing steadily the entire night.

I made my way up the stairs to the entrance, and unable to think of anything better to do, I went inside, looking around. I wasn't sure if I should ask the people behind the counter if they knew where Elizabeth was; they might not know what I was talking about. My anxiety mounted the more out of place I felt, and I almost jumped when a girl's voice called out from behind me: "Can I help you find something, sir?"

I spun around, expecting to see one of the coffee shop girls in their black aprons, the kind I'd noticed the workers behind the counter wearing. But instead, there was Elizabeth, standing there with her hands behind her back and with a cute, wide smile on her face. It was the same mischievous look that I'd fallen in love with all those years ago, and she looked more beautiful than she ever had. Her hair was shorter than I would have liked, just past chin length, but I didn't really mind. She was gorgeous, just like always.

She giggled as I let out an almost whispered *"Oh my God,"* and I couldn't help but leap forward and hug her tightly.

"Aww," she said, her voice close to my ear, the hum of it so familiar and comforting. "Did you miss me?"

"You have no idea," I said deeply, suddenly realizing that I was fighting back tears.

The hug went on for ages; I didn't want to let go of her. It had been entirely too long, and feeling her body against mine was like heaven. The softness of her hair against my cheek, the way she smelled, the cute little *"mmm"s* she was letting out as we rocked back and forth...

"Okayyy, people are staring!" she sang, and I pulled back from her, suddenly aware of our surroundings.

I laughed nervously and glanced around. "Sorry." Those who had been looking quickly averted their eyes and got back to what they were doing.

"It's okay," she said, smiling at me sweetly, the squint in her eyes making me want to dissolve into a puddle right there on the floor. She even did that thing where she bit her lower lip, and she bobbed up and down in a little dance to show that she was just as happy as I was.

"Come on," she said, taking my hand. "I've got us a table."

The layout of the coffee shop was strange; it wasn't like any place of business I'd seen before. It was almost like it used to be someone's house, and for all I knew, it had been. There were sections of various sizes that could have once been bedrooms, and the one that Elizabeth led me to was at the far end of the building. Several fancy windows lined it, and I could see the passing nighttime traffic through them.

As we passed by a black-aproned girl carrying two empty mugs, she stopped and said laughingly to Elizabeth, "Don't you get enough of this place when you're not off?"

Elizabeth chuckled. "Apparently not!"

"Oh, speaking of that," the girl continued, "I wanted to ask you about covering my shift Saturday night. I've got a Psych paper due next week that's totally kicking my butt, and I... well..."

"Should probably get started on it?"

The girl let out a somewhat guilty giggle. She was small and thin with brown hair in a sort of pixie cut, small eyes and a rather large nose, but she was still attractive. "How'd you guess?"

"Because you're Rachel!" They laughed again, and the girl hurried off saying that they could talk about it later, giving me a strange smile.

"So who's she?" I asked as we settled down at our table by the window. There were only a handful of other people in the room: a couple discussing something quietly and urgently on the far side, and what I assumed were college students sitting alone at tables, sipping coffee and reading books.

"That's Rachel," Elizabeth said with a smile. "She's great. We're like partners in crime here. People sometimes get mad when we work together, because we're always cracking each other up." I nodded. "She's also the only one here who knows about *me,*" she said more quietly.

"About...?" Then I got it and added in a whisper: "That you're a vampire?" She nodded quickly, glancing off to the side to be sure that nobody was listening in. "And she's okay with that?"

"Sure she is," she said dismissively. "She knows not to tell anyone."

"Wow," was all I could think to say. "And so... You work here?"

"Yeah!" she said playfully. "It's fun. I mean, sometimes it can be a pain in the ass, and you get the occasional customer who thinks he's like the most privileged person in the world and 'Oh my God I have to have the cream done this exact way that I'm just making up right this moment to be an asshole,' but aside from that, I like it. Sure, I don't necessarily *need* a job given how I could get money in other ways…" She said this with a sly glance to the right, then met my gaze again. "But I like it this way. It feels more normal." There was silence for a moment. I was feeling a little dizzy, still trying to take everything in. She smiled, looked down, then back up at me. "It's really great to see you again, Ray."

"You too," I said. "I kind of can't believe this is happening. It feels like a dream."

"Oh, don't," she said, reaching over the table and taking my hand in hers. "It's real. I just… I don't know. I felt it was time." She shrugged, looking down again, then peering up at me. "I really did miss you, you know."

"Then why did you…?" I started to ask, but I stopped. I wanted to ask her why she'd left me, why she'd skipped town without telling me. But I didn't know how to do that without sounding too bitter.

"Let's go get drinks," she said suddenly, releasing my hand and pushing her chair back. I sat there, dumbfounded. "We shouldn't take up a table unless we get something."

She led me back to the center of the place, and I followed her lead since I had no idea what I was doing. There were black chalkboards high up on the wall behind the counter listing all kinds of different coffee drinks that I'd never heard of, names that made no sense to me but still sounded vaguely appetizing. I'd never drunk coffee before, so I just let Elizabeth pick something out for me between her chatting animatedly with the staff. They all seemed to like her, and she got along with them as well, which made me feel strange.

I'd never seen her act quite like this before, being so sociable. It initially reminded of how she was back at school, the way she was with her two snooty friends Helen and Melinda. But this was different. She wasn't off-putting to me or anyone else, nor was she quiet and brooding like she'd been back then. She appeared genuinely confident and sure of herself, which I'd seen plenty of during our time together before she'd gone away. I just wasn't used to seeing her interact with anyone but me in that way. It actually made me feel a little jealous, but I wasn't sure why.

Back at our table, she instructed me to let the hot cup of coffee sit for a while before trying to drink it. I balked at the notion of buying something and then not being able to consume it immediately, but she warned me that if I tried too soon, I'd burn my tongue. She held her own cup in front of her and smelled it, explaining that the aroma was part of the experience. I took her word for it, feeling impatient.

I wanted to put to her all of the questions I'd had over the past year, including just why she'd left. I thought I knew some of the answers already; I'd had tons of imaginary conversations with her in my head. There were also lots of things I wanted to say to her about how I felt, not all of them good. But all of these thoughts suddenly ground to a halt when she asked me the simple question: "So, how have you been?"

I felt myself become sheepish. "Okay, I guess. Busy."

"That's all?" she asked. Her adorable smile seemed almost taunting.

"No," I said angrily, then caught myself. "I just... Where do I begin? Where do *we* begin?"

She gave me a sympathetic look, maybe an apologetic one. "Fair enough," she said, reaching across the table again and touching my hand. For some reason, I didn't grab it like I wanted to. I was starting to feel defiant, more hurt.

"Ray," she said meaningfully. "I know I probably didn't do everything right. But I did what I had to do."

"Yeah, I guess," I said.

"I'm sorry if I hurt you," she said, then sighed and rolled her eyes. "Of course I hurt you. I know. But I just had to get out of that town. It became too hard to stay. Too much... stuff."

"Stuff?"

"Yeah." She sighed again. "And sure, part of that was you. But I didn't stop loving you. I just needed to get away. I needed to start over."

"So you came here."

"Yeah. Columbia's not a bad town. It's not the best place in the world, but hey, it's not Augusta. That was what I needed."

I shrugged. "I guess I can understand that. I just wish you hadn't…" I stopped. This wasn't what I wanted our reunion to be like. "All right, enough of that. Let's stop going around in circles."

"Okay…?" she said, pulling her hand back from mine and looking surprised.

"Let's change the subject. We're getting all gloomy. How about we talk about the fact that you snuck into my room while I was sleeping and put a tape on my desk?" She laughed, relaxing. "Stalker," I added accusingly but playfully.

"Ohh… You think so?" she asked with a wicked grin.

"Yeah!" I said, wide-eyed. "Way to not freak a guy out or anything!"

"That was the poi-oint…!" she sang. I faked being indignant. "So, did you like it? The tape?"

"Of course! It was great. I keep listening to it over and over. Especially the last part."

She smiled. "I thought you might."

I laughed. She knew me too well. "Though I have to admit, I was a little disappointed that you just ended it like you did. No 'I love you' at the end or anything."

She looked a little miffed, but not really, peering at me through the top of her head. "Ray, of course I love you. That goes without saying."

I bit my tongue; I was just about to respond with a line from a comedian I'd seen who joked that the response to that phrase should be: *"Then shut up."* It was a knee-jerk thought, and I was glad I kept it in check. "Yeah, but I like when you say it," I responded more appropriately. "Anyway, yeah. I thought it was really cool. I like the way you threaded everything together."

I was about to continue, talking about how the overall, underlying message had made me uncomfortable, but she interrupted me. "You haven't even noticed, have you?" She held her lips in a tight smirk, then added, "Jeez, just as clueless as always…"

Confused, I asked, "Noticed?"

She closed her eyes, then moved her head back and forth. Her eyes opened again, and she blinked them dramatically. Finally, I got it: She was wearing make-up, though not as much as she used to when she was younger. The colors were more subtle and less dramatic, so much that I hadn't even picked up on the fact that she was wearing anything on her face. But now I could see it: the eyeliner, the subtle shading of her eyes, the light blush on her cheeks. I said as much, then added, "But how? I thought you couldn't do that without a reflection. Or did you get Rachel to do it for you?"

She let out a small laugh, then said no. "But funny that you should mention that. I did do something like that a long time ago, where I tricked this girl I met into thinking I was blind."

"What?"

The story she conveyed to me was a deceitful but clever one, how she'd approached a pretty girl one night and even had a cane for a prop, all the while not looking directly at her and pretending she'd lost her sight. After telling the girl her sad story, she said that she missed being able to wear make-up like a normal girl, like she and her sister used to do. The girl obliged by doing her make-up for her, all the while thinking that Elizabeth was blind, that she was just doing something nice for a poor little handicapped girl, helping her look pretty again, even if she couldn't see it herself.

"'I just want to have the feeling of it on my face again,' I said to her. She bought it completely. At least, almost, until the end when I screwed up and looked right at her."

"I have a feeling I know where this story is going to end up," I said, suddenly feeling apprehensive.

Elizabeth frowned at me, but I could tell she was also fighting back a smile. "I was going through a cruel phase at the time," she said. "I'm not that bad anymore. And even if I were, I wouldn't apologize for it."

I wanted to steer the topic away from her killing. "Did she… I don't know… do a good job? My sisters used to do that for each other when we were vampires. And there was this one time when Carolyn did Susanna's bad on purpose, all… I don't know how to describe it. Like smeared and uneven and stuff. And because Susanna couldn't see herself, well…"

Elizabeth laughed. "Oh, that's terrible! But kinda funny. No, as far as I know, she did it fine. I still couldn't see myself at that point, either."

"At that point?"

"Since then, I've learned how to see my own reflection." She said this with a nod and with undisguised pride, and I was shocked to hear this.

"What? How?"

"I just did. I think it goes back to that whole thing about belief shaping reality. Running water. Crosses. No reflection. With enough self discipline, you can overcome those limitations." She said this with great conviction and seriousness, but then she glanced to the side and faltered. "Took a lot of doing, though. My first experiments were with a Polaroid camera. You know, where the picture pops out and develops by itself. Didn't really work. The pictures just looked blank to me. But after a while, I was like, 'This doesn't make sense. I know I exist. I'm here. I'm real.'" She tapped the table urgently with her index finger as she spoke, then relaxed. "In time, it worked, and there I was in the mirror again. Didn't even recognize myself at first, it had been so long."

She looked sad as she said this. I told her about something I'd read in my Psychology class last year, how some schizophrenics had this condition where they'd look in the mirror but not be able to recognize their own reflection. "I wonder if that's related to the whole legend."

"Hmm. Maybe. One thing I'd read was that the entire thing was because people who were damned didn't have souls, so that's why they didn't have reflections. Not that I believe in that kind of thing, of course. Maybe that's why I was able to overcome it."

"Could be," I said. "Now that you mention it, I remember feeling something similar in '87 after being a vampire for so long. Just three weeks in my case, but yeah, that was a long time for me. Longest we'd ever done it. And when I looked in the mirror and saw myself for the first time, it felt weird, like I was seeing someone else. Though, looking back on it, I suppose some of that could have been guilt, feeling disgusted with myself for all the things I'd done." She frowned, so I decided to change the subject.

I looked at her more closely, noticing again how different she looked from before. "So you started being able to wear make-up again."

"Yes," she said, a little defiant. "I hope you're not going to say you don't approve and piss me off."

I leaned back. "No! It's not that. You look fine. More than fine. It's just... unusual, I guess. Not what I'm used to."

"Well, it's definitely less than I wore when I was younger. I went a bit overboard with it back then, I'll admit. Didn't really know how to be more restrained about it. I suppose that was kind of due to Jennifer..." She trailed off, and I felt bad for her, the mention of her dead sister putting a damper on things. But she continued on a little more brightly: "The trick is to be more subtle, to make it look like you're not wearing as much as you are."

I barely understood what that meant. "I'll... try to remember that," I said sarcastically.

She sneered at me. "Okay, so not *you*. But you know what I mean."

"I guess." I looked again at how she'd done herself up, again noticing the blush on her cheeks, and an old memory resurfaced.

"Wow," I said, "now that's something I haven't thought about in a long time."

"What is?"

I suddenly pictured myself from over ten years ago, much smaller and so much less experienced, visiting Susanna in her upstairs bedroom. She'd gotten some new blush and was trying it on, sitting in her bed with the compact in one hand and its small brush in the other. I couldn't remember why I'd come to see her or what we were talking about, but at one point, she'd pointed the brush toward me and asked jokingly, "You want some?"

"No!" I'd exclaimed. I was only six, maybe seven, but that was old enough for me to know the differences between boys and girls, at least in part. One of those was that some things were strictly meant for girls and for boys, and mixing them was anathema to me. The last thing a little boy wants at that age is to do anything girly or be perceived that way.

Susanna pushed the joke forward, insisting more, and in retrospect, it was probably my vehement protestations that egged her on. This led to her getting up from the bed and chasing me around the room with the compact, threatening to put the forbidden substance on me. This terrified me at the time, though once I was older, I felt foolish over how much I'd freaked out. Susanna, naturally, brought this incident up from time to time over the years whenever she wanted to embarrass me.

Elizabeth found the story funny, but it still made me squirm. She then brought up something I'd thought of a couple of times over the past day or two, the fact that she was now living in the same city as my oldest sister.

"What does she look like?" she asked.

"A lot like me, supposedly. People at family reunions or holidays or whatever always point that out."

"So, she's like a girl version of you. That's… interesting. If a little hard to picture."

"Well, you know, same brown hair and brown eyes, similar faces, I guess. Like our father. She's not ugly or anything; she was pretty popular in high school as I understand it. She was even on the cheerleading squad. It's Carolyn who takes after our mother. And now she's going to be a mother herself. That's a weird feeling."

"Really?"

I went on to tell her about Carolyn's recent marriage and pregnancy, but as I spoke, I began to wonder if it was bothering Elizabeth. I was describing things that she could never have. But maybe she didn't want them, either.

The conversation continued well into the night. In a way, it was like old times, the topics jumping around all over the place, sometimes serious, often not. She never drank her coffee, only stirred it with a small, flat, wooden stick. I sipped from mine occasionally once it had cooled down, but while I liked the smell of it, the taste was a little too bitter for my liking.

Elizabeth wondered if she might ever run into Susanna, which was why she'd asked me what she looked like. The thought of that made me nervous, but she assured me that she wouldn't do anything to harm her. She had in fact encountered our old classmate Tammy at one point, but because she looked so different, Tammy fortunately hadn't recognized her. "I was tempted to bite her," she added, "but I didn't. You'd have been proud of me." There was something accusatory in the way she said that, and I felt bad for being judgmental of her.

I learned more about what her life was like now, the job, her new apartment, all of that. Having the job made paying for her place easier, but she apparently still resorted to underhanded and hypnotic tricks when necessary. For one thing, she'd had to convince her coworkers that she could only work nights. I in turn told her about my own life, how I hated the job I had, was still living at home, and had taken a break from college. As I did, I felt embarrassed, but she assured me that I shouldn't. I still did.

We eventually wound up talking again about the tape she'd made for me, and I told her how I'd been thinking of one I could make for her in response. Several tunes had already made their way onto a list in my head, though none of them were vampire-related. They were more traditional love songs, particularly of the "I miss you" variety, like Richard Marx's "Right Here Waiting" and the Phil Collins song "One More Night." A couple of songs by The Moody Blues that were popular a few years back also sprang to mind, and I wondered if I still had them on tape.

While she welcomed the idea of me making a tape for her, when I began to list the ideas I had for it, she immediately shushed me. "No, don't tell me! Let it be a surprise! Surprises are good."

I then got to say something I'd been meaning to all night. "Okay, fine. I guess you're right. But I'm not going to have this thread running through that subtly says, 'I wish you could join me, become a vampire like me.'"

I expected her to be caught off guard, but she just looked at me, unfazed. "That's too bad," she said simply.

"That is what you were saying with the tape, wasn't it? I didn't pick up on it immediately, but after a few listens, I got the message."

"And?"

"You know I can't do that, Elizabeth."

Finally, she let some emotion creep into her face, and she looked down sadly. After a moment, she looked up again, more stern. "I don't believe that." She wasn't angry; she just seemed sincere.

"Elizabeth," I said, reaching for her hand. She didn't pull away. "There's so many reasons… I mean… I do love you. You know that. But I can't go through all that again. I couldn't do that to my family either, disappear on them like that. Hell, I'm going to be an uncle soon. That's a big responsibility." It felt like a stupid thing to say; I had no idea what I thought I meant by that or what duties being an uncle might entail. I didn't even know if Carolyn's child would be a boy or a girl. But maybe there were babysitting duties in my future?

She looked a little hurt, but she didn't seem angry. "I'm sorry you feel that way," she said quietly, her eyes piercing mine. My heart broke over how impossibly beautiful they were. "But I've got to tell you, I'm not entirely convinced."

Those words kept ringing in my ears long afterwards, including as we left the coffee shop together. I assumed that the next thing we'd do would be to go to her apartment, and while I was interested in seeing what kind of place she might have, I was increasingly preoccupied with the idea of finally getting to have sex with her again. This still seemed like a possibility when we paused by my car, and she turned toward me with a very hungry look, stepping closer.

Within seconds, we were wrapped in a passionate embrace and kissing deeply, our tongues dancing over each other's urgently. I wanted to convey to her how much I'd missed her all this time, how much I'd missed doing this very thing. Wordlessly, she seemed to be pleading with me to take her up on her unspoken offer, or maybe that's only what I thought she was thinking.

The kiss went on for several minutes without a break, how long I can't be sure. But it was a strange combination of the most wonderful feeling in the world and the saddest one as well. I found myself afraid to disengage from her, terrified that we might start fighting if we spoke. I was grateful that no one walked by in the parking lot to distract us or make me feel self-conscious, or for all I knew, they did and I just didn't notice.

We stopped, gasping for air, the sweat making our foreheads stick together for a second as we pulled ourselves away. "Time for you to go," she said, breathing heavily through a smile.

"Go?" I asked, surprised. "Don't I get to see your apartment?"

"Next time," she said, still smiling, her breathing beginning to slow. "This wasn't meant to just be a one-time visit, you know."

"Oh, come on," I said, deflated.

"Next time," she said more firmly, putting a finger to my chest. "I'll let you know when."

A panic began to build in me. "Please don't tell me I have to wait another month."

She giggled. "No, Ray, we don't have to do that. It's just getting late. You should go home. Didn't you say you have to work tomorrow?"

I began to get an odd feeling, the sense that she had something else to do. And then I realized what it was. "Okay," I said, not hiding my disappointment.

She pulled me close to her again, her eyes pointed down at my chest for a moment before fixing their gaze on mine again. "And just so you know, I'm not giving up on you. Not yet."

A brief kiss from her was followed by a strange sensation, that of her seeming to zoom away from me, and when I opened my eyes, she was gone. All that remained was the tiny sound of flapping wings flying off into the night.

CHAPTER TWENTY-SIX

I was a huge ball of mixed emotions on the drive home. It had been wonderful to see Elizabeth again, at least in some ways. The night hadn't gone quite like I'd hoped, which was frustrating and disappointing, but still, I loved her more than anything and was so glad that we'd finally gotten to talk. And more.

The car stereo was off for at least the first half hour of the trip. I wanted to think about all that we'd said, to run parts of it over in my mind, afraid I might forget. I even considered digging out my old journal when I got home and writing about our conversation, but I wasn't sure if I wanted to risk doing that. There was always the danger of someone finding it and reading it. But maybe, like before, I could sufficiently cloak things with code words in order to avoid writing anything too incriminating.

The fact that Elizabeth still wanted me was flattering, but what she was wanting me to be was unnerving. She'd never been that blatant about it before, but I began to wonder if this was what she'd wanted all along. Or maybe it was a recent development. Either way, it made me angry the more I thought about it: She knew how I felt about ever becoming a vampire again, so why bother bringing it up? I couldn't deny that I loved her and wanted to be with her, but I could never go that far.

Maybe, though, I could still move to Columbia. There was a Fitzgerald's there, and I wondered if it would be possible for me to get transferred from my current store to that one. I wasn't sure how that might work; it was just something I'd heard of happening to people with jobs. Perhaps Susanna could help me find an apartment, but I wasn't sure how I felt about the idea of living in the same city as her. Maybe we could reconnect, becoming closer as siblings. I'd heard of that happening, where siblings who didn't get along as children found that they finally could as adults.

Even if that worked, it would be incidental: The real reason I'd want to live there would be Elizabeth, to be close to her again. But would she even want that? It seemed like she had this whole new life of her own now, and I'd begun to feel like she didn't even need me anymore. But then, given what she said at the end of the night, well…

I didn't want to be a vampire again. If I had to hammer that point home to her and be firm about it, so be it. And then I came up with a way to: the mix tape I was planning to make in response to her own. The lyrics to Genesis's "In Too Deep" ran through my head, plus there was another song from the same album about nights spent in hotel rooms that had always made me think of her and our past.

I'd need more songs, particularly ones that conveyed the message I wanted. They could be love songs, but somehow defiant. I racked my brain trying to come up with more lyrics, but none sprang to mind immediately. I kept getting sidetracked wondering about a Robert Palmer video that I'd seen a couple of years ago on MTV. It wasn't one his more popular ones with the sultry models in them; this was a slow, black and white production, a sweet song about this wonderful woman he was in love with. I'd only seen it once and had never gotten it on tape, but I'd liked the lyrics and had thought of Elizabeth when I heard them. Hopefully I could track that song down and include it, too.

Naturally, I was distracted all day at work on Friday, my mind focused on Elizabeth. My coworkers picked up on the fact that I wasn't all there, but I just played it off as still not feeling well. That was the thing about playing sick: In order to do it right, one had to maintain the story even upon returning to work. Fortunately, my duties this day centered around restocking the candle holders on the shelves, so I didn't have to interact with people as much as usual.

This left me more time to think, the mundane work not taking up much brainpower. Getting to sleep the night before had been difficult, my mind racing with possibilities. Aside from my thoughts on the tape I wanted to make, I also kept being reminded of the things Elizabeth and I had talked about that night. Some of those were pleasant memories, but others bothered me.

When we'd talked about her apartment and what that situation was like, she'd mentioned that one annoying thing about it was her neighbors, the other occupants of the building. There was a family who lived above her that included two small children, and often, the kids would run around and play, stomping loudly across her ceiling. "But it worked out eventually," she told me. "I took care of it."

"How?" I asked.

"They were delicious," she said with a wicked smile. My jaw dropped, and then she laughed, reaching across the table. "I'm kidding, I'm kidding! Oh, the look on your face."

"Elizabeth…" I said disapprovingly, but I wasn't really mad at her. She'd gotten me.

By the time I was at work the next day, though, I began to wonder. Was she really kidding? She'd told me that she'd just talked to the landlord and had them have a word with the upstairs occupants, but was that just something she'd said to appease me? It was easy to believe her when I was in her presence. She was so damn beautiful that I couldn't help but think the best of her when she flashed her disarming smile at me. But away from her, even after all these years,

I sometimes felt suspicious of her. I didn't like it, but I could in fact envision her going upstairs and dealing with those loud neighbors in a much more brutal fashion.

The notion of moving to Columbia myself also pervaded my thoughts, and I wondered how possible that could be. I doubted that I could just move in with Elizabeth; I'd be a little too scared to do that for fear of what she might do. And she might not like my intruding on her space. But if I could just be in the same town as her again, perhaps even come clean with Susanna and tell her all about what had been going on the past few years, maybe she'd work with me on finding a way to turn Elizabeth back to human after all.

I'd all but given up on that idea, but it had resurfaced since our meeting the night before. On some level, it seemed plausible: If Susanna had been able to create the potion all those years ago that had turned us into vampires, then maybe with enough work, effort, and persuasion on my part, she could make one that could successfully turn a vampire into a human. Surely the principle couldn't be that far-fetched. Convincing her to do it would be the hard part. But I wanted it so much.

Maybe this was how it was meant to happen all along, I thought. If I hadn't been so secretive, I might have told Susanna about Elizabeth ages ago and found a way to bring her back from the hell I'd inadvertently imprisoned her in. If she could be normal again, we could truly be together, and maybe all of the horrible things we'd been through could be at least partly made up for.

I wasn't sure how to approach my sister about this, though. She might be just as unhelpful and resistant as always. I began to think that a selling point could be not so much *I'd like you to turn this vampire girl I'm in love with back* but more of a broader thing, that is, if she could develop a true cure for vampirism, we could use it to turn other vampires back. We'd be doing them a huge favor, as well as the rest of the world, giving these murderous monsters a second chance and preventing future killings.

Surely there was a way to do this. Susanna would probably balk at the idea at first, but if I could tell her about the things Elizabeth had taught me over the years — like being able to overcome the limitations like crosses and the lack of reflection and all that — she might believe it was possible. She might even find the challenge enough of an incentive. Or was she even still like that?

I'd wondered occasionally what had motivated her to make the vampire potion along with Robert in the first place, and the only conclusion I could come up with was just that: the challenge. That fit with the image I had in my head of who she'd been at that age: young and eager, curious and strong. She hadn't meant any harm at the outset. It had just been fun and interesting, but things got out of hand. Maybe now, finally, we could regain that control and make things right.

That was my thinking as I drove home from work that evening, and I rehearsed my speech to Susanna the entire way. I was going to call her, telling her that I knew a vampire who wanted to become human again, then see where it went from there. I hoped to get the chance to ask her about something that had been bugging me ever since Elizabeth and I had discovered that I could see her reflection: Had there been any times when Susanna and Carolyn had been in the bathroom together back when we were vampires? And if so, could they see each other, but not themselves? That might even be a way to start off the phone call, then segue into talking about Elizabeth.

I had a few ideas of where the conversation might go, and I tried to prepare for each of them, ways to convince Susanna to listen and consider helping. Appealing to her ego might be the best way to go; if she refused to even try, I could suggest that she wasn't up to it. I also wondered if she'd just hang up on me like she'd done before, and if so, maybe I'd try finding her in Columbia next time I was there and confront her about it face to face.

Things got derailed, though, when Susanna didn't even answer. The phone rang for a while, and I thought she'd at least have an answering machine that would pick up, but that didn't happen. So I didn't even get to leave her a message asking her to call me back. It was just as well; I hadn't planned for that.

After another attempt about half an hour later, I decided to try something else. I made my way up to Susanna's old room, something I did from time to time. Sometimes I just did that when I was feeling nostalgic, but the more practical reason was that it was the only way to get into the attic. I occasionally had reasons to go in there to look for old stuff, remnants of my family's past that had been stored away, plus it was my responsibility each year to bring down the Christmas decorations from there. But this night, I had a different agenda.

I looked through Susanna's old desk and then her dresser, wondering if I could find some of her old notes or anything even tangentially related to our time together as vampires. It was a long shot, but I hoped that I might find something related to the potion, a clue that could lead me to figure out a way to make Elizabeth human again, with or without my sister's help.

Nothing useful turned up. Some of the drawers were completely empty, while others had old clothes that she'd never bothered to get rid of. I'd start to get excited when I found pieces of paper, thinking they might be old potion notes, but they kept turning out to be miscellaneous crap that meant nothing to me.

Her closet turned out to be more interesting. As had happened with some of the stuff I'd run across in her room, I got little waves of nostalgia as I spotted things that had been left lying around, items reminding me of things I'd long forgotten. There was her old high school cheerleading uniform, plus what was probably some ex-boyfriend's letter jacket. I wondered why she hadn't returned it to him. I also found an old tape recorder on the shelf above her clothes, and I remembered being recorded by it when I was very young, fascinated with this magic rectangular box that could play my own voice back to me. Thumbing my way through the clothes on hangers revealed nothing useful, just old, poofy dresses, presumably ones she'd worn to prom or similar formal events.

A foot locker on the floor of the closet seemed to be filled with nothing other than more old clothes, outdated 1970s stuff that made me wonder why they hadn't been thrown away yet. But after a little digging, I realized the reason: They were camouflage. The first thing I found hidden beneath them was a blue spiral notebook.

Unfortunately, the notebook was erratic and unhelpful. The writing was mostly nonsensical, apparently things she'd written as a child. The later pages in the book were written in a more mature handwriting, some of them with actual dates, but even then, nothing in the doodles and non sequitur phrases meant anything to me. Maybe this had been some kind of journal, but it was so abstract and weird. There were small fragments of paper in the binding that seemed to indicate that some pages had been torn out, but beyond that, I couldn't make much sense of the book.

What I had hoped to find was her old folder with the formula for the vampire potion and its antidote in it, remembering what it looked like: a purple loose-leaf folder that she'd used for her Chemistry class in high school. More than likely, she'd taken that with her to Columbia. Then I remembered that she must have and that my clone had stolen it (or maybe just pages from it) to make the antidote for himself. I probably wouldn't find anything important in here.

That realization almost made me give up and go back downstairs, but then I spotted something else in the trunk that I recognized. It was about the size of a shoebox, maybe a little smaller: a grey, metal box with two silver-colored latches on one side. Within it were the remains of Dracula, the most famous and powerful vampire in history. We'd defeated him and reduced him to ashes back in 1987, imprisoning him in this little box, which I noticed had a few strips of duct tape added to it since the last time I'd seen it. At the time, we'd used a wild rose to keep the remains inert, and Susanna had said that she would supplement that with the more traditional garlic sometime later, but honestly, I'd never thought to ask her if she'd followed through on that.

Seeing the box made me nervous, not least because I suddenly realized that the remains of this extremely powerful and dangerous entity had apparently been sitting in a trunk right upstairs from my own bedroom all this time. That Susanna had left it there bothered me, but thinking through it, I figured that since Dracula hadn't suddenly sprung out of my sister's closet anytime in the past six years and killed me, that must have meant that he was safely contained. Still, it irritated me that Susanna had never bothered to say anything to me like, *Hey, the ashes of an undead horror are still imprisoned in a trunk in my closet. Watch out for that.*

Because Elizabeth had doubted my story about my encounter with Dracula, I considered taking the box and showing it to her during our next meetup, but I quickly decided against that. Just seeing it again made me shudder, and I didn't like the idea of somehow screwing up and releasing that monster again. The first encounter with him had been terrifying enough. In fact, I decided that I might bury the box somewhere in the backyard the next time I had the house to myself.

Leaving the miniature makeshift casket untouched, I noticed something else next to it, wrapped in plastic. I picked it up and unwrapped it, finding it to be a small, square Tupperware container. Inside was what looked like a brownie, but I quickly realized what it was. While the first version of the vampire potion had been liquid, the improved version that Susanna developed later was this, a solid form.

Seeing it brought back a flood of memories, most of them unpleasant. Whereas the original formula had transformed us instantaneously, this one was slow-acting, needing a few hours to take effect. There were all sorts of weird side effects to it during that time, particularly violent mood swings, which Susanna had failed to warn us about until after we'd taken it. The end result was us becoming more realistic and powerful vampires than before, but I remember resenting my sister at the time for how unsettling the slow transition had been.

But what was it doing here? My only guess was that this must have been left over from our time as vampires, maybe from when we had brought Damon and Nick into the group halfway through that last summer. I couldn't keep straight how many times Susanna had accidentally made too much of the potion, but it had happened more than once, and the problem was that we couldn't just throw it in the trash. Some animals might get into it and wind up becoming vampires as well; we knew already that the potion worked on them, too. So the safest thing to do was just keep it hidden away. I hadn't realized that there had been more leftovers, but apparently there were. I wanted to ask Susanna about this the next time I talked to her, but I didn't want to admit to having nosed around in her room.

It was raining when I got home from work the following night, which I hadn't been expecting, so I hadn't thought to bring an umbrella. But it wasn't like the walk from my car's place in the driveway to the carport was all that far. I was just in a bad mood anyway, mostly from things that had gone on at work, plus I'd been wondering all day when I'd be able to get in touch with Susanna. I really wanted to talk to her about curing Elizabeth, but I couldn't do that if she wouldn't answer her damn phone.

I'd asked my mother before leaving for work when the last time was that she'd heard from her, and she just said it had been "a while," which wasn't very helpful. But it wasn't unusual for Susanna to go for long periods of time without calling or visiting. Dwelling on this more than usual all day Saturday because I was anxious to hear from her did bring up some of my old resentment of her, the way we'd drifted apart over the years. I tried to keep that in check, knowing that I would need her help. That stood a better chance of happening if I approached her in a friendly manner rather than an accusatory one.

As I let myself inside, I also thought about Elizabeth, how she'd react to this idea of mine. She might be resistant, but maybe if Susanna and I could come up with a cure on our own and then present it to her, the prospect of becoming fully human again would be appealing. I liked to imagine that it would, and I had run the scenario through my head a few times while falling asleep the past couple of nights. I could picture her being surprised and happy, taking the cure, and the two of us finally being together as a normal couple. Maybe we would even get married.

I wanted to know if Susanna might have called while I was at work, so I walked back to my parents' room, thinking I would find my mother there. This time of night, she was usually reading in bed while my father stayed in the opposite end of the house watching late night TV in the red den, which we'd always called that room to distinguish it from the other den in the house, which had yellow carpet instead. But my mother wasn't in her bed, which surprised me. Maybe she and my father had found something interesting to watch together.

I made my way back through the house and to the red den, hearing the TV as I approached. I hoped that whatever they were watching wasn't terribly engrossing and that I wouldn't be interrupting.

And then my world fell apart.

I'd seen lots of death in my time, plenty of bodies. I'd been the cause of that more times than I could remember. But even then, seeing my own mother and father lying dead in front of me was such a complete and utter shock to me that I almost collapsed. I felt my legs wobble beneath me, letting out an involuntary scream of the word *"NO!"* as I realized what I was seeing. I rushed forward to where my father was in his recliner, stopping short as the grisly details became more clear.

There he was, his eyes wide and bulging, staring up at nothing. His skin was pale and his body completely motionless, as was my mother's. While I could have initially mistaken his position as normal, just him having fallen asleep in his chair, the way my mother's body was strewn across the couch was my first clue to what had happened. I couldn't see her face, which I was grateful for when I thought about it later. But it was like she'd been thrown there, her left arm bent at a weird angle along the back of the couch, the other one drooping lifeless to the red shag carpet below. She was just as pale as my father, and I didn't need to see the wound on her neck to know what had happened. The bloody puncture marks on my father's neck were enough.

I stood there, mouth open and panting, trying to will away the entire situation. My own mother and father, just lying there... But I couldn't deny it. It was real. They were dead, murdered. My mind raced, trying to comprehend everything, and as the seconds flew by, I pieced together what must have happened. The sound of the rain outside seemed to intensify, and I found myself suddenly extremely angered by the nonsensical yammering of the television behind me, some stupid bullshit about a new car that got such great fucking gas mileage or whatever...

I spun around and nearly broke my hand slamming the power button to turn it off. My seething continued, my breath rushing over and over through clenched teeth. I started to turn around, but I realized that I didn't want to. That would mean seeing them again. The image was already burned into my mind; I knew I'd never be able to forget it. They were right there behind me.

I staggered out of the room and into the kitchen, propping myself up with my arms as I almost fell against the table. *They're dead, they're dead...* The words kept running through me. I couldn't even cry; I was too upset for that. There was an urgency building within me, a need to do something about this. There would be vengeance, but on whom? And then I realized it. It all made sense. Outside, thunder rumbled, and more pieces fell into place.

Everything became a blur as I rushed to my room, tearing open my closet door. I yanked out my old backpack, last year's college books still in it, and I dumped them out onto the floor. The space within was quickly filled with every anti-vampire weapon I had, some of them having been carefully hidden away within the depths of my closet. I stomped back to the kitchen and grabbed the container of garlic powder from my mother's spice rack, briefly wondering if she might notice it was gone. Then I hated myself for forgetting, even for a second, that her lifeless body was in the next room.

I steadied myself, still hyperventilating but trying my best to stay calm. I needed to focus. Driving, especially in the rain, would be impossible given my current state of mind. But I knew what I needed to do. Then, as the thunder sounded again, something else occurred to me. It had only been raining for a short time, and if I was right about the time of my parents' death…

I shook my head. *You're no coroner on some cop show,* I thought angrily. *You don't know when.* But there was something I'd noticed. The wounds on my father's neck had looked fresh, or maybe they just did in my mind. I didn't want to go back into the den and check. I couldn't bear to see that again. Instead, I just trusted the memory, even if it might have been false. And something else was beginning to click in my head. The rain…

Ignoring how soaked I got, even feeling defiant against it, I rushed out of the front door and around the house to the basement door, which I wasn't surprised at all to find slightly ajar. Or had I not properly locked it back a few nights ago? I couldn't remember, and it didn't matter. I angrily tore the wooden flap open and nearly flew down the stairs, my stake held high as soon as I turned on the light. I fully expected a confrontation, and I wouldn't let anything stop me.

"Come out if you're here!" I shouted, looking around wildly, but no one answered. "I'm not fucking kidding!"

I looked for evidence of someone having been there, but nothing seemed out of the ordinary. Cautiously, I made my way through the dimly lit space, expecting at any moment to have to fight for my life. Then I remembered my psychic powers, and I tried to slow my breathing and concentrate, reaching out with my mind to feel if there was someone there.

There wasn't, as far as I could tell anyway. But I knew that I might be wrong. And then, plain as day, I saw it: the opening in the wall.

I recognized it immediately, a rectangular shape like a doorway, exactly like the one that had led me, my sisters, and my friends to the vampire Robert's house all those years ago. This one, though, was to my left, not the right. We'd closed that one down.

I stepped through the opening, and it was all too familiar, the boundaries of it lined with some kind of sheen, a magical substance that held the underground dirt at bay. As if to prove myself right, I touched the slick-looking surface with the tips of my fingers, and as expected, the contact with my skin caused the shiny material to crumble and let a small torrent of dirt fall down. It was exactly the same as I'd remembered. It even smelled the same, like damp soil.

I shouted a warning into the tunnel, hearing my voice echo along it but nothing else, no response. I knew what this was: It was an invitation, maybe a dare. My anger was incalculable, and if this was meant to scare me or intimidate me, it wasn't working. All it did was make me more determined. I felt so angry at myself; I'd been a fool for such a long time. I was going to follow this tunnel to its destination, and when I got there, I was going to kill Elizabeth.

CHAPTER TWENTY-SEVEN

There had been a couple of false starts into the tunnel, but eventually, I made my way inside, flashlight in hand and backpack fully loaded. Unlike the passageway from several years ago, this one appeared to head east, at least to begin with. After only a handful of curves to the left and right, it was easy to get disoriented. I wasn't sure if this one was the same size as the one from before; it felt like it, particularly the height, just out of my reach unless I were to jump up to touch the roof. But then again, I was a few inches taller now, so maybe this one actually was bigger.

These weren't details I noticed until I was well on my way, though. Initially, I'd just been a mass of panic, determination, and anger, to say nothing of grief. The conclusion I'd come to after discovering my parents' bodies was that Elizabeth had killed them in an effort to undermine my life. *I couldn't do that to my family,* I'd said to her. Or had I? I couldn't remember if I'd used those exact words when speaking to her or not. But as near as I could tell, in her own twisted way, she must have decided that if she eliminated my family, that would free me up to go be with her as a vampire. How could she think I would be okay with that?

It shocked me how much I found myself hating her. After years of admiration, longing for her, and loving the time we spent together, now all I could picture was taking her down and destroying her. She had no right to do what she'd done, and I was going to make her pay for it. Any images I had of her in my head of the pleasant times we'd had would immediately be replaced by a vision of my slaughtered parents in the red den.

This notion that she was going after my family had been what caused one of my delays. Just a short distance into the tunnel, I'd realized that Carolyn and Susanna were probably in danger as well. I'd run back upstairs and tried to call Susanna, but once again, she didn't answer her phone. All I could do was hope that she would be okay. Hopefully, Elizabeth didn't know where to find her, and maybe not Carolyn either, but that uncertainty unnerved me. This brash act of hers had driven the point home that there was so much I didn't know about what went on in her head, just how much cruelty she was capable of. Or, worse still, I'd known that all along but had pretended to ignore it. That just made me even more furious with myself.

I did manage to get Carolyn on the phone, but I didn't tell her many details. I wasn't even sure why, but I wasn't ready to tell her about Mom and Dad, nor did I want her to show up at the house and discover the bodies like I had. All I could tell her was that she needed to stay in her house and that she might be in danger from a vampire attack. She tried to question me, but I insisted that there wasn't time to explain and that she needed to be armed and protected, at least until sunrise. I'd tell her more as soon as I could. Her husband Luke was out of town, so that at least saved her the trouble of having to explain anything to him.

With any luck, I'd be back before sunrise, and my sisters and I would have to face the tragedy together then. It occurred to me later that we'd caused this kind of suffering for countless other people, and quite frankly, I didn't know how to deal with it. I knew I wasn't handling it right, but I didn't know what else to do. What was I supposed to do when I found my parents dead? Call an ambulance? The police? Maybe I should have called my sisters first? I had no idea.

All I could do was cope the best way I knew how: with a wooden stake right through the heart of the evil bitch who had done this.

My first mistake was in thinking that the journey would be as short as the ones to the old house back in the 1980s. Those walks had only taken about half an hour. It didn't even occur to me that this tunnel might be longer; I was too distracted and pissed off to think of that. I was operating on adrenaline and blind instinct, just grabbing onto something that was familiar in the maelstrom of emotion, trying to focus on what needed to be done in order to avenge my parents' death.

Being in the tunnel, walking along it in near silence, had a sort of calming effect on me, almost hypnotic. My footsteps padded quietly along the spongy floor, the weird, magical substance holding the surrounding dirt at bay. Remembering the phenomenon from my childhood, I stopped once and turned around to shine the flashlight onto the ground, seeing that as before, no footprints were being left. I shone the light at my feet, stomped one of them down and then lifted it back up, watching as the footprint quickly disappeared into the same smoothness as the ceiling and the walls.

As I continued on, I remembered another feature of these weird passageways, a characteristic Tim had speculated about once we'd realized that the distance from our house to the other one was longer than we should have been able to walk in the time we had. There was some strange warp-like thing going on, the tunnels somehow making us travel faster than normal.

I'd thought about this occasionally, but it always weirded me out when I did because it was just one more of those seemingly impossible things about our time together as vampires. Nevertheless, not long after Elizabeth and I had talked about her finding Robert's burned down house and the revelation that her sister had died there, I looked it up on a map again and figured out the distance between the two properties: about nine miles. I then calculated how fast we must have walked, or the equivalent of it anyway, which came out to eighteen miles an hour. It shouldn't have been possible, but it had happened anyway.

I began thinking about all of this right around the time that I checked my watch and realized that half an hour had passed, and there was no sign of the tunnel ending. It occasionally made sharp turns to the left or right, plus it would sometimes slope downward for a while and then go back up and level out. Fortunately, even though the strange substance coating everything glistened and looked slimy, it actually wasn't and didn't make traversing these inclines any more difficult than walking on the flat parts. I figured out that these twists and turns were probably there to navigate around underground obstacles, perhaps sewer systems or even rivers. But despite all of this, I got the impression that overall, I was heading in more or less a straight line.

My heart began to sink as I realized that this tunnel might very well lead all the way to Columbia, which would be a hell of a lot longer walk than I'd anticipated. I was still determined to do it, though, and I renewed my resolve, my anger at my former lover driving me onward. It took me a while to do some calculations in my head, plus I wasn't exactly sure just how many miles Columbia was from my house. But as near as I could guess, if this tunnel had the same warp rate as the one I'd been familiar with — and there was no reason to think otherwise — I was looking at probably a five-hour walk.

Once I realized this, I began to run, but I changed my mind and decided that there was no sense in wearing myself out. I had to keep my strength up for the upcoming confrontation with Elizabeth. I wouldn't be able to kill her if I were exhausted by the time I found her. So I had to take it slow, just walking the entire way.

That sucked, but it gave me plenty of time to think. The more time went on, the more angry I got at her, particularly how much she'd lied to me. I'd asked her about these tunnels before, if she knew anything about them or had heard of other vampires being able to create them.

She'd said no. Further speculation on the matter made me wonder if she had in fact been telling the truth back then, but she'd since learned how to make them. Had that been why she'd contacted me recently? Was this all part of her big plan?

I tried to think back to the night when I'd first listened to that stupid tape she'd left for me, how her spoken bit at the end had directed me to the basement to find her note. Had she already made this tunnel by then? Maybe I just hadn't noticed it. The note had been close to the bottom of the stairs, so maybe if I'd explored a little more…? I couldn't be sure. Maybe it didn't matter. I was here now, on my way to a showdown with her. The idea of her creeping around in my basement, which she may have done even more times than she'd told me about, felt like a violation. I hated her for that, along with everything else.

I was also disgusted with myself. All that time, letting her live and continue to feed on people, not once had I ever believed that she might turn on me like this. And that was so stupid and naive of me. She was what she was, a vampire, a killer. My parents were dead because of that naivety. How many other people were as well? Why had I been so blind? Because she was pretty, because I was in love with her? And what did that say about me, the fact that I could love such a despicable, murdering monster?

Thoughts like this ran through my head in circles, my frustration mounting increasingly each time. Once, I slammed my fist into one of the walls in anger, feeling a sense of satisfaction at the small cloud of dust and dirt that it released. I did it again and again as I walked along, eventually getting bored with the outbursts and continuing onward.

Hours passed, and I became increasingly uncomfortable, both physically and mentally. I kept getting more and more tired, but I told myself that I had to keep going. I tried not to think about how truly trapped I was, and honestly, I had no idea how far underground I might be. Was I just a few feet below the surface, walking along beneath it, or was I miles deep? Was this tunnel really going anywhere, or was it just some endless trap, a bottomless pit? I tried my best to shake off these thoughts, telling myself that they wouldn't do me any good. All I could do was keep going. Keep thinking.

Memories of my parents kept surfacing, but I continued to shove them down. I could tell that if I allowed myself to think about them too much, I'd get even more upset and possibly break down crying. There wasn't time for that; I had to get to where I was going. Still, there were more people lost to me, like Dennis, Tim, Tim's parents, Melody… even poor little Scout… I got a vision in my head of Scout running across the backyard, slowed down and dramatic like in a sad movie, and I almost lost it then.

I wished we had never taken that damn vampire potion in the first place, that I hadn't gone upstairs to Susanna's room that night ten years ago and heard about it from her. Tim may have carried the burden of guilt over suggesting that we take it, but I was just as guilty of perpetuating the whole thing. It had been fun, we thought. *Fun.* Killing people had been *fun.* We were despicable.

How many people might still be alive if we'd never done all of those horrible things? Some of them might have died by now for other reasons, but that notion was just a cop-out. And while nearly all of the endless victims over the years — either directly by my hand or by others' — had been anonymous to me, the ones that I did know hit me the hardest. Was that hypocritical as well?

Several months ago in college, I'd overheard a couple of guys between classes talking about how their dentist, Dr. Waters, had been killed over the weekend, possibly by a vampire. That was Eileen's father. I hadn't spoken to her for a long time, nor had I talked to her father all that much while she and I were dating, but it still stung to hear that. Thinking about it now, I didn't know if it was right or wrong for me to be more upset because I knew a victim. Weren't all the other unknown deaths out there just as important? Wasn't I just as guilty for all of those?

I got a strange idea, this notion that I should stop following the tunnel and head back instead. I felt like I should find Eileen, tell her I was sorry for her loss, and apologize to her. But that was stupid, I realized. I was already this far along, and I had a mission to accomplish. Finding my parents' killer was more important than tracking down someone from my past who had been hurt by my actions — *our* actions. Maybe I was going too far in trying to take the blame for everything, making it all about me. It wasn't like I was responsible for the actions of every single vampire in the world.

And I knew that I wasn't alone in this blame; I'd known that for years. Tim originated the idea, I instigated it, Susanna made the potion, and the others went along with it and continued to keep the secret all this time. Even so, there was a deeper layer, one that was completely on me: I had kept Elizabeth's existence hidden from everyone and allowed her to go on living, to go on killing. Maybe she didn't kill all the time, but she still did it, and I shouldn't have allowed that. I should have stopped her. If I had, my parents would still be alive, plus who knows how many other people.

Eventually, I had to stop and take a break. My feet hurt, and my stomach had started growling a while ago. My other delay when starting down the tunnel initially had been to go back and get some food; I hadn't eaten since that afternoon. Normally, I would have eaten dinner when I'd gotten home, but of course, I hadn't been able to do that. Even so, I'd at least had the sense to grab a couple of granola bars and a Coke, stuffing them into the outer pocket of my backpack before leaving.

I barely had an appetite, but I forced myself to eat one of the granola bars and to drink the Coke, which was kind of gross because it wasn't cold. Still, I drank it down eagerly, only then realizing how thirsty I'd become. That in turn caused me to let out a huge belch that echoed up and down the empty walls. It made my nose hairs burn and left a familiar aftertaste in my mouth, and I couldn't help but laugh at the loudness of it, though I immediately felt bad for finding any humor in this situation.

That brought back memories of when Carolyn and I were much younger, when she'd been more of a tomboy, and we'd make each other laugh with what we called "Coke burps." I sighed, hoping that she was still okay and that I'd see her again soon. I also wasn't looking forward to walking back this entire way once everything was done, but perhaps I could find a better way home once I was above ground.

I checked my watch, and according to it, I'd walked for over four hours. There wouldn't be long to go now, and that gave me the encouragement I needed to get back up and continue the journey. As I did, I brushed the dirt from my hands; the places on the floor that I'd happened to touch during my break had given way, which was a little disconcerting. I understood why it had happened, but all the same, it made me nervous, knowing that this weird substance was all that was keeping me from being buried alive.

It was at the six-hour mark that I began to get worried. As time had gone on, I'd checked my watch over and over, to the point where I was getting obsessive about it. I found myself counting the seconds as I walked along, waiting until the next time I could look at the watch, once every five minutes, I decided. Most of the time, I'd find that I'd counted incorrectly, either too fast or too slow.

When that got old, I started humming old bits of songs, just passages of them, the same repeated phrases. Sometimes they were songs from the radio; other times they were old commercial jingles. It was silly, but it was something to distract me from the mounting panic I was beginning to feel. I'd accepted that my calculations might have been wrong and that it would take slightly longer to reach Columbia than I'd thought, but by the time my watch read 6:30 a.m., I realized that I'd walked for nearly eight hours. Where the hell was the end of this tunnel?

I was worn out, and I wished that I'd brought more food. There was no point in trying to go back, though; that would be another eight hours in the wrong direction. I might not even make it. What's more, my flashlight was growing dim, but at least I'd managed to bring along some spare batteries. I considered stopping to change them, but I decided to wait as long as possible. If I shook the flashlight or smacked it with my hand, that usually made the glow from it brighten again, if only for a couple of minutes. I had no idea why that worked, but I didn't care.

Time passed. I walked. I was thirsty again. A dull throbbing built up in my head, not quite a full-blown headache but definitely on its way there. I couldn't believe the journey was taking this long. I also had to pee. Obviously, there was no one else around, so I stopped, unzipped my jeans, and peed off to one side, the light from the flashlight on the ground just barely illuminating the dark tunnel. As the urine hit the shiny surface coating the wall, it had the same effect as my skin touching it, causing the grey soil to trickle forth in quick rushes and form a small pile of dirt. I almost found that funny.

I walked a few yards farther to get away from the smell, then stopped again to sit down and change the batteries in the flashlight. Surely there couldn't be much farther to go, so I figured why not go ahead and continue on without straining my eyes. Taking the batteries out meant that I found myself in total darkness for the first time, which was a bit scary. Deprived of my sight, I impressed myself with how quickly I adapted, feeling the shapes of everything and installing the new batteries successfully.

Stupidly, I shone the newly charged flashlight right into my eyes when I turned it back on. The pain shot through my skull as I screwed my eyes shut, seeing blobs of green and red, the shape of the flashlight and its inner bulb still visible to me for several seconds. Once I could see again, I gathered up my belongings and continued onward, telling myself that there was no way this could go on for much longer.

By the time I'd reached the ten-hour mark, I just couldn't go on anymore. I knew that somewhere above me, on the surface, the sun was up. But where I was, it was darker than night. At least the night sky had stars, the occasional moon, and usually lots of electrical light scattered here and there among the streets. This was like being locked in a dark closet, but instead of four walls surrounding me, there were only two, endless and unrelenting. The thought of that filled me with despair, adding to the already impossible situation I'd found myself in.

I had to sleep, even if it meant just curling up on the ground. There was no way I could avoid it. I hated giving up, but given how exhausted I was, even if the exit turned out to be just another five minutes' walk ahead, I would be completely useless by the time I made it out. It would be suicide to try to fight Elizabeth in my current state. Hopefully sleep would restore my strength, or maybe I'd wake up just as weak. Either way, I had no choice.

I tried to use my backpack as an impromptu pillow, but the feel of the weapons inside just made it too harsh and uncomfortable. I folded my arms and used them instead, ignoring the weird feeling of the spongy magical substance coating the ground giving way and becoming soil as my skin touched it. That had been fascinating before; now I just didn't give a shit. I was too tired to care.

A random memory surfaced, how uncomfortable it felt in school as a child when the teacher would make us put our heads down on our desks as punishment for misbehaving (either individually or as an entire class). I remembered my fourth grade teacher, her harsh tone as she sentenced us to this fate on more than one occasion, but for some reason, I'd forgotten her name.

It was a warm summer day, the sun reflecting in strange but interesting patterns on the surface of the river as the ripples seemed to glow all on their own. My eyes moved up and down to focus on the patterns, necessary because of the gentle bobbing motion of the boat as we floated along. At certain spots, the sunlight caught the angles in the small waves that made little diamond shapes, dancing about wildly as we continued. There should have been a low engine noise, but then I remembered that my father had cut the engine and let us coast.

"Look! Diamonds!" I said in my high-pitched, childhood voice. I pointed, then leaned back from the edge of the boat, trying to get either of my sisters' attention. Susanna ignored me; she was lying down in the bow of the boat in a bikini, sunning herself. Carolyn just looked at me disdainfully, not falling for my ruse. Every now and then, I could get one over on her, but that was rare. I'd always wanted to be as cool and clever as she was. Maybe someday I would be.

"Diamonds are forever," my mother said cheerfully, but I just turned back, feeling annoyed with her. She was always saying trite things like that. I could no longer see the shining ripples; we must have passed them. Up ahead, I could see something else in the water, several dark shapes on the surface.

"Are those ducks?" I heard myself ask, knowing that for some reason, I should know better.

"Rocks," Jennifer said in an eerily soothing tone. She'd replaced Susanna at the front of the boat in my dream, or maybe she'd been there instead all along. The fact that she was wearing a long, flowing, black dress didn't seem out of place to me, either, despite the fact that we were on a boat in such hot weather. Maybe it wasn't hot after all. She certainly was, though, gorgeous and every bit as alluring as her sister.

"Similar, but different," Elizabeth said, having taken Carolyn's place but still wearing the same red one-piece bathing suit. I did my best not to stare, but she caught me, letting out an exasperated sigh. I felt so stupid.

When I looked back, I saw that the rocks were still there, but then they submerged, slowly and silently. They weren't ducks, though; I was pretty sure that they were alligators. I tried to peer beneath the surface of the murky water, wondering if they might be heading towards the boat.

I wanted to tell my father to crank the boat back up so we could get out of here, but he was no longer at the wheel. My mother was nowhere to be seen, either, nor were the others. The boat was empty, apart from myself. This made me very sad, plus I was feeling a mounting sense of apprehension. Were the alligators coming? Could they get up onto the boat? I ran over to the controls, but I had no idea how to operate them. I couldn't even read the gauges; they were in some weird language.

Something struck the bottom of the boat with a loud thump, and I was shocked awake.

I lay there in the dark, briefly disoriented and having to struggle to remember where I was. The strange position I was in, combined with the almost sickening eeriness of the spongy substance transforming to soil where it touched my slowly moving limbs, brought me back to reality. I realized that I'd been dreaming, then remembered what about. My parents had been there, and then they weren't. I was all alone.

I burst out crying, and I sat up, holding my knees to my chin and rocking. It went on for a very long time.

Regaining my composure took a while. It had been the first time I'd allowed myself to truly cry, to grieve over the loss of my parents. I wasn't even able to wish that it had all been a bad dream and that they were somehow okay; the fact that I was in this nightmarish, endless tunnel was proof enough of that. Checking my watch, I found that I'd slept for about five hours, which bugged me because I saw that as time lost, time that should have been spent walking. But I couldn't deny that the rest I'd gotten had helped. My legs ached, and I was stiff from sleeping without a mattress or pillow, but at least I wasn't quite as exhausted as before.

With renewed determination, I started to set off, but then I realized that I wasn't sure which way to go. Because of the nature of the magical coating, there were no footprints, so I literally could not tell backward from forward. Both paths looked exactly the same, and the more I looked in either direction with my flashlight and tried to compare the two views, the more disoriented I got. My heart raced. What if I went the wrong way, heading away from the exit instead? I knew what would happen then: I'd never make it out of this passageway alive.

Psychically, I reached out, trying to use my powers to guide me. I couldn't feel much of a pull either way at first, but then I either did or just convinced myself I did, and I chose. Cursing the weight of the backpack and trying to ignore the soreness I was getting on my shoulders from its straps, I walked.

I was hungry, but I decided to wait as long as possible before having that second granola bar. I wished I'd brought some water, but then I tried not to think about that because it only made things worse. I'd seen things in movies and on TV where people were walking in the desert and were dehydrated, longing for water and even seeing mirages of it. I really hoped I wouldn't become that desperate.

As I walked, I thought about my dream. It wouldn't be true to say that I couldn't believe my parents were gone; I knew that already. What got to me was that their death had been so unexpected. It wasn't like how I'd occasionally imagined it, the two of them — possibly years apart but still a long time from now — languishing away in some hospital room while I sat by their side, saying comforting things until they drifted away. The fantasy was the same regardless of which parent I envisioned. That's how it was supposed to be. I should have gotten to say goodbye.

I'd also heard of, or occasionally seen on TV, when someone's death was unexpected, and someone left behind would reflect on the last thing they'd said to the person when they'd seen them. But there was nothing poignant like that for me to latch onto. The last thing

I'd talked to my mother about was whether or not she'd spoken to Susanna recently. I didn't even say bye to her before I left for work. There was no reason to think that I wouldn't see her again. Ditto for my father: The last words I'd said to him were "I forgot," responding to his question about whether I'd remembered to check the oil and other fluids in my car. He'd cautioned me in the past that doing so was important, and feeling defiant but also dismissive, I'd said that to him, implying that I'd get around to it when I had time.

And that was it. The next time I saw them, they were lifeless, brutally murdered corpses. There would be no chance to say anything else to them again, profound or mundane. It wasn't my fault, not exactly. No, it was. They were dead because I'd been too much of a coward to kill the vampire that had in turn killed them. The least I could do was try to make up for that mistake by finally doing what was right.

Another regret began to surface, a somewhat irrational fantasy that if I'd just told my parents the truth, they might have been armed and ready to defend themselves against an attack. That had occurred to me a few times over the years, my wanting to warn them that despite whatever doubts they might have had, the vampire threat was real. They should have had wooden stakes. But there didn't seem any way to tell them that without admitting just how much how I knew, how deeply I was involved. *Involved? How about responsible?* The words ran through my head like a second voice, accusing and bitter. They weren't wrong.

I'd carried a stake on me wherever I went when the vampire threat had been at its worst, even in the summer months when it was harder to conceal. I knew the danger. Why hadn't I warned my parents of it to ensure their safety? *Because you were a selfish, controlling, cowardly little prick, Ray. You couldn't stand the idea of being caught out and admitting the truth.*

Growing up, I'd liked how my sisters and I had run circles around our clueless parents. We did get in trouble for things from time to time, but for the most part, we'd gotten away with so, so much. They may have been older and in charge, but we were smarter. *That's what killed them, you piece of shit.*

And not just them, but everyone else…

The fact that my mind was beginning to splinter into two warring voices scared me. What was that thing about talking to yourself being the first sign of madness? Was that even true, or was it just some clichéd bullshit phrase that people repeated because they thought it made sense?

I might have speculated on this further had I not spotted something along one of the edges of the tunnel. I guessed that it might be an animal, maybe some rogue possum or raccoon that had made its way down here. That wasn't out of the question. But then once I was close enough to see what it was, I fell to my knees, clouds of dirt bursting upwards as my hands touched the smooth ground.

It was a pile of grey dirt, and on the wall above it were little trails of the same color, now still and no longer trickling down. This was where I'd relieved myself the night before. I'd been heading in the wrong direction for at least half an hour.

My seething and self-loathing had died down by the time I'd made my way back to my makeshift campsite, and at least those feelings had done their part in keeping me from breaking down altogether. This seemingly endless tunnel, however more it had to go, had been made even longer by the fact that I'd wasted my time by stupidly walking the wrong way.

I felt a slight satisfaction as I passed that point, but it was coupled with the repeated self-disparagement over having screwed up. My feet were killing me, my back wasn't doing me any favors either, and my head felt like someone was tightening a cartoonishly large monkey wrench on both sides of it.

All I could do was keep going. As I did, my thoughts became more random, jumping all over the place. I thought about Elizabeth some more, hating myself for how much of a fool I'd been, believing all her lies. How the hell had I even loved her? Had I forgotten all those times she'd shunned me back at school?

Bethlehem… What a piece of shit that place was. All of those stupid, uptight people, terrified of everybody who wasn't exactly like them and condemning everyone to damnation because that was easier than trying to understand them. Afraid to admit that things that contradicted their beliefs might be true. Not like at my old school.

But that had been no picnic, either. I'd had friends who came and went like the weather. One minute we're friends; the next we're not. *Fuck you, Carl. Your loyalty fluctuated so much that I never knew whether to like you or hate you, and you couldn't decide whether to be my friend or to pick on Dennis.*

And Dennis was just as bad once we got to high school. But could I really blame him for that? Things started off rocky between us, got better for a while, then went to shit because I roped him into being a vampire. We had our secrets, which was fun. We let the rest of the group in on most of them.

There was Nick, who seemed so cool and rebellious, then wound up being a prick. Same for Damon.

Things fell apart when we got too arrogant. I was definitely guilty of that. We all were. What the fuck were we thinking giving that leftover potion to our cat? Crowley, just an innocent little animal, which we turned into a killer. I was so sad when he died.

Go on, I kept telling myself. *Keep walking, no matter how much it hurts.* That's what I'd always done, especially in those years after the vampire thing was over and I just had to wade through the guilt and try to move on.

It was after six more hours of walking that I finally had to collapse again and go to sleep. This time, despite how worn out and delirious I was getting, I was able to plan ahead: I staggered forward a few more feet and dropped my backpack there, using it as a marker to tell me once I woke up which way I was supposed to go. I stumbled back to my intended spot, then curled up on the sponge-turned-dirt floor, passing out while my tongue probed out the last few remaining bits of granola in my teeth.

When I got up again, I had the worst headache I'd ever had in my life. I was starving, and my whole body ached, which I didn't really notice until I resumed walking. I didn't like having the flashlight on even though I needed it; the light hurt my eyes. I did find that because the tunnel was going in a straight line — as it had been for what felt like a goddamn eternity — I could turn the light off and just keep walking. It wasn't like I was going to run into anything.

While I tried to walk straight, the fact that I was for all intents and purposes blind meant that I would eventually veer off either to the right or the left and bump into one of the walls, which of course made more dirt rain down. I'd then turn the flashlight back on, reposition myself, and continue with the light off. It made just as much sense as anything by this point, plus it meant that I was saving the batteries, which I could tell were running down.

I had slept for seven hours this time, but I'd already forgotten just how many hours I'd walked total. I couldn't believe how long all of this was taking, but that had no bearing on the reality of it: What was happening was happening, whether I liked it or not. I felt impossibly hungry, so much that I thought I could feel myself getting skinnier. More than once, I touched my hand to my belly, thinking that it felt sunken in. But when I shone the flashlight onto it the first time, it looked normal. It certainly didn't feel that way. Was this what it felt like to starve to death?

Maybe that was what was going to happen here. I imagined what it would be like to die, and I wondered if anyone would ever find my body. It had been more than 24 hours since I'd left my house, which I felt bad about; it hadn't been my intention to leave my parents' bodies there that long. I was supposed to have been back by now.

Had Carolyn made her way over there? And if so, did that mean that the police were involved? What would she tell them? What would Susanna say? What's more, what if the police searched the house and found the entrance to this tunnel in the basement?

I noticed that my heart was pounding, and I tried to will it to stop. Then I immediately tried to reword my thoughts, afraid that if I thought that too literally, my heart would stop altogether. All of this walking, this exhaustion, the dehydration… Could it actually kill me? Was I supposed to just walk myself to death? Maybe that was for the best. It wasn't like I deserved to live anyway.

I'd pondered many times over how much better things would have been had we never taken that vampire potion, but what if I'd never been born in the first place? It's not like my parents had planned to have me; I'd figured that out a long time ago. What would Susanna and Carolyn's lives have been like without me there? Would they have grown up to be completely different people without my presence influencing things? My parents' money wouldn't have been spread as thin, for one. Maybe Susanna still would have developed the vampire potion, maybe not, but there wouldn't have been me and all of my stupid little friends there egging her on to let us try it.

Carolyn's life had recently turned around and gotten better, her having gotten married and pregnant. But what about Susanna? She'd always been this older, somewhat distant figure in my life, but it had seemed like she was going places, at least at first. But after the vampire situation sort of blossomed and then blew up in our faces, she'd become a darker, bitter person, someone I could barely talk to.

I tried to picture how her life might have been different. She probably would have been happier, maybe even more successful. She'd given up cheerleading in college… Maybe if things had gone differently, she'd have stuck with that? Could she have been one of those big time cheerleaders for those professional sports teams like… what was the name… Could she have been a Laker Girl? Like that singer who used to be one… what was her name… *I should be able to remember this. Come on, think. All hot and sexy in her black tights and high heels, tap-dancing and all that... You know her name... Damn it, I can't think!*

That was another scary aspect of what was happening to me. Sometimes I'd feel lucid, but the more time went on, the more difficult coherent thinking became. It was like my brain had forgotten how to work. I tried to calculate how far I'd walked given the number of hours and the warp rate of the tunnel and how that translated into miles... But it was just impossible. By this point, I could probably walk for days and not even know it. But something told me that I wasn't going to survive that long. I wondered if Carl would come to my funeral.

Something else occurred to me, another regret. Before I'd left the house, I had briefly considered taking that leftover vampire potion that I'd found in Susanna's closet. In my rage, I'd thought that the best revenge I could have gotten on Elizabeth would be to become a vampire again and kill her that way, draining her and staking her just like she'd done with my clone. Then I would cure myself afterwards and become human again, but would I have the strength to actually do that? I then vehemently dismissed the idea, angry at myself for even coming up with it.

When I went back into the house to gather up more supplies, I paused for a moment and thought about going upstairs: Maybe I should take the potion with me just in case I needed it. It might give me an edge; I certainly would be more powerful. But again, I kicked myself for thinking of such a thing. Becoming a monster like her wouldn't make things any better. And really, I didn't need that to defeat her. I'd killed plenty of vampires as a regular human already.

By now, though, I was so hungry and thirsty that I briefly thought that at least if I'd had that with me, there would have been something to eat. It did look like a brownie, after all. As near as I could remember, the taste had been kind of smoky, like what I imagined eating a chewy piece of charcoal might have been like.

I'd had a really disgusting idea run through my head a while back when I thought about how I'd had to stop to take a shit half an hour earlier. Like when I'd had to pee, there was no reason not to just squat down and do it right there in the tunnel with no one else around. Lacking any toilet paper, I'd had to clumsily take my shoes and jeans off, and then my underwear, which I had used to wipe myself and then discarded.

A little farther down the tunnel, I remembered something I'd heard a few years ago on the news about a man who had been trapped for days under earthquake rubble, and he'd kept himself alive by drinking his own urine. I'd been grossed out by that at the time, but then I began to wonder if I could do the same thing. There was nothing to pee into, though, except maybe my hands if I cupped them. And because I was so damn hungry, maybe I could go back and find my poop...

I gagged at the thought, dropping the flashlight in the dark as I clamped my hand to my mouth, afraid that I might throw up. *Not like there's anything inside of me to puke up anyway. But seriously, Ray, what the hell?* I didn't have an answer for myself.

But what about the idea of wishing I'd brought that potion-brownie-whatever-it-was instead? All that would do would make me have to endure all of the potion's weird side effects, those violent mood swings and eventually passing out. And even though I'd then be transformed into a vampire, I wouldn't really: I'd be an artificial vampire, a chemically induced facsimile, and a starving one at that. I'd just be trading one hell for another; there was no blood down here to drink.

I stumbled along, my deplorable thoughts my only company, for what my watch told me was another six hours. This had to be some kind of joke, I'd told myself at one point. I could barely even think, so I just put one foot after the other. The tunnel's topography surprised me occasionally, going up, down, left, or right, but I barely cared. I used the ever-dimming flashlight to guide me when needed. I'd been reduced to some kind of robot, just plodding on and on for what felt like no reason. The only thing worse than that would have been stopping.

So I gave in to that. *Let it be worse. I'm done.*

I settled down as before, slinging my backpack in front of me and hearing it land somewhere ahead. That was my marker in case I actually woke up later. I doubted I would. I didn't even want to. This was my fate: the manipulative, sneaky, murderous Raymond Adrian Young, reduced to an exhausted heap of flesh, doomed to die in this endless passageway. *May he rest in peace. The end.*

I tried to drift off to sleep —or maybe death — but despite how tired I was, I couldn't make it happen. My heart was pounding again, and all I could hear was its rapid rhythm in my ears. I could feel it pulsing in my chest, just waiting to explode. My head hurt so much, as did the rest of me, and all I wanted was for all of it to stop. *Just some peace, please,* I begged. *Please, God. I'm sorry. I'm so, so sorry. I've said that a thousand times. Just let me sleep.*

Elizabeth and I had talked about God a few times. Our experiences at Bethlehem had been fodder for many a conversation about the existence or non-existence of a supreme being. We'd shared our cynicism and had philosophical discussions, sometimes laughing at the scared people — adult and our own age as well — who seemed like they couldn't decide which side of bread to butter their toast on unless they prayed for guidance first.

Bits of those conversations ran through my head as I tried to fall asleep, particularly one we'd had in Columbia the last time I'd seen her. The God-related issue was part of a larger discussion that stemmed from the notion of things working out for the best, a concept she had a problem with.

According to her, this was a human conceit, a way to assign meaning and value to events in the past based on one's opinion or interpretation of them. Phrases like "it was meant to be" or "things happen for a reason" bothered her; she felt that things just happened and people assigned meaning to them after the fact. Whether past events were positive or negative was purely subjective. Christians had their own variation on this: They'd call it "God's will." But really, it was just daily life, and they were the ones attributing what they thought God was thinking to whatever their own thoughts already were.

I got what she was saying, but I wasn't sure how much I agreed with it. That was her perspective as an atheist, but I still didn't quite know where I stood on that front. The way the past couple of days had gone, though, I figured that there must not be a God. Why would he put me through something this horrible? But maybe that was arrogance, too. *Just because he doesn't give you what you want doesn't make him not real,* I thought. *Then again, the same could be said for Santa Claus.*

Or perhaps the fact that I was here was proof of God's existence after all. Maybe this was how he sent me to Hell. I was either dying or had already died. If I woke up, I told myself, maybe I should check my sock for a lump of coal.

I wasn't sure how long I'd slept this time. I was actually surprised when I did wake up, but my vision was so blurry that I couldn't read the numbers on my watch when I tried. My tongue was clammy and sticky, the roof of my mouth hurt, and my head was throbbing. I was so miserable that I even felt pissed off that I hadn't died yet.

Defiant, I refused to get up. I just sat there on the ground, numb and depressed. What would be the point of continuing forward? Even if I made it out of the tunnel, I was so worthless now that I wouldn't have the strength to defeat Elizabeth. Maybe if I were lucky, I could emerge somewhere near a place to eat first, like a Dairy Queen. For some reason, that sounded really appealing to me. The thought of food spurred me into action, and I resumed my possibly futile underground trek.

My mind was shattered, and the disjointed, nonsensical thoughts continued to plague me. I repeated my method of walking in the dark and only using the remaining battery power in the flashlight sparingly, but at one point, I imagined that the next time I turned on the light, Elizabeth would be waiting for me in the tunnel, just inches from my face and lunging at me with fangs bared. The idea scared me, so much that when I did turn the light on, I flinched in panic, but there was nothing there. This happened several more times in a row, but eventually, I guess my mind got bored with the fatalistic fantasy.

After another hour or two of walking, I was again feeling like giving up. I thought about the way we had collapsed the other tunnel all those years ago, deliberately touching the roof with our hands to make the dirt cave in, but getting out of the way of it just in time. It would be just as easy to stand still, to reach up and bury myself. I pictured myself doing it.

Shocked at what I'd been thinking, I carried on, wondering if I would ever reach any kind of destination.

It's hard to say how much longer things went on. I'd lost the ability to keep track of time. When my flashlight had gone dead, I stopped walking and put the old batteries back into it. That sometimes worked, I knew from past experience, and it did, providing me with a bit of residual power, but not enough. I probably should have kept the ones I'd swapped out, too, but I'd dropped them in the dark and, out of anger, kicked them across the ground, not bothering to recover them.

I regretted that later once they were far behind. What were batteries made of? Could I have eaten them? Probably not. But they might have given me a little more light when the old ones ran out altogether, leaving me with nothing more to do than continue on blindly in the dark. It took a while before I realized that there was no point in carrying the useless flashlight, and I angrily threw it away as well, continuing onward.

When the tunnel sloped sharply upward, I let out a small, choked scream. It scared me at first, and I fell forward in the dark, again feeling the coating give way to sand beneath my hands as I caught myself. I tried to feel the shape of everything, but that just brought forth more dirt, and I couldn't tell what I was doing. If only I hadn't thrown away that flashlight and those batteries…

I wondered what time it was. If I really had finally reached the end of this nightmare, I wanted to know how long it had taken me. I pushed the button on my watch to use its built-in light, but I couldn't even make sense of the numbers. My mind was that far gone; it could have read 47:38 for all I knew. Then I realized that what little illumination it provided was enough, and I turned my wrist to point the watch outward and waved it around the walls of the tunnel.

It was definitely an incline, and I could just barely make out the dark shape of a hatchway on the roof. I nearly burst into tears when I saw it, but I knew I had to keep myself under control. In darkness again, I held my arms out at my sides for balance as I maneuvered my way up the incline, feeling for the door and finding it more easily than I expected. I pushed, and it offered almost no resistance.

Light seared in and almost blinded me, burning into my brain. I fell backwards and onto the ground, cursing as the door above me slammed shut. Ignoring the pain, I made my way back up again, screwing my eyes shut this time as I carefully pushed open the hatch. The sunlight still made its way through my eyelids as a wave of increasing redness, but I couldn't resist the pull of the fresh air that flooded my nostrils.

Eyes still closed, I clawed my way up through the opening, feeling grass and dirt under my hands as I did. The air felt so cool and wonderful; I hadn't realized until then how stuffy it had been in that godforsaken tunnel. I breathed in and out through my mouth with deep, painful gasps, and I cautiously allowed my eyes to open.

My head was still flooded with pain, and I was so unaccustomed to daylight that I had to cover my face with my entire arm to shut it out. I lay there on the grass on my knees, propped up with one hand, then collapsed completely, flattening. The sounds that filled my ears shouldn't have been such a cacophony, but they were: Wind gently blowing through nearby trees and birds chirping served to remind me that I'd been encased in such stark silence for so long, and what might have been pleasant under other circumstances was instead severely disconcerting.

I was so relieved to be back in the real world that I wanted to let loose and cry, but I didn't even have the strength for that. I slowly allowed my arm to pull away from my face, which was pressed to the ground. Squinting at the unforgiving sunlight, I found myself keenly aware of the individual blades of grass and grains of sand that were touching me.

I lay there for a little while — who knows how long — then managed to stand back up. My eyes still hurt from the light, but I needed to figure out where I was. What I saw barely made sense to me. It was like I was in a huge, open field, but the ground seemed to slope upwards in some directions, downward in others. The horizon wasn't where it should be; it was high in the sky, which was strewn with wispy clouds. Like the land around me, the horizon also seemed to move up and down at weird angles, and it was covered with a forest that looked impossibly far away. There were occasional trees and bushes closer to me, and I thought of trying to stagger over to one or two of them, then couldn't see the point.

Still, it occurred to me that walking was better than just standing there, so I made an attempt at it. The brief time I'd spent lying on the ground, though, had served to remind me how I'd already been walking for days (probably), and the pain that wracked through my body was unbearable. I was severely disappointed to find that I appeared to be in the middle of nowhere; there was no fast food in sight. And where the hell was Elizabeth?

As I stumbled around, it occurred to me that what I was seeing on the horizon must have been mountains. Having grown up in the mostly flat terrain of Augusta, I had never actually seen mountains in person, only on TV. And in those cases, they were usually aerial views, majestic and cinematic. They never showed things from this angle, the viewpoint of a desperate individual surrounded by nothing but wilderness. And yet, there was something...

But then there wasn't. I wasn't sure what had just happened. I caught a glimpse of a large structure out of the corner of my eye, something huge and white. But when I looked directly, there was nothing there, just more endless, sloping greenery. I took a few steps forward, and just for a second, I thought I saw it again. Then it was gone.

I wasn't sure if I could trust my senses; being so deprived of food and water might cause me to see mirages. This was kind of like that, but I couldn't be certain. I did get the sense that there was something there. When I took a few more steps forward, it was like I stepped through an invisible veil, and then there it was, large as life. But it was impossible.

What I saw — what I thought I saw — was the Bon Air Hotel, one of Augusta's prominent landmarks. It was a huge building, all white aside from its dark red, textured roof, five or six stories high and maybe three times as wide. It looked quite a bit like a hospital, I'd always felt, and it wasn't even a hotel anymore. I didn't know the exact historical details, but as far as I knew, it had once been a hotel but had since been turned into apartments. People still referred to it as "the Bon Air Hotel," though.

When I first saw it, I wanted to cry. Had I really walked for what must have been hundreds of miles, only to end up here? Had I gone in a huge circle? What would be the point of that? But then I realized that this couldn't be the Bon Air. It looked like it, but the surroundings were wrong. The place I was thinking of was located right in the middle of Augusta, roughly halfway between my house and downtown. It was surrounded by roads and neighborhoods; it didn't belong here in some anonymous, hilly field near mountains in the middle of God knows where.

As I mulled this over, the building suddenly vanished again. I cried out in shock, confused and afraid. It may not have made sense for this building to be there, but at least it was something, but now it was gone. I staggered forward a few more paces, and then I could see it again, though it looked more blurry this time. Or was that just tears welling up in my eyes?

Can't be the Bon Air, I thought. *Can't be... Then what?*

I stood as still as I could, afraid that the very movement of my body against the light wind might upset the balance somehow. Maybe if I could sneak up on it, the building wouldn't disappear again. I got the feeling that it was watching me, as ridiculous as that seemed. A sense of dread began to fill me, this notion that I should just turn around and run as fast as I could in the opposite direction. But I couldn't do that. I had to figure out what was going on here.

Inching forward, my arms held out at my sides for balance, I saw that this definitely wasn't Augusta's famous hotel. It looked almost like a castle, but then again, sometimes the Bon Air had looked like that to me, particularly when I was a kid. Another step, and the building once again vanished, which caused me to drop to the ground in despair. I risked a glance upward, fighting back a wail that was growing in my throat, and once again, the structure loomed ahead.

I couldn't take it anymore. The physical exhaustion coupled with the way this mystery was fucking with my already shattered mind was just too much. I didn't know what was happening, and I tried to tell myself that I didn't care. My last memory before everything went black was of a small trickle of drool I felt seeping out of my mouth and onto my forearm, wondering if it might reach the grass below.

CHAPTER TWENTY-EIGHT

What happened over the next few hours or so was disjointed and blurry. I woke up a few times, just lying there in the field, too defeated and weak to move. I was vaguely aware of the increasing darkness and drop in temperature as the sun went down, but this did nothing to motivate me. I was done, just waiting for my life to run out, at one point imagining myself as a wrecked car on the side of the road, idling and running out of gas. Surely it would happen sooner or later.

I wasn't even sure if the approaching footsteps I heard were real or not, if they were any more substantial than the hallucinations and delirium I'd resigned myself to. Somebody said something…

"Is that him?"

"Who else do you think it would be," someone else deadpanned.

"Here," the first voice said, closer to my ear. I thought it might be Elizabeth; the voice sounded female at least. I felt someone grab me and roll me over, and I offered no resistance. My eyes opened, and I could barely make out the two shapes looming over me. It was very dark, and I could vaguely see stars above, but they seemed to move around like grains of sand in ocean water.

"Bring me that," the woman said, and I felt her lifting my upper half, maneuvering me into a sitting position. A strange crackling sound was soon followed by the sensation of something small being pressed to my lips. Immediately, water began to pour into my mouth, and I involuntarily reacted. I started to reach up with my hands, but the woman said something that made me stop. It was similar to being shushed or calmed, but I couldn't tell if the words were even English.

I drank as quickly as I could, so much that I choked, causing water to spill down my chin and onto my chest. The water bottle was pulled away as the woman tried to wipe my face, but I lurched forward, needing more of what I'd been deprived of for so long. The skin inside my mouth hurt, particularly along the roof.

"Easy now," the woman's voice whispered in my ear, followed by a word that sounded like *vestacha,* but I didn't know what that meant or even if I'd heard it right. "More slowly this time."

I did as instructed, feeling the cool water as it filled my insides. It was simultaneously exhilarating and painful; it felt like the water was forcing its way into parts of me that had been sealed shut.

I must have passed out again; the next thing I remember was being lifted off the ground by one of the two mysterious strangers, which one I couldn't tell. Whoever it was did so effortlessly, like I weighed nothing, and it reminded me of being picked up by my mother or father when I was little. The proportions were off, though; it wasn't like I was a small child being held close to a loving parent's chest. The person carrying me seemed to be more or less the same size as me.

A realization came, and I started to struggle, but my carrier's grip tightened. "Stop it," a male voice said, and I found myself complying immediately. I craned my neck to see where we were going, and I wasn't surprised that we were headed for the strange white building, which was illuminated from within.

"Man, you stink," the person carrying me said, then let out a short, disgusted cough.

I wanted to say something like, *Yeah, you try walking for days without a shower,* but I couldn't form the words. I heard a small giggle from somewhere nearby, presumably from the woman who had given me the water.

Part of me wanted to escape, but after having been in such desperate isolation for so long, there was another, almost instinctual part of me that felt grateful just to be in the presence of other human beings. But on another level, I knew the problem with that thought: These people weren't human.

There were more lapses of consciousness. I was briefly aware of entering the building, which I supposed for a moment might be a hospital after all. But there was none of the rushing around of doctors and nurses, the random chatter, or the pages over the intercom that one might expect. The place was much more quiet, the lighting more subdued.

People were around, some of them dressed rather strangely, but mostly I was aware of their faces. Some of them looked at me with indifference, but quite a few of them looked amused, even condescending. The realization of just what these people were filled me with terror, but all I could do was lie limply in the arms of the man carrying me, who faced straight ahead as he walked past the imposing onlookers.

I couldn't keep my eyes open, but I did feel the sensation of being carried up some stairs, maybe more than once. Snatches of conversation were overheard here and there, including between the two who had retrieved me from outside, but not enough to make sense of anything. A brief glimpse of a hallway revealed carpet that was a deep color red, and the walls were off-white or beige with strangely patterned wallpaper at regular intervals. There were also occasional framed pictures, or maybe mirrors; I couldn't tell. What I thought might be flaming torches hung by the doorways, but another glance revealed them to simply be electric lights with orange, oblong shades.

I woke up again when I felt myself being dropped unceremoniously onto a bed, which prompted some chastising from the woman from before. The man, whom I saw for the first time had black, straight hair in a longish style, said something snide in response, wiping his hands on the front of his shirt as he walked away and out of my field of vision.

The woman was nicer, even affectionate and almost mothering, as she helped me into bed and removed my shoes. I only caught glimpses of her because it was too much effort to stay awake, and I was so exhausted that I barely understood her when she asked me if I wanted more water, but I managed to nod. I don't know if she ever brought it to me; I was asleep seconds later.

When I awoke, I had no idea where I was. I felt better, but that stopped when my memories began to come back. I sat up in bed with a start, then immediately regretted that as a profound dizziness kicked in. As I steadied my head with one hand and squinted, I tried to recall the events of the night before while also taking in my surroundings.

The room was dark, but I could see light spilling in from the boundaries of the thick curtains on both of the windows. I got out of bed unsteadily, surprised at how good I felt, all things considered. After my ordeal in the tunnel, it wouldn't have surprised me if I'd been recovering for days, if not weeks. I couldn't be certain how much time had passed. For all I knew, there should be a doctor here asking me if I knew who the president was.

I pulled the velvet drapes apart, the light hurting my eyes as it rushed in, but at least my headache was mostly gone. I couldn't make out much through the lace curtain, so I pushed that aside and looked out, seeing those same unfamiliar fields and mountains. I was on a higher floor, maybe two or three stories up, definitely too high to attempt an escape. I wasn't sure if I was a prisoner here or not, but I certainly didn't feel safe. A snatch of an old song fluttered through my head, something about checking into a hotel but never leaving. Or was that an insecticide commercial?

I could only remember bits and pieces of what had happened to me, but the fact remained that this hotel, or whatever it was, was full of vampires, none of whom I'd ever seen before. I tried to pretend that I didn't care who they were, but that wasn't really true. I was curious, but more than that, I just wanted to find Elizabeth and make her pay for what she'd done. But what did she have to do with all of these other vampires?

Suddenly, I realized something. With the room better illuminated, I searched all around it for my backpack, but it was nowhere to be found. All of my weapons had been in it. I checked my pockets, and there wasn't so much as a single wooden stake on me. Finding myself defenseless, I began to get scared.

What had happened to my pack? Had one of the vampires taken it, maybe hidden it somewhere? I tried to remember, but I couldn't recall if I'd been wearing it when they first found me, nor while I was being carried inside. As destroyed as my mind was at the time, I couldn't even be sure that I hadn't accidentally left it back in the tunnel.

Still panicked, I searched the room a second time. It certainly was a fancy place, much more ornate and elaborate than the comparatively spartan hotel rooms I was used to. There was a mantel with a framed painting of some blue flowers above it, along with some old books held up by brass bookends shaped like lion heads. Beneath that was a small fireplace, but it didn't look like it had been used recently. The bed had a dust ruffle and even a canopy, and it struck me that it and the rest of the room's decor looked somewhat anachronistic, more like something I'd see in a TV show set sometime around the turn of the century. But there were modern touches, too, like the electrical outlets and the lamps plugged into them. The carpet and drapes, meanwhile, were the same crimson color that I'd seen out in the hall.

I was startled by a light knock at the door, followed by the sound of a key being inserted into the lock. I drew back cautiously as the door slowly opened, and a woman with long, dark, wavy hair peered around it, a wide smile on her face. "Hello again," she said in a strange tone, almost seductive. "I felt that you were up. Or sensed, I suppose I should say."

I wasn't sure how to respond. I couldn't be certain, but I was pretty sure that she was the same vampire from before, the one who had given me the water. As she spoke, I noticed for the first time that she had a foreign accent, but I couldn't place it. The best I could guess was some kind of European, but that covered a lot of ground. As she opened the door wider and stepped forward, she asked if she could come in, but I could tell that she wasn't really asking.

"Probably don't have much choice, do I?" I managed to say, trying to cover my fear with anger.

"Don't be frightened, Ray," she said. "I'm not going to hurt you. You know I could have already if I'd wanted to." She had a point, but I also wondered how she knew my name, so I asked her. "Oh, don't worry about that," she said slyly. "My name is Mirela." It was a pretty name, particularly the way she said it, and because she was being so cordial, I resignedly made a gesture for her to come in. She paused, still holding the door, then glanced around it meaningfully at the window, its drapes still parted. Her eyes were wide, dark, and expressive, and I couldn't help but notice how beautiful she was, though I didn't want to admit that I'd even thought that. "If you would be so kind, and…?"

For a second, I felt more determined. She was referring to the daylight, which obviously she couldn't handle, so that gave me an advantage. I started to say something along the lines of *Why should I,* but then I didn't see the point. She'd already stated the obvious: She wasn't here to attack me, sunlight or not. In fact, she'd been nothing but kind to me since the moment I'd met her.

I shrugged, then headed for the window, but then I stopped. No way was I going to plunge this room into darkness with a vampire standing right there. If there did end up being a confrontation, I'd at least like to be able to see. She watched as I walked over to turn on the tall floor lamp closest to the door, still smiling at me in a knowing way. There was another one not far from the open window, so I turned that one on as well, then pulled the drapes closed quickly. It made me uncomfortable to have my back to her, even if only for a few seconds.

Turning back around — and halfway expecting to find that she'd lunged forward and was bearing down on me — I saw her move simply and elegantly as she closed the door, then glided over to one of the two large chairs that sat at either end of a dresser on the far side of the room. The clothes she wore were also intriguing: An emerald green, flowing, corseted affair with lace, flared sleeves matched the cream-colored trim of her skirt, beneath which pointed black boots with short heels on them could be seen. Again, like the decor of the room, she seemed like something out of the past.

"May I?" she asked, sitting down. She was polite, but I couldn't help but feel a sense of dread and menace, and I got an impression that she both knew and enjoyed this. She really was beautiful, but because of what she was, I still felt not only afraid of her but repulsed. "Please," she said, gesturing to the bed. I sat down, suddenly realizing how weak I still felt after everything I'd been through. My body relaxed, but then I straightened up, not wanting to let my guard down.

"I'm glad to see you feeling better," she said, her last word suddenly giving way to a yawn. She recovered, then continued. "I'm sorry. I'm not used to being up this early. The place is usually rather quiet during the day. But I'm sure you can understand why."

A strange sensation filled my head as I either psychically sensed or just imagined all of the vampires around me, probably sleeping in the dozens of rooms that were above, below, and on the same floor. I could see the whole building as some kind of vast grid, and it teemed with sleeping monsters. I also sensed or at least suspected that there were others who were awake and active in the inner parts of the building, safe from exposure to the sun. This went on for a little while until I came back to my present situation, once again aware of the gorgeous but deadly presence in my room.

"I suppose it can be an overwhelming concept for someone such as yourself," she said, still grinning knowingly. Her accent, wherever it was from, made her words sound slightly musical and even a little silly. But then I remembered something Susanna had said to me years ago when I'd expressed a similar sentiment: Just because someone spoke English with a funny-sounding accent, that didn't make them stupid. In fact, they were fluent in at least one more language than I was.

The woman nodded, and I realized that she was reacting to what I'd just thought, which made me uncomfortable. Apart from feeling caught out at being condescending, the fact that she could hear my thoughts bothered me.

"Stop that," I said, squirming internally.

She laughed, and for a moment, she seemed very young. For the most part, her face made her look like she was in her mid-20s, just slightly older than me, but still young. But even without her antiquated clothing style, there was something about the way she carried herself that hinted that she was much older, a poise and wisdom about her that belied a maturity I couldn't begin to approach.

"I'm sorry," she said. "Your thoughts are... rather loud. I was warned to watch out for that."

"Warned? By who?" Then I became more angry. "Where is Elizabeth?"

"Elizabeth?" she asked. I thought she was feigning ignorance at first, but she did seem genuinely surprised. "There's no one here by that name." She let out another small laugh, then looked off into the distance. "It's strange, but now that you mention it, of all the people here…" She looked back at me, those deep brown eyes pulling me in despite myself. "That is a very common name, but no, I don't think we have a single Elizabeth."

"You're lying," I said defiantly, but the way her expression hardened gave me pause. "You're *not* lying," I added more quietly, feeling that I'd insulted her. "Fine. But then who are you? What is this place? And what am I doing here?" I then remembered something that had slipped my mind momentarily, and I felt mad at myself for having let that happen.

"My parents are dead. She... Wait. Was it you that did it?" I stood up angrily as I said this, but I suddenly felt weak again, stumbling stupidly back against the bed. It embarrassed me, the way I'd tried to be tough but had wound up looking foolish.

Mirela watched patiently as I recovered and repositioned myself on the bed, then spoke measuredly, as if to a child. "I did not kill your parents, Ray. I am sorry for your loss, really. But you do not need to direct your anger toward me."

Trying to recover my dignity, I asked, "Then who?"

Another knock at the door interrupted us, and Mirela called, "Come in, Erica."

The door opened, and I smelled the food immediately, suddenly aware of how hungry I was. I half expected the girl entering the room to be dressed like some Edwardian chambermaid with an apron and a silly white hat, but instead, she was dressed more modernly. Her brown hair was straight and just past her ears, and she looked pretty much like someone I could have gone to college with.

But I didn't care about that. There was food, and my mouth watered at the sight of it. This new arrival carried it on a large, elegant-looking silver tray with ornate handles, and while I felt the urge to grab it out of her hands, a prompting from Mirela had me sitting back against the headboard of the bed, a pillow propped up behind me.

Erica placed the tray onto my lap, and my eyes zoomed in on the delicious steak in front of me, barely noticing the vegetables surrounding it or the glasses of water and what I was pretty sure was iced tea. "There you go," this new girl said, somewhat flatly. "Rare, just how you like it."

How did she know what I liked? And why did she seem so familiar? We'd never met, and I could tell that she was also a vampire, presumably like everyone else in this place. Moreover, when had I ever decided that rare was how I preferred a steak prepared? It wasn't something I had often, but I was so grateful for the meal that I didn't bother to question her; instead I just dug in and began eating. Erica let out a little *"pfft"* sound, and I glanced up, briefly stopping chewing and feeling self-conscious with my now-emptied fork in my hand.

"Now there's something I don't miss doing," she said, then turned her back to me as she faced Mirela, who had stood up from her chair.

"Don't be rude to our guest, Erica," she chastised, but I sensed a bit of sarcasm from her. "Let us leave the gentleman to his meal." As she said this, she gently touched the girl's arm and led her to the door.

I watched them leave, then felt a strange chill when Erica paused and smiled at me for the first time. "Again," she said cryptically. The two of them disappeared through the door and shut it, and I tried not to feel threatened as I heard the key turn in the lock once more.

There were, I knew, some people who described themselves as "stress eaters," who would eat more than usual when going through difficult times and wind up getting fat. I'd always been the opposite, though. Throughout the tragedies in my life, I'd always lost my appetite whenever I was upset, finding it difficult to force food into my body and thinking that everything I tried to eat tasted like paper. Often, I'd lost weight during these times until I got back to normal, and on those occasions, people around me would comment on it, asking me if I had or just stating it: "You've lost weight!" But I'd never really cared about stuff like that.

Memories of this ran through my head as I wolfed down the meal that had been prepared for me, and as I began to feel full, a more sinister thought occurred to me. What if the food I was eating had been poisoned? They knew I'd been starving, and now here I was stuffing my face with food prepared by people — vampires, I barely needed to remind myself — whom I didn't even know. This whole place felt like some big elaborate trap, including the tunnel leading to it, so was this how I was meant to meet my demise?

I hadn't keeled over and died yet, so the notion of that began to strike me as a bit ludicrous. But what the hell was really going on here? I was supposed to be a vengeful vampire killer, a man on a mission to avenge the death of his parents, but instead I was sitting in a posh hotel bed eating steak and asparagus. Had I known that I was going to encounter tons of vampires, I would have shown up all weapons-ready like a vigilante, eager to take out these vicious demons one by one. But that clearly wasn't what was going to happen.

These vampires, whoever they were, seemed almost amused by my presence. I definitely wasn't in control of the situation, and that frustrated me every bit as much as it frightened me. Whatever was going on, I had no choice but to play along. They probably knew that, too. The fact that Mirela — and probably more if not all of the vampires in this place — was psychic also unnerved me. Even when I was alone in this room, I felt like I was being watched.

I began to wish again that I'd brought that leftover vampire potion with me instead of leaving it at the house. At least if I were a vampire as well, I might have stood a chance against my captors. But it was a moot point: I had no supernatural abilities, no weapons, and no way out. This started to make me feel so vulnerable that I wanted to break down, but I fought the urge, again feeling embarrassed at how my thoughts were probably being monitored.

By the time Mirela returned to my room a short while later, I had placed the tray on the dresser and had explored more of my immediate surroundings. I definitely felt better from having eaten, and my mind was more or less back to normal. I still felt threatened and afraid, but I tried to believe that there must be some way out of this. At the very least, I wanted to find out as much as I could.

That meant pressing Mirela for information upon her return, this time feeling more confident and defiant. I tried to hide my disappointment over how this didn't make her falter in the slightest; she obviously didn't feel threatened by me. Instead, she just kept up her calm, patient demeanor.

"So when are you going to tell me what this is really all about?" I asked her, feeling more angry. "Why you've brought me here…?"

She laughed again, and something about her smile reminded me quite a bit of Elizabeth's. There was that same arrogance, enticing but revolting at the same time. Apparently that came naturally to someone so easily capable of casual murder. "Ray, I didn't bring you here. If I understand things right, you came of your own free will."

"You know what I mean."

She nodded, still smiling. "I do, but I think you've gotten the wrong impression of me. I am not the reason you're here." With that, her expression became more grave.

"Then what is?" I almost shouted. "Who are you? Who are *any* of you? What in the world is this… this place, with all these vampires in it?" She just looked at me blankly. "What?" I demanded.

"Maybe you're just not asking the right questions," she said, her grin returning.

I could tell that continuing to get angry at her wasn't going to get me anywhere, and the fact that she was enjoying my frustration made me force myself to pull back and not give her the satisfaction. I sat down in one of the ornate chairs, and she did the same. Something flashed across my mind, a memory of that girl Erica who had brought me the food earlier. She reminded me of someone, but I couldn't think who. So, changing tactics, I asked Mirela who she was.

"Well, she was a cook at a restaurant," she told me, "before she became who she is now, that is. That's why she was set with the task of feeding you."

I could see the logic in that, but then suddenly, another image came to me, a brief vision of Erica actually feeding me by hand, holding a fork with something on it to my mouth. Or was it a spoon? "I… remember…"

Mirela looked surprised, then intrigued. "You do, don't you?"

More memories surfaced. The meal I'd had earlier hadn't been my first one in this room. There had been at least one more, or maybe more than that? It was only a fragment here and there, but I began to recall that the two of them had fed me, though I'd been in some kind of trance. It had been some time after I'd arrived, but before I'd woken up feeling more coherent today. How much had I forgotten?

"We had to do it that way," Mirela said, interrupting my disjointed reverie. "You were very… how should I say… unstable."

I didn't know whether to feel insulted or grateful. "So you… controlled me."

"If you like," she said simply. "It was necessary."

I wanted to lash out at her again, but I fought the urge. Then I surprised myself with what I said next: "Thank you." I couldn't deny the fact that I'd nearly starved to death, and if these seemingly benevolent vampires hadn't done what they had, I might not have made it. That didn't change the fact that they probably had something sinister in store for me, though.

"You're quite welcome," she said, again somewhat condescendingly. "I have to say, though, that I'm impressed. Most people don't have their memories come back like that."

"Maybe I'm not 'most people,'" I said, starting to feel more confident. Then, unexpectedly, the image of Erica's face came into my head again, but it was attached to another memory. "Oh!" I said, smacking the arm of the chair with my hand and almost standing up, but then I sank back down. "I just realized!"

"What is that?"

"Who she reminds me of. I didn't even catch it before. Guess I was too out of it. But she reminds me of my sister!"

"Really?" She seemed quite amused by this.

"Yeah…" I laughed a little. "It didn't even click until just now. But yeah, same kind of hair, brown eyes, something about the shape of her face. Quite a bit like…" I stopped short of saying Susanna's name, suddenly remembering my surroundings. I didn't like the idea of talking about my family here; it might put them in danger.

She continued to smile at me knowingly, and I again resented the psychic insight that she had. "I really wish you'd stop that," I said.

She let out a giggle, again seeming young. But how old was she really? Decades? Centuries? I was too scared to ask. "Sorry," she said. "It's hard not to."

"Then maybe…" I concentrated, picturing a grey, translucent rectangle materializing around my body, the same shielding technique Dennis and I used to use. "Is that better?"

"Yes," she said, "it actually is. You're less… noisy now."

"Good. At least I feel like I have some kind of defense against you people now."

"The residents of this hotel are not here to harm you," she reassured me, slightly impatient but still maddeningly calm.

"So, it is a hotel?"

"I think it was once, a long time ago. Before it was moved here."

"It's not the Bon Air, is it?"

She shook her head, the black curls of her hair jostling against it. "Sorry, I don't know that name. Some of us call it Castle *Y…*" She stopped short, catching herself in the middle of a word. "No. That would be…" She trailed off, looking at me strangely. "Not for me to tell. You'll find out."

Again, I wanted to press her for more information, but it seemed like I got more out of her when I kept things less confrontational. She wasn't going to reveal anything she didn't want to, at least not on purpose. "I thought it looked kind of like a castle when I first saw it," I offered.

This prompted another laugh from her. "Oh, no. I've seen castles. This is definitely not one of them." She paused. "Though I suppose it could be the American equivalent of one."

"So where are you from? Europe? Maybe Russia? I've been trying to figure out your accent the whole time we've been talking."

She grinned at me again, this time almost seeming flirty. "Oh, here and there. I'm from lots of places. Maybe nowhere. That's what happens when you live long enough." Something in her expression hardened, and I could tell that I wasn't going to be told anything more about her origins.

I changed the subject back to the hotel, mentioning how it seemed to disappear from view when I'd first encountered it. "Was that just me going crazy or what?"

"Oh, no, that's normal," she said. "It's hidden on purpose."

I tried to comprehend what this meant. "So it's… what, magic?"

"Something like that. The master doesn't care for uninvited guests." The look in her eyes let me know that she'd just told me something important, and I felt an involuntary chill but tried not to let it show.

"The master?" I asked. "Who's that?"

She just smiled knowingly. "When you're ready."

"I *am* ready," I said angrily. Whoever this person was that she was referring to, I quickly realized that he must be behind all of this.

"No, you're not," she said firmly. "Not until you've cleaned yourself up, for one thing." She gestured to me with her hand, but I ignored it.

"I don't care about that," I said sharply. "You take me to this master-whoever-he-is right now."

"No." The charm she had exuded throughout most of our conversations had evaporated. "The master is not going to see you as you are now. You look terrible, and the smell of you is even worse. Or have you not noticed?"

I suddenly felt very self-conscious, and the fact that a beautiful woman was pointing out these flaws only made it worse. I looked down at myself, realizing that I was still wearing the same clothes from the night I'd come home from work and found my parents dead. How many days had passed since that night was a mystery to me, but I knew for a fact that I hadn't showered for days. I realized that I probably smelled so bad that my nose had shut down and wasn't even registering my own stench.

Mirela repeated her urging for me to get cleaned up, pointing towards the bathroom. I'd found that when I was exploring the place, but at the time, I hadn't remembered using it to pee earlier during my semi-conscious stay here. But once I glanced back at it, more bits of memories surfaced, and I realized that I'd been in there before.

"I…" I stood up, trying to retain some dignity, then ran a hand through my hair. It felt greasy and nasty, and my embarrassment increased. "Maybe you're right."

She pursed her lips at me in a manner that seemed to say, *I am.* There wasn't any point in arguing with her, so I headed for the bathroom. "Wait," she said, and I stopped in my tracks. "Your clothes."

I looked back at her. "What?"

"Those are just as bad as the rest of you right now. No point in you bathing yourself only to step back into those disgusting things."

I couldn't argue with that, but the way she'd started being so harsh with me made me want to do the same in return. "Sorry, I didn't pack a change of clothes," I sneered.

"We'll have to find you something," she said, looking me up and down. "You look to be about the same size as… Yes, his will probably do."

"Whatever," I added angrily. She seemed less appealing to me than she had earlier; now I just found her beauty and poise obnoxious. Even her accent was grating on my nerves. Without another word, I went into the bathroom and slammed the door behind me.

The shower was probably the best one I'd ever had; I'd never known it could feel this good to wash days' worth of grime off of me with all of that hot water, soap, and steam. I also found that, despite my nakedness, I felt safe under the relative isolation of the running water. Showers had given me this feeling plenty of times in my past; I'd noticed that sometimes my best ideas came to me when I was alone in this way. But it also occurred to me that this particular calm might have been vampire-related: Maybe the fact that I was surrounded by running water kept me safe from all of the blood-sucking creatures around me, even psychically.

As I continued to clean myself — and I couldn't help but notice that the shampoo left for me was White Rain, the same brand I used at home — I wondered about more things. The gaps in my memory were disconcerting, and the more bits and pieces I recovered, the more it worried me. I didn't like not being able to remember everything, the way that little flashes of Mirela and Erica kept coming up. It reminded me of the mind control that Elizabeth had told me — and shown — that she was capable of. Clearly I'd been a victim of that as well; these vampires could do the same thing.

And really, the potion we'd taken all those years ago had a similar effect. The first two times after we'd taken it and those summers' adventures had ended, all of us had trouble recalling details. We'd forgotten just how bad things had been and the horrible things we'd done, which left us open for naively thinking that we could just take the potion again and have fun being these cool, powerful, supernatural beings. The fact that we'd killed people, turned on each other, and committed all those atrocities was completely glossed over.

The improved potion that Susanna got us to take the third time in 1987 changed that, and once it was all over, that amnesia disappeared. The aftermath was horrible, and I found myself eerily able to recall every single thing, despising myself for all that I'd done. That guilt defined the next several years of my life, coupled with the way that our past vampire selves emerged from us and wreaked even more havoc, not least of which was my beloved Elizabeth being turned into a vampire herself.

I thought I'd come to terms with that, but I'd never been okay with the way Elizabeth had accepted her fate and even grown to enjoy the creature she'd become. Just when I'd begin to think that things might be getting better or couldn't get any worse, reality would slap me in the face. It just kept happening. People kept dying. What was occurring in this hotel now was just the latest step, and I wasn't sure how much more I could take.

I tried to regain my composure and stop crying as I got out of the shower and dried myself off with a towel. The coldness of the bathroom, despite the residual heat and humidity, quickly overwhelmed me. I tiptoed into the rest of the room hoping to find my clothes, again feeling self-conscious about my nakedness and vulnerability. No one was around, but I was simultaneously comforted and disconcerted to find that someone had placed a new set of clothes on the foot of the bed for me to wear. Whether it was Mirela, Erica, or some other anonymous vampire, I had no idea. But the thought of some stranger coming into the room without my knowledge added to my discomfort.

But the clothes were suitable enough. There was a pair of black jeans and a neatly folded, long-sleeve white oxford shirt, plus a pair of black socks and some shoes on the floor by the bed. There wasn't any underwear, which for a second made me bristle, but then I thought things through and realized that these clothes had probably been borrowed from some other male inhabitant of the place, and I wouldn't have wanted to wear some other guy's underwear, would I?

I conceded this and clothed myself, then set about brushing my teeth once back in the bathroom. Like the shampoo from earlier, the brand of toothpaste was the same one I used at home, and it bothered me even more when I realized this. Everything felt like a set-up. Even the soap in the shower had been the same kind I was used to. How long had these vampires been spying on me? And who the hell were they? Who was this "master" that Mirela had mentioned?

Again, I had to accept that the only way to find out was to go along with this elaborate game that these vampires were playing with me. But I didn't like jumping through hoops. There was an electric razor by the sink — of course, similar to the one I had at home — and though I picked it up, a glance at my face in the mirror gave me pause.

The amount of facial hair I had was an indicator of just how long I'd been in this place. It wasn't excessive; I discerned from past experience that it was probably three or four days' worth of growth. I'd gone that long without shaving before a few times in the past, but only when I'd had multiple days off of school (or later, from work). That had been due to a combination of laziness and curiosity. So this at least told me that I hadn't been here and in a hypnotic stupor for weeks, something I'd feared might have been the case. The amount of time it had taken my hosts to nurse me back to health had probably only been a day or two.

That was a small comfort, and I shrugged, thinking that I might as well go ahead and clean myself up the rest of the way. But then I changed my mind. While I wasn't sporting a full beard and looking like a lumberjack or anything, I did feel like I looked more tough and rugged the way I was. I'd already showered and changed clothes as instructed, and I was probably expected to shave as well, but the more I thought about it, I didn't want to look nice for whoever this master person was. I'd played along enough already.

Mirela led me through the halls of the hotel, which was even more elegant and fancy than I remembered from when I'd first arrived and been carried to my room. But then, I'd been barely conscious at the time. Taking in my surroundings and learning as much as I could, I did my best to hold my head up and not be afraid. It didn't help that every vampire we passed by — some in small groups, others on their own — eyed me up and down, sometimes with indifference but more often with amused, condescending looks. I wondered just how much each of them knew, if they were all in on this elaborate scheme, or if they were merely curious as to why this helpless, defenseless human was being paraded around among their ranks.

I barely spoke to my guide initially, and as we walked, I kept an eye out for anything that I might be able to use as a weapon. I hoped that I would spot something made of wood, anything that I might be able to suddenly dive for and turn into an impromptu stake, but nothing presented itself. I wondered where the kitchen might be in this vast place, wherever Erica had cooked my food, but I gave up on that idea when I figured that there probably wouldn't be any garlic in there anyway.

It wasn't long after that when I spotted Erica herself, talking quietly by a stairwell with two men. I'd noticed by this point that there seemed to be a disproportionate amount of women in the hotel; for some reason, they seemed to outnumber the males ten to one if not more. And everyone, male or female, looked absolutely perfect; there were no ordinary or unattractive people to be seen. It was like walking through a JC Penney catalog, but all of the models were undead.

As had happened before a few times already, Erica and her company stopped talking as Mirela and I passed by, and all three of them took the time to leer at me, which made me decidedly uncomfortable. I wanted to glare back at them in response, but the realization that any of these beasts could just lunge at me and drink my blood filled me with dread. I noticed once more how much Erica looked like she could be a relative of mine, maybe a sister or a cousin, and out of nervousness, I mentioned this to Mirela once we were halfway down the stairs and hopefully out of earshot.

"Oh, we're all family here," she said, her voice slightly punctuated by her footsteps down the stairs. "Some by choice, some not." I wasn't sure what to say in response. "Each of us has our own histories," she added as we reached another floor. "You see that girl over there?"

My eyes followed the white, marble tiles on the floor of the wide room until they settled upon an attractive blonde in a long, pale blue dress. There was something odd about her, but I couldn't quite figure out what it was until Mirela explained to me further: "That's Victoria. She was an actress in the '60s." I could see it; the style of her hair looked out of date but still rather pretty.

"So… What, she just stayed like who she was when she died?" I asked.

Mirela nodded, something approving in her manner. "Some of us do that. And some don't. We can stay like who we were at the time, or we can change and adapt… How do you say it now? With the times."

I started to say something in agreement, but then Victoria stopped eyeing us from afar and began gliding over, which simultaneously intrigued and terrified me. She really was gorgeous, just like everyone else here. "Oh," she said, taking my hand and shaking it politely. Hers was ice cold. "Is this who everyone has been talking about?" There was something cooing and measured in the way she spoke, her voice breathy and high-pitched.

I withdrew my hand from hers quickly, then felt bad, like I'd been rude. She didn't flinch, though, and she let her limp hand hover in the air for a moment before slowly dropping it to her side. I couldn't help but notice her abnormally thick eyelashes and heavy eye make-up, the same kind that women from her era sported back in the day. She looked like someone straight out of *The Monkees,* which brought back memories of the reruns I'd enjoyed as a kid.

"So glad to meet you," she said to me, and I felt stupid, my mouth hanging open as I tried to think of something to say. Her hair was the same golden-brown color as Elizabeth's, and while her wide blue eyes were also similar, there was something odd about her eyebrows, like they were too thick. But I didn't mind. Her smile was intensely captivating, and the fangs that peered over her bottom lip in little white points looked so sexy that I just wanted to…

"Back off, Victoria," Mirela said harshly, and she recoiled, which left me feeling profoundly disappointed. I concentrated and found myself blinking hard, like I was trying to flush my brain out. Then things felt more normal again.

"Maybe next time," Victoria called out, scurrying away delicately and looking back with a mixture of anger and mischief.

My psychic shield from earlier had gone, which was usually the case when I stopped thinking about it. Blocking out others or keeping my powers from influencing them was achievable, but only if I actively did so. And while I tried to put the barrier up again at this point, I found it difficult, like something was making it become unstable and dissipate. There was a lot of psychic energy in this place; the air almost teemed with it, giving things an increasingly dreamlike quality.

Mirela and I resumed our journey, which ended not long afterwards at a tall set of white double doors with ornate handles. "And here we are," she said to me purposefully.

I looked at her blankly. "So now what?"

"Now, you go in." She'd been being rather dramatic this whole time, even arrogant, and while some of that still remained, I spotted some softness in her newly changed expression that reminded me of when we'd first met. "I wish you the best of luck." With that, she grabbed one of the handles and turned it, then pulled the door open. With her other hand, she gestured to me to continue inside. I could tell that she wasn't coming with me.

The ballroom I found myself in was vast, bigger than any room I'd seen so far and every bit as fancy as the rest of the place had been, if not more. The floor was similar to the one I'd recently traversed, though the tiles were arranged differently, more in a diagonal fashion and also larger. Elaborate, dark-colored tapestries dotted the walls, occasionally punctuated by statues but more often with expensive-looking vases set upon small pillars. Some had flowers in them; others did not.

Two immense golden chandeliers hung from the ceiling, one at the end of the room I was in and a second at the other. I at first thought they were filled with candles, but closer inspection revealed that these were electric lights made to look that way. Countless crystals hung from them, catching the light in intricate patterns. My footsteps echoed as I walked forward slowly, and I noticed a dark, circular shape in the high, white ceiling, halfway between the two chandeliers. It was kind of like a stained glass window, but all one color, deep red that was almost black. White bars in a crosshatch pattern, just two one way and two perpendicular, seemed to hold it in place. I was certain I'd seen it somewhere before, but I couldn't remember where.

It was only when I took my eyes off of it and redirected my gaze to the far end of the room that I spotted them, two silent figures sitting in large, polished wooden chairs on what appeared to be a stage. As I got closer and took in more details, the depth of it seemed too small to be suitable for performances, but still, it was raised a few feet from the rest of the room. I realized as I approached that the set-up was more like that of an old-fashioned throne room, and my earlier thoughts about this place seeming like a castle resurfaced. And I was meeting — metaphorically if not literally — the king and queen.

I did my best to be tough as I strode forward, wanting to put this mystery to rest, but once the man's face came into view, I wasn't sure what to think. He looked vaguely familiar, with his sharp, dark brown eyes and brown hair, but he wasn't anyone I'd ever met before. His face was pale, but not uncommonly so, though I was certain upon first glance that he, like everyone else here, was a vampire, and a very powerful one. He smiled at me predatorily as I approached, my footsteps slowing as I did.

The woman in the chair to his left, whom I didn't even recognize at first, was what shocked me the most and almost made my knees buckle. Both of them were dressed in black formalwear, her dress being extremely elaborate and showing an almost obnoxious amount of cleavage. Like Mirela and some of the other vampires I'd seen, her clothing looked like it could have suited someone from a century ago, but there was a modern flair to it as well. Fashion had never been a strong point of mine, but I was at least able to pick that up.

Her long, elaborately curled brown hair slipped off her shoulders and bounced lightly as she leaned forward, saying to me with a fanged smile, "Hello, baby brother."

CHAPTER TWENTY-NINE

Susanna hadn't called me "baby brother" for many years. When we were younger, she'd used that term occasionally, but by the time I reached age seven or eight, I insisted that she stop. That just egged her on once she realized how much it bothered me; I didn't like being thought of as a "baby" in any sense of the word. She stopped eventually, but every now and then, she'd throw it out there just to make me squirm.

My heart pounded as I tried to reconcile the memories of that sister with the voluptuous, vampiric figure who sat before me in her ornate chair next to this master vampire, whoever he was. I'd had a hard enough time dealing with everything up to this point: the death of my parents, the exhausting and almost fatal journey through the tunnel, and the confounding nature of this hotel in the middle of nowhere filled to the brim with vampires. Seeing my oldest sister as a vampire and seeming to delight in both that and my confusion was almost more than I could handle.

"Susanna?" I asked, my voice almost a whisper. "What's… What happened?"

She grinned at me menacingly, a haughty look in her eyes. "What was always going to happen," she said with a purr. "Didn't expect that one, did you?" She then spread her arms and hands out in a triumphant gesture, closing her eyes and tilting her head back at an angle as if to say, *Look at me!*

"Susanna, no…" was all I could think to say. "This can't be right."

"Oh, it is," the man next to her said, bringing my gaze back to his. There was something almost hypnotic about his deep brown eyes, and I fought an urge to step back. "It was always going to come to this." His accent was strange, almost like a combination of a British and an American one.

"And who the fuck are you," I spat at him. He looked taken aback for a second, then resumed his smugness.

"You can call me master," he said, every bit the triumphant movie villain, his manner of speaking both clipped and dramatic. "More specifically, Master Youngblood."

"What? I'm not…" I was at a loss for words. I wanted to continue to be defiant, but I was so thrown by what was happening that it was hard for me to do. Regaining my composure, I nearly shouted, "Look, I don't know who the hell you think you are, or what's going on here."

Susanna — this new, vampire version of her whom I barely recognized — let out a small *"hmph,"* and I resisted the urge to glance over at her. "No, you don't," she said, and then I did turn to her. As her twenties had progressed, she'd become less stylish and more plain. But now she was so done up and well dressed that she looked a lot like she did back when she was even younger than I was, when she was in high school and used to go to things like the prom and other fancy, upscale events like that. "You never did," she added.

"Please, please," the male vampire said, holding up his hand. "Let's not be so harsh with each other. We're all family here, after all." Susanna giggled at this, but I still felt on fire with anger.

"I don't need to hear that kind of shit!" I shouted at this new antagonist. Then I pointed at Susanna, not taking my eyes off the man. "That's my sister. I don't know what you've done to her, but I'm not going to let you get away with it. Don't give me all this 'we're all family' crap."

"Ray," he said to me, and something briefly made me want to calm down, probably more psychic influence, which I pushed back against. "I meant it. We are, in fact, family. Your family name wasn't always Young. Did you know that? No, of course you didn't. That was buried along with everything else, just like they tried to do to me, to make me disappear. But I never really did."

"What are you talking about?" My anger did dissipate slightly, replaced by genuine curiosity.

"He's one of our ancestors, Ray," Susanna said impatiently. "Try to pay attention." That at least sounded like the real her, talking down to me like I didn't know anything.

Youngblood glanced at her, then back at me. "I am in fact your great-great-great… Well, I forget how many 'greats' it is; I've lost track. But your great-great… however many 'great…' grandfather was a man named Jubal Youngblood, and he was my brother."

I looked at him, and sure enough, there was some distant family resemblance. His face reminded me of the one photograph I'd ever seen of my grandfather, who had died long before I was born. What little I knew about him was that he and my dad hadn't gotten along, something about him being abusive. As for this man, the way he said his brother's — my ancestor's — name, indicated no small amount of contempt.

"And what's your name?" I asked.

His wry smile returned, and he spoke a name, something similarly old-fashioned like Zebediah or Obadiah… But then, as he continued to speak, the name quickly disappeared from my mind. Again, it was something telepathically induced; no matter how much I tried to shield myself from this man, the energy almost seemed to waft off of him like a stench. I wished my powers could be that strong, but I was nowhere near as old and powerful as he obviously was.

"But I never went by that," he continued. "When I was born, well, my poor mother didn't survive, so she didn't have time to give me a name. And my father was… absent, shall we say. So the attending nurses affectionately referred to me as 'Master.'" Seeing my baffled expression, he clarified, "It was a title for a young boy. People still use it in some circles nowadays. I suppose the modern equivalent would be if a baby were born today and, in lieu of a real name, he was called 'Mister' or 'Sir' until they settled on something more permanent.

"Regardless, the nickname Master stayed with me. I preferred it. Even once I had a proper name, I was usually referred to by that, or, once I was older, simply by my surname."

"That's utterly fascinating," I said sarcastically. "But I still don't see what any of this has to do with me or my family today. Or why you think you can just show up out of nowhere like this and fuck things up for everybody."

"But that's just the point, Ray," Susanna said, again impatient. "He didn't."

"I was here the whole time," he said, not hiding his arrogance. "You just didn't know it."

"I don't get it," I said, still doing my best to appear unimpressed.

"Of course not," Susanna said, rolling her eyes. My concern for her and what she'd been turned into was beginning to give way to increasing contempt.

"It's a long story," Youngblood said. "Please, take a seat."

"There isn't anywhere to…" I began, stopping when I spotted a plush, emerald green velvet chair behind me. It hadn't been there before; I would have walked past it in order to get to where I was standing. Surely it couldn't have materialized out of thin air… Maybe a servant had brought it in and left? I wondered if my memory was playing tricks on me again.

What followed was a lengthy explanation from Youngblood about my family's history, the first part of which I sat through with arms folded, barely wanting to hear it. I'd never been interested in genealogy, nor had my father told me much about where our family had come from. But according to the story, we'd originated in England and immigrated to "the colonies" (as he referred to them more than once) sometime in the middle of the eighteenth century. The three brothers in the family had been involved in setting up some church in Virginia, but sometime after that, some big scandal erupted which resulted in Youngblood being formally kicked out, like an excommunication.

He was vague on a lot of details, and I sensed early on that he was leaving out something important from time to time. The way he told the story made it seem like he was treated unjustly, but I could tell that he was glossing over things that would have made him look bad. Other times, he reveled in his evilness and thought himself quite clever. For one thing, he'd always been psychic, but he'd learned at an early age to keep that hidden because it was viewed as something unholy. I could certainly relate to that, but I regretted thinking so when I saw the look of recognition in his eyes. I didn't want to admit that I had anything in common with this despicable creature. It didn't seem unreasonable to me, though, to think that psychic ability could be something that ran in the family; I'd always held the belief that there must be some biological basis for it, some people more prone to it than others.

Whatever it was that he'd done that got him kicked out of the church and ostracized by the community, it eventually resulted in his death and subsequent resurrection as a vampire. In the aftermath, the two older brothers had gone their separate ways, one of them marrying Youngblood's widow and shortening the family name to Young. That man was my direct ancestor, the one who had brought the family to Georgia all those years ago. Youngblood himself was visibly quite bitter about this. But something about his story confused me.

"Wait," I interrupted. "So who was it who turned you into a vampire? You didn't say anything about being bitten."

"Very astute of you, Raymond," he said, relishing the way I narrowed my eyes at him in anger. I didn't like being called by my proper name. When I was in elementary school, Gary and some of his friends had gone through a stint where they called me "Almond" instead, then "Raymond Joy," a reference to the candy bar. It was stupid, but it still got under my skin.

"There are many ways to become a vampire," Youngblood continued. "Being bitten is just one of them."

"Another is taking a potion," Susanna added meaningfully, still looking cold and calculating.

"Hush, my dear," Youngblood said to her with a gentle hand gesture. "We'll get to that in time."

He continued to rattle on, something about a curse of some kind, but my mind wandered and I zoned out, missing some of his explanation. I was distracted by the enormity of everything, trying to think of some way out of this situation and simultaneously trying to digest what I was being told. My early thoughts had centered around some way to try to undo what had happened to Susanna, but I found myself having to accept that she was a lost cause. She was a vampire, plain and simple, and what was worse, she was obviously quite happy with that fact.

Processing this took a great deal of effort. For ages, she'd refused to even talk about our having been vampires unless absolutely necessary. She'd been ashamed of how she'd made the potion with Robert and how we'd all used it later. Seeing her perfectly content in her current role was downright disorienting. Had she just been lying the entire time?

What brought me back to paying attention to Youngblood's monologue — which was occasionally punctuated by Susanna's snide commentary — was how he explained that for the past two centuries, he'd not only kept tabs on his extended family but also actively manipulated them over the years. Every couple of generations or so, descendants would emerge who were evil enough for him to exact his influence on them, turning them into vampires and causing all kinds of trouble and strife. He delighted in this, seeing it as a kind of revenge. These vampires eventually made their way to him, becoming part of his coven, so to speak, and I realized that the place I was in now was the culmination of that.

"That's right," he said to me, sensing my thoughts. "I told you we were all family."

Then it hit me. Erica, whom I'd met earlier, didn't just look like a relative of mine; she was one. A distant cousin, perhaps, but probably part of the Young family line somewhere along the way. I pictured the other vampires I'd seen throughout the hotel, many of whom had the same dark hair and eyes that Susanna and I had, and the reality of it began to sink in. I pictured a family tree, the way it could branch out over generations, not only biologically but geographically. What was happening here really was bigger than I'd ever imagined.

"And Robert, of course," Susanna said, throwing me for a loop but simply prompting Youngblood to smile at me more broadly.

"Yes, poor little misguided Robert Trueblood."

"Wait…" I said, trying to comprehend this latest revelation. "He was a part of this, too?"

"I did tell you that there were three brothers," Youngblood said pointedly.

Robert's family, the Truebloods, had been similarly manipulated by Youngblood over time, though to a lesser extent. Some of the vampires currently in the hotel were the result of that, while still more were simply ones who fell in with the group over the years. Once Robert and Susanna met in high school, that had been the beginning of a chain of events that would one day lead us, ten years later, to this point. He hadn't realized it, but Robert had come up with the potion partly due to Youngblood's telepathic urging.

It hadn't even started out as a vampire potion; apparently it was something to do with behavior modification in mice, teaching them to do certain things. I didn't quite follow everything I was told, but there was something about a mind-altering drug I'd never heard of called peyote that was introduced into the mix, leading to both mental and physical changes. But the fact that Robert was psychic also had something to do with that, and one part in particular of this lengthy explanation did ring a bell with me: the idea of belief creating reality.

"You see," Youngblood said slowly and patiently, "whereas most hallucinogenic drugs merely alter one's perception of reality, that potion took things a step further, allowing one with a powerful enough mind to actually alter reality, even if their powers weren't fully developed. It was a catalyst, if you like. Robert had those gifts, just as you later did. That's how he was able to become a vampire. And of course…"

"Wait, wait, wait," I interrupted. "Then how did the mice they tested it on change? You're telling me they were psychic, too?"

Youngblood let out a low chuckle, and there was something strangely familiar about it. What was odd was that this was the first time he'd laughed since I'd met him, but I could have sworn I'd heard that laugh somewhere before.

Susanna threw me a snotty look. "No, stupid. Listen to what you're being told. Robert was psychic. And he, with a little prompting…" — she said this as she slyly glanced sideways at our host — "…had a long-standing interest in vampires. That in turn influenced the mice, which he began to believe could be transformed in that way. Same thing happened when he tried the potion on himself."

I recalled the story once more, how he'd turned into a vampire, almost killed Susanna, then was changed back. It scared him, so he gave the formula to my sister and distanced himself from her and the project, only to change his mind later and try to start the work up again. Eventually, his failure in that led him to the black arts, and the devil himself transformed both him and Elizabeth's sister into truly undead vampires. That part of the story had always freaked me out, plus I'd seen the outcome of it.

The parallels between that confrontation and this one suddenly struck me, and I kicked myself for not noticing before. There had been the luring through the tunnel to the big house, the legions of undead waiting for us, and then the showdown with Robert and Jennifer, who taunted me and the others by explaining everything that had led up to this, all part of their plan. It was eerily similar, but at the same time, all of that felt smaller, like a dress rehearsal compared to this.

I realized that the three of us had been sitting in silence for several moments as I worked through all of this in my head, and when I looked back up at Youngblood and Susanna, I could tell that they'd heard what I was thinking. Their smug grins indicated as much. Suddenly, a chill ran through me, and Susanna's brightened expression indicated that she knew why.

"You're…" I began, then stopped. "You're psychic, too? Or, no… hang on. It's because you're a vampire. I get it." Elizabeth hadn't had any powers like that before becoming a vampire, so presumably, that was all a part of being one.

"No, I always was," she said triumphantly, and the chill returned. "Not as obnoxiously strong as you, or those other little friends of yours, but yes. And, like our master here, I kept it quiet. Didn't need to be a little braggart about it like you."

That was unfair; Dennis and I had kept that from her and the rest of the group for a long time. Tim had kept his powers secret for even longer. But something else occurred to me, mostly a flippant thought: "Jesus Christ, has there ever been anybody in my life who wasn't secretly psychic?"

The two of them had simultaneously recoiled as I'd spoken, which was a surprise. "What?" I asked. Then I understood. "Oh…" For the first time in way too long, I smiled. *"Jesus Christ!"* I shouted at them, and they jumped, shutting their eyes briefly before staring back at me harshly. "God! Holy, holy, holy!" They continued to squirm, and

I stood up from my chair, feeling confident. It looked like I wasn't weaponless after all. In the absence of a cross to hold up to repel these vampires, apparently holy words could do just as well. I tried to recall the scenes of exorcisms I'd seen on TV, wondering what to say next.

"Stop that," Youngblood said deeply, waving a hand at me.

"By the power of *Ccc...*" I choked, unable to continue. *"Ggh..."* I tried a couple more times, but something had happened to me. I could no longer say the Christian words I wanted to. Blinking back tears from the gagging this had caused me, I staggered back and sat down in my chair, defeated.

"Nice try," Susanna said to me slyly.

"Fine," I said, folding my arms again.

"You may well wonder why it is that so many telepathic people have populated your life, Ray," Youngblood said, regaining his tone from earlier, and I could tell I was in for more self-congratulatory lecturing. "In a cosmic sense, people like us tend to clump together, sort of like magnets." He made a gesture with his hands indicating such. Then he flayed out his fingers as he continued, "The rest of the people in the world are more like iron filings, attracted to or pushed around by us. We're the important ones."

"So..." I began, but I wasn't sure quite how to articulate my thoughts, and I shrugged, frustrated. I was still digesting the fact that both Susanna and Robert had been psychic all along, but I'd never been told this. I was also getting a feeling like I was being eroded, my sense of self-importance diminished with every new revelation, each subsequent bombshell being dropped on me. I'd always seen myself as being at the center of all of these bad things, a victim of circumstance in some ways, wanting to redeem myself. But now it was becoming clear that I was more like a pawn in a chess game, and here were the king and queen of the board telling me so in painful detail.

Something else occurred to me, and it had to do with my fluctuating belief in things like God and the devil. Would it do me any good to pray to God to somehow save me from all of this? And as for the devil… "Wait," I said yet again. "You said that there were different ways to get turned into a vampire, right?"

"Yes," Youngblood said, looking pleased for some reason.

"Well, Robert said that it was Satan who turned him and… that other girl into vampires."

"And do you think that's the truth?"

It took me a moment, but then the penny dropped. "Oh, right. That was you, wasn't it? You let him believe that. Just played along with his fantasies."

"Now you're beginning to understand," he said.

The night continued on with one revelation after another, and I did my best to be defiantly nonchalant, but I knew that it wasn't working. So much had been happening that I'd never had a clue about, and I felt utterly out of my depth. They knew it, too, and all I could do was sit there and keep having things thrown in my face over and over. It occurred to me at some point that this was in fact the story of my life, expecting one thing and then being presented with another. Maybe that wasn't unusual.

The fact that the vampire potion was in fact some mind-altering drug that became reality-altering when combined with psychic powers was hard enough to take in. It made a weird sort of sense, but only insofar as anything else did by this point. I briefly recalled the werewolf potion that Robert's uncle had injected us with in 1987, and that seemed to fit. He and his partner told us that it would make us into werewolves, and so it did. Maybe they could have told us that it would have turned us into adorable beagle puppies, and the same thing would have happened. I didn't know; I felt like giving up.

There was more: My clone had known about Youngblood, having found out about him a few years ago through one of the nameless vampires who lived here. That same guy, whoever he was, had been the one to supply him with the potion that subdued vampires into a coma for long journeys overseas, the same one he'd used on Elizabeth to keep her imprisoned.

I flinched when her name came up, warning my sister and the master: "You stay away from her." Youngblood's dismissive comment that she was irrelevant and not a part of all this simultaneously relieved and disappointed me. While I was glad that he considered her nothing more than a casualty of the lifelong manipulation of me and therefore out of harm's way, I couldn't help but wish that I might see her again.

But as far as my clone was concerned, Youngblood also considered him irrelevant, just as he had Susanna's clone. Even before the emergence, Susanna had been aware of Youngblood, and the conversation we were having this night bore out the details of that. First, though, a rather frightening detail about the demise of her clone was revealed.

"Unlike the real Susanna here," Youngblood explained, "who was oh so frightened of me once I revealed myself to her…" — the two of them exchanged a sickeningly affectionate glance — "…and tried to keep her head buried in the sand in hopes that I might let her be, the astral manifestation of her vampire self was anything but shy. She sought me out immediately, wanting to be with me. But I wanted nothing from her."

"Why not?"

"Because she wasn't the real me," Susanna said haughtily.

"She was merely a shadow, part of a whole," Youngblood went on. "When she found me and tried to ingratiate herself to me, I simply did away with her."

"That was the night I felt the thread detach," Susanna reminded me, though it was unnecessary. I'd already remembered and put the pieces together myself.

"And my clone… astral projection… whatever… He never came to you?" Maybe if he had all those years ago, it would have saved me a lot of trouble and heartache.

"No, he was smarter than that, I have to say. And I think he was more concerned with staying in Augusta and tormenting you. But if he had, I would have done away with him as well, or I might have just teleported him back to where he came from."

"You could do that?"

"Effortlessly," he said. "A demonstration, if you would like…" He waved his hand, and just a few feet to my left, the air seemed to ripple. There stood Victoria, the beautiful blonde vampire I'd briefly met before.

"What?" she asked, looking surprised and disoriented. She took in her surroundings, including me. Then she smiled seductively. "Why, hello again."

I shrunk back in my chair, simultaneously unnerved by her presence but also in awe of the power I'd just seen demonstrated. Victoria turned to the stage, and she curtseyed with reverence. "Master," she said with a smile.

"That will be all, my lovely," he said to her, then waved his hand again.

"But I…" she began, but then she was gone again, transported back to wherever she'd been in the hotel before.

"Impressed?" Susanna asked me. I refused to answer, but that didn't really make a difference, I knew. My hatred for her was growing, especially the more I realized that she wasn't who I'd always thought she'd been.

She might not have been evil since day one, but the more I understood and had explained to me this night, I realized just how terrible she'd been nonetheless. The 1983 to 1987 episodes had been like one big experiment to her, with Carolyn, my young friends, and I being the guinea pigs, an extension of her and Robert's initial experiments with the potion. I'd seen it as an opportunity for us to be powerful and have fun, and she'd let me think that.

It had never really crossed my mind before what a horrific thing that was for a girl her age to do to us. At least when we'd started out, I'd had the excuse of not being old enough to know better, just how wrong all of that killing was. But she was nearly eighteen years old when we started. How much of that was due to Youngblood's influence, I couldn't say. There was a part of me that still didn't want to accept the idea that my oldest sister had always been a sociopathic killer at heart.

Further conversation revealed that she'd been aware of Youngblood's existence since 1987, and the newer potion she'd made us all take hadn't been all that chemically different from the one we'd taken before. It was in a different form, solid instead of liquid, but essentially the same thing. She'd even tested it on herself prior to that summer, "curing" herself with each trial. The erratic behavioral side effects that version had caused us were just another experiment to her, brought on by the power of suggestion and the way the potion paired with psychic power to make things happen. The whole thing was, both then and now, essentially one big mindfuck.

Even weirder than that, I was presented with another revelation that made me want to see Elizabeth again just so I could apologize to her and tell her that she'd been right. I'd already been readjusting my thinking this whole time after learning that she hadn't been the one who had killed my parents and led me here; obviously I was staring the true killer in the face as he boasted to me about all of his accomplishments. I felt guilty over how much I'd grown to hate Elizabeth under a mistaken impression, the terrible feelings I'd had towards her. I'd pictured myself fighting and ultimately staking her, thinking that it might somehow make up for the loss.

The thought had run through my head that maybe I could survive this ordeal because I'd taken part in defeating and killing both Dracula and Van Helsing, two of the biggest and baddest figures in vampire history. This Youngblood guy, for all his bluster, might not be such a big deal. But then the rug was ripped out from under me once more.

"You never did put that one together, did you?" Susanna asked, sneering, apparently picking up on my thoughts. "Van Helsing and then Dracula. They weren't real."

"Yes they were!" I shrieked back. How could she even say that? She'd been there and experienced their attacks firsthand.

"Yes, they were," Susanna repeated back to me more calmly, "but not like you think."

What had in fact happened, Youngblood explained, was that he had sent both of those characters to us to do battle with, pretty much as a game. His manipulation of Robert and Jennifer two years earlier had been a precursor to that. In each case, it had been a test to see if we could beat them, and he'd done similar things to previous generations of my family when he was manipulating them. Some had survived, some not. But the ones who did were deemed worthy of "the next step," and I could tell from his cryptic tone when he said that phrase that I would learn the rest of his plan soon enough. For now, though, both he and my sister seemed content with blathering on about their past accomplishments just to humiliate me and show me how clueless I'd been.

"Those two misguided children were easy enough to maneuver around," he said, "but I decided to raise the stakes further on. There never really was a Van Helsing, a real Dracula. They were just characters in a book. But they seemed like worthy foes for your group, and I must say you handled them admirably." His tone was a weird combination of being complimentary and condescending.

"Okay, wait," I said once again, putting my hand up. Everything I was being told this night seemed increasingly unbelievable, and while in some ways I had no choice but to accept it, things were bordering on nonsensical. "You just created this Dracula guy and the other one like... what? Like some enemies in a video game?"

"Nothing so crude," he said. "I couldn't just create them out of whole cloth; even I'm not that powerful."

What he'd done was even more sinister. In both cases, when the time had come, he'd used his powers to transform two unsuspecting men into the people he'd needed to pit against us, first one into Van Helsing and then later another into Dracula. They'd been ordinary people, but he'd worked whatever magic he was capable of to turn them into each of those, right down to the point where even they believed that they were who he'd "rewritten them into," as he put it.

The man that we'd fought and had thought to be Van Helsing, the vampire hunter, saw himself as that character, the one in Bram Stoker's novel, backstory and everything. Whoever he'd been before, those memories had been erased and replaced; even his physiology had been altered. The same was true for Dracula, whom Youngblood crafted into the powerful vampire that we almost didn't beat. It had all been part of the game. I tried not to shudder as I realized just how powerful and god-like this master manipulator truly was.

"And really, Ray?" Susanna asked. "You didn't pick up on just how hokey all that was? The world-famous Dracula comes to stupid, boring Augusta to do battle with... with *you?* That never struck you as just a little bit weird?"

"Shut up," was all I could think to say. I didn't want to admit that she was right, even though the way she was telling it wasn't exactly how it had happened. But she did have a point, not just about that but about everything: There had been something episodic, maybe even cartoonish, about those days. I hadn't noticed it back then, though. I was too young.

The situation had become so dire that I wasn't sure what I could do, and while I felt sorrow, pain, and humiliation over being so obviously outclassed, my defiant nature still wanted to hold its ground. The only defense I had now was one that had served me well when confronting both Van Helsing and my clone: acting like I wasn't intimidated by them. In this case, I was mostly faking it, but it was all I had left.

"Okay, okay," I said, putting both hands up this time and turning away. "I'm just about done with sitting here and listening to you yammer on and on about how powerful and clever you are. I get it. And you know what? I don't give a shit. Why are we all sitting here? What's the point?"

Susanna let out another *"pfft"* sound as she rolled her eyes again. "Such a teenager, isn't he?"

"Yes," Youngblood said, facing her and placing his hand on hers. "But he has potential. Just as you did." She smiled broadly, and it filled me with loathing for both of them.

"You see, Ray," he said, turning his head back to acknowledge me, "this is the point where I have to admit a failing on my part, at least partially."

"Oh, really?"

"Yes, really. What I've tried to do all these years is... well..." He bowed his head, looking genuinely apologetic. "At first it was all about revenge. Revenge on my brother, your ancestor." He looked up again, more determined. "But in time, another desire crept up in me. Jubal, my brother... damn him... He stole my wife. Made her his own. All pious and self-righteous, that one, just as always."

It was my turn to roll my eyes. I didn't want to hear more about some ancient pilgrims — or whatever they were — and their exploits.

Sensing my disdain, Youngblood hardened his voice. "It *matters,*" he said. "The curse I mentioned before, the one that made me like this... For the most part, I embraced it. That was my initial revenge. But I couldn't exact it the way I wanted. They saw to that." I wasn't sure who "they" were, and while I briefly wondered if I'd missed out on some details when I'd stopped paying attention during his earlier monologue, I didn't want to give him the satisfaction of asking for clarification.

"I wanted to kill Mary, the same way I could easily drink from and destroy anyone else. But I couldn't. Despite all of my power, even to this day, there is a limitation that was put in place. I can't harm someone who is a mother. It's just there, a definition, if you like."

At least the unusualness of this piqued my interest. This sinister, almost omnipotent being, for all his arrogant bluster, had a weakness. "How sad for you," I jeered.

He didn't flinch. "As I watched over my 'children,' as I like to call them, the desire had always been to reclaim as many as I could, the ones who were worthy. Those who are, I reward with immortality. Some come to it naturally; others have to be coaxed." With this, he smiled at Susanna again.

"I got there eventually," she almost sang, gazing into his eyes. "Just took me a whi-ile." I kept feeling increasingly disgusted with her; she was reminding me more and more of some of the bimbos I'd known in high school.

"Yes, but you were scared for a while," he said to her in a deeper, comforting tone. "Of course, I could have rewritten you as well, made you love me from the start. But I prefer my consorts to come around on their own. Some of them, anyway."

The two of them shared a laugh, some inside joke. Youngblood faced me again. "There is a certain delight I still get in bringing in the reluctant ones. There are those who touch the evil, then are appalled by it. Or so they tell themselves. There was this priest back in… oh… I forget the year. But it was roughly a hundred-odd years ago. 1870, perhaps? Around there. But oh, what a joy he was. Making him reject his faith and be repelled by the very holy objects he'd held so dear…" As he spoke, he looked up to the ceiling, seeming to forget me and what had once been my sister.

"But he came around as well. It's the pious ones who are the most delightful to wear down. Something about denying one's true nature, then embracing it… Ah, I always love that part of it." He smiled menacingly, his fangs showing for the first time.

I found what he was describing appalling, the idea of turning a holy man against himself like that. I had no great love for Christians given my bad experiences with some of them in the past, but I could at least respect their right to believe in what they wanted to or needed to. But this also made me wonder briefly what might have happened if some of the teachers at my old Baptist school, like Dr. Phillips or Mrs. Manning, had ever been forced to or simply chosen to discard their constraining belief systems. What kind of vampires might they have made? Probably pretty lame ones, honestly.

Getting back to the point, Youngblood revealed that the failing he'd mentioned earlier was in waiting too long in terms of bringing Carolyn to him. She was, according to his original plan, meant to be one of these reluctant vampires, one that he would enjoy wearing down. "Always caught in the middle, that one was," he said wistfully, "never sure of her role. She resented the two of you a great deal, never really taking the adventure to heart. But that's what I was looking forward to, changing all of that. And now it's too late."

"Because she's pregnant," I said, understanding. Then I added with a contemptuous laugh, "You fucked up." The fierce glare he shot me might have scared me otherwise, but at least for this moment, I felt some sense of triumph. He wasn't infallible, and even though Susanna was obviously too far gone for redemption, at least my other sister was safe.

"Still," Youngblood said, brightening slightly, "you're here."

I spread my arms, palms extended. "So? What now? You really think I'm going to join your big incestuous family of killers, and we'll all live happily ever after?" It struck me how the meaning of that last phrase seemed in the current context.

"Do you really think you have a choice?" he countered. I immediately felt smaller, less confident. "This is your destiny, Ray. It always was."

"Oh, don't talk to me about cheesy crap like *destiny,*" I sneered. "Besides, if you wanted a vampire-me to take up residence with you here in your stupid 'Hotel Blood-ifornia,' why didn't you just take my clone in? I'm sure that dumb little shit would have gone for it."

"I told you before. He was just a shadow. A part of you, not all of you. What I need is… how would you call it, the whole enchilada?"

I would never have put it in such a corny manner. The powerful vampire before me, ancient and intimidating, suddenly seemed like a middle-aged man trying to speak like a younger person and making a fool of himself. I started to say so, but I didn't, and I caught a glimpse of Susanna looking uncomfortably off to one side.

"Try to understand, my son," Youngblood continued.

"*Don't* call me that," I said icily. "You're not my father. My father is dead."

"Nevertheless," he said, raising his voice, "you were always meant to be here. I made you who you are, crafted your life and the lives of those around you. It was a long, slow journey, much more complicated than you can comprehend. But you will understand in time." His grave manner of speaking then gave way to his earlier, haughty tone as he added, "Once or twice, I will admit, I did have to intervene directly in order to keep you from figuring things out too early."

"Like when?"

"It's not important," he said dismissively.

It certainly seemed important to me. Had I actually met this asshole before, then been forced to forget about it? Or maybe he meant something else, some kind of telepathic intervention. But when? I looked away, trying to search my memories for anything that might have been a case of what he was indicating. But then I felt a weird surge in my mind, almost like an invisible hand grabbing me by the chin and forcing me to look my tormentor in the eye. It made me dizzy.

The sensation also reminded me of just how powerful this new foe of mine was, and my mind drifted back to an old *Star Trek* rerun I'd seen years earlier. In it, the crew found themselves on a planet ruled by these god-like beings who could completely control them like puppets, making them do humiliating things against their will. A familiar chill returned to me when I began to think that Youngblood might well do the same thing to me. He certainly appeared to be capable.

"Oh, I wouldn't be that crass," he said, hearing my thoughts. "Though I could if I wanted to," he added, narrowing his eyes at me once more and grinning.

"Maybe you should," Susanna cooed evilly. "It might teach him a lesson."

"You could be right, my dear." As he said this, my heart began to race. "But I think the more dignified thing to do would be to stop all of this talk and get to the next step."

I started to ask what that was, but I was scared to, pretty sure that I knew. "Please don't," I said, unexpectedly finding myself wanting to grovel but also trying to appear tough on the outside. It wasn't working. "I can't go back to being that way again." An eerie, tingling sensation began to build up deep within me, that kind of feeling one gets in the doctor's office when you know that something painful is on its way, like a hypodermic needle.

"Oh, but you can," Youngblood said, a predatory look growing in his eyes. "You always could. The potion never really left your system, you know."

"What?" I almost whispered, but then I remembered that he was right. Susanna and I had figured that bit out ourselves shortly before our clones emerged. Because we'd never taken the antidote, the potion was still within us somewhere, lying dormant. I'd just assumed that once my clone manifested, it had sort of taken the potion with it, but now I knew that wasn't true.

Sensing my understanding, Youngblood nodded. "I could simply reactivate it if I chose. But I think you would serve me better as a true vampire this time, not an artificial one. All of that power in you, all of that evil: That's what I'm after."

"I'm not evil," I insisted, more weakly than I would have liked.

"Don't worry," he said, leaning forward in his chair, "it won't hurt. I can turn you into a vampire with a wave of my hand; biting doesn't have to be involved."

I fought back tears, angry with myself for feeling so vulnerable despite my earlier defiance. There really was no way out of this.

"And I suppose, in a way, even though I missed out on bringing Carolyn into the fold, I can still celebrate the fact that I at least found the two of you in one generation. Two psychics, no less. That's a rare find, that many at once who are... compatible. It would have been wonderful if all three of you had come to me willingly, but I knew better than to bank on that. Still, it didn't stop us from trying to... shall we say, encourage you to leave your previous family ties behind."

The image of my murdered parents flashed across my mind, and my fear was shoved aside. "Is that why you killed my mother and father?" I spat out.

"What?" he asked with mock indignity. "Me? Oh, no. You've got it all wrong."

"What the hell are you talking *abou...*" The words died in my throat as my eyes drifted over to Susanna, who had slowly raised her hand like a student in a classroom.

"That was me," she sang, her mouth a sick grin.

I couldn't take any more. With white-hot anger, I leapt up from my chair, feeling it scoot out from under me. "What?" I shouted, staggering backward and bumping into the chair's seat cushion. That irritated me more than it should have, and I kicked behind me fiercely, hearing the chair skid backwards a few feet. "How could you even... Are you fucking kidding me? *You did that!?* "

I wanted her to look guilty, to show some remorse. But instead, she kept looking at me with complete calm and nonchalance, which was even more infuriating. "They were our parents!" I screamed at her.

"They were, yes," she said simply.

My breathing had become fast and harsh, and my entire body felt hot. I couldn't believe that my own sister could do something like this, but then, with everything else I'd seen and been told tonight, I found myself reassessing that opinion. I could picture it, even though I hated to: my mother and father, thinking themselves receiving a normal, possibly unexpected visit from their oldest daughter, who suddenly lunged at them and brutally murdered them. I wasn't sure if I was reading her thoughts and seeing what actually happened or if I was just making it up. It didn't matter either way.

"You psychotic, evil bitch," I hissed, shaking. "When I…"

"When you what, Ray?" she interrupted, slowly standing up from her chair, her elegant gown rustling as she did. She then spread her arms in a mockingly welcoming manner. "Just what is it you're going to do?"

She was right. I had no weapon. I wanted nothing more in the world than to stake her through the heart, to make her pay for everything she'd done, and not just recently, but all this time.

"Ah, sibling rivalry," Youngblood said, still seated. "I remember it well." I started to tell him to fuck off, but then he continued with a single clap of his hands, "But… I suppose fair is fair. Give the young man a fighting chance."

"What are you…" I began, then flinched when I felt something weird happen to my right hand. I looked down, and somehow, I was holding a wooden stake. It had just formed there out of nothing, but there it was, the weapon I needed. I stared at it, dumbfounded.

"Go on, then," Youngblood said to me. I looked back up at him, then at Susanna. She didn't look the least bit afraid.

"Yes, go on," she purred. "Show me what you've got. Come up here and kill me."

I gripped the stake, trying to gauge whether or not I could leap high enough to reach the stage. Would I be strong enough to knock her onto her back? I pictured this, plunging the stake down into her heart, watching her die, the blood spewing from the wound and out of her throat. I couldn't bear it. I couldn't do it. I was a failure.

"Come on, Ray," she taunted. "Don't tell me you've gone all soft on me."

There was only one way this could end, I decided. I lowered the stake, which I'd briefly raised threateningly when I'd been contemplating killing this girl I'd known my entire life. As horrible as she was, I still couldn't bring myself to attack and kill her. "Fine," I said, defeated. "You win."

Susanna broke out into a laugh, that demeaning cackle that only an older sister can deliver. Youngblood laughed as well but more reservedly, and he stood up from his chair, a pleased expression on his face. "Wonderful," he said. "You're ready to truly join us, then?"

"Just get it over with," I said bitterly. At the same time, I tried as subtly and undetectably as I could to put up a telepathic shield around my mind, hoping they wouldn't pick up on my plan.

"You'll feel much better once you've stopped resisting, I promise," Youngblood said, stepping closer.

"Whatever," I said, concentrating and holding the stake firmly. They might get their way and turn me into a blood-drinking monster, but I wasn't going to let them enjoy their victory for long. It wasn't the first time I'd contemplated suicide.

"You know," Susanna said playfully to her master, "I just thought of something. Something that would really get him. You should…" She paused, and I tried not to be unnerved by her ear-to-ear grin as she glanced back at me with a sinister glee. She then leaned in to whisper something into Youngblood's ear.

"Do you think…?" Youngblood said with surprise, and she stepped back. For a few more moments, there was some mental exchange between the two of them, but I couldn't pick up on it, possibly because of my own shield. Then he looked down at me, his smile slowly broadening. "Yes, I can see how that might… Yes. I'd never have thought of that. And I suppose it could make up for the loss of

Carolyn." He turned back to Susanna, saying, "That's why I love you, my child. You're delightfully wicked through and through, and you make me proud."

Susanna beamed at him, and now, my fear was compounded with revulsion. This sick, incestuous thing they had going on turned my stomach, making me hate them more and more. With any luck, I wouldn't have to witness it for much longer. I wasn't sure what this secret plan of theirs was, and in hindsight, I have to say that despite the fact that I was a psychic, I'd always been pretty damn terrible at foreseeing major changes in my life.

As Susanna stood by and watched approvingly, Youngblood made a sweeping motion with his hands, his arms flying out from his chest as he directed his powerful energy towards me. I'd expected something like this, and a strong wind swept through my entire body, causing me to close my eyes as I braced myself against the inevitable. The sensation that followed was very similar to the one I'd felt when taking the vampire potion, though much faster and compressed into just a few seconds. It was all there, the familiar dizziness, pounding of my heart, and the rushing thunder of my pulse in my ears. I even felt my hair whip back as the mystical power slammed through me, and I had to steady myself to keep from staggering backwards. I was vaguely aware of an unexpected sound, a little *clomp* on the floor below me.

The transformation was over, and I steadied myself, bracing mentally as well as physically for the sensations I knew would be forthcoming. I'd always feared this; I'd spent years terrified that somehow, I might wind up as a vampire again. Sometimes I'd dreamed that I had. And I always knew that if it ever did happen, I'd have all those feelings again: the thirst for blood, the enhanced strength, that feeling of invincibility coupled with a lack of conscience or reason to ever feel accountable for my actions... And despite my best efforts, I could feel them all once again. I remembered my very first transformation ten years ago and how I'd reached up to my mouth to touch my fangs, but I refused to do that this time.

But there was more, I realized as I reluctantly opened my eyes. A strange scent seemed to have filled the room, something floral. Something else made me feel disoriented, a little dizzy, like I was standing on my toes, and I felt a tightness around my waist and chest, making it more difficult to breathe. Confused, I frowned, and my face felt somewhat strange. When I looked down, I almost cried out as I saw the changes to my body and clothes, and at the same time, brown ringlets of hair toppled down into both sides of my field of vision.

"What...?" I managed to whisper, completely disbelieving what I was seeing.

"Oh, that's just perfect," Susanna said from the stage, but I was so freaked out that it sounded like she was a thousand miles away. "Well done."

"Glad that you approve," Youngblood responded.

I gripped the sides of my burgundy crushed velvet dress, shocked further by the sight of my small, perfectly manicured hands. I felt around my torso with them in panic, completely disbelieving what I was seeing and feeling. Never in my life had I expected or wanted to look down and see cleavage from this angle.

"What did you *do* to me?" I shrieked, then put a hand to my mouth, further shocked by the high pitch of my voice. And while I knew the answer to my own question, I didn't want to believe it. I pulled my hand away and looked down at it, horrified to see a small mark of dark red lipstick on it.

"See for yourself," Youngblood said, and I sensed something to my right.

I turned, first just my head and then my entire body, almost falling over not just from the sight that greeted me but also the knowledge that I was now wearing high heels. A full-length, wood-framed mirror had materialized, and there I was in it, but completely transformed into what I hated to admit was a very beautiful girl. It didn't even occur to me that, as a vampire, I shouldn't have been visible in a mirror. I was far too stunned by everything else.

I looked myself up and down, my heart breaking as I realized just what had happened to me. It wasn't like I was suddenly in drag, some campy thing like I'd seen in movies or on TV countless times, the joke either being that the guy wasn't believable in his costume, or worse still, he was, tricking other people into thinking that he was really a woman. In those cases, the joke was on them. But this wasn't funny, not in the least.

It might have been less humiliating if I'd just been a boy in a dress, wig, and make-up. Those at least could have been taken off. But that wasn't what this was. I was a girl, head to toe, just as if I'd always been one, born and raised that way. I even had real breasts that I briefly found myself unable to keep from ogling, maybe because I was still at least mentally male. But the fact that they were mine — attached to my own chest and framed perfectly in this dress I found myself wearing — freaked me the hell out and made me want to scream that all of this wasn't possible.

"Why…?" I tried to ask, still hating how high and helpless my voice sounded. I then started to cry, my body shuddering uncontrollably. The feelings of fragility and vulnerability that crept over me were overwhelming. I felt small, like a plaything.

"Aw, stop that," Susanna said, feigning comfort. "Your mascara will run."

"Don't be so cruel," Youngblood said to her, and surprisingly, it sounded like he meant it.

"Please…" I said, clutching at my newly transformed body beneath its impossibly created new clothes. "Just change me back. I'll be a vampire. I'll do anything you want. Just don't make me be like this." I glanced back at the mirror, immediately regretting doing so. The drop-dead gorgeous girl in the mirror now had a pitiful grimace, like some overly done-up beauty queen who had just lost out in the Miss America pageant.

The two of them continued to look down at me, their expressions becoming disapproving. "This is kind of fun, but it isn't really working," Susanna said with a frown.

"I agree," Youngblood said with a nod.

I then remembered my original plan. I was supposed to let Youngblood magically turn me into a vampire like he said he would, but then, I'd plunge the wooden stake into my heart, robbing them of their victory. But where was the stake? Somehow, it had disappeared during my transformation. That wasn't the only long, protruding thing that had vanished, I realized, and my resolve crumbled even further. I'd been tempted earlier to check with my hand to confirm this, but I'd stopped myself, afraid of what I knew I'd find between my legs.

Susanna and Youngblood were now facing each other, seemingly ignoring me while I suffered. "So are you going to…?" she asked him.

"Yes," he said. "Very well, then. Further rewriting." He waved his hands again.

Another rush of wind surged through me, and unexpectedly, I was grateful for it. I stopped feeling so anxious, crippled with fear over what had been happening to me. I knew that it was manufactured, but I couldn't deny the calm that I'd begun to feel. Even so, something deep within me fought back, insisting that this warm, fuzzy feeling wasn't right. I was supposed to be resisting this.

Then I let go. I thought about who I was, who I'd been, and all of a sudden, that didn't matter. It was like my memories were books on the shelves of a library, and I could see their pages fluttering as they were swept away, flying off like birds into some white, glaring doorway. There was something simultaneously heartbreaking and liberating about it. And then, in this vision, new books appeared and slotted themselves onto the shelves.

I returned to reality as the feeling of the cool breeze faded. Disoriented, I'd forgotten where I was, but the memories began to come back. High above on the small stage, there sat my master, the most attractive man I'd ever lain eyes on. He smiled at me, and there was that familiar flutter in my heart, the one I always got when he did that. I loved him more than anything.

"Hello, Renee," he said, his voice deep and resonating in my ears like a song. I'd always loved the sound of it; something about its strength made me feel warm, protected.

I'd also always liked the name Renee. Growing up, not until high school anyway, no one else I'd met had the same name, so that made me feel special. For a while, when I was a little girl and first learned what the name meant, I would introduce myself to people by saying, "Hi, my name is Renee. It means 'reborn.'" I stopped doing that once I realized how pretentious and obnoxious it was.

Seated next to my master was Susanna, whom I'd had a love/ hate relationship with my entire life. Sometimes she could be a condescending bitch, but I still looked up to her — at the moment, quite literally. She leaned forward in her chair, smiling at me as she said, "Welcome back, baby sister."

CHAPTER THIRTY

Susanna hadn't called me "baby sister" for many years. When we were much younger, I'd been fine with it, but after a while, it got on my nerves. While once a term of endearment, it eventually became a way for her to belittle me, saying that I was lesser than her. She still trotted out the term occasionally to get to me, but I'd learned to pretend that I didn't care. I started to reflect on our relationship more, but for the moment, I was having a hard time remembering what the three of us had been talking about. My chair, the empty one to Youngblood's left, was up there, so what was I doing down here on the ballroom floor?

"Are you okay?" Susanna asked me.

"Yes, I'm…" I put a hand to my forehead, then brushed a stray lock of hair from it. "What were we…?" I really couldn't remember.

"You've been through a great deal, Renee," Youngblood said to me. "I think it's time you had something to eat. You'll feel better after that."

"I… Yes." It wasn't like I could ever argue with that man. Psychic or not, there was just something about his confidence and certainty that always made whatever he said sound convincing. It was one of the many things I admired about him.

"You remember your way to the wine cellar?" he asked me, though it was more of a statement. For a second, I didn't know what he was talking about, but then it came back to me, both the place he had mentioned and how to get there.

I giggled playfully, giving him a smile. Calling it "the wine cellar" was just his little joke; what he was really talking about was the large room underneath the hotel where the human prisoners were kept, the ones we had collected to feast on later. Often, these were unwary hikers who accidentally found their way to the hotel, despite the spell that made it invisible to human eyes from far away. I could remember being down there recently — was it yesterday? Or maybe last week? I couldn't recall — and picking out a particularly delicious looking young man that I would delight in drinking from the next time I was in the mood.

"Off you go, then, my dear," he said, and I gave him a cute curtsey, then turned to go. I wasn't sure why both he and my sister looked so pleased with themselves, but the thought of drinking the hot, salty blood of my next victim was enough to keep me distracted.

I made my way through the hotel, slinking along and feeling both hungry and aroused. I pictured myself with the man chained up in the basement, toying with him before sinking my teeth into his neck. Maybe I'd even go so far as to make him think that I was setting him free at first, giving him a little something to hope for. *We'll run away together, just you and me...* I'd say seductively, pretending I loved him. Men were always easy to manipulate, especially for someone as pretty as me.

I wasn't sure why, but the rest of the vampires in the hotel kept giving me strange looks as I passed by them. I was used to being looked at, but even so, I couldn't figure out why some of them seemed surprised or even amused. I'd been here for... How long had it been? I began to feel disoriented again, my mind playing tricks on me. Part of me wanted to say that I'd only just arrived, but a conflicting memory made it seem like I'd lived here for years. It didn't make sense.

I caught a glimpse of Erica from far away, that stuck-up bitch. I'd always hated her; I didn't know why the master kept her around. She reminded me of Susanna, or at least the things about my big sister that I didn't like. When we were younger, the nine-year difference in our ages had meant that Susanna was this sort of unreachable authority figure, not someone I could relate to at all. I admired her, but she didn't seem to want me around once I got to age six or so. I didn't know if she was jealous of me or what.

People, once they found out that I was "the baby of the family," always assumed that meant that I'd been spoiled, a proper little princess and all that. But no, that wasn't how it went. Susanna was Dad's perfect little angel, or so he thought, the one who always got the best of everything. That was one thing that Carolyn and I bonded over, our resentment of her. But even she, the middle sister, seemed to have it better than I did. By the time I came along, our parents had spent most of their inheritance on them, so I was left with almost nothing.

Hand-me-downs weren't an option when it came to Susanna's clothes; anything she'd worn when she was my age was embarrassingly out of date. I wouldn't be caught dead in some of that "groovy" '70s crap she'd worn. Some of Carolyn's old clothes were okay, but I still resented the fact that I often wouldn't get nice, new things bought for me. Then of course there were the times, once I was old enough to where she and I were more or less the same size, when she and I would get into screaming fights over how I'd borrow her clothes or make-up without asking.

Whatever, I said to myself as I recalled this. *I was always the prettier one anyway.* And that had been true, which always struck me as a little weird given that Susanna and I had our father's features, the brown hair and brown eyes, while Carolyn took after our blonde mother. Too bad for her, the ugly duckling of the family. Was it cruel of me to think that? Probably.

But maybe I was feeling hatred toward Carolyn because of recent events, I pondered as I continued to make my way downstairs, lost in my thoughts and ignoring the stares of the other vampires around me. Because she'd gone and gotten herself knocked up and married to some pious Bible-beating jerk, she'd screwed up Master Youngblood's plan. It was supposed to be all three of us coming here and being his brides. If she wanted to, as some comedian I could vaguely recall had put it, become a fat-ass baby factory and pop one out every nine months, that was her problem.

In fact, it occurred to me that just because our master couldn't harm her, I still could. Maybe I would do that soon, one final payback. Then I began to wonder which would be better, to go ahead and kill her while she was pregnant, or should I wait until after the child was born? I'd never had baby blood before. Or had I? If I had, I couldn't remember. I really did need to get something… *someone* to eat. I was feeling way too distracted.

So now that Carolyn had messed up the plan, it was going to be just me and Susanna here. We got to be the ones who lived forever, side by side with our gorgeous master. And that was fine. Carolyn could die. Really, the older I'd gotten, the more I'd grown to like Susanna. When I'd been little, she and I hadn't had much in common. But later, when she was home from college on one of her visits, we'd stayed up really late one night talking in her old bedroom about how upset I was over being dumped by my first boyfriend. She'd given me lots of good advice on how to move on, and I'd always appreciated her for that. We'd become a lot closer then.

But… Wait. That conflicted with something else about her that I could recall, how she'd been distant and aloof once she'd gone off to college, especially during her later years there. Like how I could barely get her to talk to me sometimes. The two memories were there, side by side, but they didn't make sense together. Had we been close or not?

This apparent conflict occurred to me right before I passed by a mirror in one of the hallways, one that was above a small shelf on the wall, flowers adorning it. These were placed evenly throughout the halls on each floor, one every five doors or so. Just decoration, really. As I caught sight of myself, I paused. We were lucky to be the kinds of vampires who could actually see our own reflections.

I really was pretty, I knew, though admitting that felt rather conceited. But what the hell; it was deserved, even if I didn't quite measure up to Susanna. I preened in the mirror, but something at the back of my mind was bugging me, telling me that this was wrong. It wasn't just guilt over being full of myself; there was some kind of resentment in there, something to do with my oldest sister. I had some vague memory of screaming at her, fighting about something, but what was it? Why was I having so much trouble remembering things?

The memory of our recent mission surfaced, how we'd been sent by the master to kill our mother and father back at the house in Augusta. I felt pride in that, how we'd caught them unexpectedly and ended their lives so easily. It was a loose end, Youngblood had told us, one that needed to be taken care of. They deserved to die. Didn't they? Why were tears welling up in my eyes?

Stop that, I said to myself, leaning closer to the mirror and carefully dabbing the tears away from my eyes, not wanting to mess up my make-up. I did so successfully, but something was still gnawing at me. I found myself gazing deep into the mirror, focusing on one eye. There was something in there, deep within that black pupil, the surrounding iris that looked like a brown flower with green behind it…

I felt dizzy, and something made me jump back from the mirror. I shook my head quickly, trying to clear it. *Keep going,* a voice in my head said. I did, making my way down the hall. Just two more floors to go, and I'd finally be at the wine cellar, my beautiful victim waiting for me. Drinking him would be so much fun. I'd missed drinking blood.

But then, how could I have missed it? I'd been a vampire for years. That was what my memory was telling me now. I'd been such a powerful vampire, able to kill whoever I wanted whenever I chose to. I'd always loved that. No one could resist me; I was unstoppable. Soon, I was going to kill Carolyn, too, for daring to defy my master's wishes.

I avoided looking at the next mirror I passed, finding my way to the next stairwell at the end of the hall. It then occurred to me that I was taking a longer route than necessary; I should have just gone down the stairs all at once, not wasted time traversing each floor the long way around. Why was I doing that? It was like I was stalling, not wanting to get to where I needed to be in order to drink the blood of that delicious, waiting victim.

And yet here I was doing it again, down on another floor, wanting to walk the full length of the hallway to prolong the journey. What was I doing? What was wrong with me? I stopped and looked at myself in another mirror, something in me desperate to figure things out.

There she was again, the beautiful girl in the mirror. Why did that seem wrong? I flashed a practiced smile, thinking that might give me more confidence. But it didn't work. I felt like a fraud. Was I really not as pretty as I'd always believed? Was I just some despicable, horrible monster? I tried to tell myself that I was being ridiculous. This is just something that all girls go through. We're always told by magazines and other people that we're not good enough. We should be skinnier, prettier, better…

I screwed my eyes shut, not wanting to see the dolled up monstrosity in the mirror anymore. Then I opened them up again, hating what I saw. *You could have eased up on the foundation a bit…* I started to say to myself, intending to end the sentence with my name. But then I suddenly felt terrified when I couldn't even remember it. *What's my name? What's my name? Something beginning with 'R…'*

Raychel, I concluded. Yes, that was right. I'd always liked how it was spelled differently than most girls with that name, though still pronounced the same. *Raychel Elizabeth... Young?* That didn't seem right, especially the middle name. *No, no, no, Elizabeth was somebody else. That girl you knew in junior high. My middle name is...* I struggled to remember. I was also distracted by the memory of that girl I'd thought of, but I couldn't understand why. She'd been really pretty. Had I even liked her or hated her?

Adrienne, I remembered. That was my middle name. *Raychel Adrienne Young... Blood?*

I slammed my fists down onto the shelf below the mirror, frustrated with myself to the point where I just wanted to break down and cry. What was wrong with my mind? Why couldn't I remember who I was? I was starting to panic, my breath quickening through clenched teeth. I was torn between two equally compelling impulses: One was to hurry the rest of the way down to the basement to make a meal of that man, the other to run back upstairs to my master for comfort.

I pictured him, and I realized that I was doing so psychically, not just in my imagination. Or maybe those two were the same thing. Regardless, he looked concerned, unhappy about something. This made me sad, but at the same time, there was a part of me that felt an evil sort of glee because of it. Why did I like seeing my master so disconcerted? I was supposed to be loyal to him, through and through. And I was, wasn't I?

How clearly I saw him in my mind seemed pretty cool, too. It wasn't some vague impression; it was almost like my mind had become a camera, and I was seeing what was happening on that upper floor in real time. I could even feel his thoughts, plus those of my sister seated next to him.

Another memory surfaced, something Dennis had said to me when we were young. "When we get to about eighteen, maybe twenty, our powers are going to be *awesome.*" It was something I hadn't thought about for years, but the gist of it was that the psychic powers we had, which in those days were in their infancy, would eventually grow to the point where we would have superhero-like abilities and could do amazing things.

At the time, I'd dismissed his prediction as fantasy, but things did almost get to that level a couple of years later when we'd been under the influence of the vampire potion. I'd become extremely powerful, even dangerously so. But something about that memory felt wrong. It felt too… I don't know… "guy-ish." And how come all of my friends back then had been boys? Had I been some kind of a preteen slut? That didn't feel right, either.

Along with this confusion, something in my mind seemed to be inching forward, like a figure creeping out of the darkness. It was important, but I was terrified of it. Or rather, I knew I should be. I looked down at my dress again, finding myself focusing on the way the velvet caught the light from the hallway lamps in little shimmers. Something about concentrating on that made me feel a little better, sort of comfortably distracted. For the moment, I didn't feel like I was cracking up.

It wasn't as nice of a dress as Susanna's, but then, was that really a surprise? She always got the prettier stuff, got more admiration, got more boys. At least I hadn't been some cheerleading attention whore. My style had been more alternative; I'd even gone through a punk phase. I liked to think that I still had some of that, and I really was the cooler of the two sisters. There was black lace lining my sleeves, hem, and neckline. The corset I wore underneath wasn't the most comfortable thing in the world, but I had to admit that I liked the way it slimmed my waist, to say nothing of making my boobs look fantastic.

I giggled at this thought, eyeing them in my reflection. It felt immature, even naughty. Why was I so fascinated by my own breasts? What was I, some thirteen-year-old boy?

Creeping forward… closer…

No. I was a girl, and a damn sexy one at that. I was also a vampire, a killer, powerful and irresistible. I was going to stop all this nonsense and get my hot little ass down to the basement and drink every drop of that guy. I might even use my mental powers to fuck with his mind some beforehand. I'd always been good at that. And then I'd go kill my sister, the same way Susanna and I had murdered our parents.

Closer…

I tried to ignore the increasing tension I felt. What was making me act so crazy? Had killing my mother and father been too much of a shock for me? Why did I feel conflicting emotions of pride and anger over that? I should have been glad that they were gone. But something inside of me just wanted to scream.

I balled up my fists and held them up to the sides of my head, and while I didn't actually scream aloud, I did inside, and a telekinetic wave shot out from me. The mirror in front of me shattered just as if I had punched it, shards floating to the floor in slow motion. There was something almost clichéd about it, like an effect I might see in a music video. And then, as if I'd hit the rewind button on a VCR, the shimmering glass floated back up and into place, restoring the mirror as if nothing had happened.

"Our powers are going to be awesome." Dennis hadn't been wrong. Too bad he didn't live long enough to see it. How had he died again?

Remember…

I didn't want to think about it. Something about it was too painful. Had I killed him? Or someone very much like me… What did that even mean?

Almost there…

I stomped a foot down in determination, angry with myself. "Stop this right now and get down there," I heard myself saying, but it almost felt like the words had been given to me, like lines in a play. There was a familiar twinge in my forehead, a tingle that I could almost…

I am me…

What was it about that feeling? I remembered it. But my mind was such a jumble that I couldn't focus. I was supposed to be going downstairs… Something about a man… And there was another man upstairs, so beautiful…

These are not my thoughts…

I shuddered as I fought against all of the conflicting feelings. My hands slid down either side of my dress, feeling the smooth, textured fabric.

This is not my body…

I just wanted to get myself under control and stop fighting… I was a vampire… always had been… powerfully psychic… The master had made it so…

And you CAN'T… CONTROL…

"ME!" I shouted, and my powers flared up in a colossal burst of energy. My eyes filled with a bright green glow, and I could feel that it wasn't just that; my entire body was engulfed in the glare, and another rush of wind blew through me, my form changing once more, but on my terms this time.

I didn't even need to look in the mirror to know that I was back to being my male self. I could feel it; I knew who I was. Not Renee, not Raychel, not some puppet or plaything of Youngblood's. Ray. I was still a vampire, and I was more powerful than I'd ever been in my life.

I'd arrived back at the ballroom in just a few seconds, having transformed into a bat for the first time in years. I remembered everything that had happened to me, both the truth and the lies that Youngblood had implanted in me, and I felt a righteous anger unlike any I'd known before. The sick bastard had violated me in the most humiliating way he could, and I was going to make him pay for that and for everything else he'd done.

This new level of power I felt within me was amazing, and while I had a sense that the other vampires in the hotel might try to stop me, they barely even registered in my field of vision as I zoomed past them at what felt like warp speed, changing into my person form just before reaching the tall doors of the ballroom. I wrenched them both open with superhuman strength, almost breaking them off their hinges.

As I stomped forward across the gigantic room, I effortlessly used my clairvoyance to find my wooden stake, the one that had been lost to me in the tunnel. With a thought, I teleported it into my right hand, not even bothering to look down to see if it was there. I could feel it, and I absently rubbed my thumb along the back of it, feeling the plastic lid of the chamber of garlic powder.

These weren't abilities I'd had before, at least, not at this level. But Youngblood had made a grave mistake in turning me into a vampire and leaving my powers in place: The two things had complemented each other, causing my psychic prowess to increase exponentially.

He and Susanna, along with the vacant chair meant for me, sat motionless on the stage as I approached. This didn't surprise me, but I would have liked it if they'd looked mildly afraid or at least a little bit surprised. But I figured that they must have already known what had happened to me, having seen it clairvoyantly. They did their best to look unimpressed, but with my newly heightened sense of awareness, I could tell that, underneath, they were beginning to feel uncomfortable. This hadn't been in their plan.

"Welcome back, my son," Youngblood said, that same shit-eating grin plastered across his face.

"I told you not to call me that," I said firmly, not slowing my approach.

"But you are!" he insisted, putting his hand up. I felt myself stop in my tracks. It wasn't out of fear, but I was compelled to do it nonetheless. "You may have managed to resist some of my influence, I'll admit, and that's very impressive. And yet still, here you are, a vampire."

"Because I choose to be," I said, realizing the truth of the words as I spoke them. It wasn't just that my psychic abilities had gotten an upgrade, so to speak. My mind felt more focused and clear, a wisdom present that hadn't been there before. It occurred to me that it was also the lingering potion within that had given me the ability to alter my reality, just as it had always done. When I'd taken control of myself and my thoughts earlier, I could have turned myself back into a human, but I didn't. My previous self might have berated me for that choice, but here in this moment, I knew that I'd done the right thing. Only in this form could I defeat this horrible monster who had systematically plagued me and my family for so long.

"Not because you want me to," I continued, "not because Elizabeth wanted me to, and not because Susanna manipulated me to."

"Good for you," Susanna said sarcastically, clapping her hands slowly and with contempt.

"Oh, go do a cheer," I spat, and I waved a hand at her. I'd meant to do so dismissively, but I felt an unexpected rush of power go out of me, and all of a sudden, Susanna looked completely different.

She'd been sitting there in her ornate chair, looking at me smugly, but then it was like a quick breeze blew over her, and instead of being the haughty bitch in her long black gown looking down at me, she quickly jumped up, wearing a Westlake High School cheerleader's uniform. She bent her elbows and put her fists on her hips, then shouted, "Ready! Oh! Kay!"

She wasn't a vampire anymore; I could tell that immediately. She was an ordinary human girl, the one I'd remembered from when I was a little boy. Seemingly unaware of both me and Youngblood, she looked out from the stage with a fake, professional smile, then began to move her arms and legs in practiced moves as she rhythmically chanted:

"Talking about that Westlake spirit
That knocks… me… out!
What's that spirit I'm talking about?
That Westlake spirit just knocks… me… out!"

I realized what I'd done. Unintentionally, maybe because I'd subconsciously been struggling with trying to understand how Susanna had turned out to be such an evil person and never really was who I'd thought she'd been, I'd rewritten her the same way Youngblood had done to me. This vacant, wide-eyed bimbo in her red, white, and blue cheerleader uniform was what I'd mistakenly remembered Susanna to be.

"Well then," Youngblood said, standing up from his chair. "That's unfortunate."

Before I could do anything to stop him, he moved over to Susanna and grabbed her, ignoring her surprised and helpless little yelp as he sank his teeth into her neck. I screamed a pointless *"NO!!!!"* as he drained her instantly, stepping forward with my stake raised before I quickly gave up; it was too late. I stood there seething, hating him even more when he callously threw my sister's body off to one side, letting it land on the stage with a loud, echoing *thump.*

He wiped his mouth, turning to face me with a malevolent glare. "At least she tasted good," he said with a vicious snarl.

I screamed at him in rage, running forward. He swept his arm outward, and I found myself propelled backwards by a telekinetic force. I skidded on my back across the ballroom floor, stopping after a few feet and recovering. It hurt, but I stood up again, determined to kill my foe.

"What do you think you're going to do?" he taunted. "Aren't you forgetting something? Namely, who it was that made you what you are now?"

"And, what, you want me to be grateful?"

"No, but there is the small matter of… What did you call it? The 'thread.' Even if you could manage to kill me, you know what would happen to you then."

He had a point, and my first thought was to say something along the lines of not caring what happened to me; my death would be worth it if it meant getting rid of him. That would have been noble of me, but then it dawned on me that it wasn't even necessary.

"Oh, you mean this old thing?" I asked snidely, and as I envisioned the imaginary thread that linked us, it became visible, a whitish beam of transparent light. It connected us both at the chest, drooping along its middle, and I realized that it was something like a psychic umbilical cord. I waved a hand across my chest, knowing that the gesture wasn't even needed; it was more for theatrical effect. The thread severed and floated away from me, breaking into fragments before disappearing completely.

Youngblood tried to hide his surprise and anger, but then he leapt down from the stage, his expression eager and malevolent. "Very well then," he said, slowly stepping forward. "I haven't had to fight anyone for a long time. Please, indulge me."

His confidence was evident, but I still felt that I stood a chance of beating him. Even if I couldn't, I was going to give him one hell of a fight. I was reeling from the loss of Susanna; seeing her killed like that was a huge shock. But that only made me more determined.

I'd dropped my stake earlier when I fell, but I saw it on the floor nearby. With a simple thought, I made it fly through the air and into my hand. I held it high, daring Youngblood to come closer. He stopped, but it didn't appear to be out of fear.

"Bad move," he said slyly, then made a quick movement with his hand.

The plastic cap on the back of my stake popped off on its own, and the garlic powder inside flew out in a cloud that burned my skin as it touched me. I screamed in pain, dropping the stake and staggering backward. He then began to walk toward me once more.

I recovered, and instead of making the stake fly back into my hand again, this time I slung it at Youngblood, aiming for his chest. It zoomed toward him like an arrow, but just as it reached its mark, he used his own power to make it disappear into nothingness. I knew this on some intuitive level; he hadn't just teleported it away. He'd actually been able to disintegrate it.

"That was *mine!*" I shouted, angry at the loss of my prized weapon. The anger manifested in another psychokinetic burst, and I hurled him back from me, making him fly through the air. At first, he seemed helpless, but then he righted himself in midair, floating gently to the floor and facing me triumphantly.

Fine, then how about this, I thought, glancing up at the ceiling. With another thought, I wrenched one of the chandeliers from its base and sent it flying down towards him. It crashed to the floor, Youngblood having teleported himself out of the way and materializing several yards off to one side. He returned the favor by slinging one of the nearby statues at me, and I repeated his move, teleporting myself to safety and reappearing elsewhere.

"You're a quick study," he said, looking more pleased than I expected.

"And you're a prick," I shot back, trying to think of what to attempt next. It shouldn't have made sense that my powers were equally matched to his; he was well over two centuries old, and I was just a kid in comparison. But it was like I'd reached a threshold, and the more he revealed to me was actually possible, the fewer limitations there were within myself. I had less experience and control over my powers, though, which was evident given how I'd accidentally rewritten Susanna and gotten her killed.

The battle continued on in a similarly surreal fashion for quite a long time, each of us trying to outdo the other, neither of us succeeding. Hurling furniture at each other proved pointless; we could easily deflect it, shatter it into fragments, or make it disappear altogether. I found that I could make objects burst into flame and tried slinging those at him, hoping that they would ignite him, but that didn't work either. He then made a huge burst of fire appear out of nowhere and rain down on me, but I was able to throw up a dome-shaped shield that protected me until he gave up.

I tried to recall every epic fight I'd seen in sci-fi and fantasy movies, TV shows, and even cartoons, lifting tactics and adapting them for my own purposes. I shot bursts of energy at my foe, first as beams from my eyes, then as lightning-like bolts from my hands, complete with the requisite sound effects. Youngblood returned the assaults in kind, and I dodged his rapid-fire retaliations with a speed I hadn't even known I was capable of.

It even got downright silly at one point: I was fleeing an attack of fireballs from him that scorched the walls and bits of furniture that I skidded past, and I pictured myself as a hero in an action movie, complete with fast-paced, hard rock music. His assault ended, and I imagined a power chord accompanying me as I steadied myself and stared him down, ready to fight back once again.

"Oh, is that your theme tune?" Youngblood asked with a sneer, and I realized that I hadn't just been imagining the music: It had actually been playing, my mind somehow making it manifest in real life.

I briefly felt embarrassed, but I hardened my resolve and simply said, "Yes. Here." With that, I basically threw a huge cacophony of jarring electric guitar music at him, like a sonic shockwave that I concentrated at his head. He crumbled momentarily, seeming disoriented, and I thought I had finally gained an edge. He might have even gone deaf. But then he stood up and seemed to shake off the effects, back to his regular self.

His response was to attack me with a blinding flash of light, literally, in fact. I couldn't see, and I panicked briefly, afraid that he might manage to overtake me in my current state. But all I had to do was calm myself and think, *No, I'm not blind,* and that was it. I was restored.

"You're much more powerful than you should be," Youngblood said, breathing heavily from all of the exertion. I'd been doing the same.

"Sorry," I said, not meaning it in the least.

"Oh, don't be," he leered. "This has been fun. I see now that I should have focused on you a lot more, rather than your sisters."

"Don't you even mention them, you worthless waste of existence," I said, stepping closer to him.

He waved a hand dismissively, displaying that same superior attitude he'd had all along. I hated him with every fiber of my being. He may have been pulling the strings behind the scenes the whole time, but I still couldn't shake the notion that, at least as far as I was concerned, he'd suddenly popped up out of nowhere. Chronologically, at least in my life, he was an anomaly.

Our battle resumed, but the stalemate dragged on. Between blows — an energy bolt here, a telekinetic shove there, all of which would either have no effect or quickly be recovered from — I began feeling distracted. I found myself thinking about everything he'd done, wondering what he'd hoped to achieve. What would my family's life have been like if he'd never interfered? How normal might we have been? Would it have been boring? Could it have been nice and peaceful? My parents might still be alive, all three of their children growing up and becoming parents themselves, continuing on the Young line undisturbed. Instead, this loathsome monster consumed with revenge had fucked everything up, and here I was, facing him down.

What happened next took less than a second, and had I been just a little bit too slow in thinking of it, I might have been the one to lose. But the solution was so simple, and it occurred to me just in time. I had the same power that Youngblood did. Every seemingly impossible thing he'd shown me this night had proven that to me.

Once I realized this, Youngblood looked at me with a combination of shock and sadness, saying, "That's..."

I often wonder to this day what the rest of that sentence might have been, what he was going to say. But he never got the chance. I wished, or rather insisted, that Youngblood simply did not exist. It was like being in a dream and taking control, or like being the director of a play, where I could cut an actor's lines or even eliminate his entire role. And that's exactly what I did.

He was gone in the blink of an eye, and I made it happen.

I found my way out of the ballroom and into the rest of the hotel, both of which had been plunged into darkness. That wasn't a problem for me given that, as a vampire, I could see in the dark. But the entire place was in chaos; I could hear the screams of dying vampires all around me, both audibly and psychically. With Youngblood gone, the power that sustained this place had disappeared, including the electricity. That made sense, I realized; it wasn't like he would have been paying a monthly power bill or anything. The hotel wouldn't have been able to be so anonymous and hidden otherwise.

The vampires were dying because of the thread phenomenon. I'd killed their master, so they were crumbling away, but oddly enough, only some of them were, not all. I walked down to the lower floors, finding them and the hallways littered with decayed corpses and sometimes just piles of clothes and dust, the remnants of the vampires whom Youngblood had made all these years. At first, I felt a sense of satisfaction, but all of those screams I'd heard — and felt — gave me pause.

I then remembered what both Mirela and Youngblood had told me: Not all of the vampires here were of Youngblood's making. So they hadn't died. They were the ones I kept hearing, running around and screaming, terrified over how over three quarters of their colleagues had suddenly dropped dead or turned to dust before them. It was an apocalypse, one of my making.

It was tempting to just finish everyone off; I could have done it. I could have even blown this entire hotel to smithereens if I'd wanted to, taking myself with it. That thought occurred to me just before I found myself facing Mirela at the end of the second floor hallway, arms folded and looking at me sternly.

I assumed I was going to have another fight on my hands, but she just stepped towards me slowly, dropping her arms by her sides as she did so. "What have you done?" she asked me, but something in her tone indicated that she already knew. I sensed fear from her, and that gave me some confidence. I really shouldn't have found her threatening anyway; I could have wished her out of existence just as easily as I'd done to her master.

"What I had to do," I said, but the statement carried less gravity than I meant for it to. Something about this woman made me feel less powerful, like she demanded respect.

She frowned, stopping once she stood directly in front of me. "I'm not even going to ask how," she said emphatically. "Obviously, you turned out to be stronger than… well, than *he* expected."

"Yes, I did," I said, again feeling a sense of accomplishment, but something in her eyes made me feel less arrogant.

"So now," she said, gesturing with her hand as she looked around, "I expect you'll do something to clear up this mess?"

The cleaning up took a few days, and I soon settled into my role as the new "king of the castle." At Mirela's urging, my first act had been to magically restore power to the hotel, plus I had to reinstate the spell that kept the place hidden from prying eyes. As it turned out, it was her guidance that helped me quite a lot; she'd been here for ages, and while I'd sensed resentment from her early on, we'd quickly warmed to each other. I may have stumbled into the responsibility of taking over from Youngblood even though I was just an eighteen-year-old usurper, but she seemed to both acknowledge and accept that.

She filled in for me some of the gaps in Youngblood's backstory, telling me about the scandal that had deposed him from his position in that old church years ago. Aside from the fact that he'd been a heavy drinker, there had been a slave girl that he'd gotten pregnant, and he'd sent her away to try to cover it up. After she'd had her baby, she'd come back to confront him, and he'd wound up murdering her. An investigation ended up in his being disgraced, his excommunication, and the subsequent curse by the dead girl's family that turned him into a vampire. That had been what started all of this.

Apparently, he'd confided in Mirela about this at one point, and I got the sense from her that Youngblood tended to flit around in terms of the women he got close to, including her. His affection for Susanna probably would have faded after a decade, she'd said, and she wouldn't have been his consort for long.

"He would have gotten tired of her," Mirela said, her jealousy unconcealed. "We were all his 'queens' at some point."

"Tell me about it," I joked.

She smirked at me, and I told her a little more about what Youngblood and Susanna had done to me that night. I could understand some of her feelings for him, too, having briefly been a girl myself. "Don't tell Elizabeth about that when she gets here, though," I insisted, feeling nervous for the first time in a while.

Her smile became broader, more affectionate. "Oh, you'll tell her yourself, eventually. Don't be embarrassed. There shouldn't be any secrets among our kind."

I nodded. "I suppose you're right. But..." I'd picked up on something she'd been thinking. "You're not going to stay?"

"I'll stay here to greet her, if you like," she said with some deference. "But I think it's best that I move on, at least for now. Like the others. I'd like to see the old country again, the place I came from."

I'd offered the vampires who had survived my arrival and replacement of Youngblood the choice to stay or leave. Some had resented me; others welcomed me as the new master. These revelations had come about during the feast I'd arranged of the remaining humans in the basement of the hotel. The blood had been delicious, but the rejection by those who had chosen to leave left me feeling disappointed. But I'd kept my pride in check and respected their choices, resisting the urge to wipe them from existence, which I was perfectly capable of doing. I may have become nearly omnipotent, but I didn't want to be a jerk. They hadn't been the ones who had done all of those things to me and my family.

"You're always welcome here," I said to Mirela, "if you want to come back."

"I know," she said to me sweetly, standing up from her chair and leaning over to kiss my cheek. She then glanced back at the drained corpse of the woman spread out on the small table that had been between us. "I'm sure I will."

It surprised me how quickly I accepted my new life, especially given how I'd railed against the idea of becoming a vampire again for so long. But now that it was upon me, I felt differently about the whole thing. Elizabeth and Mirela had both shown me that one didn't have to be a heartless monster just because they were a vampire. Yes, there was the killing, but it wasn't just for fun. It served a purpose; it had a significance.

What's more, my life now had a definite purpose. It turned out that my branch of the family and all that had gone on in Augusta hadn't been the only project that Youngblood had been working on. There were other cities, other descendants, all around the country. They'd been experiments to him, seeing which relatives could manage to become the best and most effective vampires. If it had been a contest, I'd say that my family had won, for what it was worth. But those other ones were out there, and it was up to me to take care of them, either by cutting the experiments mercifully short or by bringing them to their proper conclusions. Perhaps some of those vampires would eventually be led here by me as well.

I didn't like the way I'd had to abandon Carolyn with no explanation and leave her behind to pick up the pieces of what was left of our family. She was basically it, left to continue the line on her own. I could only hope that she and her husband would be more involved in their children's lives than our parents were; they'd always been too hands-off. Maybe that had been part of the problem all along. At any rate, she had her new family to take care of, as did I.

With my newfound extraordinary power, I probably could have brought Susanna back to life. But what would have been the point? I'd never really known her; she wasn't the person I'd thought she was. She'd been full of more evil and hate than I'd ever imagined, certainly more than I ever was. And sure, maybe I had quite a bit of evil in me as well, but I liked to believe that I was at least more balanced. Maybe that's all anyone can ever hope for.

I now knew that it did me no good to either forget or deny my past. And because of the way I was able to repair my memory after what Youngblood tried to do to me, I could remember everything, maybe even too well. Every detail, every kill, every lie ever told, even the times he'd psychically stepped in and altered my perception of what was happening back then: It was all there. Had he made me into a monster, or was I always capable of that on my own? Maybe it didn't matter.

All of the things I'd done, both as a vampire and as a human, were a part of me. The important thing was to maintain control of myself and to take responsibility for my actions from this point on. To that end, I would also keep the other vampires in check, not letting them get out of hand either.

A week after I'd defeated Youngblood, Elizabeth arrived at the hotel. I'd contacted her telepathically, which had surprised her, but I could tell that she was glad about what had happened. I'd invited her to join me in my new life, and she'd gladly accepted. She was able to find her way here by homing in on me psychically, which I aided her in, guiding her like a beacon.

She didn't arrive alone, though. When the moment came, I went down to the front lobby to greet her, waiting impatiently. There was an unsteady knock at the door, more like a repetitive kick. I used my telekinesis to pull the doors open, and there stood Elizabeth, a small child limp in her arms.

This was supposed to be a surprise, but I'd spoiled it for myself, having looked in on her during her approach. I'd seen the violent car crash occur on the winding mountain road below her as she flew, nearing our location. She'd flown down to investigate, finding the lone survivor to be a lovely little blonde girl, no older than five. The others had died instantly or soon after, and the girl didn't have long to live, either. After taking what blood she needed, Elizabeth had used her psychic powers to calm the child, sending her into a deep sleep.

Now she stood before me, holding the girl. She strode forward, her broad, beautiful smile lighting up the room as she kept her eyes fixed on mine.

"Housewarming gift?" I asked Elizabeth, who beamed and laughed at me sweetly, her fangs showing.

"Yes," she said. "I saved her for you."

EPILOGUE:

2013

It's been twenty years since the night Elizabeth and I drank that little girl, sharing her like a feast. We hadn't been cruel about it; the girl had remained unconscious, feeling no pain. Her name had been Ashley. Our drinking of her wasn't just physical; there was a psychic element to it as well, and we celebrated her short life as we drank in her precious memories, along with her warm, exquisite lifeblood.

I won't pretend that there haven't been difficulties, but for the most part, our time together has been wonderful. Rather than lording over her and the other vampires of the hotel like my predecessor would have done, it's more of an equal partnership, Elizabeth and I ruling together. In the early days, I had a tendency to be more distant from my subjects, still getting used to my new power. But as the years progressed, Elizabeth helped loosen me up and let things become more informal. We're still in charge, but we're not arrogant about it.

The population of the hotel is more diverse as well, a more even mix of male and female vampires than in the old days. It's more racially varied, too, but that wasn't something that we engineered, at least not consciously. What we did strive for was to add people to the group who had something to offer, a purpose they could serve. In a sense, we've built our own little community, everyone doing his or her part. For example, there's Matthew, our resident techie, who keeps us up to date on the 21st century's constantly changing technology, which I sometimes have trouble keeping up with.

There's also Nigel, a DJ we appropriated from a night club in Washington, D.C. a couple of years ago. That had come about due to mine and Elizabeth's repeated visits there, which started out as what we jokingly called our "hunting trips." I hadn't been keen on dancing to begin with, but one great thing about being a vampire, particularly one as powerful as I am, is that I can drain knowledge from people as easily as I can blood. Acquiring the necessary dance skills wasn't difficult once I'd preyed on the right victims.

Fads come and go, but one thing that never seems to go out of style is nostalgia. Growing up, I'd seen a lot of 1950s nostalgia during the 1980s, then the '60s being rehashed in the '90s. These days, it's the '90s that are in fashion to look back on, and that was reflected in the "retro" theme nights at the club where Nigel worked — and still does, but only at night of course. This led Elizabeth to bring in an Ace of Base CD and convincing him to work the track "Waiting for Magic" into his set. I think it's actually a song about Snow White, but the lyrics in the chorus also sound vaguely vampiric as well.

After a while, Elizabeth decided that it would be fun to make Nigel our own. As a result, we have occasional parties in the ballroom, complete with a sound system, lights, fog, everything. Recently, he went up against another of our resident vampires, Silas, in what they called a DJ battle, Silas pitting his hip-hop tracks against Nigel's preferred genre of British electronica. It was a friendly competition, and everyone had a good time.

Some of the older vampires choose not to take part in events like this, but that's okay, too. While some, like Victoria, tend to stay stuck in the eras from which they came, others are fine with changing with the times, their styles mirroring the young people of the passing years.

Elizabeth, not surprisingly, falls into the latter category. I'll admit that my personal style hasn't changed much since the 1990s. That was when I came of age, so it's what I'm comfortable with.

I like the mix of different people, how everyone — for the most part — gets along despite their differences. I could go on about some of the others here, like Rachel, Margaret, Aiden... But it would take far too long to list everybody, and they each have their own stories.

As for the rest of our existence, I'm still overseeing everything, including the vampires around the country, even the world. While I could easily just sit on a throne and psychically spy on the rest of the world like Youngblood did, I try not to be as withdrawn and devious as he was. Some of that chess-playing is necessary, though, to intervene and pull a few psychic strings here and there. Youngblood himself knew that, I later learned from Mirela, who did return to the fold after a few years of wandering.

Had it not been for Youngblood's influence, the events in Augusta would have been thoroughly investigated by the government, possibly endangering me, my family, and my friends. Obviously, that would have upset his plans. But it wasn't difficult for him to tweak a few brains and simply make people look the other way. I've had to do similar things myself over the years, including to protect Carolyn and her family.

It was a little bit tempting to start manipulating her kids once they were old enough, maybe even to reopen the tunnel in the basement of the house that she inherited and lead them here. But there was no sense in doing that. Youngblood's vendetta against our family was over; I had no desire to continue it. Instead, I look in on them occasionally, glad to see that they're doing well. Carolyn's oldest, a lovely girl named Cathy who is the spitting image of Susanna, is currently in her second year at the University of Georgia and studying Environmental Science.

Carolyn herself is still sometimes plagued by memories of everything that went on back in the day, and when I first came to power here, I considered wiping her memory of those events in order to make things easier for her. Elizabeth talked me out of it, insisting that my sister needed those memories, those scars, in order to live her life the way it was supposed to be. Take away those lessons, and she might wind up having it too easy, neglecting her kids rather than teaching them proper morals. And she's doing just fine; the fact that her husband is a doctor and brings in enough money that Carolyn is able to be a stay-at-home mom probably helps. She's there for her kids when they need her.

The rest of the survivors, meanwhile, are getting on with their lives with varying degrees of success. I'll admit I was surprised when Carl came out of the closet a few years after high school, but looking back on it, I can see that he probably always was that way. He ended up moving to Atlanta and lives there with his boyfriend, and the two of them seem happy enough. They're active in politics, and I wish them the best of luck in their efforts in getting gay marriage legalized in Georgia. Several states around the country have passed the necessary laws in recent years, but I'm not holding my breath on it happening in my home state anytime soon. I could be wrong, though. Time will tell.

Nick became an on-air DJ working in radio, first at a station in Augusta that played alternative music, which seemed right up his alley. But as time went on, trends changed, people lost their jobs, and he's had to move from station to station in order to stay employed. He also had to change his personal style in order to match each job, one year doing the nightshift at a country music channel, the next doing afternoon drive at a soft rock station. He's stuck with it, and if he's ever felt disappointed with his career or that he's sold out, he never would admit it. Last time I checked in on him, which was about four years ago, he was doing evenings on the air at a classic rock station in Mississippi.

Damon also ended up working in commercial radio, but as a salesman, the kind who sold airtime for commercials. He enjoyed the job for a while; it was good money. But as the years wore on and his hair grew thinner, he became more bitter as his youth slipped away. The band he'd played in had split up, and he put together another one called Rhombus Room that was mildly successful for a few years, playing the bars around Augusta and in nearby cities. But he never achieved the fame and fortune he desired; no record deal ever came about like he'd kept hoping. His second wife left him when she found out that he was cheating on her with one of the women who also worked in sales at his current station, and he went into a deep depression after that. I stopped peering in on his life then; it was too much of a downer.

So here we are, me with my Elizabeth living eternally young as vampires in this hidden hotel in the mountains of Virginia. The place has become a haven for vampires of all kinds, not just the ones we've made ourselves over the years. Apart from the ones who were already here when we arrived, there are ones from around the world who come to stay with us, sometimes for only a short time, others for longer. And while the majority of the ones here are similar in power and ability to me and Elizabeth — though never quite as powerful as me; I'd never make that mistake of letting that happen — there are other varieties.

Some of them are quite old, centuries even. Most are beautiful, but there have also been ones who border on hideous, quite malevolent in their appearance, veins showing through their skin. Others have abilities and limitations quite different from what I'm used to, like the ones who can fly without changing their forms, while I've encountered others who achieve this by becoming incorporeal, like spirits. Still others have no aversion to sunlight. Honestly, I could always change my own limitations — or that of any of the other vampires — so that sunlight wasn't a deterrent, but I like us being confined to the night.

It feels like the right time for us, lurking in the shadows. There really are all kinds of vampires out there, and I've made it clear to any who visit that all are welcome as long as they behave themselves and show respect for me and the others.

There are times, though, when the enormity of my position overwhelms me. I may or may not be the most powerful vampire in the world; I'd really rather not know whether or not that's the case. But I am pretty high up there at least, and while I didn't ask for this, I accept it. Often, I enjoy it. Admittedly, I've always been something of a control freak, but now, instead of just insisting on being in charge of a small group of friends and family, I find myself responsible for a huge amount of people, and sometimes, that gets to me.

Elizabeth is very good at sensing when I'm close to melting down, at which point she distracts me. Sometimes it's enough that she insists on Nigel throwing another party, or she can lull me into comfort by sitting at the piano and performing her version of "Close My Eyes Forever," which is surprisingly beautiful. If those things aren't enough, we go off somewhere, one of our hunting trips, leaving someone like Mirela or Victoria in charge. That usually does the trick, giving me some perspective. We're thinking of going to Ireland next, particularly since Elizabeth has developed an interest in Celtic music and has taken to learning to dance to it. She's always growing and learning, and it's one of the reasons I love her. She makes my life broader and richer as a result.

The most interesting trip in recent memory was when we found a small town in West Virginia and binged ourselves on the adult population, drinking so much blood that we aged backwards. We ended up becoming child vampires, our bodies small and energetic, and even more interestingly, our sex drives vanished. We truly were prepubescent, and while in the past we'd had plenty of carnal desire for each other and had indulged in that on many occasions, we suddenly found ourselves feeling more like best friends, eager to play and have fun. It brought me back to how things had felt back in the early days of the potion, when I was an eight-year-old reveling in the power of it all, no sexual thoughts even occurring to me.

What was scary about that adventure — apart from what ended up happening to the children of the town — was that our psychic powers also disappeared along with our maturity. Had any of the vampires back at the hotel found that out, we might have been in big trouble. They could have taken over things easily. But we were lucky, and no one ever found out. The long stretch of time in which we had to starve ourselves of blood in order to age back up to our former selves hadn't been a good time at all. Still, once we got through it and back to our life at the hotel, we were able to look back on the experience with, if not fondness, then at least with wisdom.

And so we run things, ruling from on high over the other vampires and enjoying it. We hide out from the rest of the world in some ways, but our influence still carries some weight. Sometimes, we're aggressive about it, but for the most part, we're behind the scenes.

About ten years ago, our techie guy, Matthew, had a web site set up with footage of some of our vampires killing and draining victims in hotel rooms. There was a market for this, apparently, people who would actually pay to see helpless people being murdered like that. The more interesting ones featured those vampires who, for whatever reason based on their beliefs or limitations, didn't show up on camera. It had something to do with how mirrors were used in the construction of cameras; I never fully understood it. But in those, you'd have a victim seemingly killed and drained by some invisible assailant. I could at least appreciate the art of it, and that's what the web site claimed these short movies were: art pieces.

But it's not like we needed the money. Worse still, there was the weirdness in dealing with all of that, how credit card transactions might be traced to us somehow. But even if the authorities got involved, so what? I could always work my magic and wish the prying eyes away.

But eventually, I didn't think the hassle was worth it, so I put an end to the venture.

These days, most people tend to put their weird videos up online for free, something I'm still trying to get my head around. It seems like any kid with a video camera can just put their antics on the internet. Matthew noticed this, too, and he's started uploading some of the old videos, which I'm okay with. Oddly enough, the only controversy seems to be among the idiotic people leaving comments on the videos, debating about whether or not they're "fake" or "gay."

Perhaps the biggest thing I had to struggle with early on was my seeming omnipotence, something I more or less inherited from Youngblood. As I've said, Elizabeth kept me in check as far as that was concerned. But in the beginning, I had half a mind to rewrite all of history, making it so that Youngblood had never existed and never corrupted my family. But if I'd done that, where would I be? I liked who I was, who I'd wound up becoming.

I could have changed things to where my parents were alive again. I knew that it was within my capability to do so. Bringing Susanna back was pointless, but what if I changed it all around to where my family had only ever consisted of my mother, my father, and Carolyn? They could have lived out their lives happily, some kind of parallel universe in which things were better. But I always hated parallel universe stories, like those things in sci-fi where it was stupidly posited that all of the same people were there, only with beards and everyone being mean instead of nice. Reality didn't work that way.

Or if it did, I could end up royally fucking things up if I'd been arrogant enough to assert my will and make it so that certain disasters never happened, like the Challenger explosion, the terrorist attacks of September 11th, or the Holocaust. I just didn't have the right. Can you imagine how different the world might be if I'd turned those things around? I could have, but then if I had, you might not even be here. History is very fragile.

Having said that, I should admit to how I have in fact changed a few things. Cosmically, they're just relatively little bits here and there, and I've learned to be careful. Aside from in these books, do you remember reading about the massive vampire attacks in Augusta, Georgia, all those years ago? Has there ever been a historical documentary about it on TV? Of course there hasn't, and there won't be. Some people remember that, especially the people who live there, the ones who went through it. But I've had a lot of time, twenty years in fact, to do plenty of rewriting. It's something I do when necessary, and I'm willing to bet that you don't even realize how much.

Also, you may have noticed how popular vampires are nowadays. It seems like everyone and their grandmother's dog has written a vampire book, and they're all over the place in movies and TV. We helped that happen, too. Apart from the handful of vampires in our hotel who decided to put pen to paper — or these days, pixels to screen — and crank out their own novels (under pen names, naturally), there was a deliberate psychic wave that I sent out into the world, generating interest and inspiration so that the market would be flooded with the genre. As a result, some people have gotten tired of the phenomenon, and fewer and fewer take it seriously or would go so far as to actually believe that vampires are real. Even if a victim is found, the police are more likely to think that the murder was caused by some vampire wannabe rather than the real thing.

Not that bodies turn up all that often since I took things over. One of the changes I made to our parameters, so to speak, was that not only can we feed on humans without killing them, but we can also heal their wounds and make it appear as if they haven't even been bitten. Wiping their memories of the event is simple enough, or they may recall the attack but think it was a dream. I can even make it so that if a body is completely drained of blood, it can then be magically healed again, just a small alteration to reality with no repercussions. With no physical evidence and only a vague memory, if that, someone can be preyed upon without ever having known it. It isn't always done that way, though. Sometimes there is just straightforward killing.

I can see you as you read this, by the way. Not physically, but psychically. I can hear your thoughts, your doubts, thinking that I'm just making that up. I can peer directly into your soul if I choose to, rummaging through your memories. You remember that thing you did when you were five, the one that you thought nobody saw and that you completely got away with? I can see that, too, in your head.

For all you know, I've already tasted your blood, maybe even drained you completely, only to rework that event and make it so that you're alive again. I know you don't remember it; I wouldn't allow you to. If it makes you feel better, you should probably have some garlic or a wooden stake nearby when you go to sleep tonight. It might help, but I doubt it.

ABOUT THE AUTHOR

T. Marshall Bunn grew up in Augusta, Georgia, and has lived several places up and down the east coast since. He currently lives in Rockville, Maryland and works as an audiovisual preservation librarian.